THE WORD AND THE SWORD

The Word and the Sword

THEO LANG

NEW ENGLISH LIBRARY
TIMES MIRROR

First published in Great Britain by Michael Joseph Ltd. in 1974
© 1974 by Theo Lang

*

FIRST NEL PAPERBACK EDITION APRIL 1976

*

NEL Books are published by
New English Library Limited from Barnard's Inn, Holborn, London E.C.1.
Made and printed in Great Britain by Hunt Barnard Printing Ltd., Aylesbury, Bucks.

45002809 7

TO
MAURICE KIDD, W.S.

Many things do not happen as they ought; most things do not happen at all. It is for the conscientious historian to correct these defects.

Herodotus

I

Six more to be crucified this morning. The first pair had already been stripped and flung on their backs. Now their arms were being pulled outward, and a soldier waited, kneeling in the grit beside the crossbars, long square-headed nails clasped between his lips and a mallet in his hand.

Severus switched his eyes from the sweaty scene and unrolled the warrant to read again through the six names. When he came to the last name he grimaced disgust: that name made this morning's job even more unpleasant.

No doubt about it, crucifixion was the messiest way of putting a man to death. Time-wasting too. Strangulation, Roman style, was cleaner; lopping off a head was quicker; better still the swift upward thrust of a sword, so long as the executioner was a soldier experienced enough in battle to know and to find unerringly that easiest spot of entry in the yielding flesh just below the ribs. Or fire. In fact all other forms of execution were better and less tedious than this business with crosses and ropes and nails, which not only wasted so much time but also imposed on the men detailed to do the job chores almost too menial for Palestinian auxiliaries, let alone Gauls or Germans. True enough, some of those chores could be done by the condemned men themselves. As with this morning's six. They, before they had been ritually scourged last night, had been brought out here to dig, each of them, the hole into which would be planted the upright of his cross. For in this arid corner of Judaea there were no tree-stumps to which the posts could be lashed. It was also accepted routine for a man to carry his own crossbar from the cell to the place of execution. Yet some things a condemned man could not do for himself. He could not, for instance, choose on the upright the exact position for the peg which would fit under his crotch and thus, taking some of his sagging, dying weight off his corded wrists and nailed hands, keep him alive that much longer.

A German, blond hair and moustache and sun-skinned face, was fixing a peg at this very moment. As he spread the thighs apart and pushed the peg high between the man's legs he made the inevitably lewd remark. Something about the proximity of peg to anus. Or, more possibly, about the man's circumcision now distastefully uncovered. What an odious custom! It was little wonder that decent young Jews in the new Roman cities of Judaea were at pains to conceal the fact that they had suffered this barbaric mutilation. Some of them, it was said, actually paid fat fees to surgeons in an attempt to restore their members to a semblance of what they had been born with.

The Jew on the cross was hardly likely to know one word that the German was saying. But he could hardly fail to know where the German's calloused hands were groping down there, nor fail to see the grin flashed up at him by the blond face. That grin might make him understand that the words were an attempt at a joke, and he might even understand that in jerking out the obscene jest the soldier was trying to relieve to some extent the distaste which even a brutish German could feel in doing such a thing to a man.

Severus barked a command for silence. The second pair arrived on the scene.

There would be a guard to mount as well, otherwise friends of the rebels would sneak to the scene and lift them down. So a dozen or more soldiers would need to hang about until the six condemned were undeniably dead. That guard duty might last all of two days and two nights. Someone had told him that crucified men sometimes lived as long as three days and nights. But probably that was nothing but soldier's gossip. Surely not even these fierce and skinny Jews could be all that tough!

Anyhow, this morning's operation was so far going expeditiously. The detail were doing the job exactly as he had briefed them last night. Now the second pair were naked and on their backs, and soldiers were binding their wrists to the crossbars, prising open their clenched fists and pressing the splayed fingers back against the wood. One of the rebels yelped when the mallet came down and drove the first of the long copper nails through his palm. The German fumbled in his canvas bag for two more pegs.

Again Severus looked away. He stared along the track leading to the village. It was time for the last of the six to be out of the cell. Yes, there they were, just leaving the village, crossbars balanced across their shoulders, and four soldiers marching in escort beside them. As they stepped out of the shadow of the arched gateway the dawn glare lit their two heads. One head was typically Jewish with long black hair, but the other was disquietingly fair, and the sight of that one made Severus drop his eyes yet again to the names on the warrant. The first five names were Jewish; tangled outlandish names well-suited to swarthy sons of Abraham, these beings of a race and of a way of life so inferior to anything Roman that crucifixion might be considered the only way to put an end to them. But the last name! It was shocking to see a high-sounding Roman name in such barbarian company.

That name was the reason for Severus being on duty at this crucifixion. His appointment as personal aide to the Procurator, an honour so recent that he was still dazed by the dizzy leap, should have freed him from duties so routine and mediocre as superintending crucifixions. But Pilate had decided that it was essential for an officer of his personal staff to be in command at the unique ceremony at which a man of Roman birth was to suffer the form of death usually inflicted only on non-Romans, on slaves and criminals who had been found guilty of the meanest crimes. True enough, the warrant of execution had been so worded as to strip the man of Roman citizenship, but Severus felt that legal phrases, however cleverly fabricated, could never make the man's body anything but the body of a man born Roman. True enough also that at yesterday's court-martial, scrupulously just and conducted by the Procurator in person, the man had been found guilty of treason against Rome and Tiberius Caesar. He had not even tried to deny that he had consorted with Jewish terrorists engaged in acts of violence not only against Roman law but also against the laws of the Jews' own priestly government in Jerusalem, and for such crimes death on the cross might seem

9

the only suitable penalty. Nevertheless, the man had been given the chance of an honourable way out. A sword had been tossed, no one need ever know by whom, into the cell. But he had not used it. That his refusal to quit the scene in decent Roman fashion did not arise from cowardice was obvious from the way he now came stepping along the track.

Severus, keeping his head bent and pretending to study the warrant, was staring under his brows to watch the approach of this prodigy. The Roman was not wailing, as Jews, even the fiercest of them, seemed to think it obligatory to wail when confronting death, though someone had told Severus that the cries which he thought were agonising lamentations were actually prayers. Nor was the Roman dragging his feet. Indeed, the fellow strode out along the harsh gritty track quite insolently, stepping so smartly that the escorts, sweating under their helmets and breastplates and greaves, were forced almost to a trot to keep up with him. One could have imagined that he was positively eager to get to the spot: as though waiting here for him on the sandy mound were a girl and kisses, not a cross and nails. He carried his head high. His hands, draped over the crossbar, hung negligently, as though the damned thing were a battle trophy and not the plank to which those pale and elegant hands would soon be nailed. Well, if there were any comfort at all to be dredged from the situation, there was a sliver of it in the realisation that the meanest Roman, even a confessed traitor, could show men of other races how to die. Though one had to admit that his young Jew companion was facing up to the prospect of agonising death not too badly either. Taking his cue from the Roman, the boy was making a brave show of striding on equally boldly, now and again directing at the Roman profile glances which, although they were shadowed with despair and seemed each time to beg for one more dram of Roman courage, were full of adoring admiration, and culminated, when they reached the site of crucifixion, in a farewell stare of such passionate intensity that it seemed to pass between them like a sigh. To this the Roman replied with a smile grave and cool, a smile which one could imagine had been designed as the last secret communion between the two of them and which would carry into and preserve in the other world the affection that had flowed between them in this.

Avoiding the Roman's eyes, Severus kept his gaze fixed on the boy. Two weeks in captivity followed by last night's scourging had twisted the young face into lines that made it look older than

10

its years. Yet the boy's cheeks were as smooth as those of a girl, and his hair, despite all those days in a dank cellar, still gleamed in lustrous waves. In his full nakedness, when one of the auxiliaries had torn off his smock and dragged his breech-clout away, he looked pitifully fragile and young. In fact the kid could have been a twin of that Jew boy who worked in the army bakehouse at Caesarea, that boy who had become the petted mascot of the mess and whom the more randy soldiers stroked on the buttocks whenever he pressed his way between the tables with his baskets of loaves. That was the difficulty with these damned Jews: to a Roman eye they all looked so much the bloody same. If one could not distinguish between their dialects or the different stripings and foldings of their shawls, one could never tell which one was from South Palestine or which was from North Palestine; which might be from Jerusalem or southern places like Gaza and therefore likely to be an obedient subject and somewhat reconciled to Roman occupation, or which might be from Galilee and other wild places in the north and thus, if not himself a Zealot terrorist, almost certainly a sympathiser with those anti-Roman partisans.

Smartly the German curled one foot behind the boy's ankles and at the same moment gave him a punch in the chest, knocking the slender body to the ground with a slap. The crossbar shot from the boy's grip and bounced on a rock. Two soldiers grabbed it and began lashing the boy's wrists to it, and the man with the mallet, having just finished driving nails through the ankles of number four, hurried up, still dangling one nail in his lips and fumbling in his pouch for more.

Then the German turned to deal with the Roman. He strode up to him with the intention of tearing off the prison smock. But then, his hand uncertain in mid-air, he halted, suddenly aware of the enormity of a German laying his hands on a Roman for such degrading purpose. When his hand moved again it stretched out slowly, the fingertips approaching the fabric diffidently, and whether he would ever have dared to lay a hand on the Roman without the deliberate command which Severus found himself in the Roman's presence reluctant to give was doubtful. Fortunately, at that moment Fabius arrived on the scene, and, summing up the situation, solved the difficulty by shouldering the German aside and doing the job for him. It was hardly a job for an officer of Pilate's staff to do, but Fabius stripped the traitor in rapid one-two-three military movements of such anonymous indifference that it seemed he did not even see the being whom he was reducing to nakedness, an impression heightened by the fact that Fabius wore his helmet in the style favoured by the Eagles, the élite dandies of the army, tilted so low over his brow that it was near impossible to see his eyes. One was conscious only of his aristocratic nose and those handsome lips which were most times curled in a languid pouting smile but were now pressed to an impersonal on-parade tightness. The dirty job done, he stepped back and stood beside Severus.

Just then the boy screamed. One of the clumsy idiots at the crossbar had failed to hold the boy's hand firmly, and the mallet had crushed the two or three fingers curled in its path, and also driven the nail askew. The naked Roman turned and looked down at the boy. Again, surprisingly, he smiled. Then he murmured some words in Aramaic, upon which the boy, biting hard on his underlip and looking up at the Roman just as a scolded child might look at its father, tried with a twisted smile to deny his pain and the tears oozing down his cheeks.

Now that he was naked the Roman looked much older than he had earlier done. His paunch sagged and his thighs were thin. Even so, he seemed to repudiate the humiliation of his situation. He still looked stubbornly Roman. It was two weeks since he and the terrorists had been tracked down to their hiding-place in the village. He could have been strangled immediately, but the Procurator had ordered the trial to be delayed until such time as he could conduct it himself on his progress to Caesarea and thus have the opportunity of personally questioning this rogue Roman who had thrown in his hand with the Zealots. During those two weeks the Roman's hair had not grown much since he had last sheared it short in Roman fashion; and he must, in the cell, have used a flint or something to scrape his chin, for he had only a stubble of whisker, and even that was too fair or too grey to rob him entirely of the shaved Roman aspect. So, despite his surroundings of blood-spattered sand, of four men groaning on the crosses around him, of sweat and feasting flies, and even with that plank weighing on his shoulders, he somehow managed to look commandingly Roman. Like a captain, or a senator, waiting for his bath. And no one stirred to throw him down until Severus, rolling the warrant and wielding it like a baton, made a sharp downward gesture with it and then turned away and strode towards the four crucified men to make a punctilious check on cords and nails. He heard the thump of a body on the ground and the Roman's bold brave curse. The man was not pretending that he felt no pain. He was

12

honest enough and courageous enough not to attempt that farce. When the first nail went through his white hand he repeated the curse in a bellow. At the second nail he poured out a stream of imprecations on the man with the mallet. Severus, his back to the scene, commanded silence. There came back, spoken in Latin but in comically exaggerated mimicry of Severus's heavy Cisalpine pronunciation, 'What about trying it yourself, brother Captain?' and then the slap of flesh on flesh as someone's hand tried to silence the rebellious mouth. An auxiliary was just then carrying a blanket towards the rock which he had chosen for his sentry post, and Severus saw the man grinning as he passed. Severus's hand tightened on the rolled warrant. His anger was fierce relief, for it flooded away what vestiges of pity he had for the Roman. Earlier he had decided that, when the moment arrived to hoist the Roman on his cross, he would instruct the man with the mallet to drive the nails through the front of the Roman's feet, just above the toes, thus nailing them to the front of the upright instead of to the sides, and so keeping the man's legs closer together and his body less indecently exposed. But now he withheld that instruction and turned to watch the nailing. Even so, still avoiding the man's eyes, he kept his gaze down, directed only on the lower half of the Roman's body.

Two soldiers seized the Roman's feet and pressed them up against either side of the upright, making the knees and thighs splay out. The man with the mallet, plucking from his lips the first of the two nails he held in readiness there, drove it through the Achilles tendon of the left ankle. The boy, hanging on the neighbouring cross, began moaning. The Roman, even while the mallet was hammering at his ankle, again murmured something to him. It sounded like a quotation – certainly it was as tender as a verse – but at that moment the sudden clamour of crashing masonry and wailing voices in the village attracted the attention of everyone on the spot. Even the crucified men turned their agonised faces in the direction of the din.

Standing on top of the wall of the village, silhouetted against the morning-lit cloud of dust that billowed up from the collapsing houses, was a Roman soldier, stripped to his loin-cloth and his head swathed in a sweat rag. He carried a short-handled whip and as he shouted commands he thrashed the glinting metal-tipped thongs through the air above the bowed heads and shoulders of a file of villagers who, along the sloping crest of the wall, were rolling boulders into position before heaving them on to the

13

village roofs. A wisp of yellow flame spiralling up somewhere beyond the wall signalled that the destruction of the village had begun.

The man with the mallet, his fingers halted on the second nail between his lips, watched the scene for a moment, and then resumed his task. But, just as he raised the mallet, part of the village wall burst open and the dull roar of tumbling rubble again diverted his attention, so he struck the nail off-centre and bent it. He was trying to straighten the nail without pulling it completely out of the Roman's ankle when Fabius whispered to Severus, 'Your chief will be waiting. He'd almost finished his bath when I left.'

The recently promoted Severus did not fail to notice the '*your* chief'. In any other person that pointed personal linking of him with the Procurator might have indicated resentment that Severus had been hoisted suddenly from the ranks to become the Procurator's personal aide. Fabius, scion of a noble military family, rich, elegant, tall, proud of his schooling and possibly equally proud of his good looks, would have been so much more suitable for the position. But there was no jealousy on Fabius's part. He had higher, and wilder, ambitions than he could satisfy in Judaea. The present imperial policy of Judaisation, of pacification, was a bore to him, holding no promise of martial glory. Fabius did not want to pacify people; he wanted to conquer them. However, his father, because of a friendship with Pilate, had shipped him out to this dead-end hole where the most he could do militarily was to demonstrate the possession, in his own conduct and person, of that quality which these colonial troops and their few Roman officers and even, if it came to that, old Pilate himself, so noticeably lacked – style! So Fabius wore his helmet tilted forward, Eagle-fashion, and carried with languid ease the vine-embossed centurion staff his grandfather had carried in Gaul. He even affected jackboots of soft leather with gold eyelets and gold-tipped laces modelled on those worn by the Emperor's young grand-nephew Gaius Germanicus, who had worn them when he was a youngster with his father's trops on the Rhine and thus earned his nickname Caligula, meaning 'Baby-boots'.

The bent nail had now been straightened and driven true, so, welcoming Fabius's whispered message as an excuse to get quickly away from the scene, Severus turned sharply and marched off further along the track to where, in the shadow of a low sandstone cliff crested with scrub and spindly bushes, stood a big square tent dignified by standards bearing silver eagles.

The campaign tent of Proconsul Pontius Pilate, Procurator of Judaea, had been positioned with its entrance facing west so that it would not be hit by the morning sun. The tent's blind back was turned towards the village and the scene of execution. Severus arrived in the cool shadow of the entrance canopy just as a fat Negro, bent almost double, his vast ebony arse scantily veiled with a sodden scrubbing clout, was backing out and dragging from the interior of the tent a wide leather bath. He slid the bath carefully inch by inch over the bumpy ground to avoid slopping any of the used bathwater near the doorway. Severus stepped around him. The slave grinned up at him his ever-ready smile, showing his pointed filed teeth and the disconcertingly tongueless cavern beyond. A sentry, drooping during his last minutes of duty, pulled himself to moderate wakefulness. 'The Procurator has asked for you,' he said, but Severus did not pull the curtain aside until he had called out, 'Severus, sir!' and heard Pilate's reedy voice answer from somewhere at the back of the tent, 'Come in, Severus.'

Severus stepped inside. The Procurator was out of sight behind the breast-high draperies which screened his bed, so Severus took the opportunity of holding the curtain slightly open and letting some daylight filter in until his eyes grew accustomed to the dim oil-lit interior, for the walls of the tent, made in Jewish fashion of heavy and almost black worsted, kept out all sunlight. But so fervently polished was the bronze of the mules' heads on the arms of couches and chairs that even in this subdued light each leaf of their laurel wreaths and each curl of their manes glowed separately bright. And the scattered gleams of those ornaments here completely outshone by the dominating brassy glare of the Procurator's helmet and cuirass and greaves which hung on an ebony tree beside his travelling-trunk.

The back of Pilate's head came momentarily into view above the surrounding draperies, and Severus saw the upper rim of a burnished metal hand-mirror swivelling left and right as the Procurator methodically combed his grizzled short-cropped hair.

After the heat and sweat of his morning's duty, the atmosphere inside the tent was refreshingly cool and reassuring. Although the tent had been erected for only one night, the familiar furnishings and the felt rugs, thick as boards, which concealed the sand completely from wall to wall, gave the place the air of a permanent and orderly home. Every object in the tent, large or small, had been placed with military precision in exactly the same position as it occupied in Pilate's room in Caesarea and always occupied whenever and wherever the tent was used. His long narrow travelling-desk, an ingeniously designed shallow box, was always placed on its trestle legs in such a position as would ensure that either daylight or the light cast by the suspended oil-lamps would fall at the required angle over Pilate's left shoulder. The map of Judaea was always hung facing Pilate's desk at an exact height at which its details could be seen when he lifted his head. In the last few months this map, which, Severus now uneasily remembered, was due for renewal, had collected some untidy ink-strokes and chalk circles, but its ebony rollers, chased with gold monogram P's, had been scrupulously polished yesterday evening before being hooked on to the gilt eagle-claw hooks.

Pilate had apparently been doing some work before he bathed, for the wooden flaps at either end of the desk were opened, revealing two shallow trays. The stack of fresh sheets of papyrus in the left-hand tray was slightly disarranged. In the right-hand tray lay a sheet nearly covered with Pilate's beautifully clear and angular script. The inkhorn was sunk securely into a socket designed for it at the right-hand upper corner of the main writing-surface. The sealing-wax lay in its customary position. A precise inch to the left of the wax was the instrument used for melting it: a bronze oil-lamp which was neither handsome nor efficient but which was treasured because it was reputed to have belonged to Pompey and, if so, had been used by him during his conquest of Palestine more than ninety years before. The book Pilate was currently reading lay, as always, on a low table beside his day couch; a bar of ebony was planted upon it to keep the scroll open at the passage he had reached. It would almost certainly be a volume of those endless *Commentaries* of the Divine Julius. One would have thought that by now the Procurator ought to know by heart every word Julius Caesar had written, without needing to go through the tedious process of reading the work once again. But, as he constantly dotingly repeated, he was always finding new angles of vision in every sentence.

The sound of metal clinking on marble as Pilate laid mirror and comb on the table beside his bed warned Severus that the Procurator was due to emerge from his bedroom, and, knowing how rigorously Pilate avoided the ageing effects of heat and sun,

Severus let the entrance curtain fall fully into position just before Pilate stepped into view. One towel, voluminous and creamy, was draped from his waist; another, a cheap grey linen soldier's towel, was thrown over his lean but womanishly white shoulders. He acknowledged Severus's salute with a nod. This curt greeting indicated that Pilate was in one of his reflective wordless moods. The Procurator seated himself at his desk. From the right-hand tray he lifted the sheet of papyrus on which he had been writing. There was a blank space in the centre of the script. He laid the papyrus on the desk squarely in front of him, but, when he reached to the back of the desk for a pen, a swinging fold of the towel pushed the papyrus slightly aslant. He frowned, drew back his hand, put the paper square again and, this time drawing the obtrusive towel back from his right forearm with his left hand, reached out to choose a reed pen, fingered it, discarded it and chose another. Then, holding the pen over the unwritten part of the page, he said, 'The names, Severus.'

Severus unrolled the warrant and began reading out the Jewish names. He stumbled over some of the alien syllables, so he tried to clarify them by spelling them out letter by letter. With a tetchy pointing of his writing hand Pilate drew attention to the fact that his pen was keeping up with his lieutenant's dictation. He was pleased to be able to demonstrate to Severus that, far from needing elementary spelling assistance, he had already written correctly all the Aramaic names which Severus had so far mispronounced.

Pilate was proud of the progress he had made with his Aramaic. Although official and colonial business throughout Palestine was conducted in Greek, and all educated Jews spoke that language, Pilate had decided, immediately he was appointed governor of Judaea, to apply himself to the study of the two indigenous languages of the province: the Aramaic of common usage which was most useful to him in day-to-day administration, and the Hebrew used by scholars and the church. Both these languages, thought Pilate, betrayed, by their complexities and sinuosities, the dubious two-faced character of barbarian peoples. But then, the same could be said of Greek, a language which, elegant though it could be, was too often marred with subtleties of a deceitful, almost feminine, character, whereas the language of Rome, austere and virile and dignified, was so emphatically the speech of a practical people whose minds, free of womanish flights of fancy, were disciplined in public and in private, in peace and in war, to masculine courage and dignity. Nevertheless, the exercise of learning the native tongues of Palestine had been informative, and Pilate thus had an advantage over his predecessor, Valerius Gratus, fourth Procurator of Judaea, who, either because of his notorious laziness or because of sheer incapacity, had never learned even everyday Aramaic, and had thus been forced to rely on interpreters: a risky situation, for even if it did not result in one being outwitted politically, it certainly laid one open to being cheated domestically. But that fourth Procurator had been like many Romans appointed to positions of authority in foreign provinces: characters who owed their appointments not to any natural or cultivated talent as administrators but merely to their being members of noble or wealthy families. Such men, neither conscientious in their duty to the empire nor wise, used their terms of duty abroad merely to indulge in foreign entertainments and the excitements of sporadic military exercises. They considered it unknightly, even unsoldierly, to devote time to such things as books for, in their eyes, reading and writing were occupations fit only for the Greek slaves they employed as librarians and scribes and as tutors for their children. Military men were particularly prone to this prejudice, which showed their ignorance. After all, the greatest soldier the world had ever known had been a diligent reader, and also, as his *Commentaries* so brilliantly proved, a superbly scholarly writer.

Pilate wrote the names in two columns: one column in Aramaic, the other in Greek, the Greek being necessary because it was the official language of administration in the province. He would have liked to show off a little by translating the names into Latin also, but there was now only enough space beside the Greek and Aramaic pairs of names to write the crime or crimes of which each of the condemned had been found guilty.

The first names were those of two known terrorists who, after a Zealot assassination behind the Inn of the Gladiator at Tiberias, had been flushed out of their lair on the heights of Hattin and had fled south from Galilee, hoping to go underground in Judaea. They had been hunted for weeks before being tracked down to their hiding-place in a cellar in the village. As Galileans and thus subjects of Herod they were, strictly speaking, beyond Pilate's jurisdiction, but, in an effort to hide their identity, they had claimed to be natives of the village, and Pilate had decided to accept this lie and deal with them as Judaeans.

The third name was that of the householder who had harboured them. Pilate bracketed these three names together and wrote in the margin a reference to documents containing names of other partisans torn from them during two weeks' torture.

Severus now read the fourth name. This man was a goat-herd, a native of the village. Against him there was no evidence at all of previous acts of terrorism, but he had confessed to meeting two Zealots in the hills and leading them to the house where they had been found. 'Treason', wrote Pilate.

It was a merchant of the village, a law-abiding Jew, who had informed the authorities that the two hunted Zealots and the goat-herd were hiding in the house. He had been suitably paid for the information. In a night raid on the house, the three miscreants, surprised in their sleep, were easily captured. During this raid the Roman renegade and his companion, a young Jew from Galilee, were discovered on a cot in an upstairs room. The Galilean was only fourteen or fifteen. Young as he was, he was undoubtedly a Zealot, for under his robe was found a dagger of the type always carried by Zealots. This custom had earned for the Zealots, among the Jews, the nickname 'daggermen' ever since the first overt Zealot enterprise, when a band of ten of them had attempted to assassinate the late king, Herod the Great.

The five Jewish names completely filled the space which Pilate had left blank on that page of his report. Severus spat out the sixth name on the warrant, the Roman name. Pilate said dryly, 'That name I have already written. On a separate report.'

'A Roman! Why should a Roman . . . ?' The words blurted out. Severus could not hold the question back.

Severus, thought Pilate, must learn to be less demonstrative and more official. The display of feeling irked Pilate the more because the angry question trespassed on his own preoccupations. That same question had been nagging at him ever since the renegade had been marched out after yesterday's court-martial. Prior to that hour-long investigation, Pilate had felt confident that the answer to the question could be found once he was face to face with the Roman. He had, throughout his career, always considered he possessed a particular talent for uncovering truth, by personal interrogation and without torture. Torture was a blunt instrument. Under torture any man would ultimately admit anything, even the most improbable offence. That was neither just nor satisfactory. But interrogation, pure interrogation without iron or fire or wheels, was an art and, if conducted by an artist, truth would always emerge from it. Each question must be delicately fashioned. The question would sometimes be oblique and insinuating, thus relaxing the man's mind and loosening his tongue. At other times it would be direct and challenging, startling the man and tricking him into a damning admission or, even more damning, a foolish lie. The interrogator must never be too eager to put important key questions. Those would leap to his mind, brilliantly dangerous, during the interrogation, but he must resist the temptation to blurt them out there and then. He should suppress them for a time, file them away in his memory, until he could produce them suddenly, unexpectedly, irrelevantly. Completely out of context they would throw the man off balance. Above all, the interrogator must have a talent for framing questions quickly, weaving them swiftly, strand by strand, silky or barbed, until the man was finally enmeshed in the net of his own proven guilt. Then the Procurator could sign the instrument of condemnation with the certain knowledge that not only had justice been done but also it had been seen to be done.

With the Roman, however, the interrogation had not followed any logical pattern. Some questions, the 'how' and the 'when', had been answered without reserve. Freely admitting his own deeds, the Roman had shown a near-contemptuous disregard of the fate inevitably awaiting anyone making such admissions. But *why* had he done these things? Was it for greed or gain? Had he entertained treasonable ambitions to achieve power? His answers to such questions had been a hotchpotch of words such as 'faith' and 'hope' and 'love of one's fellows'; phrases so vague as to be meaningless, almost asinine. So much so that, even though he were a Roman, had he been one of lowlier birth and of less note, he could have been sufficiently punished by being sent into slavery, or into a madhouse.

The brooding silence that had followed Severus's unfortunate question was broken by the bustling entry of the Negro slave. The black giant's hips and legs were now swathed in a sheet of linen garishly patterned in stencilled squares of brilliant colour. This garment, his only article of clothing, was always good for a laugh in the mess whenever soldiers persuaded the Negro to demonstrate its multi-purpose properties. At this moment he was wearing it in decorous mode as an ankle-length kilt, but he often demonstrated how, by drawing the hem dexterously up between his thighs and tucking it in pleats around his waist, he could in two seconds convert the sheet into a pair of close-fitting breeches for working in; or by disposing more of the folds thickly around his behind

20

he could squat in cushioned comfort on the sharpest rocks. Further encouraged, he would show how the sheet could be draped open, fore or aft according to its wearer's taste, for the enjoyment of any manner of sexual exercise.

It was not necessary in this fellow's presence to observe the silence customary in the presence of body-slaves. There was no fear of this black fellow being indiscreet: he had never been able to pass on tales since the day his tongue was torn out for doing so.

Pilate held out his hand for the execution document. Severus stepped forward and laid it on the desk for the signing and sealing which would certify that six men had been found guilty of treason and related capital crimes, and had been duly hanged on crosses. The officer in charge of the guards at the place of execution could certify the day and hour of their individual deaths when those occurred.

'They were given wine?' asked Pilate.

'Yes. Enough.'

'Drugged?'

'Laced with gall, yes. Enough to numb them a bit. Except the Roman. He refused. Said he preferred a sober view of the proceedings.'

The execution warrant was dated as from Caesarea, correctly so because that city was the official seat of the Procurator, and headquarters of the Roman forces in Palestine. Pilate had no doubt that the rest of the document would be similarly correct, for the Greek he had bought in Athens was a most reliable scribe. Yet Pilate punctiliously read it, savouring the preamble 'At Caesarea, Judaea, 13th day of July, 17th of Tiberius Caesar. I, Proconsul Pontius Pilate, Procurator of Judaea, Samaria and Idumaea, by virtue of the authority invested in me by his August Highness Tiberius Claudius Nero . . . ' As the words rolled sonorously and grandly through his mind his right hand laid down the pen and strayed to his chest where his finger tips, as though touching a charm, made brief obeisance at that spot where, on ceremonial occasions, his badge of office hung from a gold chain.

When he had finished reading, he wrote his signature heavily, conscious that the firm angular characters revealed strength and authority. He affixed the seal himself. Other men in high office often delegated that job to a scribe, but Pilate enjoyed performing this final and symbolic ritual with his own hands. 'Have the scribe make six copies immediately, and have them fastened to the crosses.'

The Negro was now kneeling beside Pilate's chair. He had brought from the trunk a small phial of red ink, thick as paint, and a tiny brush, and, as the Procurator rolled the document and handed it to Severus, he dipped the tip of the brush in the ink and leaned towards Pilate's left side. Pilate waved the brush away.

'The village? Has it been destroyed?'

'They have just begun,' answered Severus. 'It will not take long.'

'Good! As for the inhabitants, I have decided . . . ' Pilate broke off and turned to the slave. 'Find Polygnotus,' he commanded. The Negro rose from his knees, laid the red ink and brush carefully on the travelling-trunk, and hurried off. Pilate reached for fresh papyrus, laid it on the desk, and, pen in hand, brooded over the blank sheet for a while, his left hand meanwhile automatically tidying into a solid stack the slightly disarranged sheets in the left-hand tray. Severus stood in silence. After a few moments of musing, Pilate wrote, rapidly but neatly, a series of notes and was numbering each one marginally when the Greek scribe arrived, carrying tablets and stilus. The Negro, following him in, took a stance in the shadows near the hanging armour, his huge blackness merging into the background of dark worsted, only his eyes and certain glistening bulges of his torso visible.

'Make a note,' Pilate said to the scribe. 'Points to be included in dispatches to Rome and Capri. I have decided: One, that the destruction of the village . . . What is the name of the village, Severus?'

The aide raised his fingers uncertainly towards his lips. 'I . . . For the moment, sir, I forget.'

'It would be as well to remember, Severus. Before it completely disappears.' Pilate handed him a piece of chalk. 'Mark its position on the map. No, more to the east. That's it; near the Gibeon road. What do you make that? Twelve to thirteen road-miles from Jerusalem? Yes, there's the escarpment.'

'There is a new map in the chest, sir,' said Severus as he drew a chalk circle.

'Replace it when we get to Caesarea. The *ink* marks must be transferred. The chalk marks are of no further importance.' He turned to the scribe. 'Make a note to get the name of the village and put a map in the record. Now, take this down. I have decided that the destruction of the village . . . No! That *by my clemency* the destruction of the village will be adjudged sufficient punishment of the inhabitants for having harboured malcontents. The inhabitants must leave the area, but those of suitable age will be provided with honourable occupation. Note two: males of military age will be attached to auxiliary forces for civilian work at Roman stations. Severus. Such men must be posted to localities at the furthest possible distance from their home region and not to any town or village where they have relatives. Marcellus will make sure of such points when he questions the prisoners at Caesarea. Nor must males be posted to any garrison en masse: they should be posted singly if possible. Polygnotus. Three: older males and also any aged females will be allowed to join any kinsfolk they may have in any town or village of their choice, providing that such town or village is not less than three days' march from this area. They may take what personal goods and chattels remain to the limit of the amount they can transport themselves. They may take any beasts, asses or goats still alive. Four: the other womenfolk, all except the aged that is, will be taken to Caesarea . . . Severus. I should be pleased if you would give my wife the opportunity of choosing any suitable ones for domestic work at the palace before they are put on the market. How many women are there?' Severus did not know. 'But you should know. You must develop the habit of compiling records of all facts on every occasion. Have the women herded for counting before we leave. But don't count them openly, of course. Remember what I told you: the Jews have some religious prejudice against the counting of persons. Have their names and ages and all relevant details registered. That is all, Polygnotus. No! Add to note four: mothers will be allowed to take with them any of their children or any orphaned children of their tribe up to the age of twelve. Three copies. Do not number the folios. They will be included in . . . What is that?'

Shouting and the sound of running feet behind the tent had interrupted him. 'Have that noise stopped, Severus, and if there is no reasonable excuse for it, have those responsible reprimanded.' Severus hurried out. 'That is all,' Pilate said to the scribe, and he too took his leave.

The Negro took the red ink and brush from the trunk and again knelt beside the Procurator's chair, whereupon Pilate lifted his left arm to allow the slave to perform the final process of his morning toilet. After dipping the brush into the ink, the Negro sketched just below Pilate's lowest left rib a small red dot indicating precisely the spot which, a physician had years ago assured Pilate, was the best position for placing the point of a dagger to ensure the easiest unimpeded entry. In this way suicide would be speedy and, being not too painful, would leave the body in a dignified posture.

By the time Severus returned, Pilate was again behind the dividing curtains, being dressed. The Negro, after rubbing him down with the big towel, handed him his loin-cloth, which he knotted around his waist, and his woollen tunic, a short military one. While he buckled the wide belt of soft leather around his waist the Negro ran dexterous fingers under the belt, pleating the fabric so that the short skirt of the tunic fell in regular folds.

On his reappearance from his bedroom Pilate looked much less authoritative than he had seemed in the toga-like swathing of towels – almost puny in fact. But the laying on of the burnished cuirass embossed with Herculean muscles gave some impression of strength. He fastened the buckles of the cuirass himself while the kneeling Negro strapped the grooved greaves over his shins. The crested helmet, which would not be put on until he stepped outside, would add the final touch of martial magnificence to Proconsul Pontius Pilate, Procurator of Judaea and Samaria and Idumaea, provinces in which he was prepared dutifully to obey Caesar's orders and ensure the peace in this eastern province of the commonwealth. Although he did occasionally dream that one day circumstances just might give him the opportunity of conducting amid the hills and valleys of Palestine military campaigns which could, should fortune favour him, be compared with the exploits of Pompey, or even those of Pompey's victor, the Divine Julius himself.

Severus explained the disturbance. One of the soldiers mounting guard at the place of execution, on going to some bushes to relieve himself, had surprised the boy who, hiding there, was gazing down on the crosses. The boy had made off and run along the ridge, but had been caught behind the tent.

'Who is he?' asked Pilate.

'A boy herding goats. From the village. Harmless enough.'

'Harmless? How do you know?'

'Oh, he is only about eight.'

'Where is he?'

'Outside. Captain Fabius says he'll have him given a taste of the whip and sent back to find his family.'

'Ask Captain Fabius to come here.'

While waiting, Pilate walked towards the helmet which glowed like a great golden flower on its ebony stalk, peered at it closely to assure himself that it had been sufficiently polished, and then with a gesture dismissed the Negro.

He heard Fabius announce himself. 'Come in, Fabius.'

The slim dandy, now without his helmet so that one saw his golden forelocks clipped and curled in a fashionable fringe, came in, dragging by the arm a near-naked child, terrified and with tear-stained cheeks.

Pilate seated himself. He found it embarrassing to be forced, when standing, to stare upward to anyone. Fabius was, like most aristocrats, too tall.

'Another Zealot for you, sir,' said Fabius, his words overlaid with a laugh. Pilate looked stonily at him; both laugh and smile faded quickly away.

'The child shall not be whipped,' said Pilate. 'Let him be taken back to the place of execution. Let him stand there for two hours so that he can see and learn what happens to terrorists.'

'But . . . sir!'

'Yes, Fabius?'

'With respect, sir. I think that's worse than a whipping. It's enough to frighten the little rat out of his skin.'

'Exactly! Better he should grow up a frightened Jew than a crucified one.'

He turned to the boy. 'Come here,' he said in Aramaic, but despite the quite gentle beckoning of the Procurator's hand the boy did not move forward until Fabius pushed him with his knee. The boy dropped his head until Pilate could see only a crown of black waves.

'What is your name, boy?' Pilate had to repeat the question before the boy whispered his name.

'Ishmael. And you lived in that village?' The boy nodded.

Pilate reached out, laid his white sinewy hands on the brown shoulders and drew the boy towards him. 'Listen, boy,' he continued in Aramaic. 'But look at me!' He slipped one hand under the boy's chin and lifted his head. 'Listen,' he said, gazing gravely into the frightened eyes. 'When you go among your people you must tell them what you have seen today. Never forget it, and then you will, I hope, grow up in peace and never need to see such a thing again.' As soon as Pilate removed his hand the boy's head fell; again the face was hidden under the thick cluster of black hair. 'How old are you, boy?' The answer was so quiet it sounded hardly more than a sigh.

'As I thought, Captain,' said Pilate. 'The boy is older than eight: he is close on eleven. Take him. But not two hours: one hour will suffice. And as you go out tell the officer of the guard that I am not to be disturbed.'

When he was alone he lay back in his chair. Severus's question still hung in the air. Why indeed, Pilate thought, why indeed a Roman? Then, with a gesture of irritation, he thrust the question away, stood up and walked quickly to the table beside his couch and lifted the scroll. An hour with the *Commentaries*! By immersing himself in that noble work he could forget trivial preoccupations, cleanse away the nagging sense of having been in some way defeated. He unrolled the scroll until he found a passage he had reached last night, and was already reading as he walked back to his desk. Pen in hand, ready to make notes, he was soon lost in the stirring narrative.

He read, 'They met in the place appointed by Caesar . . . and in the hearing of both armies Africanus spoke thus . . . that they had suffered punishment enough, but now, pent up almost like wild beasts, they were prevented from procuring water.'

'Water!' The word arrested Pilate. After a pause he resumed reading. But here again! He began copying a passage.

'Petra,' he wrote, and underlined the name. 'Here Caesar even dammed up streams, making little lakes to retain the water so that it should not trickle down its underground courses to the comfort of his enemy. The enemy could not get water on the rock, and when attempted to sink wells Caesar so diverted the watercourses that the wells gave no water.'

Pilate underlined that last word also and, with the point of the pen still resting at the end of the underline, he stared at it for a long time.

It was like a sign, like direction from a god, as though the Divine Julius were speaking to him, steering his thoughts to a decision. Courage, said this spirit, have courage in your own vision! Courage was what was needed, mused Pilate. Why wait any longer for encouragement or decision from the imperial legate, a man who spent most of his time in Rome, but even when in Asia was sunk in the lethargy of his court in Antioch, was ever too embroiled in the politics and intrigues of so vast a suzerainty to know or understand Judaea and the immediate needs of Judaea? Why, then, wait a moment longer for aid from him? The vision that Pilate entertained was beyond the legate's comprehension: so grand a scheme could be appreciated only at the summit of empire, only by His August Highness Tiberius Claudius Nero himself.

Suddenly he sprang up and went to his bedroom, and there, in the chest beside his bed, rummaged below other scrolls of the *Commentaries* for a map of the walls and wells of Jerusalem. As he carried this to his desk he called to the guard to send his body-slave. By the time the Negro arrived, Pilate was already un-buckling his cuirass. The Negro lifted it off, unfastened his greaves, and hung the glittering armour on the ebony tree. Pilate arranged the map and papyrus on the desk; before the black body had glided out he was already writing steadily and swiftly.

The hours passed. Severus had hoped for an early departure. Once they reached the sea at Joppa the coast-road north was good for quick riding, and they could be in Caesarea before midnight, by which time his wife would surely have arrived on the boat from Brindisi. But a message had come from the Procurator's tent that the plan had been changed. How changed it was not said, except that they were to leave later in the day. Around noon, food was taken into Pilate's tent, and soon afterwards a courier was summoned and was sent, with an escort of two auxiliaries, to Sebaste, north of Shechem, to inform the Roman governor of that city that the Procurator would be arriving late that night. The courier had then to go to the house of Josephus the Cohen, present the Procurator's compliments and his hope that the banker would find it convenient to receive the Procurator tomor-row forenoon.

The signal for impending departure came when Pilate called for the Negro to armour him again. It was now only two hours before sundown. Severus and Fabius were summoned to the tent. Pilate was again in cuirass and greaves. The slave was lacing his boots.

'How many men have you posted at the execution?' asked Pilate.

'Eight, and an officer. Enough for this place.' Pilate nodded agreement. 'One of the rebels has died already. The old one. Shock, I suppose. He was praying when he died.'

'To his gods, I guess,' said Fabius with a sneer. 'For vengeance against Rome.'

'Not *gods*,' Pilate corrected him dryly. 'To his god. The Jews suffice with one.'

'The householder is in a bad way too,' said Severus. 'I don't suppose any of them will last long. It has been very hot.'

'Have their legs broken,' said Pilate considerately. That was believed to hasten death on the cross.

Pilate stood up. The slave plucked the glittering helmet from its ebony stalk. When it was on Pilate's head its high crest of white horsehair made him look almost as tall as Fabius.

The Procurator issued from his tent. He frowned against the too-bright sun. But although his curtained litter was waiting nearby he declined it.

'I shall ride. The soldiers, baggage, and women can go by the coast road, by way of Joppa, but we are going north and shall stay in Sebaste tonight. I shall need only my desk and books. Dumb Black can take the rest of my things direct to Caesarea. Instruct the officers accordingly, Severus, and then catch me up. Fabius, you will accompany me.'

By the time Pilate was mounted, the furnishings of his tent were already being carried out by a squad of carriers who, instructed by grunted commands from the Negro, were loading every article in accustomed sequence into the carts. Soldiers were untying the tent cords and taking down the eagle-headed standards.

Pilate rode off, Fabius beside him, the standard-bearer and escort behind. Near the main part of the camp, where the soldiers had been lounging about all day, grumbling over their porridge at the delay in reaching the comforts of Caesarea, a group of women were herded. Some of them held children by the hand; two or three had babies in their arms.

'How many women are going to Caesarea?' Pilate asked Fabius after they had trotted past.

'Only nineteen, Severus says. One of them is pregnant.'

From the camp the track curled back on itself to climb the sandstone cliff to the crest of a low hill. Thus, when the party reached that height, they were facing east and could see in the valley the remains of the village. Pilate halted. The others drew up in a semi-circle behind him. The walls and houses of the village were all collapsed into muddled strands of rubble. By now there were no flames, and very little smoke.

'Fabius!' The captain rode up and reined his horse beside that of the Procurator. Pilate did not turn from his contemplation of the ruins. 'The pregnant woman should ride in a cart.'

'I have ordered that, sir.'

'Good.'

'She's a bit above average.'

'*Above average?* What do you mean?' asked Pilate testily, turning at last to look at Fabius. 'Height? Or looks?'

'Looks, certainly.' Fabius attempted a smile. 'But I mean in style. She's not like the others. Not like a village woman: more of a lady than them.'

'What is known of her?'

'She claims to be the daughter of a family at Magdala. She says she came here for the birth of her child. I suppose this excitement might hurry her on a bit.'

'Her husband?'

'Dead, she says. She seems wealthy. When she was captured she was wearing gold amulets and gold pins.'

Pilate shrugged, turned towards the track and then, just as he was about to spur his horse to a trot, he halted again. '*Was* wearing?' His coldly questioning stare wiped the smile from Fabius's face. 'Does that mean she is not wearing them now?'

'Well . . .'

'Well, Fabius?'

'The auxiliaries, sir. You know what they are like. Nowadays they don't get much chance for . . . for pickings.'

'Loot. We are not pirates, Captain. Romans or Germans or Gauls or Palestinians or any others who bear arms under our command represent the law and order of Rome and our empire. These provinces are governed by us in trust. Palestine is a protected kingdom, and its people are under the protection of Caesar.' Sulkily Fabius cast a glance at the ruins. Sensing the implication of that glance, Pilate went on coldly, 'The fact that we are at times compelled to punish Jews does not alter the fact that they are, as a subject race, under our protection. The ones we executed today were traitors. We knew that, but we did not crucify them out of hand. They were tried and found guilty. That woman has not been tried, nor indeed accused. Her gold will be restored to her. The man or men who took it from her or received any of it will each receive twenty lashes. If any Roman was involved he will be reduced in rank. See to that as soon as we reach Caesarea, Captain.'

'Yes, sir.'

At that moment Severus came up the track and joined the party.

'All in order, Severus?'

'Yes, sir.'

'Make sure the prisoners will not be maltreated en route. They will be interrogated by Marcellus in Caesarea.'

'With or without his metal fingers, sir?' asked Severus with a sour grin.

Pilate was momentarily taken aback at Severus presuming to attempt a joke, or having the wit to think of one. But then he laughed. Fabius however, still smarting from Pilate's lecture, remained sulky. Pilate was not displeased with this. It would do this young patrician good to feel the whip occasionally. After all, his father had packed him off to Judaea to learn the rigours of Roman discipline.

'Fabius!'

'Yes, sir?'

'What happened to Ishmael?' Fabius looked blank.

'That boy: the goat-herd you caught.'

'Oh, that kid. He was sick. Severus let him go. After only fifty minutes.' Even at this hint that an order had not been obeyed to the letter Pilate merely nodded, upon which Fabius could not resist a further dig at Pilate's favourite. 'And he also gave him a piece of silver. More than that youngster had ever seen in his life, I guess.'

'Ah well, Fabius, these Jews say that it is better to give than to receive,' said Pilate and, kicking his horse to a trot, rode ahead of the party along a spur of barren red hill northward towards Shechem and the Samaritan town of Sebaste.

Ishmael, the goat-herd, had vomited when he saw his father die. That first one to die, the one whom Severus had called 'the old one', was his father. In his last agonies the man must have believed that the Romans were deliberately adding to his torture by staging this spectacle of his son crouched, terrified and weeping, at the feet of Roman guards. The old man's head suddenly fell, as heavily as though the neck had been broken. An auxiliary strolled over with a spear and thrust the point of it into the man's flank. Blood appeared, drying quickly in the sun. 'That's one of them,' said the soldier, and the officer who was sitting near-by stopped rolling the dice long enough to ask the soldier to read the man's name from the cross, and then make a mark in the margin of the warrant. The trickle of blood stopped. The flies settled. Ishmael vomited.

Severus, walking to the scene at that moment and seeing him

retching, hauled him to his feet, turned him to face the village and gave him a gentle push in that direction. The lad, choking with sobs and wiping the vomit from his chin, stumbled a few steps away. 'Eh!' Severus called him back and, fumbling in his wallet, strode after him, seized one of his brown hands and pressed into it a piece of silver, one of the Roman occupation coins stamped with the head of Tiberius.

Half-way towards the village Ishmael halted. He dared go no nearer. The flames were dying down, but the place was ringed with soldiers. A squad of them was herding women into a group. All were wailing, some of them screaming. Was everyone to be killed? In terror he swung away from the track and ran over a low scrubby hill and into a valley beyond. The goats were there, and his staff still where he had left it leaning against a rock. One goat had given birth an hour or so ago. He took his staff, picked up the kid, and with a whistle so soft that only the animals could hear him, called the flock to follow him. He led them along the valley, eastward away from the village towards bare hills. In Jericho, twenty miles away, he would find his father's brother Simeon. Before the sun set, he had reached a point from which he could see the road to Jericho, but he kept to the crest of the hills and did not go down to the road until nightfall.

The moon rose. He could see a village ahead, but feared to go to any inhabited place. He decided that he must leave the road and climb the hills again to avoid the village. But first he would rest. He led the goats into a clearing by the road, and was about to lie down near them when he realised that he was still clutching the coin that the Roman had thrust into his hand. He opened his fist and stared down at it. It lay on his brown palm, gleaming in the moonlight. Suddenly he retched. His whole body quivered, and he feared that he was going to vomit again. Spitting with anger, he flung the coin away. It bounced on a big pebble and lay on sandy soil, still gleaming. He stole towards it, then lifted one foot and stamped on the thing, trying with his bare heel to drive it into the ground. When he failed to do that he knelt down, grabbed the pebble and hit the coin, hit it again and again as though he were trying to kill a snake.

So intent was he, so noisy with his quivering sobs and panting disgust, that he did not know anyone was nearby until a shadow fell across him. He sprang to his feet and turned round. At first all he could see against the moon was the black silhouette of a man on horseback. Seen thus, rider and horse seemed gigantic, and at first he thought the man was a Roman soldier. But when he stepped further away and the horseman shifted, he saw he was not a Roman. Nor was he a Jewish auxiliary. For he wore a simple woollen robe, and when he spoke to the boy, asking him what he was doing and who he was, he spoke in the heavy accent of a Galilean.

The boy did not answer. The horseman rode slowly forward and stared questioningly down, first into the boy's face, then at the pebble he was clutching, and lastly at the patch of beaten ground. Suddenly he slid his hand under his robe and drew flashingly out a sword. Despite his terror at the sudden blade the boy noticed the heavy gems on the man's fingers and along the hilt of the sword. Then Ishmael realised that the sword had not been drawn to menace him, for the horseman, leaning forward, was reaching the point of the sword to the ground and scratching the earth. In a moment the coin lay gleaming in the moonlight again. Again he looked at the boy, this time more intently.

'You are from Khirbet-Samaika by Bethel?' he asked softly.

The boy nodded.

'So they gave you a piece of silver, eh? One Roman piece of silver for five Jewish lives. Pick it up. Yes, pick it up.' The boy did. 'Where are you going?'

'To Jericho.'

'Who is there?'

'My uncle.'

'Where is your father?'

'He . . . he . . . ' The boy broke into sobs and fell to his knees. 'He was one of those . . . ' he whispered.

'Enough, boy. Enough. Go on to that village. Have no fear.' He pulled off one of his rings. 'Here, take this.'

The boy reached up and took the gaudy jewel without looking at it, his eyes fixed on the dark, bearded face.

'Go to the back of the inn and wait until you see the innkeeper alone. Understand? Then show him that ring and he will know who sent you. He will give you lodging for as long as you wish, and when you want to go to Jericho he will see you safely on your way. Do you understand?'

The boy nodded and, still staring up at the horseman, began backing towards the road.

'But boy, take your goats. You can sell the herd to the innkeeper. Tell him that Barabbas says he must pay you two times the price. But don't keep my ring.' He smiled, showing all his white teeth in the centre of his black beard. 'I shall need that when I come back. Give it to the innkeeper to keep for me. But keep that Roman coin to remind you always of this day. When you get to Jericho it would be better to tell no one that you have met Barabbas. Not yet. Let it be our secret. But never forget the name. Say it!'

'Bar-abbas,' the boy whispered in his different dialect.

'Barabbas. Remember it always as the name of a friend. Bar-abbas the Zealot. And what is your name, boy?'

'Ishmael son of Uzziel.'

'Ishmael, "the one God hears". You are well-named. And your father too: Uzziel, "God is strong". You have seen your father Uzziel die today, Ishmael, but be assured that God *is* strong and that on the day the trumpets sound your father Uzziel will live again. When you reach Jericho tell them what you saw in the village today. Tell them so that . . . ' His voice fell as he quoted the words of the Sons of Korah, ' "Tell them so that they might tell it to the generation following" . . . Now go, with God's blessing, and never forget this day.'

Almost, the boy thought as he led his goats towards the village, the same words that the Roman general had said to him in the tent. But this man, this stranger in the night, was the one he would obey: this one had not tortured his father to death.

II

For almost two hours Pilate had not spoken a word. Severus and
Fabius, riding beside him, had twice attempted conversation, but
both times he had silenced them with a testy gesture, and on
another occasion, when a flurry of chattering and laughs among
the escort had become loud enough to reach his ears, he had flung
a thunderous frown backward; upon which Severus, with a discreet but emphatic wave, had commanded the escort to drop
further behind. This they had done, leaving only the standard-
bearer, a Palestinian auxiliary, silently and solemnly proud on his
first spell of this ceremonial duty, riding immediately behind
Pilate and his two lieutenants.

Severus was already accustomed to his master's spells of silence
when in the saddle, but what he found different today was Pilate's
lively interest in the surrounding country. Usually the Procurator
rode with eyes fixed implacably on the road ahead, head fiercely
unmoving, chin lifted and thrust out in a theatrically aggressive
pose as though he were on ceremonial parade between ranks of
submissive or hostile spectators. But today he was constantly
turning his head to look right and left of the road, sometimes
halting to gaze intently over hills and valleys. Neither Severus nor
Fabius could understand Pilate's absorption in a landscape which,
during this first stage of their journey north, was sadly mono-

tonous and almost deserted. Such settlements as there were, huddled between eroded hills, were depressingly meagre. Patches of thirsty crops thinning upward towards barren slopes were the only signs of dispirited attempts at cultivation. Small as these settlements were, they seemed too commodious for the few listless inhabitants who sat or lay around in poverty-stricken lethargy, until, when one came near to the villages, one saw that half or more of the mud-walled cottages were empty shells from which doors and furnishings had been carried away when their occupants left. On the further hills skeletons of abandoned farmhouses emphasised the atmosphere of a defeated country surrendering to advancing desert. Yet it was in this unpromising landscape that Pilate most frequently halted, and Fabius, although too bored by these ierruptions to pay particular attention, could not fail at length to notice that the points where Pilate stopped were where the road crossed dried-up wadis or circled derelict wells. On one occasion Pilate, his attention attracted by a cistern situated above a squalid village, suddenly veered off the road, spurring his reluctant stumbling horse down a slope of loose earth and gravel towards the cistern. The escort, startled from moody silence by this sudden diversion, pulled themselves into formation and galloped to catch up with him, circling in flurries of dust protectively around him as village women, who had been filling pitchers at the cistern and washing rags of clothing, scuttled away in terror to their homes, where, from the shadows of shabby doorways, they stared in suspicious fear at the soldiers. Only one man, the very oldest of the inhabitants, had the courage to sidle up to the nearest auxiliary and ask who the distinguished officer was and then hobble back to tell the others. A whisper of awe ran from door to door. Pilate, after looking for some moments at the water trickling from the cistern, stared upward towards the rock-choked gully which, by some miracle, provided the cistern with a slaver of water. Then he turned his horse and dug in his heels to make it climb back to the road.

By the time, just before sunset, they came within sight of the Vale of Shechem their road had transported them to kindlier scenes. Clumps of woodland, becoming richer and more extensive as they rode north, were visible on the hills, until, almost abruptly, the whole aspect of the landscape changed, and ahead of them they could see in the Vale of Shechem the mingling green and gold of fertile well-tended farms and gardens. At the head of the Vale the road divided. One spur ran north, a fine quick caravan route direct to Damascus. They took the other, leading north-west towards Sebaste and then down to the Plain of Sharon and on to the sea.

When, on the outskirts of Shechem, Pilate halted at that fountain revered by Jews as Jacob's Well, an elder of the nearby hamlet, recognising the Procurator, came forward to pay his respects. Pilate chatted amiably with him. Severus, linking their gestures to the few words of Aramaic which he could understand, gathered that they were discussing harvests and rainfall and water supplies. Even at the end of a long hot summer there was no lack of water here. The whole town of Shechem, sunk between ver-durous hills, was cool with the chatter of it, and the hills behind which the sun was sinking were abundantly green with terraced gardens and orchards and vineyards.

The escort, enlivened, after their monotonous ride, by this prospect of civilisation and the thoughts it conjured up of relaxation and urban pleasures, broke out into chattering which now went unheeded by Pilate. Giving only casual recognition to the salutes of soldiers who recognised his standard as he rode past the barracks of Neopolis, he spurred his horse to a canter for the last six miles to Sebaste.

When, suddenly and breathtakingly, the city of Sebaste came into view, high and white and glittering on the crest of mighty cliffs, it seemed to Pilate that the ambitions which had coursed unsubstantial as dreams through his thoughts during all that day now took on the brilliant edge of reality. Sebaste was a symbol of all that Rome had done for Palestine and a promise of all that Rome could yet do. Those who described the site of Sebaste as the finest in the world were not far wrong, and with what magnificent bravura had Herod the Great, under Roman patron-age, used the spectacular eminence! Reactionary Jews had maligned that king, accusing him of being a puppet set up by Roman paymasters, indifferent to racial pride and ignorant of Jewish tradition. But those fulminations had not deflected Herod from his policy of steering his kingdom towards the enlightened Roman way of life. When, fifty years ago, Herod had torn down the decaying capital of Samaria and built Sebaste on that high ridge, he had had the vision and the courage to ignore old-fashioned and barbaric forms. He had built his new city in modern Roman style. With high candour he had admitted his debt to Rome by raising here a noble temple for the worship of Augustus, of blessed memory, and giving the city the name

Sebaste, the Greek form of the name of that patron. Now there it was, Sebaste, noble monument to Augustus, ruler of the world, floating in the moonlit sky, its towers and arches and its awe-inspiring impregnable wall of white smooth native stone dominating and guarding with lordly and all-seeing Roman beneficence all the hills and valleys of Samaria. If the inspiration of Rome could set such a seal on Palestine, she could do even more.

With such thoughts, running so hot and urgent in his mind that the chill moonlight seemed to take on the warmth and gold of sunlight, Pilate rode up to the city. But there, as soon as he arrived at the governor's barracks, he was chilled by vexation and anger.

His arrival created inexplicable confusion. No heralds trumpeted his arrival; the auxiliary sergeant of the guard did not even recognise his standard; the governor, aroused from wine and dice, came hurrying out without helmet or even armour. Yet the man seemed to think there was no need to apologise for strolling forward in unstrapped leather jerkin, for he greeted the Procurator jovially with many expressions of delighted surprise at the unexpected honour of his visit. Yes, he insisted, the visit was utterly unexpected, and he responded to Pilate's sharp questions with an expansive boozy grin and assurances that certainly no courier had arrived. But he assured the Procurator that a dinner fit for a king – there were cooks enough and they were especially good – could be prepared in thirty minutes. Or, he added hastily, at least in under an hour.

Pilate curtly declined this offer. He wanted no dinner, he said, no ceremonial hospitality at all. Lentil soup and bread from the soldiers' mess would suffice for his supper. It would be served to him in his room: a quiet room, for he had work to do and an important meeting in Sebaste the following morning. At the thought of that interview he turned to Severus and ordered him to go immediately to the house of Josephus the Cohen. He was explaining to Severus how to find the house when the governor interrupted with a booming laugh. 'Oh, you can't miss it. Just outside the south gate. A big villa in grand gardens. Almost a palace! Old Money Bags has the finest house . . . '

'Quiet, please!' At last the rasp in Pilate's voice and the fury in his eyes penetrated the haze of drink sufficiently to silence the man, though not yet sufficiently to wipe away that loose-lipped grin.

37

Pilate turned again to Severus. 'Inquire if the courier went to the villa to announce my intention of visiting there tomorrow morning. Perhaps he misunderstood my instructions for him to come here also.' Pilate's irritation was exacerbated at the thought that his Aramaic might not have been exact enough to make such simple orders clear.

With surly deference the governor offered the Procurator his own room for the night; but after Pilate had inspected it and seen that it overlooked the courtyard and was within earshot of changing guards and the traffic around the entrance to the mess, he walked ahead of the governor to an inner court which he remembered seeing on previous visits. There he chose a room whose doorway framed a vista of terraces of olives; through this door came only a murmur, distant and soothing, of townsfolk gossiping in the squares of the populous city.

Fabius superintended the carrying out of the personal belongings of whoever it was who normally occupied the room and the bringing in of Pilate's desk and chest of scrolls; then, having arrived in civilised surroundings with Roman voices within earshot and decent kitchen-cooked food and Roman wine in the offing, he felt in more amiable mood and assumed the personal duty of helping the Procurator to divest himself of helmet, cuirass and greaves and disposing them to the best advantage possible on a chest. The governor strolled in accompanied by a slave carrying a jug of wine. 'No wine,' said Pilate with icy politeness; then, feeling that he could not suffer for a second longer the distasteful congested stare of one who drank too freely and guzzled immoderately, he turned away with calculated discourtesy, saying over his shoulder, 'That will be all. Good night!'

How right, he thought, had been his earlier judgement of this man! On his very first meeting with him he had considered him unsuited for his post. This governor was typical of those military men who finished up in colonial posts in positions of far more authority than they could ever be entrusted with at home. Cynical nepotism had resulted in this man, who was no doubt the despair of his family and others highly placed, being given a job far enough away from Rome where he could drink and bully himself to death without them having to endure the disgrace of his brutal and degenerate inefficiency. Pilate had made the attempt, after that first encounter, to have the man transferred to some place beyond his jurisdiction. But it was soon made evident that the man enjoyed powerful patronage. The imperial legate in Antioch had indicated that the Sebaste appointment had been made on recommendations from such eminent circles in Rome that they could not be lightly disregarded. Some time later Pilate had discovered that this wine-swilling governor enjoyed an advantage over and above those recommendations: he was related by marriage to the imperial legate's former mistress, now his wife.

Severus returned to say that the steward at the house of Josephus the Cohen said no courier had been to the villa. But the steward had conveyed the Cohen's compliments to the Procurator. Josephus offered the hospitality of his villa for tonight if he wished, but was in any case looking forward to the pleasure of his visit tomorrow. He had expressed the hope that the Procurator would join him for lunch.

'Fabius!' said Pilate. 'You will lead a search for the courier. Get something to eat quickly and go back. Take two men from the escort and some auxiliaries from the barracks. Go in some strength; at least twenty. Along the road make every attempt possible to find traces of the courier and the two auxiliaries. You know their names?' Fabius shook his head. 'You do, Severus?' Sevrus nodded. 'Good; give Fabius their names, as well as any particulars of identification which may help him to describe them. Question everyone you can find, Fabius. Rouse each hamlet. People talk more easily when they are dragged sleeping from their beds. Borrow a scribe from the governor and take statements. I should say that the likeliest area in which to discover anything might be . . . Where is my map? . . . Yes, in those unpopulated hills just north of the village we destroyed. That would be the kind of place anyone planning an ambush in daylight would choose. Further north, near Shechem, there would be too many people about, and friendly ones.'

Fabius was turning to go. 'Fabius! This is important. Should you find any culprits or suspects or any witnesses who are wilfully uncommuncative, bring them to Caesarea. Alive! Do you understand? Even if you find proof of any crime, you will not take any punitive action on your own. You have my authorisation only to make arrests. Those arrested will be handed over to Marcellus for interrogation. When your mission is complete, go to Caesarea by the shortest route. Good luck!'

'You think it was an ambush?' asked Severus when Fabius had left.

'Of course. What else could it have been? The courier was one of the most dutiful and loyal I have known . . . By the way,

Severus, find another one and have him leave for Caesarea. Immediately! The palace should be informed that I am halting at Sebaste tonight and shall be arriving tomorrow afternoon . . . Who's that?'

A soldier had slipped into the courtyard and stolen quietly towards the arched doorway where he was now taking up his stance. Moonlight laid etchings of silver light on his round iron helmet and on the high cheek-bones and arched nose of his fierce Semitic profile.

'Abdeel, sir, the standard-bearer. He was so proud of being picked out for that job that now he has volunteered to do sentry duty for you tonight.'

Pilate nodded approvingly, but then, 'Not *Abdeel*, Severus. *Abdi-el*. You must get more Aramaic. Give an hour a day to it. Only an hour, and you will find it coming quickly. You know what the Divine Julius did when he could not sleep? He spent the night hours musing on the inflexions of nouns and verbs.'

'Yes, sir,' said Severus, sure in his own mind that he would not be studying Aramaic inflexions tonight: he was near to sleeping on his feet already.

'Now!' said Pilate briskly. 'Where is the map? And the Jerusalem one, too. Put them on the wall there.' Pilate watched this being done. 'If you see the governor around, head him off. Tell him I must on no account be disturbed. Have a bowl of broth sent to me from the mess: lentil preferably. A hunk of good Jewish bread. And water!'

Severus had stepped only a few paces beyond the doorway when Pilate called him back. The Procurator was pushing his desk nearer to the map of Jerusalem. 'There will be lots to do when we reach Caesarea,' he said. 'I shall immediately need your personal assistance there in a confidential task. So you might as well take the opportunity tonight of getting rid of any backlog of work.'

Severus, wondering what work Pilate had in mind, said hesitatingly, 'Yes, sir.'

'A summary of my progress this fortnight,' said Pilate, impatiently because he had noticed the hesitancy. 'The number crucified, for instance. How many were there?'

'Twenty-one!' He must check that up, but he delivered the guess with sufficient conviction for Pilate not to question it.

The Procurator seemed well contented with the figure. 'Thirty-odd years ago,' he said loftily, 'Quintilius Varus had need to crucify *two thousand* after one Zealot revolt. It would appear that,

40

despite what critics may say, I am succeeding in pacifying this country! ... And make up the accounts, Severus. A full record: executions; casualties; necessary replacements of arms, armour, horses, men; all expenditure on food and fodder. And the bribes: don't forget the bribes, nor forget either to report to Marcellus the names of those who accepted them. Such people may always be of use again.'

Severus waited for a final dismissal, but even while he had been giving the instructions Pilate had opened the trays of his desk, lifted out papyrus, ink and pens, and begun writing. After a moment or two he became conscious of his aide still standing there.

'Good night, Severus.' He murmured it off-handedly, but as Severus was slipping away, he repeated the salutation, this time very firmly and loudly in emphatically enunciated Aramaic. 'And by the way, *Abdeel*, as you pronounced it, can mean donkey.'

'The old bastard!' muttered Severus, though not without affection, as he hurried across the courtyard.

Hours later Pilate was still at work, the lentil broth chilled to a cold mess in its bowl on the low table near at hand, and a half-eaten loaf serving as a paperweight on a stack of written folios. Only once or twice had he lifted his eyes to stare out through the archway at the hills beyond Shechem, now palely lit by a sinking moon, against which background the dark helmeted profile of the Jewish sentry lay proud and still as carved rock.

At a desk in the corner of a room above the guardhouse Severus had laboured for a time at the abacus.

'Fodder: forty-seven horses for twenty days, twenty-eight mules for twenty days ... ' A guffaw from the courtyard interrupted him. He walked on to the balcony and looked down. Auxiliaries coming off duty were fooling around. 'Quiet down there!' he barked. They lifted dark bearded faces, stared up for a moment, and then hurried off to their billets, silent enough until they were out of sight, and then he heard the murmur of their grumbling.

' . . . Twenty-eight mules for twenty days. That makes four hundred . . . five hundred . . . five hundred and sixty mules for one day . . . Now: bacon and lentils and bread, and wine . . . '

At last he had roughed out the totals. Enough! At Caesarea a scribe would correct his notes and draw them up neatly. He reached for wine, drank swiftly and thirstily, then rolled himself in his blanket and slept as deeply and satisfyingly as only the young, or soldiers, can.

Dawn came with bands of saffron light slanting over the hills beyond Shechem and casting sharper shadows over the courtyards and streets of Sebaste; but in one corner of the small courtyard the smoky light of a lamp still glowed. Pilate, tired now but with his face wreathed with satisfaction, had reached the forty-third paragraph of the draft of the memorandum he was dictating for the attention of His August Highness Tiberius Claudius Nero. Bugles sounding reveille roused him from his task. He looked towards the door and was surprised to see the sky already light and some of the higher terraces of vines and olives dappled with morning's pale gold. The rigid Jewish profile, now changing from jet to bronze in deepening sunlight, looked as though it had not stirred an inch all night.

Pilate breakfasted on milk curds and a loaf crackling warm from the oven, after which he requested the governor's attendance. The man arrived, looking as though he had suffered the bad and belching night which he deserved. But at least his armour was well polished. Actually, the governor had spent the night sitting on his balcony, trying to keep awake until the light in Pilate's room was doused, in case the bloody man might think of summoning him to his presence, but he had fallen asleep awkwardly on his bench, and when reveille aroused him was full of cramps and headache. He felt weary, but out of insolence or pride tried not to show it, assuming a manner of bluff alertness to indicate that he felt no embarrassment at the memory of being caught off guard and slightly tipsy the previous evening.

'Good morning, Procurator.'

Pilate nodded. 'I remember your telling me when I inspected the new barracks a year ago that they were the work of a Jewish architect mason.'

'From Tiberias, sir. The man who planned the conduits there.'

'That's the one! Is he still working here?'

'Yes.'

'A man of considerable talent, I should think.'

'Talent! With respect, sir, that word is hardly enough. He has more than talent. He's a genius. Although he's a Jew. In my opinion he's as good as, even better than, most architects you'd

42

find in Athens, or even in Rome for that matter. In fact, he'd do well in either.'

'He can, I hope, do better here in Palestine. There is no lack of opportunity for such gifts.'

'I agree. I wouldn't let him go. Oh no! I wouldn't part with him for a sack of gold.'

'I'm afraid you will have to. And without a sack of gold. Have him sent to Caesarea.'

'But . . . But Procurator, he's at work on the extensions to the hippodrome.'

'Oh, not immediately. I shall need him only as soon as he can hand over to someone else anything that he is doing at the moment.'

'I'll see to it. As soon as . . . '

'In about a week . . . And thank you for your hospitality. And for the breakfast. I do really think your baker is better than mine. But I'll leave you *him*. Good morning! Would you be so kind, as you go out, to tell Severus to come?'

On being told that Pilate wanted him, Severus bundled up his notes and tallies and carried them with him as evidence of having dutifully obeyed the Procurator's instructions. But Pilate did not ask for them. Instead, with a little yawn, he said, 'I shall be lunching with Josephus the Cohen and we shall leave for Caesarea immediately afterwards. You will eat with the escort and parade them outside the villa to await my departure. Meanwhile, I have still some work to do. I do not wish to be disturbed for two hours.'

When he was alone again, Pilate gathered the spread folios from his desk and, occasionally yawning, put them in numerical sequence, happily dawdling over the task and at times stopping to read contentedly a favourite paragraph. When the manuscript was in an orderly stack, he carried it over to the couch, and there made himself comfortable in order to luxuriate in the enjoyment of reading through the whole of his composition from beginning to end. But the warmth of the morning flowing into his room made him drowsy, and eventually he laid the mansucript tidily aside on the nearby chest just below the sun-glow of his propped-up cuirass. He had a restful day ahead: a meal and a talk with Josephus, and after that an easy forty-mile ride, downhill to the Plain of Sharon and on to Caesarea. So it would be well to use this moment of relaxation to sketch out in his mind some kind of agenda for the conversation he planned to have with Josephus.

That interview must be handled without precipitation and with considerable tact.

Quite apart from what he hoped to accomplish on his visit to the famous villa today, however, he was looking forward to an hour or two with the banker. Josephus was always an interesting man. His only fault was perhaps his tendency to make sly and usually bad jokes. Pilate enjoyed the camaraderie which had developed between him and the powerful financier. When, as occasionally happened, persons expressed surprise that a procurator could have friendly relations with a Jew, he reminded them of the many Jews who had earned and enjoyed the friendship of Rome, particularly the father of the present Tetrarch Herod, that Antipater the Younger whom the Divine Julius himself had honoured with the supreme reward of Roman citizenship for having fought for him so bravely and successfully at Pelusium and in the Delta. Well, if Josephus assisted Rome as much as Pilate now hoped, then Josephus too might earn the honour of Caesar's gratitude.

Certainly Josephus's conduct indicated admiration of Rome and the western way of life. Instead of retiring to his native Galilee, he had set himself up in the notably Roman city of Sebaste, accepting the heavily mortgaged villa as part-payment of the even yet unassessed debts of Valerius Gratus, and had become so much accepted as a member of Roman society that everyone now spoke his name in the Roman style, Josephus. Although embittered Sadducees and the like in Jerusalem were quick to sneer and say that there were other reasons why Josephus had not retired to Galilee. In a province notoriously infested with Zealots, those fanatics might have made short shrift of a Jew so outspokenly a friend of Rome. For Galilee was where Zealotry had been spawned. The first Zealot had been a Galilean, the mischievous rebel Judas, who had proclaimed that for a Jew to pay taxes to Caesar was an affront to the one true god of the Jews, and despicable servitude to the false gods of Rome, with the result that to this day Zealots judged it their sacred duty to harass the publicans, whose job it was to assess and collect taxes, and even on occasion to assassinate Jews who collaborated with Rome.

Josephus, however, was securely elevated high above such petty terrorism and his power was too immense to be shaken by local events. It was common knowledge that, although he had supposedly retired, his many sons, strategically installed in the chief commercial centres of empire, were still dependent on his advice

44

and obedient to his direction, and in a dozen cities of the world enhanced the wealth and power of their clan. Except the youngest son, Josephus's beloved Mattathias, who, with his father's blessing, had chosen instead to follow the family's rabbiniacal tradition and was pursuing scholarly research amid the fabulous 'twenty times ten thousand books' of the library of Alexandria, as well as constantly buying and bringing to Sebaste rare books for a collection which had become famed among scholars.

Josephus was indeed typical of those enlightened Jews whom one encountered in the great cities of the world; Jews who by their commercial energy and financial courage enhanced not only their own wealth but that of the commonwealth within which they operated, and who, powerfully entrenched as an indispensable condiment of an expanding trading society, used their vast fortunes, not in the ostentatious debauchery all too common among Roman millionaires, but in wise and almost anonymous patronage and philanthropy. Such Jews willingly collaborated with Rome. Though adhering still to their peculiar monotheistic belief, they could tolerate those who differed in religious faith, because they shared the same political faith, faith in the glorious future of the prosperous and orderly commonwealth of nations which the Divine Augustus had bequeathed to the world.

How different in that respect was Josephus from that stiff-necked Temple gang in Jerusalem! How different, for instance, from a man like Caiaphas, that speechless puppet decked out in high priest's robes! How different from that even worse character, Caiaphas's father-in-law Annas, that old snake of a politician who was the most difficult and most implacably Jewish of all! Although ousted from the supreme position of chief priest years ago, Annas still wielded a power immoderately great. It was plain to see that all the other ruling Sadducees, the whole bunch of the Sanhedrin which only by Roman clemency sat in solemn session to govern the religious and domestic lives of Jews, counted for less than this one Annas. Against such an inimical personage it was fortunate to have found an ally as powerful as Josephus.

And powerful Josephus certainly was, not in his ageing body, but in his coffers. That was the most important thing. Josephus was immensely rich. Probably the richest man in Asia. Really rich. Richer, for example, than Herod Antipas, ruler of Galilee. For after all, the wealth of that showy and effete tetrarch consisted only of palaces, estates, thousands of slaves, piles of gold plate, and chests of jewels and the like, all of which could be bundled up as loot in one swoop by invasion or revolt. But the wealth of Josephus could never be so disastrously raped, for it was dispersed throughout the world of commerce, working for itself and constantly increasing itself, and so inextricably woven into the fabric of empire that the public welfare of Rome and the private fortunes of Josephus the Cohen were indivisible.

Yes, if one of the worst things Valerius Gratus had done during his term as procurator was to allow Caiaphas, son-in-law of Annas, to buy himself into power as chief priest, beyond all doubt the best thing he had done was to get himself so much over the ears in debt that he had landed himself in the hands of Josephus, and thus brought the banker into the heart of Roman affairs in Judaea.

Lapped in such thoughts, Pilate at last fell into a contented doze, during which he dreamed of rivers and streams and arches and aqueducts, and after two hours awoke completely refreshed; by the time Severus appeared he had already bathed and put on toga and sandals. As the villa of Josephus was within easy walking distance he decided to go there on foot. He was setting out and had already given a stony farewell to the governor and was crossing the courtyard when a courier from Caesarea appeared. An important visitor had arrived on the post-boat from Brindisi and was awaiting him at the palace.

'Who?'

'Marcus Gaius Paterculus.'

A shadow fell over Pilate's sunny thoughts. Momentarily off-balance, he was silent for a moment, and then, 'From Rome?' he asked.

'I do not know, sir. From Capri, we thought.'

This was what Pilate feared. 'With family?'

'No, sir. Alone.'

Pilate dismissed the courier abruptly and turned to continue his walk towards the villa. Severus took the opportunity of halting the courier and asking in a hurried whisper, 'Has my wife arrived?' The courier did not think so. There was one woman visitor at the palace, a Roman matron of whom he had heard some gossip in the mess. But she, he gathered, was some relative of the Procurator's wife. Severus caught up with Pilate. The Procurator, who seemed to have been unaware that his aide was not beside him, walked on in silence. So did Severus. Each was deep in his own worries.

Severus was not only worried: he was also somewhat angry, as angry as so young a bridegroom can be with a bride he loves. He would have been at home with her now had he not, just when he was deciding to return to Italy, been unexpectedy promoted to be the Procurator's aide. So he had made arrangements for her to come out to Judaea and was looking forward to indulging her with the comforts and pleasures that his increased pay and perks now made possible. Why had she not come out at once? She should have hurried. She was seven months gone, perhaps more.

Pilate's preoccupations were just as disturbing, but more tangled and more political. At the centre of them was Marcus Paterculus. What might the aristocrat's unheralded arrival portend? Had he come with wife and family it might have been possible to think that he was making a voyage of pleasure. But no! Tourist jaunts round the empire were becoming increasingly fashionable, but it was impossible that a Paterculus would think of taking a holiday at this moment. Now that it was clear that Tiberius Caesar was determined to stay permanently on Capri there would be in Rome too much jockeying for position for Paterculus to leave the capital for even a day, for surely it would be to the certain advantage of this son of Gaius Velleius Paterculus, favourite subordinate officer of Tiberius during his early campaigns, to stay in Rome while new dispositions of power were being made.

No, there seemed to be only one explanation for the visit, and the arrival of any friend of Tiberius was always suspect as another example of Caesar's increasing habit of insinuating into every corner of empire men who, although they conveyed fulsome expressions of Caesar's goodwill, could be described only as Caesar's spies. And now that Tiberius was marooned – yes, marooned was the word, even though the exile was of his own desire – now that he was marooned on that lump of rock in the Tyrrhenian sea, Caesar must be feeling ever more acutely the need for spying eyes and listening ears. A Paterculus, of course, would never stoop to the level of the common informers, that numerous tribe of odious creatures whom Caesar used so abundantly and whose merest whispers could weave the strangler's cord for the noblest and most innocent neck. But, at a higher level, Paterculus could certainly be used to report to Tiberius his opinion, and always such an opinion as Tiberius wanted to hear, on Caesar's servants abroad.

Yet, not so fast! There was another possibility, and the thought of it was so comforting that Pilate's step lightened. After all, he and Paterculus had one most significant attribute in common. Paterculus was an intimate and favourite of Sejanus, Prefect of Rome. And Sejanus was Pilate's own patron; indeed Sejanus was the very man who had had Pilate appointed procurator in Judaea. With such a patron, what had Pilate to fear? It was unlikely that venom even from Capri could harm a protégé of Sejanus who, as commander of the Praetorian Guard and with the voices and votes of a submissive Senate at his command was, in Caesar's absence, second in command only to Tiberius himself. After all it could be that Paterculus had come not as a spy of Tiberius but as an emissary of Sejanus to convey cordial encouragement from the prefect. If so, then his arrival at this moment was most fortunate, for Sejanus no less than Tiberius would surely look favourably on the plan now burgeoning in Pilate's mind, the plan to irrigate the parched and crumbling tracts of Judaea from which despairing and impoverished farmers were drifting away into the towns.

Thus, by the time Pilate reached the villa he had brushed away much of the disquiet which had assailed him when he first heard of the patrician's arrival. Now he found the news acting as a stimulant, a timely spur pricking him to keener appreciation of the importance of this morning's talk. Now he must be prepared to go further and more quickly with Josephus. He must be prepared to take, sooner than he had planned, the risk of inviting the banker fully into his confidence in man-to-man fashion, to put his cards on the table, to unbend, to ingratiate himself with his powerful ally.

The villa was situated in one of the choicest spots in Sebaste, its pavilions and gardens occupying the whole of a natural terrace just outside the southern wall of the city but within protective sight of the barracks. The banker, being a Jew, was not standing in the portico, Roman style, to welcome his guest, but his steward was there, demonstrating in his elaborate oriental courtesy the graces he had learned in service at Herod's court. This functionary ushered Pilate, with Severus following some steps behind, across the entrance-court towards a garden of a gentler and more secluded character than that of the formal gardens around the principal part of the villa, and Pilate realised with pleasure that he was being led towards that wing of the villa where Josephus entertained only intimate friends. The private garden was traversed by a grove of cypress through which Pilate glimpsed a profusion of rhododendron and azalea and hibiscus. Further beyond were small plantations of pomegranate, and beyond those, at the furthest limit of the garden, a frieze of fig trees, their bas-relief of silvery limbs and suppliant hands espaliered against a sky of palest blue. At the end of the cypress-grove was an arcade, beyond which Pilate descended three shallow steps to the terrace. These immensely long steps were little short of miraculous: they ran almost the entire width of the terrace, yet each one was a monolithic unflawed slice of yellow Numidian marble. At the southern end of the terrace, surely the most beautiful retreat in all Asia, was a balustrade along which noble urns overflowing with blossoms framed a succession of views of the hills beyond Shechem, each view a vignette of exquisite perfection. Through shadowed arches to left and right of him could be seen mosaic floors, painted and gilded woods, richly sombre rugs and hangings, and the Etruscan mirrors of Josephus's private apartments. The air, captive under a green and sun-dappled ceiling of vines, and odorous with lilies and sun-warmed vine, was refreshingly cooled by the splash of water falling into a central pool where carp grew fat and succulent. One of the first things Josephus had done when he took over the property was to remove from the centre of the pool a statue of Poseidon, which, although it was the beautiful and deservedly renowned work of a Delphian sculptor, was an inadmissible 'graven image' in the household of a Jew. Yet, in sensitive appreciation of the Grecian character of the supporting columns, Josephus had been at pains, when seeking a substitute for the statue, to find something appropriately Hellenic and, being always just that little less rigidly orthodox than his fellow Jews, had eventually commissioned from Mallia in Crete a magnificent bronze sufficiently stylised not to offend Jewish eyes, though if anyone particularly censorious did choose to recognise it as vaguely representing a winged lion, he would admit that at certain angles it could possibly be seen as vaguely reminiscent of one of the lions of King David's throne.

On hearing his visitor approach, Josephus, who had been bending over the pool and crumbling bread for his fish, straightened up and walked towards Pilate. Sun and shadow dappled his white cap and his hair, which flowed from it snowy white but still enviably thick, as he passed below the vines holding his hands outstretched and palms upward in a lavish gesture of openhanded welcome. He halted however, momentarily nonplussed, when Severus came into view, marching behind the Procurator, stolidly upright with his plumed helmet grandly displayed in the crook of his arm. When Pilate presented Severus to Josephus, the banker ceremoniously welcomed them both in Greek, then added in an undertone the Judaic formula for greeting guests.

Josephus was a tall man. Indeed, for a Jew he was singularly tall. Had it not been for a slight stoop of age he might perhaps have been as much as a hand's-breadth taller than Severus. So Pilate, under pretence of wishing to examine the famous bronze at closer quarters, edged away and mounted the steps to the rim of the pool, and stayed at that elevation until Severus, after exchanging civilities with Josephus, took his leave.

Pilate and Josephus settled on to couches in a shady recess beside a table of yellow bevelled marble already laid with food. By the standards of the abundant hospitality for which Josephus was renowned, the food was simple, but, he explained, he had felt that the Procurator would prefer a simple picnic over which, unhindered by servants parading a succession of hot dishes, they could discuss whatever subject was the reason for this unexpected but welcome visit. He shifted to one side the bowl of Egyptian roses which interrupted their view of one another, waved his hand over the array of chopped meats, pickled fish, cheeses, eggs, fresh and dried fruits, sweet chestnuts, almonds and wine, and invited Pilate to choose any delicacy he wished.

Josephus, now that they were alone, now that the young soldier – how formidably serious he had been! – had departed, regained the smile that he had beamed upon Pilate on his initial appearance. Pilate responded. The atmosphere, with no servants around, apart from a wine-steward within easy call, was suitably intimate and relaxing, and Pilate found himself increasingly at ease in the presence of a host on whose face geniality and goodwill were so rosily apparent. Yes, indeed, how different this Josephus was from Caiaphas and Annas and their priestly kin! The faces of those Jerusalem Sadducees were etched with all the miseries and rancours of their racial history. With eyes narrowed and lips compressed with bitter memories and corrosive resentments, they looked as grey and dull as their books of law. But Josephus was cosy and expansive, his face ruddy, like the face of someone who had lived always in sunlight all his life, or in the glow of a generous oven. Whereas the only light that ever flickered in the eyes of Annas was the glint of malevolence, the constant light in the eyes of Josephus was the light of joy.

Josephus slid across the table a flat, freshly baked loaf on its wooded trencher. Pilate smiled across at his host. 'This morning,' he said, 'I had the best bread I have ever tasted, even in Judaea.'

'Who's the baker?'

'That I shall not tell you,' said Pilate, pouring icy-cold water from its jug of thickest earthenware. 'If I did you would be buying him.'

'But I know,' said Josephus. 'The baker at the barracks. He was the best baker in Sebaste. But then by a most unusual coincidence . . . ' He bent his head until he was peeping at Pilate through the lowered fringe of great white eyebrows, a pose he always adopted before one of his mischievous jokes. '*By a most unusual coincidence,*' he repeated, 'he was conscripted for military duties. So he now bakes for the governor. Were you comfortable at the barracks? I should have been delighted to entertain you here.'

'Thank you! But it was desirable to give the governor the honour,' said Pilate with a pinched smile. 'You know him, of course?'

'I have made his acquaintance, yes. But he made it obvious that he did not care to strengthen it. I fear he resents the fact that a Jew has acquired this modest piece of property. He doesn't take kindly to the idea of a *Jew* living in a *Roman* villa. But . . , ' He flung back his head and laughed ' . . . there are Jews in Jerusalem who are equally peeved by it!'

Pilate withheld comment. The crisp manner in which he tore some bread from the loaf indicated that conversation about the governor was closed.

'Take some wine, Procurator,' invited Josephus. 'But you must! It was opened specially for you.' He pointed towards the amphora standing on a tripod sheltering from the sun's rays in a niche. The clay stopper had been prised out, and some wine from the amphora had been strained into the wide-necked two-handled decanter of Phoenician glass which Josephus now proferred. Josephus was notoriously eccentric about wine. He did not look on wine as did most people, as merely a convenient accompaniment to food. He was one of those odd people, and Pilate knew a few Romans who had similar affectations, who cultivated what they called 'a taste in wine'. One of the hobbies of the old man's supposed retirement, along with such extravagancies as collecting Egyptian and Etruscan bronzes, ancient red-figured pottery from Apulia, amber from the Baltic and rugs from India, was that of tracking down selected wines in every corner of the Empire. Rumour had it that he had in his cellars no fewer than ten thousand jars.

'This is from Sicily, Procurator,' Josephus said as he poured some into Pilate's goblet. 'A Potitian. So named after its original grower.' He held the goblet up so that Pilate could admire the clarity of the wine against the light. Indeed, it was like peering through an enormous ruby. And it was typical of Josephus, thought Pilate, that the goblets were of carved crystal. Nothing so base as silver, nothing so vulgar as gold for this epicurean.

'It looks good,' agreed Pilate.

With a proud smile Josephus put the goblet before his guest and poured wine into his own. 'Potitian is one of the Mamerines grown near Messina.'

Pilate, after adding a good measure of water, sipped. 'It tastes good, too.'

Such words were hardly indicative of a knowledgeable palate, so Josephus reached to the amphora and flipped the leaden tag on the neck to show Pilate the date of the vintage. 'The same year . . . ' But dare he repeat the joke he had tried out quite successfully on Valerius Gratus some years ago? He peered under his white eye-brows. 'Laid down in the same year as Augustus Caesar.'

The deep creases at the sides of Pilate's mouth deepened as he pursed his lips. 'Not laid *down* in that year, Josephus. Elevated,' he said, though so dryly that it was impossible to tell whether the words were intended as a garnish to the banker's joke or a rebuke.

Josephus feared that he might have strayed a little too far into irreverence. Himself, he had long ago escaped from any fear of the Deity. Indeed, he was now on what he felt nodding terms with his God, and, after all, the God of the Jews was a far more terrible Being than any one of the plethora of minor deities which Greeks and Romans had dreamed up to populate their rather childish theisms. But perhaps he did sometimes go too far along the road of thinking that God, far from being invariably terrible, might be given the credit for occasionally having a sense of humour. And these Romans, he well knew, could sometimes be touchy about the divinity of their Caesars. So, seeking for something to say which would mitigate against his *faux pas*, he added hurriedly, 'But a noble wine is worthy of a noble anniversary. What was it Horace said? "Oh, jar of wine, born when I was born, worthy to be brought forth on a glad day." ' Pilate seemed to relax again. 'There is spring water or sea water, whichever you wish. We could not provide snow at such short notice, but the wine was chilled overnight in the well.' So that, thought Pilate, could well be the reason why it seemed to be somewhat insipid. Like any military man, Pilate preferred a grog. 'But, tell me,' insisted Josephus, 'how do you find it?'

'Excellent.'

Josephus savoured his delightedly. 'Of Italian wines, I find this more to my taste than your famed Falernian or even that favourite of Augustus Caesar, Rhaetic. I have also acquired some Ligurians. Very fine, but . . . Of course perhaps it is my Jewish taste that is at fault . . . but they are too resinous for me.' Ah, thought Pilate, perhaps lack of resin was what made this wine so tasteless. 'So,' said Josephus, 'I decided on a Memertine for today. Appropriate for you, Procurator. For as you will certainly know, Julius Caesar spoke of it so highly.'

'Indeed!' And after that, on his host's insistence, Pilate was persuaded to taste some of it with as little as only one-third water.

'I was delighted to have news of your coming,' went on Josephus. 'So was Mattathias, my youngest son. You have not met him yet.'

'He is here?'

'Indeed, yes. If he does put in an appearance before you leave, I hope to have the pleasure of presenting him. But, this morning . . . ' Again that mischievous stare from under white eyebrows. 'This morning he is very occupied.'

'Among his books?'

'Books! Books might be around, but for the moment . . . ' Josephus laughed again. 'He was married only two days ago. A charming girl. A delightful daughter-in-law to gladden these old eyes. And so well-matched for Mattathias. She has claims to be . . . What strange changes happen nowadays! Women are liberating themselves from domesticity. Even among Jews, abroad but also in Judaea and Samaria, you find girls and women who are thinking of vocations, actually planning careers. My son's wife shows signs of being a scholar. I imagine such a mother and father could raise a whole tribe of historians. Which makes me think of your son, Procurator. I always remember . . . ' He smiled with affection as he recalled the scene. 'I always remember the time you brought Julius here, and we suddenly realised we had been talking for an hour or more and he had slipped away. You were sure Julius was stealing fruit or up to some mischief, but we found him in the library buried in history books. How is he?'

'Still at university in Athens. I get good reports.'

'Then we really might see him a historian.'

'I hope something more. I had rather my son created history than merely recorded it. A general perhaps, who will write, if he writes anything at all, commentaries on his campaigns.'

Josephus peered under white brows. 'A father is happier when he does not farm out his own ambitions to his son. I speak from the rich experience of many sons. But if Julius has military ambitions, then would it not be more useful for him to learn his craft here in Judaea with his father?'

'When he is older. I would wish Julius to be with me, of course, for not only do I love him, but also a son benefits by the presence and example of his father. But I am too often either engrossed in state affairs or away from Caesarea, and if he were alone at home he would be in danger.'

'Danger?'

'Yes. The danger of too much domestic feminine influence. It is not desirable for a boy to be alone with his mother most of the time.'

'But,' said Josephus, 'Rome is renowned for its great mothers. Cornelia, the mother of the Gracchi; Atia, mother of your Emperor Augustus; and, of course, the mother of the Dictator Julius himself.'

Pilate smiled slightly. 'I am afraid that my beloved wife, the Lady Claudia, talented though she is, is hardly cast in so heroic a mould as those three ladies.'

The expression on Pilate's face gave Josephus the impression that once again he had trespassed too far into personal Roman sentiments; so, after drinking more wine, he asked, 'And now, Procurator, to what do I owe the pleasure of this most welcome visit?'

Pilate did not answer immediately. The words he had prepared were the better for being tossed off lightly, after a smiling hesitation. 'I suppose,' he said eventually, 'mine is the usual reason for a visit to the Cohen.'

Preparing a laugh, Josephus flung back his head. 'Money?' he asked, and the laugh came dead on cue when Pilate nodded.

'But not to ask for it,' Pilate said quickly, suddenly thinking with some embarrassment of the still unravelled tangle of debts, personal and public, of Valerius Gratus. 'Not as yet. At the moment I am seeking only financial advice.'

'Now what does poor old Josephus know about finance?'

It was Pilate's turn to laugh. '*Poor old* Josephus knows more about money than anyone else in this country. Not only how much there is, but *where* it is. By all accounts not half a shekel can drop in the sand without Josephus hearing it. That is why I come to seek the advice of Josephus. And, I hope, his collaboration at a later date.'

'Advice! If my advice is of value, Procurator, it is always at your disposal. As for my co-operation . . . well, that is limited only by a few shekels in my purse.'

'I have in mind a certain project. It is one which will need money. A lot of money. Perhaps even more than those few shekels Josephus has in his purse.'

'What is the project?' asked Josephus, and before Pilate had time to reply, asked, 'Building? I guess it must be. That or new roads. The two passions of the Romans.' As Pilate was about to speak, Josephus restrained him with a genial wave of his hand. 'Don't misunderstand me. Rome has done some fine building in this country. Any sensible Jew has to appreciate the cities the Herods have built with Roman aid, but . . .'

'Cities!' Pilate broke in. 'I am thinking of something bigger than cities. I want to build more than a city: I want to build a country. I see no longer any need for more grand palaces and temples and gymnasiums and theatres. I am not planning to give Judaea more monuments: I am planning to give it new life.' Pilate paused. Josephus settled himself to listen. He was pleased to see how Pilate's manner had completely changed. Now that he was speaking on a subject which had captured his enthusiasm, he was no longer a buttoned-up stickler for Roman and military proprieties. He was expanding, speaking with less caution. 'I envisage a scheme not of private glories, but of extensive public works. I see possibilities of making Judaea one of the richest and most prosperous provinces in Asia. I want to make its deserts bloom.' Pilate waved his hand towards the prospect of verdant hills. 'All Judaea could become as rich and beautiful as that. But to become so the country needs a scheme of irrigation planned on a scale only possible by national enterprise.' He paused. 'However, I shall not go into details at the moment, Josephus. Later I shall show you some plans and sketches. But in essence my project is for a series of acqueducts, a grid by which water, which now runs to waste down useless ravines, can be carried on acqueducts to irrigate the dry and at present increasingly deserted valleys of the south.'

Meditatively Josephus poured wine. He drank it this time without adding water. At last, 'I admire your ambition, Procurator. It is visionary, and, I believe, practicable. But . . . ' He shook his head. 'But, I imagine, the money needed would be immense. What would be necessary would be long-term investment. That, I fear, will not attract anyone at this time.'

'Why not? There must be scores, even hundreds of men with money stacked away: men as rich as . . . as rich as . . '

'As rich as Josephus, eh?'

'If that were possible. Surely they would see that the possibilities of future profit were vast?'

'*Future* profit! There's the rub. With the way money is going nowadays, constantly decreasing in real value – in short inflation – financiers are not attracted by *future* profit. They know that ten shekels today will be worth only two in a few years' time. That makes them chary about investing, unless, of course, you can offer them a ruinously high rate of interest. As much, for example . . . ' Again that mischievous glance under the white eyebrows. 'As much as your compatriot Brutus asked of the people of Salamis when he lent them money. Forty-eight per cent, wasn't it?'

Pilate, with a wry smile, nodded.

'But, seriously,' Josephus went on, 'too many of us have capital already tied up in places like this: in Sebaste, in Tiberias, in Caesarea, in all the new cities. So nowadays, if anyone has any fluid capital at all, he doesn't look for more long-term investment: he wants short-term investment. He wants small profits, but quick returns. Trade and shipping; buying and selling; importing and exporting: day-to-day profit.'

Pilate sat silent. He tried not to frown too heavily, but Josephus could see how vexed he was at the slightest hint of opposition to his scheme. Obviously this typically grandiose Roman project was very dear to him.

At last, 'If the financiers will not help,' said Pilate, speaking very slowly, 'there is one alternative. Taxation!' Josephus pursed his lips and shook his head. 'Why not?' snapped Pilate. 'The people will benefit and profit by it eventually. They must be persuaded to see that.'

'*Persuaded?* Rome does not usually persuade, Procurator. Rome usually commands.'

'And justly so, Josephus. Have no doubts. If necessary it will be commanded. But commands are more readily obeyed when people can be persuaded that the commands are framed for their own good.'

56

'Jews do obey, if they are able to do so. But taxes here are already too onerous. The total of Roman and Jewish taxes is near to crippling. Twenty-five per cent! I have long thought that for the sake of poorer people there should be some reform towards a progressive and fairer tax. As it is, taxation falls equally, and thus inequitably, on rich and poor alike. Present taxes are as heavy as most people can stand.'

'Tax-payers always say that. They say the same throughout Palestine. And in Greece. And in Egypt. As well as in Rome.'

'Yes, one thing tax-payers never can stand is taxation. But you have to realise that Judaea is still a poor country. No, what I really mean is that it is still a country of poor people. I admit that the Roman administration has raised the standard of living. But a higher standard of living costs money, and the small farmers and country folk are just about scraping the barrel. That is the cause of what is one of the most disturbing things happening in Judaea today: the drift to the towns. They can only scratch a meagre living in those hill villages. Any extra demand is the last straw, and they give up their holdings and they come into the towns in the hope of a better life. Some of those little people are so poor that they are hard put to find even their half-shekel every year for the Temple. Tithes on crops and cattle; tithes even on the few handfuls of herbs they grow at their doors; tithes on cumin and mint ... '

'And dues for every little deed of their daily lives,' broke in Pilate. 'Half-a-shekel to the Temple as a thanksgiving for any haphazard piece of good fortune or family luck. Half-a-shekel as a bribe against heavenly punishment for some trivial human sin. Half-a-shekel for shew-bread. Even half-a-shekel *for circumcision*! Every shekel going to the Temple so that men like Caiaphas and Annas can grow fat!'

'I haven't noticed much fat on Annas,' said Josephus with a laugh, and even Pilate forced a smile. 'But, Procurator, the tithes you mention are sacred dues. The Jews who pay them do so as an act of faith. They are paying them not to Annas but to God, and they are prepared to render unto God the things that are God's. But then comes Caesar demanding payment of other taxes: taxes on houses and land and fruit trees, on fishing-boats and carts, on cattle and salt.'

'For which they get good value: sound administration, law, good roads and ports, increasing trade ... '

'Yes, yes, Procurator. Sensible Jews would agree with you there.

And sensible Jews try to pay for such things. But can they pay more?'

'Perhaps they would need to pay no more at all if the taxes they do pay were not whittled away by the corruption of the tax syndicates and the local collectors. The publicans who assess the taxes and collect them are often no better than petty thieves. How much of the taxes farmers and townsfolk pay rub off on to those hands before it reaches the treasury? What is more, townsfolk and farmers and villagers have only the vaguest idea of the eventual destination of the taxes they pay, and no idea at all of what is done with the money when it reaches that destination. But if they were paying for an aqueduct irrigating their own valley, if they could see something being done within sight of their own homesteads, then surely they would gladly pay.'

'An idealistic idea indeed, Procurator. You young Romans . . . Forgive me, Procurator. I mean no offence. But one of a race so ancient as mine, a race that can remember the time when Rome did not even exist, tends always to see Romans as a young people who have suddenly erupted on the scene. And your ideas seem also surprisingly youthful and new. Such a system of decentralised taxation as you have suggested, local taxes for local needs, does seem to me to belong to a future that can be achieved only after a radical, indeed revolutionary, change in methods of government.'

'Decentralisation could begin in the centre, Josephus. That is not contradictory. What I mean is . . . well, take Jerusalem. In one place in that city is immense treasure which could be used and *should* be used for the good of the people of Jerusalem.'

If these words indicated what the banker suspected, then, thought Josephus, danger threatened. Anything tending to encourage such thoughts had better be avoided. 'You have asked my advice, Procurator. I am bound to say that if you raise taxes at this moment, or introduce any new ones . . . if you are going to add water taxes to, for instance, the road taxes which Jews resent . . . you are going to have trouble on your hands.'

'Trouble with the Zealots? I have the measure of the Zealots by now. I can contain them.'

'But, Procurator, what if new taxes create new Zealots? As you know, it is not because of lack of money that Zealots refuse to pay taxes. They refuse because they believe it is a sin to render unto Caesar. Now ordinary everyday Jews do not think so. Sensible Jews recognise that good government must be paid for. But . . .

58

and this is the important factor . . . if you are going to demand from those law-abiding Jews more than they can pay, if it seems that Caesar is making them poorer than they already are, then even they will begin to listen to the Zealots. In short, you would risk furthering Zealot propaganda and thus creating more Zealots.'

'Not if law-abiding Jews can see immediate benefit. One aqueduct for Jerusalem, only one, could make that city one of the most prosperous in the Empire. The few gardens and orchards you see around the city now could be extended for miles. Wouldn't the people of Jerusalem, for instance, rather have a decent water supply than more gold on the Temple domes? They have been building that place for fifty years now. How many thousand builders did they anoint as priests to work on that monument? So many that there are merchants in Jerusalem who have made fortunes mass-producing sacerdotal robes for builders' labourers!'

Josephus shook his head gravely. Again Pilate was coming close to dangerous thoughts better left unspoken. 'If you ask such questions in Jerusalem, Procurator, you will be reminded that the Temple is being raised to the glory of God.'

'And some would tell me that it is being raised to the glory of the Herods. Those are people who would rather have fresh water at their door than an altar for Herod. It is a case of first things first.'

'To a devout Jew,' said Josephus softly, 'the first thing might be a Temple to the Lord.' He looked grave, but then, attempting to lighten the atmosphere, he ducked his head and peeped under his brows. 'Indeed, I imagine that the economic misery endured by the poor and the social unrest it engenders encourage them to sacrifice to God what little they have left after they have paid their taxes. Probably they believe that religious salvation is the only hope for the future. In short, if you risk making them miserable in this present life, they might listen with dangerous fervour to any preacher who promises them something better beyond the grave.' He poured wine into Pilate's goblet. The Procurator laid his fingers around it, but did not drink. Deep in thought, he gazed at the wine, swirling its ruby light in the dappled sunlight, and then said in a whisper, 'Yes, there is a logical way of raising money.'

'What way?'

Pilate looked up quickly, as though surprised that he had spoken his thoughts aloud. He shrugged the question aside, and attempting a joke, said, 'I could always increase the tax on imported wines.'

Josephus laughed heartily. 'Of course! But Josephus will shed no tears. I have enough laid aside to see me through. Ten thousand jars! So people are fond of saying. Josephus cannot count.' But even as he laughed he was wondering where Pilate's thoughts were leading. To Jerusalem obviously, as his next words revealed.

'Jerusalem seems prosperous enough. As busy and crowded as Rome itself.'

'With the advantage of a better climate,' said Josephus. 'Though I haven't been for almost a year. Really, I get lazier and lazier. I need a change. I must stir myself beyond these walls.'

'I should like you to visit me in Caesarea.'

'Now Caesarea is just about far enough for my idle bones. I owe a visit to an equally idle friend of mine there and could stay with him.'

'I should be honoured to entertain you at the Palace.'

'Tut, tut, Procurator!' Josephus raised his hands in mock horror. 'That would be asking for real trouble. What would be said if it were known that I were living with Gentiles? I am in ill favour enough with the orthodox even for drinking wine like this, wine made by Gentile hands.'

'Of course,' said Pilate with embarrassment. 'Forgive me. I had forgotten . . .'

'Oh, there's no need for excuses, Procurator. I am notoriously careless about such matters. One out of every seven of those eggs on the table was probably laid on the Sabbath. And you cannot know how my mouth waters at the temptation of eating the products of your Gentile kitchen.'

'We have Jews working in the kitchens.'

'No doubt. Though I wager that every time they go off duty they ritually purify themselves. But I am sure I should not be defiled by calling at the Palace on business and paying my respects to you and your lady.' Josephus, still curious, steered the conversation back to Jerusalem. 'Did you see many people in Jerusalem?'

'I did not entertain. I never left the Antonia. I was working all the time. I saw Caiaphas, of course.' He made a sour face. 'But that was merely procurator and chief priest discussing routine matters of state.'

'And what had Caiaphas to say?'

'Nothing!' The grin dawning on Josephus's face became wider

when Pilate continued, 'Annas did the talking. There were moments when it did seem Caiaphas might speak, that an answer to one of my questions was rising up his throat and might reach his lips. But when he realised he was on the brink of actually saying something, he turned to father-in-law, and of course it was Annas who spoke. Always Annas. The old pigeon-fancier!'

At that Josephus laughed outright. Pilate's nickname for Annas was a neat one, encapsulating as it did the whole scandal of the deal Annas had made with the Temple to sell the 'sacrificial flesh' of his own pigeons.

'He's still finding sufficient doves,' said Josephus. 'And cleaning a pest from his estates at the same time. I suppose you know what a plague doves are in Galilee. There is actually one valley called . . .'

'Yes,' interrupted Pilate. 'I've heard of the Vale of the Doves. But that country of Galileee seems to be a place rich in plagues: if it isn't doves it's Zealots. Does trouble always begin in Galilee?'

'They're a tough people up there, I agree. Those are the kind of people, Procurator, farmer and fisherfolk, who are ripe for causing trouble if taxation stings them. Remember, Procurator, it was Rome's attempt to make an economic census in Galilee which gave rise to Judas the Galilean and fourteen years of assassination and war.'

'If Annas would only snare Zealots and put *them* in crates,' said Pilate sourly. 'Then he would be doing a greater service to his people than selling a brace of doves for every circumcision.'

'Doves are easier to net than Zealots.'

'And easier to recognise! But a Galilean! A Galilean can always look as meek and mild as a dove, but ten to one he has a Zealot dagger under his robe. But why is it, if Annas hates Zealots, he is not more friendly to Romans who also want to see the end of them?'

The sigh with which Josephus met this question was not, as Pilate might think it was, a sigh at the impossibility of answering the question. For that was easy to answer. Annas was anti-Zealot. As a Sadducee, a man of the Law, he had to be. But Annas was a Jew; the Zealots were Jews; Pilate was not. It was as simple as that. No, the sigh was conjured up at the thought of the western innocence of these Romans. Pilate's question showed how sadly inept these simple souls could be when confronting the complexity of eastern politics. They came starry-eyed from the West, a new and infant nation, technologically clever, full of ideas of reform, passionate in their ambition to show the decadent old-fashioned East the Roman way of life, but they were altogether too ingenuous, too young to grasp the ancient and tortuous wisdom of the East, a wisdom fabricated by centuries of racial inheritance and racial prejudices. Indeed, these Romans were not even conscious of what race really meant. To them race was something that could be assumed by law and contract and oaths: like, for instance, making Herod a Roman citizen and thinking that by so doing they had wiped away all traces of his Jewish forebears and Jewish culture. They could not grasp the fact that people could not be changed by the stroke of a pen, particularly people of a culture that was centuries old at a time when Romans were still being suckled by wolves.

But he could not say that now. He would have to know Pilate for a long time before he would venture to insinuate such thoughts into him. Instead he said, 'You must always be cautious with Annas. He is the power. He is not only father-in-law of Caiaphas. There is that son of his, Eleazar, who was also chief priest, and two others already entrenched in the Sanhedrin.'

'Yes. Jonathan and Theophilus.'

'And another two sons, Mattathias and Annas the Younger are being trained as high priests.'

'A family concern,' commented Pilate. 'Typical Pharisees,' he added with a sour smile. This smile was against himself. 'Do you remember that mistake of mine: when I first described Annas as a Pharisee? I know better now.'

'I suppose it was Procurator Gratus who minsinformed you. He was notoriously careless, or not sufficiently interested. He never could get his Pharisees and Sadducees right. But, poor man, that is probably not all that surprising. Jewish politics can be difficult even for a Jew to unravel. No, certainly Annas never was at any time of his life anywhere near becoming a Pharisee. Annas is a typical Sadducee; a born conservative. He could never, like a Pharisee, believe in demons, angels and life hereafter. Nor be content, as a Pharisee is, with the promise of glory when he is resurrected: he wants power here and now on earth. He doesn't trust in holy promises: *he wants it in writing*.'

But Pilate was by now hardly listening. The heat and the peace and, probably, the wine had lulled him into a dreaming mood. Silence enwrapped them, until, far away, the single cry of a bird engraved the air, and amid the roses, the buzz of an insect embossed the quiet, upon which he roused himself, stood up and paced towards the balustrade. 'This view, Josephus,' he said over his shoulder, 'reminds me so much of a certain view in Tuscany. Oh, the colours are different; the flora is different; and, indeed, the temperature is different. But the view has the same shape. And the villa in Tuscany, oh, not like this one, a far more modest retreat, looks out on to it at about the same height.'

'Your home?'

'Not yet. But I hope to acquire it. For my retirement.'

'Retirement! I imagine Procurator Pilate would find retirement dull.'

'The time will come when I shall be tired of work. Then those who come to me will not be suitors and officials: they will be dear friends. I imagine myself sitting with them on that terrace, sharing my view with me.'

'And with your family, of course.'

'Ah, Julius! But by then he will be one of the big world. His visits will be precious.'

'It is hard to imagine Pilate as a simple country gentleman. Won't you miss politics, state affairs, high position?'

'I hope not.' Pilate laughed softly. The laugh was against himself. 'I hope to remain known, of course. I hope that travellers passing through the valley may point up to my roof and say, "There lives Pontius Pilate, one time Procurator of Judaea." ' He turned urgently to Josephus. 'Well, to achieve such fame I must, must I not, make some mark on history here? I must do something for which the name of Pontius Pilate will be remembered.'

Josephus was struck, even disturbed, by the fervour of ambition which came into his visitor's eyes at that moment.

'You will be remembered for your acqueducts, Procurator,' he said gently teasing.

'I could have worse fame,' said Pilate smugly, and then, preparing to take his leave, thanked Josephus for his entertainment and advice. As they walked through the gardens, he repeated his invitation to Caesarea. Josephus promised to come.

Severus was awaiting Pilate in the entrance court. The escort, the standard-bearer at the head, was drawn up in formation outside. On the head of the standard were the brazen features of Caesar. Tolerant though Josephus was of the customs of other peoples, he did find graven images of this kind somewhat distasteful. He was not so rigidly orthodox as to consider it sacrilegious to copy God's work, but he did feel it sacrilegious to make mortal and not very creditable gentlemen into gods. Well, each man to his taste, and he had to admit that the Romans did allow other races to practise their own faiths, and in Judaea they showed sufficient regard to Jewish susceptibilities not to display such 'graven images' in God's Holy City of Jerusalem.

He took genial leave of his guest and then walked back to his terrace where slaves were already clearing the table. He snatched a chunk of bread and crumbled it for the fish. He was not a bad fellow, this Pilate. As procurators went he was certainly better than his lazy predecessor. But he was so very Roman. Not very subtle. Rather brash in fact. Like all his fellows from that prosperous energetic go-getting western world, he lacked the sophistication which only the heritage of ancient culture could give. Yes, there was only one word for it: ingenuous. And being ingenuous could always be dangerous.

As they rode out of Sebaste, Pilate said, 'It was not twenty-one we crucified, Severus. It was twenty-three.' And did not speak again until they reached the Vale of Sharon.

III

In the golden light of afternoon the Plain of Sharon stretched hazily before them. The sheep on the hillside pastures and the cattle beside the streams were fat, contented, half-asleep. Farm cottages stood ankle-deep in lavish herbs. Villagers, lounging at doorways and wells shadowed by oak and cedar, gazed without alarm or curiosity at the Procurator's cavalcade. Some even waved. People and landscape alike were placid and amiable. No farmer nor shepherd here would carry a dagger under his robe, nor was there here any sign of that drift to the towns of which Josephus had spoken.

A clever old man, that Josephus. He had, of course, the deficiencies of age. That laugh of his: it came too loud and too easily. But that was the way with some old folk, and assuredly much of the cunning which had built his vast fortune must surely remain in that old head. He was worth keeping sweet for the sake of that wealth and for the influence he still could exert on equally wealthy cronies. The hint had been dropped, the seed had been sown. Josephus would brood over what had been said and pass it on to others. Josephus had not refused aid; he had said only that it would be difficult. With so cautious a financier that was near to acceptance.

At the village at the crossroads near Caesarea their horses were slowed to a walk amid crowds in the market square. A rabbi, recognising Pilate, detached himself from the group at the well and stalked across to greet him. The tall proud young fellow smiled confidently up at Pilate, and the villagers stood around, watching the encounter with genial interest.

'Welcome back, your Excellency,' said the rabbi in passable Greek.

Pilate replied in clearly enunciated Aramaic and heard appreciative murmurs from the onlookers.

'Your Excellency!' The rabbi placed his hands together in exaggerated pose of humble supplication, but there was friendly candour, no trace of timidity, in his voice. 'Can one ask when the work at the palace will be finished? We need our men back at the village for the harvest.'

'If you would send us good builders and plumbers instead of saboteurs, rabbi, the job could be finished tomorrow,' said Pilate. The rabbi and the others laughed. The party moved on amid smiles.

Just beyond the village two auxiliaries were sent galloping ahead to inform the palace of the Procurator's approach. Caesarea and the sea came into view. Pilate halted, as he invariably did at this spot, to gaze on the grandiose and beautiful prospect. From the eminence on which the Temple of Augustus Caesar was poised like a glittering crown, tiers of marble and limestone buildings, white and orderly, stepped down to a magnificent harbour lively with shipping: fishing-boats darting out beyond the mole to a sunset sea, huge merchantmen loading and unloading the produce of empire at the docks, and graceful triremes and quinqueremes of the navy. The breakwater, one of the wonders of the world, had transformed what had once been but a primitive settlement on a wasted coast into the finest and safest harbour in the East. Two hundred feet wide and up to twenty fathoms deep, it was ennobled by massive towers, the loftiest of which was named Drusion in honour of the stepson of Augustus. Herod had devoted twelve years to building this city, which was now the capital of Judaea. The cellars of Caesarea, even its drains, had been engineered with as much care as had the arcaded and terraced Temple, theatre, amphitheatre, baths and palaces above ground. And beyond it all lay the Great Sea, the centre of the earth, that sea which Rome had tamed to a lake, on whose shores, north, south, east, and west, the Empire flourished.

Pilate, filled with pride that his authority as Procurator should be represented by a capital of such magnificence, stayed gazing at the inspiring prospect until the auxiliaries came back from the city, leading at an easy canter the caparisoned horse he was to use for his entry; a short-limbed, broad-chested but noble beast, its hide freshly polished for ceremonial duty. It trembled slightly, as though stiffening with pride, when Pilate mounted, stared haughtily around and pawed the ground with imperious impatience. Pilate handed his helmet to an auxiliary. The man flicked a rag over it, breathed on it, polished it gently, and then combed the plumed crest before placing it back on the Procurator's head. Another man dusted the Procurator's cuirass and greaves. Pilate rubbed his signet ring in his palm. Among the ranks, soldiers straightened their jerkins, buckled and tightened straps, polished hilts of swords, and then moved into processional position. At last all was in order and the cavalcade moved off towards Caesarea, leaving behind it asses and porters and baggage carts, which would follow much further behind so that their bulky clumsiness would not detract from the martial grandeur of the Procurator's entry.

Pilate, holding his chin high and thrusting out his lower lip, stared implacably ahead, the hand which held the reins disposed in such a way that the gold signet, catching the light of the westering sun, was boldly displayed. So blank-faced he appeared that those who watched him pass might have thought he saw nothing, but actually he was savouring the approach to the city, delighting in the way in which, as they came nearer, it unfolded to his gaze its separate noble buildings. Severus attempted a similar military posture, but his eyes roamed over the shipping in the port, seeking the familiar lines of the packet from Brindisi. Tonight, or if he were not free tonight, then certainly at dawn tomorrow, he would make an offering at the Temple to beseech a safe voyage for his wife and his unborn child.

The cavalcade entered the arcaded avenue which cut through the heart of the city to the port. The evening crowds fell back, left and right, and gathered in archways to watch the arrival and to stare at Pilate's profile. The horse, drilled to press its way without shying through the pressure and noises of the most tumultuous crowd, also showed only its profile to the spectators lining the route and occasionally flared its nostrils in imperial disdain.

The crowds were mostly Greek, and many of them workers from the dye-works, their forearms stained with expensive Caesarean purple. But there were some Jews, easily distinguished from the others by their tight-fitting cotton caps and the horizontal stripes at each end of shawls which they wore like cloaks. The atmosphere was urbane and relaxed, very different from the tetchy and sometimes threatening atmosphere of the alleys of Jerusalem. Indeed, Caesarea had the ambience of any city in Italy or Greece. The vista of sea beyond and the flow of foreign merchandise through its streets recalled such Roman ports as Ostia and Brindisi. As for the palace, formerly the palace of Herod but now the praetorium of Pontius Pilate, Procurator of Judaea, that grandiose complex of arched entrances and sweeping staircases populated with statues was as majestic as a corner of Rome itself, and on Pilate's appearance the helmeted sentries on the esplanade stiffened to such immobility that they looked like Roman statues carved from gleaming brass and walnut.

The escort wheeled away towards the barracks as Pilate, Severus close behind, rode through the arch of the principal gateway into the main courtyard, paved with marble and surrounded by porticoes, and as thronged as the square of a small but busy city. In one portico a queue of people waited outside the tax offices; in another a bunch of suitors were demanding appointments with the administration; in a quieter one scribes and other members of the secretariat could be seen bustling from office to office. On Pilate's arrival, the murmur of voices faded away and a hush fell over the scene. Everyone stopped in his tracks to watch Pilate and Severus ride towards the arch leading towards the Procurator's household quarters, and slaves who had been washing mosaic paving slipped out of sight until the Procurator had entered the archway to the inner courtyard.

At the end of that archway Pilate was forced to a sudden halt. He could ride no further. Access to the inner court was cut off by a mound of rubble and paving-stones lying before his horse's feet. He stared into the court with a deepening frown. The place was in even worse disorder than it had been when he left Caesarea almost three weeks earlier. Since that departure a ditch had been dug diagonally across the whole court, and at the far end of this ditch a gaggle of labourers were lowering clay pipes and mixing mortar. Pilate dismounted. To cross the ditch he had to step on a plank serving as a temporary bridge, and beyond that he had to find a path between stacks of new bricks and pipes before he could reach the foot of a staircase which, breaking into two monumental curves, rose grandly to the arcaded terrace of his apartments on the first storey. The lowest step of the stair, a gigantic slab of marble, had been wrenched away and was leaning askew on a mound of gravel nearby. A labourer ran forward with a spade and hurriedly battered a pile of clay into rough shape for Pilate to use for reaching the second step. Having gained that spot Pilate swung round, and, spotting among the labourers the foreman builder who was bending over the far end of the ditch and instructing the pipe-layers, he sent the labourer to tell the man to come to him. The foreman, still bending, glanced over his back and waved acknowledgement of the command, but then turned his face again to the workmen and was another minute giving them further instructions before he straightened up and, shaking his head in a pantomime of exasperation, walked unhurriedly and sulkily towards the Procurator, wiping sweat and dust from the back of the hand in which he was clutching a creased and mortar-splattered plan.

'What is going on here?' demanded Pilate, pointing to the ditch. 'Is that for the water pipe?' The man nodded. 'Why is it crossing the court? This court is to be planted as a garden. My instructions were that the pipe should follow the line of the wall. Where is the architect?'

'He said it couldn't be done, sir. Not near the wall. Unless he altered the whole line of the building.'

'Nonsense. A mere hand's-breadth.'

'Yes, sir.' The man sighed. 'But he found that a line following the wall would take the pipe through the central-heating ducts we put in last year.'

'Then it could be laid deeper: under the ducts.'

'No, sir. Further down there's rock, supporting the retaining wall. If he cuts into that he will have to divert the water supply for the gardens. If he diverts the water supply, the orchards will need a separate irrigation canal. If he builds that, then . . . ' The man scratched his chin with the rolled plan.

'Then what?'

The foreman shook his head. 'Then . . . I don't know, sir. But there *was* something else.'

'It seems, Pontius,' a woman's voice said from above, 'that if you want that water-pipe moved, you will have to change the whole face of Judaea.'

Pilate looked up. His wife Claudia was leaning over the balcony at the far end of the arcaded terrace. She smiled down and waved. He nodded towards her, the frown still on his face, and turned to the foreman. 'How long would all that take?' he asked.

'With local labour!' The man shrugged elaborately. 'In Rome you could do it in four days. But here! I'd say three weeks.'

'It will be done more quickly, or someone will suffer. Find the architect and . . . No. Severus, you go. Tell Lucius I want to see him in an hour's time. With all the plans.'

His wife's words nagged him as he mounted the stairway. Her interrupting, in the presence of slaves, was unseemly. That too aristocratic accent of hers gave her words a tinge of mockery, the more so because what she had said seemed all too true. 'Change the whole face of Judaea!' Indeed it would seem more simple to do that very thing than to knock this one stubborn building into Roman order. The fact needled him, deflating the grand visions he had entertained today and inflaming his resentment of Claudia's intrusion. Already he could feel cocooning around him the entanglements of domesticity. They reduced his stature. Imprisoned amid home and family and in the presence of a wife who was familiar with every wrinkle of his skin and had witnessed him in every ludicrous posture of human passion, a Procurator could all too easily become but an ordinary man naked of the trappings and dignities of high office. By the time he had reached the top of the stairs he felt that gnawing digestive pain which always nagged him when he tried to damp down irritation. He belched.

His wife's tire-woman was hurrying along the corridor with the alabaster box crammed with pots and jars of liniments and pomades and paints.

'Lucia! Inform the Lady Claudia that I have returned. I shall await her in half an hour.' He swung abruptly in the other direction and marched into his own quarters. There the Negro had already filled a foot-bath with hot herb-scented water and was laying out a freshly laundered toga. He turned to welcome his master. A huge smile spread over his face, but Pilate's answering frown closed that tongueless grin.

'Find Polygnotus. Immediately.'

The big black body slid silently from the room, and, unaided, Pilate began unbuckling his cuirass. Warned that Pilate was in a testy mood, the scribe came in quietly, tablets and stylus at the ready.

'A note, Polygnotus, presenting my compliments to Marcus Gaius Paterculus. By the way, where is he?'

'In the tower apartment, sir. The Lady Claudia thought . . .'

'A note presenting my compliments to him and asking him to

70

attend on me an hour before dinner. Here. Alone. Have my chest of papers sent up immediately. And have the Young Barber come . . . as soon as you can find him.'

By the time Claudia appeared Pilate had washed and changed into fresh loin-cloth and toga, had drunk a whole beaker of pomegranate juice and water, ridding himself of the dust and sweat of the journey and the acidity of Josephus's wine, and now felt so much recovered that his sense of irritation with her had utterly gone. He rose and kissed her on the cheeks, and then, holding her at arm's length, looked her over appreciatively.

'We have a visitor,' she said.

Yes, she had dressed herself with even more than special care. A fillet of gold instead of the usual silk bandeau was threaded in her hair which was piled in a pyramid of close-packed curls – the fashionable style, though Pilate did not care for it. It tended to make her appear slightly taller than he, which was ridiculous, because she was a finger's breadth shorter; rather tall for a woman. However, the hair-style suited her long face. Her ear-rings, collar and pendants were all of emeralds. He wondered if he had seen them before. Emeralds seemed somewhat too cold against her whitened skin, but those which lay against the purple of her knotted scarf gleamed luxuriously.

'Yes, I have heard about our visitor. You put him in the state apartment.'

'*Him?* Oh, you mean Paterculus! Yes, I thought the tower the best for such a grand person.'

'Yes,' agreed Pilate. 'And he will be saved the necessity of having to cross the courtyard and risk breaking his neck in that drain.'

'And more convenient,' went on Claudia, 'because he brought so many slaves.'

'How many?'

'Eight, I think, as well as a huge escort. I don't know how many guards. The guards are in the barracks, but among the slaves in the tower are his secretary, his body-servant, his librarian, and a Greek architect.'

'An architect?' She nodded. 'Are you sure? Why an architect?'

'It must be that he is studying architecture. He has a whole chest of books. All ten volumes of Marcus Pollio.' Then, as Pilate silently pondered over this news, she went on, 'But the visitor I am talking about is a visitor of our own. A house-guest.'

'Who?'

71

'Sextia!'

'Sextia!' Claudia smiled at his exaggerated consternation. 'But
. . . but it seems only days since she left.'

'Five months.'

'But she was going on a tour of the Empire. At least, so she
said.'

'Yes. She's been. She is on her way back to Rome.'

'I did not know the Empire was so small. I could wish it were
ten times greater.'

'You don't appreciate my sister . . .'

'Sister-in-law,' he corrected her. 'And not even that since her
last divorce. *Former* sister-in-law.'

'Sextia is so kind. She thinks of everything. She has found a
teacher to help Julius with his languages. She bought him in
Alexandria. It cost her a lot: he was a librarian there.'

'Has she already sent him to Athens?' Pilate asked quickly.

'No. She has him waiting in Alexandria.'

'Good! I had rather see my son's tutors before they are
appointed.'

'And she brought me these,' said Claudia, fingering the
emeralds. 'She bought them from one of her agents in Carthage.
They had been his wife's. She brought you a gift also: a charming
oddity. A troop of elephants.'

'Elephants? Did she drive them herself, or ride on them?'

'Ivory elephants. She bought them in Sabratha. They were
carved in Fezzan; most ingeniously, from a single tusk.'

'Is she well?'

'I've never seen her better. She is in tremendous form.'

'Worse and worse.'

Claudia laughed. 'She has been very good company. And I was
glad that she was here when Paterculus arrived. She knows him.'

'Is there anyone she does not know?'

'And she has been entertaining him.'

'In bed?'

'Pontius!' she exclaimed, pretending to be shocked, and happy
to see him in joking mood. 'You always make Sextia out to be
so . . . so . . .'

'Yes. *So!* And she is.' He heard footsteps and saw his master-
of-works and architect, attended by the surveyor, crossing the
anteroom. 'Lucius is ahead of time. Or you are late?'

'It is I who am at fault, Your Excellency!' Her curtsey of mock
obedience offended him. Often when she indulged in this play-

acting, affectedly emphasising her aristocratic accent, he found himself comparing her with his first wife. That woman had never put on airs and had spoken humbly and only when spoken to. 'Yes, it is I who am late,' Claudia went on, 'but on your account. Because of your arrival I had to alter the kitchen roster. Some of the slaves cannot work after sundown this evening.'

'You should know by now that Jews cannot work on their Sabbath. Or won't. You could do with a higher complement of Greeks in the kitchen. Or Gauls or Germans.'

'Please! Not Gauls or Germans. They are insensitive with food. And dirty. Nor would you, Pontius, suffer any but a Jewish baker nowadays, would you?'

Her smile attempted to coax back his good humour. He did not return it. 'Did you see the women they brought yesterday?'

'Only two were suitable. One is a baker's widow, incidentally. The other will be good later. She's pregnant.'

'That one! Why choose a pregnant woman?'

Conscious of Lucius awaiting him Pilate only half listened to Claudia's characteristically enthusiastic description of the woman: a ladylike person, intelligent, speaking good Greek and belonging to a religious sect into which she had been baptised.

The last word caught his attention. 'Baptised! By that wild man whom Herod beheaded?'

'No. By some other prophet, apparently.'

'You must be cautious, Claudia. The woman is a Galilean. She will have to be interrogated.'

'Not while she's pregnant, surely?'

'In that condition she might speak before the lash touches her.'

Claudia Procula made a gesture of distaste. 'If she is to be questioned, you should do it. Without whips and things.'

'I am afraid the Procurator has not time to devote to questioning slave women,' said Pilate stiffly.

'Well, then please give the Procurator's lady credit for some judgement in such matters,' she retorted and, swiftly slipping away from the subject, said, 'Shall I ask Sextia to come along? She's eager to see you.'

'There's no hurry, Claudia. No hurry, so far as I'm concerned. How long is she staying?'

'That depends. She is not taking the boat she came on. She is waiting for one of her grain ships from Alexandria.'

'Never could grain be more urgently awaited,' said Pilate. 'But just now I have Lucius waiting; then the barber; and I want an hour before dinner with Marcus Paterculus.' He pushed her towards the door. 'However, present my compliments to your sister-in-law, your *former* sister-in-law, Sextia, and tell her I shall be indescribably charmed to receive her in half-an-hour.'

They had nearly reached the door to the anteroom when he halted her. 'By the way, Claudia, it is not in keeping with the Procurator's lady to make jokes about Judaea in the presence of slaves.' Not until she was half-way along the balcony did she realise what joke he referred to.

'Go in, Lucius,' said Pilate to the waiting architect, then turned to shout to the Negro along a corridor, 'Find the Young Barber right away.'

Before the barber boy appeared Pilate had become somewhat reassured. Lucius had explained that the laying of the pipe would not prevent planting the court with trees and vines and flowering bushes. The pipe was being laid in a brick tunnel high enough for men to crawl through, so that they could inspect it and keep it in repair without disturbing the garden.

At this stage they were interrupted by an invasion, one slight boy filling the whole room with the noise of his singing and the flash of brown limbs and white teeth and flowing black hair as he capered around, a silver bowl full of water dexterously balanced on one palm and a cloth enfolding razor and scissors in the other. This was the Young Barber. He was known by that title by all Romans in the palace, for Pilate was the only one who could get his tongue around the cacophony of syllables that built up the boy's Edomite name. Perhaps for that very reason this pretty scamp could always win an indulgent laugh from the Procurator. He was allowed almost unlimited licence. Pilate had even agreed, although the boy was a bought slave, to pay for every haircut and shave as though the boy had a barber shop of his own, and Pilate paid at the rate he would have paid in any Roman tavern. Of course, the Young Barber was still only a child, and could be treated as such. About the same age, Pilate was thinking while he watched the boy caper around, as that little Jew whom Fabius had dragged into his tent yesterday morning.

'Come on!' said Pilate. 'Quickly. And stop singing! I am busy.' When the boy came within reach he grabbed a handful of the long silky hair. 'You've still got that,' he said with mock severity. 'When are you going to cut it off and become a Roman?'

'Roman! Bah!' The boy stuck out his tongue. Smiling, Pilate leaned his head for the shears.

'There would probably need to be one manhole near the centre of the water-course,' went on Lucius. 'But it could be camouflaged. A circle of bushes, perhaps. Or a statue.'

'Or something better,' said Pilate suddenly. He leaned forward, though he had to lean back again when the young fingers authoritatively gripped his chin and pushed his head into its former position. 'A fountain! What is easier? Above the water-course itself! With a statue of Poseidon. There's the very thing stacked away in Sebaste, looking for a buyer.'

'How tall?' asked Lucius, looking at his plan. 'It needs to be pretty big to have any effect in that large area.'

'It is big. And a famous piece too.'

Lucius nodded. 'That solves it. A beautiful idea!'

Pilate smiled contentedly. The boy's fingers delicately pressing and massaging ahead of the well-sharpened shears had a delightful soporific effect. 'And building the tunnel, you say, would take less time than following the line of the wall.'

'Oh, a lot less.'

'Well, it must be done quickly. Severus will fix up the details about the statue and have it brought.'

When Lucius left them, the boy began chattering. He was a born barber: full of gossip, and most of it scurrilous. He was still telling his tales when he had finished with the hair and was dampening Pilate's jowls for the razor. Pilate let him go on. The boy's chattering was no more intrusive than that of a sparrow, and probably no less bawdy, and Pilate's thoughts were not interrupted until he heard a man's laugh in the anteroom. He glanced round. Ah, he always made the same mistake. It was not a man: it was Sextia.

'I'm here, Pontius,' she growled. 'Don't mind me. It won't be the first time I've seen a man shaved.'

'From the next chair, I suppose,' said Pilate. And then regretted the words. Not that such reference to her shadowy upper lip would offend her, but because indeed it would amuse her, and he regretted having betrayed himself into that inane game of tossing insults back and forth which was common in the Roman society she frequented.

She slumped herself inelegantly on a couch, and her brocaded dress bunched up stiffly, showing her sinewy ankles. The boy, scraping away at the hairs behind Pilate's ears, fell silent; not because he knew too little Latin to understand what was being said, but because this strange lady awed him. The boisterous self-

75

confidence with which she sat down in the presence of a man without a by-your-leave made her fearsomely different from the modest women of his own race.

Pilate, swivelling his eyes to peer between the boy's hands, stole glances at his wife's former sister-in-law. How on earth, he wondered, and he wondered the same every time he saw her afresh, had such a monster managed to ensnare three . . . no, now *four* husbands, and to retain even after divorce their jovial friendship? Certainly they had not married her for money. In fact, each one of her husbands had been more vulgarly rich than his predecessor had left her. It was, of course, possible that these plutocrats had queued up for her because of her proved ability to manhandle vast fortunes into even vaster ones; to wave a wand over two boats and transform them into a fleet of grain ships; to buy anything, it could even be a crocodile from the Nile, for one dinar and sell it for a hundred. One thing was certain: it was not physical charm that had enslaved her suitors, for she was positively ugly: black-browed, almost moustached, and short. Though short was not quite an exact description. He had once described her to Claudia as half a big woman and half a small. For her body was that of a dwarf and her legs those of a giantess. The girdle she was wearing at this moment accentuated this disparity: vividly coloured and ablaze with a king's ransom of gems, it shamelessly drew attention to the fact that her waist was under her chin. And when viewed in profile she seemed to have just the suspicion of a hump. Yet despite those woeful handicaps she had attracted men by the score: not only four husbands but a whole bevy of whispered lovers. She throve on scandal. Perhaps one could not believe that she had attended Games dressed as a man, but it was common knowledge that she frequently went alone to private houses to dine with men who were not even relatives. In short, she was that deplorable thing, an emanicpated woman: a would-be Clodia, a symbol of that permissiveness which was eroding the morals and the decent severities of the Augustan era. Some argued that emancipation of women was but a reaction against earlier Augustan conventions. Surely it was the other way round. Emancipation of women was one of the root causes of the present degeneration of society. Why, only some thirty years ago Augustus Caesar had considered adultery sufficient reason for banishing no less a personage than the wife of his heir Tiberius. How was it, thought Pilate, that Tiberius Caesar could suffer conduct which to his predecessor and tutor, the Divine Augustus, would have been anathema? Could it be that, among the reasons for Tiberius retreating to Capri, was his distaste for the evidence of decadence which must continually assail him in Rome? Though, if that were so, it would have been more honourable for the Caesar to stay in Rome and apply himself to the labour of cleaning up the mess. In forty-four glorious years as Caesar, Augustus had moulded society to the sober dignity of his own noble mind. It was sad to see that grand morality being eroded under the rule of a lesser . . . With sudden disquiet Pilate saw the trap into which his thoughts had led him. 'Enough!' he said sharply to the Young Barber who had now for some minutes been lovingly massaging cream into his chin and cheeks. 'Enough! You'll have me as scented as a dancing girl! He pushed the lad away.

'I see now,' said Sextia, 'why the Procurator risks baring his throat to a Jewish razor. You use the boy for practising your Hebrew.'

'Aramaic, not Hebrew,' said Pilate, and then in Aramaic explained to the boy what Sextia had said, particularly her comment about throat-cutting. The boy laughed and pointed the shears at Pilate's throat; then shook his head and, pretending more serious purpose, pointed them at Pilate's body, directing the blades to that position below the ribs where he had seen the red spot.

'Off with you, you rascal,' Pilate ordered, but the boy, after folding his instruments in a towel, waited until the Procurator had taken a coin from a box on the table and tossed it to him. 'Add that to your fortune, Ephir. At this rate you'll soon have enough to buy your freedom.'

'Ephir? What does that mean?' asked Sextia.

'It's his name. Ephir Iphthahel Bar-Hadad Oholibamah!' Pilate found his way through the syllables with relish.

'A big name for a small boy,' said Sextia.

'It tells his whole lineage and geography. It means the gazelle, the first-born, the son of a god, born of an Edomite clan. Ephir, gazelle, for short.'

With an indulgent smile Pilate watched the boy caper out and, still smiling, listened to the young voice impudently breaking into song in the anteroom and fading away along the balcony.

One of the few things Sextia liked about Pontius was his affection for young people. He would be a more agreeable and perhaps a more successful man if he could be as warm and understanding in his relationships with adults.

He turned to face her, and she sensed he had difficulty in retaining his smile. 'You are back sooner than we expected,' he said. 'I hope you enjoyed the tour.'

'As much as I expected. Which wasn't much. Interesting, though, in patches. Gaul: unspeakably dreary, except for Vienne. The theatre there was doing a Plautus season. Vulgar as vulgar: really delightful. Mauretania was pleasant. Lovely people. I bought one of them. A dancing boy. You must see his act before I leave. Incredible.'

'There are few occasions here for acts by dancing boys,' Pilate said stiffly.

'More's the pity.'

'You visited Carthage, I hear.'

'Horrible! More and more prosperous, and I had useful talks with the wheat merchants. But provincial. So, *so* provincial. Even worse than here. Perhaps that's because Carthage has even more governors' wives and soldiers' wives than Caesarea has.'

Now the attempted smile had completely collapsed. He was sitting staring at her with what she called his buttoned-up look. If only the man could be warmly angry for once instead of merely stony! She tried her best.

'Colonial wives are death,' she went on. 'All of them flailing sharp elbows to get to the head of the queue for a crumb of Roman gossip. Hungry as hens chasing corn. They peck it up and chew it over, then gabble it out at their dreary dinners as though they've just brought it back from a week-end in Rome.'

'I take it that you did not care for Carthage?'

'Ugh! Alexandria was fun though. Lecherous. But awful food. And they smell. The men as much as the women. I suppose it's the climate. Damp. Like a steam bath. I got a cold. Though even with a streaming nose I was chased.' She chuckled throatily. 'There was always one man at least with his foot pressing under the table. Probably they were trying to get their own back for Cleopatra. The library's marvellous, though. And it's not just a monument. Alexandrians certainly do read. That Jew Philo is all the rage at the moment. They lionise him. Romans as well as Egyptians. One hour with him makes you think Romans are ignorant. It was he who put me on to a tutor for Julius. Did Claudia tell you?'

'Thank you, she did. But I have reservations about the idea. Julius's course at Alexandria has already been planned.'

'Yes, but he'll need a mentor. Some intellectual company outside the gymnasium. The young man I've found is brilliant. Actually he is Greek, of quite a good family. But, unfortunately for them, they backed the loser. I mean they fought *against* the Dictator, so they were sold into slavery. He knows every eastern language one can think of.'

'My son will not be short of tutors, Sextia.'

'I guess not. But he might as well have the best. I can afford it. I can afford anything for Julius. Anyhow I'm paying the fellow to wait until Julius needs him. He's charming. He'll win any boy's heart.'

Pontius frowned. 'I cannot say I find that altogether a satisfactory recommendation.'

'Have him brought over, Pontius, and vet him yourself. I know he'll take your fancy because he's done two translations of the *Commentaries* already.'

'Interesting.'

'Yes. It is.' She hesitated. She must make sure of warning the Greek about that invented tit-bit, but she hoped it had put Pontius into good humour for another thing she was eager to propose. She thought it had. 'I'm looking forward,' she said casually, 'to seeing Julius when I get to Athens.'

'I do not want his studies interrupted.'

'But he'll be almost at the end there now; packing up.'

'He'll be some weeks in Athens yet.'

'I know. That's excellent. I plan to take Claudia with me.'

'Claudia! To Athens?'

'Yes. I haven't told her yet. But I'm sure she would love to see Julius.'

'She will see him when he comes home from Athens, on his way to Rhodes. He is going to Rhodes for rhetoric, before Alexandria.'

'Is that what he wants?'

'It is what he *needs*.'

The coldness offended her. 'What are you trying to make the boy, Pontius?' she asked seriously.

'A true Roman, first of all, Sextia,' he said, holding his head high. 'In the *best* sense. After which he can decide his future. Though I hope he will be a worthy son and continue my work, here or elsewhere.'

'I hope he'll do much more than that,' she retorted savagely and, despite a stare stonier than ever, continued, 'I hope to see him something better than a provincial governor.'

79

'Can I, as his father, ask what?'

'An artist. A poet.' He grimaced. 'Yes. Not just a soldier or politician dealing merely with today, but someone who could mean something for all time. Julius has it in him, Pontius. He has inherited Claudia's brains.' She waited, but even in the face of that Pilate only shrugged. 'Anyhow, what is worrying me more at the moment is Claudia. She needs a change. She's too young to be cooped up in this dead-end with a pack of colonial housewives. I'd like her to go on to Rome with me.'

Pilate flushed with anger. 'I had rather Claudia stayed in what you call this "dead-end" than join the company you keep in Rome. Or, from what I hear, in Baia.'

Sextia slapped a knee and laughed. 'You mustn't believe half you hear about goings on in Baia. Most of it's wishful thinking. Midnight orgies on the beach and such like. They're dull, deadly dull. A trip to Rome would give Claudia something to do, something to freshen her up a bit.'

'She has plenty to occupy her time with, here.'

'Looking after you? I suppose that's what you mean by plenty to occupy her? Organising kitchens. Getting dressed for colonials. A woman like Claudia wants more out of life than that. I warn you, Pontius. One day, if you try and keep her locked up like an Augustan matron, she'll suddenly break out and do something foolish.'

'Like you?'

She guffawed at that. It was a pleasure to hear some edge in his voice. 'No, not like me. Claudia's not my type.'

'It's comforting to know that.'

'She is like me in only one respect. We both take after our frustrated mothers. My mother consoled herself with wine and men. Like me. When she cut down the former she had more time for the latter. But when Claudia's mother retreated from that dull senator husband she retreated into endless reading and writing. If she hadn't died so young, the gods alone know what would have been the end of that. And what she wrote no one, except her husband who thought it wise to burn it, knows either. Claudia's *that* kind. If I find life empty, I fill it up with . . . well, you know what. Unfortunately Claudia has too much brain to be satisfied with that. So, Pontius, I'm warning you. If you don't let her have interests in life outside the kitchen, she'll do what her mother did: find a life of her own. She might even turn to politics. Or worse. Religion.'

Pilate, his lips tightening, could feel his whole body stiffening with suppressed rage in the face of this impudent and intrusive chatter. He resented the insinuation that Claudia, by being wife of the Procurator of Judaea, was exiled from stimulating and intellectual society, marooned in what Sextia in her stupidity saw as a provincial backwater of empire. But he bit deep on his anger: he would not give the woman the pleasure of seeing that she was capable of arousing it. He was determined also not to accept her past generosity and future promise as a bribe giving her the right to interfere in the affairs of the family she had so abundantly subsidised.

To Sextia the storm signals were clear: his buttoned-up ferocity told her that she had gone as far as she should for the present. She loved Claudia and was determined to do everything she could to ensure her happiness. With equal warmth she loved the lovely Julius, that handsome and sensitive boy who had by some miracle been spawned by this cold fish Pontius. Though she did not despise Pilate. She could even see him as, within his lights, a decent fellow even if bone-headed. She was, if anything, sorry for him, as she could be for anyone so encased in tradition. The renowned cool-headedness which many people admired in Pilate signified to her no more than absence of emotion and imagination, an inability to free himself from the strait-jacket of discipline which he had knitted around himself during his mildly distinguished military career. His successes in the field, trivial but seeming so great to him, had been sufficient to inflate his ambitions but not to increase his wisdom. Nurtured on petty triumphs, his egotism had laid such scales of self-satisfaction over his eyes that he could not see that the men he indiscriminately idolised – that viper, Dictator Julius, and the opulent hewer of marble, Augustus – won their eminence not by run-of-the-mill ability to win campaigns and frame codes of law by foot-rule, but by their rankly human capacity to deceive, and to circumvent any code of conduct they judged restrictive of their ambitions. Pilate, his head buried in dusty histories and such feeble passions as he possessed curbed by military orders and legal precedent, imagined that the truth of life could be sucked out of a text-book, and was not something that had to be hammered out in agony on the anvil of doubt and self-questioning. By now he had, behind his tinpot Procurator's breastplate, become so impervious to doubt that he would never be moved even to ask what truth really was. However, no crisis big enough or pointed enough could ever arise in

6

this backwater of Judaea to face the little man with the question of truth. He was just big enough for his job: to carry out orders like a man in a kitchen, to keep the pots simmering until he had served his spell of duty, after which he would honourably retire and settle himself, complacent and satisfied, in a villa in Campania or any similar retreat favoured by retired army types.

She was resolved to rescue Claudia and Julius from so humdrum a destiny. However, she had said as much as was wise at this moment. She had dropped into Pilate's mind a hint of her plans; she would revert to them at some time when she had him in a more receptive frame of mind. Meanwhile it would now be good policy for her to be more amiable. So, casting around for some way of demonstrating a milder and less contentious attitude, she hit upon the subject which must now be engaging his thoughts and on which, she felt, she might offer a few words of advice. 'An old friend of mine is visiting you,' she said, with the smile of a secretive but friendly oracle.

Pilate welcomed the change of subject. Here was a matter in which Sextia could be of some use. 'Marcus Paterculus, yes. I understand you know him well.'

'Yes, very well. He and Cassius were bosom pals for a time.'

'Which Cassius?' asked Pilate. There were two men of that name notoriously prominent in Sextia's life.

'The one who didn't get away. My second husband. He took full advantage of the Paterculus family connections. Also he was rather gone on Marcus's wife. But who isn't? She is still unbelievably beautiful. I saw her in Rome early this year with her two children. Pretty girl, fine handsome boy. Both in their teens now, but she looking like their virgin sister. When we are being bitchy we call her Immaculata. Men still go overboard for her. They send her gold boxes and jewels. She virtuously sends them back or gives them to the slaves. Caligula was far more clever. He sent her spring flowers packed in moss, grapes from the Black Sea, and suchlike. People said he was hard-up or mean, but he said that gems were too used and tawdry for her. She deserved only the first fruits. Probably he meant himself. Those gifts she did not send back. She put the flowers in her bedroom and ate the grapes.'

'But Gaius is far, far younger than she can be.'

'Oh yes! Young enough to be her son. But probably Caligula is looking for a substitute mother, his own being in exile. Paterculus and his wife are a powerful couple socially. Related to about everybody. Even to the Claudii and old man Tiberius himself.'

'Aristocrats!'

'Of course. Right back to the wolf, one would think, from the airs they put on. But you attach too much importance to family, Pontius. I suppose it's understandable, but . . . ' She broke off, then shrugged apologetically to excuse the gibe, which was, on this occasion, unintentional.

To Pilate the implication was offensive. He was sensitive on the subject of his origins. The gossip that one of his forbears had been a slave was mere slander, circulated by those who were envious of the noble position he had reached and the marriage he had made. He took care not to refute that slander: to do so would be to take cognisance of it and thus inflate it. But, if taxed, he would admit with a show of pride that a grandfather who, although only a humbly-born veteran in Caesar's wars, had been granted land in return for outstanding and faithful service to the Republic was of greater merit than a grandfather born in the stew of some decadent and possibly incestuous noble house. It was true that Claudia's aristocratic connections had helped his advancement. But, after all, Claudia's family were not above suspicion. They had suffered reverses under Sulla. It might be true, as some people said, that Sulla's treatment of them during the course of his harsh but nevertheless necessary reform had been unjust. Yet the fact remained that they must have been either careless or rash to incur the displeasure of that dictator.

Sextia's gruff voice broke in on these thoughts. 'His coming here worries you, I suppose.'

'Worries me?' He stood up abruptly. 'Why should it?' As he walked past her he exaggerated the difficulty of stepping around her sprawled ankles. He strode on to his balcony and, staring out towards the sea, asked, 'Why should it worry me?'

'I was thinking you might attach too much importance to him because of who he is. Don't let his family connections impress you, Pontius. Those old sticks who cluster around Tiberius are already half dead. Whoever succeeds Tiberius – Nero or Caligula – will have little time for them. Let's hope it's Caligula. There's one who'll crack the whole lot over his knee. Not separately. All at once. One dried-up bunch. But, if it's any interest to you, I gather that Marcus Paterculus is desperately anxious to win your favour.'

'Caligula? Does it seem that . . . ?' Pilate flinched at the danger of putting it into words.

Sextia had no such inhibition. 'There's no doubt. He's in Capri now. The old man personally invested him with his toga of manhood.' She guffawed. 'Bit late in the day. And gave him an augurate and a priesthood. Everyone's sure he'll soon name him his heir.'

Caligula! Gaius Caesar! Pilate pondered. Nero, younger and thus more amenable to advice, would have been better. Gaius had already shown himself too sympathetic to the aspirations of his own unschooled generation, too liberal by far. Yet, that being so, he would almost certainly be a more amiable, less suspicious, less malevolent ruler. Yes, Pilate could hope it might be true.

His musings were interrupted by a noise in the anteroom. A young Roman and a slave were carrying in a chest. Behind them came Paterculus in person.

Pilate was exasperated that Sextia should be present when he arrived. Instead of meeting the aristocrat in the dignified silence of his room in a manner befitting a procurator giving audience, he was caught hob-nobbing with a bizarre woman whose feminine chit-chat hung around the room like the smell of armpits and who now began bouncily effecting introductions as though the meeting of Procurator and Paterculus were a trivial social encounter instead of a state occasion. Therefore when, after the inevitable cataract of social inanities, she said, 'Well, I'll leave you two alone to chew over politics,' although he found that choice of words insufferably unbecoming, he was sufficiently relieved by her impending departure to say almost with warmth, 'We shall meet at dinner Sextia, I hope.'

'Where else, Pontius?' she said. 'I can't see myself being tempted to plunge into the night-life of Caesarea,' and, as she swayed long-leggedly across the anteroom, laughing like a tipsy centurion, the fringe of her brocaded gown caught on the corner of the trunk and she berated the attendant slave for depositing baggage in such an awkward position. The man deserved a rebuke, but Pilate thought it presumptuous for a guest to take it upon herself to administer it.

'If ever,' said Paterculus as the clip-clop of her heels reverberated along the balcony, 'we do see a woman senator, Sextia will be it.'

Pilate could think of no rejoinder to that observation. In any case he preferred to forget that Sextia had been there at all and, to exorcise memory of her presence, he tried to invest the meeting with proper ambiance by formally expressing the pleasure the

Procurator experienced at welcoming to Judaea the son of an illustrious father.

He seemed older, this son, than Pilate had expected, not in years but in manner. Paterculus had, it was true, the figure and stance of a young soldier, but his face seemed tired, or, rather, over-disciplined, as though enamelled by experiences much older than its flesh. There was also something contradictory in the blank pale-grey eyes. The stare was typically patrician, directed haughtily from behind the bridge of a beaked nose held aristo-cratically high. Yet this lofty regard had in it also a tinge of wariness: one might also call it slyness. His mouth had a cor-responding duplicity: the lips curved in a line of apparent amiability, but the line had frozen.

Pilate ushered his guest out of the room on to his wide balcony overlooking the port. This balcony, under a coffered roof sup-ported by thin columns and screened at both ends by windowless walls, was shielded from sun and wind and also insulated from intrusive eyes and ears, and was therefore Pilate's favourite out-door nook for intimate conversation.

The sun had set. Shafts of light from anchored boats rippled water to the shore. Along the quay more diffused and smokier light issued from taverns from which drifted also the murmur of voices and occasional laughter. Paterculus murmured appreciative comments on the scene and chose a couch. The languid manner in which he stretched himself indicated that his sole intention was that of relaxing in the velvety warmth of the evening, yet Pilate felt there was some significance in the fact that Paterculus had chosen a position where his face was hidden in the shadows. That pose of relaxation might well be masking an attitude of watchful-ness, camouflaging the alertness of a spy who from the darkness would stretch his web to capture the slightest vibration of any thoughts that might be ensnared in it.

'Yes, Procurator,' said Paterculus, 'you have chosen a beautiful corner of the world.'

The nasal drawl imbued the words with a flavour of con-descension, but Pilate warmed to the word 'chosen'. That gave him the credit of having possessed the power to select any theatre at all for the exercise of his talents.

'I am glad you like Caesarea,' said Pilate. 'I hope you are free to spend some time with us and see more of Judaea.'

'Indeed I am. That is the reason for my coming here. I plan to go north eventually to Antioch.'

'You know the imperial legate?'

'I meet him occasionally in Rome.'

'I confess myself somewhat surprised that he remains there.'

'More than surprised, I suspect, Procurator.' Paterculus laughed softly. 'As a conscientious proconsul you must deplore an official who leaves his administration to deputies. I venture the opinion that were you in such an exalted office you would devote your presence and energies to it.'

For a moment the wildest hopes dazzled Pilate, but he cautiously refused to rise to the bait. 'You have friends in Antioch?' he asked.

'I have many friends in Asia.' Was this a boast? Or a warning?

'Is your visit a kind of holiday? Or a tour of duty?'

'Duty,' Paterculus said with affected weariness. He stared out at the harbour. 'At the suggestion of the prefect. Sejanus thought the time was opportune for me to come out here to strengthen contact with personalities of importance and in positions of authority in Asia. People like yourself, Pilate.' He turned his head in Pilate's direction. The eyes were invisible, but Pilate was conscious of a grey gaze probing towards him. He nodded slightly, accepting the compliment. Paterculus turned to look down on the harbour again. 'He is anxious,' he continued, and the drawl was now accentuated as though each word had to be dredged up and slowly turned over for examination before being released, 'the prefect is anxious to establish, because of the increasing responsibilities of empire now being imposed on him, to establish a closer association, even one might say friendship, with officers of state on the periphery of empire. Though only with certain officers. One must restrict such favour to proved men of vision, to men possessed of more than usual administrative talent. To men . . . I know the prefect's mind so I can say this sincerely . . . to men like yourself.' The words fell voluptuously, like tempting plums. 'Men, also, of ambition. High ambition. Like you, Pilate!' Now he most pointedly waited.

Careful, careful, thought Pilate. This is the test. Ambition! A dangerous word.

'I have ambitions,' he said heartily. 'Big ambitions. In fact your arrival actually coincides with the formulation of one of them.'

'Indeed!' Interest was noticeably aroused in the shadows. Paterculus was now leaning forward, his silent questioning so intense that it could be felt like a breath on one's cheek.

'Not a personal ambition, of course,' said Pilate with a light laugh. 'An imperial one.'

'I appreciate the distinction,' said Paterculus with marked lack of enthusiasm, and as he sank back on to the couch his interest seemed so deflated that one could have suspected he almost sighed. When at last he did speak again his voice revealed some impatience. 'Let us not fence, Pilate. Let us be frank. Personal ambition is not something we should deplore. We should recognise it as a necessary condiment in men most suited for high destiny. How, for instance, would one distinguish in the person of the Divine Julius the borderline between personal ambition and devotion to the public good?' He paused for a comment from Pilate. None came. So he went on, 'Even in a diligent servant of empire, lack of personal ambition could be judged not as a virtue but as the symptom of a mediocre mind, an indication of the servile obedience one demands only from the lower ranks. I should appreciate some elucidation of the nature of your ambitions.'

'I was referring to a plan which I am now formulating for submission to Tiberius Caesar. As it concerns the development of Judaea it should be attractive to him.'

'Hm!' The interest in the shadows seemed now completely snuffed out. Pilate felt he had dexterously skirted around a trap. There was silence now for quite a time. Paterculus was apparently considering a new line of approach. Then, 'But, Procurator, I presume that the realisation of what you call an imperial ambition would inevitably advance your personal interests.'

Pilate felt he dare now adopt an attitude of bluff candour. 'Personal interests, of course, Marcus Paterculus. But my personal interests are not, I flatter myself, the common ones of gain or political advancement. As one deeply interested in history, I see myself as somewhat like the general who hopes to win a battle not for the reward of loot but in order that his name may be recorded in the annals of history.'

'An admirable sentiment,' drawled Paterculus. 'But can you see yourself satisfying such grand desires as Procurator of Judaea?'

'I can. I hope that one day I may do something in Judaea by which my name may be remembered.'

Again the soft laugh. 'My historian father, in his more cynical moods, says that history is woefully indiscriminate in the bestowing of her favours. Winning fame, he says, is as haphazard as winning at dice. And, as at dice, the prize can go to the meanest creature. A deed by which a man wins immortality in history need not necessarily be a noble one. For example, if an otherwise insignificant character with a dagger in his hand should choose a personage of sufficient eminence for assassination, he enters the pages of history along with his victim.'

Choosing to acknowledge this as a pleasantry, Pilate directed an amiable laugh towards the shadows. 'I should prefer to enter history without blood on my hands.'

'Unless, Pilate, the blood is that of the enemies of Rome! But, as I see it, those who win fame in history are those who happen to be in the right place at the right time. Let us hope, therefore, that Judaea may be the right place and the present be the right time for Pontius Pilate. But, Pilate, that depends on you. Enjoying as I do the high privilege of your patron's confidence I am able to assure you that loyalty to Sejanus in the immediate future can provide you with ample opportunity for ensuring that the name of Pontius Pilate will be inscribed indelibly on the pages of history.'

'Thank you, Marcus Paterculus.' The invitation was exquisitely oblique, the temptation to respond to it and immediately assess the profit of it was intense. Yet until the patrician's purpose could be seen more clearly caution was still advisable. However, so as not to give Paterculus the impression that he was ignoring an offer of influential aid, he said with every semblance of eagerness, 'I should be most grateful if you would engage the prefect's interest by presenting him with a copy of the memorandum I am drafting for submission to Caesar.'

But this offer obviously did not excite Paterculus. 'I was thinking more of matters of imperial policy than of domestic affairs in Judaea,' he said stiffly. He shifted on the couch, and then, leaning forward and with something like urgency in his voice said, 'Procurator, at this time it is necessary for all of us, for men like ourselves, men in key positions, to face up to the fact, a sad one but inescapable, that because of Caesar's increasing years the time is fast approaching when certain shifts in political power have to be envisaged. Men of vision, men of ambition, cannot afford to wait too long. They must be prepared to assume responsibilities greater than they have hiterto assumed. They may even need to assume such responsibility without, as it were, waiting on imperial authority. They must act, in a way, autonomously and ahead of time, thus making sure that they will be in control of affairs before the change, sadly inevitable, in Rome.'

The change? It could mean only one thing. 'Gaius?' Pilate breathed.

Paterculus started. 'Caligula . . . or Nero. Or even some other,' he said sharply. He seemed irritated: either at the interruption, or because he was plagued by the dangerous speculations which the murmuring of Caligula's name had stirred. He recovered his composure. 'The change I am speaking of, Procurator, is of greater significance than the one you visualise. It is one which demands that men of vision take up their positions *now*. We cannot plan for *years* ahead: we must act in *weeks*.'

Very clever, thought Pilate. He was feeling easier in mind now. Tiberius's spy was playing the game which Pilate could play much better. This slanted cross-examination by a questioner who had, as the sky darkened, become almost invisible, had assumed that pattern which Pilate himself was competent in weaving or unravelling. It reminded him of that first crucial occasion when he had faced the necessity of parrying questions designed to beguile and entangle him; an occasion more fraught with danger than this. Then, standing in a tent facing Caesar's inquisitors, he had been fighting for his life. It was during the mutiny in Pannonia. Tiberius had sent his son Drusus to Pannonia. Ostensibly the prince was there to suppress the revolt, but the real architect of that exercise was the man who stood in the wings; one at that time little known to the public but already whispered about as a man of high ambition and ferocious talent. That man was Caesar's favourite, Aelius Sejanus, and his assumed role was no more than adviser to Drusus, which seemed reasonable enough. Drusus could justifiably be considered as somewhat young to handle alone so delicate and dangerous a situation. But the truth was that Tiberius trusted Sejanus more than he trusted those of his own blood. In fact when Drusus later died of slow poisoning, it was generally assumed that it was Sejanus who had been entrusted with that necessary execution. So in Pannonia, while Drusus enjoyed the glory of parading at the head of loyal troops, Sejanus laboured behind the scenes. Sejanus it was who insinuated *agents provocateurs* and spies among the dissidents, and Pilate was one of those who had been forced to assume a role which could be seen by Drusus as treasonable or, at least, ambiguous. When Pilate marched in to face the inquisitors he was, he knew, in mortal danger. Claiming that he had intrigued on behalf of Sejanus would not save his life: the silencing dagger of a Sejanus hireling would be as lethal as the hands of Caesar's strangler. Yet from the moment the first questions were posed Pilate knew he was in a position of strength. His questioners were hampered by ignorance. They knew only one side of the situation: he knew both. With this advantage he could fabricate each answer in such a manner that it inevitably drew from his questioners the very question he wanted. At every turn he was one step ahead of them, and remained so during a whole gruelling hour. He escaped unscathed, utterly cleared of suspicion and, more important, he had earned the certain patronage of the ever-increasingly powerful Sejanus. Compared with that probing in Pannonia the present exercise by Paterculus, dangling smooth invitations so palpably designed to lead him into expressing treasonable speculations, was pitiably ingenuous. In fact, as the aristocrat's next words proved, worse than ingenuous: positively crude.

'Pilate! Sejanus was instrumental in your being appointed as Procurator of Judaea. He is noted for his ability to choose the right man for the right destiny. Obviously at that time he relied on you. Equally obviously he relies on you now.'

Then abruptly, as though determined to allow Pilate time to weigh those significant words in silence, he sprang to his feet, walked across the balcony, and, leaning over the balustrade, gazed down on the port.

'I am honoured by the Prefect's confidence in me,' said Pilate.

Paterculus stared out to sea. 'A beautiful night,' he said. 'I suppose the packets from Brindisi arrive regularly.'

'At this time of the year it is usually an easy crossing. Though, as you know, the Great Sea can change its temper quickly.'

'I hope not to be inconvenienced by any delays while I am here.'

'You are expecting someone?'

'Dispatches. One must keep in touch. And what about communications between here and Antioch?'

'Excellent. The road is best: it is quick and good.'

'And safe, I hope. It seems there are still rebels in Galilee and the north.'

'Very few. Rumour exaggerates.'

'Hm! The Lady Claudia was telling me . . . ' Paterculus broke off. He roused himself from his contemplation of the sea and turned to face Pilate. 'Your charming wife has been most informative, Procurator. She is, I must say, somewhat over well-disposed towards the natives, though one must of course make allowances for feminine sensibilities. The dear lady went to some effort to enlighten me on sectarian tangles in which these Jews are perpetually enmeshed. Have you heard about this new Galilean baptiser?'

'The preacher? Galilee produces preachers by the score.'

'I know. More worrying is the ease with which they recruit followers.'

'Religious cranks. They come and go.'

'But don't you think, Pilate, that their success in Galilee indicates a dangerous undercurrent of disaffection in that province? We found it with the druids in Gaul. A preacher can be dangerous in a disturbed province like Galilee, a province notorious for those . . . what do you call them . . . Zealots?'

'There are far fewer of those than there used to be. During the years of my administration I have had need to execute, I think, no more than a couple of hundred. Quintilius Varus crucified two thousand in only days.'

Paterculus laughed. 'A critic of your administration, Pilate, might argue that such a comparison merely reveals a less rigorous pursuit of Zealots rather than there being fewer of them. I wish I could share your optimism. But my suspicion is that any Jew, with or without a dagger, is a Zealot at heart. A Jew is by nature an enemy of Rome. He has to be.'

'Facts disprove that, Marcus Paterculus. Throughout the empire there are Jews who are loyal subjects of Rome.'

'These loyal subjects once murdered every Roman settler in Judaea.'

'That was eighty years ago, Paterculus. Things have changed. Present imperial policy is to integrate Jews into the commonwealth, as has been successfully done with other subject races.'

'With some races integration might be possible. But not with Jews. In that opinion I find myself in wholehearted agreement with the Prefect. He sees Jews as a special case. The dangerously exclusive religious belief to which they adhere prevents them from being assimilated into other races and other cultures. Oh yes, I know that in any city of our Roman world you find your Jew making a good pretence of being a law-abiding subject and working with characteristic Jewish industry. Though his real aim is that of amassing a fortune for his clan, and although he outwardly bends his knee to Caesar, in his heart he remains an alien being. First and foremost his allegiance is not to Caesar but to his God.' Paterculus abruptly relaxed again. 'But, Pilate, I am sure you have heard the Prefect say all that. And also I am sure you share your patron's opinions. Otherwise, of course, you would not be here.'

'I am indeed fully aware of the Prefect's opinions,' said Pilate quietly. 'And he, I am sure, understands that my duty in Judaea is to administer it in accordance with the policy of Caesar. That policy is to encourage prosperity in the province, and by so doing cultivate the peaceful acceptance of Roman administration. Tiberius Caesar expressed this with characteristic wit when he said . . . '

'Oh yes, that!' interrupted Paterculus impatiently. 'Everyone repeats that. "My sheep are to be shorn, not flayed." And one can understand why Caesar treats Judaea as a buffer state. On this periphery of empire we need a bastion against the ambitions of Parthia and other eastern adventures. But all the more reason why in Judaea we must keep alert. We must guard against being lulled into lethargy by an ambience of peace. A calm surface might be no more than camouflage. In fact, the calmer it is the more likely that under the surface these devious Jews may be working as silently and industriously as ants to undermine Rome, in the same way as those preachers who proclaim peace with their lips and have daggers in their hands. The wall we have built against Parthia needs cement. I mean direct rule from Rome. And direct rule would be best enforced by Roman soldiers.'

'The auxiliary forces at my disposal are adequate and well trained.'

'In present circumstances, I am sure they are. But in a crisis? What might these mercenaries do should they be forced to choose between service to Rome or the call of their Semitic blood and racial sentiments?'

'Conflict of so drastic a nature I do not envisage. If the bulk of the population is content and prosperous, it could not happen.'

'You overlook something, Pilate. The root of the crisis might not be in Judaea. Nor in Asia. What would be the position if the storm centre were in, for instance, Rome? Some violent shift in power there? You of all people, Pilate, cannot surely forget that after the assassination of Julius Caesar the destiny of empire was determined not many miles from this very spot. Nor would you, I am sure, be reluctant to have command in Asia of legions of seasoned Romans rather than a horde of alien mercenaries.'

It was a tempting bait. Quite dazzling in fact. But if this really were an offer of generalship, Pilate preferred to wait for it to be made less ambiguously.

'I should be eager,' he said, 'and proud to assume at any time any office to which I might be elevated and in which I might further the glory of empire. But the most immediate need in Judaea is not increased force but increased patronage: not soldiers fighting for an empire, but civilians building one. At the moment we do not need soldiers, we need builders. Yes, builders. And architects.'

Paterculus forced a smile. 'Architects! Well, if that is all you want,' he said condescendingly, 'I can satisfy the need at this very moment. I have one for you there.' He nodded towards the ante-room. 'Let me show you.'

Ahead of Pilate he walked into the anteroom. The lamps had been lit. The slave was still standing beside the corded trunk, and Paterculus gestured to him to open it.

'A little gift, my dear Procurator. From Rome, with the compliments of myself and my wife. In fact it was she who in conversation somewhere learned of your deep interest in such things.'

'I regret she is not here to hear my thanks. I have heard much about her that would have made me most happy to receive her.'

'She left Rome with me, but I left her at Paphos where she has family connections. She is fond of Cyprus and will winter there with the children.'

The box was now open. It was packed with scrolls, lavishly bound with gold and ivory. Paterculus lifted one out. 'All ten volumes,' he said. 'The whole works of Marcus Pollio. A nice addition, I hope, to your library here.'

'Not for the library, Marcus Paterculus. These I must have at hand in my study. A most fortunate gift. You can hardly appreciate how useful it is at this very moment.'

'Ah! Then, my dear Procurator, I believe I can guess what your present ambition is in Judaea. Building?' He laughed slightly again. 'Fortresses, I hope.'

Pilate was glancing through the first volume, and to his delight there leaped immediately from the page a phrase which he could use with great effect in his memorandum, though he must first take the precaution of finding out whether Pollio was currently in favour with Tiberius Caesar or not. Sextia might know.

Then something suddenly occurred to him. Pretending to be absorbed in the inspection of a diagram, he said, as offhandedly as possible and without looking up, 'You brought it from Rome?

I had understood that you came direct from Capri?'

'I was invited to Capri along with a number of senators. Tiberius was wanting to discuss certain routine matters. It was also necessary that I should come here . . . I am pleased my gift interests you. You might find equally interesting the Greek architect who will be travelling with me to Antioch. He is recognised as an authority in his field: fortifications.'

When Paterculus had left him, Pilate laid the scroll in the box and, with the slave carrying the gift from Rome behind him, walked to his workroom deep in thought. What had Paterculus said exactly?

Pilate settled himself at his desk. In such moments of doubt it was his method to write out conversations, word for word, while still fresh in his mind. Nuances which one's ear might have missed could thus be recalled and studied objectively.

'I was invited to Capri . . . ' That was how Paterculus had said it. He had not answered the question. He had evaded it. Indeed, that evasion seemed almost as positive as a lie. What lay behind such caginess? It would be useful to question the captain of the boat in which Paterculus had come to Caesarea. Severus must be sent on that job. Or might it be better to entrust such a task to Marcellus? For the questioning must be oblique: nothing must be asked in so direct a way as to make Paterculus suspect that he was being investigated. Anyhow, before the boat left Caesarea that question must be put: from Rome or Capri?'

Meanwhile there was still time before dinner to recall every word of the conversation with Paterculus. It was as well to put everything that had been said on record. One never knew: such records could at times be useful.

Although many Jewish customs did seem bizarre to western eyes there was one which Pilate thought most commendable: that Jewish custom of excluding womenfolk from meals at which distinguished guests were being entertained. Such a custom would have freed him from the social necessity of inviting Sextia to dine with Paterculus. It was strange that, despite the quite recent examples of the dangers of allowing women – Agrippina and others of similarly vicious disposition – to intrude into public affairs, Romans had not learned to exercise sensible control of their women.

Not, of course, that Sextia was dangerous politically. Fortunately her ambitions were confined to the world of commerce. No tyrant would consider amassing wealth as treasonable, so long as she poured increasing taxes into the treasury. Yet Pilate would have preferred to dine alone this evening with Paterculus. Not out of fear of Sextia's indiscretions – after all, she was intelligent enough to know how far it was politic to go with the aristocrat, and Paterculus, on his part, was sufficiently sophisticated to recognise the difference between social pleasantry and subversive slander – but Pilate felt that were he alone with Paterculus he could more properly maintain masculine dignity than he could in the cloying atmosphere of dining *en famille*. He could have made the dinner less of a family occasion by summoning some Caesarean notables to dine with the important guest, but he had decided against that. In Carthage or in Alexandria Sextia's reckless irreverencies might be laughed at as merely the inanities of a wealthy but politically unimportant socialite, but in Caesarea, capital of a politically sensitive province, they could be taken seriously as subversive opinions emanating from the Procurator's palace. There was in Caesarea, as in any other city in the Empire, the danger that among the Romans there would be one who nursed hopes of joining the ranks of Caesar's notorious public informers. Such a one would collect any scraps of conversation which could be manipulated into disparagements of the dignity of Caesar. A store of such scraps could earn the informer a considerable financial reward for uncovering the dangerous crime of *laesa maiestas*. Under that heading even accidental acts of irreverence could be judged as treasonable – for instance, an indecency committed unwittingly before Caesar's effigy, even if that effigy was no more than that on the ring one wore or a coin lying unnoticed on the table, and the indecency of nothing more than stripping a slave for chastisement or oneself for a bath. In such a climate, some of Sextia's jokes, if picked up by an informer, could be enough to bring a whole household to the strangler.

Pilate had also rejected the idea of increasing the dinner-party by inviting some of his senior officers. The only two who had their wives with them in Caesarea were red-necked oafish veterans. Their brutish wine-sodden silences allied with their wives' uncultured twitterings might be even more offensive to the aristocratic guest than Sextia's *risqué* indiscretions. No. All he could do was to have a word with the lady before dinner and warn her against excessive exuberance.

Just at the moment when Pilate had made this decision, Fabius was announced. Fabius had solved the mystery of the missing courier. Pilate had taken it for granted that the courier and his escorts had been ambushed by Zealots and butchered. The truth was worse. It was the escorts who had cut the courier's throat.

His corpse had been found beside a dried-up water course in the arid hills to the east of the great north road. His hands were tied behind his back. Bruises on his wrists showed they had been tied for some time before his death. His face revealed that he had been beaten up before his throat was cut. Fabius and his squad had been led to the body by a herdsman and his wife, an old couple, too old to be suspect and in fact too savage to understand what was happening around them or even to appreciate any difference between Zealot or Roman. In terror they had watched the murder from the shelter of their goat-pen on a hill, and had not dared to approach the body until Fabius and his men arrived. They had seen the two assassins making off over the hills towards the eastern deserts.

'We sighted them an hour later,' Fabius told Pilate. 'They had apparently bivouacked for the night not far away from the scene. They still had the courier's horse. We kept track of them. I hoped, sir, they might lead us to a Zealot hideout in the desert. They were not hurrying. For a long time they had no idea they were being followed. Then, unfortunately, the courier's horse broke loose. It was when they turned back to round it up that they caught sight of us. Then they made a dash for it.'

'Were they captured?'

'No, sir. They are dead.'

'But I ordered . . .'

'We caught up with one and brought him down. But he was killed, either in the fall or in the struggle to subdue him.'

'And the other?'

'He took refuge in a deserted shack. We encircled it. When we moved in he was dead.'

'Dead? How?'

'With his own sword, sir.'

'Hm! They do seem to learn *something* from the Romans.'

'They were both traitors.'

'Obviously, Fabius. But inept ones. What point was there in killing only one man? Or, if they had wanted to defect, they could have done so some other time, more safely and without murder.'

'Probably they thought the escort carried an important dispatch. They had searched his wallet and his body.

'I think it more likely that somehow the courier had discovered that they were traitors. Probably they began by trying to suborn him. Then, when he refused, they assassinated him because he knew too much.'

'That is possible. He was a loyal soldier.'

'His family will be compensated. They need not know the exact circumstances of his death. You have reported all this to Marcellus, of course?'

'Fully, sir.'

'And where are your men?'

'Marcellus has taken them over for the time being.'

'Not into his dungeon, I hope,' said Pilate with a grimace.

Fabius laughed. 'No. He's confined them to barracks, incommunicado. He wants to brief them against saying too much.'

'This incident, Fabius, shows how you must always be alert to the danger of Zealot sympathisers infiltrating into the ranks. And remember always, anyone with any connections in Galilee is always suspect. Incidentally, Fabius, there is a guest at the palace. A certain Paterculus. I should not wish news of this incident to reach his ears. It could disturb him more than it merits. Understand?'

'Marcus Gaius Paterculus, sir?'

'You know him?'

'A little. His wife is a relative of mine.'

'Indeed!'

Here, then, was the solution for this evening. The presence of the young 'Eagle' would add a patrician ingredient to the dinner party. It would also demonstrate to Paterculus that a family, quite as grand as the Paterculus clan, thought so highly of the Procurator that they had entrusted their son to him to teach him the art of empire building. Admittedly the father of Fabius was known as an uncompromising critic of the Prefect Sejanus, but that he could be so and keep his head showed how powerful he was.

'Fabius,' said Pilate, 'you will dine with us this evening.'

'Thank you, Procurator.'

'And, Fabius! Those men who took the woman's gold. Have they been flogged?'

'Not yet, sir.'

'See to it. That will be all.'

Pilate ran Sextia to earth as she was striding up from the

kitchens where she had been bullying the cooks into preparing some oriental delicacies as a surprise for Pilate and Paterculus.

'We shall have one of my captains at dinner with us this evening, Sextia. I hope you will bear his presence in mind and not . . .'

'I know what you mean, Pontius. But don't think all women are fools. Such things as I say in private I only *think* in public. I will say nothing that will bring a blush to the cheeks of young Severus.'

'It is not Severus who will be dining with us. It is Fabius Caelius Rufus.'

'That young beauty! How nice. Well, you have no need to worry about him. For all his patrician airs I should say he is the very essence of loyalty. It is Paterculus you have to watch. I have news for you about him! I sent down to the boat he came on to make inquiries.' Pilate frowned. 'Oh don't worry. My inquiry was only to ask if they had some produce from Ostia or Puzzuoli. That was enough to find out that the boat had not come from there. Paterculus joined the boat at Brindisi. He came overland, Direct from Rome: not from Capri.'

The architect Lucius had refrained from telling the Procurator why the work on his courtyard garden was behind schedule. The real reason was that Marcellus had appropriated six of the best masons. He had taken them off to do some building for him in that remote eastern corner of the palace which he had for some time treated as his private terrain and which he was now, so he said, 'improving'. He did not specify what the improvement was. Marcellus had requisitioned the builders out-of-hand because he had no wish to go through the normal procedure of having his 'improvements' vetted by the palace secretariat. If he had made a formal application, someone might have mentioned it to the Procurator, and Marcellus always took pains to see that Pilate was not worried with details which he might find burdensome or even distasteful. When the masons had finished the improvements, Marcellus paid them well and succeeded in having them sent off to Jerusalem without fuss. There was no point in having them gossiping around Caesarea; there was always need of good builders in Jerusalem. When architect Lucius first discovered that six of his builders were missing he began protesting. Then he heard who had taken them and he said no more. That was the effect Marcellus had. Although he was seen around so rarely, his presence permeated the establishment, chillingly, like a superstition. No one wished to intrude into his part of the palace; invitations to visit it were not considered pleasant.

When in a gossipy mood, which was rare, Marcellus found pleasure in repeating a joke made about him years ago. Someone had said that the javelin which had pierced his neck in Pannonia had made him not only crooked in body but also crooked in mind. There was, Marcellus admitted, some truth in that. Had the javelin been sharper or more accurately aimed it would have cut off his head: being blunt or ineptly aimed it had merely twisted it. Marcellus hid the scarred area of savaged flesh and muscle by arranging a scarf high under his ears before he donned his cuirass; but however tightly he wound the scarf it could not pinion completely erect a head which, because of severed tendons, slanted quizzically towards his enfeebled left shoulder. But the wounds which had so enfeebled his frame as to put paid to his fighting ambitions had proved an exquisite asset in the exercise of the work which Pilate had entrusted to him: confronted by a visage which seemed to droop perpetually in an attitude of bitter disbelief, prisoners tended to start babbling answers before questions were even asked. So the joke about crooked neck and crooked mind was like the javelin. The joke had been aimed in malice: it also had gone awry and been received with profit.

For extra effect Marcellus sometimes pulled his peculiar metal-and-leather gauntlet off his left hand and placed the hand palm-down on the table. He had found that the sudden sight of a hand with three fingers missing gave added point to what was hinted at by the rods and pincers and chains and wheels beside the ever red-hot brazier in the room beyond. The missing fingers had been caught between beams and wheels of a siege engine when it was being trundled up to a city wall in an earlier engagement in Pannonia. Hoisted in mid-air and suspended by three fingers Marcellus had presented an attractive target for enemy darts and boiling oil from above. He had escaped from this predicament by lopping the fingers off with his sword and dropping to safety amid the bundles of brushwood protecting his comrades at the base of the engine. After the town had been taken he and his squad spent some time looking for his fingers. He had wished to give a macabre twist to that Roman custom of sending home a dead soldier's finger to his bereaved family. He intended to send three separate fingers to three relatives who would be overjoyed with the memento and as correspondingly cast down when later they learned that the rest of him was still alive. But around the broken and discarded siege engine there had been such a litter of fallen stones and so many corpses bursting and stinking that he never found his fingers.

This evening Marcellus was walking about the rebuilt cells and surveying new walls with bended but satisfied gaze. He was well pleased with the work. Previously this part of the palace had been reached through a spacious archway at the foot of a flight of shallow steps. Marcellus had felt that a wide archway bathed in morning sun gave the wrong impression to his visitors. The new entrance, a slit just wide enough for two guards with a roped prisoner between them, was more suitable. The slit, formidably high and dark, could be closed with a grille of iron teethed with sharp spikes. Though the inner walls had always been monstrously thick, another layer of masonry had been added. This had made the rooms much smaller, but there was now no danger of any noise in those rooms being heard in the secretariat or even, as had happened on one occasion, by a nervously sharp-eared guest in the household apartments. For it was, of course, of little use stifling the groans of a man or woman with a gag when one wanted the truth out of them. There had been one big central dungeon. This he had had converted into separate cells, for he considered the practice of dumping a mass of prisoners together and letting them rot old-fashioned. It was a waste of space. Worse, it was a waste of time. It also caused smells. And it had been proved time and time again that, even when lying amid the bilge and mud and excrement thrown back by the sea, men could strangely find comfort and courage merely by being together. Marcellus judged solitary confinement more effective. He allowed two in a cell only when one was an informer. Most often that situation was the more delicious because neither was very sure which was which.

Yes, he was satisfied. His 'improvements' would result in a quicker turnover. Suspects could now be dealt with expeditiously. When they had told all they could tell, they could be dispatched or discharged, and the kitchen swill that had been wasted on them could be used more profitably to feed poultry, geese and pigs.

In the room which Marcellus had fashioned for interrogations a scribe was busy, happily setting up his table and writing materials. Marcellus sat down at his own table and, laying his gauntleted hand on it, assumed the attitude he would assume before a prisoner. High in the wall behind him was a tall window. For an hour in the morning the sunlight streaming into it would slap his victim full in the face. As that sunlight would be the first light he had seen for three days or more it would almost blind him. The hour was long enough. If nothing of value could be got out of him in an hour, preferably less, the interrogation could be continued more profitably in the room with the brazier.

He sighed. The satisfaction faded from his face. He jumped up, walked moodily into that other room, and mournfully inspected the waiting instruments. All his cleverly conceived improvements were too good for the primitive victims usually sent to him. He would never have need for them so long as the army went galloping over the country, blundering into villages to round up those few pathetic dolts and peasants whom the real partisans had left behind as expendable and bringing them back to Caesarea in the bland belief that they had captured important terrorists. A waste of the army's time. And of his.

A household slave appeared. If Marcellus was disengaged, the Procurator would like a word with him. Before dinner if possible. Marcellus brightened up. For the first time he could now use on an errand to Pilate the stair which he had tunnelled through the walls to give him direct access to the corridor outside Pilate's study. He envisaged circumstances when it might be advisable for him to go to the Procurator unobserved, and this staircase enabled him to bypass the guards at the end of the corridor. In fact, he could reach the door of the study without even Pilate himself being aware that he was there. He had not told Pilate about this improvement. Not yet. No need to trouble the Procurator with details. Indeed, in order that the noisy labour of quarrying out the staircase should not disturb the quiet of Pilate's study, the work had been done during Pilate's absence.

As he slipped quietly up this stairway Marcellus was preparing what points he would make in discussing this affair of the assassinated courier. Here was something, he thought, which he could use to reinforce his arguments that terrorism must be combated by methods more sophisticated than blatant posses of soldiers.

But, as it turned out, Pilate wanted him on a very different matter, a more personal problem.

'I have a visitor,' Pilate began.

'Marcus Gaius Paterculus,' said Marcellus quickly. 'Son of the historian. Aged thirty-eight. Wife and two children, whom he has left with relatives in Cyprus. The wife is a cousin of Fabius.'

Pilate smiled at the satisfaction in the leaning face. 'And he came from where?'

'From Rome, via Brindisi.'

'Good!' Pilate sat silent for a while, and began, almost shamefacedly, to ask if Marcellus might possibly devise some way, with the utmost discretion of course, to . . .

'To find out what he's up to,' Marcellus interrupted with brutal impatience, and, indifferent to Pilate's gathering frown, went on, 'I've already been trying.' He knew the Old Man might resent his taking the initiative in such a matter, but he saw it as his duty to be informed. One could not have too much information about anyone. No one was above suspicion, least of all the unsuspected. 'Paterculus's guards are a tight-lipped bunch. That's what makes me the more suspicious. They are altogether too cagey. I'll let you know what I can.'

'Do so. But, I emphasise, you must be discreet. After all, Paterculus is a guest. He does, in a way, represent Caesar.'

All the more reason to be wary, Marcellus thought, but although he knew the same thought was in Pilate's mind he did not put it into words. Instead, he introduced the matter which he considered of more urgent interest. 'That courier affair, Pontius. It does show, doesn't it, how the Zealots can get under our guard?'

'I've warned Fabius on that point. He will take steps.'

Marcellus sighed. 'Draw the auxiliaries up on parade perhaps? All Zealots one pace forward.'

Pilate met the heavy sarcasm with a smile. 'I think Fabius will cope. And you, I think, will adequately interrogate any suspects he finds. Good night, Marcellus.'

Marcellus hesitated before accepting this dismissal, but, after reflecting for only seconds, judged that even yet the moment had not arrived when Pilate would accept that terrorism could never be stamped out by the feet of military men. Fabius was just the same as all other Roman officers: enraptured with the spit and polish of military dignity, too ossified in armour and tradition ever to go down on his belly to seek out terrorists and sting them to death in their breeding-grounds. So, 'Good night,' said Marcellus, and, gliding so quietly towards the curtained door that the guard at the far end of the corridor heard not a movement, disappeared down his staircase.

Pilate still found it somewhat discomfiting, although it was by now the accepted custom, to see women reclining on couches in masculine style at dinner. He could remember the time when a woman always sat upright, a posture proper to a Roman matron. Claudia, he was pleased to see, adopted the new style with decorum: by leaning only slightly on the cushions she retained feminine modesty. But Sextia positively stretched out, and with her right hand continually clutching a wine goblet and her left hand waving some half-bitten tit-bit to emphasise a point, she looked like some raddled millionaire rigged out in women's silk. To complement the spicy Asian dishes which she had engineered for this evening she was wearing an eastern gown, ridiculously diaphanous for her grotesque frame, and displaying a mass of jewellery she had bought in Alexandria, including a triangular contraption of three enormous grey pearls which she wore dangling on her brow as though she were a slave girl. Nevertheless, Pilate appreciated the tact – sometimes it smacked of cunning – with which she steered the conversation through the pitfalls which Paterculus, either by design or accident, opened up. She was indeed so adept in the exercise that somehow it always turned out that the slightly irrevernt jokes came from the patrician's lips, never from hers.

As when a conversation on building led inevitably to the sensitive subject of Tiberius's mania for building villas on Capri. This interchange began when Pilate told the party of Paterculus's gift of Pollio's work.

'Oh, I must see it,' exclaimed Sextia.

Paterculus smiled condescendingly. 'Are you also interested in architecture?' he asked.

'In anything to do with building. At the moment I'm thinking mainly of property. My husband had a miserable experience a few months back. He saw a house his father sold twelve years ago sold again for ten times the price.'

'One deplores how quickly money has depreciated in value,' said Pilate.

'Deplore it! I'm scared to death by it,' exploded Sextia. 'It's driving me out of commerce. The sea has been cleared of pirates, but now we are being robbed ashore. Every year slaves cost more and demand better living-conditions. Sea captains want higher pay each trip. Harbour dues go up. And then any profit you manage to make is worth about half the amount in a few months. But property! That's the thing to put money in now. The produce of a thousand slaves you've to coax one day and whip the next won't earn you as much as you can make by selling two rooms. Well, I've made my fortune secure forever.'

'How, may I ask?' Paterculus showed lively interest.

'As I say: by buying property. I've bought an inn, two shops, a bakehouse, four villas and two whole streets in Pompeii.'

The sheer size of the purchase impressed them.

'And,' she added triumphantly, 'anything in Pompeii is bound to double in value every five years.'

'Do you intend to settle there?' Paterculus asked.

'No, no! It's too popular. Crowded with Romans, and not the best type. I'm seeking a parcel of land in the country where I can build.'

'In the Apennines, I suppose,' said Paterculus, parading his knowledge of her family origins. 'The healthiest climate in Europe.'

'Healthy!' Sextia shivered. 'Maybe. But too cold and frosty in winter for me. And farming is so difficult there. The soil's so hard you've to plough it nine times before it's broken in. No. At my time of life I want the sun. I'll go south. I do like the coast near Naples, but so many people are building there.'

'On Capri particularly,' said Paterculus with a smile.

Sextia laughed. 'How many villas has Tiberius built there? Is it six already? Or more? Before long, building villas on Capri will be quite the thing. But not for me.' She shot her gold bangles back with an emphatic click. 'Living on an island, no. Having to cross the sea every time. I like the sea only to look at, not to lose my dinner in. And certainly a rocky perch like Capri would not suit me. Too austere for a gadfly like me. Only someone who is very tired of people could want to live in a place like Capri.'

'Are you suggesting the Caesar is tired of people?'

'Oh no! A Caesar needs a retreat. Tiberius obviously finds an island provides him with the atmosphere he needs. Cut off from the noisy world, he can study the problems of empire. Don't forget he's done it before. In the reign of Augustus. Then, at one crisis, he retired to Rhodes. But those Capri cliffs! I've seen them from the bay. They are quite terrifying.'

Paterculus took the bait. 'Gossips in Rome say that the Caesar finds the cliffs very useful.'

She pretended ignorance. 'Useful? How?'

'For throwing people over.'

She laughed again. 'Oh, that old story! I heard something

104

better.' Pilate felt uneasy. 'Cocceius Nerva told me that after three days on Capri Caesar has no need to *throw* anybody.'

Pilate breathed easily. Sextia had neatly put the dangerous words into the mouth of one who, as legal adviser to Tiberius, was the most powerful lawyer in the world, and at the same time she had underlined her intimacy with Caesar's intimate. An irreverence from Nerva had to be accepted as a joke; the patrician had to accord it a laugh. Nevertheless, Pilate thought, the point that it was only a joke should be underlined. 'Gossip of that nature,' he interposed, 'can soon become almost folklore. Why, in Jerusalem they actually accuse me of mingling the blood of Galileans in my sacrifices.'

'But, Pontius!' said Sextia between gulps of wine, 'I thought... I thought that one was true!'

Now they all laughed. Pilate joined in, feeling at last so much at ease that, when Sextia drew Fabius into the conversation by asking how long he was to serve in Judaea, Pilate took the opportunity of teasing the young man.

'Oh, Fabius finds it dull here,' he said with a genial pout. 'Not enough action. His heart is set on the wild west. He is wanting to emulate the exploits of his grandfather by capturing a few more of those rain-soaked rocks they call Britain. He is young enough not to care that those naked woad-smeared savages will suck Rome dry for generations before they make any contribution to the Empire.'

Fabius grinned. The Old Man had never before referred to his ambitions: it was pleasant to see him taking them in such good part.

As for Sextia, the reference to Britain enabled her to launch into a description of the coasts of Gaul as she had seen them during her tour. Before long she was well launched on her travelogue. She described, with a wealth of sighs, the weariness of the road to Cadiz.

'The rest-houses were not so bad,' she said. 'They make a fuss about passports, though, because they are run by the military. And the booths are loaded with tourist trash. Imagine! Silver beakers designed like the milestones on the road, engraved with the distance from Rome. If you pay extra, you can have your name and date put on them. Well, I suppose some tourists find them useful: they can remember where they have been.'

'Did you buy some?' asked Claudia mischievously.

Sextia guffawed. 'Of course. Lots of Romans will love 'em.'

By some leaps of narrative she arrived on the new road built across North Africa by Tiberius. 'A good road, and nice places on it. Sabratha and Leptis Magna. Though too few inns as yet. As Aristophanes says in whatever you call it, "roads without inns are no better than life without holidays".'

Admiration for her broke through Paterculus's haughty languor. 'But your journey really is an Odyssey, madam. However did you plan it all?'

'I didn't plan a thing. I booked the whole lot in Rome at that agency near the Palatine. Inns, rest-houses, carriages, horses, guides, boats. I bought an itinerary. It showed the lot: lakes, rivers, mountains, night stops and interesting sights.'

Soon she was sailing up the Nile to see 'those tombs of the Egyptian kings. Like that tomb of Gaius Cestius on the Ostiensis in Rome.' She attempted to illustrate the shape by pressing her fingertips together and splaying her wrists in a triangle.

'Pyramids,' said Pilate helpfully.

'Yes, that's it. That visit was expensive. Thirty pieces of silver: the accepted price of a slave in the East.'

By this time, with the conversation safely steered away from more sensitive areas such as Rome and Capri, Pilate was able to look the marble bust of Tiberius in the eye with the certainty that not a word had been said out of place before Caesar's effigy.

Bronze gleamed softly; mules' heads on stools and couches; helmet and breastplate and greaves on the ebony tree. Every object, large or small, had been placed with military precision in exactly its accustomed position. Pilate's desk was placed so that daylight or the light cast by the suspended oil-lamps would fall at the required angle over his left shoulder. A new map of Judaea, stretched on ebony rollers chased with gold monogram Ps, hung on gilt eagle-claw hooks on the wall facing the desk. The sealing-wax lay one inch to the left of Pompey's ugly oil-lamp. On a nearby table a scroll of the ten volume architectural manual of Marcus Pollio lay open, a bar of ebony planted upon it to keep it open at the passage Pilate had reached. This room which Pilate had chosen for his workroom on the first day he had moved into the palace of Caesarea was no larger than the interior of his campaign tent and, with only one window and that too small to allow disturbing intrusion of sunlight and too high on the sea-ward wall to distract him with a view, the walls looked almost as dark as that tent's black worsted.

It was mid-morning. Pilate was working industriously. He had exchanged social pleasantries with Marcus Paterculus and, after carefully briefing Severus on what the patrician ought to see and what he should or should not be told, had seconded his aide to accompany the visitor on a tour of the port and the city. Then he had retired to his workroom with strict instructions that he was on no account to be disturbed.

His task this morning was to remodel the draft of his introduction to the long memorandum he was submitting to the Emperor. In the light of his conversation with Paterculus, he thought it expedient to show that he was fully aware of the preoccupation felt in Rome and Capri about current events in the province. Consequently he must make some reference to recent executions and the wiping-out of a Zealot-contaminated village, and thus impress Caesar with the vigilance his Procurator was showing in stamping out disaffection. Normally the execution of six rebels would not be considered important enough to merit the attention of His August Highness, but the fact that there had been been a Roman among those crucified gave the event more than trivial importance. As he refashioned that sentence, he remembered the doubts Paterculus had expressed about the ultimate loyalty of auxiliary soldiers. At this point he made cross-reference to an earlier memorandum in which he had described his reorganisation of the lines of command in the Judaean forces, explaining how a core of Roman personnel was being threaded through those forces to ensure that any whispers of disloyalty would be overheard long before they became mutinous. He had introduced into the auxiliary forces the Roman system of dividing every command between six officers, each officer being in command for two months of each year. Such a system kept a recurrent check on both officers and rankers.

Now to civilian affairs. He was pursuing in Judaea, he emphasised, a policy which he could best call Judaisation. He was on the one hand winning the friendly acceptance by Jews of Roman government and western customs, and at the same time he was encouraging them to stand on their own feet and themselves resist attacks from rebellious partisans in the north. The native priestly government in Jerusalem was gradually becoming more amenable to collaboration with Rome. It was therefore an opportune moment to encourage this collaboration by increasing Roman Patronage to assist them in developing Judaea, making it so prosperous and peaceful a province that it would become a faithful client, a buffer state against any menace, military or political, from the east. One of the first measures he envisaged towards the attaining of such a vision of the future was . . .

The voice of Severus disturbed him. He looked up angrily.

'What is it?'

'Forgive me, sir. I have a request.'

'Later, Severus. Later!'

'Forgive me. But it is urgent.'

'Yes?'

'I wish to ask for leave to go home.'

'Home?'

'Yes, sir. My wife . . .'

'Ill?'

'Dead, sir.' Severus choked on the word. As the young man came nearer, Pilate saw his face was grey with sorrow. This disquieted him. He turned to his manuscript, fiddled with his pen, and waited. 'The child came early, sir.'

'The child?'

'Alive, sir. A son. That is why I want to go home.'

Thoughtfully Pilate sorted the leaves of manuscript into order, noticing a passage against which he had scribbled the name of Severus to unearth the date of a memorandum. 'It is unfortunate,' he said.

'Yes, sir.'

And inconvenient, thought Pilate. But the young man was obviously so racked with sorrow that he would not be clear-headed enough to be much use for days.

The sorrow embarrassed Pilate. How long ago was it that he himself had been young enough to feel an individual tragedy of sufficient moment to tear the heart and divert him from his true work and his real destiny? For just a moment he found himself envying Severus: not his sorrow, but the agonising single purpose of youth. But the fellow would soon get over it. Young and virile as Severus was, he would soon find an outlet for those passions which, it must seem to him now, had perished with that girl in Lugano.

'You ask only for leave? But I suppose you really wish to stay in Cisalpine.'

'No, sir. I want to come back! My sister has found a nurse for the baby. I could bring them back here. I want to serve with you, sir. As long as ever you wish.' Then added, with a ghost of a smile, 'And my son too!'

Pilate stared up at him. The fellow really meant it. Pilate was moved by the thought that he could inspire a soldier to such loyalty, even, it seemed, to admiration.

'I appreciate that, Severus. You have my assurance that if you are not delayed by any further family complications your post will be kept open. So you will go as on furlough. When will you be leaving?'

'The next boat to Brindisi leaves tomorrow night, sir, weather permitting. Or the following morning.'

'Good. Forget duties for today, Severus. But I must ask you to be with me tomorrow morning to hand over outstanding things to Fabius . . . By the way, Severus, I am sorry to hear the news.'

'Thank you, sir.'

Severus turned and was about to walk out when Pilate suddenly halted him. 'Severus!'

'Yes, sir.' He did not turn to face the Procurator. Now, after having spoken the news to someone for the first time since he had heard it at the port, there were tears on his face, and he did not think it correct to present such weakness to his commander.

Pilate, drumming fingers on his manuscript, reflected on an idea that had come to his mind. 'Yes,' he said at last. 'You can perform a valuable service, Severus. It will entail a diversion on your route home. But it will add only a day or so to your journey.' Severus waited. 'You can take my dispatches to Capri. It is an ideal solution. They are of too great importance to risk with any ordinary courier. You will ride from Brindisi to Puzzoli and get the first available post-boat to Capri. You will present the dispatches to His August Highness yourself, personally. Indeed, the sending of my personal aide might emphasise, if such emphasis is needed, the vital importance of my dispatches. Your departure will thus serve both our ends, Severus.'

'Yes, sir.'

'Do not mention this arrangement to Paterculus. He kindly suggested that I might use one of his couriers. I shall explain the change of plan in my own words. Understand?'

'Yes, sir.'

'So I must work longer than I intended today. Probably tonight, too. I think I can get through the job by tomorrow. Send Polygnotus to me. Warn him that he is in for a full day's dictation. Tell the household I regret I shall not be joining them at table today. Thank you, Severus. I shall see you in the morning.

109

And, by the way, Severus, it would be useful to you, and take your mind off other things, to pack your Aramaic grammar.'

By the time Polygnotus appeared, loaded with a pile of fresh tablets and styluses, Pilate had finished his introduction. In a neat stack on his desk were notes and extracts from the work of Marcus Pollio, arranged in sequence to be included in his plan for the development of new water-supplies in Judaea.

Hours later Claudia saw the scribe hurrying down to the kitchen and, hoping to find Pontius enjoying a moment of relaxation, slipped into the room. But he was bent over the desk, and so absorbed in work that she was at his side before, startled by her silent approach, he turned quickly. He looked up at her abstractedly.

She laid a hand on his shoulder. 'I am going to bed, my dear,' she said. 'Don't work too long. You look tired.' She smoothed back his brush of grey hair. 'I shall wait for you.' She was bending to kiss him on the lips, but he, half-risen from his chair and bowing as much as he could in such a position, took her hand instead and lightly pressed his lips to the knuckles. 'Good night, my dear,' he said. He was already back at his notes before she reached the door.

Sextia had also seen Polygnotus somewhere outside. She came in less silently than Claudia.

'Still at it, Pontius?'

He sighed heavily and, pen still in hand, looked towards her. He nodded, hoping that this wordless recognition would be enough to indicate that he did not want her stamping in on his train of thought.

'I heard about Severus's wife,' she said. 'Poor lad!'

'Yes.'

Cold-blooded, it seemed to her. 'There's a ship of mine due in Caesarea tomorrow. It's crossing to Brindisi as soon as it's unloaded. Severus can go on that.'

He was angry at the thought that Severus had already been blabbing about his trip. 'Did Severus tell you he was going?' he asked.

'No. But I took it for granted,' she said blandly. 'Surely he has to go home. For his son.'

'Yes. He has to go home,' said Pilate, and began fiddling with his notes.

'Pontius!' He looked up again. 'Can you spare me just a crumb of your attention for a few moments? Please!'

110

He laid his pen down. 'What is it, Sextia? I am busy, you know.'

'So it seems. Is it always like this?'

'You mean my being busy. Mostly it is.'

'You've been back two days and I doubt if you've spent more than four hours with Claudia.'

'She knows I must work.'

'Yes. I see that. You've got her well trained. But why, when you see so little of her, cannot you let her have a holiday? Why not let her go with me? At least as far as Athens.'

'I have been thinking about that suggestion, Sextia. I also mentioned it to her. I have decided to let her go.'

She seemed somewhat taken aback. She had worked herself up into a rare old rage, determined to bully the fellow into submission, and here he was offering her what she wanted on a plate! She was pleased. But she was determined not to show herself over-grateful.

'Thank you, Procurator!' she said, and then barked, 'Sir!', centurion fashion.

He ignored her pantomime. 'I shall for the next few weeks be more than usually busy. My work might involve me in another progress to Jerusalem and further afield. It would be nice, therefore, to think that Claudia should have some company.'

'Even mine!'

'I am planning to give a dinner to some local nobles. I am hoping you can stay on so long. For that dinner we could well make use of your dancing boy.'

'Boiled or roasted, you monster?'

'But I must ask you, Sextia, to bear in mind what I said about Julius. I don't want you to drag him around Athens. I do not wish his studies to be interrupted.'

But she was hardly listening. She was pacing about looking disparagingly at the armour, the map, and every object in the room. Then she came near to him. She faced him sternly.

'Pontius, tell me something. Do you love Claudia?'

His hand trembled. She went too far. 'Why do you think I married her? For her family? Or for her money?'

'For both, I think,' she said brutally. 'But I wasn't talking of marriage. I was talking of love. A quite different thing. Anyhow, you have answered my question. If you really loved her, you would have used very different words. Good night, Procurator, sir!'

111

It took Pilate several minutes to subdue his anger. Perhaps, he thought, it would have been better after all not to let Claudia travel with that stupid woman. But he must push all thoughts of women away. He turned to his work.

Soon afterwards Polygnotus returned, but was sent away immediately to wash away the stink of grease and garlic. He came back sheepishly and the dictation began again. It was almost dawn when at last the scribe left the room with his pile of scribbling. Pilate leaned back in his chair. He was not at all tired. He was still too excited, too buoyed up at the thought of a good job well done, to feel weariness. Soon Severus would be placing his inspired work in the hands of His August Highness Tiberius Claudius Nero.

Thought of Severus made him remember the sad scene when Severus had told him the news of his wife's death, and now Pilate recalled the occasion when news had reached him of his first wife's death. At that time he also had been on foreign service, fighting on the Rhine. And also, as with Severus, the news had reached him when he had just been promoted. He had not asked for leave. In his case there had been no son to consider, but in any case there seemed little point in going back to Etruria merely to bury someone. He could not now remember whether the news had greatly distressed him. Perhaps the heat and danger of active service had cushioned him from sorrow. In any case, things had eventually turned out for the good. His first wife belonged to a humble past, and her death had made it possible for him, when he advanced under Sejanus, to make a brilliant match. Thus was the pattern of a career woven. Obviously Severus had loved his wife deeply, but he too might live to profit similarly. He was a good fellow.

Would Claudia still be awake? After drawing the bolts on the inside of the door to his workroom he left by way of a small archway which gave access to the narrow private passage leading to Claudia's bedroom. She had not, it seemed, waited for him. At least her door was not ajar. However, to make sure, he gently opened it and looked into her room. She must be asleep, for the curtains around her couch were drawn. He decided not to disturb her.

He went along to his own room. There was pomegranate juice and water there. He drank thirstily. He sat on his couch for a while, then stood up, stretched, and walked to the wall on which, between frescoed panels, stood a cupboard. He fiddled with the

112

lock for a while – it was purposely difficult to open – and swung back the door. The cupboard was lined with mosaic, so that the statue standing there looked, Claudia had teasingly said, like the statue of a god standing in a shrine.

He carried the statue to a table and sat before it. His gaze softened with affection. This was a moment when he did not need to act the procurator. When he was actually in the living presence of his beloved son he was compelled to assume the authority and dignity of a Roman parent, but this was only a statue of the boy.

The sculptor, whose work did betray perhaps a rather too obsessive affection for the subject, had somewhat idealised the boy, giving the statue an almost feminine grace and delicacy by depicting Julius in milder and more reflective pose than was usual with him. He was leaning against a pillar on a sports ground, his left leg lightly crossed over the ankle of the right leg which bore his weight. The body and arms were covered from neck to knees with a short cloak, the type Julius would throw over his shoulders when resting between sweaty rounds of boxing. The calf muscles were defined so boldly that they looked as though embossed on the limbs, like simulated muscles on armour. This, which might have been suspected as the sculptor's exaggeration, was actually true to life, for the boy's fervent athleticism had developed a pre-cociously mature physique, and his arms and shoulders, here hidden by marble drapery, were similarly muscular. In his modelling of the cloak the sculptor had succeeded in giving the impression that the boy had flung it on only a moment before. A bunching in the folds showed where, below the fabric, his left hand was holding the cloak to his right shoulder; a vertical fold showed where the exhausted but triumphant right arm hung inert. The carving of the fine square brow, wide gentle eyes, full lips and strong dimpled chin was accurate, yet the sculptor, allowing sentiment to get the better of him, had persuaded the boy to hold his head downbent in a meditative and studious pose quite unlike the direct head-high gaze most characteristic of Julius. And the smile, soft and pensive, did not have the frank vigour of Julius's customary boyish grin. Nevertheless, despite the sculptor's doting idealisation of youthful beauty, the statue was on the whole a true portrait of a lovely son.

Pilate reached out to it and caressed the short-cropped waves of hair. Then he ran the tips of his fingers down one marble cheek and under the chin, as though trying to lift the head and make this thoughtful lad look his father in the eye. Pilate smiled, indulgent to the stubborn shyness of the downcast head, and sat before the statue for some time. At last he carried it back to the cupboard, replaced it in its mosaic-lined shrine, closed the door on it, and went to bed.

IV

How could anyone, thought Severus as Capri came into view, how could anyone, least of all a Caesar who had all the world to choose from, choose to live on an ugly lump of rock poking out of the sea like a sore thumb with bitten stumps of finger-bones rotting round the base of it? Unless Tiberius really was what gossips said he was, a twisted tortured man, and had deliberately sought out an eyrie as malevolent in shape as his own mind.

Severus was dazed with heat and immeasurably tired. In this sullen south the nights were warm as bakers' ovens and the days so breathless, so steamy, that the very flies flopped, heavy with clotted wings. Along the Appian Way from Brindisi to Capua, all through scorched Apulia and the wearisome tangle of the Samnium Hills, he had snatched an hour's sleep, sometimes less, each time he had changed horses at post-houses. 'Queen of All Roads' they called the Apulia. Some Queen! Counting that boring succession of six-foot-high marble cylinders, each one of which laid one more burning mile behind him, he had craved for the north, for the green and lovely land of cool grandeur, for his native mountains and deep cold rivers and sky-high curtains of forest which would be balm to his sun-blasted mind, and where he could unhurriedly and decently mourn his wife and find joy in the first sight of his son.

There had been some respite from metalled road and some shelter from glaring sun after Capua, when he was cantering down towards the sea through the terraced groves and vineyards of Campania to take the post-boat for Capri at Puzzuoli. But he had experienced unexpected difficulty getting aboard. It was to be expected that the port for Capri would be heavily guarded nowadays because of Caesar being on that island, but Severus was surprised to see how many soldiers were around, and, although he appreciated that he had arrived unheralded, the questioning to which he was subjected before he was allowed on board seemed unnecessarily stringent.

'I am carrying important dispatches,' he explained. 'If this boat is too crowded, then I can catch the next.'

At this the officer gave him a long mocking stare. 'You'd be better taking this boat,' he said at last, and then, in an undertone, added more genially, 'though they might not let you land on the island. Anyhow, you can deliver your dispatches to the guard over there.'

So Severus had jumped aboard and, stretching himself under the shade of the awning, sleepily watched the activity on the quay. The port itself, shielded from the full glare of the sun by cliffs terraced with fruit-trees, was rather pretty in its disorderly Greek fashion. There were a lot of townsfolk around. Some of them were fishermen, but only a few of those were fussing about with their nets and floats. Most people were standing about gawking, though the loading of the boat did not seem to interest them. They were all staring at the soldiers. So it might be that today there were more of those than usual.

Passengers arrived. These, it was clear, were expected, for they were shown aboard without fuss. First aboard was a pompous but obviously shit-scared man in the purple-banded toga of a senator. He was an old man, but his slave, probably a faithful slave of long service, was even more ancient; so dodderingly old that he was for a moment in danger of going arse-over-tip into the sea with all the bags, and the senator himself was decent enough to grab one of his shoulders and steady him aboard. It was as well that he did so, for at that moment no one would have helped an old slave, the attention of everyone being attracted to the latest arrival.

A remarkable fellow, this newcomer. He was, one could see at a glance, a personage confident of high distinction, so markedly so that soldiers and centurions, immediately alerted by it, shuffled hastily into position to form a guarded corridor along which he, his gait so crippingly upright that it looked downright painful, strutted down to the quay. He was a lean man, and little, though his peppery dignity made one overlook, or forget, that he was below average height, with lips pressed firmly together as though against the danger of any smile ever softening the prissy severity of his martial visage, and with narrowed, switching eyes which, even while he was stepping so quickly towards the quay, seemed to have time to search each and every soldier in the file from top to toe; and one had the impression that he was storing, no doubt with marginal comments of acid disapproval, each fault of face or stance or uniform or weapon in an inspection so pointed that one could imagine his eyes were sharp enough to probe even under a man's kilt and note if a soiled loin-cloth harboured a louse.

From a distance the slight figure, sheathed in sheen of leather and flash of brass, had appeared inordinately well turned-out, quite dandified in fact. So it was a surprise to see, when he came nearer, that his gear was old and, on the whole, as modest as that of a foot soldier; not one leather strap without some scar of sword or javelin, not one brass boss or buckle without the dent of a blow. Indeed, his outfit was so battle-worn that it made him quite unique amid soldiery who had thought it proper on this Capri duty to sport smart virgin gear. Though it was, on reflection, noticeable that every inch of leather and every curve of brass, all flamboyantly registering past encounters in battle, had been polished and polished and polished His difference from all others was emphasised by two features of his costume, features so unusual that they must surely be eccentricities of his own fashioning: his boots and his buckles. The boots, calf-high and of soft kid, were made so that they could be pulled on instead of being laced, and thus, having no laces, would be impervious to sand; they now proclaimed, with each step they took, a proud history of desert campaigns. The buckles were even more illustrative of arrogant pride in a military past. Although his cloak was ostentatiously that of a common foot-soldier – in fact one would have found it impossible to buy a cloak more cheap, more simple and more rough – it was clasped to his shoulder not with the usual single brooch but with *two*. One brooch was of regulation type, bearing Caesar's effigy, but the other was adorned with what appeared to be an Asian decoration, and, probably some trophy he had won or been awarded in some foreign campaign, was now worn, in utter disregard of military convention, as a reminder of successes in the East.

Following him was his retinue. This comprised two markedly spick-and-span officers; a slave with a travelling trunk balanced on his shoulders; four others carrying a corded crate which was not very large and seemed hardly heavy enough to need so many bearers; and, superintending these four, a youth who seemed, in such martial company, somewhat of an oddity, perhaps because of the bold colour and excessive ornamentation of his tunic, which he wore Greek style, very short, with the fluted folds below the jewelled belt jutting out and barely concealing his buttocks. The military personage, waving away members of the boat crew who had leaped ashore to help in the embarkation, said that this boy – he referred to him as his secretary – would personally attend to the safe disposition on board of the precious crate. The man had a high-pitched voice, but it was a compelling authoritative voice; the words came out sharply in clipped little yelps, though apparently down his nose, so nasal did they sound and so little did his lips appear to open. The lad, stalwart and broad of shoulder but becoming rather plump, had a sulky expression. His hair, one could suspect, was not by nature either so golden or so curly. The two officers were also very young, quite outstandingly handsome. One of them, catching sight of Severus lying on the bench beside the gunwhale, began, after running his eyes boldly over Severus's travel-crumpled gear and sweat-smeared legs, a friendly and markedly collusive smile. Severus yawned in his face, pulled down his kilt and turned his back.

The operation of disposing of the crate continued for quite a time. The distinguished gentleman was not satisfied until it was placed, well roped-down, in the position which he judged safest for it but which was damnably inconvenient for the passengers' legs. But at last they were off.

There had been, just off Puzzuoli, a cool breath of sea breeze, but that lasted only a few minutes, and now, as they neared Capri, they were ploughing through heat so scorching that one could almost hear sun-battered Capri frying in its oily sea. Towards that island the distinguished gentleman kept his critical frown steadily directed, and on one occasion, noticing that his secretary, indifferent to the important view, was falling into a doze, he laid sinewy brown fingers on the plump cheeks so fiercely that one could see the young flesh flush and pucker under the grasp, and swivelled the lad's head around to direct his sulky gaze to scraps of buildings now becoming visible on the ravaged brows of Capri's cliffs. These, he proclaimed, loudly enough for others to hear and thus appreciate his intimate knowledge of the place, were new villas built by Tiberius Caesar.

Severus pulled himself up and leaned out beyond the awning to look at these fabled dwellings. All he saw was white shapes, scattered along the tops of the cliffs like dead bleached eagles, a few black feathers of cypress still sticking up from the corpses; so he drew his head back into the shade and was dozing when the boat grounded on the shingle of a cove near those tattered needles of rock.

It was a long business getting ashore. A captain of the boats was on the beach to superintend the arrival. This was customary, one of the boatmen told Severus, but, the man said, it was unusual for there to be so many guards around. 'And by all accounts,' he said later, 'we're not going back to Puzzuoli this evening. We have to stay the night.'

Even the distinguished gentleman seemed somewhat taken aback by the array of force on the beach and by the scrupulous examination of passengers and baggage, particularly when, despite his flourishing of papers and protests, an officer insisted on two boards of the crate being prised off so that soldiers could probe down into the straw and feel the contents. Severus, being unexpected, was subjected to the longest questioning. He managed to establish his identity, but not until he had produced the rolled manuscript with Pilate's seal and his questioner had weighed that in his hand, and even thrust fingers between the folds, was he given permission to jump on to the shingle.

'You will leave your arms,' said the captain of the boats. Severus drew back, laying his hand on his sword hilt. But, '*You will leave your arms,*' the captain repeated flatly, holding out his hands for sword and dagger.

Accompanied by two guards wearing the insignia of the Imperial Guard, one going ahead and one coming behind and neither speaking, Severus began climbing the first of the succession of staircases which zig-zagged towards the sky.

Severus had been delayed so long that the puffing senator and the military gentleman were far ahead of him. Once, faintly, he heard their porters break into chattering, but they soon stopped that: the steep climb knocked the wind out of them. It was hellishly hot: not with the dry and burning and exhilarating heat of Judaea, but clammy and sweat-making. Every now and then a few yards of horizontal pathway along boulder-buttressed terraces allowed one to walk instead of climb and gave one a breather, but for the most part it was up and up; prickly bushes stabbing over the steps to scratch calves, lizards scuttling, and occasional glimpses of a sea which became flatter and bluer as it fell below. No sight, as yet, of any villa.

Eventually a gentler stretch of stairway brought them on to a wide natural terrace. Here at last were signs of civilisation: some vegetables trying to hold their heads up in the shade of newly-planted cypress, and, further ahead, as welcome to the sight as the first humans glimpsed after a trek through uncharted forest, some labourers building pergolas for vines. As he and his guards plodded towards these signs of life, parts of the villa suddenly came into view overhead: sections of balustrading and urns and flowers and balconies and tiled roofs glimpsed through gaps in the trees. It still seemed damnably high above them.

The slaves working on the pergolas looked happy enough. They were of every type and colour, as though someone had gone round the whole Empire picking them one by one like flowers from different beds. Negroes, round-headed or long-headed but all burly, swathings of stencilled loin-cloths making their behinds look like enormous painted gourds; blond long-haired and moustached Germans wearing scraps of fur which could have been remnants of the skins they were wearing when they were rounded up; low-browed muscly Gauls; even, thought Severus, some Jews. And, of course, lots of Greeks. What language all these spoke among themselves only the gods knew, but their chattering was animated enough and there was a lot of laughter. They did not seem to be taking their work at all seriously, and the four kneeling around a brazier trying to blow the embers to life to heat up a mess of sausages and lentils were spending more breath laughing than blowing.

There was only one person of authority present: a bent old man with a mason's cap perched on his bald pate and leathery neck and wearing a mortar-splattered smock too long for him. He was showing a dumb-faced but half-similing Gaul how to lay a brick. 'Like this!' he snapped in an authoritative Roman voice. 'This way up!' He tossed the brick expertly in a hand which was decorated, too gaudily for a foreman, even a Roman one, with a massive signet ring of gold – probably only gilt. With his other hand he deftly twisted the trowel and landed a dollop of mortar slap in the middle of the last-laid brick. When he slapped the brick down, mortar oozed out from under it like soft cheese from a sandwich. He scraped these remnants up with the trowel as smoothly as peeling apples and flipped them on to the hod. 'See?' The Gaul nodded. 'Then in future do it properly!' said the foreman and, like a conjuror finishing a trick, tossed the trowel to the Gaul. The stupid oaf dropped it, but for him fortunately the foreman, hearing the approach of Severus and the guards, had now swung round to face them.

At which the guards, as though hit on the forehead by rocks, came to a shuddering halt. They stiffened to quivering attention. And so did Severus, struck dumb by the sudden revelation. For two slaves who had come running forward were now hoisting over the 'foreman's' head the stained overall which, like a curtain ascending on some scene of grandeur, rose to reveal the purple and white robes of His August Highness Tiberius Claudius Nero, Caesar.

Old and thin and gnarled Tiberius was, yet more terrifyingly impressive than Severus had ever imagined. The face, drooping forward on a lizard neck, was like a leather purse. The scars disfiguring it, scars left by those expensive but over-zealous Egyptian surgeons who, cauterising ulcers, had pressed the red-hot irons so deep that they burned into the bone, made it look as though the purse, repaired too often, had been carelessly stitched. The mouth was like old leather, too, puckered and pulled down at the corners, fallen in because of few teeth behind it, with the lips drawn so tight that the thinnest coin could not have fallen out. The eyes, however, were not the eyes of an old man. They were neither cloudy nor rheumy, but sharp and clean, the lids above them so full and heavy that they looked as if they could slide down and cover all the secrets of the world. Severus saw those eyes, glinting with suspicion and irritated surprise, glance quickly to where his sword might have been, and then, in milder inquiry, course over his armour, seeking some insignia which might reveal the newcomer's identity and purpose. Severus was agitatedly thinking whether it was proper for him to proclaim himself, when the Emperor suddenly asked doubtfully, 'From Rome?'

Still speechless, Severus shook his head, and, hoping that this might be the correct thing to do in the Presence, sank on to one knee, opened his satchel and pulled out the sealed bundle, holding it out with both hands towards His August Highness as one offering up a sacrifice, or one's very life, to a god. It seemed, though he could not have sworn to it, that the Emperor sighed with relief. Certainly the leather face relaxed a little, but he stared down at the proffered bundle some moments before he accepted it. At last he lifted it cautiously and then, more confidently, turned it over and examined the seal. The thin lips slightly wavered. The purse had not opened, not a crack. But the movement was, Severus hoped, a smile.

The Caesar turned round, made a quick gesture which might have been a beckoning, and walked away towards a point where some steps led upward. 'You're to follow him,' whispered one of the guards. Severus did so. But by the time he caught him up, Tiberius, after climbing only two steps, was turning sharply right into a shady clearing, where two slaves who had been stretched there gossiping on a patch of parched grass leaped to their feet to assist Caesar into a massive battered armchair. The chair was a most peculiar contraption. It took some moments before Severus understood its purpose. It had been fitted, in rough-and-ready fashion, with large wheels which, one eventually noticed, were resting at the beginning of two narrow wooden troughs which stretched uphill, disappearing into the trees and presumably leading up to the villa. A beam had been roughly nailed to the front legs of the chair, and to this a ship's cable was tied. One of the slaves hollered. From somewhere up above came an answering holler followed by the sound of a winch, which, as it turned, began taking up the slack of the cable. When he had taken his seat, Tiberius Caesar looked across at Severus with another of those closed-purse smiles. Probably the thing was his own invention.

'Go up the steps, Captain. I shall beat you to the top,' said Tiberius, leaning back and breaking the seal of the documents. He was already reading before the rope tightened. The chair jolted. The wheels creaked and turned. The chair rumbled upward. The slaves grinned. Like a god fashioned from old leather, Tiberius Caesar ascended.

The Old Man had been right about winning the race to the top. By the time Severus had run up the last steps leading to the villa gardens, the chair had already reached the terrace, and Tiberius, his bald pate now concealed under an embroidered purple cowl, was kicking off his mortar-encrusted shoes. A kneeling slave was sliding bootees of gilded kid on to the imperial feet before their soles descended bare upon the paving, but then, when his impatient master had levered himself out of the chair, he had to slither after him on his knees, making ineffective grabs at the gold-tipped laces as he tried to thread them. Two slaves came hurrying out of the villa with bowls of scented water and towels as Tiberius seated himself on a marble bench, his back to an awesome panorama of razor-edged cliffs cascading dizzily thousands of feet into the sea. He handed the bundle of manuscript, opened at a selected passage, to one of the slaves, instructing him to hold it open so that he could continue reading. The other washed smears of brick-dust and mortar from imperial fingers and big gold ring. The kneeling slave was still fiddling with the laces. Tiberius pushed him off with one foot, and, his hands now dried, took the manuscript and began flipping through it. Sighing, he wearily slung his legs along the bench and lay back. One bootee fell off. The slave scooped it up and attempted to slip it on again. Caesar's white foot, blue veins standing out on it thick as cords, shot out again, this time to greater purpose, for the lad rolled over. The lad retreated and, in the shade of a magnolia, sat on his haunches, sulkily wiping dust from gilded leather.

Tiberius read on, then gave another sigh and looked up and around until he made out the form of Severus still standing at attention, rigid with awe, against a wall in the shadow of a brick stairway curving up to a ground-floor entrance of the villa.

'Sit down, boy,' said Tiberius. He returned to his reading. So far, he thought, it was nothing but preamble. If only this man Pilate could come to the point, and, having reached the point, would stick to it! But soldiers were notoriously afflicted with pomposity once they got a pen into their hands. If this Pilate ever became a general, which the gods forbid, he would write his memoirs, and surely among the most lamentable results of any war was the wrack of autobiographies written by generals! He stared across at the young messenger from Judaea.

Severus, in the full glare of oppressive sunlight, was now perched stiffly on the very edge of a marble bench. In Capri even marble was hot. Despite the awesomeness of the company in which he found himself, he was near to nodding off in the sticky heat.

'Have you read this?' asked Tiberius.

Severus shook his drowsy head.

No, thought the Emperor. This lucky lad had to do no more than lug the Julian epic across the seas: it was not his task to read the thing. Daunted by prospects of how long it would take to do that, Tiberius held the documents breast-high as though he were weighing them, then let his hands sink, miserably overburdened under the load. It had to be read. Who could do it? That kind of labour was what Sertorius would have to perform before long, but he was too busy at the moment. Nerva? No, the lawyer was interested only in the legalities of administration, not in its performance. In any case Nerva was at the moment fully occupied in drawing up that urgent mass of death-warrants and sentences of exile. Yet some answer, even if no more than a delaying one, would have to be sent to Pilate.

'When are you due to return to Judaea, Captain?'

Now, for the first time, Severus had to speak to His August Highness. He found his voice dry and strained. 'Your Highness . . . Your Grace . . . ' Which was right? 'The Procurator has granted me some days' leave to go home. My wife . . . my wife has died, giving birth to a son.'

'Your first child?' Severus nodded. 'It lives?'

'Yes, your Grace.'

'You are lucky, Captain. You have a son.'

'I . . . Your Grace, I loved my wife,' said Severus in a whisper, his voice hoarse with this first spoken confession of his sorrow.

'That I do not doubt. But you have a son. And a lad like you will not be long finding another wife. Nor in loving her also.' For a moment the hooded eyes closed, and he brooded over memories. Better a loved wife dead and beyond desire than a loved one exiled and still desired, as his first wife had been by the command of Caesar and the dictates of dynastic necessity. 'Where is your home?' he asked as he opened his eyes.

'Lugano, your Grace.'

'Ah, of course!' That throaty Celtic accent was unmistakable. It also might explain why this lad, rather raw and possibly not over-bright, had found favour with this Pilate who worshipped the memory of Julius Caesar. For had not Julius, his Divine Self, always said that the best soldiers came from Cisalpine Gaul?

'Then We shall send our reply to this,' he said, tapping the manuscript, 'by other hands. You have Our permission to leave immediately for Lugano.' But then, as Severus was about to stand, he halted him with an uplifted hand. Caesar had suddenly remembered something. Severus crouched, taking his weight on his hands. 'But, of course, there are no post-boats until . . . No. Report immediately to the captain of the guard and let him arrange supper for you. You will eat alone in a room of your own. Keep to vegetables; and no wine. Always avoid wine before a journey. You look in need of sleep. Tell the captain you must have

124

a room of your own. You will not sleep in the dormitory, and you will not talk to the guards. The captain of the watch will come to you when it is time to leave. Tell the pantryman to pack a hamper with all you need for a long journey. I advise fruit and cheese and bread. When you report to the captain of the guard ask him to report to me here. Sleep well!'

'I thank your Grace,' said Severus, getting finally to his feet. He stayed there some moments, wondering whether it was protocol to await some imperial gesture of more positive dismissal from the Presence, but the Emperor was now reading steadily. Hardly daring to breathe, Severus stole away.

The glare of the sun was decreasing, but the air was still oppressively hot and clammy. The slave had fallen asleep under the magnolia, still nursing the gilded bootee. Tiberius skimmed through a page. And another. He yawned, and when he had wiped his eyes there came back teasingly into his mind memory of a passage he had earlier scanned too hurriedly. He scrabbled among the papyrus until he found it. A wicked smile twisted his lips as he mercilessly dissected the rhetoric; and when he reached the closed words he mouthed them histrionically, though in silence. After which, staring at the bench where the young captain had been sitting, he mused for a long time. The smile slowly faded, and the lips sank into their customary downward curve.

Yes, indeed, this communiqué of Pilate's, ambitious but pathetically mediocre, was nothing but a palimpsest of a Julian epic. That last passage for instance: jerry-built from words filched one by one from the *Commentaries*. But so bemused was the Procurator by myopic plagiarism of his god that he could not see the wood for the trees. In all this load of words there was so little of immediate application to immediate problems. Such real trouble as assassinations and guerrilla raids was accorded only passing mention. Even the crucifixion of a Roman was dismissed in a curt paragraph and marginal reference to an attached warrant of execution. Perhaps that Roman really had been a rascal, but some data about the nature of that rascality and some explanation of the causes of it would have been instructive. The punitive measures Pilate had taken were misjudged: they were either not severe enough or too severe. They were not severe enough to annihilate rebellion at a blow, but just severe enough to inflame Jewish animosity. Admittedly Julius Caesar's destruction of a cluster of tribal huts in the valley of the Rhine had probably been sufficient to awe savages like the Germans, but a proud and anciently civilised race like the Jews could not be cowed by wiping out a hamlet. Pilate saw things on too local a scale. The nearest he came to showing any appreciation of politics was in his discussion of administrative difficulties, and even those he illustrated only by trivial personalities, reporting meanly on the incompetence, lack of education and senseless brutalities of wine-bibbing Roman governors. A man worthy of the position of governor of a province should have the courage to show initiative and eliminate offending personnel, Roman or otherwise, without worrying Rome with petty details. On Galilee Pilate was deplorably vague. Admittedly Galilee was outside his province, but he seemed unaware of the dangers threatening from that disorderly country. Dispatches from the legate's secretariat in Antioch, so much farther from Galilee than was Judaea, showed that Antioch was far more observant than was Pilate of the activities of the seditious fanatics who wandered the hills of Galilee, exhorting farmers and fisherfolk to revolt against Rome. Why, according to Antioch, even in the towns now, in places like Nazareth and Tiberias, crazy preachers were inciting townsfolk against the law-abiding rulers of Judaea. To such sinister presagings of a storm that could at any moment burst over his head Pilate gave only the scantiest attention. Instead, at this moment when, though Pilate of course was not to know this, the very existence of the commonwealth was in peril, when events soon to take place in the heart of empire, in Rome itself, could plunge the world into a civil war as bitter as any in the past, this Pilate, strutting around his terrain on the fringes of empire like a busy but bewildered ant, went on and on like a stream. No! More like a dripping fountain. Prating about water-supplies and aqueducts and irrigation as though the whole destiny of the world depended on an artichoke. Oh, this Pilate! The man could not look on his own piss without seeing a Rubicon.

'Do you know what they are saying in Rome about the Old Man?' said one senator to the others. The senator, who had just arrived on the post-boat from Puzzuoli, shifted nervously on the bench and peered timidly down through the trees to where he could see, on a terrace far below, a purple cowl and gilded feet. But the other senators, who had been hanging around at the villa for days, knew enough by now about the disposition and acoustics of the place to know that up here on a terrace as high as the roofs they

126

could gossip freely without one word reaching the ears of Caesar or any of his staff of eavesdroppers. In any case Tiberius must have long ago lost any sense of offence at being called 'Old Man'. He had been called that even when he was a youngster.

Yet no one asked the speaker what it was that people were saying in Rome about Tiberius. No doubt it was that barber's joke one heard nowadays in the chair at any tavern: the one about Sejanus being now emperor of Rome and Tiberius only governor of Capri. The gossiping senator had been boring them for days with such chestnuts. At the moment they were in no mood for more. They were oppressed by the heat as well as by the knowledge that they were at last to dine with Caesar. A vegetarian meal, of course, which would almost certainly be accompanied by a lecture.

The senator began again. 'They say in Rome . . . ' But the yapping of a dog interrupted him and attracted the attention of them all. Along the terrace, at the furthest end of it where it abutted on an olive grove, Gaius Germanicus, balancing on the uppermost of three benches piled one on top of the other to form an improvised dais, was teasing a greyhound with a bone dangling on a cord. Below him a young Greek, smooth and gleaming brown, was stalking earnestly around, chisel and mallet poised, trying to capture glimpses of Caligula's sunlight-and-shadow profile and decide on the next stroke to be made on the statue he was carving. It was a life-sized portrait of a young warrior, naked except for shield and sword and, of course, boots.

'I must say the Greek lad is making a good job of it,' said another senator.

'Except for the hair,' sneered another. 'Marble's too smooth for Caligula's body; goatskin would be more suitable.'

'Though not for his head,' tittered another. 'So young. Nineteen, eh? And already getting thin on top.'

'Baldness runs in the family.'

'Truer to say it runs under the diadem. The Divine Julius, for instance. They say he spent hours laying each strand in place with his forefinger. And look at Tiberius: head like an egg.'

The oldest senator, the one who always sat so silently and never gossiped, cleared his throat loudly. He had not intended it as a warning, but it did remind the others that they had touched on two forbidden subjects in fewer minutes: baldness and hairiness. Tiberius had exiled a man for joking about baldness, and the usually amiable Caligula had once knocked someone down who

127

had made a quite innocent remark about goats which Caligula had thought was a calculated reference to his hairy torso.

'Please, Gaius,' the sculptor pleaded. 'Please keep still. Just a moment.' Caligula resumed the pose, leaning back with arms aloft as though holding sword and shield heroically high. The thrusting forward of one strong hairy thigh shortened his skimpy tunic immodestly.

'I think Caligula ought to run quickly to the nearest fig-tree,' said another senator, and smirked with a superior air when they gaped at him uncomprehendingly. Having travelled so much in Asia he liked to air his knowledge. 'Like the Adam of the Jews,' he explained. 'To cover his nakedness.'

'Ah!' said another and turned to examine more closely Caligula's bold display. Then, comparing it with the statue, he commented, 'The Greek is exaggerating even *that*!'

'Being Greek he probably has ambitions.'

'Well, I hope his ambition won't be too high or too hard,' said the bore and chuckled obscenely.

At that moment the statuesque group was joined by a uniformed personage stepping stiffly erect between the olives. The newcomer stopped a yard away from the dias and, gazing up at sunlit Caligula, struck an attitude of condescending admiration.

'Good afternoon, Gaius Germanicus,' he barked.

Caligula dropped his arms quickly and pulled down the skirt of his tunic. 'Good afternoon, Vitellius,' he said and again began dangling the bone just out of reach of the leaping dog.

'Our inspired Greek has chosen a handsome subject,' said Vitellius.

Caligula flushed, then flung the bone towards the trees, which sent the dog bounding away and afforded Caligula the excuse of vaulting lightly to the ground and striding after it. Not that he disliked his physique being admired: he was used to that in the baths. But he could not abide the kind of look that slid over his body like oil in masseur's palm.

'Gaius!' Vitellius was following him through the lemon-trees. 'Have you a moment? I have something to show you.'

'Nothing you have to show could be of much interest to me,' thought Caligula vulgarly, and grinned. But he stopped, pulled further down his tunic, and turned. 'What?' he asked curtly.

'A present for your uncle. I should like your opinion on it. It is being unpacked downstairs.'

'All right.'

They walked down two stairways and across the garden court to the arcaded entrances. In an anteroom just off the main stairway two slaves were clearing up a litter of opened crate and straw. The present for the Emperor had been placed in a prominent position on the black marble table near the door. The table was one of Caesar's beloved treasures, so sacred to his eye that only objects of his own careful choice were ever placed upon it. Now sunlight fell full on Vitellius's gaudy offering. It was a bowl held aloft by the figure of a dancing boy. The bowl was exquisite; of jade, and quite large. It must have cost a fortune. Its price, of course, would be what had impressed Vitellius. To men like him cost was the only criterion. Ambitious courtiers who offered gifts to the Emperor's art collection always made the same mistake. All they could appreciate was the size of the vast prices Tiberius was sometimes forced to pay for the treasures he coveted. Impressed by those legendary purchases, they overlooked his bargains. They would talk endlessly of the fifteen thousand dinars he had paid for one picture by Parrhasius of Ephesus, but completely ignore how little he had paid when he made off with the Lysippus which Agrippa had gifted to the baths in Rome. Though Tiberius had lost that treasure. The Old Man had been furiously angry when the populace had protested against this 'piracy' of a public statue. Compelled to put it back in the baths, he had grudgingly admitted that it appeared that Romans did after all have some taste in the arts. Nevertheless, the costly gift from Vitellius was perhaps sufficiently an oddity, flagrant combination of the exquisite and the banal, to interest the Old Man. The figure, upon which the lovely bowl must have been fixed at a later date, was atrocious. The form of the pirouetting body was lively enough in its conception, but utterly vulgarised by being heavily encrusted in enamels. It was, in short, in the worst style of depraved Greek – just the kind of bauble to attract the eye of a Roman millionaire.

'What do you think of it?' asked Vitellius impatiently, stalking proudly around it.

Caligula did not think he knew Vitellius quite well enough to say what he thought. He nodded judiciously.

'Do you think the Caesar will like it?'

'One never knows that, does one?' said Caligula diplomatically. In all probability, he thought, the Old Man would same day detach the bowl and put it tenderly in one of his cabinets of

129

treasures; then stow the offensive figure away somewhere out of sight.

At that moment Tiberius himself, followed by a slave carrying a bundle of manuscript, mounted the stairway. Now bathed and robed in purple magnificence the Caesar looked very different from the bricklayer Vitellius had seen two hours earlier. Vitellius made the briefest of bows, for it was known that Tiberius loathed any obeisance that had the slightest suggestion of flattery. He had once so forcibly pushed away an obsequious courtier kneeling to kiss the imperial knees that the two of them had ludicrously rolled over. Vitellius, anxious to present his gift and encouraged by having been accorded a quite amiable nod, ventured the joke which would have been more appropriate among the vines but which he had not thought of until a few moments ago. 'Hail Caesar!' he declared, 'Builder of empires; builder of pergolas!'

How idiotic military men could be! And how peculiar, thought Tiberius, that this Vitellius, a soldier of acknowledged brilliance, but also, so surprisingly, famed for political sagacity, chose to affect posture and dress and mannerisms which only an actor would consider anything like those of a general. It was possible that Vitellius was merely attempting to disguise himself, though Tiberius was inclined to suspect some ambiguity of character, the nature of which he could not precisely diagnose. This irked him. Tiberius liked to know what people really were. When he knew that, he could tolerate even rascals, even potential assassins, up to a point, the point when it was necessary to hand them over to the strangler. Which reminded him of events imminent in Rome. Pushing aside these thoughts, he said to Vitellius, 'You will dine with Us,' though in such sombre tones that it did sound more like a sentence of death than an invitation. He would have passed on had not Vitellius at that moment stepped aside to allow Caesar uninterrupted view of his gift.

Tiberius halted. 'Who put that *thing* there?' he asked.

'It is a gift, sir,' said Caligula quickly. 'From Vitellius. The bowl is very fine jade.'

'Hm! Thank you, Vitellius.'

'I am glad the Caesar is so pleased with it,' said Vitellius.

'Thank you,' repeated Tiberius sharply. 'But I hardly think that is the right place for it, do you?' He was on the point of turning away from the gift and giver altogether, then suddenly halted. He looked towards the piece again. Slowly he stepped to the table. He bent down and peered closely at the bowl. He ran

130

a fingernail along the bevel of the jade. 'Hm!' he said reflectively. Then he lifted the whole piece aloft and swung it over in the sunlight so that he could see just how the splayed hands had been fixed to the base. 'Hm!' he said again. 'The bowl is from Asia, I suppose?'

'The figure too, I believe.'

'Could be. The bowl is a gem. You are still interested in that part of the world, Vitellius?'

'Always. Once one has acquired a taste for the East one never loses it.'

'In that case,' Tiberius beckoned the slave towards him and took the pile of dispatches, 'in that case you will find these dispatches absorbing. Go through them, Vittelius. Make me a digest of them. In fact, knowing Our mind on Asian policy you might well draft Our reply. Make it short, though.' He handed the load to Vitellius and repeated, but this time in warmer tones, 'You will dine with Us,' then swept on towards the corridor which led to his private apartments. Caligula took the opportunity of escaping from Vitellius by pretending that he must follow his greatuncle in equal haste.

Meanwhile, on the high terrace, where there had been a deep-breathing somnolence for a long time, the senators watched the sculptor shrouding his work for the night. Except the bore: he was sleeping, and his snores added to the boredom and inertia of the hour.

'I wonder what the Caesar is paying for the statue,' mused one senator. 'I heard someone downstairs saying that he has decided to send it to Rome and have it put on the Capitoline just to let the Romans see their next Caesar.'

'They'll certainly see all of him,' said the critic.

The newly-arrived senator, seeing that the blue cowl and gilded feet were no longer on the lower terrace, dared now to whisper, 'Do you think it's all settled, then?'

'No, no, no! It's still a toss-up. There's Nero in the running too.'

'But he's so young.'

'Precisely. It depends, I suppose, on how long Tiberius lives.'

'And how long Caligula lives,' said the Judaean expert. 'Tiberius might have brought the youngster to Capri to do a Herod act.' He could not resist the temptation of airing his knowledge of Asian politics, but those with whom the fig-leaf joke had fallen flat could not fail to see the significance of this last remark, and felt the senator was going dangerously far to talk in this context of the Herod who had strangled his heir. One was aware, of course, of the slanderous rumours surrounding the deaths of Caesar's heirs. His son, Drusus, for instance. Poisoned by Sejanus, they said. But one did not say such things. Now, himself regretting his impropriety, the Judaean expert laughed his remark away as the stupid joke it was and continued, 'Don't you think the question of the succession could well be the reason why Tiberius has summoned us to Capri?'

'Which might be why Sertorius is here,' suggested another.

'Macro Naevius Sertorius?' asked the newly-arrived, his voice full of awe.

'None other. But don't be scared. You'll not be meeting him. He's not shown his face all the time we have been here. No one sees him except the Old Man and lawyer Nerva.'

'Caligula as Caesar!' sighed the newly-arrived. 'That would change things, wouldn't it?'

'For us, yes,' said the oldest senator, at last breaking his long silence. 'I think he would consider us rather ancient.'

'He certainly would,' said the notorious cynic of the gathering. 'He would bring in all his young friends. All that tavern and theatre society that run after him.'

'Don't be misled by appearances, my friend,' said the oldest senator. 'Just because they wear their hair long and dress in fancy clothes doesn't mean they lack brains and courage. We have to face facts, my friend. The Augustan age is dead. We can't go on living on its fat any longer. Something must take its place, and there could be worse things than Caligula. At least he is liberal.'

'Yes, liberal! If by that you mean one who is always talking about reform. That's what the Caligula set are always preaching. Reform, reform, reform. Down with corruption! Down with capitalists! Down with nepotism! And kick out the old fogies!'

The old senator smiled. 'If one lives long enough, one always hears on other lips the songs one sang when one was young. The young are ever rebellious against the ways and the laws of the old. It is the nature of youth. But actually it is not our *laws* they wish to overturn: it is our *presences*. Once they are in our seats of power they do very little different. I suppose every new generation always thinks itself born to sweep up the mess left by the old. Although,' he added after a long pause, 'they most times bend their energies to the sweeping with such enthusiasm that they do not realise that their brooms are only dispersing the mess, not cleaning it up.'

'Anyhow,' murmured the timid newcomer, 'it will be some time before Gaius Germanicus or Nero or anyone succeeds. How long . . . ?' He mused fearfully. 'How long do you think Tiberius might wear the diadem?'

'How long might he live?' said the cynic, putting the question more brutally. 'If you were gifted as an oracle you might find the answer to that question by counting the ulcer-scars on his face.'

Stung to anger by that offensiveness, the oldest senator retorted, with a lack of discretion which he immediately regretted, 'Or find the answer on the face of Sejanus.'

At that there was a momentous silence, full of suspicions and personal terrors, until the bore, awakened by one of his own snores, again began asking, this time in a desperately determined voice, 'Do you know what they are saying in Rome about the Old Man?' No one rose to the bait. He pointed to the dizzy fall of fierce rock below the villa. 'If Tiberius has to "throw anyone over", then he throws them down that cliff.' He shook his head. 'After three days in Capri . . .'

But just then everyone began scrambling to their feet, and in their haste to get downstairs for dinner no one heard the last words of the stale joke.

The silence was oppressive. Since dinner began the Caesar had not uttered a word, and no one thought it proper to speak before he did. They stole nervous glances at Caesar's face on which the scars, shining pale in the lamplight, looked like slivers of dead fish stuck haphazardly on the old brown skin.

The senators munched their way stodgily through heavy polenta and under-cooked greens. Now, not satisfied with being vegetarian, Tiberius had decreed that vegetables were spoiled by over-cooking. So everything was only parboiled. The only tasty thing on the table was the asparagus. It was said that one gardener was kept fully occupied from dawn to dusk shifting around the wheeled boxes in which it grew, keeping the asparagus in the shade so that it would grow pale and tender as Tiberius liked it. Yet even the asparagus could have done with a few more minutes in the pot. As for the wine! Only the newly-arrived senator had been foolish enough to put water in it: the others knew that the steward had already done that, and had not stinted, either. Which was just as well. The wine was from Sorrento – the cheapest that could be found even there and sour as acid. Tiberius himself called it 'my good vinegar'. This evening the Caesar was nibbling his favourite food, radishes which were always sent direct from Germany. He had once quarrelled bitterly with his son Drusus for refusing to eat these vegetables. Usually he ate them with wine and honey, but this evening he had waved the wine aside and was drinking only water. A bad sign. A drop of wine might possibly have mellowed him. But he who had once been nicknamed 'Biberius' by his troops was becoming increasingly abstemious. And, as with a convert, he was fanatical; pompously righteous against wine-bibbers and sourly bad-tempered in his deprivation.

The Caesar's diet was in tune with his surroundings. There was not a senator there who did not at home live in greater comfort and luxury than Caesar did on Capri. The dining-room was austere. Admittedly it was not completely finished: the obligatory bust of the Divine Augustus was already *in situ* but the lesser niches were as yet unpopulated. One, in fact, was still bare brick without as yet marble frame or mosaic lining. But the dining-room showed no promise that even when it was finished it would be any better than one could find in a modest country house. There was not so much as one slave to wait at table: one had to reach for dishes or ask a neighbour to pass them. The whole villa was run like one belonging to someone who had retired on a not too adequate pension. The place was absurdly under-staffed. There was a whole pack of Chaldeans of course: Caesar always had to have those astrologers nearby for consultation. Lots of scribes as well. But domestic staff was cut to the minimum.

Chasing shreds of radish around his teeth-stumps with a viperish tongue, Tiberius gazed with unconcealed boredom at the array of dumb and chewing senatorial faces. His 'Conscript Fathers'! They were like nothing more than cattle brought to the trough, masticating the abominably half-cooked vegetables, which some expensive quack from Egypt had years ago told him were required diet for a sedentary man, and swilling down his watered vinegar.

He had placed Vitellius on his right hand. The honour had taken some of the sting out of that unfortunate affair with the gift and was also some recompense for unloading the Judaea dispatches on him. The oldest senator, the only one of the gang from Rome for whom Tiberius could summon up the merest flicker of trust, was on his left.

A glint of amusement, however, softened the heavy-lidded gaze when his roving eyes fell on yong Gaius at another table. Caligula, in animated argument with his sculptor friend, was illustrating a point by modelling a figure with lumps of bread which he damped with spit and pressed deftly into shape. Neither he nor the Greek was eating. Tiberius guessed they had sneaked into the staff-kitchen earlier and gorged themselves on sausages and lentils. He cleared his throat loudly. Caligula smiled at him. Was this, the smile asked, the signal, the call for help which Tiberius sometimes sent across the room, beseeching Caligula to initiate any conversation that might break the constipated silence? The boy's grin was frankly impudent. Yet the impudence had a comradely flavour, managing somehow to convey at one time both impertinent intimacy and affectionate reverence. Tiberius shook his head. Don't speak just yet!

You rascal! Young as you are, you are old enough to read my mind, though not, I hope, able to read it too closely at this moment. That which I know is soon to happen to you had best be innocent of until the deed bursts on a startled world.

But when, oh when, could he rouse himself this evening to conjure words instead of bestial champing from his 'Conscript Fathers'! So many things he might say. A hundred thoughts and opinions and plans coursed through his head. Yet any one of them could lead too dangerously close to that one thing which he must not say: not yet.

How he hated this bunch from Rome, with a hatred constant and intense: a hatred fierce enough to dry up even his venom, leaving his mind scorched and bored! They saw themselves, he knew, as a gathering of trusted senators summoned to confer with Caesar on imperial affairs. He hoped to be still alive after the next few days, and able then to tell them the truth. Then they would learn that they were here not because they were the most trusted but because they were the most suspect. How he craved the power to throw the lot over! Were it not for the fact that singly each one represented a family of wealth and collectively they represented a great chunk of popular will, he would do that. Would throw them over. Those Capri cliffs could tempt him to make legend a reality.

They, for their part, hated him equally. That he knew. But he did not find hatred of him all that offensive. He was used to hatred: many who had loved him little had served him well. No, what curdled his anger was their fawning duplicity. Were he at this moment to strike any one of them with his glowering frown he would receive in return a full false smile. Such smiles he had seen for years. Some here tonight had been among those who, sixteen years ago, fell on their knees imploring him to assume the diadem. He had not craved that honour. When Augustus died, the need for an emperor also died. Augustus had completed the job to which history had called him. He had done all that needed to be done to stabilise Caesar's conquests, to subdue unruly children and make a great family of the world. After that there was no need any longer for a father. Father Augustus's passing had been a fitting moment at which to restore the power of an enlightened populace and to realise once again the ideal of a republic. But the senators would not have that. Were they frightened of the people? Or were they such lazy infants that they craved a father figure who would make the decisions they were incapable of making and the mistakes they feared to make? Whatever their reasons, they had lauded him and elevated him. Well, they had had their way, and, by entrusting the weal of millions into the hands of one mortal man, had saddled Rome with a Caesar, salving their consciences by professing to see their Caesar as immortal. By thus transforming a free republic into an absolute despotism they had established the precedent. Now the concept of Caesar would persist. For how long? Until the time when some irresponsible and noxious tyrant would be too much for men to stomach and Rome would be forced to overthrow him, even if, by so doing, she brought the whole fabric of empire around her ears.

That reverence which they paid to the memory of the deified Augustus was a measure of their hatred of Tiberius. In retrospect they looked back with longing to the Augustan age. Augustus had had the knack of wreathing with roses the chains he laid upon his subjects; under Tiberius the senators felt the iron. And although every one of his 'Conscript Fathers' who so obsequiously munched at his table would, were he to demand it, grovel to kiss his feet, in their hearts they despised him. They imagined themselves as statesmen, wise in politics and sophisticated in philosophy, and saw him as one upon whom the purple had fallen merely through luck and not by virtue of talent. In their eyes he was a lucky ignoramus, his only gifts his brutal energy and devious cunning, attributes which they lauded with political euphemisms in public and poked fun at in private. They looked down on him, in the same way perhaps as he himself, a couple of years ago, had been looking down on that little man in Judaea. It was well to remember that a Caesar's performance on the world stage might be a bigger, but was after all no better a performance than that of a Pilate in a provincial playhouse. Any Caesar was only a Pilate to whom accident of birth had given greater suzerainty.

He must curb his tendency to think others were stupid. Only a fool ever said a man was a fool: a wise man never did.

A Caesar could be as guilty as any other of the error of imagining that his transitory shifts and improvisations were immortal wisdom. We would think any sailor mad if he imagined that it was his sail that controlled the winds. Politicians, even Caesars, were just as mad when, not accepting that the most they could do was to shift sail, they imagined they were actually creating the gales and convulsions of history.

Of all the senators present there was only one he loved and whom he could trust: that oldest one now sitting on his left. He was the only sincere one of the whole bunch. Too sincere sometimes. So sincere that in private he dared tell Tiberius the truth about Tiberius. There had been moments during such interchanges when Tiberius had felt that he hated the old man for the cruelty of his truths more than he hated all mediocre others for the honey of their lies.

He cleared his throat again, and this time when Caligula glanced in his direction he nodded. Caligula, eager as a ringmaster giving the signal for the game to begin, seized on the first subject that came to his mind and asked, 'What news from Judaea, sir?'

'Our friend Vitellius can best answer that question,' said Tiberius. 'He has just read all the latest news.' This would show whether the rogue had done as he had been asked.

'News!' Vitellius drew himself erect, speaking haughtily, yapping the words out as though he were reading a proclamation. 'As much news as Proconsul Pilate vouchsafes to insert in his exhortation for a scheme of public works. His only news as such, at least the only news that sticks in my mind, is that the Procurator has . . . ' He grimaced and then hissed out the words like a spitting snake. 'The Procurator has crucified a Roman.'

There were gasps.

'I thought that fact might catch your eye,' said Tiberius with a mildness calculated to make Vitellius bridle. It was quite exhilarating to see honest indignation cracking the military mask.

'But, Caesar! A Roman! Crucified along with a bunch of

137

Jewish rebels and, what is more, crucified within the sight of Jews!'

There were more gasps. Now none of the company was eating. One, with his mouth full, had left it hanging disgustingly open.

'Our Procurator in Judaea,' said Tiberius, 'is at some pains to emphasise that the man was not technically a Roman when he was put on the cross, but had been, by formal instruments, deprived of citizenship.'

'A mere device. Whether legally viable or not, I do not know.'

'Nor is it necessarily important, Vitellius. It is not the first time that a Roman, a real Roman, has been crucified.'

'Yes. There was at least one regrettable occasion in Sicily, and others, I think, in Spain. But with all respect, August Highness, I beg you to recall what Cicero had to say about that. No word, said Cicero, no word was too terrible to describe a man who could condemn a Roman citizen to such an end.'

'Our Procurator in Judaea is no doubt also fully cognisant of Cicero's opinions: might even be moved to any act contrary to the opinions of an avowed enemy of the Divine Julius and his successors. Though I am inclined to think that Pilate was attempting to emphasise by crucifixion that a traitor, even more so if a Roman, is too perfidious to enjoy the gentle Roman privileges of being nobly strangled or decorously disembowelled.'

'But what . . . ? With the uttermost deference, Your August Highness . . . ' began one senator and then fell silent.

'Go on. Speak out, Afranius. Try to forget that you are a guest enjoying the lavish munificence of my table. Imagine you are in the Senate where it is customary to tell Caesar where he is wrong.'

'Not wrong, Caesar. I seek only to resolve my doubts. I am trying to reconcile my mind to accept that the most heinous Roman imaginable could be crucified.'

'One reason could be that the Roman chose crucifixion.'

'Chose it?' whispered Vitellius in bewilderment.

'Yes. By his own acts. By becoming a Jew. For it appears he did become one, by renouncing his Roman gods and accepting the one god of the Jews. Though Pilate omits to tell us whether or not the Roman went to the lengths of becoming a Jew physically. The Procurator, out of modesty no doubt, denies us the pleasure of such intimate details. But the man did indulge in a rite called baptism in a Judaean river. This, more than active malice, seems to have landed him into the company of Jewish terrorists, those guerrilla fighters known as Zealots. He professed that he had come south on a mission of peace. He said he had hoped to dissuade these creatures from violence. But the facts are against him: the boy with whom he was found in bed was armed with a Zealot dagger.'

Tiberius reached for a radish. He seemed to be awaiting comments, but the only sound in the room was his champing.

'I take it,' he said at length, 'that my senators now see that the punishment fitted the crime and was suited to the criminal. But I am not particularly interested in the treason and delusions or the fate of one individual. I have been cogitating over this trivial affair in Judaea for quite other reasons. I see it as a symptom of our time. Only a symptom, no bigger than a pimple pricking the skin, but equally significant of a disease in the body politic. It is a significance which I find historically fascinating. It is a clue to the future: a future which none of our generation will live to see.' His eyes rested on Caligula. 'Nor your generation either, Gaius Germanicus. No, that Roman in Judaea is the forerunner not of the immediate but the distant future. We have inherited from the Divine Augustus a commonwealth of peaceful nations. I admit that peace is, in political terms, desirable. But I can envisage that, in a world in which national rivalries no longer exist, our successors might hear voices which have previously been muffled by the clash of arms and the tramp of legions. Can you imagine such a world, senators? A world in which man will no longer have the need and therefore no longer the desire to fight for the nation in which he happened accidentally to be born? When a man will no longer kneel before a Caesar to offer him his sword, but will kneel before a cause and offer it his life? When a man will no longer fight for his country but will fight for an idea? I see the Roman who was crucified in Judaea, this man whose name, as Our Procurator has rightly suggested in his instrument of debasement, must be erased from all published records, as a scout of that vast army which is assembling beyond the frontiers of our time. He did not die for Rome. He did not die for Judaea. He did not even die for his treasonable confederates; he died for something he believed in. What a novel notion! Something completely new to the world! You were saying, Vitellius?'

Vitellius pulled himself together. 'I can only compliment you, humbly, August Caesar, for having used a sordid incident as a text for a sermon of such . . . well, I can only say such grandeur. I would hope that others have the ability to see the event in historical perspective. Though I fear such an exercise is beyond the capabilities of mortals like this Pontius Pilate. His lengthy memorandum to Your August Highness suggests that, faced with the task of assessing the oriental mind and administering Asian affairs, he has no more vision than had his predecessor.'

'Don't be too hard on Pilate, Vitellius,' growled Tiberius. 'You yourself said when his predecessor . . . what was his name?'

'Valerius Gratus.'

'When you were there and saw what a mess Gratus was making of things, you excused him by saying that Judaea must be about the most uncomfortable province any governor could have wished on him.' His eyes, ranging along the faces to discover any senator who might be showing signs of an intelligent understanding, fell on one that was pouting heavily. 'You can inform us, Titus Roscius. You were in Judaea recently. You met Pilate. How did you find him?'

The senator, startled by being plucked out of silence, stammered, 'Oh, looking older.'

'Any taller?' asked Tiberius and, contemptuously discarding the senator's inept contribution to the discussion, turned again to Vitellius who was now recollecting some of Pilate's phrases.

'He is virulent in his criticism of governors,' said Vitellius.

Tiberius nodded. 'Pilate describes them as bull-headed brutes, self-indulgent, wine-swilling sots, with less intelligence than the average corporal.'

Some senators, imagining that Tiberius could repeat Pilate's adjectives only in disapproval of them, made conventional murmurs of outrage. This brought a smile to Tiberius's face. That smile further tricked one senator. Thinking it indicated the Caesar's approval of the senators' mumbled protest, he whispered loudly to a neighbour senator, 'Pilate is giddy: for one with the blood of slaves in his veins he has climbed too high too quickly.'

Tiberius glowered at the whisperer. Vitellius tut-tutted. The remark was unbelievably tactless. Could the old fool really be unaware that Tiberius's favourite, his confidant Macro Sertorius, now labouring at this very moment in mysterious secrecy with lawyer Nerva somewhere in this very villa, was actually the son of a slave?

It was several moments before anyone dared break the prickly silence. At last one senator daringly attempted a pleasantry which might take everyone's mind away from the gaffe. 'This man Pilate reminds me of Cicero,' he said with a frail laugh, and won the accolade of renewed amusement in Caesar's eyes. Tiberius, everyone knew, was continually being plagued by Vitellius's quotations of Cicero.

'The senator speaks nonsense,' Vitellius snapped. 'Had he had the misfortune of being forced to wade through Pilate's prose, he would have found it vastly different from Cicero's precision. Furthermore Cicero, though often in error, believed he was attacking great wrongs: he would never have wasted so many words on trivial targets.'

'I wasn't speaking of Pilate's language, Vitellius,' said the senator. 'I was referring to Pilate's self-obsession. He imagines that every little thing he does out there must be of formidable interest to us in Rome. And what I was remembering was that story of how Cicero came back from foreign service asking everybody, "What are people in Rome saying about what I have done?" to which someone replied, "But *have* you been away, Cicero? Where? You must tell us all about it." '

There were smiles. Vitellius shrugged. 'The comparison is not apt. For a governor of such petty importance as Pilate to criticise in such gross terms officers who are, after all, servants appointed by Caesar, is, I think, presumptuous.'

'It is!' Tiberius nodded sombrely. 'Atrociously presumptuous.' The senators nodded with him. But their nods jerked to a halt when he added, 'And atrociously true. Pilate has apparently discovered the common fault of colonials: of conducting themselves without tact. They fail to remember the nature of the people they are dealing with. Jews are a prickly lot. They are religiously sensitive, and above all, they are sensitive about being subject to Roman occupation.'

'They did invite us there,' said Senator Roscius. Having now pulled himself together, Roscius was eager to show Caesar that he was well informed on Judaea. 'It was the Jews themselves who sent delegations to Rome begging us to go there and get them out of the mess they had been plunged into by Aristobulus and that incestuous horror Janneus. It was in the Senate in Rome, not in the Sanhedrin at Jerusalem, that Herod was proclaimed king of Judaea. And it was our Divine Augustus who saved the Jews from their own Jew tyrant, Archelaus.'

'You should go further back than that, Roscius,' interrupted another. 'Rome made its first treaty with the Jews two hundred years ago. Rome sent Judaea military advisers. It followed up with Roman arms. But, let's face it, these Jews should be reminded that

141

Judaea isn't their country at all. The Jews are the invaders there, whether we are or not. The Jews stole that country from the Canaanites in the first place.'

'That is a long time ago, Senator,' said Tiberius. 'All of seven hundred years ago.' His attitude now, leaning forward with hands clasped on the table and those leathery eyelids almost closed as he sought for words, indicated that now had arrived the moment for the lecture. 'We had better not enter into discussion of what part of the world belongs originally to whom. If we do that, some of us Romans might find ourselves being sent back to some mighty strange places. We should be honest. We should admit, between ourselves only of course, that we offered to help Judaea in our own interest as much as in theirs. Both races would perhaps be happier if they accepted that truth. It was to the interest of Rome to have a friendly power sitting between ambitious states like Syria and Egypt. We must still see Judaea in that light: a buffer state. East of it is Parthia. "In all the wide world",' he quoted, ' "Rome fears no foe save Parthia." That collection of barbaric military states beyond the Euphrates poses a potential menace which we must never ignore. The day may indeed come when the whole of the western world will have to resist the threats and pressures of emergent and ambitious peoples on its frontiers, particularly from the vast hordes of the East. This man Pilate does show, within his limits, some perception of that political concept when he advocates peaceful extension of Roman patronage in his province. One of the last and wisest actions of the Divine Augustus was to warn Rome against adventuring beyond the confines of its now established commonwealth of peoples. He urged us to restrain the temptation, to which Rome is by its nature particularly prone, gloriously to expand. It was the wise advice of a wise ruler. And in pursuance of that policy it is Our Imperial intention to encourage the prosperity of client states upon the periphery of Our commonwealth and thus cultivate their solid friendship in maintaining peace throughout the world We have inherited.'

Having delivered himself of this pronouncement of imperial policy, Tiberius turned instinctively to his familiar critic on his left. The lines gouged on that aged visage were too deep to be erased by flattery, and the lips had crinkled into a mocking smile at Caesar's praise of Augustus. The old man knew how deeply Augustus had detested Tiberius. Yes, Tiberius knew how much Augustus had detested him, though perhaps that dislike had been the kind which a father could bear for an unloved son: an unloved one he had been forced to adopt as heir, because he could find no better, to inherit the empire he had created. So, sternly but dutifully, Augustus had educated Tiberius; and Tiberius, unloved, but, despite that, admiring and revering, had learned well. Perhaps one does learn better from a teacher who hates one: with such a teacher there is no danger of sentiment intruding on wisdom.

'Why don't you say it, old cynic?' Tiberius growled at him in an undertone, mimicking the mocking smile with his pursed mouth. 'You are old enough to dare. At your age you have few years to lose.'

'Under your beneficent rule, Augustus Tiberius, I have indeed experienced the rare happiness of daring to *think* anything I please. I must be content with that. It would be folly to hope for the further happiness of daring to *say* it.'

Tiberius laid a hand on the old shoulder. 'Well said,' he murmured. 'And enough said.'

The oldest senator sipped his wine and made a sour face. 'Though one thing I dare say, August Caesar. In one respect at least you have not followed the glorious examples set by your divine predecessor. I remember with a wine-lover's nostalgia how Augustus Caesar cultivated the fashion for drinking that mild ambrosial Setinian from the hills beyond the Marshes. His august heir goes only as far as Sorrento for his vinegar.'

'Enough, enough, I said,' growled Tiberius with a thickening in his voice that the senator recognised as the nearest to a chuckle the Caesar could ever attain. As with any man of eccentric frugalities, references to and even jeers at his economies delighted him more than praise for grander virtues.

'But we must consider other things than arms and trade,' said Vitellius, encouraged to sudden boldness by the apparent joviality of the Caesar. 'Rome should attempt to introduce these Judaeans to a fuller appreciation of the Roman way of life: not only laws and military disciplines and commercial dexterity, but also Roman culture.'

'Roman habits have been the very thing these stubborn Jews have most resented,' growled Roscius. 'Why, they scream denunciation against any of their own youths who adopt Roman dress and Roman customs.'

'They scream even more when the boys try to put back that bit of flesh,' murmured the bore, who, having now drunk as much

143

Sorrento wine as he could stomach, at last entered the conversation.

'I am not referring to Hellenisation,' said Vitellius stiffly. 'Clothes and baths and statues are only the trimmings. There is no need gratuitously to offend them by forcing such things upon them.'

'Was Herod's eagle only trimmings?' retorted Roscius. 'A gang of rabbis inflamed the students to drag that down from the Temple and chop it to bits.'

'That was a mistake on Herod's part. He, although only half a Jew, should have known better than to affront the susceptibilities of a touchy race. I am certainly not proposing that we introduce the *mores* of Roman culture in defiance of Jewish racial prejudices. We must not *impose* culture: we must *insinuate* it. We should patiently display it and be content gradually to enlighten others to its riches. Just as we pursue a policy of Judaisation in the hope that eventually Jews will learn properly to conduct their own affairs in the free world of Roman civilisation, we should allow them the liberty of choosing such features of our western culture as appeal to them. We cannot, we must not, attempt to drive them to such things. We must merely provide them with free access to our art, our theatres, our literature and our way of life.'

'Well spoken, Vitellius,' said Tiberius. 'You make it evident that we need in Judaea not merely military and commercial executives. We could do with a cultural one as well. I must think of that.' He cast his eyes over the assembly. 'Gentlemen, We thank you for your attendance on Us this evening. We shall shortly have decisions of imperial importance to communicate to you. We shall call you to Our Presence at the appropriate time. Good night.'

It was still night, with not a glimmer of dawn, when Severus was awakened. He awoke completely refreshed: he had slept well in the quiet of a sturdy little stone cabin near the beach. Last night, eating alone in a room in the guard-house near a lower entrance to the villa, he had heard the bustle in the guards' mess and the murmur of conversation. The talk, he thought, was more muted here than was customary in a soldiers' mess. Then, just when he was preparing his cot for sleeping, there had been a change in plan. The captain of the boats had appeared and told him he would have to sleep at the beach. It seemed to Severus that he was

144

being treated as a very important person when none other than that captain himself led him down the stairways; though the man did give the impression that he considered Severus's presence somewhat of a nuisance that night, and confirmed that impression by bolting the door of the cabin on the outside after showing Severus in, as though Severus would want to escape or something. All Severus wanted to do was to sleep; he was soon doing that.

It was again the captain of the boats, no less, who was now shaking his shoulder to awaken him. 'Get ready quickly,' he said, 'but stay inside until you are summoned.'

A great deal of coming and going and tramping of feet and whispering could be heard outside. Eventually, after waiting quite a time, Severus ventured to open the door and peep down towards the sea where rowing-boats were taking soldiers to somewhere beyond the Needles. 'You are to stay there until summoned,' hissed someone just outside, and sharply pulled the door to. So there was even a sentry posted at his door.

Eventually he was summoned. Again it was the captain of the boats, and now he led Severus down to the beach where only one rowing-boat remained, a waiting boatman bent over the oars. 'Get in!' ordered the captain curtly. 'Your arms will be given to you when you leave the boat at Puzzuoli. Have a safe journey, Captain.'

As they rowed towards the Needles the other boats were coming back empty. 'Where is everyone going?' asked Severus interestedly. The boatman made no reply, but Severus soon saw where all the soldiers had got to. At sea off the Needles was a trireme, a fine new one with sixty oars; and along all the length of all three decks Severus could see the soldiers' iron casques gleaming dully, looking like strings of round beads punctuated at regular intervals with the horse-hair tufts of officers' helmets. He was hauled aboard and bundled along to one of the remotest niches of the lower deck where, special treatment again, he was seated out of contact with all but the captain of the guard who gave him a nod of greeting but did not speak. In fact, no one spoke all the way to Puzzuoli. It was the most silent voyage Severus had ever known: everyone seemed to have had the last murmur squeezed out of him by some enormous pressure from above.

At Puzzuoli Severus and the captain of the guard were, obviously by some pre-arrangement, the first off the galley. Not until they stood on the quay and the captain handed Severus his sword and dagger did the captain speak. 'There is your firman,' he said, handing Severus a small but heavily sealed document. 'It will see you past all posts and guards from here to Lugano. You are advised . . . you are *commanded* to avoid Rome. You will go north through Ostia and will not leave the coast road until you reach Pisa. After that it should be easy.'

'After that!' thought Severus. After that he would be nearly home. They had provided him with a magnificent horse. It looked in fettle enough to do the whole journey without a change. There were two panniers of provisions, vegetables much in evidence but no wine visible, and even a bed-roll. So it was true, then, that the Old Man thought of everything. He had often heard how Tiberius Caesar would sometimes put his own doctor, even his own cooking-utensils, bath and biscuits, at the disposal of a soldier in need of them.

Contentedly Severus mounted and rode off, accompanied by an escort of two guards who had been detailed by the captain to see him to the limits of the town. It looked, as dawn now broke, more like a barracks than a town: there was not a sign of townsfolk on the waterfront, and the end of every street was blocked by soldiers. His escort saw him through the north gate. Now the open road, empty and morning-cool, was before him. Joyfully he spurred the horse; the long strong legs broke into a canter. At last he was on his way to his beloved north and his son.

At about the time when Severus was passing through the town gate the last and most important passenger from Capri was coming ashore. At the sight of him the guards drew up in close array. The passenger walked between Macro Naevius Sertorius and the imperial lawyer Cocceius Nerva, clasping their forearms as he stepped along the file of guards towards his waiting litter, his leathery face almost hidden by the purple cowl, and his lips already pressed into that line, thinner and more virulent than usual, which they would retain throughout the next grim days. His August Highness Tiberius Claudius Nero, the Roman Caesar, was on his way to the villa of Lucullus at Misenum on the mainland, where, protected by a cordon of devoted troops, he would await the outcome of the most exquisitely dangerous and most decisively bloody exploit of his old age.

Dawn broke over Capri. One by one the snores of the senators guttered to a stop. The senators turned over in their cots, listening to the noises coming up from the kitchens and the general bustle

146

of a populous household beginning the day. One by one they issued from their cells and climbed the staircase to the high terrace.

The sculptor had already coaxed Caligula back on to the improvised dais and was again beseeching him to hold the heroic pose for just a little longer. The Greek, in the last frenzy of completing his work, seemed bent on finishing it that very morning.

It was not until mid-day or thereabouts that one or two of the senators noticed anything different in the atmosphere of the villa. A lack of something; the withdrawal of a presence. At first the emptiness of the terrace far below, the continued absence of a figure which had during three days become on that balustraded shelf as familiar as a domestic ornament, was something which they did not consciously think about. But it could have been that empty terrace which eventually intruded on their senses sufficiently to make them finally aware that there seemed today to be none of that coming and going of servants and slaves and soldiers to and from the Emperor's apartments. There were far fewer soldiers about than usual. In fact, the complement was apparently so much reduced that the captain of the boats was today having to do stand-in service for the captain of the guard. But it was the singing of a boy that suddenly revealed the truth: the impertinent singing of a boy, blithely carolling some vulgar ditty as he sauntered carefree along the corridor leading to the anteroom of the Caesar's apartments. Then came realisation. Tiberius was not in the villa.

They speculated in whispers about where he could be. They comforted themselves for as long as they reasonably could with the supposition that the Caesar had retired to some other cliff-top on the island, either to brood alone there or to choose still another site for yet another exercise in building. One senator essayed uneasily a joke that Tiberius might even have gone to the mainlain to consult the Cumaean Sibyl, and would eventually return with some fresh oracular inspiration. 'I hope he may give us it clear, not on laurel leaves,' murmured another. It was a custom, so people said, for the Sibyl, housed at the shadowy end of her grim tunnel laced into the cliffs, to deliver her pronouncements in single words impressed on laurel-leaves and then scattered before her devotees. Tiberian pronouncements, full as they were of hints and *non sequiturs* dropped here and there for the listeners to sort out and piece together into some pattern according to their intelligence or hopes, had something of the same quality.

But as the hours passed, another singular and sinister feature of the day intruded itself upon their consciousness. It dawned on them that for hours the bay had been utterly empty. For hours not a boat of any kind had disturbed the placid sea: no post-boat, no galley, no trading-vessel. Then at last they were aware that they were marooned on a rock. Capri was cut off from the mainland. Capri was frighteningly isolated from the whole world.

One of their company did not join in their preoccupied whisperings. The oldest senator had sat somewhat apart from them through the whole day. He seemed to prefer it so today. He showed most emphatically his desire to sit in meditative loneliness. But, placid though he attempted to appear, those who looked in his direction began to get an impression that he had some difficulty in keeping from his face that smug content which suffuses the features of those who know and will not tell. At this some of them began to see significance in the memory that this oldest senator had been the earliest to arrive at the villa. They recalled that he had left Rome several days before they were summoned to Capri. They recalled also that he was actually closeted with the Caesar on the day they reached the island and had remained so closeted for several hours before they got a glimpse of either of them. But none of them dared now to summon up courage to question him directly. They did not even venture to question any of the household staff or soldiers. The Caesar's villa was not a place in which to ask questions: one merely waited to be told things. If things were not told, it was safer to satisfy oneself with guesses, safer still to keep those guesses to oneself. In any case, the few members of the household staff whom they encountered seemed to disregard them, or at best to regard them as no more than so many mouths to be fed, as though they were some herd of sacred animals to be adequately stuffed and comfortably stabled until the day of sacrifice. In this simile they could, when they looked down the sharp cliffs to the mysteriously empty sea, find somewhat disquieting connotations.

They did, however, take one advantage of the situation: that of collaring the wine steward some time ahead of dinner and inducing him to leave the water alone. Thus they were able to sway back to their cells in somewhat tranquillised mood, and were soon snoring in their cots.

They kept to this regimen for a number of nights until a dawn when they were awakened by a stir louder than that of recent mornings and were drawn to the balconies of their sleeping-

148

quarters by the sounds of shouting and occasional cheers on the beach. The bay was alive with boats. They could distinguish in those boats a few metal-clad heads, but most of the soldiers' heads were bare, their casques on their laps or dangling from their hands as they lay about in postures of ease, hailing each other joyfully and singing snatches of song. A short time later each senator separately received a summons: the Caesar would be pleased to have his presence at dinner that evening.

The silence was oppressive. The senators munched their way stodgily through the familiar menu: the wine was liberally watered. Caligula was the first to speak. 'What news, sir?'

Tiberius did not reply to the question. Instead he looked round the room at the assembled company. He performed the operation very slowly, letting his eyes rest on each senator in turn, staring at him until the senator, nervously embarrassed, stopped chewing and pushed his platter away. One by one they suffered this intense scrutiny. One by one they stopped eating. One by one they fell quiet and still like candles snuffed out in turn. Only when his whole audience was completely silent and motionless did Tiberius, after a quick and wryly conspiratorial glance towards Caligula, speak.

'Gentlemen, We now have time to devote Our Person to the performance of a task which events of the last few days necessitated Our postponing until today. We are now free to attend to a series of dispatches sent to Us by Our Procurator in Judaea and to express Our opinions on certain recommendations he has thought fit to submit to Us. In making Our reply We have decided that it can form the basis of an exposition of Our future policy for the government and development of all subject provinces on the periphery of empire. This being so, We think it would be instructive to Our senators to hear this policy defined when We dictate Our reply to Judaea. You will therefore attend this dictation in Our library. We ask you to listen to it carefully and to bear its terms in mind until such time as you each receive a fair copy of it and then have it at all times beside you for reference. You are not asked to make any comments or suggestions during, or for that matter after, the dictation. There will be *no* interruptions.'

He paused. One or two of the senators, who felt they had been holding their breaths throughout the whole of this preamble, let forth audible sighs of relief. This was better than they had, during the last few days, ever dared to hope.

The Caesar heard those sighs. They seemed to please, perhaps even amuse him. The thin lips twitched as, in a conversational tone, he added, 'I am grateful to the gods that I am now able to proclaim these imperial policies in an atmosphere of safety. A moment of acute danger is past.' He looked over the company, and when his eyes again rested sternly on each senator each in turn became one by one less sanguine.

He reverted to his official voice. 'We have returned this morning from Our villa at Misenum. It was considered strategically advisable for Us to go there and thus be on the mainland during a period when Our Person and the whole destiny of Our commonwealth was in danger. News of the peril which threatened Our Person was first sent to Us in Capri some weeks ago by Our beloved sister-in-law, the Lady Antonia. The communication was carried by a courageous and loyal scribe. She sent the message and he delivered it at the risk of both their lives. We are grateful to the Lady Antonia. The slave, Pallas, will be rewarded by being raised to the dignity of Roman citizenship. We must also extend gracious thanks to that one member of the Senate who at some risk to himself acted as intermediary in engineering these secret communications.'

His eyes, looking for a moment as benign as they ever could, rested on the oldest senator. The oldest senator modestly lowered his head and fingered bread-crumbs.

'Acting on the information contained in the messages, We ordered the arrest of those who threatened Our Person. Their leader was, to Our great distress, a man who had been Our friend: a man who, although a mere provincial, had, under Our patronage, been raised to a position of power, but who abused Our friendship and, impelled by pernicious ambition, sought to usurp Our Divine Authority by the assassination of Our Person and the seizing of Rome. We ordered this man and his pernicious associates to be handed over to the Senate. Last night at Misenum We received good news from Our imperial capital. Sitting in solemn session your colleague senators, by which I mean those members of the Senate left in Rome because they enjoyed Our trust . . . ' He paused again and repeated his slow scrutiny of his ashen-faced guests before he added, 'We mean by that those senators whom We allowed to remain in Rome because they were not weak men. We could rely upon those senators not to bow

150

their knee when the would-be tyrant cracked his whip. Those senators heard Our accusations against the would-be regicide and usurper and found him guilty. He was executed within the hour. Unfortunately the miscreant's daughter, a girl of only tender years named Junilla, had of necessity also to be put to death. But, gentlemen, We hasten to assure you that the sacrilege of executing a virgin was avoided. She did not die a virgin. She was deflowered by a sturdy and obedient soldier before she was strangled. The traitor's eldest son lies in prison awaiting execution. All his known friends have been imprisoned, with only one prominent exception. Orders for the arrest of that one have been issued.'

He pushed his goblet towards Vitellius, nudging him to fill it. Sipping his good vinegar he peered around the company.

'Gentlemen, I shall not rebuke any separate one of you. Some of you were acquaintances of that man. Some of you have accepted favours or hoped for favours from him. Some of you are even rumoured to have been friends of his. But I prefer to think, I prefer to *imagine*, that you are at all times so conscious of your senatorial oaths that you may have remained loyal to me, at least so far as your powers of endurance against threat could sustain your loyalty. Only because I suspected, probably mistakenly but with necessary caution, that your endurance might not survive the would-be usurper's show of power, did I summon you here to the safety of Capri to enjoy, in this lovely island, my personal and loving protection.

'So now we can proceed to the library for the dictation of imperial policy. The danger is past. The menace is removed. He is dead. I refer, of course, to Our late lamented Consul and former friend, Lucius Aelius Sejanus, one-time Praetorian Prefect of Rome, who is now succeeded in that appointment and in the enjoyment of its attendant powers by Our devoted Macro Naevius Sertorius.'

He rose abruptly, bringing the senators scrambling hastily to their feet to form across the room a straggling avenue of white or bald bowing heads through which he moved towards the doorway. One of them seized his hand and kissed it; the Caesar used the hem of his toga to wipe the man's tears off his fingers.

'Gaius Germanicus,' he said as he neared the young prince, 'you will also attend the dictation. Indeed you, because of what I have decided, stand more highly and gloriously in need of instruction in imperial policy than any of these others with shorter and lowlier destinies. No, your sculptor friend cannot attend so solemn an occasion. He can busy himself during your absence with packing that statue. I am well pleased with it. I shall send it to Rome. Ahead of you.'

V

The sun, bold and red, sank into the Great Sea, and dusk, warm and languid, flowed over Caesarea. From the esplanade of the palace and from the arcaded streets higher in the city one could see the lights come on one by one around the harbour. Sailors, happy to get away for an evening from swaying decks and to walk on solid ground, clambered ashore. Those who had been sleeping in the seamen's dormitories in the arches below the promenade joined them to stroll with the townsfolk in the cool of the evening.

The inns were crowded. The stalls were doing brisk trade in salted fish and pastries. Pickle-vendors, pushing their barrows through the throng, helped to enliven thirsts and appetites. There was an unceasing melody of friendly noises: conversations exploding into shriller notes of greeting and laughter, the incessant slap of bare and sandalled feet, the trundling of wheels, and the tinkle of water-sellers' bells. Then, quite suddenly, the pleasant murmur of a contented city was shattered by yells and oaths bawled by a mob of men struggling around the entrance of one of the taverns. Then fighting began, and the noises grew harsher. At last the brawl became so noisy that it could be heard throughout the palace. It penetrated even to the Procurator's bedroom.

Pilate had retired early that evening. He was placidly writing a letter, smiling with satisfaction each time his pen obediently sculptured some choice phrase, when the din reached his ears. He stopped writing. Frowning, his pen poised over the folio, he waited for the noise to subside. When it did not, he jumped up impatiently and stalked through corridors and anterooms, to his balcony and stood there, gazing out towards the harbour, spreading his arm magisterially on the balustrade, and flinging his head back, expressing with uplifted jutting chin and pouting lips his displeasure.

Busy port though Caesarea was, filled every day and night with men of many races and the wildest and most adventurous of the world's sailors, clamour of an angry nature was seldom heard in it. The commerce of its streets, though always strident with the cries of wagoners and pedlars, usually had a good-natured note. Rare indeed was it to hear the polyglot voices of the inhabitants raised in anger, rarer still to see them milling about in disorder as some were doing in the port at this moment.

In the shafts of light cast from open doors on the waterfront, Pilate could discern a press of people around the entrance of the tavern. At times some individuals broke away from the swaying bunch and ran off out of the range of the light. But others darting after them apparently overtook them and grappled with them; for Pilate could hear, detached from the central uproar, the gasps and cries of scuffles in dark corners. He could not determine what class of people were involved in the brawl. Most of the shouts he could distinguish were Aramaic, but once or twice he heard a Roman oath.

Household slaves who had flocked to neighbouring terraces to watch and listen eventually became aware that the Procurator had issued from his room, and those who should have been on duty at the doors of anterooms and corridors hurried back to their posts and stood there awaiting the Procurator's commands. Pilate was on the point of ordering the nearest of them to go below and summon an officer from the guard-room to report on what was happening, but then he heard Fabius, out of sight along the palace esplanade, barking commands. A moment later Pilate saw a platoon of guards, broadswords and shields at the ready and accompanied by torch-bearers, rapidly filing down the staircases to the port. Whatever the disturbance was, Fabius was attending to it. Pilate turned away and walked back to his room. As he passed through each door he gestured to the attendant slave to close it and thus insulate him somewhat from the irritating noise.

He resumed his letter. He was writing to his son, and the statue of Julius stood on the table. He had begun with the intention of writing only a brief note which Claudia could take to Athens with her. This would convey affectionate greetings to Julius and the advice that the boy must not allow the visit of his mother and the Lady Sextia to interrupt his studies. Though, of course, Julius must be dutifully attentive to the ladies: he was now old enough to assume the dignity of host and make arrangements for their comfort and entertainment. That was all that needed to be said at the moment. But, having said it, Pilate took the opportunity of adding further fatherly counsel, and the letter was now developing into a lengthy homily which Pilate, as he moulded his phrases into Julian cadences, began to think worthy of a wider public. It deserved publication as an example for other fathers writing to their sons. Whenever he paused to cogitate on his next words he glanced at the statue, and then, when he resumed writing, he had the feeling that the pensive downcast eyes were watching his pen with filial devotion, and he feared that affection too indulgent might be seeping into the communication. So he repeatedly found it necessary to delete phrases which lacked the grave dignity proper in a letter from a father to his heir. At last the draft of the letter was finished. Tomorrow he would have a fair copy made of it. Or he might even take time off to perform that pleasant task himself.

Claudia came in. When she saw the statue she smiled and, walking to the table, bent over Pilate's shoulder and read some passages of the letter. He turned and drew her towards him. She looked down into his face which appeared, she thought, more youthful and less tired tonight than of late. At most times his features, particularly that wide mouth with its stubbornly pouting underlip, seemed to be carved in unrelenting marble, but at this moment his face seemed more mobile and sensitive. The wrinkles around his eyes and even the deep folds from nose to jaw were more relaxed. He smiled up at her, bending his head back for the kiss which her lips seemed to promise, but instead she moistened a fingertip and ran it over his eyebrows, pressing each hair into place with a touch as soft and caressing as though she were tracing the contours of his brow in the dark. This was for both of them a memorable gesture. That same caress she had performed when, with exultant sighs, he had drawn away from her after their first copulation. So that now, whenever she repeated it, the caress recalled the joy and mystery of that first time, the joy of taking possession of one so beautiful and so young, and the mystery that any woman could arouse such tumultuous passion in him. Through the years the joy had become habitual: the mystery remained. And the mystery engaged him now as he reached up and untied the gold fillet and watched her hair fall slumberously around her shoulders. He stood up, took her hands in his and led her to the couch. They lay down together still clothed. They remained clothed for a long time; so happily assured were they of what was to follow that they felt no need to vulgarise with haste the caresses with which they slowly reduced each other to nakedness.

Later, bending over her, her murmurs of pleasure still sounding in his memory, he watched her eyes open drowsily again and again to smile up at him until, finally surrendering to the pleasure of content, they slept. He lay back. He was immensely satisfied. He was also proud that he could perform this most intimate exercise of life with vigour and that he still possessed authority enough to control the passion of another. Lapped in that pride, he lay looking at the beloved son who had been born at his will. Then his eyes fell to the letter curled at the boy's feet and in his mind he began recasting some of the phrases he had written in it. As he thought of words and of the writing of words, his thoughts drifted appreciatively to phrases he had coined in the massive memorandum now in the hands of Tiberius Caesar.

Claudia stirred. He drew her head into the crook of his arm and pulled the cover over her shoulders. Her presence beside him tonight seemed to set the seal on a succession of sanguine days. After his recent progress through Judaea and his work on the memorandum, he had felt that he needed a rest, and deserved one. He had reduced his official activities to the minimum, even postponing the trials of the few prisoners in the jail in Caesarea. Delegating routine matters of administration to Fabius, a young man who was proving himself increasingly energetic and reliable, Pilate had retreated to his private apartments where, in the vast palace, he could feel peacefully remote from the praetorium's multifarious activities, from the labours of its multitude of clerks and slaves and workmen, the parading of guards, the queues and suitors and petitioners, and the daylong activity of its secretariat and tax-offices. During this respite from public affairs he could, he felt, await with confidence expressions of imperial encouragement from Capri and, he hoped, assurance of financial assistance from Josephus. So he could relax and enjoy private life which, as the presence of Claudia in his bed deliciously demonstrated, had its pleasures.

In what was for Pilate a rare season of content, even the chatter of Sextia had seemed less obnoxious. In any case, he did not see that lady too frequently. Her days were now consumed with superintending dressmaking and with other preoccupations which she had assumed in order to prepare Claudia for their trip to Athens.

He saw even less of Marcus Paterculus. That glacial patrician remained most of the time closeted with his secretary in his apartments in the tower. Paterculus had excused this withdrawal by saying that he was busily engaged on confidential work of imperial importance, an excuse which seemed to be borne out by the impatience with which he sent his secretary hurrying to the port whenever a packet arrived from Italy. After their first conversation he had conferred with Pilate on only three occasions. During the first and second of these three interviews he had again insinuated oblique and probing questions, but on the third occasion he had carried with him a dispatch which had just arrived from Italy, and Pilate detected in the drawling voice an uncharacteristic note of urgency. On this occasion the aristocrat's questions were more pointed than hitherto. After some tentative remarks about Herod Antipas, the patrician admitted that he was anxious to know all he could about the Tetrarch.

What kind of a man was he, Paterculus had asked.

'The Fox!' Pilate had smiled. 'That nickname about sums him up. He's cunning. He has not the greatness of his father. Nor the madness. Indeed, the only thing he seems to have inherited from Herod the Great is the peculiarly Herodian passion for building.'

But, Paterculus had gone on, was the Tetrarch popular in his kingdoms of Galilee and Peraea?

'Popular?' Pilate had ruminated and then, cautiously, had replied, 'A ruler who is appointed by Rome and supported by Roman power and who has the added disadvantage in Jewish eyes of being racially only half a Jew might find it difficult to be popular with Galileans.'

This reply appeared to have pleased Paterculus. Antipas, the patrician suggested, probably had little sympathy for Jews or for their aspirations. In fact, were circumstances to demand it, he would probably be prepared to use his power against Jews?

'Power? His power is as much as Rome allows him,' Pilate had replied sharply. 'Ostensibly he inherited the tetrarchy of Galilee and Peraea under his father's will. But the Fox is wise enough to know that he can enjoy that inheritance only under the sanction of Rome.'

Fingering the dispatch, Paterculus had pondered over this for a moment and had asked Pilate if he met Antipas frequently.

'We meet when necessary,' Pilate had replied ambiguously. Then, 'Is there something in that document you wished me to see?'

Upon which Paterculus had hastily rolled up the dispatch, assuring Pilate that it was of only personal importance, and had hurried off without asking further questions.

After that conversation the patrician's withdrawal from the household had been complete. Was he disappointed, or indifferent, or even hostile? Seeing nothing of him, Pilate could not judge, but thought it advisable to keep track of his movements through Fabius and such members of the secretariat as could be trusted to watch such things discreetly. Thus it was not from Paterculus but through an informer whom the Procurator employed in the court of Herod Antipas at Tiberias that Pilate learned that the Roman was seeking an audience with the Tetrarch. It was discourteous of Paterculus to by-pass the Procurator in such a matter, but Pilate was less offended by this breach of protocol than by the secrecy of the approach. However, he did not tax Paterculus with this. If only the man had asked him outright, he would have been pleased to arrange the audience himself. He had nothing to fear from such a meeting. In fact he found himself hoping that, if Herod did agree to meet Paterculus, the audience might be staged not in Tiberias but during one of Herod's visits to Jerusalem. The Roman spy would then have the opportunity of seeing how that Jewish capital, formerly so tetchy and explosive, had under Pilate's administration become positively tranquil, going about its daily life so placidly that nowadays a Roman soldier, who in the past would have been the target for glowering stares, could push his way through Jew-crowded streets almost unnoticed.

Such an experience would teach the patrician a lesson he obviously needed. Like many Romans newly arrived in the province, Paterculus seemed prone to fear hostility where none need be expected. But unlike other Romans he never seemed to lose this fear. Instead he seemed to grow every day more nervous. He was always armed, parading about in cuirass and greaves like an officer on campaign, and always accompanied by a complement of guards. These unnecessary guards irritated Pilate. They were obviously picked bullies but, scrupulously turned out, and proud, aggressively so, of their martial kit. They were a surly bunch and caused repeated offence among the auxiliaries in the barracks by their braggart boasting of racial superiority and their contemptuous treatment of non-Romans. Their devotion to Paterculus was unpleasantly like that of a gang of bullies; their hands were always hovering at their sword-hilts as though ready to draw their weapons at his slightest nod. One could have imagined that the man went in constant dread of some violent assault on his person – a fear which was, in peaceful Caesarea, absurd. This excessive show of military force annoyed Pilate not only because it was inappropriate to the patrician's status as a guest at the Procurator's court but also because it could be offensive to the susceptibilities of a law-abiding and friendly populace. Furthermore, it could give the impression that Paterculus was not the civilian emissary he claimed to be but was conducting some kind of military expedition in the province. Pilate's hints that such behaviour was inappropriate had, however, been disregarded. Pilate refrained, nevertheless, from making an issue of the man's pretensions. After all, Paterculus was now preparing for an early departure, and by the time he returned from his visit to the court of the imperial legate in Antioch Pilate might be in the happy possession of an imperial mandate for his project, in which case it would perhaps be politic to let Paterculus have a copy of the memorandum to take in person to Pilate's patron, the Prefect Sejanus.

Meanwhile Pilate looked forward eagerly to the impending visit of Josephus. The statue of Poseidon had arrived from Sebaste. The bowl and its supporting columns would soon be on their way from the same quarries from which the most beautiful of Caesarea's thousands of columns had been hewn. He was hopeful that when Josephus did arrive he would bring assurance that finance could be raised for his irrigation project, so that within a month or even less he might be able to instruct architects and engineers to begin work on the first of the new aqueducts, the one which would carry water into Jerusalem from the Pools of Solomon outside Bethlehem. With a vague but glorious vision of its conduits and running water filling his mind, Pilate fell asleep.

All sanguine dreams were roughly blown away the following morning when Fabius, presenting himself for the orders of the day, gave his report of the disturbance on the waterfront. The facts were disquieting.

The tumult, which but for prompt action by Fabius could have flared up into a minor riot and spread throughout the city, had been caused by guards from Paterculus's company. Off duty for the evening, they had drifted from tavern to tavern. Sozzled with wine and revelling in that lack of discipline common to soldiers in a foreign city, they had become rowdy. With their arms interlaced and provocatively bawling out barrack-room songs extolling Romans as the master race, they had swaggered roughly through the crowds at the booths, jostling passers-by and shouting bawdy familiarities at women. It seemed that they had deliberately singled out Jews for their dirtiest insults. They had actually seized one old Jew and defiled his shawl by scrawling on it with blood from a butcher's slab some obscene anti-Semitic symbol. Eventually they flocked into the tavern. There they ordered the innkeeper about as though he were a helot, shouting for wine and, to make a show of avoiding any physical contact with a Jew, they had paid for their drinks by tossing their coins on the floor and bawling to him to pick them up. Customers attempting to leave the scene quietly were hustled and insulted. One of the guards, taking up his post at the door, had bawled, 'No dirty Jews allowed!' No Jews had been foolish enough to seek entry, and one man who was picked up and thrown across the street was actually a Greek sailor. This action stirred the growing crowd outside to anger, upon which the drunken soldiers thought, or pretended to think, that they were about to be attacked by a mob. They picked on some individuals who, they claimed, were instigators of this attack and began chasing after them. By now some of them had drawn their daggers. Fortunately Fabius and his party arrived at that moment. The only serious casualty was the Greek sailor. He had landed on his head. He was dead. The Soldiers were then restrained, some forcibly, from doing further mischief.

'They are in cells now?' asked Pilate.

'No, sir. When we got them back to the barracks, one of them insisted on Marcus Paterculus being informed.'

'And?'

'He objected to his men being disciplined by auxiliaries or put into cells. He rebuked the guards, but said they must be allowed to go to their quarters. Some of them were now so drunk that they had to be carried. All of them were spewing. Later Marcus

160

Paterculus sent for me and complained that my men had used undue force at the tavern and that it was disgraceful that Romans should have been handled in such a way in the presence of Jewish witnesses.'

'Present my compliments to Marcus Gaius Paterculus. Say I wish to see him. And, Fabius, have a full report of the incident prepared and filed. Get all testimonies possible, particularly from your men.'

When Fabius had gone, Pilate cleared his desk of dispatches and sat down behind it, drew himself erect in his chair and stared towards the entrance arch, his chin uplifted and his lips set in a formidable pout. He felt grimly satisfied. At last the patrician had put himself irremediably in the wrong. The conduct of his personal guards and his interference against their punishment was a breach of discipline. But, far more important, he had revealed himself as indifferent to Caesar's policy of attempted pacification of Judaea. The Prefect Sejanus was, unfortunately, somewhat notorious for his anti-Semitism, but Tiberius Caesar had made it evident that racial prejudices should not be offended. Pilate looked forward with some pleasure to making it clear to Paterculus that in any issue impinging on the conduct of Judaean affairs the Procurator must conform with the desires of Caesar, even if in so doing he might offend the opinions of his own patron, the Prefect Sejanus.

Pilate heard footsteps approaching. He placed his hands on the desk and lifted his chin even higher, with the result that Fabius, when he entered was greeted with the stony stare prepared for Paterculus.

Fabius had returned to the Procurator with unexpected but welcome news. Josephus was on his way to the palace. He had come to Caesarea at short notice with his son Mattathias and his daughter-in-law to see them aboard a boat for Alexandria, and had sent a message expressing the wish that he might call on the Procurator after the boat had left.

'Marcus Paterculus will attend on you shortly, sir,' added Fabius.

'He must await my convenience,' said Pilate and, hoping that the banker would not have heard any gossip on the waterfront about last night's brawl, he hurried down to do the banker the honour of welcoming him in person in the entrance court. When he saw Josephus approaching he stepped forward with a wide smile and, addressing him as 'my dear friend', greeted him so

11   161

warmly that Josephus discarded the formality of title and, in return, addressed the Procurator as 'Pontius'.

'We had best go by way of the secretariat,' said Pilate as he took Josephus by the arm to steer him in the direction of the portico leading to the secretariat. 'The inner court is still in disorder.'

'But, Pontius, among my reasons for calling was to see Poseidon's future home.'

So they picked their way through the paving-blocks beyond the arch, and when Josephus saw the position of the fountain in the inner court he declared enthusiastically that the branching stair and colonnaded balconies formed an appropriately Greek setting for the statue.

'I have not yet asked the price of the statue, Josephus. I fear it will bankrupt me, but I was determined to have it.'

Josephus shook his head. 'Nor will you hear a price, Pontius. It is a gift. Yes, yes, yes, I insist. But, mark you, a gift to you in person: not to the palace, not to Rome. And I give it with one proviso. If ever you do leave Judaea, I should wish that you take it with you to that home which you have chosen for your retirement. It will serve as a memento of Judaea and of Sebaste, but more, I hope, of the friendship of old Josephus.'

'I am deeply moved. I shall always treasure it.'

Josephus avoided further thanks by turning his attention to the corner of the courtyard where part of the garden had been laid out and where gardeners were raking the soil. He stepped towards some shrubs which were now *in situ*. Their twigs and leaves, which had drooped after transportation, were already showing signs of lifting. Josephus fingered a leaf and then stooped down and ran his fingers through the soil. 'You are lucky, he said, 'to have so many horses. But don't be too liberal. The blooms of Judaea, like its people, thrive best on a frugal diet.'

They moved towards the staircase. The ditch was now filled in. The first step of the staircase had been laid in position, but it had not yet been underpinned and cemented, so that it tilted slightly under the considerable weight of Josephus. Embarrassed, Pilate grabbed the banker's arm to steady him, but was surprised at the agility with which the old man recovered his balance and strode upwards to the second step.

They arrived on Pilate's balcony just in time to see the boat for Alexandria hoisting sail beyond the harbour and veering south.

'I did not know your son was leaving so soon,' said Pilate.

'Nor did I. But I decided it was necessary, and, for his bride's sake, safer.'

The banker's smile faded. For a moment a worried frown made him seem very old, but when Pilate was on the point of asking what was wrong Josephus stemmed further questions by saying, with a renewed smile, 'However, he will be carrying a message with him to a business associate of mine, a Jerusalem merchant who trades in Alexandria. He is a man who has just made a good sale of some big estates. He is in the unusual position of having a lot of idle money which needs a good home.' Pilate was again about to speak, but Josephus held up a restraining hand. 'No. Don't let us count our chickens before they are hatched. But I am hoping that if I make it known that I am advising him to put money into public works in Judaea, other men with capital may be attracted.'

The arrival of Claudia and Sextia interrupted this encouraging conversation. 'We must speak about it later,' said Pilate, as Claudia stepped forward to welcome the banker and present Sextia. The banker, his amiability characteristically coming into fuller bloom in a family atmosphere, settled himself expansively on a couch and draped the striped ends of his shawl over his knees. When Claudia had seated herself modestly on a low stool beside him and Josephus, his white hair tumbling from the cap, bent his wise old head to listen to her, he looked, Sextia thought, the very prototype of a Jewish patriarch.

What delighted Pilate most about the scene was to hear Josephus, who had begun his conversation with Claudia in Greek, change suddenly to Aramaic and compliment her on the progress she had made in that language since they last met months ago. Claudia, thought Pilate, was indeed becoming noticeably more fluent in that language. It was largely because of this that Pilate had not objected to her showing special favour to the Galilean woman, whom she had removed from the slaves' quarters and promised to appoint as her personal maid when the child was born. The association was obviously what had helped Claudia with the language. It seemed also to have given her some insight into Jewish affairs, for he now noticed how quickly she turned the conversation away from domestic trivia to engage Josephus in discussion on political and religious matters. Josephus, displaying candidly that affectionate admiration which an old and distinguished man can direct without offence on a young and beautiful matron, chatted happily with her, and Pilate was delighted to see the banker's wise head nodding as he gravely acknowledged her remarks.

Sextia sat listening to it all. She was, Pilate contentedly noted, refreshingly silent. It appeared to him that she was as intrigued as he was with Claudia's growing interest in the religious problems of Judaea and Galilee. Claudia was retailing to Josephus news which she had picked up from the woman about the emotions aroused in Galilee by the execution of that wild skin-clad fanatic known as the Baptist, and she seemed to have learned much also about another wandering preacher who, she claimed, appeared to have assumed the role of baptist. At this point the conversation was interrupted by a servant bringing a message that the Egyptian doctor had arrived and was awaiting the Lady Claudia. She abruptly excused herself and, promising to return quickly, hurried away. Pilate turned to Sextia with a questioning frown.

'Nothing to worry about,' said Sextia, though she too was frowning. 'Claudia called the doctor to examine the woman.'

'The Galilean?'

'Yes. Claudia has the idea that the woman's pregnancy is not progressing favourably.'

Pilate shrugged, then, turning to Josephus, he explained, 'A slave in whom my wife is taking kindly interest.'

Noting the irritation underlying the words, Josephus nodded understandingly, for he was aware of the Roman attitude to slaves and could sympathise with Pilate's annoyance with what must seem too concerned a preoccupation with a serving-woman. It was different for a Jew. In a Jewish household slaves were indulged with as much kindness and fatherly care as one devoted to one's own children, and Josephus could not refrain from making the point. 'The Lady Claudia is most gracious,' he said, looking at Pilate through his eyebrows. 'By such concern she shows admirable understanding of Jewish susceptibilities.' Then, turning to Sextia, he asked, 'Is this Galilean woman the one who has told the Lady Claudia so much about that country?' Sextia nodded. 'And her husband?' Josephus went on. 'Is he also a slave?'

'Dead!' said Sextia. She looked away. Her flat reply made it pretty obvious that she did not wish to continue the subject. She had her reasons for avoiding it. She knew – Pilate did not – that the woman had no husband. She had in fact never been married. The woman had told Claudia this. She seemed to be the kind of person who could not resist telling the truth whatever the consequences. Claudia excused this uncomfortable habit. Telling the truth, she explained, was one of the tenets of the sect with which the woman had become involved. The woman had confessed to Claudia that before she got mixed up with those people she had been a harlot. Her career had followed a fairly usual pattern. As a girl she had been sold as concubine to a merchant who, when he tired of her, had profited by handing her over to an official at the court of Herod Antipas. That one was presumably the father of the child she was bearing, and he would probably have brought the child up in Tiberias had she not met the baptising folk and been persuaded to escape from the licentious mob around Herodias and her daughter Salome. The initiatory rite which her sect indulged in, that of dipping themselves in the Jordan, was supposed to have washed away her past. Baptism, she believed, had made her a new woman – in fact, she claimed, a woman born again. She had travelled south to Judaea to live with relatives until her child was born. But the village where her relatives lived had been destroyed by the Procurator. She was still suffering from the shock of that event.

Sextia had advised Claudia that it would be better not to tell Pilate all this. She was beginning to think this advice had been unwise. Claudia, as Pilate had just hinted, was becoming far too involved in the welfare of this one slave. In fact she was fast becoming a bore. One could not venture any opinion on any subject at all without Claudia quoting some precept or parable which the woman had heard from the lips of those Galilean preachers. Claudia was betraying an unhealthy interest in the woman's religious beliefs. Indeed, it was almost akin to sympathy. This was the very danger Sextia had warned Pilate about, though she had not expected it to become evident so soon. It was plain to see that Claudia, thirsting for any new interest which might fill the vacuum of her empty life in this dreary Judaea, was ripe for infection by any mumbo-jumbo. It was just as well that she would soon be leaving Caesarea. Pontius ought to be pleased. Without her to think about, he could surely do his job better and more conscientiously if his mind was not burdened with the presence and demands of his wife. That was why governors and the like were not usually allowed to take their wives abroad. It showed what a special favourite Pilate was of the Prefect Sejanus for that dour man who loathed Jews so much to have allowed Pilate to bring a Roman matron out here.

Well, thought Sextia, the sooner Claudia got away from Jews, away not only from their problems and their dangerous ideas but also from their insidious influence, the better. In Athens she would forget gloomy Jewish religions and find livelier things to engage her mind. Because her thoughts were running on these lines, Sextia was anxious to avoid risky talk about the Galilean woman. So, overhearing Josephus mention Alexandria, she seized on that name as her cue. The high spot of her visit to Alexandria, she declared, had been her meeting with the Jewish philosopher Philo.

'You were lucky, my lady, to meet Judaeus,' said Josephus.

'You know him?'

'Indeed I do. I am happy, and honoured, to number that excellent and learned Judaeus among my dearest friends.'

Sextia beamed. This Jew Josephus really was a nice old boy.

Pilate leaned back happily. Yes, he had to admit, Sextia did at times have a way with her. Although she was at the moment stooping forward in a most inelegant posture, her elbows planted on her widespread knees and her innumerable bracelets jangling, her enthusiasm was so vibrant that one quite overlooked her unfortunate ugliness. Indeed, Josephus seemed almost charmed by her.

Pilate was content to listen, but at that moment the sound of heavy tramping beyond the anteroom heralded the approach of Paterculus. Pilate went pale with anger. It was preposterous for Paterculus to come escorted. Did the man, even in the palace itself, not dare to move without his bullies tramping beside him?

From where he sat, Pilate could see Paterculus enter the anteroom. The two guards immediately behind him actually had their hands at the ready on their sword-hilts. After stepping a few paces into the empty room, Paterculus halted and then looked warily around.

'I am out here, Marcus Paterculus,' Pilate called. Paterculus appeared in the archway. He seemed surprised to find Pilate placidly reclining amid company. At least the patrician had the decency, Pilate observed, to signal to his guards to stay in the room, but when he stepped on the balcony he had not the courtesy to vouchsafe Pilate's guests more than a fleeting examination, and then, ignoring their presence, addressed the Procurator as though there were no one else there.

'Fabius informs me that you have expressed a wish to see me, Procurator.'

'The matter can wait. In the meantime I should be pleased if you would join us.' As he made this invitation Pilate forced a smile, but icily added, 'Without your bodyguard, if you please.'

Paterculus dismissed the men with a wave of the hand. Their heavy-footed departure seemed to relieve him from his martial stiffness, at least sufficiently for him to pay his respects to Sextia with condescending politeness.

'Marcus Paterculus,' said Pilate. 'I should like you to meet my guest, Josephus the Cohen, who is visiting us from Sebaste.'

Paterculus lifted his nose one inch higher to look Josephus over. His grey gaze lingered for a significant moment on the Jewish cap, then fell for a similar slow inspection of the distinctive bands of colour on the shawl. The handsome lips curved in a smile so manifestly fabricated that it was close to being a sneer.

'Josephus is a friend of mine,' Pilate's voice quavered slightly with the effort of giving due emphasis to his words. 'And, I might add, a friend of Rome. One of our most valued friends in Palestine.'

Paterculus inclined his head. 'I am always pleased to meet a friend of Rome. Particularly in Palestine, where I find them singularly rare, at least among the native population.'

Josephus remained seated and he acknowledged the patrician's words with the slightest of nods. But then, assuming his air of elderly amiability, he asked, 'The son of the writer Paterculus?'

'Of Paterculus the tribune and soldier,' the Roman retorted stiffly.

'Of course.' Josephus smiled expansively. Anyone who knew the banker well would know that such a widening of smile heralded mischief. 'Of course, I know well enough that your father served with distinction under Tiberius; though being myself a civilian I tend to honour him more for his greater achievements as a historian.'

'Do sit down, Paterculus,' said Pilate uneasily.

After the patrician had chosen a high stool on which to sit erect, Josephus went on, 'He served in Germany, I believe. But also in Pannonia. Of that I am certain, for when I was on the Danube some years ago I met some friends of mine, men of finance, who rendered him valuable service.' Josephus lowered his head and peered around at the company under his eyebrows. 'Romans are known for their genius in conquering territory by force of arms, but when it comes to financial battles they must recruit Jews as their allies.'

Paterculus flushed. There was a chilly silence. It was broken by

Sextia, who, with a desperately exaggerated laugh, turned with an impulsive show of friendliness to Josephus to ask, 'Is there any country in the world you have *not* visited, Josephus? Or anyone you do *not* know?' She looked quickly across at Paterculus. 'For instance, Marcus, I have just learned that Josephus is a friend of Philo of Alexandria.'

'That does not surprise me,' drawled Paterculus. 'If I may say so,' he said as he fastened his eyes again on the striped shawl, 'wherever a Jew goes in the Roman world he can find a friend of his own race. One can find Jews everywhere.'

'Yes, indeed,' said Josephus mildly. 'We rather pride ourselves on that.'

'Yet wherever they are,' went on Paterculus, 'they bemoan their exile and dream of returning to their homeland. What is it your people say? "By the waters of Babylon" . . . '

' "By the waters of Babylon they sat down and wept when they remembered Zion",' quoted Josephus helpfully. 'Oh, I grant you, we are much addicted to nostalgia, but for our past as much as for our homeland. We also sat down and wept by the Waters of Merom when we remembered Egypt. Yes, we Jews have done a lot of sitting down and weeping, and an immense amount of remembering.'

Everyone laughed except Paterculus. He persisted in driving on to the point he wanted to make. 'If the Jews love their homeland and their holy city of Jerusalem so fervently, why don't they stay there?'

Josephus laughed again. 'If a Roman asked a Jew such a question, the Jew might be tempted to ask the Roman a similar one.'

Sextia slapped her knee in appreciation, and Pilate said to her coldly, 'You were talking of Philo, Sextia.'

'I was.' She gave Paterculus a hard stare. 'Do you know him?' she asked.

'I have heard of him,' said Paterculus loftily.

'I mean have you *read* him?' she snapped. Incensed by the patrician's arrogant and insensitive attitude to the pleasant old man, she had lost all patience. Whether Pilate was right or not in thinking Paterculus was politically important, she saw him now only as someone who needed putting in his place, and she bent her energies to performing that operation. 'Perhaps, Marcus, like most Roman politicians, you read only historians. And Philo is not a historian. He is not parochial enough to be a historian. Philo is universal.'

'I am not unacquainted, my lady, with the casuistry of your Jewish Alexandrian acquaintance,' retorted Paterculus and swung his gaze away from her to point his nose at Josephus. 'The Cohen will correct me if I am wrong, but I understand Philo to say that if we do accept the existence of a deity, then that deity can be only one god, and that one god is the god of all mankind.'

Josephus nodded. 'Broadly speaking, Marcus Paterculus, that is the essence of Judaeus Philo's philosophy.'

'So why do Jews not stone him to death? That is the Jewish method of executing blasphemers, is it not? For surely it is blasphemy to question the Jewish claim that Jews are the chosen people and their god the only true god?'

'You would need to study the Mosaic laws more objectively, Marcus Paterculus, to understand that the view you express of them, the gentile view, is exaggerated,' said Josephus gravely. 'So far as Philo is concerned, I can assure you that one thing he is not is a racialist. So far as I understand his basic philosophy, it attempts to reconcile the wisdom of Plato with the Mosaic revelation. Therefore, you might be correct in some small measure in your presumption that his ideas could offend the stricter Jew. Yet I think, and I hope, that for both Jew and Gentile Philo is only a little ahead of his time. His belief that all humankind can have and should have a common god, common aspirations and a common destiny may seem today the wildest idealism, but surely tomorrow it will be accepted as a human truth. After all, your Stoics welcome that aspect of Zeno's philosophy. But I beg you to excuse me. I must refuse to adventure at conversational level into such deep matters. I am not a philosopher. I am, only a banker.'

'And,' said Sextia, leaning towards him again and lifting a hand almost as though she were going to pat his knee, 'a banker, if he is wise and if he is a Jew, no doubt thinks it more economical to sacrifice to one god and not pay tribute to a host of branch-managers.'

Pilate stiffened with anxiety. This must sound near to blasphemy in devout Jewish ears. But Josephus smiled admiringly at Sextia. 'You put it excellently, my lady. Any banker, and certainly a Jewish one, must be appalled at the cost of supporting the many deities so expensively cherished by other races.' He stole a glance at Paterculus. 'A god of the sea and a goddess of hunting,

A goddess of love. Even a god of intoxicating liquor. Pan, Mars, Zeus, Cupid, Venus, Apollo . . . oh, so many! You must not expect an old man to remember all their names. I wonder if even Gentiles know them all? Forgive me for repeating irreverent gossip, but I have heard it said that in some cities there are so many deities that one is more likely to meet a god in the street than a man. Yes, my lady Sextia, if I may copy your banking terms, setting up so many gods does tend to depreciate the currency.'

'One must respect the religious beliefs of others, Josephus,' said Pilate. 'That has always been the policy of Rome.'

'And could never be the policy of the Jews, Procurator,' said Paterculus. 'Their god, they claim, is the one true god, and they make him inaccessible. A Roman will allow a man of any race to worship Roman gods and continue worshipping his own. The Jew says a man must disown all other gods before he can worship the god of the Jews, and that god is, says the Jew, a god of war in whose name Jews must destroy all who worship false gods.'

'That is the Gentile view, I suppose,' said Josephus, but, turning away from Paterculus, who was obviously working himself up into an aggressive mood, took up Pilate's remark. 'Religious tolerance, Procurator, *was* Roman policy. But it does seem that the sheer multiplicity of religious beliefs has exhausted the patience of Rome. For instance, your Caesar Tiberius has felt it necessary to suppress Druids. And only some ten years ago he expelled the worshippers of Isis from Italy. The priests of that cult were crucified, were they not, on the banks of the Rhine? And even in his attitude to what one might call the official and traditional religions of the Romans, Tiberius shows scant sympathy – so little sympathy that one could suppose his philosophy is much akin to that of Judaeus Philo.'

'You have got it wrong, Josephus,' Paterculus said. 'A true Roman must ever render honour to the gods of Rome. That is *pietas*, and without it no Roman can be pure and strong and confident. When Caesar rids the world of fanatics, he is not acting against their religion: he is suppressing political factions. It is the duty of Romans to cleanse the world of those who use racial superstitions to foment rebellion against the Roman way of life. A Roman must do that also when priests of certain religious beliefs encourage their believers to remain a separate racial entity. That is why Tiberius Caesar once found it necessary to transport four thousand Jews to Sardinia.'

'Thank you, Marcus Paterculus,' Josephus's smile widened

again. 'It is refreshing to hear the truth so frank on Roman lips. At the time that happened – you are too young to remember it – Roman propagandists explained the event very differently. They told the world not that the Jews were being banished to Sardinia but that they were being established there in the hope that their civilising influence would pacify that bandit-ridden island. I must confess we Jews never believed it.'

'Nor did anyone else with any sense,' growled Sextia. 'We all knew Tiberius wanted to concentrate the Jews in one camp. And I heard it said that secretly he hoped that Sardinia's foul climate would kill 'em off!'

Pilate winced. Pleased though he was at Paterculus's discomfiture, he felt that Sextia was going too far. So it was a relief when Claudia appeared in the archway. He stood up quickly to lead her to her stool. Her return, he hoped, had created a diversion which would put an end to an argument which was fast becoming a vulgar quarrel. Paterculus seemed also to wish it ended. He had stood up, and, after staring coldly at Claudia sitting so amicably at the knees of Josephus, walked to the balustrade, where, half-turned away from the company, he stared moodily down to the port. However, Sextia, refusing to let the matter drop, casting her voice in the direction of the aristocratic back, said loudly, 'I agree with Philo. One god is enough for anyone. I don't say, of course, that he should be a Jewish god. I don't very much like what I've heard about that one. But even he is better than gods other races have dreamed up. That Anubis, for example!' She shuddered. 'I saw him. Imagine worshipping a god with the head of a jackal. Or is it a dog? After all those stories about gods! Most of them disgustingly incestuous, or worse. Women falling in love with bulls. One with a swan. And Minerva born through the head of Zeus. Even if you could believe that, can you believe she came out already in full armour bawling battle-cries? And even gods born of virgins!' She smirked. 'Well, perhaps I'm not in a position to judge about *that*. Though I guess that if I ever live to see a virgin mother, I'll have seen about everything.'

'Sextia!' said Claudia in a distressed whisper. 'Some beliefs are sincerely held and are very precious to their believers.'

Josephus looked down at her benignly and then, addressing himself to Sextia, 'As a Jew, my lady, I suppose I ought to applaud your strictures on alien gods. But as an old man I find myself more and more sympathising with man's search for some-

171

thing to believe in. And it is a natural hope, one common to many races, that God might be born of mortal loins. Your great Roman Vergilius Maro envisaged, I believe it was in his *Fourth Eclogue*, the birth of a child who would bring back the Golden Age.'

'I hope you know your Virgil, Marcus,' said Sextia brightly. 'When one talks with Josephus one must know the world's writers. And know the world too.'

Paterculus turned. 'One's knowledge of the world is measured not by the miles one has travelled, my lady, but by one's wisdom, and by one's discretion. Procurator, if you will excuse me, I have work awaiting me. I shall attend on you at your convenience when you are less occupied.'

The great sigh Sextia breathed out as he walked away must have been audible to him, and he would still be within earshot when she said loudly, 'I measure my knowledge by my ears. Those are considerable enough.' After that she relaxed. 'When you were in Alexandria, Josephus, did you make a trip up the Nile?'

'Unfortunately, no. I am afraid my old bones could not endure the rigours of such a voyage.'

Pilate could relax. Sextia had returned to her favourite subject. He would permit her to enlarge on it in the hope that her torrential flow of anecdote would wash away from the banker's mind memory of the patrician's more inflammatory anti-Jewish comments.

'Oh!' said Sextia. 'The boat was uncomfortable. The food was dreadful.'

'But the wine?' Josephus asked.

Sextia licked her lips. 'Divine! Ah, the Egyptians are masters. You know Egyptian wine? But, of course, *you* would.'

'I have a modest store of some good Egyptian at Sebaste. It will be an honour to send you a few jars to take home with you.'

'It is an honour I shall most graciously allow you, my dear Josephus. I shall drink it in your memory. And in memory of one evening on that barge.' She lay back and closed her eyes, blew a kiss to some remembered companion, and then, 'But I won't remember the smells, I hope. Nor recall the price. Those Egyptians are devils. Can you guess what it cost me for a boat trip to see those triangle things?'

Before long the party were listening with amusement as she enlarged on the delights of Alexandria. 'The theatre is wonderful. The audience remarkable. So quiet. No shouting and brawling.'

'They leave that to the actors I suppose,' said Pilate.

'I mean there are none of these claques. No yelling for favourites and booing the others. Not like in Rome. Did you know, Josephus, that the audience fought so at one show in Rome that it became a riot? Some soldiers were killed. Worse, a centurion was killed. *And* a tribune! The Egyptians are not so silly as that.'

At last Josephus indicated that he must leave. Pilate accompanied him to the main courtyard.

'I hope . . . ' he began hesitantly.

'Please, Pontius. I know what you wish to say, but do not worry. As a Jew I am accustomed to being assailed; usually by the same type of person as that raw young Paterculus. But, Pontius, we Jews are terrible rogues: we never let abuse deflect us from good business. And for my part, perhaps my referring to my friends on the Danube was a little offensive, for Paterculus's father hasn't finished paying those debts yet. No, Pontius, be assured. Words do not injure me. I could wish they were the only things thrown at me.'

'What does that mean? What is it that is worrying you?'

'The same thing which has made me send Mattathias and that very young bride of his away earlier than I had planned. When one gets old one becomes less timid, at least I hope so, about oneself, but more concerned about the welfare of others. I did not want those two young people to be exposed to any unpleasantness in Sebaste.'

'What unpleasantness? What has happened at Sebaste?'

'Only a day after your visit, Pontius, I was the target for a rather weighty pebble. Someone threw it at me from over a wall. Oh, it was a bad aim: it missed. And perhaps if it had hit, it might not have hurt me: Jews are very thick-skinned. But the pebble was a significantly unpleasant variety. On it someone had scratched the outline of a dagger.'

'A Zealot dagger!'

'Undoubtedly! No Zealot is likely to be pleased at my having been the host of the Roman Procurator. But that bit of hooliganism alone would not have induced me to send Mattathias away. Yesterday, however, something worse happened. One of my slaves . . . not a Jew, a Numidian who is completely ignorant of all our Jewish quarrels . . . was stabbed to death outside the bathhouse.'

'By a Zealot?'

'I could not say that, but . . . '

173

'It could have been a personal brawl.'

'I wish I could have thought that. But the corpse was mutilated in a way which made it plain that the murder was political. Added to which someone had daubed on the man's robe, in his own blood, words which, so far as one could read, were "Josephus, Friend of Rome".'

'But this is outrageous. Did you inform the governor?'

'Of course. As a law-abiding resident of Sebaste that was my duty.'

'What did he say?'

'I hardly expected a reply. I had not received one by the time I left Sebaste.'

'I shall see to that.' Pilate pondered. 'I shall also order a stricter watch to be kept for Zealots in the neighbourhood. And there must be a guard posted at the villa.'

'A guard. Oh, no! A Roman guard around the home of Josephus will be considered no honour for the inhabitant, and I fear, Pontius, that it might further inflame my enemies. They would see me as sheltering behind the power of Rome.'

'But it is obvious that you need protection.'

'Nor do I very much relish the prospect of Roman soldiers stamping around my gardens.'

'Whatever you say, Josephus, you cannot object to my having them posted in the street.' He forced a smile. 'I could even order them not to wear boots, or at least not to stamp. Have no fear, Josephus. I shall make every provision for your safety.'

'Thank you, Pontius. I hope to have the honour of receiving you soon at Sebaste again.'

'I too hope that may be soon. I shall call at Sebaste on my next progress to Jerusalem.'

'By which time I shall, I am sure, have good news for you.'

They took affectionate leave of each other.

The news that his treasured banker was being persecuted stoked up the anger that had smouldered in Pilate through the morning. After sending a message to Paterculus that he wished to see him immediately, he stood on the terrace. From there he saw Paterculus crossing the courtyard, one of the two bodyguards harshly ordering labourers out of the Roman's lordly path. Paterculus glanced up. Seeing that Pilate was alone he halted his guards at the foot of the stair. As he reached the top of the stair Pilate turned his back on him and walked along the corridor.

'The Jewish gentleman has left?' drawled Paterculus as he

followed the Procuator into his study. 'An interesting character, as Jews go.'

Disregarding the comment Pilate seated himself at his desk. 'I suppose you know why I wished to see you.' Paterculus stared down at him blankly. 'I have had a report regarding the disturbance in the port last night.'

'Oh, that!' The shrug was elaborate. 'It seems that my men indulged a little too liberally in Judaean vinegar.'

Pilate looked up into the blank bored eyes. 'Sit down, Paterculus,' in a tone more of command than invitation. The patrician disposed himself on the chair, again stiffly upright. Pilate took a chair opposite him, seating himself equally erect. 'Yes,' continued Pilate. 'Your men were drunk. But that, though deplorable, is not in itself the offence. The offence is that they conducted themselves in a riotous manner in a public place.'

'My dear Procurator! It was, I agree, a regrettable incident, but with all respect it was six of one and half-a-dozen of the other. These Jews, these natives, are a hysterical bunch. My men are Romans.'

'They seem to have forgotten that fact last night. They proved themselves unworthy of the name.'

Paterculus drew back as sharply as though he had been slapped in the face. 'May I ask, Procurator, what that comment implies?'

'That they were a drunken undisciplined mob who were conducting themselves not as Romans but as barbarians. They abused the hospitality of this city and thus indirectly insulted me.'

'With all deference, Procurator, you take it too seriously.'

'Conduct of that nature cannot be taken too seriously. Without apparent reason and certainly without orders from any officer, they used force against civilians.'

'I repeat, Procurator, that my men are Romans. Those whom you refer to as civilians are not Romans. Furthermore, it is they who were insultingly riotous.'

'Paterculus. As I have already tried to make clear to you, the successful administration of this province demands peaceful collaboration between the Roman command and its native population. There are still occasions, unfortunately, when force must be used. But force is used only when political or legal necessity demands it. And it is never delegated to a pack of drunken bullies.'

The young face remained haughtily impassive, but the voice quivered with suppressed anger. 'My men were not too drunk to recognise that the dignity of Rome was being insulted, and not too drunk to defend that dignity.'

'A wine-sodden brute, whether Roman or not, has no dignity. But what particularly offends me is that you refused to allow offenders to be put in cells where they might have regretted their deeds and loss of Roman dignity in the squalor of their own vomit. I assure you, Marcus Paterculus, that had I been present last night I should have had each and every one of them flogged. I insist, Marcus Paterculus, that these men of your personal guards shall conduct themselves in accordance with the laws of this province. As Roman soldiers they must be considered as being, even if indirectly, under my command.'

'Perhaps technically under your command, Procurator. But their prime duty is to Rome. With respect, Pilate, I suggest that your immediate patron, the Prefect Sejanus, would think first of Rome, only second of Jews.' He stood up suddenly. His grey eyes were now cold with undisguised hostility. 'My dear Procurator,' he drawled with affected indifference, 'there is something at the root of last night's little scuffle which I might not have mentioned had you not taken so harsh a view of the conduct of my men. They were already in an angry mood when they left the barracks. I can understand their feelings, for they had overheard some gossip among your native auxiliaries. That information must have loomed large in their minds when, in the tavern, they found themselves the target for abuse and threatened attack by a pack of Jews.'

'What information?'

'During our first conversation, Procurator, you confessed to the hope that you might at least live long enough to do in Judaea something by which the name of Pontius Pilate would ever be remembered. I think you have already done the deed. Certainly it is something which your patron the Prefect Sejanus will not easily forget. That deed was in the minds of my Romans when they faced a bawling Jewish mob. Can you blame them for being shocked by the news that Pontius Pilate, Procurator of Judaea, had crucified a Roman?'

'You should be more accurate. The man was not a Roman when he was crucified.'

'A mere legality, as I see it.'

'And the crucifixion was done with a purpose. It was designed expressly to demonstrate the impartiality of Roman law, to show that under Rome anyone guilty of treason, whatever his birth, will suffer the punishment applicable to that crime.'

'I dare to suggest, Pilate, that you understand these Jews less than the Procurator of a Jewish province should. The first essential is that the Jews, and all subject races of Rome, should recognise that we Romans are a master race. The crucifying of a Roman can only lead to Jews imagining that Romans are no better than other mortals.'

'Enough, Paterculus. I refuse to tolerate your questioning my judicial decisions. Only Caesar has the right to do that. Here in Judaea I represent Caesar. I speak with his voice.' Pilate's hand strayed to that position on his breast where, had he been sitting in state, his badge of office would have been lying.

'May I point out, Pilate, that you are also answerable to the personage to whom you owe your appointment as Procurator, your patron and friend the Prefect Sejanus.'

'Who, despite his great eminence, is also answerable to Caesar. Listen, Marcus Paterculus. I must now speak to you not as your host but as the governor of a province in which you are merely a visitor. My command is that until your departure for Antioch, your guards are confined to barracks.'

'As you wish, Proconsul Procurator. So that the order will not unduly incommode them or me I shall leave for Antioch to-morrow.'

'Good. Furthermore, I am taking steps to ensure that your bodyguard do not blunder into further trouble. You and they will be accompanied to the limit of the province by soldiers commanded by a Roman officer. Goodbye, Marcus Paterculus.'

Paterculus stood up. 'Goodbye, Pilate. I thank you for your hospitality. Please convey my respects to the Lady Claudia.' He turned smartly on his heel.

Pilate chose the moment when he was almost at the door to call his name.

'Yes, Procurator?'

'Please be so good as to tell the Tetrarch Herod, when you enjoy the audience you have sought of him, that I hope to have the pleasure of using his palace when I go to Jerusalem for the festivals of Yom Kippur and Tabernacles.'

Late the following evening Pilate was alone with Claudia when a message came from Marcellus requesting to see him urgently. Pilate dressed and went to his study and unbolted the door leading into the corridor. The guard summoned a slave who hurried in to fan the brazier to life. Marcellus appeared, but did not speak until the man had gone. He closed the door after him and produced a folded sheet of papyrus.

'I have an interestingly unpleasant document here, Pontius.' He handed it to Pilate.

It was slightly damp. Pilate unfolded it. On it were five lines of writing. The characters were blotched, though not so much so as to prevent their being read, but the groups of letters were a code. 'The writing is that of Marcus Paterculus,' said Marcellus. 'The message was found on the body of one of his guards.'

'On his *body*.'

'Yes. The man is dead. He was seen leaving the tower after sundown. Being officially confined to barracks, he should have been challenged. But as he was behaving in a suspiciously secretive manner it was thought advisable to follow him rather than halt him.' Marcellus smiled. 'One could always say that for the fellow's sake we had to follow him to make sure he came to no harm on the waterfront.'

'I get the point, Marcellus. No need to embroider the alibi. Go on.'

'When the soldier arrived at the port he went to a tavern where he contacted the captain of a merchantman due to leave Caesarea tonight for Cyprus. Incidentally, it transpired later that arrangements had already been made for his passage. He was carrying letters from Marcus Gaius Paterculus.'

'How did he die?'

'When he was stepping aboard he slipped and fell between the quay and the boat. Rather foolishly someone pulled the boat nearer to the quay thinking that might help him. At last I realised that actually this was holding the poor fellow under water.'

'Ah. So you were there yourself, Marcellus.'

'As it happens, yes. Bearing in mind last night's disturbance I had thought it best to go down there also.'

'Go on.'

'In the man's wallet were letters written by Marcus Paterculus, to his wife, to his steward, to others. They seem to be merely domestic letters. Quite personal.'

'So you read the personal correspondence of Marcus Paterculus?'

'That was necessary. We had to establish who the man was and for whom he was acting as courier.'

'There I see an inconsistency in your story, Marcellus. After all, you knew the man was one of Paterculus's guards and he was seen to leave the tower.'

'Yes. But it was necessary to establish that he had told the truth to the sea-captain. For the sake of Paterculus. Why, the man might have been stealing something.'

'Hm!' Pilate pondered for a moment. 'I suppose it could be argued that way. And this?' He tapped the document. 'Was this with the letters?'

'No. It was stitched in his vest.'

'Then how was it discovered?'

'When we stripped him.'

'How can you explain stripping and searching him?'

'Someone suggested we might press the water out of his lungs. I thought it would be better to strip him for that.'

'It could be a reasonable explanation.'

'He was past saving.'

'Poor fellow!' Pilate tapped the document again. 'I take it that this has been deciphered?'

'Quite easily. I am surprised Paterculus should use such an elementary code.' Marcellus produced another sheet and handed it to Pilate.

Pilate read. ' "As I feared. Pilate not to be relied upon. Not only sympathetic to Jews, but also up to his neck in them. Probably in their power financially. Consequently I shall take the action I previously advocated." '

Pilate laid the translation neatly on the original.

'It bore no address?'

'No. I suppose the man or Paterculus's wife knew where it must go.'

'Does Paterculus know that his courier is drowned?'

'Of course. I thought it best to tell him immediately.'

'Quite right. I hope the news reached him expeditiously. I should not like him to think you had been reading his correspondence.'

'He was notified immediately. While the letters were being read I sent a message telling him of the tragedy, but assured him that we would soon be able to recover the body. Later we reported the finding of the wallet and offered the services of a courier. He accepted the offer.'

'Did he ask for the man's vest?'

Marcellus smiled. 'No. But when I promised that the man

179

would be given decent burial in Caesarea he had a better idea. The man's home, he explained, was in Cyprus. He felt he owed it to the man's family to send his body there for honourable burial. He would pay expenses for a coffin.'

'Is the corpse being sent?'

'Yes.'

'In full armour, I suppose?'

'Paterculus was considerate of the family. He ordered that the man should be sent just as he was, fully clothed in martial style.'

'But without vest?'

'Oh, no! I saw to it that the poor lad got his vest back.'

Pilate lifted the translation, read it slowly through again, then stared meditatively at Marcellus.

'Paterculus is leaving us soon.'

'Yes. Tomorrow. For Antioch. But calling at Tiberias *en route*.'

'So he told you that?'

'I learned it.'

Pilate smiled. 'Well, I think we ought to honour Paterculus by providing him with someone of rank to act as personal escort on his progress.'

Marcellus nodded appreciatively.

'What about you?' Pilate asked.

'No,' said Marcellus firmly. 'He knows my function here. He wouldn't say a word to me.'

'Hm! I suppose you are right. Well, then, what about Fabius?' Marcellus pouted doubtingly and his right shoulder stirred. 'Paterculus is quite impressed with Fabius,' Pilate persisted. 'Far more than he could be with me. Fabius is an aristocrat.'

Marcellus nodded. The idea was not too bad.

'And what would your briefing be?' asked Pilate.

'That Fabius should himself approach Paterculus and say he would like to get away from the damned Procurator for a while. Fabius would ask Paterculus to request your permission to allow Fabius to be in charge of the escort. During the trip Fabius should make himself as agreeable as possible to Paterculus.'

'And,' Pilate interrupted, 'if, to do that, Fabius found it necessary to make uncomplimentary or even seditious remarks about Pontius Pilate, those remarks will not be taken amiss. He should make sure, wherever protocol allows it, of being present when Paterculus meets personages of importance.'

'But,' said Marcellus, 'Fabius must be warned not to commit anything to writing. He must store everything he hears in his

180

head. I guess there's plenty of vacant space in that handsome skull.'

Pilate laughed. 'Don't underestimate Fabius. Give him a good briefing, and give him a chance.' He reached to a box on his desk, snapped back the lid and produced a key. He handed this to Marcellus with the two sheets of papyrus. 'Have these documents, together with a note of the date and relevant circumstances, put in the strong-box. Polygnotus will need to go with you: he wears the companion key round his neck. But, just a moment, Marcellus.' He leaned back and stared at the leaning visage. 'It was surely strangely opportune, Marcellus, that you should have found yourself on the scene at such a crucial moment?' Marcellus shrugged non-committally. 'But what I find even stranger is that Paterculus's guard, a young and agile soldier, and, I presume, sober, should be so careless as to fall into the sea with an important dispatch.'

'Yes. The poor fellow was unlucky. It was a fellow from the tavern, a clumsy lout and probably drunk, who stumbled against him just as he was stepping aboard.'

'What a remarkable coincidence!'

Marcellus stared back crookedly. 'Yes, indeed. A most remarkably coincidence.'

'I hope Paterculus thinks the same.'

'I hope so too.'

'Well, thank you, Marcellus. Good night.'

Marcellus went out vastly pleased. He clasped the key firmly. It was the first time he had been entrusted with that.

VI

Simeon the balsam-grower awoke as the first light of day, filtering through the trees around his cottage on the outskirts of Jericho, filled the low-ceilinged room with cool green light. Beside him his nephew Ishmael was also awakening. Simeon drew the boy's taut body nearer. These first moments of morning, the time when the boy awoke to the awareness that the arms around him were not his father's, were the worst moments of the day.

'Are you awake, Ishmael?'

Simeon pushed the long hair from the boy's forehead, and the head drew back; and when Simeon laid his hand on the thin shoulders he felt the muscles tighten under the skin as though resisting the caress. Simeon sighed. Each dawn he hoped that this might be the day when the boy would emerge from his lonely anger and surrender to sympathy. But he was beginning to think that somehow the chance of that had passed and that now sorrow was hardening around Ishmael like a shell.

The boy had found his way to his uncle's home two days after fleeing from the scene of his father's crucifixion. Simeon, coming home from work in the plantation, had found him curled into hiding beside the barred door of the courtyard. After he had carried the boy indoors, Ishmael, dazed with weariness and choking with sorrow, told him how his father Uzziel had died.

Saddened though Simeon was by the news of his brother's death, and revolted by the manner of that death, he was pleased that it was to him that Ishmael had fled for refuge. Simeon was a hard-working and moderately happy man, but he was a lonely one, and so he was happy to offer the boy a new home, and cherished the prospect of nurturing him as though he were his own son. But as the days passed, every offer of fatherly affection withered before the wall of the boy's stubborn loneliness. He tried to talk the boy out of that. Perhaps against such impassioned sorrow words might not of themselves bring solace, but always he hoped that just the sound of a voice might do so.

'It is God's will, Ishmael.' He had said that often, perhaps too often. But it was his attempt, within the limits of his know-ledge of such things, to comfort Ishmael with the wisdom of the prophets. Yet how did one teach the very young to accept death, teach them to see death as part of the pattern of life, something which came at some time to everyone one loved, even as it must come inevitably to oneself? No. Only when one had seen death many times did one learn to wear mourning with dignity like a robe, and to honour the dead by remembering with joy the love they had bestowed, not indulging in paroxysms of selfish grief as though their love was nothing but a treasured toy snatched untimely from one's hands.

'Ishmael,' he had tried to say, 'it is right for a son decently to mourn his father. But sackcloth should not be worn in solitary pride. Nor in anger. Uzziel lives on in you, for you were born of his seed. And you do greater honour to his memory by being joyful in the life he gave you than by sitting in the ashes of sorrow.'

If only the boy would speak, even if he did no more than tell again in gasping anger his story of how the Romans had sought out the son of Uzziel to make him kneel and watch his father die on the cross. The shock of repeating that story might cauterise the wound, scorch poison from the memory and leave only a scar. Or if only the boy would look into his eyes, instead of staring always beyond him, staring so fixedly that even in the light of day it seemed as though he were trying to see something in darkness.

'Ishmael!' As the strengthening sunlight warmed the room he grasped the thin shoulder more firmly and turned the boy towards him. Slight though the body was, it weighed against his hands as heavy as a stone lifted from a stream, and as unresponsive.

183

Despite this rejection he settled Ismael's head into the crook of his arm and smiled a morning greeting. Ishmael's eyes under smooth childish brows were wide open, big and black, but hard, not looking at him, but staring beyond.

The Roman coin slid across the boy's brown chest, glinting in the sunlight. The day after his arrival at Jericho the boy had found a nail to drive a hole through the coin, and then had hung it around his neck on a leather lace. Simeon had murmured objection against a Jew wearing a bauble decorated with a human head, but it seemed that the coin had some personal significance to the boy, and as the thong was long enough to allow it to dangle out of sight under his robe during the day, Simeon said no more, though he always found the sight of it distasteful. The boy, noticing his eyes on it, covered it with one hand. As his fist closed around it, his mouth tightened.

Simeon sighed again. He reached for his robe and got up from the bed. 'Come along, Ishmael,' he said as heartily as he could, 'we have a lot to do today.'

Every morning Simeon took Ishmael to work beside him in the balsam plantation. Simeon, proud of his small but profitable holding, enjoyed the fragrant labour amid shadows heavy with the odour of resin and gaudy with the fluttering of countless butterflies. He hoped the boy would learn to be equally happy there. Balsam had grown in the valley, he told Ishmael, since the days of the great Solomon when the Queen of Sheba brought the first precious root in a caravan of rich gifts from her southern kingdom. He showed the boy how to cut the stems with a sharp stone and how to harvest the pearls of resin which oozed out like tears.

Their task today was to clean a season's accumulation of silt and dead leaves from one of the irrigation ditches. The boy, intent on the job, worked well, but wordlessly. At midday they walked down to a reed-fringed pool to wash dirt and sweat from their bodies. Simeon called on the boy to admire the beauty of their surroundings, asking him to look along the regiments of palms which stretched in sun-dazed rows towards the river Jordan. The boy looked for a second where he was told to look, then turned to sluice the last of the mud from his limbs. When he had finished he slung the coin round his neck and put on his robe.

They walked towards the town to eat at the house of a neighbour. In a courtyard roofed with vines, the family were crowded on benches around a long table of rough wood. The air was filled with the scent of fresh bread, and the sweet tang of cumin rose from the big bowl of stew. Simeon brought the boy to eat here every working day, feeling that lively company was better for him than the quiet of the cottage, just as he believed that life in populous Jericho and work in the balsam groves, being so different from herding goats on parched hills, would help Ishmael to forget the past.

He was wrong. Each day that Ishmael worked in the lush plantations and each evening that he walked along the opulent palm-shaded streets of Jericho, the boy recalled his native highlands with fiercer longing; each day his rage against those who had driven him away from those hills burned deeper. It seemed that everything he loved had been destroyed when, by Roman command, the mud walls and wattle roofs of his village had been crumbled to ruins. Faithful to his homeland, he hated this scented valley which men called 'the Garden of the Lord' and where even in winter, when snow was falling on the highlands, it was warm enough for soft city-dwellers to walk in linen.

His uncle Simeon had pointed to the road which snaked up the deep ravine between the hills to the south. They called that road, said Simeon, the 'Ascent of Blood' because bandits and Zealots had butchered so many victims along it. But, said Simeon, at the end of it, beyond Bethany, was the Holy City of Jerusalem. One day, he promised, they would make pilgrimage to the Temple together.

When, as a child in his highland village, Ishmael had heard the rabbis talk about Jericho and the river Jordan and Jerusalem, City of David, they had seemed to him not the places of today but places of legend, belonging to the past glories of Judah, belonging to the days before the Romans, when the tribes of Israel had marched free and victorious into their Promised Land and the singing trumpets of Joshua had brought down the walls of Jericho. Also from his father Uzziel he had heard of Jerusalem. Uzziel, coming home wide-eyed with wonder from a Passover pilgrimage, had told of a golden Temple and a maze of a thousand streets piled high with all the treasures of the world. Ishmael had listened as one listening to travellers' tales. The picture his father painted dazzled the boy's imagination, but he did not see it as anything real, only as a vision vouchsafed his pilgrim father by an angel of the Lord. For Ishmael had found it impossible to believe that beyond his familiar horizon of threadbare pastures and rock-choked wadis there could be anything other than more hills and more goats and grass no greener than his. Nor had he ever wanted the world to be otherwise; certainly not like this Jericho, this Sheol, this valley of the dead in which servile farmers and handwashing merchants, cringing like slaves before their Roman masters, grew white and fat as corpses. So each day as he worked beside his uncle, bending to his task in the cloying warmth of the plantation, he dreamed of his own hills, baked and cracked in summer and scoured by freezing dust in winter; each night, when at last he had fallen asleep, his soul wandered those beloved highlands, and each morning he awoke to the memory of his father dying on the cross, and his hand closed hard on the coin at his breast.

His uncle Simeon was much younger than his father, and not like Uzziel at all. Uzziel had been austere and brave and proud: Simeon was soft and gentle as a woman. Even the evil news of Uzziel's death seemed to move Simeon to nothing more than submissive and unmanly sadness. A true Jew would have shown anger. A true brother would have sworn that when the power and the weapons were at hand the death of Uzziel would be avenged. Did not the Book of the Law decree that a life should go for a life? But all that Simeon had said was, 'It is God's will!' That was not true. The murder of Uzziel had not been God's will: it had been the will of a Roman general, sitting bathed and shaved in his cool black tent while Uzziel, streaked with blood and sweat, died in the sun. Neither was it God's will that Ishmael had been sought out and made to kneel to watch his father die: that had been the will of Roman captains.

It was Simeon's custom to walk into town each evening. He went always by the same route and to the same place: past the handsome Roman baths where, it was said, Herod the Great had had his son Aristobulus strangled while swimming, to a little inn where there were tables and benches on a terrace shaded by palms. There Simeon sat for hours gossiping with his cronies. When there was nothing to talk about there was much to see. Opposite them were the walls of the old town, at the base of which the pastry-stalls kept open late, and arches through which one could see into the narrow streets where there were other, less reputable, drinking-dens and eating-houses and, at a bend in one street, a notorious house where women with painted faces would peep at passers-by through barred windows and sometimes flutter a gauzy scarf to catch the eye of a likely man.

Now each evening Simeon took Ishmael with him, and whenever he saw a friend or neighbour or anyone whom he knew passing by with a son beside him, he would call the father over, and thus give Ishmael the chance to make contact with the boy of his own age, hoping that the prospect of friendship might tempt the boy from his fierce shyness. Ishmael merely mumbled ritual formulas of greeting and ignored further friendly advances. In fact, the boy never seemed aware of the chatter going on around him. The only time he did show a spark of interest in the gossip, and Simeon noticed it with disquiet, was one evening when the innkeeper was telling two of the customers that 'the Romans' had been raiding inns in the town the night before. Well, not Romans exactly, he admitted. They were auxiliaries from the barracks. But they had been under the command of a Roman officer newly arrived from Caesarea. They had questioned innkeepers about their lodgers. One of the customers shrugged and laughed. 'Hunting Zealots, I guess.'

'Yes, that's what they were after. They didn't bother me, though. They know no Zealots will come here. Too many of my customers are from the barracks.'

'They've little chance of finding any Zealots here in Jericho,' said the other. 'They should go into the desert. That's where Zealots hang out.'

'True enough,' said the innkeeper. 'And better for all if they stay there.' He broke off then to serve other customers. The two men resumed their grumbling about the taxes on garden produce sent to Jerusalem market. The boy turned away.

Nor did Ishmael appear to have the slightest interest in his surroundings, apart from those moments when, with head bent and narrowed eyes, he peered at the young Jews who strolled around the arcaded square or gathered in chattering groups at the lighted stalls. These Jews were unlike any Jews Ishmael had ever seen before, but his face registered no surprise, only contempt. The petted dandies wore laundered robes, and their hair was clipped so short that it showed their ears. Had it not been for their Jewish caps they would have looked no different from the gentile Greeks and Romans with whom they mingled in sickening amicability.

Simeon saw the boy's glances and, recognising the hostility in them, decided that Ishmael needed wiser coaching in city ways than any he could give. With this in mind he took the boy with him to visit a rabbi whom he frequently went to for advice on family and business affairs. A visit to so fine a house – it had three courtyards and was in the best part of town, close by the monumental race-track built by Herod in Roman style – would at least give the boy some idea of the graces of city life.

It was not a successful visit. The fine furnishings and gleaming ornaments seemed to do no more than make the country boy ill at ease; the learned man's kind questions were met by cold responses. The rabbi did, however, remark that Ishmael's replies, curt though they were, revealed that his schooling in the village had been sound, although meagre.

'My father taught me,' said Ishmael.

The rabbi smiled indulgently when he heard the bold pride in the boy's voice. ' "He who had a father was taught the Law by him",' he quoted. ' "He who had none did not learn the Law." '

He tested Ishmael's knowledge. Yes, the lad was well versed in the Law and had a retentive memory. He could recite from the *Shema* without any prompting. ' "Hear, O Israel, the Lord thy God is one God." ' He spoke it clearly and well. But it was apparent from the fervent emphasis he gave to certain verses that the Mosaic exhortations which he most fiercely cherished were those which could support his vengeful thoughts against the enemies of Judah. ' "If someone comes to slay you, you slay him first." '

As they walked through the courtyards on their way to the street, the rabbi took Simeon aside and attempted some advice. For a time, he suggested, it would be wiser not to risk inflaming the boy's thoughts with further schooling. Work in the open air and the company of youngsters of his own age would be better than synagogue teaching. Healthy activity would sublimate the pent-up sorrows and angers which secretly plagued him.

'I have tried all that,' said Simeon miserably.

'Keep on trying. You must have patience. It may take a long time.'

An encounter later that evening made Simeon hope it might not take a long time after all. They were walking back from the rabbi's house along the road beside the race-track, the boy's hand lying obediently but utterly unresponsive in Simeon's, when a passer-by halted to tell him that a friend of his had that afternoon come home from Galilee.

Simeon's face lit with pleasure at the news. The returned traveller, son of a rich merchant in Jericho, was his dearest friend. What was more, Simeon delightedly thought, he was the very man likely to coax Ishmael out of his brooding miseries. A boy who had expressed himself so fearlessly to a rabbi would certainly admire a Jew who, though his patriotism might be a little too wild, dared to criticise High Priest Caiaphas and the Sanhedrin, and who, without regard for his father's importance and wealth, had turned his back on worldly things and thrown in his lot with a band of preachers teaching their new concept of the Law in the hills and villages and along the roadsides of Galilee.

'Come along Ishmael. You must meet this friend of mine,' said Simeon, hurrying along to the merchant's house, drawing Ishmael behind him, and, as he entered the courtyard, calling out eagerly.

A young man appeared on the roof. He was still wearing his travelling mantle, a robe of unbleached wool, the hood thrown back from his dark head. 'Simeon!' he shouted joyfully, and then ran rapidly down and embraced him affectionately. He looked questioningly at the boy.

'This is Ishmael,' said Simeon. 'Son of my brother Uzziel.' The glance accompanying these words indicated that there was something more to be told, but later and not in the boy's presence.

Ishmael, standing with head bent in his habitual awkward silence, stole a glance at the young man. His robe was a fine tough country one, his black hair covered his ears, and his eyes were narrow and eager, like those of a man who had stared long over high hills. The young man put his arms around their shoulders and led them into the house, inviting them to stay for supper. 'Yes, Simeon,' he insisted, dropping his voice as they approached the door, 'stay this evening. That I still have friends makes my father happy.' Then, with a wry glance, he added, 'And company stops him thundering at me.'

The mother and father welcomed Simeon warmly. The mother, overjoyed that her son was home, was bustling happily from stove to table, urging one slave girl to fan the embers and another to gather more herbs.

The father, grey-bearded and thin, sat quiet and grave. He was a wealthy man, but his house was simple, frugal in traditional style. In his plain gown and cap of rough linen he was, Ishmael thought, much like Uzziel. The boy suddenly felt very much at home. Feeling so, he looked with envy at his uncle's friend.

That young man was at the moment answering Simeon's questions about his activities in Galilee. At first he kept his voice low, obviously in deference to his father, but he could not hide the light in his eyes nor keep the vibrant enthusiasm from his engaging, expressive face. Soon, as though forgetting or challenging his father's disapproving silence, his voice rose. This was when he was describing his companions and the preacher from Nazareth who had inspired them.

'Don't believe the stupid nonsense you hear about him,' he urged. 'Wait until you hear him for yourself. Then you will believe him: then you *must* believe him.'

When the Nazarene preached, he went on, all critics were silenced. At his words the saddest became joyful, the most timid were filled with courage. Although, the young man continued, the preacher's influence could not be gauged merely by the words he used. His language was beautiful, yes, and full of wise and happy sayings. But far more compelling than his words was his presence. For he did not speak, like a scribe or rabbi, with his nose buried in the Book of the Law, picking out the words with his finger. Instead he spoke with the authority of personal wisdom.

'He knows the Law, Simeon. He knows it inside out, better than any Sadducee or Pharisee ever did. But on his lips the Law is not the dead thing it is in their mouths: it is a living thing. His Law doesn't sound like the mumbling of ancient dogma and old-fashioned prohibitions: he shows it to us as something that we can live by every day of our lives.'

The old man broke his silence at last. 'The Law should be preached by those appointed to preach the Law,' he said sombrely. 'Yet at least it is good to hear, if all you say is true, that he preaches according to the Law.'

'Dear father,' said the young man, 'he does. But, please, wait until you hear him. And you wait also, Simeon. You will hear him soon, when he comes south, as he must, and the sooner the better. Jerusalem stands in need of such a man. Jerusalem will welcome him like a saviour, like a king. He will conquer the City of David and make it glorious again as a city of God.'

'He has certainly taught my son to preach,' said the father, 'and also, it seems, how to win disciples,' he added with a nod that drew attention to Ishmael. The others, turning to look at the boy, saw him leaning forward, his hands clasped on his knees and his face glowing as though reflecting the fire of the young man's enthusiasm. Laughing, the young man patted Ishmael's shoulder and ruffled his hair, and just then the mother called out, 'Come along and eat. We can't live only on words.'

'By the way you talk, one would think this Nazarene is raising all Galilee,' said Simeon as he took a place at table near his friend. 'But you are only . . . how many?'

'Twelve. All Galileans, except me. Yes, only twelve. But, Simeon, numbers are of no importance. His words give men such courage that twelve can seem like an army. In his presence how many we are does not seem important. Nor how we live. He tells us to take no thought for our lives, neither what we shall eat nor what we shall drink. Seek first the Kingdom of God, he says. That is his message, Simeon. He is a man of destiny. And he is moved by the spirit of the Lord God to Establish the Kingdom of the Jews.'

Simeon was hardly listening, for now he was entranced by the glow in Ishmael's eyes. He had never seen them so alive. Then he glanced towards the head of the table. The young man's last words had reduced his father to heavy and embarrassed silence. How many other times, Simeon wondered, had the old man bitten back rebukes? Simeon guessed how fierce must be the arguments in that house between a patriarch, famed as wealthy and devout, and a son who had so unaccountably left his father's house and surrendered his life to a rebel mystic from the hills of Galilee. What good, the old man would ask from the heart of his Judaean prejudice, ever came out of Galilee? The son, following Simeon's glance, also saw how his words had disturbed his father, and fell silent abruptly, sending towards his father a dutiful smile which attempted to convey his apologies for having, at his father's table and in the presence of strangers, expressed sentiments which, to an old man conditioned by a lifetime of orthodox worship, must seem near to blasphemy. Simeon broke the uncomfortable silence by turning the conversation to the perennial subject of taxes.

Ishmael kept his eyes on the young man. Here at last was a real Jew. Here was someone different from any Jew he had met in Jericho. So strong and beautiful a man would never grovel to Romans.

'Meet me tomorrow night at the inn,' said Simeon's friend as he walked into the street with them. 'Will you come also, Ishmael?' he asked. The boy nodded eagerly.

'Not tomorrow,' said Simeon. 'The day after. We are going to Jerusalem tomorrow.' Ishmael looked up with surprise. Simeon grinned at him, and then said, 'Tomorrow Ishmael is to become a landowner. I am buying a plot near the plantation for him.'

The plan had been forming in his mind for some days; the ambience of this moment had made him decide to put it into effect without delay. He was determined to capture the boy's mood of happiness and nourish it. A patch of land which the boy could call his own would give him a stake in the valley. This, together with the friendship that had been born during the last two hours, would encourage him to see the possibilities of happiness in his new life.

'You have done us both a world of good,' Simeon said to his friend. 'I do not know whether to thank you or the Nazarene.' He meant that. At that moment he was thinking that some of the reputed magic of the Galilean preacher must have rubbed off on to this young disciple from Jericho. Certainly the manner in which his friend had lifted Ishmael clean out of his brooding melancholy was like a miracle. ' "If thou seest a man of understanding",' Simeon quoted softly, ' "get thee betimes unto him and let thy foot wear out the steps of his door." '

'Well, I hope that I am a man of understanding,' said the young man, glancing back towards the house. 'But I fear that when I get indoors, my father may quote something else from the same chapter. "He that spareth the rod hateth his own son." '

Then, with a laugh of pleasure, he embraced Simeon, briefly caressed the boy's head and left them. Ishmael watched him until he was out of sight across the courtyard before he joined his uncle. They walked home without speaking, but tonight their silence was a happy one.

Simeon and Ishmael left for Jerusalem before dawn. As their donkeys trotted up the Ascent of Blood, Ishmael fixed his eyes on the crest of the dark hills outlined against a sky greyly lit with a sinking moon. Beyond those hills lay Jerusalem, and now he was eager to see the Holy City because now the young man's words had transformed it from a dream into the City of David, the shrine and symbol of Jewish freedom.

The nearer they came to Jerusalem the more people there were on the road, coming down to the road from villages and farms. Some rode donkeys that overflowed with garden greens and fruits; others trudged along on foot, the bowed women showing only thin tireless ankles under great bundles of bayleaf boughs and sacks of herbs. By the time they had reached Bethany, three miles from Jerusalem, the road, like every road converging on the city on market-day, was so crowded with farmers and gardeners and craftsmen and families of children that they had to slow to a walk, as though in a procession.

Ishmael had a purse slung at his waist. Simeon had insisted that the boy should have the responsibility of carrying the money for the transaction they were to make today. In the purse was the money the boy had got when he sold Uzziel's goats, and money which his uncle had added. Simeon wanted to make sure Ishmael would have sufficient to pay for the land and something left in his purse after the purchase. For the old man who owned the land was well disposed towards Simeon. Ever since he had become too old and ill to work it himself and had moved to Jerusalem, he had been urging Simeon to buy it at a modest figure.

Lapped in these pleasant thoughts of today's good business, Simeon had paid little attention to the familiar road, and was half asleep when he was startled out of his reveries by Ishmael suddenly halting his donkey. They boy sat transfixed. They had reached the last bend in the road, the bend which skirted the olive-gardens on the Hill of Gethsemane, and the Holy City had burst suddenly into view.

All those gaudy visions of Jerusalem which Ishmael's father had conjured up were outshone by the wonderful reality. High and cool, embowered in hills, the dazzling treasure of roofs and terraces and palaces of marble and glowing brick which flowed down to the Kidron valley was now emerging tier by tier into the strengthening light of dawn. There was no need for Simeon to direct his eyes to the Temple. It proclaimed itself with spires of alabaster and gold, and at that moment, as ruddy light of the rising sun flooded down the holy mountain of Zion and flushed with pink the marble of the many-pillared porticoes, three blasts of the silver trumpets sounded through the chill air to proclaim the dawn of a new day and the opening of the Temple doors.

They entered the city at the Fountain Gate and after leaving their donkeys at a stable in the Valley of the Cheesemakers they joined the pilgrims and city folk now flocking through the gates in the battlemented outer wall of the Temple. They pushed their way into the Court of the Gentiles, and there they were engulfed amid a tumultuous and noisy crowd. The scene was one of startling contrasts: the nobility and beauty of marble, the squalor and stench of human traffic. The vast court was surrounded by colonnades as lovely and majestic as the halls of Heaven. Hundreds of pillars, all dazzlingly white, each single one hewn from a solid block of marble and seven or more times the height of a man, and bursting at the top into a glory of intricate interlacing, supported ceilings lined with carved and gilded panels of cedar-wood. Yet in a setting of such divine magnificence rose the stink and dust of a surging mob, the moans of condemned cattle and the bleating of sheep. Hawkers of sacrificial flesh bawled their prices, while the money-changers tossed Roman coins into their bowls and doled out Jewish money, the only money acceptable as payment for sacrifices. There were stalls of pastry too, and of dried fish and other snacks, and hawkers pushing around with prayer shawls and caps and girdles. The mosaic paving was scattered with droppings, the air heavy with the tang of dung.

A gaudy Jew, beside him his silk-swathed wife and attendant slaves waving feathered parasols officiously to keep flies and also people at a distance, was bargaining with a deferential dealer who was selling oxen and sheep as offerings to God. Simeon joined the poorer worshippers who were queuing to buy, more economically, pairs of doves. One greybeard in the queue mumbled something about 'the bazaar of the Sons of Annas'. That description of the Court of the Gentiles was a worn-out old joke, but the irreverence brought appreciative grins from those nearby. Like the old man, they all knew about the profitable deal Annas had done with the Temple. He had been chief priest himself until fifteen years ago, when, said the gossips, he saw a chance of going into business in a big way, had seen that there was more money to be made in the mass-market than in the luxury trade. As money got tighter, fewer and fewer Jews could afford to buy cattle and sheep for sacrifice. But what about doves? The poorest worshipper could scratch up a few pennies to buy a couple of doves. There were thousands who could do that, and Annas could easily supply that market. His estates were infested with doves. So Annas was sitting pretty. By having thousands of doves captured and sent daily in crates to be sold in the Temple, he could not only keep a pest under control but also put a fortune into his pocket. It would hardly be right, however, for the chief priest to be so openly making money at the Temple. So he gave up that office. But he did not relinquish power. He persuaded the Romans to appoint his son-in-law Joseph, popularly known as Caiaphas, as chief priest. Also he pushed four of his sons on to the Sanhedrin: two were already high priests, and the other two were in line for becoming so. That was how Annas became at the same time the real power behind the throne and the richest trader at the Temple. And that was why everyone called the Court of the Gentiles 'the bazaar of the Sons of Annas'. Even the timid law-abiding Simeon, waiting in the queue to buy two doves and watching the dealer tossing the pennies into the bowl, was moved to tell Ishmael that Annas's doves were going cheap today but at Passover the price would go up by as much as fifty times.

Ishmael saw lots of Gentiles in the crowd. Some, obviously visitors to Jerusalem who had come here to see the sights, were walking around vulgarly gaping, grinning with contemptuous amusement at the Jews bargaining at the stalls. Some were Greeks; a few were Romans. One could not get away from Gentiles in this city. Even in sight of the Temple there were flagrant reminders of Roman occupation. Just below the Temple plateau, in the Kidron valley, was the grandiose race-track built by Herod for Roman sports, and on the western hill, beyond the bridge and overlooking the Temple, the Hasmoraean Palace, the Jerusalem home of the Herods; a typical Roman palace, with courts and pleasure grounds built on terraces sweeping luxuriously down to the Kidron valley, and with three ornate towers built in memory of three of King Herod's wives. Just beyond the bridge which crossed the valley to the Temple entrance was the Roman gymnasium where Gentiles, though it was hard to believe that even they could be guilty of such sacrilegious indecency with their bodies, ran and boxed and wrestled in utter nakedness.

But of all reminders of Roman domination of Jerusalem the most brutal was a hated fortress which cast its looming shadow over the whole scene. This mighty square keep with lofty pinnacles at its corners was the Antonia fortress, so named by Herod in honour of Mark Antony. The fortress served as head-quarters of the Roman garrison and as official headquarters of Procurator Pilate when he came to the Holy City. The two stair-cases of this fortress swept arrogantly down to the outer court of the Temple, so that Roman guards could clatter out at a moment's notice to 'discipline' the Jews with staves or even swords when they thought the 'natives' were getting out of hand.

There were two soldiers on one of the staircases at this moment. Hateful in their leather jerkins and iron casques, they were leaning over a balustrade, chewing olives or dates and with their thumbs flicking the stones into the crowd. The sight of them brought back like vomit the anger Ishmael had for some hours almost forgotten. Turning away from the sight, he hurried ahead of Simeon and climbed one of the flights of fourteen steps which led from the unclean rowdy court to the terrace of the Temple proper. He felt freer and less defiled when, reaching those sacred precincts where only Jews could tread, he passed the balustrade where slabs of stone bore inscriptions in Hebrew, Greek and Latin forbidding anyone not of the true faith to step beyond them on pain of death.

There were many gateways into the Temple, their double doors covered with silver and gold, but he and Simeon entered by the grandest gate of all, the East Gate, built entirely of Corinthian brass. Worshippers were streaming in, dropping their offerings of pennies into trumpet-shaped boxes, and beyond their heads Simeon could see in the distance the magically shimmering veil of embroidered Babylonian silk which hung over the golden doors of the inner sanctuary, that sacred House of God in the secrecy of which the chosen priest of the day would now be offering sacrificial flesh to God.

When the priests emerged and incense from the offerings thickened the air, Ishmael raised his voice along with hundreds of worshippers in the prayers he had learned from his father and, each time the trumpet sounded, prostrated himself fiercely and devoutly. The prayers and exhortations of his childhood, chanted now by priests and cantors in sumptuous vestments and echoing under a sky of embossed and gilded cedar, seemed invested with fresh purpose and more glittering promise, and he was so lost in the throbbing murmur of adoration that he was still walking in a fervent dream when he and Simeon came out into the morning.

The Court of the Gentiles was now almost quiet. The money-changers were tying their sacks of coins; the dealers were packing their produce; ragged old men were sweeping up litter and dung. Simeon and Ishmael joined the stream of worshippers leaving the Temple to cross the bridge into the western half of the city, where, in the seven markets of Jerusalem, a multitude of people jostled along cool canyons of streets ceilinged against the sun with striped and tattered canopies and lined with stalls and booths where all the produce of the world was piled for sale in prodigal abundance: fine cloths and veils from India and further east; earthenware baked in nomad ovens in southern deserts; baskets and sandals and robes from Arabia; ivory and ebony from Edom; myrrh from Arabia; rare woods and spices from Parthia; fruits and apples from Crete; dusky grapes from the hillsides of Samaria; cheeses of every size and colour from every village of Judaea and live birds and vegetables from the slopes and gardens of the Jordan Valley. At every corner pickle-vendors and water-sellers clashed their bells.

They halted at an eating-house for a snack of pastry and fried locusts and refreshingly cool Egyptian beer, then made their way towards the Fish Gate, where Simeon pointed out to Ishmael the pompous portico of the house of the famous High Priest Annas. Through its archway they could see a crowd of tradesmen and suitors waiting in the outer court. At a doorway beyond, soldiers were lounging. In the fish-market Simeon pushed his way to the stall of a fishmonger whom he knew. He wanted to treat Ishmael and himself to a brace of the famous fat-bellied carp from the Sea of Galilee. These could be bought any day in the market at Jericho, but it was Simeon's belief that the choicest and plumpest always found their way to the higher-priced market at Jerusalem. The stall was covered with fish of every description, daintily arranged in stars and friezes of white bellies and brown backs and pink gills. On a stall nearby were dried fish and salted fish, and underneath, pushed almost out of sight, were baskets lined with seaweed amid which strange shell-backed creatures, black and grey and smeared with green like the depths of the abominable crannies in which they had been found, heaved and clambered over each other, thrashing their tied but menacing claws and waving long obscene antennae. Some Gentiles stopped to inspect these monsters. They turned them over with expert fingers, and then, in their version of Aramaic, began haggling about prices. They were actually buying them! 'But what will they do with them?' asked Ishmael. 'Boil 'em,' said Simeon with a laugh. 'Boil them? Why?' 'To eat them of course.' Ishmael yacked with disgust and, turning quickly away, rubbed his hands on his robe as though trying to clean the memory of the things from his fingers.

Their route to their appointment at the landowner's house took them uphill along the winding street of the silversmiths and gold-workers, where slanted trays in the doorways of the booths tempted passers-by with jewels from Babylon and golden trinkets from Parthia, displayed in apparently careless profusion, though each piece was cunningly anchored with an invisible pin to the rich fabric on which it lay and which enhanced its charms. Then along an alley where the air vibrated with the beat of tinsmiths' hammers working on silver and tin from Britain, and eventually into a court of cutlers where grindstones squeaked as craftsmen sharpened knives and scissors and scythes. On one stall in this court a pruning knife, curved like a dagger and its blade glittering sharp, caught Ishmael's eye. 'Better for the balsam than a sharp stone,' said Ishmael. Simeon picked it up, weighing it in his hand and turning it round to admire the fine bone handle. He ran an appreciative thumb along the blade. 'Good!' he said, but laid it back on the stall, saying, 'Stones are cheaper.'

Beyond this court was the landowner's house. The old man welcomed them with much ceremony, and after a long ritual of greetings and munching of bread and sipping wine and a torrent of Jericho gossip Simeon and he got down to discussing the sale of the land. The price was fixed. Ishmael produced his purse. When he had counted out the price of the land he had still a few pieces left. 'Those are yours,' said Simeon, and Ishmael put them back in his purse, which, on the old man's advice, he put into safe hiding under his robe. When a slave was sent to bring a scribe for preparing the document of sale, Ishmael asked his uncle's permission to go out. 'All right,' said Simeon. 'But don't get lost. And don't spend all your money at once.'

By the time the boy came back the deed was awaiting his signature, and Simeon, delighted that the deal had gone so easily and so cheaply, smiled with joy as he thrust into the boy's hand the document which made Ishmael son of Uzziel owner of a strip of land in the valley of the Jordan. The landowner insisted on their staying to eat with the family, so it was late in the afternoon when they walked down through the city to collect their donkeys and ride out of Jerusalem, and night was falling when they came in distant sight of Jericho.

Pilate reached Jerusalem before dawn, accompanied by only one officer, the scribe Polygnotus, and a small escort. He had programmed the journey so that he would ride into the city before daybreak. With no standards flourishing, and Pilate wearing a dark cloak over his armour and an iron casque instead of the plumed and glittering helmet, the small party trotted into Jerusalem almost unregarded by the pilgrims and market-folk plodding beside the hedges and high walls of the gardens and orchards at the approaches to the city.

Normally Pilate came to Jerusalem only on the eve of Jewish festivals, and on those occasions he arrived in state at the head of a massive column of troops. The ostensible reason for those visits was for him to perform the ceremony of handing over to High Priest Caiaphas and his court of priests the robes and insignia with which they decked themselves for festival events in the Jewish calendar. The priestly vestments, a treasure of richly embroidered robes and girdles and jewels, including Caiaphas's violet mantle lavishly studded with gold, and with golden bells and pomegranates dangling on its fringes, were kept under Roman lock and key in a chest, appropriately ornate, in the treasury of the Antonia fortress. They had been stored there for more than a hundred years, ever since the dangerously rebellious days of John Hyrcanus the Maccabee. The ritual of formally unlocking the chest on the morning before high holy days and handing the gaudy collection over to the priests suitably underlined the fact that, although Jews were free to adhere to their religious beliefs and indulge in their exotic rites, they enjoyed such freedom only by the clemency of Rome. However, the real reason for the Procurator's festival visits was expressed in the impressive number of troops he brought from Caesarea to reinforce the cohort permanently stationed at the Antonia. For there was always the danger that the emotions aroused at Jewish festivals – at Pentecost, or the Feast of Tabernacles, or, above all, at Passover when as many as three hundred thousand fervent and excited pilgrims crowded into the city – could stir these Jews to extravagant frenzies. Some hooligan or some preacher or some other fanatic might easily inflame the mob and transform religious hubbub into political revolt. The formidable display of Roman military strength was designed to dissuade the Jews from such folly, or, if the worst came to the worst, batter them to silence with clubs and swords.

This morning Pilate had arrived to confer with Chief Priest Caiaphas. It was always impossible, of course, to have any private talk with Caiaphas during festival visits. On those high holy days no lesser figure than the chief priest himself could officiate at Temple sacrifices, and the rigours of Jewish superstition prohibited an officiating priest from contaminating himself by contact with any unclean object, including any Gentile, even Caesar's procurator himself.

Pilate had allowed the stubborn and slow-moving Jewish administration a week in which to consider the project for the irrigation of Judaea, and today he expected to receive the Sanhedrin's official acceptance of the plan. He could, and, if necessary, would, carry the scheme through without their compliance. But work would proceed more smoothly with the Sanhedrin's approval. It would proceed even more smoothly with some of the Sanhedrin's money. The money was more important than the approval, and the principal aim of today's conference was to make it plain that the Procurator expected the Sanhedrin to provide a considerable proportion of the necessary finance. The news that private financiers were ready to help would perhaps induce them to lend some of their immense treasure.

The guards who had been posted at the approach to the Antonia in preparation for the Procurator's arrival sprang to position when he approached. As he dismounted, Fabius ran down to accompany him up the stairway into the fortress.

Pilate smiled warmly at Fabius. 'You saw Paterculus safely over the border?' he asked. But the din billowing up from the rowdy crowd in the Court of the Gentiles drowned his words, and he had to repeat them when they had passed through the archway into the comparative calm of the entrance hall.

'Yes. Eventually.' Fabius pulled a face. 'There was some trouble with the auxiliaries, though.'

'Trouble?'

'Yes, sir. The auxiliaries were near to mutiny when . . . '

'Later, Fabius, later,' said Pilate, for at that moment the steward of the Antonia had appeared to welcome Pilate and to inform the Procurator that Chief Priest Caiaphas had suggested that the discussion should take place at the house of his father-in-law Anna. Pilate frowned at this.

'I took the liberty, Procurator,' the steward went on hurriedly, 'of expressing some doubts as to the suitability of such a venue. I suggested that a better place for the meeting would be the Hasmonaean Palace. He agreed.'

'Excellent! Is Herod in residence?'

'He arrived two days ago. He was aware of your intended visit and, to some extent, the purpose of it. He expressed the hope of entertaining yourself and the high priest at midday.'

'Does he actually intend to give us food?' said Pilate with a laugh. He turned to Fabius. 'We can kill two birds with one stone: Caiaphas and the Fox. You'll find Herod an interesting rogue. I don't expect him to part with a shekel, but he'll enjoy the spectacle of the Jews doing so.'

The gloom of the sombre hall was suddenly lightened above by a rosy glow as the sun rose over the sacred Mount of Zion and a shaft of light streaked through a high window, and at that moment there came to their ears the shrill blast of the silver trumpets, followed immediately by the thunderous rumble of the Temple doors being flung open for the morning service.

'They say that din can be heard as far as Jericho,' said Fabius when the reverberations had ceased.

'I can believe it. Let's find some quiet.'

Pilate and Fabius, followed by Polygnotus lugging his bulging satchel of maps and documents, walked through a succession of stony corridors to Pilate's audience chamber. It was a vast room, at this moment of the morning an expanse of shadowy distances and emptiness. The cavernous depth of the three embrasures, where latticed doors opened on to the narrow balcony directly overlooking the Court of the Gentiles, revealed that the walls were immensely thick, built for strength rather than beauty. But some efforts to modify the stern aspect of the place had been made. The walls had recently been covered with boldly coloured frescoes and the floor laid with a mosaic of variously tinted marble. A false ceiling of coffered panels and gilded bosses had been installed. This was supported by two rows of pillars which, owing to the reduced height of the chamber, looked rather squat and fat. In the wall facing the windows two niches had been carved to contain, in over-decorated frames, statues of Augustus Caesar and Tiberius Caesar; the mass-produced similarity of their visages was made the more emphatic by their wearing identical wreaths of laurel. But at the farthest end of the room, near the dais on which was mounted the Procurator's chair of state, was an object of real value. It was a bust of the Divine Julius, reputedly the work of a Greek sculptor of great distinction, though there were some doubt about that. Nevertheless, it had cost the Prefect Sejanus a great deal of money, and experts agreed that it was one of the most accurate portraits existing of the first Caesar. This expensive gift had been presented to the Antonia by the prefect shortly before his protégé Pilate was appointed Procurator of Judaea. To avoid offending Jewish susceptibilities on the matter of 'graven images', it had been smuggled into Jerusalem at night in a grain-chest addressed to the victualler of the soldiers' mess. When Pilate moved in as procurator he had the bust mounted on a pedestal whose utmost simplicity he considered a suitable compliment to the dictator's legendary austerity. He had also had it placed in such a position near his dais that anyone who entered for audience with the Procurator would, throughout the whole of his walk along the unnerving length of the gleaming empty floor, see ahead of him two awe-inspiring figures: the small figure of Pilate raised to grandeur by his chair of state and the height of the dais, and, on his right hand, the omniscient marble countenance of the Divine Julius. On a bar above the bust, as also above the busts of

Augustus and Tiberius, drapery was arranged curtain-wise, so that if the visitor were a Jew of note the graven images could be politely hidden from his eyes.

The steward hurried to one of the embrasures and opened the lattice. Morning light flowed into the chamber, but with it came also the tumultuous babble of the crowd and the cries of traders and dealers. Turning quickly away from light and noise, Pilate made for a corner beyond the dais where, behind thickly embroidered curtains, were the carved and gilded double doors opening into his workroom.

Like his study at Caesarea, this workroom was a frugal cell. Here also there was only one window, high in the wall, and a desk situated to allow daylight to beam down over his left shoulder. He took off his casque and cloak and seated himself on a leather couch, rubbing his thighs to disperse the stiffness and chill of the long hard ride. Polygnotus busied himself at the desk, laying on it the stack of plans and documents, groping in his wallet for Pompey's lamp and putting it in the accustomed position, and then making sure that pens and ink and sealing-wax were in their accustomed position.

'What was the trouble with Paterculus?' Pilate asked Fabius.

'His standards. The auxiliaries objected to them.'

'But Syrians do not usually object to images of Caesar.'

'It wasn't objection to a graven image, Procurator. In fact I'm sure there would have been no trouble if the image had been Caesar's. But it wasn't.'

'Whose was it?'

'Prefect Sejanus's.'

'Hm. Of course!'

'The spokesman for the auxiliaries argued that his men were prepared to march under standards proclaiming their obedience to Caesar but they objected to the glorification of Sejanus. They seem to hate the prefect.'

'It's not his person they hate. They hate his racial policies. But did you get out of this, Fabius, any indication how their hatred of the prefect affects their attitude to me?'

'They are good soldiers, sir. I am convinced of their personal loyalty to you. I know that they do not hold it against you that Sejanus is your patron. They take that, if I may say so, as just one of the normal misfortunes in the chain of command.'

'Hm! Nicely put, Fabius. Did you straighten out the trouble?'

'I threatened them with the lash if they persisted in their objections.'

'And did that work?'

'After some persuasion, yes. I think they consoled themselves with the thought that they would suffer the display only as far as the frontier.'

'So it turned out satisfactorily?'

'More than satisfactory. It was fortunate that Marcus Paterculus was present during the argument. Up to that time he had been very distant and suspicious with me. When I bullied the auxiliaries into accepting the Sejanus standards he became markedly more friendly.'

'So you won his confidence?'

'Not completely. But who could? He's as close as an oyster. But he did eventually talk more freely about you, sir.'

'He did, eh? In what way?'

'Only by hints at first. But I did as you asked. I encouraged him to go further.'

'Did he do so?'

'Yes.' Fabius suddenly sat down on a nearby chair and, leaning languidly back, adopted a pose so superbly mimicking the patrician's customary attitude that a smile suffused Pilate's tired face. 'He began by confessing his surprise,' drawled Fabius, looking over his nose, 'that a man of such talent as myself and of such noble lineage should be content to serve in subordinate position to a man ...'

'A little man whose ancestors were slaves, etcetera, etcetera,' Pilate interrupted grimly. 'And he dangled before you temptations of advancement?'

'Just so.'

'Write a full report. I shall enjoy reading it.' Pilate grimaced. 'It will be as salutary as looking in a mirror.'

Pilate, accompanied by Fabius, the scribe and a posse of guards, rode to the Hasmonaean Palace. The passage of a company of horsemen through the city at this hour of the day caused considerable stir. The Procurator was still incognito, his casque low on his forehead and the dark cloak pulled up to muffle his chin and mouth, but the furious efforts of the guards to protect him from the press of people and clear a path before him made everyone aware that here was a Roman of high importance, though that did not overawe drovers who were crossing the bridge. They, with their habitual insolence, yelled surly protests when they had to pull or push their laden asses to the side to allow room for the cavalcade. But a few minutes later Pilate's party had ridden past the hippodrome and entered the shadowy peace of the fragrant stream-laced gardens of the Hasmonaean Palace.

Awaiting the Procurator's arrival, Herod Antipas, Tetrarch of Galilee and Peraea, was agreeably passing the time in stroking the bejewelled necks of his favourites among the gaudy-plumaged inhabitants of his aviary.

He was looking forward to today's encounter with Pilate. He had come specially from Tiberias for the meeting. Not that he liked Pilate, or enjoyed his company. Not a bit. He disliked the man. He disliked all men without blood; cold men, austere men. He disliked even more men lacking in social graces, and, really, Pilate was so plebeian in manner, so downright ordinary. One could well believe that his forbears were slaves. Compared with his predecessor, Valerius Gratus, who had been so recklessly hospitable a host and always ready to fix a deal, whether in land or rents or women, Pilate was a dull stick. He was a man of such appalling rectitude: there was no profit, nor any expectation of profit, in him. He was, one had to face it, so frightfully Roman: a stickler for law and order, and always pontificating on the dignity of Caesar and the glory of empire. He seemed unaware, this popinjay spawned by slaves, that the Herods, of ancient lineage, were real royals, far more royal than those modern upstart Caesars. Some talent Pilate must have, one supposed. Otherwise Sejanus would not have sent him to Judaea. But Herod would be glad to see the back of the little martinet. And that he might be doing very soon. At least the Roman Paterculus had hinted at such a possibility. So, with this prospect enlivening him to mischievous anticipation, Herod, hearing soldiers brought to a halt below the terrace, kissed a parrot's beak, received a nibble and a squawk in return, put the bird on its silver swing, and left the aviary.

From the end of the terrace Pilate saw the Tetrarch emerging from the golden cage like a sumptuous doll. He caught a glimpse at the same time, on a balcony above, of a flutter of silks and scarves. A woman with a tower of black hair bound with ribbons dodged out of sight into the shadows. He hoped that the woman might be a concubine and not Herodias. He hoped not to endure this morning the wearisome social process of meeting that ageing but still coquettish bitch.

Herod, he noted as the Tetrarch bobbed towards him, was

honouring today's meeting with a display of regal splendour. His robe, stiff with embroidery and encrustations of jewels, enclosed his effete figure in a box of solid dignity. The golden fringes at the hem were so heavy that one could hear their whisperings on the mosaic as he glided towards Pilate.

One glance at the yellow raddled face was sufficient to put Pilate on his guard. It was wreathed in smiles. His greeting was flowery too. Slaves appeared on the scene immediately. One carried away Pilate's casque and cloak; another raised a feathered parasol to shield his grey head from the sun; a third flapped an ivory-handled fly-whisk. Pilate presented Fabius. On him also the Tetrarch bestowed effusive greetings, and then, his wealth of bracelets flashing and tinkling, he seized Pilate's elbow in an excessively friendly clasp and led him through arcades into a courtyard where a succession of fountains spouted into marble conduits prettified with floating blossoms and crossed by pretty marble bridges.

The preparations in the courtyard confirmed the suspicions engendered by Herod's expansive smile. Herod was laying on hospitality thick – a bad sign. He smiled so broadly and entertained so richly only when he was sugaring a pill. The hand clasping Pilate's elbow was another clue. The grasp was all too familiar, all too friendly. Here, it said, is a man in our grasp, in power: let's give him a banquet before we have his head.

Taking advantage of the pleasant warmth of the morning, Herod had decided to entertain his guests outdoors. An awning with purple and silver fringes and supported by ebony posts anchored with saffron-coloured cords had been set up over a table on which was arranged a parade of golden goblets and platters. Pilate recognised the table as the famous one from Herod's private dining-room. Its simple elegance would disguise from the uninitiated the fact that this table, constructed of rare African cypress, was one of the costliest pieces of furniture in the world, one of the many treasures transported to Palestine from Egypt when Cleopatra had seduced her Roman lover Antony into giving her the town of Jericho and its rich terrain in the Jordan valley. Near each end of the table, golden braziers had been placed on tripods of golden snakes, and at this moment slaves were sprinkling on to the glowing charcoal shavings of rock which, after flaring slightly, gave off sleepy spirals of aromatic smoke.

Herod was making solicitous inquiries about the health of the Procurator and his dear Lady Claudia, but his ceaselessly shifting eyes noticed Polygnotus hovering awkwardly in the background with his leather satchel, and as the Tetrarch, his soft fingers still clasping Pilate's elbow, led his guest towards a couch he murmured a command in Egyptian to one of the slaves. The slave, a Nubian in brocaded waistcoat and crimson drawers, hurried off.

Before sitting down, Pilate stood looking over the city, a magnificent prospect of which was framed by the pillars immediately behind his couch. In the centre of this panorama was the Temple, and at this moment the immense bunch of grapes of solid gold on its eastern wall was magnificently ablaze in the morning sun. As Pilate sat down the Nubian came back, accompanied by one of Herod's own scribes, tablets and stylus in hand. At a gesture from his master the scribe squatted on a bench some distance from the table, but within earshot. Polygnotus took the hint and took a seat beside his fellow professional.

Herod seated himself opposite Pilate. He leaned back and looked complacently at his guest. He smiled widely again. Pilate was aware of an attitude of condescension in the man again. He resented the puppet putting on such airs. Yet he would bear with it. One had to play this gilded fish carefully. Herod was a bundle of Asiatic cunning and dishonesty upon which the lacquer of Greek elegance lay very thin. Yet, during nearly thirty years on the throne, this client of Caesar had served Rome not too badly. After all, he had built Caesarea; had rebuilt Sepphoris in Galilee after the Romans had sacked that nest of Zealots; had built Betharamphtha in Peraea; and was now glorifying Tiberias. Yes, the Herods were great builders. That at least could be said for them.

Herod nodded towards the head of the table. There a chair of exceptional magnificence had been placed. 'Our friend Caiaphas will be here shortly,' he lisped. 'With his father-in-law, of course.' He smirked, but when Pilate rejected this invitation to share a well-worn joke his eyes skidded quickly away. It could, thought Pilate, have been those eyes which earned Herod, long before he became notorious for cunning, his nickname of the Fox. Tinged with green, like jasper, and looking just as hard, they really were like the eyes of a fox, unnaturally close together and feverishly wary. Though a better nickname for a man so sinuous and with such a sibilant voice would have been the Snake. His tongue, always flickering its tip as he awaited replies to his pleasantries, was a smooth as that of a reptile.

His cheeks had been rouged in an attempt to give his sagging jaundiced skin some semblance of life; his short square beard was freshly crimped; his lank black hair was still damp from its morning henna. He reeked of patchouli. He waved a hand enormously burdened with gems to invite Fabius to seat himself on a couch at some distance from the one upon which he had placed Pilate. Pilate waited for something to be said. Herod caressed his beard. Except for the creak of an ebony post taking the strain as the breeze pushed the canopy, and the occasional sigh of a fly-whisk, there was silence.

At last Herod said, 'I had the pleasure of giving audience in Tiberias to a compatriot of yours.' One could hardly imagine that Greek could be so full of sibilants. 'One Gaius Marcus Paterculus.'

'Ah. So he reached you. I suppose he was gratified to be received by you?'

'No doubt! No doubt!' Herod fixed his eyes on one of the largest of his rings. He twisted it round, watching the shafts of light spring from its gems. 'I shall be seeing him again,' he went on. 'He requested the pleasure of visiting me again when he comes south. I got the impression that he felt that after his visit to Antioch he might have some positive reason for enlarging our acquaintance.' The fox eyes slid a quick glance in the direction of Pilate's profile. The Tetrarch was awaiting some comment. None came. He stretched his hand forward, fingers splayed, and amused himself by pivoting the wealth of his jewels in the sunlight. 'You did not send Paterculus to me for any particular reason, Pilate, did you?'

'He came of his own wish.'

'So he said. I might have suspected that the distinguished young Roman had come to recruit my interest in the ambitious project which you have proposed to the Sanhedrin and which Caiaphas, at your request I presume, has outlined to me. But Paterculus made no mention of that. I suspect he has little interest in domestic matters, only in imperial ones.'

'How do you mean?'

Herod tittered. 'I should like to know. Really I should. He has powerful friends.'

This time Pilate turned in time to catch the quick green eyes. Before they switched away he had time to see in them not their habitual wariness but something not far removed from contempt. Whatever Paterculus might have said, it had apparently been sufficient to impress the Tetrarch with Paterculus's importance

207

and, to that extent, diminish Pilate's. 'Of course,' lisped Herod, who had now abandoned playing with his rings and was inspecting the toe of one gilded boot, 'you and he have a mutual friend.'

'Naturally we have mutual friends,' said Pilate sharply. 'We are both Romans. We have the same friends. We also have the same Caesar.'

Herod at last looked at Pilate directly. 'Have you news of him? Of his August Highness? How is he?' The tip of his tongue fluttered over his lower lip.

'Why do you ask?'

'It is natural to ask, Pilate. One worries. Our beloved Caesar is of great age. At this time of life anything might happen.'

Pilate was saved from expressing any comment on that by the sound of others approaching the courtyard. Herod stood up. Under a flurry of bobbing parasols, Caiaphas and Annas emerged from the arcade. Herod glided forward to greet them. He bowed slightly to them both, then lifted the fringe of the high priest's girdle and brushed it slightly against his lips.

Pilate saw Caiaphas's lips moving, but could catch no sound from them. The voice of Annas, on the other hand, grated vibrantly through the air as he delivered formal greetings like a proclamation. 'Let the King live. Peace be to this house. And on you be the peace of God.'

'And on you the mercy of God and his blessing,' Herod murmured casually as he turned to lead the two pontiffs towards Pilate and Fabius.

Annas, an angular and stooping figure in a black robe devoid of decoration of any kind, darted an inquiring glance at the two scribes scrabbling to their feet, and then strode quickly forward. Rolling behind came Caiaphas in full sail of billowing draperies. His fleshy lips writhed with soundless greetings as he approached Pilate, but his round watery eyes, popping out in their habitual expression of perpetual surprise, seemed unable to focus, and gazed instead at some heavenly vision around or beyond the Procurator.

The face of Annas was a grid of wrinkles, so criss-crossed with their deep lines that his cheeks and jowls were a mosaic of tiny squares. But his brows and the ridge of his great beak of a nose, where the weathered skin stretched taut over his narrow Semitic skull, gleamed like ivory. Aged though Annas was, he conveyed an impression of vibrant energy, and there were still strands of black amid the grey of his hair and beard. Caiaphas, on the other hand, was, for a Jew, unnaturally bald. His cap was capacious, but, even so, patches of his pink scalp were visible; the few locks of hair protruding from the rim were snowy fluff. His beard, however, was formidable – a frothing torrent of white which gushed out from his chin to surmount a bosom as vast as that of a milk-filled mother and to cascade over his protuberant belly. The girdle which encompassed him, a wondrous confection of purple thread and jewelled embroidery, would have gone three times around the haggard waist of Annas and even then there would have been enough for the golden tassels to dangle at his ankles.

'Peace be with you,' said Pilate in Aramaic. In some recess deep in the rotundity of the High Priest a murmur was born and fluttered up to the heavy lips. It could have been a reply, or it could have been, and certainly looked more like, a belch. After which Caiaphas sailed grandly into position and berthed himself on the chair at the head of the table. The rest of the company took their seats. A file of slaves immediately appeared. The first carried golden bowls of water into which all but Caiaphas perfunctorily dipped their fingers and then brushed their hands over towels which they tossed back to the slaves. Caiaphas executed the purification more elaborately, immersing his plump hands lingeringly in the scented water and drying each separate finger and the great boss of his signet ring with loving attention. Other slaves were placing dishes on the table, some with covers from which fragrant steam arose, the others open and piled with varied delicacies. When those slaves had finished that task, others came to stand, two for each guest, to hand dishes and proffer fresh towels on demand.

There came suddenly to their ears the sound of plucked strings and the first experimental pipings of flutes. A troop of musicians, six boys prettily attired in ankle-length kilts of Egyptian style, with tasselled caps perched on their curls, had assembled in one of the porticoes. Two of them stood at harps, impressive instruments, taller than the players, their boat-shaped bases, extravagantly carved, coated with countless thin gold leaves which overlapped like the scales of a fish.

'We are not going to have dancers as well, are we, Herod?' rasped Annas.

Herod lifted his glittering hands in mock horror. 'I had not thought of arranging such for you, High Priest,' he lisped.

The boys played softly, the gentle strains not competing with but complementing the plash of fountains. Caiaphas, who seemed

14

not to have heard the music – at least he had not so much as glanced in the direction of the players – had already torn a wedge of bread and, after pulling back his wide sleeve, was using it as a scoop to gather up a generous mess of stewed meat and leeks. When he chewed he closed his eyes, and the expression of pop-eyed surprise was transformed into one of munching reverie. Annas fiddled among the small dried fish on a platter to find one to his taste.

Pilate took an olive. It was not that he wanted to make a show of refusing Herod's food. He had not had much appetite for some time now. Too many preoccupations, Claudia had said. And even the long ride had not made him hungry. In fact he felt rather queasy.

'There is Italian wine for you, Procurator,' murmured Herod. 'And for Captain Fabius. Or, if you prefer, my own Signa from Galilee. Also Judaean.'

'Thank you,' said Pilate. 'But not so early in the day. Water, please.' Wine, he felt, would bring back to his stomach that acid burning.

'But,' said Herod, ' "it is the duty of a man to mellow himself with wine until he cannot tell the difference between cursed and blessed",' and, when Annas curled his lips in testy disapproval of irreverent quotation, he smirked impudently in the priest's face.

'Some Judaean for me,' said Annas.

'Hattulim,' Herod announced as a slave poured it into Annas's goblet. Caiaphas pushed his forward to be filled.

'But our Procurator is abstemious. His mind runs ever on water,' chattered Herod. He reached for a joint of lamb, licked the sauce delicately from the bone and then, before sinking his teeth in the meat, went on, 'And water is, of course, the reason for the Procurator's presence with us today.'

'As we of the Sanhedrin are aware,' said Annas, tossing the unchewed fragment of dried fish away and beckoning a slave to bring to his side a loaf of bread, choosing that bread in which bean meal had been mixed with the wheat, and also a platter of quails and the dish of cucumber salad. 'But, Procurator, do not deprive your lieutenant of wine. That young Roman will no doubt appreciate the treasures of our King's cellar.' A slave poured wine for Fabius. 'And, Captain Fabius,' added Annas, 'you must taste this quail. Quail is also much appreciated by Romans, is it not?'

'Far more tender, Captain Fabius, than pigeons,' said Herod, smiling slyly at Annas. Annas glared at him, and then sent his eyes ranging over the loaded table. He nodded with mock surprise at the array of dishes. 'This is a memorable display, Herod. Are you staging it to impress the Procurator or to bribe your poor relations from the Temple?' He looked to the head of the table where Caiaphas was chewing on a leg of kid encrusted with cumin. 'Quite a feast, Joseph, is it not?' Caiaphas blinked and nodded.

Herod waved a deprecating hand over the table. 'A man's tongue needs nourishment as much as his limbs need oil, Annas,' he said. 'I find one talks more easily at table than in a conference chamber.'

Annas tossed a half-eaten quail away. A slave scooped it up and proffered the salad. Annas waved it aside. 'If what we have to say is to be measured by the wealth of food on our table we shall be talking for a week.' He again peered across at Pilate. Then, sharply, to a slave, said, 'Water for the Proconsul Procurator.' The boy leaped to fill Pilate's goblet. 'There is actually so little for me . . . for us of the Sanhedrin to say.'

Pilate did not ask what that little was. He was not prepared to ask questions as though he had come as a suitor to Herod's court or to the Sanhedrin. He had done enough by outlining his project by letter. Now it was up to Herod and Annas to offer their comments. He waited.

'All that need be said is that the Sanhedrin . . . ' But Annas broke off, and, the immeasurably wrinkled face nodding approval, said, 'But first one must compliment Proconsul Procurator Pilate on the imaginative character of his project and the convincing manner in which he has presented it. It is indeed encouraging to have confirmation that a governor appointed by Caesar has the welfare of our people so much in mind.'

'Thank you, Annas. I am pleased to hear so warm an appreciation of my intentions.' Pilate turned to Caiaphas and addressed that dignitary directly. 'I can take it, then, that the Sanhedrin looks upon the project with favour.'

Caiaphas sucked the last morsel of meat from a bone and let it drop. He took a towel from a slave and wiped his fingers. He cleared his throat. His lips stirred, but then he covered them with a towel and, his pop-eyes appealingly on Annas, spent time wiping his mouth until Annas took up the conversation. 'The Sanhedrin,' said Annas, 'looks upon the project with the greatest approbation, of course. If I may speak bluntly to you, Procurator . . .'

He broke off and slowly shifted round to look behind him to where on their bench the two scribes were sitting. He turned to face Pilate again. 'We have people taking minutes of this conversation?' he asked.

Pilate shook his head. 'My scribe carries plans. Also a draft of the programme of the work and an attempted estimate of the cost of material and labour for each stage of the necessary constructions. Full details of design and cost have already been drawn up for the first aqueduct. This will bring the city an abundant supply of water from north of Bethlehem . . . But my scribe will provide you with copies.'

'And my scribe,' said Herod, 'I summoned merely to be at your service, Annas, should you need to dictate any decisions.'

'Decisions?' Annas lifted his hands and held them out across the table like two battered begging-bowls in an attitude of bewildered helplessness. 'Decisions? But we of the Sanhedrin are not in a position to make decisions. The Procurator's project is a Roman project. Its execution is a Roman affair. Thus any decisions can surely be made not by us but by the Procurator. We of the Sanhedrin an assume only the role of spectators of this grandiose Roman exercise in public works. It is an exercise which we, as spectators, shall sincerely applaud – when, and if, it is ever executed.'

Pilate forced a diplomatic smile. 'Applause will be welcome,' he said crisply. 'But applause does not build. Applause does not bring life to deserts. It is my hope that the Sanhedrin will be more than spectators. Indeed, it is my intention that they will be more.' When Annas, begging-bowls still extended, made no reply to this except to shake his head, Pilate again faced Caiaphas, this time determined to wring some reply from him. 'High Priest Joseph!' he said sharply. 'Surely I made it clear in my communication to you that I expect the active participation of the Judaean government in the project?'

Caiaphas shifted hugely. His eyes protruded further as he focussed Pilate in their range of vision, and slowly he dipped his head. The movement could, with some imagination, have been interpreted as a nod of agreement, but by performing it he caught sight of crumbs on his beard. Uneasily he brushed these away and gazed uncertainly down the table towards his father-in-law. Annas, still retaining his attitude of imploring inquiry, was waiting for further words from the Procurator.

Pilate turned from Caiaphas with testy contempt. 'It is time to stop playing with words, Annas. If High Priest Caiaphas prefers not to give us the benefit of his wisdom, it is up to you to give me a clear expression of the Sanhedrin's opinions. A moment ago you were beginning to speak bluntly. Pray proceed. As *bluntly* as you wish.'

At this Annas let his hands fall slowly to his lap. 'What I was on the point of telling you Procurator, was the opinion expressed by my colleagues. This opinion,' and at these words he inclined his head with excessive reverence in the diretion of Caiaphas, 'is shared by the High Priest Joseph. The Sanhedrin is grateful to the Proconsul Procurator, and of course to Caesar, for inviting us to participate in a Roman project. We of the Sanhedrin are even more grateful at the prospect of Rome at last showing herself prepared to make some return for the onerous taxes she has exacted from our people for nearly one hundred years. The Sanhedrin sees the Procurator's project as merely a modest token of Rome's indebtedness to Judaea and its people.'

Pilate stiffened. The half-smile which he had laid on in an attempt to convey an expression of patience and amiability completely disappeared. 'I find your words offensive, Annas. The Sanhedrin's attitude, as you describe it, is insulting to Rome and to Caesar. And false. You should teach your colleagues to appreciate that, far from Rome having any indebtedness to Judaea, it is the Jews who are in debt to Rome and have been so for more than a mere one hundred years. It was at the behest of the Jews that Rome sent military aid to this country, and Rome has given Judaea what it never had since the days when Moses brought its people out of slavery in Egypt: stable government, just laws, and sound administration. Judea enjoys Roman protection, sharing the peace that Rome has laid upon the world. You share Roman prosperity and trade. Her roads and transport and communications have opened up new markets for your agricultural produce, your fruit and wine. You have freedom of religion and, within the Roman commonwealth, national and racial autonomy. And do not forget, Annas, that you owe your very existence to Rome. If we Romans pulled out of Judaea you would not last beyond tomorrow. Either the Arabs of King Aretas would engulf you or those Jewish brethren of yours, the Zealots, would string you up by the roadside. For it is Roman law and Roman justice that keep you in office. And without much profit to Rome. You describe the taxes you pay to Caesar as onerous. Those taxes are no more onerous than the taxes paid by any client state in the commonwealth. Some of those states are rich; they pay accordingly. Judaea is, however, a poor country, and in assessing the taxes levied on its people Rome has shown compassion.'

Herod tittered. 'Caesar, having shorn the lamb, tempers the blast.'

Pilate waved the impertinence away testily. 'But Judaea,' he continued, 'should not be a poor country. It could be a rich one. If its people are encouraged to work, if they are given independence and pride in their homeland, if we resettle Jews on those deserted uplands, they can make Judaea one of the wealthiest provinces in Asia. My plan for irrigating the uplands is the first step in bringing that dream to fruition. Every Jew stands to profit by such development. The poorest farmer will share in that wealth. As will,' he added with icy emphasis, 'the richest priest. But to initiate such a plan a price must first be paid. The taxes now collected are utterly insufficient for that price. In fact, they are at the moment barely covering the cost of the benefits and services Judaea receives from Rome.'

Herod interrupted again. 'You can't increase taxes at the moment, Procurator. I can tell you that from my own experience. In my kingdom of Galilee I find it difficult nowadays to gather up even rents due to me, let alone taxes.'

'Then you should try keeping pigeons instead of parrots,' snapped Pilate.

Annas glowered at them both. 'I suspect the Procurator has ideas other than taxation,' he said. 'I believe he has hopes of finding Jewish gold by different means.'

'That is so, Annas. I have hopes of considerable investment from private financiers.'

'From Josephus the Cohen? Oh yes, I do happen to know something about that. We enjoy scant communication nowadays with that Jew who has turned his back on us and chosen to live beyond his homeland, but even so we in Jerusalem can hear whispers from even so far away as Sebaste.'

'There is no need, Annas, to keep your ear to the ground. There is no secret about my discussions with Josephus. On the contrary, I wish them to be bruited abroad so that they will inspire other financiers to follow his wise example. For his part, the Cohen is even now seeking help from others.'

Annas's grid of wrinkles puckered with distaste. 'Those others will no doubt be his commercial associates in Alexandria.' Seeing questions hovering on Herod's lips, Annas turned to the Tetrarch to explain. 'Josephus the Cohen has powerful brethren in Alexandria. His closest friend there is the writer Philo, named Judaeus. And this heretic Philo happens to be the brother of the alabarch, the chief magistrate of the Jewish community in that city.' He turned to face Pilate again. 'We Jews, who, as you so pointedly remind us, long ago escaped from slavery to Egypt, can hardly be expected to welcome selling ourselves back into it. Even if this time our Egyptian buyers would be Jews.' He looked at his son-in-law. 'That is how we feel on that score, is it not?'

Caiaphas nodded profoundly.

'I should be surprised to see Jews refuse gold,' said Pilate. 'Even if it does come from Alexandria.'

'Jews always welcome gold,' said Annas. 'We are always in need of it: to pay our dues to Rome. But we should be loath to accept gold which would inevitably lay upon us the burden of paying interest to a notoriously covetous people.'

'Then, Annas, it is obvious that the more money we raise here in Jerusalem the better. My scribe will hand over to you the provisional estimate for the first stage of the work. The Sanhedrin will study those estimates. And the Sanhedrin will bear in mind that I expect the Judaean government to provide a substantial proportion of the necessary finance.'

The begging-bowl hands were again extended over the table. 'As I have said, the Sanhedrin applauds the Procurator's Roman ambition. So much so that if we had gold lying idle, we would be prepared to further Roman plans. Unfortunately there is none.' He sadly shook his head.

'If I were a merchant from Babylon, you would not say that,' snapped Pilate. 'Not even if that merchant were offering less interest than I do. The Temple lends vast sums every day.'

'Not *every* day,' said Annas with a sour smile. 'But every day, certainly, we receive requests for loans. Those requests we try to meet, for those who make them have been our clients for generations. But in these difficult days even some of those must be refused.'

Pilate sprang to his feet and, turning his back on Annas, pointed between the pillars to the Temple. 'There is gold there in the Temple, even if your bankers' coffers are empty. Gold lying idle. A toiling people sucked dry of sweat and pence to gild that one place! How many millions of shekels have still to be laid on that alabaster?'

'As many millions as the prayers that ascend each day to God,' said Annas.

'Those prayers could best be answered by bringing work and comfort to the peasant farmers and the poor. While the coffers in that monument bulge with money, the land it lives on dries up into a desert.' Pilate lifted his hand again and pointed to the Temple's eastern wall. 'The lives of a generation of Jews could be changed by only a few grapes from that bunch.'

'Pilate!' exclaimed Annas. 'You must understand the nature of the Jews and their devotion to the true God. Those grapes are the symbol of God's sacred vineyard. Not one Jew begrudges the adornment of the House of God. That Temple is the treasure-house of all the hopes and all the beliefs and all the destiny of our people. One inch of its alabaster . . . no, one chipping from its humblest block of stone is more precious to a Jew than twenty Roman miles of aqueduct.'

Having delivered himself of this outburst Annas also stood up. 'I regret we must end our conversation when we are, as it were, in mid-stream. But I have a heavy list of hearings to conduct before sundown.' He bowed solemnly to his son-in-law. 'With your permission, High Priest Joseph, we must take our leave.'

Two slaves ran forward to grasp the chief priest's elbows and lever him to his feet. Annas bowed to Pilate. 'Thank you, Procurator, for honouring us with this visit to our Holy City.'

'The estimates, Annas,' said Pilate. He gestured to Polygnotus, and the slave jumped up and pulled a scroll from his satchel.

'Ah, yes, the estimates,' said Annas. He beckoned a slave to take the scroll and carry it to his litter. 'The Sanhedrin will study the figures with grave attention. We will let you have our considered opinion when it pleases Your Excellency to come to Jerusalem again.'

Herod accompanied the two priests to the terrace, and then glided glitteringly back to Pilate, his yellow face shining with wicked amusement. 'You won't get a shekel from them,' he said.

Pilate smiled. He was tempted to tell Herod something, but refrained from doing so. What he could have told Herod was that, inserted in the estimates, was a note about the rate of interest to be paid on investments, public or private. That interest was high enough to make even Annas think twice about refusing. But all he said was, 'Thank you, Herod, for your hospitality. I must leave you. After riding all night, I am tired.'

Herod cast his eyes over the table. Slaves were taking away

platters of untouched food. 'More wine, Captain Fabius,' he said. 'And you, Pilate?'

'Hm! Well, yes. I'll try that Judaean. Caiaphas seemed to like it. He certainly drank plenty.'

A slave poured wine. Herod sat down, but Pilate remained standing, and, after examining the heavy golden goblet in his hand, turned once again to gaze at the Temple.

'I think that is, even when one remembers Caesarea, and Sebaste, and all else, the most extravagant edifice your family will be remembered by.'

Herod laughed softly. 'After having built so many houses for Herod it is perhaps wise to build one even more grandly for God.'

'Even so you are still embellishing Tiberias,' said Pilate somewhat enviously. 'You Herods spend lavishly.'

'Fortunately we can afford to. Thanks to Caesar we were given a prosperous province. As they say, it is easier to raise a legion of olive-trees in Galilee than to raise one child in Judaea. Nor are we in Galilee troubled by lack of water.' He smiled smugly. 'We have plenty of that. A whole sea of it.'

'You are to be envied. That, Herod, is why I find it difficult to understand why so fruitful and prosperous a land should be so unhappy. Why is there constant unrest in Galilee? You have indeed lots of water, a whole beautiful sea of it, but also lots of Zealots on its banks.'

These comments did not wipe the smile from Herod's face. 'Not so many Zealots nowadays. Our police are active, and we've rustled most Zealots out of the towns. Most of them have scuttled off to the desert. Where they will go from there, who knows?' He shrugged. 'I know it is selfish of me, but I hope, if they do move, that they will come south: to Judaea. After all, that would be logical. For their real objective is Jerusalem. Perhaps they'll try once again to take the Holy City by storm. Well, if that happens, they'll be your problem, not mine.' He sipped wine and grinned. 'At present our problem in Galilee is not so much Zealots as preachers.' He sighed. 'We have to keep watch on that lot. We are always afraid of finding ourselves with another John on our hands. We got rid of that crazy one without too much fuss, but . . . The trouble with Galileans is that they have ready ears for preachers. As my steward at Tiberias has found out.' He laughed loudly as he raised his goblet to his lips. 'Steward Chuza has lost his wife to a preacher.' He choked on his wine. After he had wiped his beard he went on. 'Yes, Chuza's wife, Joanna, has packed up and left him. She's run off to become a disciple of another wild man, a preacher from Nazareth.'

Pilate had planned to spend the afternoon with the architect from Sebaste who, now installed in an office in the Antonia, had begun some prospecting and drawing, but after he had climbed the stairway to the entrance of the Antonia he was seized by a fit of dizziness. He saw the paving heaving under him, and Fabius, who was staring at him with perturbation, seemed to be swaying. Pilate, felt that he was about to lose consciousness. He drew air in gaspingly and forced himself to walk into the fortress. 'I am tired,' he said. 'I shall lie down.' Ashamed of his weakness, he gestured Fabius away: he did not like the idea of that young man thinking the night ride from Caesarea had been too much for him. He stayed on his couch all afternoon. But he did not sleep. He dozed off frequently, but was repeatedly awakened by pain in his guts. 'Curse that Judaean wine!' he said several times.

Every evening now, by the time Simeon and Ishmael had walked into town and joined the knot of gossipers under the palms, the young man from Galilee was already the centre of the group, the chosen target for questions and arguments. The young man had always been popular in Jericho, and his decision to join the preachers in Galilee had lost him neither popularity nor friends. Most considered it as one of the wild things brainy young fellows did. Eventually he would grow out of it and come back to settle in Jericho and finally inherit his father's business and fortune. So those who argued against him, even the older ones, did so with good humour. In refuting their arguments, he often quoted his Galilean leader to show them how that preacher could confound both Pharisees and Sadducees by turning their own pronouncements against them. Some of the quotations were witty, and as Jews always love a good argument, especially when it pokes fun at pomposity, the young man's audience enjoyed the interchanges. They laughed, most of them heartily, and only one or two, the older and more orthodox, a little uneasily.

Ishmael laughed too. Not that he always understood very clearly what the laughter was about. He was merely amused when his young hero made the soft Jerichoans look foolish, and did not bother to puzzle over the play on words. He seized only on those phrases which, to his ears, blared out like trumpet blasts. 'The City of David'. 'The Kingdom of God'. 'King of the Jews'.

Those words dazzled him. They waved like banners, conjuring up scenes of marching men and butchered Romans. When he gazed at the young man he imagined that his leader in Nazareth must be such another. That 'man of destiny' must also be a man of vigour and courage, a man who would lead the Jews to victory and freedom and strike the Gentiles with the lightning of God.

During recent evenings two labourers, members of a gang who were working under a Roman architect on a new stretch of road north of Jericho, had come regularly to the inn. These strangers had sat apart, quietly chatting to each other as they contendedly slaked their dusty thirst after a hard day. One Sunday evening, however, they burst suddenly into the argument. One of the group under the palms had been questioning the young man about something the Nazarene had said about Caesar. To give spice to the argument the questioner laughingly baited the young man, and, after cautiously glancing around to make sure no soldiers from the garrison were in earshot, said that, for his money, only Zealots had the right idea. Only Zealots knew what should be done to Romans and to Jews who collaborated with the occupation forces.

'That's what I say!' one of the labourers suddenly bawled out, banging his tankard on the table. Surprised by the angry interruption, everyone turned to look at the fellow. He was quivering with rage. When he saw their questioning stares, he went on to tell them what incensed him. Work that afternoon had taken him and his mate to a village near the road. There a Roman soldier – they described him as an ignorant lout full of wine – had lurched out of an inn and, casting his bleary eyes over a group of villagers, had beckoned one towards him. 'Carry my pack to the camp,' he had ordered. The Jew he had summoned was old, a respected figure in the village. A lad offered to perform the service. The soldier had slapped the lad aside and insisted on the old man shouldering the pack.

The questioner in the group turned to the young man. 'What would your Nazarene say to that?'

Ishmael waited anxiously for the reply. He was disappointed when the young man shrugged and murmured, 'It is the law. I agree it is offensive. It is something that should be changed. But for the time being it is the law that any Roman has the right to command a Jew to carry for him.'

'Law!' sneered the labourer. 'Law, it is. But not Jewish law. Roman law!'

'Though the Romans are very kind,' his mate added with angry sarcasm. 'It is decreed that the Jew must not carry for more than three miles. That Jew was old. Old enough to be the bully's grandfather.'

Somebody nearby murmured, 'The Sanhedrin agreed to these laws.'

The young man nodded. 'We must have patience. The time will soon come when these laws will be changed.'

The labourer banged his tankard again. 'Bad laws can never be changed into good laws. If a law is bad, it should not be obeyed.'

'The Romans have Caiaphas and his crowd in their pockets,' said the other. 'Oh, yes, Pilate says Jews can have religious freedom, but what does that freedom add up to? Only to keep Caiaphas and Annas in fat jobs. We have a Temple. We have a Sanhedrin. But we pay taxes to Rome. And what for? To build amphitheatres and hippodromes and baths.'

'Are you a Zealot?' asked someone in an eager whisper.

'Not yet,' said the labourer grimly, and his mate added with a laugh, 'Only because the Romans haven't left enough in his pocket to buy a dagger.'

At that the two drained their tankards, got up and walked off. Ishmael looked around the group under the palms. They were silent. The incessant arguments about words had been shattered by the noisy intrusion of reality. Soft Jerichoans had been silenced by two men telling the truth about Romans.

The two labourers had walked across the square towards the old walls, and Ishmael saw them halted in the shadow of the gateway that led to the narrow crooked street. There they had encountered another man and had stopped to talk with him. He was a tall man, but although his head was almost hidden by his hood, he seemed to Ishmael to be a familiar figure. Then the man's hand gestured through a beam of light and the light of jewels flashed. It was Barabbas.

Ishmael jumped up quickly and hurried across the square, but by the time he had pushed his way through a group of elegant young Jews who were promenading in the evening air, the men had disappeared. He ran into the narrow street. Ahead of him in the darkness he heard voices, but when he caught up with the speakers he discovered that they were a family chattering in the courtyard of their house. He turned back. Most of the courtyard gates were closed and dark. At the open lighted ones he peeped in, but failed to find Barabbas. When he got back to the palms his uncle, anxious to set off home, was looking around for him.

The following day Ishmael surprised Simeon by asking if he could go into Jericho and spend the afternoon there instead of working in the plantation. Simeon agreed delightedly. The request indicated that the boy had at last emerged from his sullen loneliness and was finding pleasure in his surroundings.

All afternoon the boy wandered through the streets of Jericho. So often did he walk the length of the crooked street that one of the women peering through a barred window eventually recognised him and waved. Embarrassed, Ishmael hurried past this house, through the doorway of which men with their faces heavily shadowed by their hoods slipped furtively.

Evening fell. By now his uncle would have arrived at the inn. Tired and disappointed, Ishmael wandered back in that direction. He was walking into the square through one of the arches when he heard his name called. It was the young man from Galilee. He was standing in the shadow of the old wall, just beyond the lights of the nearest pastry-stall. With him was Barabbas. Ishmael ran eagerly up to them.

'Greetings, Ishmael son of Uzziel,' said Barabbas.

'You know Ishmael?' exclaimed the young man.

'We have met,' said Barabbas.

'Where?'

Barrabas did not answer. Instead he reached out his hand, slid his fingers under the boy's chin and into his robe, and, finding the thong, pulled out the coin and let it dangle bright against the dark cloth. 'I knew you would do as I told you, Ishmael son on Uzziel. Good! When next we meet I shall give you a gold chain from a Roman's neck.'

Frowning, the young man again asked Barabbas. 'Where did you meet?'

The smile with which Barabbas had welcomed the boy faded from his face. He looked at the young man sternly. 'We met on a road on the evening of the day when Uzziel father of Ishmael died, the day when Uzziel father of Ishmael was hanged on a cross by Romans. Your Nazarene asks us to forgive murderers, does he not? Let him ask this boy to forgive those who killed his father.'

Placing his arm around Ishmael's shoulders, the young man drew him away from Barabbas. 'It is wrong for you to talk about that in the boy's presence.'

'Do you think if we do not talk about it, he will forget it? Or forgive it?'

'You forget something, Barabbas. On that day when Uzziel was executed the Romans also crucified a Roman.'

Barabbas sneered. 'That Roman! A traitor. I am not fond of traitors. Not even those who would serve our cause. I think I prefer a Roman honest enough to fight against me to one who betrays his own people. No; all I remember of that day is what this boy remembers: that Uzziel and four other sons of Judah were murdered.'

'And what is the Zealot answer to that? More murders?'

'Zealots do not murder: Zealots execute. Until the sons of Judah are free, the Zealot dagger is our only instrument of justice. Violence is the language Romans understand.' Barabbas thrust his hand below his robe and drew out his dagger. Its curved blade trembled in the uncertain light. 'This is the tongue I use when I speak to the enemies of God, be they Gentiles or Jews.'

'Put that away, Barabbas. For your own sake, and in the memory of our past love, I beg you to have done with the assassins. If you do not, then sooner or later the Romans will find you. As I've told you tonight, I have heard your name whispered in Jericho. They know about you.'

'I am not afraid of Roman search-parties, my friend. They will meet many daggers in the dark between them and me. And I am well hidden in this town.' He pointed the dagger back along the street. 'I lodge in a house where the coming and going of men is not much remarked on by day or by night. Like the spies of that Joshua who brought down the walls of Jericho, I lie in the house of the whores.' He laughed softly. 'And this blade has won me my freedom many times.' The dagger flashed downward. It seemed almost to hiss as it severed a beam of light. Then its gleam was doused under his robe. 'The Nazarene has taught you how to preach, my friend. It is now time that you learned how to fight. In preacher's robes you disgrace your heritage. You bear the name of a man who led the Jews to glory, and also the name of that other, the first Zealot.'

'And both of them brought disaster in their train. What they did thrust us and our kings into the arms of Rome and laid the chains heavier around our necks.'

'Will the Nazarene's soft words snap those chains?'

'When the time is ripe, Jesus of Nazareth will lead an army more powerful than we have ever known.'

'Another Messiah, eh? Yet another! Another like that crazy fool John who came out of the wilderness wearing camel's hide and with honey on his tongue as thick as on a bear's. Where did he end up? His head served up at a whore's banquet. Tell me, how is your Jesus going to topple Pilate? With the blast of trumpets? Or will he blow kisses?'

'By leading us to God.'

'Let him first lead us to Jerusalem. Let him lead us to the Temple. To Herod's palace. To the battlements of the Antonia. That way he can prove himself the true Messiah, not by healing sores with soft hands and doling out comfort with soft words. If he would show himself as a Messiah, let him leave his little hidey-hole in Galilee and dare to show his face in Jerusalem.'

'He will come.'

'The sooner the better. If he can do half as much against Rome with his words as the Zealots have done with their blood and daggers, even I might be there to welcome him.' He shook his head. 'But, my friend, I fear you will be disappointed in him. Jesus of Nazareth will find Jerusalem folk tougher than a few green countryfolk in the villages of Galilee. Would I could wish him well, for your sake. But I see no hope in him.' He glanced across the square. There were more people flocking across it. 'I must go. I am leaving Jericho tonight. Back to the desert, to speak words of courage to my friends who await me there. The voice of yet another man shouting in the lonely desert "Get God's road ready, make his paths straight." Soon we too shall be coming to Jerusalem.' As a group of people passed close by he pulled the hood further over his brow. His voice fell to a whisper. 'My friend! We, my comrades and I, need men like you. And I think you will join us sooner or later, when you have seen your Messiah put to the test. If this Jesus dares to come to Jerusalem, if he dares to say on the steps of the Temple all he has dared to say in Galilee, then we shall see whether he is a leader or not. If he is all you say he is, neither Caiaphas nor Annas nor even Pilate can harm him. But if he is snuffed out like another John, then, Judas, you will know he is only another impostor. God be with you, Judas.'

Barabbas turned away quickly and disappeared into the darkness of the narrow street. Judas took Ishmael's hand. They walked towards the inn where Simeon, amid his cronies, welcomed them, pleased to see the boy in the company of his friend.

'I must hurry home,' said Judas, 'for my father is waiting

supper for me. But I have something to tell you. I shall come to the plantation tomorrow.'

As they walked home hand in hand Simeon asked Ishmael how he had spent his day in Jericho. The answers were vague, and the boy was soon sunk again into brooding silence. Perhaps he was tired. It certainly seemed so, for as soon as they reached the house he hurried off to bed.

In the darkness Ishmael felt deep into a cranny in the wall and drew out a long thin bundle of oiled rag. He unwrapped it, uncovered the curved pruning knife he had bought in Jerusalem and slipped it under the sheepskin. When he lay down he could feel the bulge of it near his cheek, and he put his hand over it.

'Are you asleep, Ishmael?' Simeon asked when he came to bed. The boy breathed heavily, as though he were.

Two hours later Ishmael slid, inch by inch, from under his uncle's arm, slipped his hand under the sheepskin and drew out the knife. He snatched his robe from the bench and silently stepped across the rough floor. The bar holding the door creaked only slightly as he carefully lifted it, and in a moment he was outside, slipping his robe over his head. He trotted quickly through the plantations, keeping out of sight amid the bushes as he followed the road leading to Jericho and Barabbas.

When dawn was filtering green into the low-ceilinged room, Simeon awoke. Where the boy's head usually lay, the corner of the sheepskin was turned back. Ishmael had gone.

VII

'Up to two thousand Jews . . . ' Polygnotus slanted the dispatch nearer the lamp. 'Yes, it does say *two thousand*! . . . Up to two thousand Jews are assembling at Herod's Gate with the intention of marching from Jerusalem to demonstrate in Caesarea. The Sanhedrin is meeting in special session. At the . . . ' Polygnotus paused.

'Well? Go on!' said Pilate immediately. He was sitting up on his couch, clutching under his chin the toga he had flung over his shoulders. He was shivering.

'Captain Fabius uses the code clumsily,' Polygnotus murmured, then added apologetically, 'But he was probably writing in haste. Or in the dark.'

'He was writing on horseback,' said the courier. Pilate looked across to the auxiliary. The man drooped in the doorway, dazed after his formidable ride from Herod's Gate in Jerusalem to the palace in Caesarea. His face ran with sweat; his leather jerkin and kilt were sodden with rain.

'Sit down, man,' said Pilate. The man slipped on to a stool. 'You saw the demonstrators?'

'Yes, Proconsul. They were moving off when I left. Further along the road there were more waiting to join them.'

'Were they carrying arms?'

225

'Ah!' said Polygnotus. He had decoded the next words. 'At the Hasmonaean Palace the Roman standards are still in position. Paterculus's soldiers have beaten back a mob moving towards the gardens.'

'Does Fabius say that the Jews are armed?'

' "Some threw stones",' went on Polygnotus, haltingly reading the scrawled message. ' "I dispatched auxiliaries in civilian dress. Mingling with the crowd . . . " '

Pilate nodded approvingly: Fabius was working well.

Polygnotus corrected his translation. '*To mingle* with the crowd,' he read. 'These report they encountered no people speaking with a Galilean accent, nor were any Zealots found. A number of young Jews threw stones: they were arrested.'

'None of those on the road were carrying arms,' said the courier. 'At least none that I saw. Many were wearing sackcloth. A few old ones had sprinkled ashes on their heads.'

Polygnotus read on. ' "I have detached fifty auxiliaries from the Antonia under command of Captain Gaius to marshal the procession. I have withdrawn the rest of the cohort into the Antonia, feeling that the presence of soldiers in the streets could provoke disturbances which we would have difficulty in controlling. There is still a lot of noise in the city, yelling and wailing, but no sign of further violence." ' Polygnotus looked up. 'That is all, sir,' he said with a sigh of relief.

'He says nothing further about Paterculus?'

'No, sir,' Polygnotus replied, but looked on the other side of the papyrus to make sure he had missed nothing.

Pilate turned to the courier. 'All right, man,' he said wearily. 'Go and get some sleep. Ask the duty officer at the barracks to awake Marcellus. I want him here immediately.' The man pulled himself to his feet and tramped off. 'Polygnotus! Have you your tablets?' He had. The scribe had been shaken out of his cot in the early hours of the morning to decipher an urgent dispatch, but even so he had not omitted, when he grabbed his gown, also to gather up tablets and stylus before running to Pilate's bedroom. The old professional probably slept with them, thought Pilate. 'I shall be dictating orders. Make a full note.'

Pilate leaned back and sighed heavily. He shivered. After tucking the rug under his legs he reached to the table for the phial of linctus. He took a sip of its dark and glutinous contents, then wiped his lips with distaste, trying to remove the stickiness and the bitterness of what the doctor had told him was bdellium.

That, together with sulphurous water from the hot springs of Callirrhoe beyond the Dead Sea, comprised the medico's latest specific against the violent pains that had stabbed Pilate's guts for three days. Polygnotus poured water from an ewer, handed Pilate a towel, and watched the Procurator anxiously as he retched. Having heard these sounds – they were now customary in the sickroom – the Negro roused himself from his cot in a nearby room and padded in.

'Bring me a mantle,' said Pilate. 'I feel cold.'

The Negro opened a closet, brought out a robe of soft furs and tenderly draped it around the Procurator's shivering shoulders.

'All right; that will do,' said Pilate, pushing away the hands that were attempting to fasten the robe under his chin. He reached to the table again, this time lifting from it an earlier dispatch from Fabius which had reached Caesarea just before midnight. It was annoying that this crisis had occurred when he was feeling so physically low.

Claudia, swathed in a dark gown, appeared at the door. She looked worriedly at her husband. 'Have you still got the pain, Pontius?' she asked.

'No, no, no! Go to bed, Claudia.' He saw the look of surprise she cast when she became aware that Polygnotus was sitting in the room with tablets on his knee. 'Don't be alarmed, Claudia.' He smiled. 'It is not my will that I am dictating.'

'You're not worse, are you, Pontius?'

'Not I. It's only Judaea that is worse. No, I'm working.'

'But must you? Can't it wait?'

'No. It cannot. Good night, Claudia,' Pilate said dismissively, but she came over to him and laid a hand on his forehead. Feeling the dry heat there, she shook her head. As she bent to kiss his cheek lightly she murmured, 'Get some rest as soon as you can.' Then she left.

Awaiting Marcellus, Pilate marshalled his thoughts. He again read through the first dispatch from Fabius. That one Fabius had not written in code, for at the time of writing it he had not appreciated that what Paterculus had done in Jerusalem could spark off a major revolt, tempting out of every valley and village throughout Judaea those terrorists who always, in their secret liars, dreamed of full-scale guerrilla warfare. Pilate could not blame Fabius for failing to see the danger immediately. It was only after years of experience with these bloody Jews that one learned that the most trivial and quite accidental disregard of their superstitions could be seen by them as an insult to their god, an offence to be atoned for only in blood and agony.

Marcellus arrived speedily. There had been no need to awaken him. He had learned enough from the earlier courier to feel sure that Pilate would be needing him, so he had been fully clothed and only dozing on his cot when he was told that a second courier had arrived in sweating haste and that Polygnotus had been summoned to decipher a coded dispatch.

'Marcellus! We've a big problem on our hands. Two thousand Jews are on their way to Caesarea. In this dispatch which I received from Fabius a few hours ago he reports that Marcus Paterculus has arrived in Judaea. He did not report to the Antonia but went straight to the Hasmonaean Palace, which had been placed at his disposal by the hospitable Tetrarch Herod. Fabius draws particular attention pointedly to the fact that Paterculus was attended by a considerably augmented escort of guards: all of them Romans detached from the legion at Antioch. Out of ignorance or stupidity on someone's part the troops marched into the city displaying standards bearing *graven images*. They have raised these standards at their bivouac outside the gates of the palace. At dawn yesterday a Levite delegation came to the Antonia alleging a flagrant breach of the treaty between Rome and Judaea, that treaty by which Caesar, in consideration of Jewish prejudices, promised that graven images should not be displayed in public in the Holy City. The Sanhedrin alleges that standards bearing the image of Caesar have been brought into Jerusalem under cover of darkness.' Pilate paused. His throat felt sore. He sipped more linctus, but when Polygnotus and the Negro began fussing with a towel he waved them testily away. He cleared his throat. 'Probably the offending images are not images of Caesar at all. But then, I do not imagine that Jews see much difference between the profiles of Caesar and Sejanus. That, however, is immaterial. We must admit, between ourselves only, that an offence has been committed. Now! I have just received more serious information. News about the standards spread throughout the city. After morning service, crowds from the Temple crossed the valley to the Hasmonaean Palace. The Roman guards bivouacking near the gardens attempted to disperse them. Stones were thrown. However, pressure in the city has relaxed, at least for the time being, because Jews howling in the Court of the Gentiles for some word from me learned that their Procurator is here in Caesarea. So a couple of thousand of them are making their way here.'

'But not armed,' said Marcellus.

'No. Apparently not. The demonstration promises to be a passive one. I hope we are right. No. The real danger still lies in Jerusalem. Now, these are my orders.' He cleared his throat again, and Polygnotus posed the stylus.

'By my hand at Caesarea etcetera etcetera. Until my arrival in Jerusalem I appoint Fabius Caelius Rufus as officer in supreme command of all troops there, auxiliary and Roman: both those stationed at the Antonia fortress and *any others in any other part of the city*. A proclamation to that effect will be posted at the Antonia. A copy will be delivered to Marcus Gaius Paterculus at the Hasmonaean Palace or, failing personal delivery to him, will be handed to the officer in charge of his escort. By the authority of the Proconsul Pontius Pilate, Procurator of Judaea, the said Fabius Caelius Rufus will make such military dispositions as he thinks fit and will take such political decisions as necessary in accordance with my known policy. Now, Polygnotus, a separate note for the eyes of Fabius only. Captain Fabius will bear in mind that nothing must be done to exacerbate the situation. He will convey to the Sanhedrin merely formal acknowledgement that the protest has been received, and will inform them that it has been forwarded to the Procurator and that the Procurator will later come to Jerusalem in person to investigate the validity of the allegations made against a Roman gentleman and his escort.'

Pilate leaned back. He lifted his hands and pressed them over his face. With his eyes covered he read in his mind all that he had said. 'Yes,' he said at last. 'That will be all.' He uncovered his eyes. 'But we must send troops.'

'At least a thousand,' said Marcellus. 'Some will be needed to marshal the demonstrators along the road to Caesarea. The rest can go on to Jerusalem.'

'But not enter the city. Their doing so could spark off full-scale revolt.' Pilate turned to Polygnotus. 'The reinforcements will be dispersed outside the city near each gate. The strictest camp discipline will be maintained. There will be no fraternising with civilians, male or female. Nor any harassment of the populace.'

'I shall go myself, Pontius,' said Marcellus.

'I shall follow. When I am well enough . . . ' began Pilate, but hurriedly covering up this confession of illness, added, 'I shall deal with the demonstration here first. I suppose it will take them a couple of days to reach Caesarea.'

'At least.'

'Right. Assist Fabius all you can. I shall expect regular dispatches.'

'Of course.'

'Now, Marcellus! Who is the officer here most fitted for special duty? I mean a man of utmost discretion. Also a man of courage and in good shape for a long hard journey.'

'To Antioch?' Pilate nodded. Marcellus pondered over the request for some moments, then named a certain Sextus Afranius.

'I shall see him immediately.'

Polygnotus was about to hurry off with Marcellus, but Pilate called him back. 'There is something more.' He looked round. The Negro was standing in the shadows. 'Leave us, Dumb Black. Come back when I am alone.'

The Negro padded out. Pilate pulled the toga closer around his trembling shoulders and sat thinking for a while, then dictated, 'To the Tetrarch Herod Antipas at Tiberias. The usual compliments. But make them coldly formal, Polygnotus. No flowery affectations. Tell him that the Procurator has received with displeasure . . . No. Scrub that out. It is *reported* to the Procurator that Marcus Gaius Paterculus is at present in residence at the Hasmonaean Palace by the Tetrarch's permission. It is reported that Marcus Gaius Paterculus, probably in ignorance of the treaty obligations of the Roman administration in Judaea, entered Jerusalem with standards bearing the image of . . . No. With *standards offensive* to Jewish susceptibilities. The Procurator intends himself to go to Jerusalem as soon as he can detach himself from official business in Caesarea, but suggests that it would be advisable for the Tetrarch to go in person to the Hasmonaean and make clear to his guest the implications of his conduct. Meanwhile, the Procurator awaits urgently the Tetrarch's comments.' Pilate paused. Then, 'That is enough. Leave it like that. Now another, Polygnotus. No addresses. Nor any indication, Polygnotus, of the source of the communication. This is the message: Your sister-in-law in Judaea is angry . . . No! . . . is *sorry* to have received no letter from you, and is particularly anxious to know everything about the reception of her beloved Roman friend at the legate's court. That is all, Polygnotus.'

Afranius reported. He was fastening the last strap of his leather jerkin as he came in. He was a stocky, muscular fellow with black hair cropped so short that his scalp showed. His grey eyes were deep-set, but they were, although he had been jerked out of sleep, piercingly alert. Pilate liked the look of him.

'Sextus Afranius?'

'Yes, sir.'

'You are to carry two important dispatches. Polygnotus! Do those two first. As quickly as possible.' Polygnotus hurried out. 'Afranius! You will take a small escort. Four. They must be the most reliable and toughest you can choose. You will not display Roman armour or standards. In fact, you and your men had better cover yourselves with Jewish robes. Use mules instead of horses. One dispatch you will deliver at the palace of Herod at Tiberias. Inform the secretariat there that it is urgent. The other dispatch you will take to Antioch. When you leave Tiberias let no one there know you are heading north. At Antioch you will contact the brother of the legate's chamberlain. You must meet him away from the court, secretly. The man's name is not written on the dispatch. You must remember it. Lucius Turpilius. Repeat it.'

'Lucius Turpilius.'

'Keep repeating it to yourself. Do not on any account write it. You will find his villa easily. Your arrival at his house will not cause remark. He trades in balsam and has many callers from Judaea. Now go and collect your escort. Then report back here.'

When he had gone, Pilate reached for the phial again and took another sticky sip. The stuff might be doing his stomach good, but his head was thumping.

Polygnotus was soon back. The old man was a commendably quick worker. He brought a pen to the bedside for Pilate to sign the dispatch to Herod and, having asked Pilate for his signet, sealed it. The other one he rolled and sealed with wax, but did not impress the seal.

'You have made copies of both, Polygnotus?'

'Yes, Procurator.'

Afranius came back. 'The men have been roused, sir. We can leave within minutes.'

'Excellent. Polygnotus, give Afranius the dispatches. Now, Afranius, listen. You . . . ' He broke off. 'Polygnotus, leave us a moment. Close the door.' When Polygnotus had gone out and the door had closed, Pilate continued. 'Afranius, to no one in Antioch, will you ever reveal that you have come from me, or even from Caesarea. Understand?'

231

'Yes, sir.'

'Not even under torture.'

The grey eyes stared at him without a flicker of fear. 'No, sir.'

'Anyhow, Afranius, there is no reason, unless you are inept, that it should come to that.' Pilate glanced towards the door. 'Come closer.' His voice fell to a whisper. 'There is another matter, Afranius. If in Syria, or anywhere in the north, you see troops on the way south, or hear anything at all to indicate that troops are moving, you must let me know. Detach one of your escort to bring me such information. Verbally. Nothing must be written.'

'I understand.'

'Right, Afranius. On your way. And good luck.'

'Thank you, sir.'

Afranius marched out: Polygnotus slipped in. 'Anything else, sir?'

'Of course, Polygnotus,' said Pilate with irritation. 'The orders and dispatches for Jerusalem.'

'They are being drawn up now, sir.'

'As soon as possible. I do want to sleep.'

The scribe darted off. Pilate was sliding under the covers when the Negro padded in softly. He straightened the covers and then, when he lifted the fur mantle, saw sweat cold and greasy on Pilate's shoulders. He shook his head at Pilate severely, then, holding up his vast hands, turned their pink palms to Pilate, and, with a pantomime of stroking gestures, invited the patient to submit to the therapy of his massage. Pilate shook his head. 'No! I think . . . yes, I need the doctor. Tell him to come at once.' Alone again he murmured, like one praying to himself, 'I must have sleep.'

On the evening of the following day news came to Pilate that the demonstrators were approaching the city. He arrived on the battlements just in time to see the first of them appear over the brow of the low hills to the east and trickle slowly down the road leading to Caesarea. More appeared, and soon the road was a stream of robed figures plodding on towards the city.

Even from this distance it was possible to see that they were travel-weary. They were making no noise at all. This was no victory march: it was a begging procession. When they reached the outskirts of the city and flowed into the main avenue, they

232

livened up a little. Chanting, wailing protests against Roman sacrilege in their Holy City, they tried to shove their aching feet forward more briskly and assume an air of confidence. But when they saw how many soldiers had been posted along both sides of the colonnaded avenue leading the Palace Square their mood changed again. Their chanting and shouts became less challenging, their looks of defiance less rebellious and more despairing, as though they felt like men marching towards certain death. For they were flanked on both sides by a chilling display of Rome's military might: soldiers in leather jerkins and casques leaning on hungry spears, officers with plumed helmets with polished breast-plates wielding thirsty swords. But the soldiers did no more than stare at them, and the officers' eyes, almost invisible under helmet-rims, seemed to gaze with indifferent contempt above and beyond them. A few of the younger demonstrators, stirred to indignation by this indifference, shouted insults. One or two spat at soldiers' feet. One brandished a shepherd's crook in an officer's face.

There were fewer than had been originally expected. Reports brought regularly by couriers along the route had informed Pilate that many of the demonstrators who had left Herod's Gate had soon thought better of it and, daunted by the prospect of the long tramp, had stopped and, after shouting encouragement to the hardier souls who pressed on, gone back to Jerusalem. Further along the route others, who had halted to rest at wayside hamlets, had not resumed the march, but stayed where they were to fill the villagers' ears with wild exaggerations of the happenings in Jerusalem.

The footsore ones who had come the whole way moved on through the files of soldiers to the palace. There were several hundred. When they reached the Square they surged expectantly into it, excited now by the momentary exhilaration of having reached their goal and of seeing, many of them for the first time, the alien magnificence of Pilate's palace. The leaders halted in the middle of the Square and gazed at the high walls and marble porticos. But the pressure of others marching into the Square pushed them forward towards the vast arched entrance. The great bronze gates stood wide open, but across that entrance guards stood, three deep and swords drawn.

Within an hour the Square was packed, and those who were still arriving, seeking other vantage points to view the palace, filtered into nearby streets. At the ends of those streets they found further progress blocked by guards. Townsfolk, flocking in the direction of the palace to see the happening, found cordons of troops barring their way. Debarred from seeing the spectacle at close quarters, the townsfolk hurried back to their homes and went up to their roofs to look down on it from a distance. The more prudently-minded of them closed the gates of their court-yards and barred their doors. Seamen coming up from the port were halted before they could reach the centre of the city: they went back to the taverns. The whole area around the palace was cordoned off.

Evening shadows flowed over the Square. A last ray of a stormy sunset bathed the roofs of the palace with a sulky yellow in which the demonstrators in the Square saw the occasional glint of armour and spears as the Praetorium Household Guards patrolled the battlements. Their attention was so taken up with this march-ing and counter-marching of guards that those in the Square paid no attention to the three figures grouped on the battlements near to an archway which led into the roof. Indeed, as the shadows deepened, this group could scarcely be seen, let alone recognised. In its centre was a man enveloped in a fur mantle, his face almost covered by the hood drawn low over brow and ears. A Negro slave was draping an extra blanket over the man's shoulders, and a doctor was urging the patient to return indoors.

The chanting faded. Some shouts were raised, but soon even these were stilled. All that could now be heard was the murmur and fidgeting of a bewildered crowd. The demonstrators were uneasy, and their uneasiness grew when they became aware that the soldiers, having made sure that the last bunch of demonstra-tors had passed down the avenue, began closing in behind them, laying across the avenue of retreat a formidable barrier of iron casques, plumed helmets, spiked shields, spears and naked swords. The soldiers at the gates of the palace began running impatient hands up and down the shafts of their spears; their officers fingered the hilts of swords and daggers. Those demonstrators who knew the palace stared into the courtyard over the heads of the triple file of guards towards the first-floor balcony. They had expected to see that balcony draped with purple and en-crusted with shields and to see Procurator Pilate appear on it, strutting into view with his chin tilted up and thrust out, and then standing there, arms stretched on the balustrade, staring down on his audience for a few moments of impressive silence. But the balcony was bare and empty. Was there to be any speech at all? Now fear began to slide and congeal in the unnatural silence that had fallen on the scene. They began to think that, if Pilate did appear, it would need but the lifting of a hand for the ring of spears and swords to tighten around them, and massacre to begin.

The leaders of the demonstration turned their backs to the guards and huddled together. Pilate could see them gesticulating as they argued among themselves. Some of these leaders were elderly men; one or two wore shawls of a quality which denoted they might be men of substance.

Then the rain which had threatened all afternoon began to fall. The doctor became more insistent that Pilate should move back indoors, but the Procurator did not do so until he was told that an officer had arrived with a report from Marcellus.

Pilate went down to his study. The room was snug, but somewhat smoky because, although the paving was warm, a brazier had been brought in for greater comfort. After he had thrown off his mantle, Pilate allowed the Negro to rub his head and shoulders dry with a rough towel and change his damp bootees for lambswool shoes, the kind of shoes, Pilate reflected sadly, that old men like Josephus had to wear, even in bed. He submitted also, though with curdled lips and a massive groan, to another spoonful of bdellium linctus and another cup of that foul Callirrhoen water. Then he shooed doctor and slave away and received the officer, one of those who had accompanied the procession into Caesarea. The report was on the whole reassuring. Whoever it was who had organised the procession had apparently insisted that the demonstration must be a passive one. The order seemed to be being obeyed. Spies in Jewish costume had been infiltrated among the demonstrators. They had not come across any overt Zealot sympathisers, nor any Galileans. Some young males who looked potentially dangerous and others who had been a little too rowdy had been discreetly detached from the procession and smuggled away for interrogation. Only three of these, however, had been found to be wearing daggers. These were being sent to the Antonia for interrogation by Marcellus.

The officer seemed well pleased. 'A lot have gone back to Jerusalem,' he said. 'So not so many have reached Caesarea after all, sir.'

'I'd rather have had them all here,' said Pilate. 'Better here than in Jerusalem. Good night!'

Was he feeling better? Well, for the first night for weeks bed seemed welcoming. He really might have slept tonight if the city had not been full of Jerusalem Jews.

Just then an officer of the Praetorium Guard presented himself. The leaders of the demonstration, he reported, requested audience with the Procurator. They wished to present a petition.

'Tell them the Procurator receives petitioners only in the forenoon. If business allows I shall accept their petition in the morning,' he said and, when spots of rain blown in through the high window fell hissing on the brazier, added, 'I hope they can keep it dry. And now I'm turning in. I don't want to be disturbed. Unless, of course, news comes from Jerusalem. I must see any dispatch from there immediately it arrives. Good night!'

Throughout the following morning Pilate conducted normal business in the secretariat with unhurried attention to detail. After which he ordered that the guards at the gate should allow a deputation from the crowd in the Palace Square to enter the courtyard. Twelve Jews, most of them elderly, were admitted. The oldest, who bore the petition, was shivering so violently that he had to be supported by two of his companions, and when an officer of the secretariat took the scroll from his hands, he collapsed whimpering on his knees. Pilate, watching the scene from the ceremonial balcony overlooking the courtyard, summoned a guard. 'Get that old man somewhere warm. See him fed, if he will eat anything from our Gentile kitchen.'

The scroll was brought up to him. To run his eyes quickly over it was merely a ceremonial formality. The protest against the offending standards and the demand for their removal was written in Hebrew. He could have found his way through it well enough, but he had no need to read it. He knew the wording of it already, because a copy of it had been made by a Marcellus informer at the time when it was being dictated at Herod's Gate.

With the scroll rolled in his hand like a baton, Pilate walked from the balcony into the audience-chamber. The Jews must wait. They would assume they were waiting merely at his heartless pleasure. They would not know that he was playing for time. The latest dispatch from Fabius, received an hour before, had told him everything he expected, but nothing that he hoped. The proclamation announcing that Fabius was in supreme command in Jerusalem had been handed to the captain in command of the cohort encamped in the gardens of the Hasmonaean Palace, but Paterculus had made no reply. By virtue of his present authority Fabius had followed up with a demand for the standards at the camp to be lowered. They had not been: they were still raised in full view of the shocked city.

This defiance confirmed all Pilate's fears. He had at first been tempted to imagine that Paterculus had carried the standards into Jerusalem merely in sheer stupid ignorance of treaty obligations. His blank disobedience to orders from the Antonia showed that his act was one of neither stupidity nor arrogance: it was an act of deliberate mutiny.

The force from Caesarea was strong enough to march into the city and overwhelm the cohort at the Hasmonaean. Pilate knew that, and so did Paterculus. But Paterculus, lording it at the palace behind his guards and standards, also knew that Pilate could not risk such a confrontation. The spectacle of Roman fighting Roman in Jerusalem could inflame the whole city, and within days the whole of Judaea, to rebellion against Rome.

At the back of Pilate's mind were questions far more sinister. What had encouraged Paterculus to this flagrant challenge? On whose authority was he acting? On authority from Antioch? From Rome? Or, worse, from Capri? Until those questions were answered, any attempts to winkle Paterculus out of Herod's palace could be dangerous. Even if they were answered satisfactorily it would be dangerous to attemp to dislodge him by force.

There were some gleams of comfort in the dispatch. The Jews, although still milling about in disorderly groups and wailing their lamentations throughout Jerusalem, had still not resorted to violence. The knowledge that a thousand troops lay just outside the city's gates was probably enough to restrain even the bravest fanatics from foolhardy attempts to attack the palace and remove the standards with their own hands. There had been, but this of course was inevitable, a few incidents in the Court of the Gentiles. Frustrated and incensed Jews had insulted and jostled non-Jews, but these scuffles had been minor, quickly damped down by the clubs of guards from the Antonia, and Fabius had now posted guards near the outer entrances of the Court of the Gentiles 'to discourage' non-Jews from approaching the Temple. Annas had sent several emissaries, each one demanding with greater vehemence than the last, the immediate removal of the standards. Fabius had replied that any decision about the standards must await the expected arrival of the Procurator at the Antonia. Fabius had not made the mistake of revealing that he had ordered the removal of the standards and that the order had been disobeyed by Paterculus. Good! On no account must Annas and the Sanhedrin, nor even an ordinary Jew in the street, know that Roman was quarrelling with Roman.

Pilate unrolled the petition again and gazed at it. It was rather beautifully worded. It read like a prayer. These Jews were good at declaiming. He would respond with even loftier eloquence when he replied to their protest. He had that speech already composed in his head. He even knew precisely where appropriate and dignified gestures would punctuate his noble phrases. He would not attempt the speech in Hebrew. He could, of course, have easily delivered it in that language of scholars, but he would soften their hearts with colloquial Aramaic. However, that speech could not be delivered yet. He could not yet declare that Rome, in her might and clemency, had looked with compassion on the petition of the Jews and, in sympathy for their religious prejudices, the Roman standards, precious though they were to Roman hearts and dear to Roman loyalties, would be removed from Jewish sight and, decently veiled, brought out of the Holy City.

What a lot of names the leaders of the demonstration had collected! Many of the names, by their grand collection of patronymics, indicated that those signatures were of men of ancient and important family. Two, Pilate actually recognised. The names ran on and on, covering leaf after leaf of the scroll. Ah! That populous collection of signatures had given him an idea! It was an idea that would allow him a breathing space. He hurried into the secretariat and summoned the officer who had brought the petition. He handed it to him.

'Give this back to the leader of the deputation. Tell the deputation that I have read it with interest and not without sympathy. But I understand that only *twelve* Jews have presented themselves at the palace. Yet there are scores of signatures here. I insist that all, not merely twelve but *all* who signed this document, should show the courtesy of presenting it to me personally.' He dropped his voice. 'It should take them a day at least to rustle up that crowd, or longer. Some are probably in Jerusalem.'

Returning to the balcony, Pilate watched the twelve old men go out through the arch to the square. He saw them waving the scroll to those nearest the gate. He heard names being called. He stood there for a while watching twos and threes of Jews coming forward.

The rain began again. The sky darkened. He shivered. The pain began bumping in his innards. The doctor, as though the damned man had actually heard this thumping, appeared at his elbow with a sticky phial and the bottle of sulphur water. The doctor pressed his fingers on Pilate's temples.

'You should not be walking around,' he said.

Pilate felt pain leaping up to his throat and screwing at his neck. '*Should* not!' he gasped. 'I don't think I *can* be walking around. Not for an hour or so.' As the whole floor undulated before him he leaned heavily on the doctor's arm and made his way back to his bedroom.

He dozed for the rest of the morning. Claudia came at midday, along with a bowl of lentil broth, very welcome, and Sextia, less welcome. But Sextia did not chatter overmuch. Her grain ship had just docked.

'When is it sailing?' he asked with comically exaggerated eagerness.

She laughed. Pilate was almost bearable when he was ill.

'It will wait. It depends when I can get out of the palace, doesn't it? I'm besieged, am I not?'

'We are not besieged: it is the Jews who are besieged. There's no danger, Sextia.'

'I know. I'm probably trying to find an excuse for staying.'

'I'll see you safely aboard.'

'I bet you will.'

They all laughed. Pilate looked at Sextia's moustache but then dropped his eyes to her jewelled collar. 'Where on earth did you get that barbaric rig-out?'

'Don't you like it? It came from Carthage. When I bought the emeralds for Claudia.'

'It's rather ornate. But then, Sextia, so are you.' He looked all over her saffron high-waisted robe. 'I'll miss you, Sextia.'

'For my jewels? Or for my impudence?'

'For both, Sextia.' He turned his face to Claudia. He reached out and took her hand. 'I'll miss you too.'

'But, Pontius, I am thinking of not . . .'

'Come along, Claudia. Don't start arguing just now. Leave the man in peace. He needs rest.'

He made no protest against Sextia bustling Claudia out. He was pleased to be alone. The lentil broth warmed his belly. There was less pain. He rested for nearly two hours more before getting up and going to his study.

That afternoon's dispatch from Jerusalem reported everything the same, and more protests from Annas. Meanwhile the secretariat had set up a booth at the gate, and the names on the petition

239

were being checked against those seeking entry. They were coming in very slowly. As Pilate had hoped, some of the signatures were those of aged demonstrators who had fallen out *en route*.

'Good!' said Pilate, and willingly signed a firman allowing two of the demonstrators to hire mules and leave Caesarea to find the missing petitioners.

He was relaxing in his study, official documents shoved aside and the *Commentaries* unrolled on his desk, when the officer from the secretariat reported again. As the door opened Pilate heard rain battering the roof of the corridor and porticoes beyond his room.

'The Jews in the Square, sir.'

'What about them?'

'An elder of the Jewish community says some could be offered hospitality in Jewish homes in the city.'

'I'm sure they could. They could be dried out and fed and warmed up to demonstrate again. No. They will be contained in the Square.'

'It's a foul night, sir.'

'It is Judaean rain.'

'But not Roman rain, sir. The guards!'

'Are *they* grumbling as well? Are they not as waterproof as Jews? . . . All right. Alter the roster. Make it only one hour on and three hours off. Our numbers will allow that?'

'Yes, sir.'

'And tell the elder of the Jewish community that I shall allow his hospitable compatriots to send food into the Square.' As the man was turning to go, he added, 'Just a moment!' He pondered. 'Any really sick or elderly Jew in the Square can be given leave to go to a house. But the householder receiving him must stand bail. Good night, Captain.'

'Good night, Procurator.'

When the officer had closed the door Pilate bolted it and walked along the corridor to his bedroom. He sank gratefully on to his couch and lay down. His biggest worry at the moment, he felt, was a grinding headache. Had it not been for that, an hour's reading would have taken his mind off immediate worries and relaxed him. The *Commentaries* lay temptingly at hand. But, no, his eyes were too tired. The Negro came in with a lighted brazier. 'No. I don't think I need that tonight.' But as the Negro was carrying it out he said, 'Just swing it round a moment.' The

Negro did so, and the air was filled with the aroma of the resin sprinkled on the charcoal. 'I'll undress myself,' said Pilate. 'Good night.'

When the Negro had gone Pilate got up and walked across to the cupboard. He lifted out the statue of Julius. How weak his illness had made him. The statue felt quite heavy. He placed it on the table. Like an actor dressing a scene, he adjusted two lamps to shine upward into the boy's reflective face, and then went back to his couch. Two hours later he was lying there, his headache gone, contentedly gazing at the portrait of his son, when Claudia opened the door. She stood smiling at the tableau, and then stepped to his couch. She looked down at him. 'Why Pontius!' she said. 'You are looking much better.' She felt his forehead. 'Much better. All my patients are doing very well.'

'All?'

'Yes, all three! The woman from Magdala has had her baby. A son!'

'Oh, no! No, no! Not *another* bloody Jew!'

As she laughed he grasped her hands. 'Stay here tonight,' he commanded.

Afranius and his escort had halted at a tavern nearly two miles beyond Kafr Kana on the Nazareth-Tiberias road. They found the innkeeper an oafishly stupid fellow.

They had pulled up at this spot, having made good time, to water their mules and drink fresh milk. It was late afternoon, with still enough light in the grey lowering sky for them to discern the Sea of Galilee below them, fading away, sullen and grey, to the east. One of the party strolled up a goat-track to stretch his legs, and came back to say that from an outcrop of rock he had been able to see the outline of the buildings of Tiberias on the shore of the Sea. Ahead of them now were six or seven miles downhill to the Sea and another easy seven miles along its shore to Tiberias.

They relaxed. They were warm after riding, so they sat outside, preferring the evening air, damp though it was, to the smoky inside of the grubby building. In any case they preferred to talk among themselves without being overheard. Not that there were any customers there. One could not imagine that the innkeeper did much trade at this spot. Within sight there was nothing but a huddle of mean little cottages and a few shepherd huts on the surrounding hills. And the innkeeper seemed unaccustomed to travellers. So much so that when they ordered milk he shook his head, expressing ill-tempered failure to understand their dialect. The party's spokesman, despite his command of Aramaic, had to mime the action of milking a goat before the man understood what they wanted and went scowling to the outhouse. Eventually he came back with a jug of frothing milk and some clay beakers of different shapes and sizes. Two of the beakers were cracked, one of them with the dry deposit of earlier milk encrusted on the crack. It took some time to explain to the man that he should bring a clean beaker. He did it eventually, banging it on the table, and went indoors. Afranius, who knew no Aramaic, cautiously said not a word in the innkeeper's presence.

The escort conversed in undertones. None of them had ever been to Antioch. They were excited by the prospect. There were wonderful women in Antioch: not just whores, but Greek women, even Roman ladies, who went out alone to pick up hungry men from the desert.

'Well, you're not from the desert,' murmured Afranius with a chuckle. 'You can find women just as good in Caesarea. Anyway, you'll have no time for women in Antioch.'

'We shall have tonight in Tiberias. If we lodge at the Fighting Gladiator I know a whore who lives nearby . . .'

Afranius interrupted this hopeful discourse. 'We shall not be lodging in Tiberias tonight. We need somewhere quieter. We'll push on to Magdala. Come on. Let's go.'

'How long to Tiberias now?' asked one as they mounted.

'We'll be there before nightfall,' said another optimistically.

As they rode off, the innkeeper came from behind the door and watched them trot off towards the Sea of Galilee. As soon as they were out of sight he ran, pulling his robe up to his knees, quickly towards the cottages, stopping at one which looked even more broken-down and deserted than the squalid rest and banging on its bolted door. A swarthy fellow opened the door. Another man was standing behind him.

'Five Roman soldiers have just passed.'

'So what?'

'They were disguised. They wore Jewish robes and shawls.'

'Then how do you know they were Roman soldiers?'

'They talked of nothing but whores. And when one was getting his purse out to pay I saw his breastplate: part of it. Anyway, two of them spoke Latin to each other.'

242

'You heard what they said?'

'Yes. I was near enough: but they didn't know I was. They didn't even know I knew anything but Galilean.'

'What did they say?'

'They are going to Tiberias. They seem to have some need to call there. Then they intend to lodge at Magdala. They are on their way to Antioch.'

The man at the door looked back at the other. 'What do you think?' The other shrugged indifference.

'But they're on some secret mission,' said the innkeeper eagerly. 'Perhaps they're carrying dispatches.'

'And in disguise too,' said the man at the door.

The man behind him shrugged again, but then, in a grumbling voice, said, 'Well, perhaps we should . . . ' He broke off. 'Thanks,' he said to the innkeeper. 'Thanks,' he said again and closed the door in the man's face. The two slumped down on an improvised bench where they had been eating supper. One scooped up the last of the mess of cold beans with a lump of bread. The other tapped his fingers on the wood and eventually he said, 'I suppose that man's right. It might be important. We should let the Tiberias group know.'

The other wiped his mouth. 'That's miles extra to our road,' he grumbled. 'I need a sleep. At least two hours.'

The other got to his feet. 'You're always sleeping! Come on! I'll pack up. You call the boy.'

The tired one went out. He tramped round to the back of the cottage where a makeshift ladder reached up to a fodder store built into the roof. 'Ishmael!' he called softly. 'Ishmael!' There was a scuffling and then the boy's face appeared at the opening, peering down through the gathering darkness. 'We're off, Ishmael. Get the mules.'

Ishmael rubbed sleep from his eyes and, ignoring the ladder, swung from a roof beam and dropped lightly into the yard. He tightened the cord round his waist, shifted the hidden dagger into a more comfortable position, and leaped over the low wall where three mules, tethered to a post, were sleeping. He kicked them awake, and they scrabbled moodily to their feet.

'I wish I were that age,' said the tired one as he went back into the cottage to help with the bundles. 'He's as bright as a lark.'

They drew the bolt over the cracked door, hung a chain on it, and in a few minutes all three of them were trotting downhill. Behind them, the sky to the west was black with rain-clouds rolling in from the Mediterranean, but above the Sea of Galilee the clouds were thin enough for them to see the glow of the full moon. Light rain was falling, but as they approached Kinneret, on the south-western shore of the Sea of Galilee, they rode out of the rain. Villagers were strolling around the stalls in the main street.

'We can get to Tiberias before the market closes,' said one of the men.

'I suppose so,' the tired one growled. At that moment they were approaching a tavern. It stood at a fork in the road. On its left was the road leading north to Tiberias; on its right the road to the south of the Sea. The tired one nodded to the right. 'That's the way we should be going.'

'We'll be back here in little more than an hour. Or less,' the other consoled him.

The tired one scowled. 'An hour's an hour.' Ishmael, who had reached the fork long before them, had reined his mule to a halt and was waiting for them, his impatient heels raised to urge the beast on. 'I know what,' said the tired one suddenly. 'Send the boy.'

'Where?'

'To Tiberias.'

They brought their mounts to a halt. The other one shook his head.

'Why not?' asked the tired one. 'Barabbas said we'd to show his little pet the ropes. Put the boy to the test, Barabbas said.'

The other thought about it, frowning. He glanced towards the tavern.

'Then we could have at least one hour's kip,' the tired one tempted him.

'There's one good point about the idea,' the other conceded. 'No one will notice that lad in Tiberias. Whereas if *we* go back there . . . '

'I was thinking the same,' said the tired one.

'All right,' the other said suddenly. 'Ishmael! Come here. You can do something useful at last. An important job.' The boy's eyes shone. 'We're going to wait here. You are going alone to Tiberias. Go to the meat market. You'll find a beggar there. His name is Ikkesh.'

The boy grinned. 'A crooked one?'

'Yes, Ikkesh; his legs are as bent as a grasshopper's. But he's not really a beggar, Ishmael. He's an important man. He's our

244

postman: he'll pass on a message for us. He sits by the north arch of the market. If he's not there, go to the man at the first stall on the right and ask where Ikkesh is.'

'And what is the message?'

'Tell him that five Roman soldiers wearing Jewish costume have just come up this road. They have come from Caesarea on some secret mission. They plan to spend tonight at Magdala and then go north to Antioch. Can you remember all that?' Ishmael nodded. 'Repeat it.' He did. 'Right, off you go. God be with you. We'll wait here for you.'

Ishmael dug in his heels. In a minute he was out of sight. The two men dismounted, tethered their mounts, and strode to the tavern to buy a drink before they slept. 'We should have taken that dagger from the lad,' said one. 'If by chance he catches up with the Romans they might stop and search him.'

The other laughed. 'If so, that young firebrand would take all five on single-handed. But don't worry. The Romans are twenty minutes or more ahead of him.'

'Are they still there?' Sextia asked as, drawing her hood over her head against the chill and rain of a Caesarean dawn, she stepped out on to the palace roof. Pilate, hooded also and swathed in an ankle-length cloak, was leaning over the battlements and staring down at the sodden Jews in the great courtyard of the palace.

Surprised at hearing her voice, Pilate swung round quickly. It was unusual to see Sextia astir so early in the morning. He also wondered how she had persuaded the guards to allow her access to this eyrie on the roof, but did not bother to ask her about that. 'Yes, still there!'

The Jews had now weathered two rain-slashed nights in the courtyard. A few were moving around, stamping their feet and blowing on their hands, but the rest, bunched closely together for warmth, kept below the rugs and sheepskins sent by the committee of Jewish residents of Caesarea. They lay still as death, though probably some of them were peeping out and, seeing the yellow gleam in the unpromising sky, hoped that today the clouds would part and let down at least a little sun.

Sextia craned over the wall. 'They've lit no fires this morning.'

'They cannot. It is their Sabbath. Even if I went down now unarmed and bared my throat and said, "Kill me", some of them would say they could not. Not on the Sabbath.'

Sextia drew back. She shivered. 'Poor beasts. I've always heard that Jews were stubborn, but . . . How long are they going to stay there?'

'Until I grant their petition.'

'When will you do that?'

'When it is practicable.'

'But why don't those out there, in the square, pack up and go home?'

'They can't. The guards will not let them pass. But even if they were free to go, I doubt if they would do so. They will stay now to support their comrades in the courtyard. Yes, stubborn's the word. But what brings you up here? And so early?'

'I wanted to talk to you before Claudia is about.'

'About her? Or about that woman's baby?'

'That baby!' She grimaced. 'Claudia goes on about that brat as though it were her own. It's a pity Severus is not back with his as well. She could set up a nursery, and that Jew woman is full enough of milk for a litter of wolves. No, I wanted to talk about the trip to Athens.'

'When are you leaving?'

'I can't delay the boat any longer. Not even for Claudia.'

'How do you mean?'

'She has kept putting it off. Last night she came pretty close to saying she did not want to go to Athens.'

'Because of the baby?' Sextia shook her head. 'Because she is worried about me?' He smiled. 'But I'm almost better.'

'It's partly because of you, Pontius. She feels you are having a lot of difficulty here, and she might help.'

He smiled again. 'I admit that Claudia is sometimes a comfort. Sometimes. But I can manage to govern Judea for a spell without the assistance of a wife.'

'Claudia doesn't think so, Pontius. Not now.' Sextia made a gesture of exasperation. 'It's happened. Just what I feared.' Pilate frowned questioningly at her. 'She's gone political. Or religious. Or both. She's listened to that Magdala woman as though the whore were a priestess. So much so, that I really think Claudia sees herself as a priestess herself, or at least as a Roman lady who can bring comfort and peace and love to a suffering people.'

'I think you exaggerate, Sextia. It's all this baby business. Women do get sentimental when babies are around.' He laughed. 'But that you wouldn't know.'

'I wish I could think sentimentality were all it is. I can't. She'll be at you, Pilate, as soon as she thinks you are free to listen. She'll be telling you she is not coming to Athens with me.'

'You *are* exaggerating. She's not so much as hinted that.'

'Well, if she does, persuade her to come with me. Bully her. Tell her she cannot offend me by changing her mind. Anything! But if she insists on staying here, what will you do?'

'I certainly should not send her away against her will.'

'I was afraid you would say that. Then, if she stays, promise me you will do something, Pontius.'

'What?'

'Have Julius come home.'

'That is not possible for some time.'

'For her sake. If Julius were here, Claudia would find interest and happiness in his company. He would give her something to think about instead of damned Jews.'

Pilate shook his head. 'Claudia would not wish it either. She is as concerned as I am that Julius should continue his studies in a western atmosphere.'

An officer from the secretariat appeared with another dispatch from Jerusalem. 'Excuse me, Sextia. Let's talk later.'

Pilate opened the dispatch without much hope. His pessimism was confirmed. Everything was the same in Jerusalem, except that the Sanhedrin, in the name of Caiaphas of course, had sent an envoy to the Legate's Court in Antioch beseeching the Roman Legate of Asia to take the action which his Procurator in Judaea was refusing to take.

Pilate went down to his private apartments. He was feeling decidedly better. After an hour in the steam room he felt even lively, and by the time the Negro had pummelled him and almost jerked his head out of its socket he felt fitter to face the world than he had felt ever since that night ride to Jerusalem to meet Herod. As the Negro rubbed him murderously with a towel as harsh as a grater, Pilate was asking himself when the lethargic Tetrarch would reply to his dispatch, and at that very moment a courier appeared with the very thing. Pilate swung himself to a sitting position on the slab and read Herod's communication while the Negro dried his feet. It was as chillingly formal as the one Pilate himself had sent. Herod expressed only mild surprise at the news about the standards. It was inconvenient for him to leave Tiberias immediately. However, he was due in Jerusalem with Her Majesty Herodias within a few days. He saw no urgent reason for changing his plans for that progress.

The Negro swathed big towels around his master and bustled him upstairs from the baths to his bedroom.

'Get the Young Barber,' Pilate ordered.

Ephir came dancing in, gay as ever, flourishing towels and implements. 'Have you the salve, Ephir?'

'I'll get it,' the boy carolled, and in moments was back with a pot full of the pomade made, so the Roman barber had vowed, from the same recipe as that used by the Divine Julius. Though it had not apparently, the barber ruefully confessed, kept the Dictator from going bald. But Egyptians used it; and look at their hair. As the boy rubbed the pomade into Pilate's stubbly grey hair, the Negro knelt down and, his filed upper teeth biting his lower lip in the intensity of concentration, painted the red spot just below Pilate's lowest left rib.

Would he, Pilate thought, ever have to use that guiding point? Or would a Zealot dagger, or even a Roman assassin's sword, choose some other entry? He thrust such morbid questions away and leaned back for Ephir to scrape his chin. His whiskers were so softened by steam that he could hardly feel the blade. He watched the boy's face. He watched the young brows pucker into a frown as the eyes followed intently the course of the blade. The boy was suddenly conscious of being stared at. He flashed a glance. Their eyes met, and the boy's frown was swept away in the bewitching wave of smile, and Pilate found himself gazing into two dark pools full of joy and devotion.

Pilate was dressed and lying relaxed on his couch before going to his workroom when Claudia came in.

'You look well,' she said. He held out a hand, and she walked over and laid her hand in it. 'And you're stronger too,' she added when she felt his clasp. 'You look happy, too.'

'So, Claudia, you can leave for Athens with a light heart.'

'The trip is off. I'm not going. I've just told Sextia.'

'Wasn't she offended?'

'Immensely.'

'That's a pity. Why not go?'

'I'm too busy.'

'Busy? What with? Babies?'

She shook her head smilingly. 'It's not that. The baby doesn't need me. Nor does the mother. But I am going to do some studying. I've asked Polygnotus to find me a teacher of Hebrew.'

'I'm pleased,' said Pilate doubtfully. 'But what is the object?'

'I feel that as the Procurator's wife it is time I learned more

248

about this country, about its people, its history. And its religion.'

'I see. Such knowledge can have some interest among ourselves, Claudia. But you must not mislead yourself. In Judaea it is not considered proper to allow women to use their intellectual attainments in public affairs.'

'There is Herodias.'

He grimaced. 'There is, indeed. And that bitch uses more than her intellect. Anyhow, I am not against your interesting yourself in such things, but go to Athens first. You'll see Julius.'

'There is something I want to ask you, Pontius. Isn't it time Julius came home? He could help you too.'

'In time, he might. But, for the moment, no. He is better where he is.'

At that moment the officer from the secretariat appeared, and Pilate drew himself up to a sitting position. 'Procurator! Forgive my interrupting you. A matter of urgency.'

'What is it?'

'A courier.'

'Well then, where is the dispatch?'

'He insists on delivering it in person, sir.'

'He *insists*!'

'Yes, sir. He is from Capri.'

For a moment Pilate sat completely motionless. Then very slowly he stood up. 'I shall receive him in my study. Tell Polygnotus to go there at once.'

The man waiting in the study wore the armour and trappings of a centurion, but his manner suggested someone of greater rank and much greater importance. He stared with ominous gravity at Pilate. Then he looked towards Polygnotus. 'Proconsul, we must be alone.'

Pilate faced the solemn stare with a frown. 'If the matter is something demanding urgent attention, it is better to have a scribe at hand.'

'What I have to say, Proconsul, must not be heard by any other than yourself.'

'Very well, then.' Pilate walked to the other side of his desk, and sat behind it, facing the man. 'Prepare a pen, Polygnotus.' While the scribe did this, Pilate reached to a shelf below the desk and from it lifted on to the top of the desk some sheets of papyrus. While he fiddled with these, his head bent over them, he glanced under his brows at the man's sword. For a private audience the man should have been disarmed. However, he could feel, beside his knee, the dagger which had lain under the papyrus. Polygnotus, his back to the courier, handed the pen to Pilate. As he did so his eyes passed a message. Polygnotus understood. 'Leave us, Polygnotus,' said Pilate.

The scribe went out by the door leading to Pilate's bedroom and closed it behind him. Only Pilate, knowing the sound of the scribe's feet, could hear how quickly they slid over the marble of the corridor. Within a minute the guards summoned by the scribe's whispers would steal along that marble just as silently and, hardly breathing, wait behind the door.

The courier closed the other door, the one leading to the anterooms, and faced Pilate. After unlacing a strap of the leather jerkin below his breastplate he drew out a rolled and flattened dispatch and laid it on the desk. The seal was immediately recognisable: pressed into the wax was the signet of His August Highness Tiberius Caesar. Even as Pilate broke the seal and unrolled the document, his mind raced through a dozen probabilities. But one thing was certain: this was not the communication he had awaited so eagerly from the Caesar. Anything handed to him with such forbidding secrecy could certainly not be merely a report on his Judaean project.

He began reading, his practised eye skipping the formal introductory addresses to leap straight to the essence of the dispatch communication. He paled. The catastrophic words made him feel dizzy. Lucius Aelius Sejanus . . . Former Prefect of Rome . . Accused by Caesar . . . Arrested on orders of the Senate . . Judged guilty of treason . . . Strangled.

His patron strangled! The man who had elevated him to the post of procurator strangled! Strangled by order of Caesar! Inwardly Pilate shuddered. But he kept himself rigid and erect at his desk, his face impassive as he read on.

When he read the second part of the dispatch his immediate fears, the fears that he might be implicated in the Sejanus treason, were partially dispelled. The instructions now being given to him indicated that he was, at least for the time being, still considered trustworthy enough to obey Caesar's commands Though even this, he thought, when he had finished reading but kept his eyes on the dispatch, might be merely putting him to the test.

At last he looked up. 'You have another document, so it says here.'

'Yes, sir. But I am ordered to keep it on my person until . . .'

'Yes. So it says. But you know all that is ordered here?'

'Yes, sir.'

'In that case!' said Pilate and, standing up and walking to the brazier, he laid the dispatch on the charcoal. The papyrus writhed in the heat. Being damp with the man's sweat it burned slowly. The seals melted and flared. Both of them watched until the papyrus broke into flaming segments which died away in grey ash.

The courier drew his dagger and with the point stirred the ash into the cinders.

Pilate smiled. 'Hardly necessary to do that, captain.'

'Probably better that your scribe should not see that anything has burned.'

'I should think he will guess.'

'I await your orders, sir.'

Pilate nodded. Everything was clear now. So many questions answered. The Jerusalem affair could be settled in a way he had never expected. The operation would demand discretion and exquisite intrigue, yet now, knowing where he stood, he could do it. And after? Well, after Jerusalem there were dangers. Personal dangers. But if in Jerusalem he did capably what Caesar now ordered him to do, he could rid himself of some of the odium of being the protégé of a would-be regicide. Forcing a confident smile to his lips, he faced the officer.

'Your name, captain?'

'Ennius Naevius Nerva.'

Pilate pursed his lips extravagantly. 'I guessed you were no centurion. You are of the family of the lawyer Cocceius Nerva.'

'He is my uncle, Proconsul.'

'We are entertaining at Caesarea at this moment a friend of your uncle's, a sister-in-law of my wife. You will find the office of the household steward along the balcony, Nerva. Tell him to make you comfortable. Tell him to give you the apartment in the tower. Have you slaves with you?'

Nerva shook his head. 'Only the boat crew. They will lodge in the dormitories in the port.'

'The steward will supply you with servants. You can use my private baths. Make yourself comfortable. We must talk later about what was asked there.' He pointed to the brazier. 'The operation is more difficult than you might expect. But I'll fill you in with the details later. At the moment, have a bath and a rest, and join us at table in an hour's time.'

When Nerva had gone, Pilate opened his private door. Along

the corridor were Polygnotus and four guards with swords drawn.

'Thank you, Polygnotus. Our courier is now a distinguished guest.'

By now even Ishmael was tired. Finding a track across desert lands at night is exhausting, and, after one has found it, keeping on it is equally exhausting. The tired one – he seemed always tired – grumbled about having to make the trip 'in this stinking dark', and he kept on with his grumbling even after the other had reminded him a dozen times that they were forbidden to cross the desert in daylight for fear Roman patrols might spot them and mark which way they were going.

Constantly Ishmael tried to show them how one could best follow a track. One must not look down at it and try too nicely to guide's one's mount. One must keep one's head up and look ahead. If one did that, one could see, even in the meagre glow of the night sky, the beaten strip where sand and stones had been trampled down and smoothed by beasts and men winding their way between scrub and rock or trekking straight across bleak and stony plateaux. Although he had never crossed the Desert before, Ishmael was soon feeling quite confident. In the first few miles he had realised that desert tracks were not all that different from those along which he had led his flocks in the highlands above Gideon. Tracks and paths, however twisting, were logical. They twisted only where it was necessary to do so, to avoid an obstruction or skirt a danger. After all, a track, any track, was originally beaten out by beasts, and then by herdsmen and their flocks, by caravans of camels and troops of horsemen, with the result that a track flowed through a landscape as a stream flows. When animals or men had to go from one point to another they did it in the same way as water did it: they found not always the shortest but always the easiest way. So sometimes, Ishmael soon found, it was easier to let the mule find its own way. Sure enough, when, after his eyes had drooped for a few moments, the mule's swerving to left or right awakened him, he would find that the beast had turned to avoid some gully or some rocks and was still following the track. The two men had eventually realised that Ishmael was better at finding the way through this kind of country than they were. Also, being soft city men, they wanted to sleep. So finally they sent him to ride ahead. He took the lead proudly. But now, at dawn, he was feeling weary; so weary that, although the sulphurous band of light over the eastern horizon was not all that bright, it stung his eyes.

'We must be nearly there,' said one of the men. 'We've done seven hours from Kinneret.'

'We are there,' said the boy. 'Look!'

They looked down into the wadi where he pointed; then looked back at him with blank bewildered faces. The stupid fools could not see anything. They probably thought they were looking at another scatter of rocks, for the whole landscape was littered with these slabs and triangles of sand-scoured stone, sticking up from the earth's crust like big broken teeth. And, as dawn's light strengthened, one could see in the distance clusters of these stones which earlier travellers had piled up, and then stuck a big sharp-pointed stone on top of them, to guide one across the wild waste. These pointed piles of stone with their pointed tops did look like men who had squatted down beside the track, heads hanging but peaked hoods sticking up.

'Look!' said Ishmael again, still pointing down into the wadi. Even then it was not until one of the peaked hoods stirred and a man who had looked like a sliver of rock sat up and stretched his arms and yawned that the two men realised that they had reached the camp. Ishmael was disappointed, even a little critical, that they had been able to ride down upon it unchallenged. What if they had been a Roman patrol? But when he turned to look back at the two men he felt he had been almost as stupid as they were, for now he saw that six Zealots with their daggers at the ready had sprouted up out of the rocky outcrop which he had just passed.

The two men flung back their hoods, and Ishmael saw grim stares suddenly crack into smiles of recognition as the sentries ran up and the two men dismounted. Then everyone was hugging and slapping backs and kissing. They took no notice of him, who had led their comrades into the Desert for the last six hours.

'Ishmael, son of Uzziel!'

Ishmael nearly fell off the mule when he heard that voice. He swung round. 'Barabbas!' Now he did fall, but on purpose, falling into the jewelled embrace, feeling the beloved hands gripping his shoulders and the fierce black beard scrubbing his cheeks.

'Well, Ishmael, you've made your first expedition. How was it?'

'I've bloodied my dagger,' said Ishmael and laughed at Barabbas's look of surprise. 'No, I haven't killed anyone yet. They made me stay at the cottage when they went to get the tax-collector. But one of them promised to use my dagger.' He brought it from under his robe. The blood lay on it like rust.

'You must clean it, Ishmael.'

'Don't you like blood?' Ishmael teased.

'It spoils the blade.' They laughed together and strode down the litter of rocks to the camp-site hidden in the wadi. Warm as he was with the ride, Ishmael had not realised, until he saw the waking men blowing on their fingers and flapping their arms, how cold the morning was. This desert was colder than his highlands: the wind from the east had a sharp edge. One of the partisans had got a fire going. He and Barabbas sat beside it, watching the cook brewing a grog of wine with herbs and water.

'And I took a message to Ikkesh in Tiberias,' said Ishmael as he dunked bread in his grog. The two men, joining them at that moment, told Barabbas about the five Roman soldiers travelling north in disguise. Barabbas said it had been wise to alert the group in Tiberias. There might be enough time and enough partisans to ambush the party in the Golan Heights.

The tired one pulled a purse from under his robe and tossed it over to Barabbas. It fell heavily. 'We found it in the tax-collector's bed,' said the man. 'Look. There's his blood on it.'

Barabbas lifted the purse and turned it over, weighing it in his hands. They all heard the clink of coins. 'Fodder for a month or more there,' said Barabbas with a satisfied smile. 'Put it in the saddle-bag, Ishmael.'

As more partisans gathered around the fire, Ishmael heard talk of the stirring things that had happened since he had left Barabbas to go on his first Zealot expedition. Jerusalem was in tumult against the Romans. One man who had come from Jerusalem said hotly, 'The whole city would rise at a word,' and added, though in the tone of voice which one uses when one has been saying the same thing for days, 'if only we gave them that word.' Then, as he drank, he frowned over the rim of his cup at Barabbas, challenging a reply but getting none.

Throughout the morning, others arrived at the camp, among them two who grumbled that they had been given wrong directions for reaching the rendezvous. 'The directions were clear enough, comrades,' said Barabbas. 'Listen more carefully tonight when I tell you the place for our next meeting.'

All those arriving brought news and heard news about the partisan groups in towns and villages throughout Judaea and Galilee. Some dictated names to Barabbas, names of new and tested recruits, names of notorious collaborators with Romans. Some brought roughly sketched plans of public offices and private villas where tax-collectors or wealthy Jewish collaborators could be ambushed, robbed and burned. Two more brought purses of tax money.

Just before noon a party of four horsemen arrived. Barabbas addressed three of them by name. Others, who knew them as coming from Bethlehem, gathered around them to ask if they had news from Jerusalem. They said that they had heard that the standards still stood outside the Hasmonaean Palace and Pilate had sent troops from Caesarea. The others already knew that. But what else? Had there been fighting? The men from Bethlehem shrugged off these questions: they had more personal worries. The fourth one, the stranger, announced himself to Barabbas as Malachi son of Emmanuel of Bethany.

'The brother of Joseph son of Emmanuel who died in Bethany?' said Barabbas.

Grief contorted the man's face. 'Who was *strangled* in Bethany,' he said harshly.

'Yes, Malachi. But better that others strangled him. If they had not, you might have had to do it. Would you have done so?'

Staring at the ground, the man nodded. 'He was my brother.'

'And once you loved him. But he betrayed you.'

'It was not me he betrayed.'

'He betrayed comrades of yours. It is the same thing. Remember how Judas the Maccabean had to kill a Jew he had loved. Have you heard the story?' The chattering nearby died away. Everyone was listening, everyone looking at Barabbas. He saw them waiting for his next words, and, responding to his audience, he stepped back on to slightly higher ground. He drew himself up, lifting one beringed hand in the gesture of a preacher demanding silence, but leaving the other hand on the jewelled hilt of his sword. 'The Syrians tempted Judas the Maccabee,' he said, by some trick in his voice making them actually hear the subtle tongues of tempters. 'The Syrians offered to Judas the wealth and power of the East, if only he would relinquish his faith; if only he would deny his God; if only he would worship Greek idols. You know how Judas answered that. With his own hand he slew the first Jew who stepped towards the altar of idolatry. Even though he loved the Jew as a brother.' Barabbas beckoned Malachi to approach him and took his hands in his. 'Malachi! Mourn no more. Look around you. See how you are surrounded by true brothers,

255

brothers who love their country, as you love it. Brothers who are devoted to *Torah*, as you are devoted. Brothers who, like you, are ready to fight and die for both. Brothers who love you.' He embraced Malachi; others stepped forward and did the same.

'Ishmael! Come here, my boy.' Barabbas put his hands on Ishmael's shoulders. 'Look at this boy, Malachi. This is Ishmael son of Uzziel. After your brother had sold himself for Roman pieces of silver, the Romans went to Ishmael's village. Ishmael saw the Romans nail five Jews to the cross and leave them in the sun until the vultures came to peck out their eyes. One of those five Jews was Uzziel, father of Ishmael. Ishmael will live to see that murder avenged. You, Malachi, will live to see your brother's death avenged. For he too, although he was a traitor, was in his own way a victim of the evil that Rome has brought to our land, setting brother against brother and friend against friend. Think only of that. The time is near when we will strike a blow which will topple Pilate and Caesar from their seats of power.' He lifted his hand again and addressed them all. 'Remember all of you, always, the words Mattathias the Zealot used to the oppressors of Judah. "We will undergo death, we will undergo any sort of punishment which you can inflict upon us, and we shall suffer all with pleasure. For we shall suffer in the knowledge that we do not die for any unrighteous act but die for our faith in God." Our only enemies, brothers, are the enemies of our God. In whatever guise those enemies come, they must die as enemies. For such there is no forgiveness, only death. Never forgive them, brothers. Spit with contempt on those rabbis and preachers who exhort you to forgive your enemies. Beware of those who beseech you to turn the other cheek. For the Law of God, the Law taught by our prophets and written in the Book of the Law, demands an eye for an eye, a tooth for a tooth.'

In the late afternoon, when the desert was taking on the ruddy glow of a reddening sun, Barabbas had named the place and time for their next desert rendezvous and the partisans, after packing bundles, had gathered round the fire for a final hot drink before the fire was stamped out. Then another partisan from Jerusalem reached the camp. He seemed, to Ishmael, a most unlikely figure for a partisan. He was much older than any of the men in the camp; his silky, well-combed beard was quite white. His ample robes were rich, his hands soft. He had two servants with him. Any Roman seeing him riding along the road would have guessed him to be a wealthy merchant. He was, a partisan told Ishmael, a cheese-maker. To his Jerusalem store in the Valley of the Cheese-makers came herdsmen from miles around. They brought milk: they brought information. Barabbas sometimes lodged at his house. the partisan said. The partisan was excited by the hope that the old man had brought vital news. Surely such an important partisan would come out to this desert rendezvous only on a matter of vital importance. But the matter of importance, so far as Ishmael could see, was money. For heavy purses were taken out of the saddlebag, and the old man's servants hid them in their bundles. This newcomer also had brought names for Barabbas. They were for the most part names of associates who had contributed or promised funds for the resistance movement, but there were also names of two wealthy Jews who were assisting Pilate so openly for personal profit that they had become notorious as powerful collaborators with the Roman régime.

Those partisans who questioned the cheese-maker about developments in Jerusalem were told that the situation was unchanged. No, there was still no fighting. A brawl or two near the Temple, but nothing of consequence. The questioners turned discontendedly away and left him and Barabbas, sitting away from the rest, talking quietly together, nodding their heads as they agreed about strategy in the city. But interest was aroused again when Barabbas raised his voice to say, 'Our brothers here are ready to march on Jerusalem this very day.'

Their eyes lit up; one or two sprang to their feet, but the cheese-maker shook his head, and, 'Patience, brothers,' said Barabbas. When they scowled he added with a laugh, 'Oh, how you hate that word patience. I know.' His laughter ceased abruptly. His voice fell. 'Comrades! To march on Jerusalem now would be playing the Roman game. Rome would welcome an excuse to use its legions against Judaea. You must understand the cunning methods western people use to extend their power, not only in Judea but anywhere in the world. The first thing these men from the West do is to enter into a solemn treaty with a state. Once they have got their foot in the door, their secret agents do everything to foment unrest, and when disorder comes they intervene on the pretence that Roman honour is involved. But they do not support the governing power. They work against any true government. In the name of justice they help the opposition, which is weak and dependent on Roman arms, to overthrow the government. And when the government has fallen they replace the legitimate rulers with a king of their own creation, as they did in Judaea. They give their puppet the status of an ally. Then they goad him in turn to rebellion. When he does rebel they have the excuse they need. He has broken a sacred treaty. They seize the country and make it a conquered province under a Roman governor. Comrades, if we strike now, before we are strong enough to make the blow decisive, and fail, then Rome can destroy hopes of Jewish freedom for generations. Once again I ask you to remember Judas the Maccabean. Two hundred years ago his sons and partisans came as we have done into this desert. Here they waited; waited until they grew strong enough to descend into the villages and cities. Then they destroyed the Greek idols. They circumcised the children. They restored Jewish faith. And finally they won back from the idolators the Holy City of Jerusalem. They purified the Temple and made it again the House of God. So, brothers, I must repeat that word "patience". We have done much already. We have sown the seeds of unrest against Rome. We have used our daggers to show our secret strength. And all we do is done with the knowledge that our ultimate aim is to gain mastery of our capital Jerusalem. Yes, I know you would march on the city tonight were I to ask you. There is not one of you who would not, if needs be, go alone: just one man and a dagger against the might of Rome. But this is not the moment for heroism, nor for martyrs. Pilate has up to one thousand soldiers ringed around the city.' There were mutterings at this. 'All right, all right,' he said, holding up his hand to stem the interruption. 'I know that we can muster a thousand more. But when we have defeated Pilate's thousand, when we have seized the Antonia, when we have invested the city, we shall have declared war on Rome. Rome will throw in all her forces, from Caesarea, from Antioch, to drive us out. We shall need more than one thousand men then to fight Rome.'

'How many more?' growled someone.

'One hundred thousand,' said Barabbas with calculated softness. 'Yes, one hundred thousand. And it is my plan that some day Pilate himself will let that one hundred thousand enter Jerusalem. He will not even know they are assembling.'

Most of them, waiting for his next words, wore questioning frowns. Though a few nodded, and one of these murmured, 'At Passover.'

'Yes, comrade. At Passover. On the eve of every Passover three hundred thousand men and women of the faith flock into Jerusalem. At the Passover which we await, when we are sure there will be one hundred thousand Zealot daggers under one hundred thousand robes, and not before, we shall be ready to drive the Romans out of the Holy City for ever!'

'At the *next* Passover?'

'The next. Or the next to that. Or the one after. What difference does a year or two make when one is planning for eternity?'

The sun was setting and the chill evening wind was tearing up flurries of sand when the partisans left the camp. They left in groups heading north, west and south. These groups thinned out as ones or twos broke away for their different routes to towns and villages and hamlets of Judaea. When the moon rose and shone down into the wadi its rays fell on slabs and pointed stones that looked like sleeping or squatting men.

Those demonstrators who had been allowed into the courtyard of the palace at Caesarea became aware that one of the Roman officers who had appeared on the balcony was Procurator Pilate. Turning towards him, they knelt down, stretched their hands out and pressed their faces to the paving.

'What are they doing?' exclaimed Nerva. 'Praying to you?'

'Praying is something the Jews have not done to me as yet. No. They are *baring their necks.*'

That submissive posture, Pilate explained, signified that a petitioner was prepared to persist in his petition until it was granted or until he was put to the sword.

'And would they be prepared to die?'

'They would. They are stubborn in their faith.'

'How long have they been now?'

'Five nights. I think they should by now be in a mood of obedience.'

As Pilate said this, guards, marching out of the palace and moving among the prostrate figures, began kicking them to their feet. In the Town Square beyond the entrance gates other soldiers were marshalling the Jews into a rough column to march them out of the Square.

After five nights of rain and cold, the demonstrators were in a sorry state. The oldest had to clutch the arms of younger ones as they hobbled stiff-jointed through the city. Even the youngest looked haggard and hungry. The skies had cleared, but the morning sun was not warm enough to dry the shawls and robes which hung sodden and chill around them. Some of those lying in the courtyard refused to rise even when they were kicked, and clawed the ground in attempts to remain prostrate before Pilate, and had to be peeled from the paving before they could be whipped towards the gateway. Even then they stepped backwards, turning agonised faces to the Procurator and flinging beseeching arms towards him.

'And those,' said Pilate, 'are only passive resisters. You can imagine how dangerous Jewish fanaticism can be when it is armed. We are fortunate that there have been no Zealots in this demonstration. The Zealots are actually greedy for death. They make light of dying any kind of death if it is for their faith. Nor are they deterred by punishment of their relatives or friends or sympathisers..'

'A kind of courage.'

Pilate shook his head. 'No! Stubbornness. So stubborn they are that they get beyond fear, so stubborn in their racialism that they neither recognise nor give obedience to any master who is not of their own race.'

By now the courtyard was empty. The guards had rounded up the last of the Jews, and, fencing them in on both sides with spears, were herding them towards the hippodrome.

Two litters and an escort of palace guards arrived below the balcony. 'Let us go,' said Pilate.

At the race-track the Jews had been pressed into a mass in front of the principal balcony. In the centre of tiers of marble benches and under a fluted cupola was the proconsular box with several ornately carved seats of honour. Two of these chairs had been draped with velvet, and cushions had been laid on their seats.

The Jews clustered together. The soldiers now circled them three deep, their spears pointing towards them, and the officers' swords drawn. In the eyes that stared at them through the gaps between the casques and tops of brass-studded shields the Jews saw no pity. Some of the Jews prayed; the older ones shivered, and a few of those wept; but the younger ones drew themselves upright and tried to outstare the soldiers.

But all the Jews, old and young alike, were so reduced in spirit by the five-day vigil that they had reached despair, finding sad solace only in the thought that if it were true, as some alarmists said it was, that Pilate had given orders for a massacre, death by sword and spear would be quicker and more bearable than by crucifixion, for they could not see along the long curve of the race-track the posts they had feared to see there, nor any crossbars piled in readiness. And if they died protesting against sacrilege they would die as martyrs in a holy cause and such death would be a noble death.

When Pilate and the grim-visaged Ennius Nerva, both wearing armour and high-crested helmets shining brighter than the weak sun, marched to the cushioned seats, the Jews prostrated themselves again. There was a long silence. Piate and Nerva seated themselves. An officer walked towards Pilate carrying a scroll. It was the petition. Pilate took it solemnly and laid it on the marble ledge before him. A scribe and another officer appeared. The scribe handed another scroll which Pilate unrolled slowly. He cast his eyes over it and then stood up.

Before he read the proclamation which announced his decision on the fate of the Jews, he stared over them. Those who lifted slightly their prostrate heads to look at him saw a pale visage, with deep furrows running down on either side of a pouting implacable mouth, and a chin thrust out dictator-style. They waited for the sentence of death.

Pilate read. The preamble was in Greek, which many of them did not understand, though they could recognise the style and titles of Tiberias Caesar and Proconsul Pontius Pilate. After the preamble Pilate paused, then read it again, this time in Aramaic.

The thin voice came clear to them. The Procurator, the voice continued, had taken notice of their petiton and its report that Roman standards had been displayed in the city of Jerusalem. The petitioners had claimed that this was contrary to the treaty existing between Caesar and the Jewish government of Judaea. It was necessary to remind the Jews here gathered in Caesarea, and to remind all Jews throughout the province, that Judaea was a client state within the Roman commonwealth, and therefore all people within its frontiers, of whatever race or creed, be they Jews or Syrians or even citizens of Rome itself, enjoyed equally the benefits of Roman rule and the protection of Roman law. Rome, in her desire to endow Judaea with good government and establish peace and prosperity in the province, has not hesitated to assume the burden of protecting its people from danger at home or abroad, from injustice, from persecution, from corruption and anarchy. The highest-born in the land enjoyed that protection. For instance, it was no longer possible for any Jew to suffer death, as it had been possible in the past, at the whim of a barbaric governor or sectarian priest. By the wisdom of Caesar the power to pronounce sentence of death or agree to capital punishment was now vested in Caesar's Procurator in Judaea. This ultimate authority demonstrated Caesar's overall supremacy in Judaea. To accuse Caesar of error, as the petitioners had done, was to deny Caesar's supremacy. The petitioners had besought the Procurator to act in accordance with the treaty existing between Rome and Judaea. Caesar and his officers always honoured treaties. But not even Rome could honour a treaty unilaterally. A treaty was a bond between two parties. The failure of one of the parties to honour a bond made a bond null and void. The Jews should search their hearts and ask themselves if they had kept faithful to their treaty with Rome. Did they not even now harbour in their midst and give succour to rebels and terrorists who sought by stealth to plunge Judaea once again into the anarchy from which Rome had rescued her? Could the Jews honestly claim to have honoured the treaty? Until they had weeded out from their midst the disobedient and the rebellious, they could not. Rome was not indifferent to the sensibilities of Jews in matters appertaining to their religion. Rome had allowed the Jews freedom to worship their own god in their own way, and Rome recognised that to the Jews certain objects were sacred and certain other things profane. It was so with the Romans. To the simple soldier of Rome and to all those who served in the armies that had liberated the countries of the East from petty tyrants and brought them into the community of nations, the standards borne by those troops were also sacred. In their clamorous protest against the Roman standards, the Jews had failed to consider sentiments as dear to Romans as any superstitions were to Jews. But the greatest error of the petitioners was in the manner in which they had attempted to petition Caesar. They had not petitioned Caesar in a decent and legal manner. Instead they had plunged the city of Jerusalem into disorder. They had marched threateningly in large numbers on Caesarea. Nevertheless, they had not been put down with force. Their peaceful reception in Caesarea was due entirely to the clemency of Rome. Now, in the name of Caesar, the Procurator was moved to extend that clemency even further. The demonstrators were to be allowed to return unharmed to their homes. They were to be allowed to go back to Jerusalem without hindrance or molestation.

The Jews did not stir, except for a few who moved to press their faces even closer to the ground and stretch their hands another agonising inch forward.

'They are not getting up,' whispered Nerva. Pilate shook his head. 'Why not force them to?'

'They have bared their necks,' Pilate murmured. 'They would rather die. They still wait for some declaration about the standards.'

'The Procurator of Judaea further declares,' the thin voice went on dispassionately as though reading something of no moment or interest, 'that the standards as described in the petition will be removed from public display in Jerusalem.' The crowd sighed. It seemed one could actually see that great sigh running like a wave through the prostrate bodies. Heads began to rise. 'The Procurator has decided to make a personal progress to Jerusalem to see this decision put into effect. Petitioners to Caesar, depart in peace. Return to your homes in decent order and be grateful to Caesar for his clemency.'

Pilate rolled the proclamation, handed it and the petition to the officer, then turned quickly away and marched off the balcony. Guards kept the Jews cordoned off until he and Nerva had entered their litters and returned to the palace.

'You should have been a lawyer, Procurator,' said Nerva. 'My uncle would have appreciated your argument and particularly your escape clause: *the standards as described in the petition.*'

Pilate acknowledged the compliment with a self-satisfied nod. If the worst came to the worst, the petitioners' mistake about 'standards bearing the images of Caesar' could be used to gain more time.

Though he hoped that the standards would be down by tomorrow and the heat taken out of the situation by the time the demonstrators got back to Jerusalem. He and Nerva would reach the city tonight. So would Herod. Pilate had told Fabius to order the Tetrarch to hold himself in readiness for audience with the Procurator tomorrow morning.

Pilate and Nerva reached Jerusalem late that night. Near Herod's Gate a strong detachment of the troops from Caesarea was bivouacked. Pilate emerged from his litter. He felt quite relaxed. He had even slept a little during the journey. He chatted with the officer in charge until Fabius and a small escort from the Antonia arrived; then, with Nerva beside him, he rode to the Antonia. Herod, Fabius told him, was to attend service at the Temple in the morning, after which he would be happy to receive Pilate at the palace.

'I must talk to him before he goes back to the palace,' said Pilate. 'Some way to do that must be found. Send Marcellus to me.'

For more than an hour that night Pilate and Marcellus discussed how Herod could be entangled in a *coup* against Paterculus.

Before going to bed, Pilate went up to the battlements of the fortress. The city below, wrapped in darkness, was reassuringly quiet. On the western hill the bulk of the Hasmonaean and its three white towers looked tranquil. Much as he strained his eyes, he could not discern the offending standards below its walls. The peacefulness of the scene seemed a good augury, held promise that tomorrow's grim business would be executed without fuss.

He awoke before dawn. He was dressed and was standing with Marcellus and Fabius on a balcony overlooking the Court of the Gentiles by the time the silver trumpets shrilled and the Temple doors thundered. They saw Herod arriving, a gaudy swaying figure with a retinue of slaves clearing a path for him. The slaves wore coloured ankle-length tunics and their gaudy head-dresses were so bulky that they almost covered their faces.

Marcellus counted the slaves. 'Eight! I could have hoped for more. But eight should suffice, Fabius.'

Fabius nodded. The slave carrying the parasol was a burly Negro. 'Dumb Black could carry the parasol,' suggested Fabius.

'A good idea,' agreed Marcellus.

'But can he use a sword?' asked Pilate.

'He can throw a dagger and pierce a target forty feet away.'

'Forty feet!' said Pilate. 'That could be useful in one of Herod's smaller rooms.'

By the time the service at the Temple had ended, Fabius was standing in the Court of the Gentiles with an escort of seven guards and the Negro. The little group stood out like a rock amid a torrent of Jews which, flowing down the staircase, broke and surged around it. Still gripped by the fever of emotions stirred by prayers and chanting and sacrifice, the more passionate of the Jews saw the presence of guards as an aggravation of the insult their Holy City had suffered at Roman hands. There were shouts and hisses; the bolder Jews raised their fists and spat; but even the fiercest kept wary eyes on the hands that gripped the hilts of swords, and as they stormed angrily past they took care to keep out of swords' reach.

Fabius ignored the clamour with stinging indifference. With his helmet cocked forward and not glancing to right or left, he kept his impassive gaze directed up the staircase at the top of which stone slabs threatened death to the uncircumcised who stepped beyond the balustrade. At last Herod, who had stayed within the Temple until the press of common folk had left, stepped out in regal calm. The eight slaves assembled around him, his Negro servant raising the fringed parasol above his head.

The Tetrarch's eyes had already caught sight of the group of guards. Then, his smile widening expansively when he recognised Fabius, he came grandly down, clasping his hands in a gesture of greeting so extravagant that the bracelets on his forearm clashed.

In phrases of elaborate politeness Fabius conveyed the Procurator's invitation that the Tetrarch should attend him at the Antonia before proceeding to the palace. Herod turned his gaze towards the fortress, his eyes slowly climbing the staircases as though counting each step and each guard. He retained his smile as he said that he had hoped to entertain the Procurator at the palace.

The Procurator, Fabius replied, was looking forward to that entertainment, but wished first to discuss with the Tetrarch a matter of urgent importance. 'Away from the palace,' Fabius added.

'Away from . . . ' Herod began, but then decided that it might be better not to mention the name of Paterculus. He did not know how much Fabius might know, and with these Romans, who kept their secrets insulated in separate packets of their involved chain of command, one could not be too careful.

Pilate appeared at the head of the staircase. He was not in armour; he was wearing only a toga, and when he lifted his hand to beckon Herod he did so in a manner which Herod diagnosed as calm and without threat. Herod mounted the stairway. At the entrance Pilate introduced to him his companion, Ennius Naevius Nerva. 'The nephew of Cocceius Nerva,' added Pilate.

'Indeed!' said Herod blandly. 'Dare I express the hope that your distinguished uncle has sent the Procurator some sound legal advice?' Nerva made no reply.

As Herod was about to step into the entrance hall he gestured to his slaves to wait outside, but, 'No,' said Pilate, 'Let them come in. We shall have need of them.'

'Need?' Herod seemed puzzled, but as Pilate made no further comment, he shrugged and walked with an attitude of indifference into the stony chill of the fortress and through the stony corridors to the pillared audience-chamber.

'Are you also expecting the High Priest, Procurator?' Herod asked.

'Not, I hope, today.'

'I asked because I notice you have drawn the curtains over your Caesars. If that was done for my sake, I must thank you. Though it is not necessary for me. I am not, I am happy to say, disturbed by graven images. Though for that, as you well know, Annas and some others consider me grossly lax.'

'Graven images are what I want to discuss with you now,' said Pilate.

'I guessed so.'

'I suppose you have been informed of the situation which developed here in your absence: dangerous disorder in the city and a demonstration by several hundred Jews in Caesarea?'

'Yes. In that dispatch, Procurator . . . ' He broke off. 'By the way, I have something to tell you. The day after your courier left the dispatch at my secretariat, strange news was received from Magdala. There had been a fire there.' He stole a sideways glance at Pilate to see what the reaction was to the mention of Magdala. There was none. 'The fire was at an inn on the outskirts of the town.' Still no reaction: in fact Pilate seemed impatient for the story to be finished so that he could return to the problem of the standards. 'The innkeeper reported that five travellers arrived and asked for a quiet secluded room. Eventually they chose a loft above the stable where they tethered their mules. During the night the innkeeper heard a brawl in the yard and was alarmed to see the stable surrounded by a considerable number of men. He did not dare to come out until they had made off. Before they did so they had set fire to the stable. They took the mules, of course. The lodgers were moaning in the loft. But they had probably been bound and the trapdoor had been chained on the outside. When the place had burned down there were five corpses. Beyond recognition of course.'

'And you said you were free of Zealots in Galilee!'

'You think it could be Zealots, Pilate? So do I, actually. But the incident is mysterious. The travellers who went in were Jews, or pretended to be. But the corpses that came out had metal adhering to them which indicated that the five who died were soldiers. If they were, then they had been foolhardy pretending to be otherwise. And also impolite to me in passing through my territory in the manner of spies.'

Pilate stared back at him without expression. 'I should advise you to prosecute earnest inquiries in the area,' he said calmly. 'But now let us turn to the more urgent matter which I raised in my dispatch to Tiberias.'

'Yes. In the dispatch which you sent me in Tiberias, Procurator, you seemed to hint that I should do something about it. But . . . ' He shrugged elaborately and spread his ringed hands apart in a gesture of helplessness. 'What could I do about it? Marcus Paterculus was a guest of yours in Judaea.'

'And a guest here of yours, Herod.'

'Indeed. I had invited him to enjoy the hospitality of the palace if and when he returned to Jerusalem. I did not, of course, expect him to return in such strength. Nor to commit the indiscretion which he has committed.'

'Have you reproved him for the indiscretion? The standards are still displayed.'

'Reproved him?' The bejewelled hands spread even wider. 'What could I do about it? Can I command a Roman what to do? I am the ruler of Galilee, not of Judaea. In Jerusalem I am merely a private resident.' He turned to Nerva. 'You, I am sure, will appreciate my legal difficulties there.' Nerva made no reply.

'Marcus Paterculus,' said Pilate, 'has been more than indiscreet. He has been mutinous.'

The smile flooded back to Herod's face. The uncovering of a Roman quarrel gave him mischievous delight. Also he could hope that Pilate would burn his fingers badly this time. 'You have a problem, Procurator,' he lisped. 'But perhaps you are a braver man than I am, and dare take stronger action than any I should dare to take. Perhaps you will not be deterred by the forces which Paterculus represents. I have been oppressed by the knowledge that he enjoys not merely the support of the Court at Antioch but also the patronage of the most powerful man in the empire.'

'The most powerful man in the empire is His August Highness Tiberius Caesar.'

'Of course, of course!' Herod smiled weakly. 'That goes without saying. I meant the most powerful after Caesar. And after all, Caesar is ageing. We must always bear in mind the possible calamity of Caesar's demise.'

'You show your ignorance of Rome, Herod,' said Pilate harshly.

'You make the mistake of thinking that Caesar can die. Tiberius can die, but Caesar does not die.'

Herod bowed smiling acceptance of that point, and did not pursue the argument. This man Pilate would soon see what did happen when Caesar died. Meanwhile he waited for Pilate to come to the point. The little man was bound to ask the Tetrarch to help him out of the present impasse. Herod was determined not to help. Although, of course, he would not refuse his good offices, he had already prepared his tongue for the pitiful phrases with which he would confess his dislike, even fear, of causing offence to Aelius Sejanus, Prefect of Rome. So, his hands meekly clasped at his girdle and his yellow visage moulded into a mask of sorrow, he waited for Pilate's plea.

Instead, 'The offending standards will be lowered this morning,' said Pilate baldly. 'They will then be destroyed. The cohort from Antioch will be ordered to return.'

Herod kept himself steady. The slightest tightening of his hands was the only indication of his surprise. 'You are aware, Procurator, I suppose, that the standards are the standards of Aelius Sejanus.'

'I am.'

'I take it that Paterculus carries them by permission of the prefect. I should think that if you ordered them to be lowered and . . . do I hear you aright? . . . destroyed, you will earn the displeasure of your own powerful patron, Sejanus.'

'Sejanus is dead.'

'Dead!' The serpent's tongue flickered over the black beard as though trying to dampen lips which had suddenly gone dry. 'How?' He glanced fearfully at Nerva.

At last that grim-visaged man spoke. 'Aelius Sejanus was strangled in Rome. As a traitor. By order of His August Highness Tiberius Caesar.'

'The Sejanus conspiracy is ended, Herod.' Pilate's words, full of significance, came like a whiplash. 'Aelius Sejanus and others in Rome and elsewhere who supported him have been executed.'

There was a long silence. At last, 'What now?' Herod sighed.

With barely concealed contempt Pilate said, 'I cannot ask Herod, who reminds me he is ruler only in Galilee, to take any action in Judaea. But I can command that Herod, as no more than a private resident of Jerusalem, does not give succour to the enemies of Caesar. You can demonstrate your loyalty to Caesar by assisting us this morning.' Herod waited for instructions. 'I intend to go to the palace and shall there give necessary orders to Marcus Paterculus.'

Pilate saw the agate eyes darting quickly right and left. The Fox was desperately looking for an escape.

'Would it not be better,' Herod suggested, 'to summon Paterculus here?'

Pilate shook his head. 'Such a summons might encourage him to some act of folly. I wish to avoid any disorder, at the Hasmonaean or in the city.'

'Then,' said Herod, 'I shall go now and make what arrangements I think fit.'

'No, Tetrarch! You will please go to the palace in my company.'

Fabius came in. To Pilate's questioning glance he replied with a satisfied nod. The slaves were ready.

Herod was becoming alarmed. 'But if you march on the Hasmonaean . . .' he began.

'I shall not *march* on the Hasmonaean. I and Ennius Nerva shall go with you as your guests, without any escort.'

'Then what . . . what if Paterculus resists?'

'I do not think he will. The one danger is that his bodyguard might react idiotically. That is why we needed your slaves, or, rather, needed their clothes. I understand from Fabius that the transformation has been effected. Seven of my guards and my Negro body-slave are now wearing those clothes. I am sure neither Paterculus nor any other Roman patrician could distinguish one dark-skinned slave from another, nor will Paterculus see the swords below their gowns. Don't worry, Herod. The men I have chosen have carried out more dangerous exploits than this before without mistake or fuss.'

'No! No!' Herod protested. 'I prefer not to take part in this. I cannot involve myself in plotting of this kind.'

'Do you refuse to help us, Herod?'

'I am afraid I must.'

'Is it in memory of Sejanus that you refuse? I warn you, Herod. If you do not help us now, then it will be known that you are no friend of Caesar's.' Pilate waited until the words had sunk in. Herod's resistance collapsed under the weight of them. 'Let us go,' said Pilate. In the entrance-hall seven slaves in long tunics and coloured head-dresses and a giant Negro with a parasol awaited them.

'Don't worry about your slaves, Herod,' Pilate said amicably as they descended the staircase to the Court of the Gentiles. 'They will be kept safe, though naked, until their clothes come back.'

A posse of guards escorted the party through the crowds around the Temple, but only as far as the bridge. There the guards halted and the party went on unescorted. There were crowds here too. Many of them were visitors to Jerusalem who had flocked there to stare at the disputed standards. They parted sullenly but without resistance to allow Herod and his party to pass through them. Two or three in the crowd recognised the Procurator. His presence confirmed the rumour that had reached the city that the Procurator had declared in Caesarea his intention of removing the standards. Was it true? They would wait and see.

Beyond the crowds were the guards from Antioch, encamped on sloping ground below the palace gardens. Behind them, silhouetted against the retaining wall of the gardens, were the standards of Aelius Sejanus, former Prefect of Rome. As the party entered the palace, news spread through the encampment that the toga-clad figure with Herod was Pontius Pilate, Procurator of Judaea. On hearing the news, the officer in charge of the cohort abandoned his wine and dice and began putting on his armour. He supposed that if Pilate really had arrived, he had to be ready for anything.

'The best place for talking with Paterculus would be the courtyard,' Herod suggested to Pilate. If there was to be trouble, he thought, it would be better for it to happen outside.

'No. Indoors. Where is Paterculus lodged?'

'In the south pavilion.'

'Then there.'

As the party ascended the garden staircases, Pilate saw a solitary figure on the terrace. When they came nearer he said to Nerva, 'There is Paterculus.'

Paterculus was now leaning over the balustrade, watching the group coming up from the garden. After recognising Pilate and seeing him accompanied by only one centurion, he turned away and disappeared from view. When the party reached the terrace he reappeared. Now he was not alone: four of his guards swaggered closely behind him as he strode quickly towards Pilate.

Paterculus was a little surprised but hugely delighted to see the Procurator arrive in this casual social fashion. Since early morning he had been expecting what he had thought inevitable in the circumstances: a summons to the Antonia. That command he would, of course, have had to disobey, for now he had to hold out at the Hasmonaean until he received news from Rome and the promised reinforcements from Antioch. Herod, despite the armour he had piled up in Galilee, had refused to make a move until he had assurance that the prefect had taken over in Rome. However, it appeared that the Tetrarch had done something useful: it seemed that he had talked Pilate over. The Procurator's modest arrival could be seen as a token surrender. By coming with only one officer Pilate showed his reluctance to do battle; by coming at all he showed his weakness.

So Paterculus could afford to be genial, and he smiled grandly down on Pilate. 'I informed the Tetrarch that it would be convenient for me to receive you here, but I had not hoped you would come so soon.'

'There was need to come at once,' said Pilate stiffly.

'I am glad you realised that.' The little man was still trying to retain his petty air of authority. Well, for such time as remained to him, he could be allowed to enjoy the fiction.

Pilate turned to Herod. 'Will you please accommodate us, Herod? A quiet place, for private conversation.'

Herod led the way towards the southern portico. As Pilate and Paterculus followed, the slaves mingled clumsily with the patrician's bodyguard. At that moment Herodias, having heard visitors arriving, appeared in the arcade. Herod quickened his pace. He hurried ahead of the others to reach her before she spoke, for he had seen the question gathering on her lips when she spotted the unfamiliar face of the grinning Negro who carried the parasol. Herod reached her in time to murmur something that stopped her speaking. Pilate could not hear what Herod said, but he could see the look which passed between husband and wife. How often had those eyes met in such glances? So experienced were these two in the arts of conspiracy and betrayal that they could concoct the most devilish plot without speaking a word, their faces alone transmitting all the vocabulary of treachery. After this little interchange, Herodias greeted Pilate with more warmth than she usually accorded him, even laying a hand on his arm as the party moved on towards the south pavilion, and Pilate felt that he could detect in those furtive smiles she cast at Paterculus a stirring excitement, an almost lustful expectancy.

The south pavilion was approached by way of a small courtyard which blazed this morning with an abundance of exotic plants which had been carried from the hot-houses to grace the arched recesses during the day.

'We shall use your reception room, Marcus Paterculus, if that

271

pleases you,' lisped Herod.

'Most convenient,' said Paterculus.

Pilate looked into the room. It was spacious, but not too vast for anyone to reach any part of it with a skilfully thrown dagger. 'Yes, thank you, Herod. Quite convenient,' he said and stepped indoors, Herodias, still smirking, on his arm.

Herodias looked somewhat bewildered when the slaves also bustled in. Even the Negro came in, though he did have the sense to leave the unnecessary parasol outside. However, when the slaves showed reason for their presence by drawing couches towards the sunlight and piling cushions, she paid no further attention to them, and settled herself on an elaborate stool. She sat erect, a pose to which she was regally entitled and which, she felt, concealed the sagging age of her withered frame, and let her wide sleeves fall so that their fringes, reaching to her painted nails, covered too-sinewy hands. Her hair, too much of it and too lustrously black to be all her own, was built up from her whitened brow in a tall cylinder intricately interwoven with ribbons on which tiny exquisitely wrought butterflies held their enamelled and gem-dusted wings quiveringly poised for flight. Her other jewellery was simple; six or eight gold amulets, two of them serpents with emerald eyes, and a necklace of plain minute links of gold, so long that it wound at least thirty times around her neck, thus forming a collar which hid most of her drooping muscles. Her eyebrows had been shaved; her eyelashes were heavy with kohl; and her yellow skin was coated with a mask of white which she took care not to crack by over-animated smiles. How amazing it was, Pilate always thought, that Herod could be so besotted with this painted hag that to consummate his union with her he had divorced his first wife, daughter of Aretas, even though he knew that by so doing he would earn that Arabian king's undying enmity. There had not even been need, by Asian custom, for Herod to divorce the daughter of Aretas. He could have married Herodias as well. But Herodias, who would hate any rival, had obviously insisted cn that divorce. How could such a woman so enslave a man? In manner and, it seemed, in some of her promiscuous habits she was a kind of Asian version of Sextia. But Herodias was evil, which Sextia never could be, and ungenerous, which Sextia never was.

Seeing Pilate looking at her so intently, Herodias peeped coquettishly at him. 'We had expected you later in the day, Procurator,' she said. 'But you will, I hope, stay to dine with us.'

'That, your majesty, I am unfortunately unable to do today,' said Pilate and glanced impatiently at Herod. The Tetrarch took the hint and, bowing to his escort and offering her his arm, said, 'We must leave our guests to discuss state affairs.'

'Well, please let us see you soon, Procurator,' said Herodias. She rose regally, neatly kicking aside her long gown, a movement which gave a glimpse of jewelled slippers with thick cork soles to give her height, and walked out, resting painted fingernails on the brocade of her husband's sleeve, the false buttocks of padded kid beneath her gown swaying like shifting heaps of sand. One slave followed close behind.

Paterculus chose a couch away from sunlight and sat down. 'Now, Pilate, what have you to tell me?'

'I prefer to speak to you alone,' said Pilate, looking pointedly at the bodyguard.

Paterculus's lips curled. 'I know your opinion of my soldiers, Pilate,' he said and then looked, equally pointedly, at Pilate's attendant centurion, letting his bleak gaze rest on armour and sword.

'Leave us, please,' Pilate said to Nerva. Nerva drew a folded document from under his breastplate and handed it to Pilate. Paterculus had time to notice that it was heavily sealed. Nerva turned to leave them, but did not move away until Paterculus, with an off-hand gesture, had dismissed his bodyguard. When the men tramped out Nerva followed them. So also, in some haste, did six of the remaining slaves. The only slave now left in the room was the Negro, but now he padded into the courtyard, retrieved the parasol and walked off, but only into an arcade where, out of sight of the occupants of the room, he was still within earshot.

As soon as they were alone, Pilate laid the document on the table near Paterculus and, resting his hands on it, looked down at the patrician. 'You were, I imagine, expecting news from Aelius Sejanus?'

If this approach did cause Paterculus any surprise, he restrained himself from showing it. 'Naturally I am in constant communication with the Prefect.'

'You will receive no further communications from him. He is dead.'

Paterculus was jerked from his languid posture. He sat up suddenly. 'Who told you that?'

'Caesar! At Caesarea I received a dispatch from Tiberius

Caesar. It announced the execution of the former Prefect Aelius Sejanus. He was executed. For treason. As were others involved in his conspiracy.'

For the first time Pilate saw the grey eyes looking up at him instead of slanting down at him over the bridge of a tilted nose. Those eyes were still blank, but not now with indifference. They were blank with shock. Pilate also saw the patrician's hand sweep to his sword. Ignoring this, he broke the seal and unfolded the warrant and read it through silently. The accusation against Marcus Gaius Paterculus had been written by lawyer Cocceius Nerva at Capri. The Senate in Rome had found it proved, and the signature of Tiberius had approved sentence of death by strangulation.

While Pilate was reading, Paterculus stood up. He leaned over the table and, resting his weight on his left hand and keeping his right hand on his sword-hilt, tried to see what was written on the document. Pilate looked up from his reading.

'The correct procedure,' he said quietly, 'would be for this communication from Capri to be read aloud to you at the ceremony it demands. However, I accord you the favour of reading it for yourself.'

He twisted the document around on the table. Paterculus read it without touching it. Inch by inch, as his eyes coursed down from preamble to signature, his head drooped, so that eventually the principal features presented to Pilate were the crown of a bowed head, the fair curls scrupulously brushed, and a hand clasping and unclasping on the sword-hilt.

The room seemed suddenly deathly silent. Then, from somewhere in the distance, from far along a corridor or from behind closed doors, came the faint sound of clashing metal, some muffled noises that could have been oaths or gasps, and then, once again, silence.

Paterculus's head, still bowed, switched surreptitiously left and right as he stole swift glances to the two doors. Then, at each doorway, a slave appeared. Both carried swords. On one sword there was blood. The Negro, his filed teeth opened in a great tongueless grin, sauntered in from the courtyard. He also carried a sword.

Paterculus closed his eyes and breathed deeply several times. The last breath was a heavy sigh. He withdrew his hand from the table and stood quiveringly erect. His handsome lips curved in a sneer, and, lifting his nose high, he directed his grey gaze on each

274

occupant of the room in turn: first at the two soldiers tricked out in the falsity of Herod's livery, then at the Negro, and finally at Pilate, linking the four of them in one aristocratic gaze of contempt and fury.

Pilate retrieved the document and neatly folded it. 'To rid your mind of any thoughts of violent resistance, Marcus Paterculus, I should inform you that by now your bodyguards are under restraint.' He looked towards the bloodied sword. 'Except perhaps those who were foolish enough to resist arrest. As for the cohort from Antioch, the officer in charge of them will have now seen documents explaining your present situation, and my order that the force must strike camp and leave the province of Judaea as soon as practicable.'

By now Paterculus had command of his lips. 'I demand, Procurator, as a Roman citizen, the dignity, the privilege, of being allowed, before my arrest, of writing a will expressing my last wishes and making testamentary provision for my family.'

'You *demand*?' said Pilate. He smiled. 'I admire your choice of words. But, yes, I grant your *request*.'

'I can do it more composedly when I am not overlooked. Can I be alone, Procurator?'

Pilate stared down at the folded document for some moments before he replied. Then, looking deep into Paterculus's eyes, he said, 'Yes. You can be alone.'

'Thank you, Pilate!' Paterculus spoke with sudden warmth. 'It is the only favour I have ever asked of you. It is the greatest I have ever had granted.'

'These three,' said Pilate, indicating the impostor slaves, 'will accompany you to your room and guard the door. Listen,' he said to the three, 'guard the door of the room, but it will be closed to allow Marcus Gaius Paterculus to prepare himself undisturbed. Allow him fifteen minutes.'

'A further request, Pilate. I should be pleased, should it be possible, for you to send through any channels petitions which will ensure the welfare of my wife, my son, and my daughter.'

'I shall see what I can do.'

'Thank you. Goodbye Pilate. I hope you will find the works of Marcus Pollio useful.' He laughed lightly, and swung away, but suddenly halted and, facing Pilate again, added venomously, 'And please express to the Tetrarch Herod Antipas my regrets that I am unable to thank him for his hospitality in person or condole with him on the sudden death of his adored friend the Prefect Sejanus.'

'Goodbye, Marcus Paterculus.'

Paterculus marched stiffly out of the room, the two soldiers and the Negro walking close behind him, wary eyes on the sword which swung at his hip.

Pilate sat down. He opened the folded document and read it again. How magnificently worded, as befitted a warrant for the execution of a patrician of such a family! Would a death-warrant for Pontius Pilate, Procurator of Judaea, read quite so grandly as that? Perhaps: if it were written by lawyer Cocceius Nerva or, for that matter, by Nerva's nephew.

A few minutes later Nerva and Fabius hurried in. They halted with astonishment when they saw Pilate alone.

'Where is he?' asked Nerva, and for a moment the fierce face looked alarmed.

'In his room,' said Pilate mildly.

'Alone?'

'Yes. But the door is guarded. He is writing his will.'

Nerva looked at the table, at the couch where Paterculus had sat, and then under both. 'His sword?'

'He has it with him.'

'But . . . He will . . .'

'Yes,' said Pilate. 'He will. It is better that way.'

'The warrant,' said the lawyer's nephew in a lawyer's voice, 'specified strangulation. In public.'

'Which in Jerusalem, or anywhere else in Judaea, would have been unwise to the point of idiocy. I think even your uncle would agree on that. The Jews would have been convinced that he had been executed for raising the standards. That would have established a dangerous precedent. In any case, the exercise of getting Paterculus out of this palace as a prisoner could have been hazardous to public order.'

Nerva was striding about irritatedly when the soldiers rushed in. While standing guard they had heard what sounded like a violent struggle in the room. On opening the door they had found Paterculus twitching in his death throes. He had fallen on his sword.

'Ah, well,' said Nerva. 'What's done, is done.'

'And well done. It will be salutary to leave Herod Antipas the job of cleaning up messes made by his guests.' Pilate handed the warrant to Nerva. 'You can make the necessary marks on it. And don't be worried. If you examine the warrant closely you will notice that the word strangulation is encircled by a faint ink-line. The line is rather wavering, as though someone was a little dubious about that form of death. The ink is the same as that used by Caesar for the signing. I take it that Caesar was himself doubtful about the manner of executing a Paterculus.'

'Or thought the Procurator of Judaea might choose crucifixion.'

'Oh dear! So you also have feelings about that!' moaned Pilate in mimic distress, and then, with a bite in his voice, added, 'That was something to which Marcus Paterculus strongly objected. And see what has happened to *him*.' He rose. 'Let us go. I do not think that today we shall be accorded the pleasure of taking leave of the Tetrarch. The Fox will have gone to earth.'

But they did see Herodias. As they were walking from the south pavilion they glimpsed her tottering jerkily along, her skirt held high as she hastened, panting and hungry, to feast her eyes on the corpse of her handsome Roman guest, and too expectant of that sight to notice them.

As Pilate and Nerva walked down through the gardens, Fabius and an escort were entering the palace to collect the soldiers and their prisoners. At the gateway the officer from Antioch greeted Pilate obsequiously and informed him that the troops were packing and foddering the beasts, and within two hours would set off back to Antioch.

Nearby, an escort awaited Pilate. As he crossed the bridge and walked uphill towards the Antonia fortress, surrounded by loyal guards, he felt, this short figure swathed in the nobly traditional folds of a Roman toga, like the Divine Julius walking victoriously up the Capitoline Hill in the sunlight of a Roman morning.

'Nerva,' he said. 'Paterculus besought me to do what I could on behalf of his wife, son, and daughter. They are, I have been told, three singularly beautiful people.'

'They were executed,' Nerva replied. 'Eight days ago. In Cyprus. I halted there on my way here. They, of course, were strangled.' He looked keenly to see how Pilate took this news and then continued, 'Paterculus should have known that the hand of Caesar reaches everywhere. Those who reach high office give their families as hostages to Caesar.'

Pilate reached Caesarea in time to see Sextia before she sailed. He gave her a message for his son. Julius was to leave Athens. He was not to wait to finish his studies there. He was ordered to come home to Caesarea at once.

'Why this sudden change?' asked Sextia.

Julius, Pilate explained off-handedly, had in recent letters expressed his regret that he would not be in Caesarea for the Games. As the Caesarea Games took place only every four years and the boy was so keen on sport, it did seem a pity that he should miss them this time. But not merely because some of the finest wrestlers and other athletes in the world would be coming: several highly distinguished Romans were also expected to attend. Julius could help in some capacity in the preparation for the event, and would thus learn a little about administrative procedure and at the same time meet important personages in an official capacity. Pilate knew Sextia did not believe a word of it, but her nod of agreement assured him that this was the explanation she would retail to others.

VIII

Rumours from Sebaste, first of a riot in that city and then of the sack of the villa of Josephus the Cohen, trickled into Caesarea by the usual route for rumours: the grape-vine of carriers and tradesmen who every day collected local produce and also loads of local gossip from the farms and gardens of Samaria and the Plain of Sharon. The result was that at first only the Jews in Caesarea and the Jewish slaves in the palace heard the story and they, arguing its rights and wrongs in fearful whispers, kept it to themselves.

So Pilate, for whom this period was one of returning confidence in the future, did not hear the news. He had again removed himself from day-to-day administration, and worked contentedly day-long in his study, around the walls of which architect Lucius had fastened plans of projected routes for aqueducts across the landscape of Judaea. Pilate's confidence was buttressed by comments, muted comments but mildly approving, which he had received from Italy, not, it was true, from Caesar himself, but from a most influential politician – from none other than Publius Vitellius who, since the fall of Sejanus, was, it seemed, stepping ever higher in Caesar's regard. To this Vitellius, Caesar had delegated the task of replying to Pilate's memorandum. The reply was somewhat disappointing by being lamentably brief and thus lacking Pilate's literary eloquence. Nevertheless, it did commend the Procurator on his concern for developing the natural resources of Judaea. 'Such development,' said Vitellius, 'could convince Jews of not only the amenities but also the profits coincident with the Roman way of life.'

The only fly in the balm of this soothing communication was the last paragraph. This informed Pilate, somewhat pompously, that Tiberius, graciously honouring Vitellius's wide experience in Asian affairs, was sending him on a tour of Asia as Caesar's personal plenipotentiary. Pilate sighed. There would be a powerful favourite of Tiberius breathing down his neck, watching every move he made. However, the fact that Vitellius so candidly proclaimed the terms on which he was coming did suggest that it was unlikely that he was coming with an imperial demand to question or even remove from office a Procurator appointed by the disgraced Sejanus. And the postscript to Vitellius's letter, so casual, took Pilate into his confidence in a manner quite reassuring. Vitellius had scribbled this postscript in his own hand, as though it were an afterthought. He would prefer, Vitellius said, to begin his tour of Asia at Caesarea rather than at Antioch, for no other purpose than that he looked forward to attending the Games, for, as it happened, he had at the moment a more than usual interest in athletics: a young protégé of his was a promising wrestler.

So the name of Publius Vitellius must go high on, if not at the top of, the list of the very important persons being invited to the Games. Julius was now drawing up that list.

The boy had been installed in an office of his own in the secretariat. There, assisted by a young scribe recommended by Polygnotus, he was learning administrative procedure, flexing his young talents on preliminary arrangements for the great event. That office would soon need to be vastly extended, and many more clerks recruited. No effort must be spared to make these Games memorable. Credit would always go to Herod for being the first to institute the Caesarea Games in honour of Augustus, so it was all the more desirable that on the forthcoming occasion Pilate should be seen as responsible for making them more than usually spectacular, even grander than those other Games regularly staged by Herod in Jerusalem. By doing this, Pilate would not only glorify the Roman presence in Judaea but also increase his own prestige throughout the commonwealth. To this end, now that he was confident of financial backing from Josephus, he had earmarked a considerable proportion of this year's tax receipts to meet the cost of lavish entertainment at the Games and of tempting prizes. Proclamations were being prepared to advertise the Games throughout the Roman world, so that the harmony of all peoples under Roman rule would be demonstrated in the friendly multi-racial competition of commonwealth Games. The prizes had of course to be lavish enough to lure to Judaea the world's star wrestlers, boxers, runners, discus-throwers and charioteers, as well as musicians, but also the glory of the Games had to be proclaimed loudly enough to make victory at them seem to the athletes even more important than the gold they could win.

Julius, responding with delight to his father's trust, had bent himself with a will to the preparatory work, and by his charm and enthusiasm had won the hearts of all members of the household who came in contact with him. Even the Jewish architect, that dour and conscientious worker, had stolen time from his drawing and planning of Jerusalem aqueducts to make sketches of the auditoriums at the amphitheatre and hippodrome and theatre. On these sketches Julius was plotting, with inks of different colour, the seating of spectators according to precedence of importance and rank.

Pilate had first delegated this holiday task to Julius merely to keep the boy occupied until a decision could be made about his further studies. Until it was certain that there was no likelihood of another political convulsion, Pilate had thought it best to keep his son within sight. But now, as he saw how happily Julius had adapted himself at Caesarea, Pilate was thinking the boy might stay on in Judaea. The young tutor whom Sextia had bought in Alexandria could be brought to Caesarea, and with Sextia's financial aid other scholastic talent could be bought.

Pilate was struck by how much Julius had grown during the eighteen months he had been away. The infant smoothness portrayed in the statue had almost gone, as also had the awkward shyness of a young boy. His body, like his voice, was rougher. In so short a time now he would be a man. In fact, in the eyes of the Young Barber, who without invitation or command had attached himself to Julius as devoted body-slave, Julius already was a man. The Young Barber came dancing into Pilate's room one morning with the proof. He carried it in a little cedar-wood casket, which, after disposing his bowl and implements on Pilate's table, he solemnly showed to the Procurator who lay stretched in his chair for shaving.

'Look!' whispered Ephir.

He opened the casket. On the lining of the white fabric was a tiny heap of what to Pilate looked like dust. He pulled himself up and leaned forward to peer more closely into the box.

'What is it?' Though even as he asked he was beginning to know.

'Julius's whiskers!' said Ephir and let out a whoop of joy. 'His first whiskers. Julius is a man!'

'Did he pay you for shaving him?'

'No!' The boy laughed. 'I do not charge Julius anything.' Then his face went suddenly grave. Solemnly again, he placed the casket centrally on the table. 'You will put it in your temple, no?'

Pilate laughed. He was, if anything, indifferent to puberty rites, feeling that such remnants of primitive and barbaric superstitions had no place in modern and enlightened society, although, as he well knew, there were many Roman families who, when a son was shaved for the first time, invested the occasion with solemn ceremony and carefully collected and enshrined the first sprouts of the boy's manhood.

Suddenly he smiled and jumped up. 'Come on, Ephir! Bring Julius's beard with you. I'll show you where to put it.'

Walking into his bedroom ahead of the boy, he unlatched the door of the cupboard and flung it open. He heard Ephir gasp. Turning round, he saw the boy backing away, the casket clasped to his breast. Shock and joy mingled tormentingly in Ephir's enormous eyes: shock at the sight of a graven image so appallingly faithful to the god-created original, joy at this confirmation of the startling beauty of the young master he had claimed as his own. Pilate pointed to a space below that pillar against which the statue leaned. 'Put it there, Ephir.' Timidly the boy stole forward, keeping his eyes bent to avoid the statue's too human gaze, and gently laid the casket in the place indicated. But then, unable to restrain himself, he lifted his face to gaze at the statue.

'Julius!' he sighed. 'In marble! Beautiful!' He reached out.

Pilate was touched when he saw the lean brown hand caress the carved waves of hair in the same way as he himself so often did. He closed the doors, and then ran his hand roughly under the Young Barber's chin. 'And when shall we have hair from that?'

The boy shook his head fiercely. 'Never!' he said, pouting stubbornly. 'I am an Edomite.'

'So you will grow a beard?'

'Yes.' The boy laughed. 'And will not cut it until I trip over it.'

'Well, come now. Back to work and shave off my whiskers. They are, unfortunately, not my first.'

To Claudia also Julius's presence in Caesarea was a constant pleasure. Out of love of his company she had invited him to join her Hebrew lessons. This, thought Pilate, was good for the boy, for he felt sure that Julius was now mature and level-headed enough not to pay too much attention to the somewhat rarefied views of Jews and their religion which Claudia had learned from her Magdala slave. By now Claudia had quite a family to look after. When Severus returned she had immediately taken a motherly interest in his baby son. She declared that the nurse Severus had brought from Lugano was completely unsuitable. Poor Severus, she surmised, had been duped into buying someone's cast-off. The girl, Claudia said, was full-bosomed, broadbottomed and certainly healthy, but coarse and vulgar in the worst Celtic manner, and ignorant and raucous-voiced into the bargain. Claudia bored Pilate for some days with these complaints, but then solved the problem in her own way. She married the nurse off to a Gaulish mercenary whose fancy for a girl from Lugano was stimulated by the gold Claudia offered along with her. Then she handed the baby to the woman from Magdala. 'Two baby boys are happier together than separate,' she said.

'You are,' Pilate said with a tolerant smile, 'encouraging fraternisation between Roman and Jew at an early age,' and left it at that.

Pilate found it good to have Severus back, although at present the young man was still in the woefully sentimental mood of a young father with his first son. Twice he had reported late for duty, wiping baby kisses from his mouth. But Severus was a loyal and obedient fellow, easier to work with than Fabius. Severus did what was asked of him readily without that questioning attitude, that suggestion of knowing better, which one had to admit, Fabius was inclined to betray. It had to be admitted that Fabius was the type who could be relied upon to act with superb *élan* in an emergency, but when there was no crisis he drooped with boredom. In fact, it was with the intention of giving this restive soul the feeling of having something to do that Pilate, on the day after Severus returned, called Fabius in and told him, 'I've been thinking that after what happened in Jerusalem recently we need someone there of quick wits. Not that I fear another *invasion* from Antioch, but, the Jews being what they are, I do feel the need for someone in Jerusalem who can be relied upon to take appropriate action in emergency.' When he paused, Fabius began suggesting names of likely officers. 'No, no!' Pilate interrupted. 'It needs someone of higher rank. I know there is only a cohort stationed at the Antonia, but the importance of the command should not be judged on that. It is a key position, militarily and, in some measure, politically. So I am sending you.'

'Yes, sir,' said Fabius and marched out without comment; though just before he left for Jerusalem he told Pilate that he had written to his father telling him that he felt he had now learned about as much as he could in Judaea and asking him to get him preferment in some more active theatre of operations where he would have more possibilities of advancement.

Each morning, after his session of audiences, Pilate spent an hour or so with Claudia before hurrying happily to a aqueduct-lined study, though sometimes when he left her he took time to walk along the balcony overlooking his courtyard and admire the way the garden had developed. The plants and flowers around the base of the fountain into which Poseidon poured glittering water already looked as though they had been there for years. The furthest end of the garden, however, the part where shrubs had not yet been planted, was trodden bare, and Julius had annexed this retreat to use as a make-shift palaestra.

One morning Pilate saw him there with Ephir. Julius was teaching the Young Barber some wrestling tumbles, trying patiently to impress the little savage with the need for disciplined grasp and throw instead of wild flurries of useless struggling. The two bodies, one golden fair and the other bronze, Julius naked but the Edomite in a gaudy loin-cloth, and both gleaming with sweat, circled in attack and defence. Pilate laughed when, for about the sixth time, the Edomite, too excited and too impatient to await the tactical moment, flung himself violently at Julius and was caught expertly, twisted into helplessness and flung on his back, letting out yells of mock rage and simulated agony.

'Julius! Time's up! Back to work!'

Julius looked up when he heard his father's voice. He protested in dumb show at the interruption in the game, but only for a moment, and then reached for his robe, and as Pilate walked out of the sunlight to his room and desk the two lads were racing each other towards the baths. What inexhaustible energy they had! The holiday did seem to be doing Julius good. He would give the boy a few more weeks away from his books, apart of course from his daily session with the *Commentaries*, and then send to Alexandria for the tutor. Yes, he would keep Julius here. He was finding the joy of having his son beside him.

All this domestic tranquillity was shattered by the atrocious news from Sebaste.

It was from the Young Barber that Pilate heard the first hint of trouble. During shaving sessions the boy always chattered, barber-fashion and most times scurrilously, and Pilate, soothed by the caressive fingers and his mind on other things, rarely listened. But this evening the name Josephus got through to him. In the face of Pilate's vehement questions the boy's tongue faltered, and his information was revealed as merely scraps of half-understood gossip. Pilate pushed him aside and summoned Severus.

Severus shook his head dumbly. The contentment on his face suggested he had just come from the nursery. No, he had heard nothing.

'Find out immediately what is known. Use Polygnotus if you still need an interpreter.'

During the next hour Severus reported back with different stories. They added up to a conflicting muddle of gossip, but everything indicated that there had been a nasty incident in Sebaste. Pilate ordered the immediate dispatch of a courier to Sebaste. 'But,' he added emphatically, 'he must make inquiries at the villa and in the city without contacting the governor.' For in the hour of inquiries Pilate had become increasingly disquieted by the fact that the governor of Sebaste had not thought fit to send a report of the event to Caesarea. During a restless night while he awaited news from Sebaste he began formulating plans for the action he would take if that news was as bad as he was beginning to fear it might be. It was. Before the dawn Pilate was aroused from uneasy sleep by the announcement that the courier had returned.

'The villa was attacked by Zealots,' said the courier. 'It is utterly destroyed. Some of it was still smouldering when I saw it. What would not burn, statues and things, they smashed. There is blood everywhere, and wine.'

'And Josephus?'

'No one knows for certain. Some of the household escaped on horses. They were seen heading south, to Jerusalem, it is thought.

Some slaves, and all the women, were carried off. Those who put up a fight were butchered.'

Pilate summoned Severus. By the time Severus appeared, Dumb Black was laying on Pilate's armour. Pilate gave orders in a flat lifeless voice. 'We are going to Sebaste. We shall need an escort of . . . How many Romans would you say there are at the barracks at Sebaste?'

'Six or seven. Certainly no more than eight, including the captain of the guard.'

'And auxiliaries?'

'A cohort. Probably under strength.'

'We shall take a large escort, Severus. A cohort. Men with campaign records, with full armour and baggage for an expedition. They are not to be told where we are going. And, yes, in case hospitality is not offered me in Sebaste, my tent. See to that, Dumb Black.' The Negro hurried out. 'The plan is, Severus, for us to reach Sebaste before anyone knows our intention. I do not want any Zealot slipping out of Caesarea with the news. So have the cohort marshalled and marched out quietly to a rendezvous outside Caesarea. You and I will meet them there. I shall leave the palace as quietly as possible. No formal leave-takings. Act with the utmost dispatch, Severus. Send Polygnotus to me.'

Dumb Black was packing pens and ink and Pompey's lamp in the travelling-desk when a young scribe hurried in with tablets, papyrus and stylus. Polygnotus was ill. He had been vomiting all night and was now in some kind of coma.

'Has he been drinking?'

'Oh no, sir. He is very ill.' The young man put on a sad expression. 'And very old.'

'Yes, indeed. A short note: my compliments to the Lady Claudia. My regrets that I must leave early without seeing her. But I am going to . . . ' He looked speculatively at the young man who was now writing industriously, and, after thinking it over, said. 'No! Leave it at that. Draw that up and let me have it quickly.'

'It is already written, sir.'

Pilate took the sheet of papyrus which the scribe handed to him. 'So it is.' The lad worked more quickly than Polygnotus: he had made shorthand scribbles on the tablets, but while Pilate was cogitating he had already written the message in clear script on papyrus. 'Good! Have that delivered to the Lady Claudia's apartments. But, no. A moment. My seal.' Pilate pointed to the chest.

While Dumb Black and the scribe brought seal and wax and lit the lamp, he added a secret message. 'I am going to Sebaste, but in the absence of Polygnotus I send that information under seal. Keep my destination secret, even from Julius, until late today.' He sealed the letter himself and impressed it with his signet. 'Rouse the Young Barber and send him here,' he told the scribe as he handed the letter to him.

Despite the hour, Ephir came dancing in as gaily as ever, but halted with surprise when he saw Pilate already dressed and in armour.

'Where do you think I am going, Ephir?'

The boy cast another glance over the armour. 'To Sebaste?'

'Yes. I thought you would guess that.' He studied the situation for a moment. He trusted the boy, yet what barber could hold his tongue? 'And you are going with us, Ephir,' he said suddenly.

'And Julius?' the boy asked happily.

'No, not Julius.'

The boy's face fell. 'But who will shave him?'

'With luck we shall be away for only a couple of days. I don't imagine Julius will grow a beard in that time.' Severus came in to report that the auxiliaries were leaving in groups for the rendez-vous. 'Good! And take this young imp to his quarters. See he packs what he needs without him chattering to the slaves.'

Fifteen minutes later Pilate and Severus went down to the courtyard where Ephir and Dumb Black were waiting with the Procurator's personal escort. The six soldiers were all men well known to Pilate; the standard-bearer was that same Palestinian who had so proudly carried the Procurator's standard on the day Pilate rode to Sebaste to see Josephus. Pilate mounted. The party moved off through streets still wrapped in the hushed half-hour before sunrise, and the few drovers coming into town for the morning market stared at them without curiosity. Beside the Jerusalem road the cohort of troops was waiting in an orchard. They fell in behind the escort.

Pilate rode in silence. He did not assume his usual all-conquering posture. Oppressed with anger against the terrorists who had harassed Josephus, and even fiercer anger against the governor who had not even thought it necessary to send news of the event, he rode with his head bent, his face muffled against the chill wind.

Not until they reached the foothills at the limits of the Plain of Sharon did Pilate call a halt. At a farm he ate dates and bread and drank water from the well. The escort seemed to be infected by his silence, munching and drinking wine without their customary chatter, all the time stealing questioning glances at the Procurator's impassive profile. All of them apparently realised that something unusual, probably nasty, was afoot.

When they reached Sebaste the cohort were halted just outside the principal gate to the town and within sight of the barracks. Pilate rode straight to the villa. The outer walls looked very much as he had seen them when he had last visited Josephus. They were singularly unscarred, which made the scene of desolation and destruction behind them all the more terrible. Throughout all the garden ribbons of char showed where swathes of straw had been spread to carry fire to every part of the villa. The roof of the library had caved in when the beams of carved and gilded cedar had burned through. Scorched remnants of scrolls, from which the gold and ivory covers had been torn off as loot, were all that remained of the fabulous books. Pilate walked through the private garden. The trees, except for a few leaves shrivelled by the blaze, had survived, but when he passed through the smoke-smeared arcade to the terrace, that once loveliest retreat in all Palestine, he saw that those magically long marble steps had been deliberately fractured. The urns that had been used for that vandalism were lying smashed, earth and trampled roses spread around. On patches of paving not covered by char, rusty blotches could be seen. It might be wine, as the courier had said, for there was a vast litter of smashed amphorae, though some of it could be blood. The supports of the fountain had been smashed, the bowl of the pool cracked open. The bronze lion was too sturdy to have suffered: it lay, grimacing, foolishly, on its back. Something squelched under Pilate's foot. It was the corpse, now stinking, of a carp below dried mud. He walked along blackened arcades to the recess where he had lunched with Josephus. The stench of burned rugs came out of rooms into which he avoided looking. The table was smashed into three jagged wedges of rosy marble. Sunlight glinted on half a crystal goblet.

'To the barracks, Severus. Have a message sent ahead that I am calling on the governor.'

He was mounting the three devastated steps when he heard voices in the distance. He turned and, looking beyond the wreck of balustrading and tumbled urns and withering flowers, saw some soldiers coming down a hillside towards the woodland path which skirted the retaining walls of the villa, to reach a minor gateway into the town. Before they went out of sight he saw they were carrying a cross with a corpse still on it.

With Severus and the escort ranged around him, Pilate waited in the town gateway until the soldiers with their burden came into sight. They were shouting to each other. Some, excited by having found what they had been searching for during nearly three days, were laughing. When they saw the Procurator and escort they fell silent.

Naked and bloodied though he was, Josephus looked strangely undead. When the soldiers lifted the cross and held it erect, his white head drooped down in that familiar way, and his eyes, still open, peered under white eyebrows as though he were about to crack a joke.

Above the white hair a legend had been nailed to the cross. 'A Roman death for a friend of Rome!' The murderers had had the gall to write that in Latin.

Severus saw the Procurator's gesture of anger and revulsion, and translated its meaning exactly. 'Lay it down, you men,' he barked. 'And cover the corpse decently for proper burial.'

Pilate stepped towards Josephus. With head bowed he murmured a prayer in Aramaic. He hoped he remembered the words aright. Even if he had not, no doubt that one god of the Jews would accept a Roman's supplication that the soul of Josephus would rest in peace.

The governor, all smiles and swaggering pride, and faultlessly turned out in polished helmet and armour, was awaiting Pilate at the entrance to the barracks.

'I heard you were coming, Procurator,' he said grandly.

Pilate frowned. 'How?'

'From the Jews.' In the reply was a hint that he resented having got the news by the grape-vine rather than by a courier. 'Two soldiers in the market heard a drover saying that the Procurator was on his way to Sebaste.'

Pilate suppressed his annoyance at this leak. It was disturbing. Investigation would have to be made at the secretariat. Security must be tightened up. 'So you know why I am here?' The man looked blank. 'I have come to inquire in person what has happened at the house of Josephus the Cohen. How was it allowed to happen?'

'How?' The governor shrugged extravagantly. 'How indeed?

289

It's one of those things. How does one keep one Jew from another's throat?' He grinned, but at last he became conscious of the cold enmity and censure in Pilate's eyes. He set his features in a wooden stare. His voice dropped. 'I can tell you about it at dinner.'

'I prefer to eat alone this evening. But you will make your report to me at once. Is there somewhere we can be alone?'

Frowning and with less swagger the governor led the way to his room.

'Severus,' said Pilate, 'you will stay with us.' He turned to the governor. 'We shall need a scribe too.' And when the man looked blank at this request he added, 'Such an incident as this must be properly recorded.'

The governor, his frown and puzzlement even deeper, went himself for the scribe and came back with an elderly Greek, a little man in a tunic so creased that he had obviously just been sleeping in it. Crouching on a stool in the shadow of the burly governor he looked cowed and nervous, like a dog regularly whipped, but he had quick intelligent eyes and he could, Pilate noticed when he had dictated titles, place and date, write swiftly and easily. The governor, not having been invited to sit, stood stiffly in front of the desk. It was perhaps better, Pilate judged, to put him more at ease. 'Take a seat, Governor. And you too, Severus. Now I want a summary of the facts.'

The governor sank on to a chair, putting his helmet on the floor beside him. He leaned forward, resting his leather-bound forearms on his knees, breathing heavily and his face congested. 'Still full of wine,' thought Pilate and then asked, 'Now what happened?'

'I knew nothing about it until it was reported that the villa was in flames.'

'What did you do?'

'There were a lot of people milling about the streets and around the gate of the villa. I had them dispersed and sent to their homes. Then I instructed a corporal to take a squad and investigate at the villa.'

'You did not go yourself?'

'No.'

'What time was this?'

'During the night. In the early hours.'

'Then you were in bed?'

'As a matter of fact, no. I was in the mess.'

'On duty?'

'Well, yes. In a way.'

'What does that mean?'

'On duty and . . . entertaining. An officer, he was once a comrade of mine here – he's now at the imperial legate's court – was visiting Sebaste. It was his last evening with us and we had sat up late discussing reports and such things.'

'Alone?'

'No. He had expressed the wish to meet some of the local people, people he knew when he was stationed here.'

'Greeks, or Jews?'

'Oh, no Jews! Greeks. And an Egyptian.'

'People of importance?'

'Not exactly important. But useful.'

'Who, for instance?'

'Well . . . With respect, Your Excellency, does this matter?'

'I have no idea. I am merely trying to get some idea of the occasion. I am trying to understand what prevented you from immediately making personal investigation. I presume your company must have comprised persons of singular importance and your entertaining involved discussions of matters also of importance to detain you from going to the scene of an incident of quite obvious gravity.'

'Grave, yes, I agree. Worse than I thought at the time. It's a pity about the house.'

'A pity about Josephus, too.'

'The old Cohen. Yes, that's also a pity, I suppose.'

'Only *suppose*?'

'Well, he was an old man, and after all he was a bit of a problem.' He stopped, waiting for the next question.

'Continue, Governor.'

' . . . A problem. I mean he wasn't popular in Sebaste. In fact, a lot of people resented him being here at all.'

'Did you resent it?'

The governor lifted his big red hands and flung them wide. 'I'd no feeling in the matter at all, one way or the other. To me he was just a rich old Jew whom I'd seen no more than a couple of times.'

'One of those times was when he came some months ago to tell you he had been threatened by Zealot terrorists, was it not?'

'Yes.'

'Did you provide protection for him and the house?'

291

'When I got your orders to do that, I did it. After a week or so things quietened down and I withdrew the guards. I'm short-handed here. I did advise him, however, that it might be better for all concerned if he went to live in a less lonely spot. And among his own folk. He had a house in Jerusalem.'

'But he did not take your advice?'

'No. He was stubborn. Like the rest of them. And . . .'

'And?'

'Rich. He was so rich that he thought he could do just as he liked. That was what people resented.'

'What people?'

'Zealots might resent it, I suppose. But even people around here talked against him. Yes, even in Sebaste.'

'Like your visitors on the night of the fire?' The man looked blank, puffing his lips. 'I mean, did your visitors of that night talk against Josephus?'

'I don't recollect the Cohen being mentioned. Not until the fire. When the news came everyone rushed out to watch. One or two of the women were alarmed. They were screaming. I had to calm them.'

'Women! So you had women guests too?'

'Friends of my colleague. Yes.'

'Who were they?' The man puffed out his lips again. His face went redder. 'Street women?'

'Oh no! No. Quite respectable girls. Two of them were daughter's of a local tax-collector's widow.'

'Were the two respectable girls the ones who screamed?'

'No. Or perhaps they were. I couldn't say. We were all rather confused.'

'So I can imagine,' said Pilate with a grimace. Then, after a moment's thought, he asked, 'Were those who screamed screaming in fear? Or distress?'

'No. Or . . . I couldn't say. They were probably frightened. They might have thought it was a Zealot attack on the town. There was that mob building up in the street.'

'So you called the guard to control the tumult.'

'Yes, sir,' said the governor with a sigh of relief.

'But did not write a report of the event.'

'I instructed the captain of the guard to enter it in the log.'

'I mean a report to me.'

'I didn't want to worry you, Procurator. Not with such a matter. After all, it was only a local incident.'

'A very valuable property is destroyed by fire. Its owner is carried off, and is now found to have been crucified. His servants are slaughtered. Is that your opinion of a *local incident*?'

'I mean by "local" an incident between *Jews*, sir! That's how I see it. I know these people. I've had experience with them for years: in Syria, when I was attached to the legate's guard, and for seven years here in Sebaste. I've handled situations like this for a long time.'

Pilate sensed the hint, the near-threat, in that little speech. The governor had been appointed before Pilate's time, and not by the preceding Procurator but by the personal favour of the Imperial Legate of all Syria.

To the governor, Pilate's silence now indicated that the stuffy little man had taken the hint and was at last seeing the thing in its proper perspective. Pressing his advantage, he went on, 'With respect, Your Excellency, I suggest you might ask other people about this event. You would find their opinion the same as mine.'

'I am more interested in your opinion. What is it?'

'Well, I should say that the Cohen rather asked for what he got. It was stupid his staying here. So rich. And an outsider.'

'How do you mean: *outsider*?'

'Well, for one thing he wasn't even a Samaritan. Judaeans aren't very welcome in Samaria. Jews who do not need to come here avoid this place as much as possible. Though he wasn't any longer a real Jew. At least, some Jews said that about him. I guess they mean he wasn't very orthodox. That might have been why he left Jerusalem. Yes, the Cohen had lots of enemies on both sides of the fence. And, as I've said, he was so rich.'

'Yes, you have said he was rich, Governor. The fact seems to annoy you.'

'I mean he did flaunt it. Ask them in Sebaste.'

'I think we can confine our questions to ourselves and to this headquarters, Governor. There is no need to spread our difficulties throughout the town. Is your colleague, the officer who was visiting you, still here?'

'No, sir. He decided not to stay the rest of the night. He left immediately.'

'Dictate his name to the scribe,' said Pilate, but the scribe had written it before the governor spoke. 'Thank you. Now, Governor, I should like a word with the captain of the guard.'

The captain of the guard was less of an ox of a man. He was a lean, nervous type.

'It was you who reported the fire to the governor, Captain?'

'Yes, sir.'

'You can sit. When did you first see the fire?'

'One of the sentries said he had noticed a glow in that direction. I went up on to the battlements and saw a flame or two . . . '

'A moment! Do I understand that at that moment it seemed like a small fire? Only a flame or two?'

'Yes, sir. At first that's all it was.'

'But I understand from the governor that when it was reported to him *all* the villa was aflame. Quite a big conflagration.'

'Yes, that would be so. It spread quickly, I imagine. And . . . well, it took me some time to get to the governor's house.'

'And some time to gain his attention, I suppose?' Pilate waited. The captain shifted uneasily. 'Of course, he was entertaining. It would take some time for him to disengage himself from his guests.'

'Yes, that would be it, sir.'

'Was he dressed?' Pilate waited. 'I mean was he clothed by the time you were admitted to the dining-room?'

'Oh, yes, sir. Everyone was.'

'And what did he do?'

'He . . . He instructed me to have soldiers clear the street because there was a mob of people bawling outside. While I was superintending this, I sent a corporal and a squad to the villa.'

'To give assistance?'

'Well, to investigate first.'

'Along with a fire-brigade I suppose? With fire buckets etcetera?'

'No, sir. Not at first. The governor said the men must first investigate.'

'Of course,' said Pilate. His savage sarcasm set the man trembling. 'To go and stare at flames for a while and then come back and report what everyone could see: that there was a fire.' He resumed his level questioning tone. 'Did they do that?'

'Yes, sir.'

'Did they report anything else?'

'They had heard screams in the gardens of the villa. They saw some men dropping over the wall and running down the ravine.'

'Did they follow them?'

'No, sir. They were Jews.'

Pilate turned to the scribe. 'Insert a note. Not only omitted to . . . Not only failed to afford protection and render assistance, but, in grave dereliction of duty, did not pursue malefactors and bring them to justice.' He looked back at the captain. 'Do you understand what I have just dictated?' The man nodded, but not very comprehendingly. 'Meanwhile,' went on Pilate, 'what was the governor doing?'

'He was on the balcony, sir. With his guests.'

'I asked what was he *doing*?'

'Er, nothing, sir.'

'Nothing?'

'Well, he was watching the fire.'

'Did he speak?'

'No, sir.'

'Do you mean he stood there staring at the fire speechless. Was he drunk?'

'Oh no, sir.'

'But did he give no orders at all?'

'No. Well, he had already given me some orders. He had ordered the street to be cleared and a squad sent to the villa.'

'Were those the only orders he gave to you?'

'Yes, sir.'

'And he gave those orders to you immediately you reported the fire?' The captain nodded. 'Were those orders the first words he said when you reported the fire?'

'Yes, sir,' said the man hesitantly.

'What I am wanting to know, Captain, is what were his *first* words when you went in to him.'

'Those orders, sir,' said the man even more hesitantly.

Pilate analysed that hesitation. He stared penetratingly at the man and, choosing the very moment when the soldier flinched under his stare, said sternly, 'I do not think you are telling me either a true story or a full story, Captain. I can question others who were present, and, if needs be, I can use means to make those others answer me fully. Have no doubt that by piecing their answers together I can get the full story. It would be regrettable, and it would be unpleasant for you, if their story was not fully in accordance with yours. I give you now your opportunity to tell me what were the *first* words Governor Laecus said when you eventually broke into his midnight party and told him that a fire had begun at the villa of Josephus the Cohen. Go on. What you say is to me alone. Should this scribe repeat it he will lose the tongue he uses to do so.'

The man shifted in his chair, dodging the Procurator's stare by bending his head, but then lifted it again, cleared his throat, and, 'The governor said, sir . . . The governor said, "Old Josephus has put on a light for us. Let's continue our dice on the balcony".'

Pilate closed his eyes. He shuddered. He stood up suddenly and turned his face away from captain and scribe. His lids were wet.

'You can go, Captain,' he said. Then, his face still turned away, he asked 'A moment, Captain. Have you thought over this incident since it happened.'

'A little, sir,' said the soldier uncertainly.

'And what is your opinion of it.'

'Well, I've no real opinion, sir. Only, that . . . Well, the old man seemed to ask for it.'

'Did you ever meet Josephus the Cohen, Captain?'

'Oh, no sir.'

'That will be all.'

When the captain had gone Pilate swung around. 'Scribe, you will write that out verbatim. Severus, see that the scribe works under guard.' He looked down at the desk. 'Paper? Pens? Yes. Severus, have my seal and wax brought to me. And then leave me alone for one hour.'

In exactly one hour Severus presented himself. On the desk was a rolled document, sealed. Pilate handed it to Severus.

'Take this, Severus. Keep it sealed until you make the arrest. Meanwhile, have a room chosen for me as far as possible from the governor's. Have a light supper sent to me there – something cold that I may eat later, if I can. You will wait until the governor is alone. If he already has sentries mounted now, wait until that guard is changed. Then replace them with men from Caesarea. Should the captain of the guard or any officer object to this, say that it is done on my orders and that any resistance will be met with force. When *your* sentries are mounted, serve this warrant on the governor. Have sufficient men at hand to quell any disturbance, for I wish it all done quietly and as expeditiously as possible. Take four men with you when you go in to the governor. Read the warrant. Have his armour and helmet removed from the room. Leave him his sword. If within an hour he has not honourably dispatched himself, have him taken out and beheaded in some quiet spot.'

'And the captain of the guard, sir?'

'He is only a fool. It is the governor who is the rogue. What happens tonight may teach that captain a lesson. But, should he interfere, you will have to kill him. In a case of armed resistance no warrant is necessary. Is that all clear, Severus?'

'Yes, sir.'

'I rely on you implicitly, Severus. A dirty job. But such must be done to avoid dirtier. Come to my room when it is all over. I shall not be sleeping.'

Until an escort came to conduct him to the room where a bed had been prepared for him, Pilate sat silent and alone. He saw a white head bowed, eyes full of wise mischief peering under bent brows. And he kept his eyes resolutely turned away from the balcony where Romans and their whores had played dice while an old Jew had been dragged from his blazing home and crucified.

It was after midnight. Pilate, lying wrapped in his cloak on a cot, heard outside his door a sentry challenging and heard Severus reply.

'Come in, Severus. How did it go?'

'He would not use his sword. We beheaded him.'

'And the captain?'

'He did resist. He is dead.'

'As I said: the captain was foolish. But had not thought quite as foolish as that. Do the barracks know what has happened to their governor?'

'Yes. They have taken the news calmly. Some even seemed pleased.'

'Pleased? In that case take statements from those who were pleased. Comments from such could be useful. Good night, Severus.'

'Shall we be leaving for Caesarea early, sir?'

'No. I am not returning to Caesarea immediately. I shall tell you later. Thank you, Severus.'

When Severus had gone, Pilate lay staring up into the dark. He hoped Severus had taken that hint and would know what kind of statements might satisfy Antioch that the governor had deserved summary execution. In Antioch the events in distant Sebaste would be seen as primarily a Zealot outrage. People there would ask how it was that a flare-up of Jewish terrorism could result in the execution of a Roman governor, for that bully's failure to protect one wealthy Jew would not be seen in Antioch as a particularly heinous crime. Therefore the report must boldly allege that the governor had, by his indifference to the fate of that Jew, revealed himself as still sympathetic to the anti-Semitic policies of the disgraced Sejanus. Yes, that was one way to approach it. Even so there was the fear that people would say that the Procurator was being soft on Jews. He must prove he was not.

Above all it was essential that the report to Antioch must be phrased in such a way as to throw a smoke-screen over the truth that Pilate had been moved partly by personal anger. To himself he confessed that anger. Although he cherished the opinion that no man in high office should ever allow personal passion to over-ride impartiality, he did not regret what he had done. The horror which had convulsed him when he saw the crucified body of Josephus still raged within him. Even so, amid the sorrows and angers of that memory, more mundane thoughts were taking shape. As the shock ebbed he saw more clearly the loss he had suffered. The death of the banker at this crucial moment meant the drying up of powerful aid for his beloved project. No mention of even that reverse, however, must leak into the dispatch to Antioch. The Governor's failure to pursue marauding Zealots was what must be made the most of, and, in case that did not seem sufficient justification for a death-penalty, the indictment must be buttressed by such evidence of dereliction of duty in the past that discontented soldiers could recall.

Meanwhile Pilate must demonstrate that he was determined to stamp out Jewish terrorism; so fiercely determined that he would even execute a Roman governor, not for allowing a Jew to be assassinated but for showing himself incapable of resisting Zealots, and furthermore launch a full-scale drive against the partisans. That operation must begin immediately, and with sufficient severity to show the Procurator's determination to stem rebellion at its source.

As for the question of finance for the aqueducts? He had now made up his mind. Annas would have to pay up. The way he would be forced to do so would shock him.

He turned over and closed his eyes. He hoped to sleep, but did not.

Before dawn he summoned Severus to the bedroom. 'You will base yourself on Sebaste,' he said. 'You will take temporary command of the barracks. Additional troops will be sent from Caesarea to reinforce the cohort here. Later I shall send Marcellus to assist you. In the meantime I want the presence of Rome to be seen, and felt, in every village and valley. Go in strength. Any Zealots run to earth must be jailed to await interrogation, trial and crucifixion. Villagers believed to have housed them or given them succour will be held on suspicion. Their houses will be searched. If arms are found, or any objects that could be used as arms, the houses will be destroyed. Understand? Good! I shall put these orders in writing before I leave this morning. I am going to Jerusalem. You will send reports on progress to me at the Antonia and to the secretariat in Caesarea. Incidentally, report to Marcellus that news that I had left Caesarea got here ahead of me. You investigate that leak here. Two soldiers in the barracks heard it from a drover in the market. They might be able to identify the man.'

Pilate sent many messages to Caesarea that midday. One was a dispatch from Pilate ordering a force of five hundred troops to arrive at Herod's Gate in Jerusalem in four day's time. Another was a demand that the architect must bring immediately to Jerusalem completed plans and final estimates for the first aqueduct. Another was to Marcellus asking him to make all haste to Jerusalem to meet the Procurator there. Severus managed to insert into the bundle a letter humbly requesting Lady Claudia to let him know if his son had recovered from the gripe.

A dispatch was also sent to Jerusalem to inform Captain Fabius that the Procurator was on his way, would enter at Herod's Gate and proceed to the Antonia in full state. Soldiers should be posted along the route through the city and clear the streets for the cavalcade. The High Priest Caiaphas was to be informed of the Procurator's impending arrival and invited to an audience at the Antonia tomorrow.

On the well-built road Pilate's litter did not sway overmuch, and he managed to doze for an hour or so. Fabius, his grand-father's vine-embossed baton in hand and his helmet tilted lower than ever over his eyes, was awaiting Pilate at Herod's Gate with a grandly caparisoned horse, stalwart and lusty but trained to docility for ceremonial processions. Dumb Black unwrapped the Procurator's armour and gave a last breath and a rub to it as he fastened it on. Pilate, with Fabius and two escorting officers ahead, rode into the city. The sight of soldiers being stationed along the route had attracted a large crowd. Soldiers, laying their spears horizontally, pressed the spectators back into the narrow streets off the processional route. Those who moved too slowly out of the way, as well as the scampering excited children who tried to slip under the spears, were hurried off the street by the threat of raised clubs or, if necessary, not too severe blows.

The sun was setting, so that those who gazed up at Pilate saw him against the light and had to lift their arms and shield their eyes to see the Procurator's visage. All they saw was an upraised chin, jutting fiercely forward, a pouting mouth drawn down at the corners, and eyes staring implacably ahead from the shadow of the glittering high-crested helmet. Behind the Procurator rode more officers in armour; behind them, in iron casques and leather jerkins, marched Palestinian auxiliaries who had come from the Antonia fortress to accompany the cavalcade. At the tail of the procession came Pilate's litter, followed by a baggage-waggon stacked with chests on the top of which lolled a fat Negro, and, balancing precariously upright, a long-haired Edomite slave boy.

There were no shouts or insulting gestures. Indeed, Pilate sensed nothing more than the excited curiosity any crowd would evince at a procession which added some distraction to their day in town Only at one point in the whole progress did he see any open expression of hostility. This was when the cavalcade was slowing to a halt at the base of the steps leading to the Court of the Gentiles. At that moment Pilate, relaxed from his rigid posture, was looking casually around, and his eye was caught by two persons in the front rank of a group held back by the spears. Of these two persons it was the man who first attracted Pilate's notice. He was a tall, dark-visaged Jew with a black beard and fierce eyes. He was probably a desert type, one accustomed to carrying all his wealth on his person, for the hand which clutched his robe under his chin was studded with flamboyant rings. His other hand rested on the shoulder of a boy whose hood had fallen back far enough to show a wealth of hair. The hair was as glossy and wavy as the Young Barber's. The boy's eyes were also like Ephir's: big and black under smooth brows. But this boy's eyes were not glowing, as Ephir's did, with love and admiration, but with a hatred that burned like a madness. When he saw Pilate's eyes on him, the boy, as though by some reflex which he could not control, spat towards him. At this the man pulled him violently back into the crowd, saying sharply something that could have been a rebuke for the petty display of irrational hostility.

Pilate sighed, dismounted and walked up between a file of guards to the fortress. The little incident had disturbed him. It was sad to see hatred, so without cause, in one so young. It proved how the Jewish young were suckled on racialism. How many more years would it take to woo these stubborn Jews from their frantic superstitions?

Fabius, who scented in this heavy military arrival the promise of action, was openly delighted to see Pilate. Dutifully he forced his features into lines of sympathy when Pilate told him of the death of the old Jew at Sebaste; then brightened up when he heard that massive reinforcements were coming from Caesarea and that he was to be put in command.

Caiaphas had sent a Levite with a message accepting the Procurator's invitation to the Antonia the following morning. He was, he said, 'free on that day from sacred offices at the Temple'. After thus emphasising that the Procurator was fortunate in finding the chief priest disposed to visit him, he managed to phrase the acceptance of the invitation in such a manner as to suggest that although he, Chief Priest Caiaphas, was coming to the fortress it was he who was granting the audience.

'And he made a request, sir,' added Fabius, trying not to smile too broadly. 'He asked that his "cousin-in-God" the High Priest Annas might accompany him.'

'Of course.' Pilate shrugged contemptuously. 'We shall need the financier father-in-law, for I have come here for money. I hope it may be given willingly. If not . . . ' His face settled into stubborn lines. He strode out on to the balcony. 'If not, then I shall take it by force. The troops from Caesarea will be here in three days. I intend to keep the city quiet with a show of strength.'

As he said this, he was looking down into the Court of the Gentiles. Gleaming pale in the dusk were the staircases leading up to the great doors of the Temple, now formidably closed against the night. But Pilate was seeing another scene: a table dappled with sunlight that filtered through leaves; wine like rubies being poured from a two-handled decanter of Phoenician glass; eyes peering at him under white brows as Josephus, who had guessed the dangerous thought in Pilate's mind, expressed with the slightest pouting of his lips disapproving warning. Well, Josephus, the moment you feared has arrived after all!

Marcellus reached the Antonia during the night. He was told that the Procurator had asked to be roused as soon as he arrived and he had waited only moments in the study when Pilate came in, wrapping a fur robe around him. He told Marcellus of the death

301

of Josephus. Marcellus shrugged. The murder, the shrug said, was a typical Zealot deed. He was more taken aback by news of the governor's execution. He looked at Pilate keenly, questioningly, like one looking at someone he had not known sufficiently before.

'As a result of the events at Sebaste,' said Pilate, 'I have decided to allow you to put into effect your plans for intensifying secret operations against terrorism. I have left Severus in charge temporarily at Sebaste to make search-and-destroy forays in the area. More important, I have asked Fabius to form and train detachments exclusively concerned with assaults on terrorist hide-outs. All prisoners taken during those operations will in future be handed over to you. Interrogation of them will, I hope, uncover valuable information of guerrilla activity.'

'I should prefer the opportunity to form a corps of my own and track down some prisoners myself. My methods might be less gentlemanly but should be more productive than anything Fabius does.'

Pilate frowned dubiously, but then, 'After Sebaste,' he said grimly, 'I shall not be over-nice about the methods used. I have told Fabius that you will discuss with him ways of tracking down terrorists.'

Marcellus stood up and paced about for a moment or two. Then, holding his left hand to his breast and pressing the gauntlet heavily over it, he faced Pilate. 'I am prepared to give Fabius a little advice. But I am not prepared to give him much. I can use men of my own choosing better than he can.'

'How can you be sure of that?'

'Let me prove it. I can do it only in my own way, without Fabius or any other officer knowing what I am doing or why I am doing it.'

'That is asking a great deal.'

'I am asking it for the sake of security. I dare claim, Pontius, that had I had such powers earlier Josephus might be alive today.' Pilate winced. 'If Fabius and the army know what I am doing, half the effectiveness of my operations is lost. I am prepared to report only results. How I get them I need tell no one.'

'Not even me?'

Marcellus directed his leaning gaze on Pilate. 'Not even you, Procurator.'

Pilate accepted the challenge. 'Right, Marcellus. But I do expect results.'

'You will have them.'

A few hours later Pilate awaited Caiaphas and Annas in the pillared audience-chamber. He sat in his high chair on the dais. He wore a toga, but the two guards flanking the dais were in full armour. Immediately in front of him was a long table at which sat two scribes detailed to make a full record of the proceedings. Facing Pilate beyond this table were two chairs with tassels and ample seats of gilded leather.

Fabius came in from the balcony to announce that two litters and a group of Levites were crossing the bridge. On hearing this, one of the scribes jumped up hastily and began drawing drapery across the graven images of Augustus Caesar. 'Leave them uncovered!' said Pilate curtly. The scribe scuttled back to his bench and made a face at his companion.

Pilate pulled himself higher in his chair, grasping the carved acanthus leaves which formed its ornamental but uncomfortable arms, and fixed his eyes on the distant doorway when he heard the tramp of guards escorting Chief Priest Caiaphas with stamping ceremony along the echoing corridors. Caiaphas and Annas, attended by six Levites, entered. Caiaphas, his stubby fingers holding beard over stomach, waddled across the vast expanse of paving. A few modest paces behind him strode Annas. For a moment he directed a glowering stare at the Caesars, then averted his eyes and shrugged distaste.

'Pray be seated,' Pilate said, without rising from his chair but bowing slightly.

Annas murmured formal greetings in an undertone; Caiaphas's lips mimed.

Pilate acknowledged the greetings with a brief 'Thank you', and then, 'You will know that I have come from Sebaste?' Caiaphas stroked his beard and turned his pop eyes on his father-in-law; Annas inclined his head. 'And you will no doubt have heard the lamentable news from that city?'

Annas nodded. 'Yes. We heard of the death of Josephus the Cohen.'

'I hope you also heard,' said Pilate emphatically, 'of the execution of the Roman officer whose negligence, if not responsible for the outrage itself, was responsible for the Zealot perpetrators of it going free?'

Again Annas nodded. 'Though I could not help speculating, Procurator, whether any Roman would have suffered similarly if the victim of the Zealots had been a poorer and more humble Jew.

However, I venture to hope that the execution may indicate a change of heart on the part of the Roman administration. Can it be that it is beginning to be more conscientious in protecting Jewish lives and Jewish property than it was during the Sejanus régime?' But, when he saw Pilate bracing himself for a retort, he went on hurriedly, 'We are, of course, conscious that you must feel denuded of a powerful friend by the death of Josephus. For our part we pray that before he died our departed brother saw the error of his ways and made his peace with God for his many omissions in faith.'

'Such expressions might have been used by the governor of Sebaste himself,' said Pilate hotly. 'It seems that you share that brute's opinion of Josephus, for neither did he consider Josephus a good Jew. He might have thought his murder could go unpunished. For that mistake he paid with his life.'

'Other Jews have perished in Judaea,' said Anna, sighing heavily. 'Not always have the Romans who murdered them been punished.'

'I remind you that Josephus died at the hands of Jews.'

'That he died at the hands of Jews is sadly so,' said Annas unctuously. 'But in the final accounting between a Jew and his God the instrument by which the man perished is not of prime importance.'

'Do I understand then that you condone the crime?'

Annas shook his head sombrely. 'But as a believer I must accept death as God's will.'

'Do you see Zealots as the agents of God's will?'

'Zealots are men of violence, and we deplore their deeds. But it must be admitted that the fanaticism they display is the result, a deplorable one but an inevitable one, of Roman excesses in our country. The manner in which they put Josephus to death demonstrates that. Did they not crucify him, as Romans have crucified other Jews?'

'The Romans crucify only lawbreakers.'

'Jews.'

'Lawbreakers is the word I used. Jews whom we have crucified were not put to death because they were Jews: they died because they were found guilty of treason and terrorism. Roman policy is not infected with the racial prejudice to which, I am sorry to say, you people are, because of their religion, notoriously prone.'

'I would agree, Procurator, that Jews are proud of their race. They are also more observant of the commandments of their one true God than Gentiles are of the commandments of their many false ones. But the angers which you see only as manifestations of racial prejudice do not spring from anti-Roman prejudice, but from the mistakes your administration has made in Judaea. During recent years Romans have shown themselves more racialist than Jews by glorifying what they call the Roman way of life and attempting to impose that alien culture on our people. And when Jews have refused to surrender their racial identity, they have suffered the anti-Semitic excesses and repressions which characterised the policy of your former patron. But, Procurator, I hope that soon you may satisfy those hopes which the Sanhedrin is now encouraged to entertain following the disgrace and death of Sejanus. We know that you were appointed governor of Judaea by the notorious anti-Semite, but we hope you were not specially chosen by him because you shared his vicious opinions. We await reassurance that Roman policy in Judaea is now to be cleansed of racialist oppression. Failing that reassurance, we of the Sanhedrin have decided to petition Caesar for a change in policy.'

It was an ultimatum, and in delivering it Anna smiled. Pilate recognised the smile of victory. Annas was convinced that Pilate's teeth had been pulled by the downfall of his patron. From now on the procurator would either have to placate the Jews or be himself smudged out along with all other remnants of Sejanus's political mistakes.

'You repeatedly refer to Sejanus: you over-rate his importance,' said Pilate icily. 'The policy I have pursued in Judaea was not dictated by Aelius Sejanus, it was dictated by Caesar. And by my conscience. The Sanhedrin must not make the error of thinking that the execution of a traitor has changed the world. That event has neither diluted my power nor diverted my intentions.' He turned to Caiaphas. 'High Priest Joseph! It was I, Pontius Pilate, who on my appointment as Procurator confirmed you in your office as high priest. I did so because I prefer to see continuity of responsibility. I should regret to break that continuity. But if it were necessary, regret would not make me hesitate.' Caiaphas made no reply to that. Pilate addressed Annas again. 'You are right in remarking that the death of Josephus has deprived me of a powerful friend. His loss will also also affect you. You are aware that I hoped for valuable financial assistance from him. As that assistance is now not available, the assistance that I shall require from the Sanhedrin is correspondingly increased.' Annas gestured to one of the Levites. The man tripped to his side and handed over scrolls. Annas laid them on his lap and waited for Pilate's next words. 'I see that you have thought fit to bring the plans and estimates which I presented to you at Herod's palace. I wish to hear the decision your Temple bankers have reached.'

Annas cleared his throat. 'I regret, Procurator, that in the present disturbed political situation . . .'

'The political situation is not disturbed,' Pilate interrupted sharply.

Annas spread his hands in his begging-bowl posture. 'We see it as so,' he said in a mild tone of helplessness. 'Or, if not disturbed, at least uncertain,' he added and shook his head in a gesture intended to show compassion for the uncertain tenure of office enjoyed by a Roman procurator. 'Therefore, we have decided that for the time being it would not be representing the best interests of the people of Judaea to invest in what is fundamentally a Roman project.' He gestured to the Levite again. It must have been a pre-arranged signal, for, without a word of command being uttered, the man lifted the scrolls from the high priest's lap and solemnly placed them on the table. The whole process was symbolic of the plans being discarded by the Sanhedrin.

Pilate did not hurry his reply. He savoured the pause, seeing Annas's look of inquiry growing more intense and Caiaphas's eyes protruding further. 'Then,' he said with a sigh. 'I must change my plans. I must look elsewhere.'

Annas clasped his hands. Victory had come more easily than he had dared to hope; the Sejanus débâcle had taken more iron out of Pilate than he had expected. Pilate's next words made him less sanguine.

'So be it! As the Temple bankers refuse to loan funds to me despite my offer of a higher rate of interest than they receive from Asian traders, then I must resort to other means.'

'Taxes?' Annas shook his head vigorously. 'I must warn you against increasing taxes. It is already rumoured that a quarter of this year's taxes are to be used to finance the Roman Games in Caesarea. That event, the Procurator must know, is at best offensive to the sensibilities of devout Jews. To increase taxes in the climate engendered by that impost is asking for trouble.'

'Not taxes,' said Pilate mildly. 'I have decided to put to good use a vast sum of money that is lying idle in Judaea. That money is in the possession of your son-in-law, the Chief Priest of Caiaphas. I refer to that Temple treasure which you call the Corban.'

306

Annas leaped to his feet, quivering but speechless. The Levites broke into shocked whispers. Even Caiaphas spoke. 'The Corban!' he moaned, and in an extravagance of emotion he clutched his beard.

Annas was still trying to find words. At last he found them, but he choked on them. 'Impossible! Sacrilege! Blasphemy!' he gasped and had to draw a deep breath before he could speak again. 'You must understand, Pilate, that the Corban is not a negotiable part of the Temple's wealth. The Corban is a sacred treasure. Untouchable. It is built up of the votive offerings which Jews surrender to God. Once given, such offerings are beyond man's disposition. They can be used only in the service of God.'

Pilate leaned back and smiled savagely. 'The Corban is the pence Jews have paid to wash away the sins they have committed or the sins they wished to commit. It can be well spent to provide God's gift of water.'

'Beware, Procurator!' boomed Annas. 'If you touch that treasure, you violate the sanctuary of God. Such an act will bring Judaea thundering about your ears. Not only Judaea, but Galilee will also rise against you. I warn you.' He turned to Caiaphas. 'Chief Priest, with your gracious permission, we shall take our leave.'

'No, Annas. Not just yet. Before you go I must tell you that the plans for the Jerusalem aqueduct have been finalised, and work on it is to begin immediately. I have already drawn up the necessary instruments ordering the annexation of the Temple treasure.'

'You would rob the House of God, Procurator Pilate, to build an aqueduct? You would commit sacrilege to fill your Roman baths?'

'And fill Jewish baths also, I should hope. Yes, Annas, I would rather govern clean Jews than crucify dirty ones. Pray be seated, Annas.' Annas, either from weakness or shock, did sit down. Pilate again pulled himself erect on his high chair, thrust out his chin and stared down at him. 'Understand this, High Priest Annas. I am resolved on this course. Therefore, it is for you to decide whether the Corban gold will be transferred decently and peacefully or taken by force.'

Annas waved his hands violently. 'Dare you threaten to trespass into the House of God? Such an act will let loose bloody rebellion.'

'Only if you will it, Annas. And if that should happen, I shall hold you, and the Chief Priest Caiaphas, and all the Sanhedrin responsible.'

'We shall appeal to Caesar. We shall *protest* to Caesar.'

Pilate stood up, flung a hem of his toga over his shoulder and stood with one hand clasped to his breast. 'In Judaea I represent Caesar. I have declared my will. I give you forty-eight hours to devise the means by which the transfer can be made without disturbing religious susceptibilities. You have forty-eight hours in which to convince the Sanhedrin that this can be done. You can remind them that "on the third day God gathered the waters under heaven unto one place", and tell them that Pontius Pilate, Procurator of Judaea, is to bring God's blessed gift into God's Holy City. Your Levites can use that same forty-eight hours in counting gold. Our audience is ended.'

He swung away and walked quickly down the steps towards the door leading to his study, and Annas, leaping up and rushing after him to make further protest, found his way barred by Roman breastplates, shields and spears. With a gesture of disgust against this contact he drew back and with long strides that flapped his long black robe around his ankles marched the length of the audience-chamber and out of the distant door. Caiaphas levered himself heavily to his feet and, surrounded by sympathetically whispering Levites, followed at a slower pace.

Late that afternoon messages in the name of the High Priest Caiaphas were sent to the sons of Annas and to two other members of the Sanhedrin summoning them to an urgent conference at the house of High Priest Annas. It was to be a secret meeting. No scribes or Levites were to attend. Not until Annas's 'Inner Cabinet' had been briefed could the matter be brought before a meeting of the full Sanhedrin: political strategy was too delicate to be tossed about in public debate.

Dusk was shadowing the streets of the city before two of those Levites who had attended the Antonia conference were able to slip away from the Temple unnoticed. Swathed in mantles which completely covered their Temple raiment they made their way to the Valley of the Cheesemakers and hung about near one of the booths until they saw the portly owner come down from his house to collect the morning's takings. They caught his eye. He nodded. The two Levites slipped past traders and customers and followed him to the upper landing. There one of the Levites gabbled out an account of what had happened. The cheesemaker's face quivered with excitement. As he listened, he darted glances towards a door leading to the inner apartments of his house.

'So it has come to this: Procurator Pilate is threatening sacrilege,' said the Levite fervently when he came to the end of his story.

The other Levite, who had not said a word, shrugged, and it was to him that the cheesemaker turned to ask, 'What is Annas going to do?'

Again the Levite shrugged. 'That is obvious. Why has he not summoned a full meeting of the Sanhedrin? Because at this moment he is priming his creatures with arguments to convince the Sanhedrin that they must accede to Pilate's demand.'

His companion gasped. 'But they cannot! They must stand firm against sacrilege.'

The other sneered. 'Can't you understand? Can't you see that Annas dare not oppose Pilate? Not yet.'

'Our friend is right!' said another voice. The door leading to the inner apartments had opened and a man had appeared. 'Our friend is right,' the man repeated, and as he strode into the light the Levites recognised Barabbas. 'Annas will whine. He'll tear his gown and pull his beard and go through all the motions of sorrow, but he dare not confront Pilate. He will go on, behind the scenes, doing everything he can to weaken Pilate's position and unseat him. But Annas dare not fight Pilate in the open. If he did so, the whole of Judaea would see it as war between the Temple and Caesar. There would be a full-scale rebellion.'

'A rebellion in which, with Zealot help, Judaea would win her freedom,' declared the fervent one.

'And in such freedom where would Annas be?' asked Barabbas. 'He and Caiaphas would be lost in the dust of revolt. Annas does not seek martyrdom. He seeks wealth and power. He can hold on to those only at Caesar's will. No, not even for the treasure of God will Annas risk his future or his skin.'

'Then let him be destroyed. Jerusalem will rise as one man against Pilate. He has only a cohort of troops at the Antonia. With Zealot aid we can take the Holy City in a day.'

'Pilate has only a cohort at the Antonia today. Within forty-eight hours he will have five hundred troops at Herod's Gate.'

'Then what are your orders?' asked the other Zealot. 'What do we do?'

309

'Nothing,' said Barabbas flatly. 'The Zealots are not to move until they are sure of decisive victory. That time is not yet. For my own part, I shall leave Jerusalem tonight. There will certainly be disorder in the city, and I don't want to risk being swept up with the débris.' He turned to the cheesemaker. 'Let our group here know that they must keep out of trouble. We do not want Zealots rounded up and crucified. We must conserve our strength, and we can find comfort in the fact that Pilate's latest crime against Judaea will bring more patriots flocking to our ranks.'

Barabbas had judged the situation aright. Pilate had frightened Annas. The high priest had gone to the Antonia that morning with high hopes. He had expected to find the Procurator, weakened by the downfall of his anti-Semitic patron, conciliatory. The Sanhedrin's rejection of Pilate's plans had been staged in a contemptuous way to emphasise that Judaea had lost all respect for Pilate's presence and all confidence in his future. Pilate's air of strength had thrown Annas off balance, and now the high priest faced the task of convincing the Sanhedrin that the time was not yet ripe to oppose Pilate. He must explain that even if, by defying him, they brought him down, they would be swept away in the storm. The Sanhedrin must of course protest against the sacrilege, but it must do so with the formal dignity befitting a priestly government. It was to be expected that the protest of the common people against the seizure of the Corban would take a more violent form. Well and good. That would serve to show Pilate, and eventually Caesar, how odious the action was. The Sanhedrin could enlarge on that in their complaints to Caesar. Through various channels, including the Herods, they would make known in Rome and Capri their opinion that Pontius Pilate was undermining Caesar's policy by repressive and illegal acts, and was proving himself sympathetic even yet to the abhorrent anti-Semitism of Aelius Sejanus. Meanwhile Annas would comfort the Sanhedrin with the assurance that the treasure now being confiscated by Pilate would have to be repaid fourfold when a more amenable procurator was appointed.

Throughout the evening this statement of policy was diligently circulated among all members of the Sanhedrin. Even so, when the priestly parliament met in full session next morning, extremist Zealot-minded members argued that the sacred treasure must be protected against Gentile robbery. The arguments of these few were brushed aside by the obedient majority, and the Sanhedrin agreed to accede, under protest, to Pilate's demands. No attempt was made to keep this decision secret. News of it swept through the city.

On the morning when the deed was to be done crowds began building up along all the streets leading to the Temple. In the Court of the Gentiles almost the whole complement of troops from the Antonia were drawn up in two shoulder-to-shoulder files which stretched all the way from the Temple to the stairway leading to the fortress. At the foot of the Temple steps a strong guard encircled the group who were to check the transfer of the gold – members of the Procurator's secretariat and some sour-faced Levites.

Pilate looked down on the scene from his balcony. Beside him were Severus and Marcellus. Marcellus, who had accompanied the reinforcements from Caesarea, had also brought with him a complement of his security corps. These, wearing tattered mantles, darned shawls and a variety of Jewish caps, had filtered into the city unnoticed, some actually driving asses loaded with garden produce. Some, as Marcellus pointed out to Pilate, were at this moment dutifully buying Jewish pence at the money-changers' stalls. They were not armed, though some did carry, hidden under their robes, useful clubs, and others openly carried shepherd's crooks.

There was the possibility, Marcellus had learned, that the people of Jerusalem might after all accept the Sanhedrin's decision and meekly submit to the provocation of seeing the sacred Corban being handed over to the Romans. If this was so, if these Jews seemed unlikely to make trouble, then Marcellus was determined to rouse them. A few strategically placed security-men could easily stir up a riot in which, Marcellus hoped, Zealots would be flushed out. When the riot reached its height, the reinforcements waiting at Herod's Gate would march in and arrest the rioters. A sophisticated twist to his plan was that the troops should arrest the spies along with the rest. They too would be carted off to Caesarea. En route the spies would be bound to pick up some information from arrested Zealots.

There seemed, at the moment, no prospect of any trouble. The only worried people in the Court of the Gentiles were the money-changers and the dealers in sacrificial flesh: business that morning had been unusually slack. The packed crowd was, disappointingly, not a profitable one, for everyone was standing around rather bemused, staring at the files of soldiers and the gates of the Temple.

311

The people were bewildered. When news of Pilate's intentions first reached their ears they had been excited, but news of the Sanhedrin's craven compliance had deflated the excitement. Their priestly government had apparently decided in its wisdom that the votive offerings which the faithful had rendered unto God must now be rendered unto Caesar.

At the Temple doors appeared a troop of Levites surrounding those who carried two cedar chests. At the sight of the treasure leaving the Temple a great sigh rose from the crowd. But nothing more. The Levites came down the steps, their faces full of grief. Those carrying the chests contorted their features into expressions of strain, exaggerating the weight of the treasure they carried. Some of the soldiers fell back to allow them to bring it towards the Levites and Roman clerks detailed to exchange the instruments of transfer.

The crowd, irresolute, even stopped murmuring so that they could hear the finance officer from Caesarea reading the agreement drawn up by the Sanhedrin and the Roman administration for allocating funds from the Corban to finance works planned to better the conditions and increase the wealth of the population of the city and the province. Those who had at first believed that appropriating God's money was sacrilege were now beginning to believe that the Sanhedrin did not see it so, and glumly but peacefully watched the chests being hoisted on the shoulders of Roman guards. Even the Zealots, it seemed (for surely there must be some of those in this vast throng), were not protesting; so those watching the chests being carried towards the staircase of the Antonia and hearing not even Zealot voices raised against the deed felt their secret angers must be inappropriate.

In fact, what seemed a crime against the House of God would have been executed without turmoil had not one tall fellow drawn a club from under his robe and, brandishing it, yelled, 'Sacrilege! Blasphemy! Woe on Jews who allow the plunder of God's Holy Temple!' At that another man nearby also drew a club. 'Rescue the sacred Corban!' he cried. And yet another, whirling a shepherd's crook like a flail about him, flung himself against the backs of the soldiers who barred his path, thrusting them aside in his wild attempt to reach the chests. Before he was overcome he managed to fling his crook like a spear. It hit one of the Levites full in the chest and flattened him.

The money-changers and dealers in sacrificial flesh had obviously been prepared for possible trouble. Within seconds they

312

had cleared their counters and slid them out of danger in crannies below the terrace and were scuttling away from the scene with bowls and sacks of coins, baskets of pigeons and livestock. But the crowd paid no attention to these deserters. All eyes were now turned to other men waving clubs and rallying those around them to rescue the Temple treasure. So the Zealots, for surely these men could be none else, were at last making their presence felt! The soldiers faced the clamour of the crowd and tried to hold them back with a fence of spears.

'Rescue the sacred Corban!' yelled those with clubs. 'Rescue the Corban,' the crowd echoed, and, awakened from its stupor, now rushed forward with wild cries and grimaces of mingled ecstasy and rage.

On the balcony Marcellus raised his hand. The signal was seen by two horsemen posted near the bridge. The galloped off, people scattering from below their hooves, towards Herod's Gate.

The first file of soldiers in the Court of the Gentiles was too weak to withstand the immense pressure of the crowd. Their line broke and a mob surged towards the second file drawn across the staircase. The soldiers there were a tougher crew, and drew their swords and bashed spiked shields in the faces of the attackers. Even so, some of the crowd got beyond them. A few even gained a foothold on the staircase of the Antonia and rushed up only a few steps behind the slowly ascending chests of treasure. Some of these were seized by the extra guards running down from the fortress. Others were beaten back. One of them, too old a man, really, for such frantic exploits, fell backwards down the steps. Even in the tumult the crack of his head on the paving could be heard, and those nearby drew back and looked down pityingly at his broken twisted body and the blood flowing from his skull. But those behind suddenly heaved forward and in a second the mob was surging over the corpse, treading it flat as grapes and forcing more blood out of it.

Now there were soldiers also under their feet, thrown down, despite their swords and shields, by the massed weight and fury of the unarmed crowd. Even some soldiers who had kept their feet had lost their casques, and these were kicked around by the mob until some rioters, recognising their usefulness, snatched them up to wield as clubs or, rammed on their heads, to take the brunt of Roman blows.

The soldiers were driven back, retreating step by step. The rioters redoubled their violence, some already entertaining visions of leading the rest in triumph up the steps into the very heart of the hated fortress. So exhilarated were they by these extravagant ambitions that they were slow to realise that the pressure and support behind them had slackened and that fewer were coming forward to take the place of comrades beaten down beside them. But at last, hearing piteous wailing behind them, they turned and saw that those behind them were now facing an attack at the rear as three enormous metallic animals drove into the crowd. These fearsome creatures were built up of scores of foot-soldiers, the men in the centre ranks holding shields horizontally above their heads and those on the outer ranks overlapping their shields to form impenetrable walls, so that only the soldiers' feet were visible as they marched on relentlessly, breaking up the mob into helpless groups in which only the luckiest escaped the beating clubs. Behind these war engines came other troops, and the crowd, now hemmed in on every side, lost heart. Those now fighting most desperately were those fighting for nothing more than escape from the scene. They were hurried on their way by clubs battering their heads and shoulders. Those who stumbled were kicked down the steps. The ones who had shouted loudest or fought most violently were thrown face down on the paving and their wrists tied behind their backs. Among these were some of those who had first sparked off the revolt by brandishing clubs and crying 'Sacrilege!' and 'Blasphemy!' By this time the original cause of the tumult, the chests containing the Temple treasure, had long since disappeared into the stony maw of the fortress, and Pilate and Marcellus and his officers had left the balcony.

Within less than an hour the Court of the Gentiles was quiet. Fabius gave permission for the family of the old man to scrape his remains from the paving and carry them away for burial. Only a handful of others had been killed, and those mostly on the steps leading to the bridge. Only one auxiliary had been seriously wounded. His face had been kicked in after he had fallen: now he was dying. The dungeons in the cellar of the Antonia were crowded with a motley collection of prisoners, moaning over their bruises and lamenting their incarceration. Even the soldiers guarding the prisoners, Marcellus said with satisfaction, did not know that some of them were his agents. Surprisingly, only two of the arrested Jews had been found to be carrying daggers, but rigorous questioning at Caesarea would undoubtedly uncover other Zealots among the mob.

Pilate was already in his study conferring with the architect, an engineer, a treasurer and the two Jerusalem builders most capable of recruiting journeymen and slaves. 'Offer good pay,' Pilate said. 'We can now afford the best workers.' He indulged himself with a final loving examination of the plans and sketches, and then, handing the bundle over, told the architect, 'Have the wording drawn up for a commemorative slab.'

'In the name of Proconsul Pilate?'

'No. In honour of Tiberius Caesar. The slab will be installed before Passover, by which time there will be, I hope, an impressive portion of the work already built. At the ceremony we shall have a party of distinguished visitors from Rome, even from Capri. And,' he smiled broadly, 'let us remember to invite High Priest Caiaphas.'

IX

With a wad of warrants bunched in his gauntleted hand,
Marcellus came slowly up his staircase. The Procurator's door
stood open, and Marcellus could hear the shifting of stools and
an outburst of murmurs which signalled the breaking up of
Pilate's conference with the army commanders.

Pilate was seated at his desk. His map of Judaea, scrawled over
with ink and chalk marks denoting recent Zealot incidents, had
been taken from the wall and lay before him. Over a table nearby
was stretched a map of Palestine. The arrows which someone had
been chalking on it cut deeply across the frontiers of Galilee and
Nabataea. Standing around his map, staring down at it, plucking
lips and fingering chins and exchanging end-of-conference
second thoughts, were the commanders: grizzled Antonius,
Master of the Horse, and red-cheeked Aemilius, commander of
the Jerusalem cohorts, prominent among them. All had arrived
for the conference in full fig of martial splendour. Their cuirasses
gleamed gloriously; on stools and chests their helmets shone like
beacons; and they sailed as high and ornate as armoured ships of
war around the slight toga-clad figure at the desk.

As Marcellus went in he could feel their on-parade eyes checking the untied laces of his leather jerkin, his sweaty tunic, and the
charcoal smuts smeared on his brow and the back of his bare

hand. He laid the warrants with a solemn flourish before Pilate and pressed them flat for signing. That stack of documents was evidence that during this morning, while those swaggering warriors had been lounging in burnished finery and arguing grandly about strategy and frontiers, he had been doing the real work of keeping the peace in Judaea. He was exhausted, and, proud of looking so, exaggerated his posture of weariness, hoping the officers might see how a man's strength could be drained more dry by stretching his brain than by wielding his sword-arm. But could they ever understand that? Even if they did, their bullheads could never appreciate the fine truth that whispers plucked out by pincers could signal victories more valuable than those proclaimed by exultant battle-cries.

Pilate glanced down at the warrants. The top one was for the crucifixion of a Jew involved in the murder at Sebaste last year of a certain Josephus the Cohen. He winced, pushed the warrants aside, and covered them with the map. 'Marcellus! We have discussed the general situation in the light of the information you have uncovered in Tiberias.'

Marcellus responded with his slanted nod. He knew why Pilate had staged this conference today. News had arrived three days ago that Caesar's confidant, Vitellius, was on the last stage of his journey to Judaea. He had sailed from Brindisi for Cyprus, where a new trireme of the Roman fleet was waiting to bring him in state to Caesarea. Also from Antioch were coming rumours that Tiberius was sending Vitellius to Asia as legate-designate to succeed the absentee Legate of Syria, Aeilius Lamia. Pilate, obsessed with the idea of Vitellius thus becoming his superior, was determined to impress upon the army that Caesar's favourite must see Judaea peaceful, or at least outwardly obedient.

Pilate had been disturbed by news from Rome that his seizure of the Corban gold had been described there as a recklessly rash act, though by now he was thinking that his critics would have to admit that he had judged the temper of the Jews better than they could. The act had been so well executed and so well timed that it had passed off with little more than a morning brawl outside the Temple, and protests elsewhere in Judaea against the 'sacrilege' had been agreeably few, weak and ineffective. So far, so good. But one had to plan against any untoward incident happening while Vitellius was in Judaea. The presence of a plenipotentiary known to be an intimate of Caesar's might induce Jew partisans to stage demonstrations or even terrorist acts during his

317

visit, in the hope of thus bringing more directly to Caesar's ears their abhorrence of a procurator still known as the creature of that enemy of Jews, Sejanus.

There were two events in particular which the Jews might choose as an arena for riot. The first was the Passover festival. Vitellius would certainly want to attend that. Every tourist always did. The second was the Caesarea Games. Games in any case were abhorrent to the Jews. Not only were Jews offended by sacrifice to Gentile gods in particular, but also to their dour and frugal minds any communal jollity was disgusting debauchery. The Zealots might attempt some outrage to sully the joyous glory of the Games.

Marcellus guessed, because of the far from friendly looks the officers cast at him, that Pilate had brought his name into the discussion that morning. Pilate would have been advising the commanders that any information which Marcellus had collected from Zealot prisoners could help the army to stamp out sparks of revolt at the source before they flared up into dangerous incidents. The commanders would not have liked that suggestion.

They had not. Aemilius, Commander in Jerusalem, had made no attempt to hide his antagonism and had puffed out his red cheeks at the hint that his renowned military expertise could benefit by advice from a non-combatant who was so crippled that he was fit only for dirty work in the palace cellars. Aemilius was prepared to admit that Marcellus had handled that Corban affair siklfully. But Passover was a bigger problem and, traditionally, an army one. For years Aemilius had faced the possibility of a full-scale revolt flaring up among the three hundred thousand pilgrims who converged upon the Holy City for that high festival. During those years he had learned just where to parade his troops to show the exuberant crowds a cautionary display of Roman strength. Even if that bent-necked Marcellus was right in suspecting that this year's Passover could be more critical than usual, Aemilius could handle it. He had been doing that long before this little man Pilate had come out to Judaea. He had no need for fussy advice from a procurator. After all, what was a Procurator of Judaea or any other province? Nothing more, as his title indicated, than Caesar's butler, appointed to look after the law and finances of what was an imperial estate. He should keep to his job of administering the law and gathering the taxes, and leave military matters to military men, and not strut around, as this Pontius Pilate seemed to love doing, like some new-age Julius

Caesar, trying to teach to the army lessons which it had mastered before his forbears lost their slave-rings.

Antonius, Master of the Horse, preparing to leave, swung round and picked up his helmet, but then, catching sight of Marcellus's sooty forehead, looked down at the man and, with the helmet cradled like a goodly treasure in the crook of his scrubbed and scented arm, could not resist saying, 'The Procurator has been telling us some of the information you have scraped up in Galilee. Particularly about the army which, according to your information, the Tetrarch Herod has built up. I have been able to assure the Procurator that your information is out-of-date. I have not been idle. I have also secured information, more up-to-date. Actually, Herod has recently been disbanding troops.'

Marcellus nodded. 'I know. Herod has sent men home. But what does that mean? I also know that he has piled up arms and armour sufficient to put sixty thousand in the field in the few days it needs to call men back from farms and hills.'

'I must confess, Marcellus,' Antonius retorted, 'that after that business at Magdala, the murder of Afranius, I begin to doubt the reliability of some of your informers.'

Marcellus nodded glumly. He did not reply, only raised the back of his gauntleted hand to cover a yawn which, had it been left uncovered, might have looked impolite.

'The more information Marcellus collects,' said Pilate sharply to Antonius, 'the more hope we have of avoiding outrages like the Magdala one. Marcellus has discovered a number of bases in Galilee from which the terrorists operate.'

Antonius sneered. 'If the Horse could move on Galilee,' he lamented, 'we could wipe out these bases at a stroke and establish a Roman peace over all southern Palestine.'

Pilate waved this aside testily, though his exasperation was caused not so much by the futility of the words as by the fact that they struck such a responsive chord in his own suppressed ambitions. He could sympathise with the frustration an Antonius suffered at not being free to solve a vexatious problem in traditional Roman fashion. Only a few nights ago Pilate himself had been reading how Julius Caesar, ignoring all the envy and animosity his adventure might arouse in Rome, had marched a slender force against guerrilla mountaineers in Spain and triumphantly performed the kind of mopping-up operation that Antonius now spoke of. But that was close on one hundred years ago. The age for grandly simple military exploits was past, alas.

Nowadays everyone was so enmeshed in the web of imperial politics that one could not stamp on even a buzzing insect like Herod without endangering the whole fine-spun political fabric of empire.

'Why doesn't Herod clean out the Zealot bases himself?' asked Quintilius, the youngest of the group and recently arrived in Asia. 'If he fears, as he says, an attack by King Aretas, he should be putting down the Zealots before that happens. Otherwise he could find himself fighting on two fronts, against Zealots as well as against Arabs.'

Again Pilate did not answer. He merely looked impatiently at the lad and, to emphasise that the conference had finished, began rolling the map.

It was Marcellus who answered. 'The Zealots would not help the Arabs against Herod, though I would not put it past them to team up with Aretas if he were trying to drive Rome out of Palestine. But if Aretas attacked Herod, the Zealots would rally to the Tetrarch to protect their sacred Jewish homeland from Arab invasion.'

Pilate tossed the map aside and drew the warrants towards him. The officers took the hint, gathered up their helmets and sailed out. Pilate, as he reached for his pen, heard them break into whispering along the corridor. They would spend the rest of the day grumbling in the mess. But they would obey. Reluctant to acknowledge his authority they might be, but they were Roman soldiers and loyal. The name of Josephus confronted him again. He signed that first warrant, and then to shift from his mind the sad memories the name aroused, he asked, 'How many Zealots were found among the Corban protesters?'

'No Judaean ones. My trap sprang on none of them. They kept out of the affair, which confirms my suspicion that they are lying low for something bigger. But there were four Galileans among those arrested.'

The second warrant was for another murderer of Josephus. Pilate looked up. 'Galileans? What are you doing with them?'

'Interrogating them. No more. When they have recovered from that, we can send them back to Herod. Galileans are, as he constantly reminds us, his subjects.'

'And see that they are sent back with an impressive escort. Make a big show of the operation. I shall use the occasion to write to Herod and tell him once again that we hold him responsible for any Galileans who cross the border to commit crimes in Judaea.

Let me have the names of the base or bases from which those four came. It would be good to make Herod aware that we know the locations of those camps.' He brooded. 'I wonder how many Zealot confederates he has? Look how quickly he knew all the details about the assassination of Afranius. The escort you will send with the Galileans to Tiberias could be used to make some inquiries about that Magdala affair.'

Marcellus frowned down at his gauntlet. He wished that the Old Man would drop this habit of concerning himself with such details. In any case Marcellus did not see the murder of Afranius as a tragedy. Not at all. The lives of Afranius and his escort were a cheap price to pay for the promising leads their deaths had provided. It would not, of course, be politic to put it to Pilate in that way. So, to divert Pilate's interference, he said, 'Two of my agents in Galilee are on to that already,' and added with a grin, 'they are operating in the meat market at Tiberias, of all places.'

'Well, I hope they will be more careful than Afranius seems to have been,' said Pilate testily. 'If they are also caught, we shall have Herod complaining about Judaean agents operating illegally in his kingdom.'

'He could hardly do that in this case. My two agents are not Judaeans. They are Galileans.'

'But can you rely on Galileans?'

'On these two, yes. They are expensive, but they have not failed me yet.'

'Hm! That Galilean woman who is nursing Severus's baby. She came from Magdala. Have you questioned her?'

'Not directly. Hardly worth doing so. The Jews do not let their women mix in politics. They are not so foolish as the Romans in that respect. But I did make some inquiries about her. She's harmless.'

'Harmless? I do not believe any Galilean, even a woman, can be harmless. After all, she is a subject of King Fox.'

'She doesn't think herself so. She was a follower of that desert preacher John, and when the fellow was beheaded she left Herod's court.'

'And then, the Lady Claudia says, she joined some other preacher.'

'A carpenter from Nazareth. The transfer was logical. They say the Nazarene was baptised by John. It is established that he began preaching in Galilee as soon as John was arrested.'

'Then why doesn't Herod lock him up as well? Particularly if he preaches the same kind of nonsense as alarmed Herod about John: common ownership of land and property.'

'The Nazarene doesn't seem bothered about such things. He's actually been heard to say that it is a duty for people to pay taxes to Caesar.'

'Well, that's a change. So he is not a Zealot.'

'To be honest, Pontius, I'm not all that sure. I suspect there could be Zealots associated with him. He did spend some time in the Desert. He is a rather mysterious character. Some Galileans say he is merely crazy, as John was. His own family – he has four brothers and two sisters – are reported to have said that they thought him out of his mind. Yet reports indicate that he has some talent for attracting big crowds.'

'Naturally! The crazier the preacher, the bigger the audience.'

'Some Galileans talk about him being the awaited Messiah.'

Pilate sighed heavily. 'How often must I repeat that Messiahs are a regular crop in Judaean superstition? Anyhow, this one is in Galilee, so he is Herod's problem.'

'He could be our problem. We can't entirely overlook the political implications of this Messiah belief. The Jews expect their true Messiah, when he comes, to drive foreign oppressors out of Judah and establish God's rule.'

'They've talked that way since the days of Solomon.'

'And there is always the possibility that, in an inflamed situation – a Zealot revolt or even an Arab invasion – any so-called Messiah moving into Jerusalem could be troublesome.'

'If he comes to Jerusalem, Marcellus, you'll be able to cope with him. You'll find the dagger under his robe,' said Pilate and put an end to further talk on that point by giving the warrants intenser scrutiny. But, after he had signed two more, he began looking through the others. 'You have not put the dates for the executions,' he complained.

'No. The dates will be inserted later. I hope to visit the Sebaste ones and persuade them to say a little more before they die.'

Pilate pondered for a moment or so, but then, aware of Marcellus looking impatiently at his poised pen, began signing again, shoving each warrant quickly away as he hurried through the distasteful job. However, he halted when he came to the last three warrants. He looked up sternly. 'On these three you have not even written the names of the men to be crucified.'

'They have yet to be identified.'

'When?'

'When they have been arrested.'

Pilate tapped the uppermost of the three warrants. 'According to this, the person condemned has been found guilty of treason. How found guilty if not yet arrested? Without trial?'

'He will confess his guilt. Or the sight of a warrant on the table might make him collaborate more readily.'

'So you would use a warrant for crucifixion like an instrument of torture? Or as a bribe?' Pilate tossed the pen aside. Clasping his hands before him he stared down with an air of disquiet.

Marcellus had been expecting this moment. It was a crucial one. The point he must make now was essential to all his strategy. 'Such methods are necessary, Pontius,' he said persuasively. 'I must be in a position to act quickly, without referring every case back to you, without, if needs be, the law's delay. But, I can promise you one thing: there are going to be far fewer crucifixions in Judaea.' At this Pilate looked up, keenly questioning. Marcellus, avoiding the direct stare, busied himself assembling the warrants into a neat stack. He counted them. 'Fifteen,' he murmured. 'Fifteen small fry whom the drama of crucifixion will glorify.' He slapped his gauntlet on the stack and faced Pilate. 'Today we crucify these fifteen: but tomorrow fifteen times fifteen will buy daggers to avenge the martyrs we have exalted as heroes on the cross. And there is something worse. Because it is you, Pontius Pilate, Procurator of Judaea, who has signed these warrants, it is Pontius Pilate who is accused of murdering another fifteen Jews. For the sake of getting rid of fifteen utterly worthless criminals you suffer odium as a brutal and oppressive governor, and your policy is seen throughout Judaea as anti-Semitic. It is seen so also in Rome. *And in Capri.* Why should you pay so high a price for smudging out a handful of oafs? Public execution is too noble an angony to accord to them. Perhaps we could learn a lesson from the Jews. They don't make a public show of their executions. Most times they stone their condemned to death or burn them at the stake in back-yards. Or strangle them in cellars.'

'We are not Jews!'

'Well, at least let us reserve the high drama of crucifixion for worthy foes. If we reserve the ceremony for real Zealot leaders, it might have some value as a demonstration of Roman victory. But we weaken the impact of crucifixion when we use it indiscriminately for run-of-the-mill rebels. We have seen that crucifixion does not act as a deterrent. It merely inflames Jews to greater frenzies. Each time you crucify one man no one has even heard of, you make him a national hero.'

'Justice must be seen to be done.'

'No Jew partisan can see Pilate's justice as just. A Jew sees Roman justice only as the instrument of Gentile oppression. We cannot fight partisans with justice: we must fight them with their own weapons.'

'Daggers, eh? Would you have me wear a dagger under my toga?'

'Excellent, Pontius!' Marcellus smiled brilliantly. 'You have put it superbly. Yes, I do suggest that you wear a dagger under your toga. But let me be that dagger. You are Caesar's procurator; you represent Caesar's law: you are also a Roman officer. Leave it to your dagger Marcellus to fight in the way you cannot.'

'You are a Roman officer yourself, Marcellus.'

'But I can forget that.' He fingered his scarf and grinned. 'The battle against terrorism cannot be fought with cohorts and standards on a battlefield. It must be fought in the mind of the enemy. In that fight I cannot wear either armour or toga: I must forget I am a Roman. Against terrorists a parade of cohorts is not strength: it is weakness, for it shows the enemy where we are. Our battle must be fought in the dark, in cellars and bedrooms and sewers, and in the mind of the enemy. They fight in secret: so must we. They hide and kill at night: so must we. At all times we Romans fear that any civilian Jew smiling at us might have under his robe a Zealot dagger: I want now to make every terrorist fear that his fellow partisan might have a Roman one. The night raid, the knock on the door at midnight, the sudden disappearance of a neighbour, the finding of a body, the question "Who has killed and why?" With such a war of nerves we can riddle the terrorist ranks with uncertainy and suspicion.' He gathered up the signed warrants, rolled them and held them before Pilate like a baton. 'There are fifteen here, but there should have been sixteen. That sixteenth would have been worth all these fifteen put together. But he got away. Because we moved too slowly, in legal Roman fashion.'

'Who was that?'

'A Zealot in Jericho. He was hiding with the whores. By the time the posse had polished their helmets and lined up on parade and marched to the town he had skipped into the Desert. In fact, he probably got wind of what was to happen even before orders for his arrest left Caesarea.'

'How many of those fifteen were concerned in the murder of

... in the Sebaste affair?'

'Four. One of my best agents tracked them down. He is doing good work in that area. He got himself established as a carrier, and now he is popular, in a not too obtrusive way of course, at many of the village inns. He hears a lot.'

'The Sebaste four: have they been proved guilty?'

'Yes. They confessed. But they have not yet given much information.'

'Do you think they will do so?'

'With persuasion.'

'And you will give them that persuasion when you go to Sebaste?'

'Yes. With all respect to Severus I think my persuasion might be more effective than his.'

'I don't doubt that,' said Pilate bleakly. Even yet he could not avoid a sense of distaste when he tried to imagine the kind of things Marcellus might do to bodies. The criminals deserved, of course, all they got. What happened to their fingers, toes, eyeballs, or more tender parts of their anatomy was of no significance. What Pilate found offensive was that Marcellus, who was after all Roman and born of a moderately good family, seemed to take pride in skills which were really in the province of brutes like public hangmen or stranglers. Anyhow, it was fortunate that Marcellus was prepared to superintend such operations. When a tortured man did speak it was obviously advantageous to have within earshot a man agile enough in mind to pick out grains of truth from the garbage of groans. 'Will that young Titus be going with you to Sebaste?'

'Yes. I am glad you approved his taking over there.'

'You spoke so highly of him. Though, as I say, he is very young.'

'And consequently can learn quickly. Better young men in such jobs than old army throwouts without an idea in their heads.'

'It is our duty to train young men to responsibility.'

'Yes.' If Pilate preferred to see the appointment of Titus as commander at Sebaste as an opportunity for fashioning a lad for imperial administration, well and good. Marcellus saw the appointment in a different light. Titus was not only young and capable; he was beautifully fierce. There were one or two others of the same kidney whom Marcellus hoped to insinuate into the administration when the time was ripe.

'Let Severus hand over to Titus as quickly as possible,' Pilate

325

went on. 'I need Severus here as soon as possible. In any case he'll be wanting to hurry back to his child.'

The three blanks were still unsigned. He was still reluctant to put his name on them. To do so seemed in some measure a surrender of control. Marcellus saw the reluctance. Thumbing through the fifteen warrants he said casually, 'Two of these were actually the men who nailed old Josephus to the cross.'

Pilate reached to his pen again, wrote his signature quickly three times and handed the blanks to Marcellus. 'There you are. I hold you on your honour to use them justly.'

'On my honour,' said Marcellus. 'On the honour of a Roman officer.' Then folding the three warrants with the others he went out, closing the door softly and stepping noiselessly towards his staircase.

Severus had completed the formalities of handing over command at Sebaste to young Titus. Now he was eager to get back to Caesarea. A message from his son's nurse had said that the boy, completely cured of his tummy upsets, was in good health and growing sturdier every day. Tomorrow morning, after the crucifixion of the four Zealots, Severus and Marcellus would be leaving for Caesarea.

Marcellus came in and dropped four warrants on the table. They were already signed by Pilate. 'Put today's date on them,' he said.

'Today? But the execution should be at dawn tomorrow.'

'Better today,' said Marcellus, and while Severus was writing the date he took up another pen and used its point to scrape two flecks of dried blood from the leather of his gauntlet.

Severus would have preferred that the crucifixion should be done tomorrow, because then Titus could superintend the operation. But when he went to the spot customarily used for crucifixions at Sebaste, a hilly plot too stony for any more productive purposes, and saw the first two being dragged to it he understood why the ceremony could not have been delayed. Those two could not have lived until tomorrow. Indeed it seemed no more than a formality to nail the younger one to the cross at all. 'A tough lad,' Marcellus had said of this one, something akin to admiration in his voice. 'We got next to nothing out of him.' The boy's fingers curled slightly as the nails drove through the palms, but apart from that movement the rest of a youthful and once wildly beautiful body seemed incapable any longer of recognising pain. So far as Severus could make out, the youngster was dead by the time he was hoisted aloft and his feet were nailed. The second one was in slightly better shape, but gabbled senselessly as vomit and blood gushed from his mouth. After seeing these two positioned Severus thought up some further details he must attend to at the barracks and asked Titus to supervise the ceremony. The young fellow accepted the duty blandly, almost eagerly.

Next morning Severus was glad to turn his back on Sebaste, and during the ride to Casearea he ventured to express to Marcellus that opinion which he had never dared to voice to Pilate. Crucifixion, he said, was a messy, time-wasting form of execution. Marcellus smiled. Severus always made him smile. The fresh-complexioned face, northern and square and solid, was so earnest and honest. The guttural Celtic Latin rumbling out of it was similarly homespun, equally without guile. Severus, taking the smile as a signal of accord, was encouraged to add that in his view participating in the barbarous ceremony was demeaning to Roman honour. Marcellus agreed, so warmly that Severus was surprised. Marcellus added that Severus, as personal aide to the Procurator, should not have to deal with such unpleasant and trivial things as crucifixions. Even less, went on Marcellus, should Pilate. The Procurator needed to be free to devote himself to higher things: to political strategy and the like. 'You and I, Severus, must do all we can to insulate Pilate from dirty work.' Severus, flattered by prospects of partnership with Marcellus in such a laudable exercise, fervently agreed.

As soon as they arrived at the palace Severus knew there was a busy time ahead for him. Before he had crossed the great courtyard no fewer than three of the many members of the secretariat who halted to greet him told him that the Old Man, who was working everyone day and night, had been asking if he had arrived. There was scaffolding over all the south face of the palace, and a host of builders and painters and tile-workers swarming around. He met architect Lucius at the foot of the staircase. The entire south wing, said Lucius, was being refurbished to lodge the guests expected for the Games. Some of the larger halls were being converted into private apartments for very important visitors. For Vitellius half the whole first floor was being transformed into a kind of self-contained palace with a pool and fountain in the entrance hall; vast tanks, one for freshwater fish and one for shellfish, near the newly built kitchens; and, below, a private steam bath for him and a larger one for his entourage.

'Near the hippodrome,' went on Lucius enthusiastically as he unrolled the plans he was carrying, 'there will be an athletes' village.' It was the biggest project Lucius had ever designed in his career, and he was vastly proud of it. 'An arcaded building, you see. Two storeys high, with a canteen there, and baths, all enclosing a courtyard big enough for tracks and stages for training. Then, curving out from the building, you see, two single-storey wings for the dormitories and day-rooms for the teams. Look! The whole concept is oriental. Those dormitory wings are a series of separate pavilions, Asian in style. Each team from each country has its separate pavilion, and all the pavilions are linked by porticoes with national emblems in mosaic over each entry.' It all looked vastly impressive, thought Severus. And vastly expensive. The Jews would grumble like mad at their taxes being used for such extravagance. Lucius rolled the plans with a flourish. 'The Old Man is asking for you,' he said and hurried off.

But before he went up to the first floor to report his arrival, Severus slipped through the gardens to his quarters to see his son. He was surprised to find the Luganese woman once again installed as nurse. The Magdalene, said the girl, had left and had taken her baby. No, she did not know why. The Lady Claudia had not told her. However, young Severus Secundus seemed happily indifferent to the change of nurses and was obviously bursting with good health. When Severus lifted him up the child stared entranced at the blazing cuirass and ran plump inquiring fingers along the curves of embossed muscle. Severus swung him aloft, playing peep-bo by tossing him behind and before the horsehair crest of his helmet. His son's laughing screams and joyful excited eyes swept away all memories of yesterday's squalid scene at Sebaste.

But the memories were summoned back when he went into Pilate's study. For there was a young Jew there, a courtly richly-dressed fellow, rather small but of great dignity, with a thin face and cavernous dark eyes, whom Pilate introduced as Mattathias of Alexandria, son of Josephus the Cohen, and then asked Severus, 'How are things at the villa now?'

'All the débris has been cleared away,' said Severus. 'An engineer and slaves from the barracks are restoring the pergolas.'

'The workmen are at your service, Mattathias, for as long as you want them,' said Pilate. 'My desire is that the villa shall be completely restored to its original state. As near as possible, or in any other style according to your wishes. The city of Sebaste is being taxed to provide the materials and labour necessary. Numidian marble is being quarried to replace the steps.' Mattathias waved aside this generous offer with a gesture which plainly indicated that the damage to the villa was a matter of indifference compared with his greater loss. 'It is the least I can do,' Pilate said quietly. A young scribe who had been writing a document jumped up and brought it to Pilate for signature. 'It will add further strength to your position in Sebaste, Mattathias, if you present this to the Roman command on your arrival. Incidentally I have written to a relative of my wife, a woman who has many contacts in Alexandria and elsewhere. I have asked her to busy herself and her friends in collecting books which can form at least the nucleas for a restored library.'

Mattathias thanked him and took his leave.

'Have you drawn up the letter for Herod?' Pilate asked the scribe.

'Yes, Procurator. Copies are being made.'

'Let me have them. And Julius? How is he getting on?'

'Excellently, Procurator. He gives me a lot of work.'

Pilate smiled happily and when the young man had left said, 'A very capable scribe. Works amazingly quickly and has command of about seven languages. Though I still miss old Polygnotus.'

'Is he still ill?'

'Dead,' said Pilate. 'He never recovered from the illness that struck him the day before we left for Sebaste.' His face saddened. 'Josephus and now Polygnotus. First an old and faithful friend; now an old and faithful slave.' He brooded over the losses for a moment, then, drawing himself sharply erect, began, in a voice faint and dry with weariness, to bring Severus up-to-date on work facing him at Caesarea.

Severus, he said, must take over all routine matters from now on until Passover. 'By the way, I shall proceed to Jerusalem rather earlier than usual this Passover. I want to get the ceremony of inaugurating the aqueduct out of the way before the height of that festival. The engineer suggests that the most impressive spot for the ceremony will be at the Pool of Siloam where the line of the aqueduct can be seen to the best advantage. Vitellius will represent Caesar at that event.' He frowned. 'Sacrifice to Caesar and to the gods must be made. We have decided how that can be done without offending Jewish susceptibilities. We shall erect a pavilion, a temporary but dignified structure, to serve as a temple for the ceremony. After that, Passover; then, only four months later, the Games. So we have much to think of. By the way, Severus, look at the list of guests which I have given to Julius. He is already sending invitations. If you can think of any dignitary whom I have missed out, let me know. Lucius has come up with a promising sketch for the athletes' village. From now on, Severus, I want to be free of details.' Just what Marcellus had said, thought Severus. Pilate leaned back, yawned and rubbed his chin. 'I need a shave. Have the Young Barber sent, Severus. You can have the evening free. I suppose you are anxious to see your son.'

'Yes, sir.'

Severus hurried away. The Old Man really was looking tired. Poor old Polygnotus.

A slave told Severus the story of the old scribe's last days. Each time Polygnotus came out of his coma he had been given medicine, but each time, convulsed with pain, he had vomited again. At last, apparently knowing that he was dying, still unable to speak, he had indicated that he wished to write something of great secrecy. The young scribe had rushed into the sick-room with tablets and stylus. But a few minutes later he came out. 'Polygnotus is dead,' he said.

When Severus ran the Young Barber to earth, the boy was clipping the grizzled hair of Antonius but when told that the Procurator was demanding his attention the boy hastily finished tidying the Master of the Horse and raced up to the first floor. As he tripped gaily into the room the new young scribe was there and Pilate was signing the final version of his long severe letter to Herod. Pilate was about to hand the scroll to the scribe for sealing, but then drew it back. He had decided to add a postscript telling the Tetrarch that the Procurator would be arriving in Jerusalem earlier than usual this Passover for the purpose of inaugurating the aqueduct, and that Vitellius would accompany him. Pilate added this mainly because he felt that a few words written in his own hand might sugar the pill of a letter expressing Pilate's displeasure about known camps in Galilee from which partisans were crossing into Judaea on terrorist forays. Having written this postscript, Pilate asked for wax and laps to be brought to him so that he could seal the letter himself. 'It will be sent at dawn tomorrow by the Tiberias courier,' he said to the scribe and then, as the scribe left them, cast his eyes over the implements spread out by Ephir. 'Where's the pomade?' he snapped. The boy flung up his hands in shocked apology: again he had forgotten. He darted out.

Pilate shook his head with only mock exasperation and leaned back in his chair awaiting Ephir's return. He waited an unusually long time, yet without annoyance, for the quiet loneliness of the empty room was conducive to reflection, and in peaceful mood he could arrange in his mind tomorrow's work. He relaxed, so much so that he was actually dozing when Ephir came back.

Ephir's manner, slipping into the room so stealthily and tiptoeing towards him, alerted Pilate to the sense that something was wrong. He pulled himself erect. The boy held out a scrap of papyrus.

'What is it?' asked Pilate, taking it and trying in the dim light to read it.

The boy leaped lightly on to the desk and lit the suspended lamp above Pilate's left shoulder. Now Pilate could read the words. It was a translation into Aramaic of the postscript he had just written in Greek on the letter to Herod.

Ephir waited until Pilate, having finished reading, lifted his eyes questioning him. The boy stole forward. Straining on tiptoe, he put his excited face close to Pilate's, and, his eyes darting all the while towards the door, he whispered, 'When I ran out for the pomade the scribe was at the foot of the stairway. He was looking at the letter. I watched him. He was trying to open the seal before it hardened. I followed him without him seeing me. He did not go straightaway to the secretariat to find the Tiberias courier. He went first to his room. He closed the door and locked it. But I climbed on to the portico where I could see through his window. Now he had the letter opened, and he was writing. Then he sealed it again and went off to the secretariat. He locked the door again when he left, but I'm thin enough to get through the window.' He pointed to the papyrus. 'That's what he was writing.'

'Call the guard,' said Pilate. 'No, don't go down, Just call him.' Ephire called from the doorway, and when the guard appeared Pilate ordered him to fetch Marcellus immediately.

While they waited Pilate, gazing at the bright-eyed boys, occasionally shook his head in mingled bewilderment and admiration. Marcellus arrived.

'Tell Marcellus what has happened,' said Pilate.

Marcellus listened. The smile of triumph which suffused the

331

boy's face as he began telling his story faded under the fierce leaning stare.

'And how did you get this?' asked Marcellus, pulling the papyrus back and forth through leather fingers.

'I broke the box open.'

'Curse you, boy!' exclaimed Marcellus. He darted to the door and yelled to the guard to go with others and seize the scribe. 'Curse you, boy,' he repeated when he came back and glowered down at Ephir. 'You should have come to me before you did anything.'

Pilate defended his Young Barber. 'I think the boy acted very expeditiously.'

'Novices always spring traps too soon,' grumbled Marcellus. 'Anyhow, Pontius, this answers the question you asked when you went to Sebaste. How did they know that you were on your way? From the sealed note which you gave the scribe to take to the Lady Claudia.'

Pilate nodded. 'But who did he use to send the news to Sebaste?'

'We'll make him tell us that.' Marcellus read the postscript again. 'I suppose he has already copied the whole of the letter as well.'

'He had ample time to do so during the drafting of it. Anyhow, there was no information in it of any value to terrorists.'

'It names three Zealot hide-outs we have discovered in Galilee.'

'That doesn't tell the Zealots anything they don't know themselves.'

'It tells them that we have discovered those camps.'

'They would have learned that soon enough from Herod.'

'I know. But I was planning for certain things to happen at those camps before Herod got your letter,' grumbled Marcellus. 'Anyhow, knowing that the information has leaked, I have time to recall my men.'

There was a sound of scuffling in the corridor. Marcellus hurried out. 'No!' he could be heard shouting. 'Take him downstairs.' He reappeared looking more cheerful. 'We've got him.' He pulled the gauntlet tight on his hand. 'I must go. I have a busy night ahead.' As Marcellus passed him Ephir felt two leather fingers tweak the nape of his neck. 'Good work, boy. You're wasting your time as a barber.'

'But, you haven't brought the pomade yet,' said Pilate, and Ephir, dragged suddenly from his dizzy height as a spy, became Young Barber again and scuttled off.

'The scribe was a good capture,' said Marcellus three days later. 'We now have a whole list of names. Most of them we can keep tabs on. A few we can deal with quietly. The biggest prize is in the centre of Jerusalem. Right on Annas's doorstep: in the Valley of the Cheesemakers.'

'So the scribe confessed?'

'Confessed? Oh, yes. In the first few minutes. But he tried not to tell anything more.'

'Who carried his messages from the palace?'

' A water-seller. The one who sells to the queue outside the secretariat.'

'You managed to catch him also?'

Marcellus shook his head. 'If you go out on to the balcony you can hear him still rattling his bell. I'm keeping him in reserve. He might lead me to someone more important.'

'All right. But the scribe should be crucified.'

'He died an hour ago. He collapsed under interrogation.' Marcellus saw the familiar pucker of distaste on Pilate's face. To stem criticism he quietly added, 'By the way, it was not mussels that poisoned Polygnotus: it was the scribe.'

Each time the icy breath of the night wind sneaked down the wadi Ishmael awoke. Shifting himself nearer to the niggardly fire, he pulled the sheepskin more tightly around him. This was the smallest desert gathering of partisans he had yet attended, but the intensity of the whispering of the robed figures huddling around the carefully shielded embers told him that it was probably the most important. Even so he could not keep awake. A sixteen-hour ride from Jerusalem to this desert rendezvous on the frontier of the mysterious dominion of the Arab king, Aretas, had so exhausted him that he kept dozing off, awakening only each time the sheepskin slipped and let in chilling wind. Each time he stared for a few moments at the grave faces, tried to link up their urgent questions and answers, and then nodded off again.

On one occasion, however, it was not the cold that awakened him but the growled laugh which always heralded some bitter jest from Barabbas. 'Can people really believe in such a man?' Barabbas was asking contemptuously. 'Can they believe that a Messiah promised by God will come armed with a chisel? A carpenter!' He spat into the embers. 'One things, as a worker in wood the Nazarene ought to know what kind of carpentry the

Romans would give him: the beam for a cross.'

When Ishmael next awoke he heard the reedy voice of the cheese-merchant from Jerusalem complaining about men being bound and burned alive in an inn at Magdala. 'Why was that done? Barbarities like that do our cause harm.'

'It is sometimes necessary to shock one's enemy,' Barabbas argued. 'To show him that we can be as cruel as he. Remember: "He who is merciful unto the cruel is destined some day to be cruel to the merciful." '

Soon after that Ishmael was again awakened, this time by the clatter of hooves on sliding stones, and saw three horsemen riding down the wadi and, as they approached the group, flinging back the peaked hoods and skirts of their dingy brown robes, and they looked to Ishmael like a dream springing into life from the dark sky: like three Kings from the East in splendour of jewelled turbans and velvet vests and embroidered pantaloons tucked into boots of gilt-sewn kid. Their gem-encrusted scabbards lit the night. They were young. Their nut-brown faces were sharp and keen with fiercely level brows like pencil strokes, glinting narrow eyes, straight noses and clipped black beards. They were small men, but their beauty, tight and vigorous, made them impressive, like their horses: thin-legged beasts with small square heads, flaring nostrils, coats smooth as silk, and eyes that glowed like the carnelians of Edom. The few words they spoke before Barabbas drew them away further down the wadi for private talks were in a language Ishmael had never heard before.

'Who are they?' he whispered.

'Arabs,' said one, without much enthusiasm. 'From Petra; from the court of King Aretas.'

Barabbas was away with them for close on an hour. Ishmael, eager to see the wondrous visitors again, forced himself to keep awake. Now and again, when the argument down the wadi became animated, he heard Barabbas's voice raised in its familiar clipped and angry tones; but once or twice Ishmael heard a voice he could hardly recognise as that of Barabbas: a wheedling muted wail. When they came back to the fire, hot wine and water were awaiting them, but the Arabs downed the grog quickly without squatting, and, vaulting on their horses, said they must leave at once to make sure of getting back across the frontier by daybreak. From his saddle-bag one of them drew out a long thin bundle wrapped in a scarf and handed it to Barabbas. Barabbas thanked him, and they rode off.

The cheese-merchant looked questioningly at Barabbas.

'Aretas will not move until we have drawn the Roman strength,' said Barabbas. 'Not unless we can hold Jerusalem will he move against Herod again.'

'Which is reasonable strategy,' said the merchant.

'For him, yes,' said Barabbas and gloomily nodded. He turned the bundle over on his knees. 'Well, Aretas did send me a gift. A trophy of his last battle with Herod.' He saw Ishmael eyeing the bundle. 'There, Ishmael! A present for you. From the East; from beyond the Euphrates; from a battlefield in Parthia.' Ishmael unfolded the scarf. He gasped. What he saw seemed the richest and most beautiful thing he had ever owned. 'Better than a pruning knife, eh, Ishmael?' laughed Barabbas.

Ishmael felt cold no longer. The blaze of the dagger's jewelled hilt and curved blade ran through him like a flame. He sprang to his feet, carving murderous arcs against the dark sky, and when he heard the chuckles of the partisans he shouted the words Barabbas so often quoted: ' "If someone comes to slay you, you slay him first." '

One of the partisans stretched out his hand for the dagger. Ishmael, letting him take it, stood looking down proudly as the man sighed admiration and weighed balance of hilt and blade on a finger. 'That is too good for any throat but Pilate's own,' said the partisan and handed it back.

Ishmael's eyes grew big with ambition. 'Yes. Let this blade taste Pilate's blood.'

'Ssh!' hissed Barabbas. 'Not so loud, Ishmael. Even deserts have ears.'

After warming themselves with grog, the partisans resumed their talk, and Ishmael busied himself with altering the loop of his leather belt so that he could hang his treasure upon it. Here in the desert he could wear the dagger boldly above his robe. When he got back to Jerusalem it would have to be hidden. But not for long; only until that day soon to come when all Jews would wear Zealot blades proudly shown. He swaggered up the wadi, delighting in the gaudy glitter swinging at his waist. When he came down again, Barabbas, in that voice he always used when he was summing up what had been agreed at a rendezvous, was repeating the plan for the attack on Procurator Pilate and his party.

'So, Imeer, as soon as the Roman party have left the city for the ceremony you will leave the Valley of the Cheesemakers and go to the Pool of Siloam and make your way to the cabins of the builders. Wait until the ceremony is over, until Pilate and his party are preparing to leave; then shout the word for attack. There are only a few Zealots among the builders, but enough to create a diversion. All they need do is to draw Pilate's guards towards them. When that happens I shall bring my men up the Kidron and attack the guards from the rear.'

Ishmael flourished his new dagger. 'This will kill Pilate. This will avenge my father's death.'

'Quiet, Ishmael,' said Barabbas angrily and, when Ishmael had drawn away in sulky silence, went on, 'Our main force will be camping among the pilgrims in the olive-groves around Gethsemane. They will wait until I have engaged the guards. By then the Antonia fortress will have been aroused and will be sending reinforcements. The armed pilgrims will come down from Olivet, their daggers hidden, and crowd around the city gates. They will not engage the troops coming out. They will enter the city when the troops have gone out. Then they will close, or barricade, the Fountain Gate. I and Imeer will retreat through the Dung Gate and then close that one. Our first objectives are the Court of the Gentiles and the Temple; our eventual aim is to invest the city.'

'How long must we hold out there?'

'Perhaps four days. Or less. The cavalry of Aretas will arrive first, and his foot will be with us before Roman reinforcements can move up from Caesarea.' He turned to Imeer. 'Comrade, a lot depends on you. It is you who must choose the right moment to attack Pilate's party. Anyhow, you can hardly forget the word, can you?'

'Messiah!'

'Messiah!' Barabbas only whispered it, but it sighed through the night like a battle-cry. 'What better battle-cry could we have? Messiah!'

The others, beginning to stamp out scattered embers, laughed softly.

Imeer laughed too. 'It will be really odd if that Galilean does arrive at the same time.'

'If he does, he can carpenter a coffin for Pilate. The Nazarene is welcome to the scraps of our victory.'

Imeer swung himself into the saddle.

'God be with you,' said Barabbas.

Imeer bent down to embrace him, then spurred his mount. The horse clattered up the wadi and disappeared in the silence of sand and the blackness of night.

Soon the others left by their separate ways, until only the old merchant remained with Barabbas and Ishmael. He got stiffly to his feet and clambered on to his mule. Anxiously Barabbas said, 'But you cannot get to Jerusalem before dawn.'

'I shall not try. I shall be near Jericho before daylight, and I shall spend the day there on business so that I reach Jerusalem unobserved at nightfall.'

'God be with you!' said Barabbas.

'God be with you!'

The merchant watched Barabbas and Ishmael head down the wadi towards the northern trail. When they were out of sight he turned his mount up the wadi, and turned south. The animal followed the track obediently, and the merchant, ample and sedate like any prosperous trader returning contentedly from profitable deals, dozed most of the way until he reached a village north of Jericho. There he breakfasted at the farm of a kinsman and slept through the morning. During the afternoon he called on merchant friends in Jericho, and later sat with them under palm-trees outside their favourite inn which faced the pastry-stalls below the walls of the old town. He arrived in Jerusalem in the dark, as he had planned. For although as a merchant he could always advance legitimate business reasons for going out of town, it was wiser not to be seen leaving the city or returning to it too often. He stabled the mule in the cabin it shared with the mule of a neighbour and then quietly made his way unobserved into the Valley of the Cheesemakers. He rapped on the shutter drawn across his booth. An upper window in the house opened. He whistled softly. The window closed. He walked then into the deep archway giving access to the courtyard, waiting there for his wife Ruth to slip down and unbar the door. He yawned and rubbed his plump belly. He was looking forward to a bowl of fresh curds and some of his own wine. A light glinted behind the door, and he heard the bar being levered up. 'Quickly, Ruth,' he whispered under a laugh. I'm hungry, I'm cold, I'm thirsty!' The door swung open, and he saw, uncertain in the jigging light of one small handlamp, the outline of her beloved face slanting round the edge of the door. She looked pale. Her mouth was hanging open as though with surprise or fear. Murmuring reassuring and tender words he stepped quickly towards her. He had reached the doorway, was

337

actually stepping inside, before he saw why her face was pale. It had no body attached to it. It was dangling by its hair, the white tresses bunched in the fingers of a gauntlet curiously fashioned of leather and metal.

X

Not Caesar himself, certainly not the parsimonious Tiberius, could have put on a grander show! Pilate had guessed that Vitellius would glorify his arrival in Caesarea with trappings befitting a favourite of Caesar, but as soon as the trireme was sighted rounding the mole he realised that this visit of Caesar's plenipotentiary to Asia, this return to the area of his past successes and future ambitions, was to be more impressive than anyone could have foreseen.

It was a sunlit windless morning. The sea had but the kindliest swell, which the new-built vessel, a lovely confection of clean fresh timber, unsullied paint and virgin cord, breasted languidly, its brilliant prow rising and dipping in slow and regal nods to acknowledge the tribute of massed standards and fluttering pennons, and guards glittering stiff along the quay. The vessel's upper deck, furnished with an extravagance of painted bucklers and stencilled hangings and many sumptuously fringed awnings that swayed on garlanded poles, blossomed like a bouquet, its hues so brilliant that reflections of it were scattered like petals over the glassy sea, and as the trireme came nearer Pilate could hear, flowing ahead of it across the undulating sea in rhythm with the oars, fragments of music played by a band of pipers in the stern. Members of Vitellius's entourage could be seen moving through the velvety shadow of the awnings. Some of them wore helmets and cuirasses burnished to a brightness that rivalled the sun. But others, obviously in enjoyment of a sunlit and peaceful cruise, had decked themselves out in crisp tunics and dainty kilts, and sported a wealth of jewelled belts and golden collars and glittering bracelets.

Aroused by this lavish display, Pilate sent for Severus, at that moment due to leave for the port to marshal the guard of honour, and instructed him to have every available man who possessed military gear of suitable magnificence rounded up immediately and marched down to the waterfront to endow the reception with extra glitter.

By the time Pilate himself reached the port the last wrinkles were being smoothed from the heavy rugs laid all along the quay, and the trireme, its oars slowing, was gliding across the smooth water of the harbour. And now Vitellius, for surely that figure seated on a high draped chair must be his, could be picked out. Sitting in the very midst of the magnificently colourful throng, so enclosed by it and yet so immeasurably cordoned off from it by his intransigent austerity, he was, in his ostentatiously simple habit, uniquely impressive. The ornate canopy raised above his throne shadowed the whole of his rigid figure, except for one bronzed and sinewy arm which flashed out again and again into the Asian sunlight as, with a silver-wreathed and silver-eagle-headed baton, he pointed out landmarks of the city to members of his court who, clustering at the rail or sitting low around him on trestle stools fashioned of fretted wood and scalloped leather, swung obedient eyes to each building or monument of his choice.

The dockers and tradesmen who frequented Caesarea's waterfront were so accustomed to the coming and going of important personages from Rome and Greece and Alexandria and Sidon and Tyre that they usually accorded little more than passing attention to formal receptions at the port. But this morning's spectacle of colour and music was so exceptional that it brought them crowding towards the quay, and also stimulated the pickle-vendors and water-sellers to an ecstasy of clashing bells, though that must have been more out of excitement than from any hope of attracting customers, for the townsfolk had little time for pickles or water as, jostling each other aside and crouching down or craning up, they peered above the shoulders or between the knees of soldiers to catch glimpses of this visitor whom Pilate was honouring with his presence and with such a prodigal array of soldiers.

The oars swung upright, scattering sunlit jewels. The music shrilled to a higher note. The mooring ropes were cast down. The vessel bumped gently to its berth. A railed gangplank was hoisted into position. And Vitellius stood up.

Vitellius descended. He came down gently. Yes, he was, as Pilate had been told, slight and lean, no taller than Pilate himself – and as slender of figure, as the Divine Julius. Yet he held himself so erect and was, to outward appearances at least, so corseted in imperious self-confidence, that he did not seem markedly diminished in height by the two taller officers who accompanied him. These two, who had quickly detached themselves from the rest of the entourage to march closely beside him with the air of being his chosen intimates, were remarkably young: so youthful that one must suspect them of possessing most precocious talent for them to have risen to such favour at such an early age. They were outstandingly athletic, though in a supple, graceful manner.

Vitellius looked serenely amiable as he paced over the rugs, extending both hands with regal geniality towards Proconsul Pilate. Pilate recited the words of greeting he had rehearsed that morning, introducing, as though spontaneously, reference to his guest's distinguished career in Asia. Vitellius responded by jerking his head in stiff military acknowledgement, and then inspected his host. Though this inspection was of the briefest duration, it seemed to Pilate that even in so short a time those experienced eyes had executed an all-embracing inventory of every inch of his appearance and sucked up his very thoughts, so that behind the intent stare were now stored all the relevant facts, particularly the disappointing ones, pertaining to Proconsul Pilate, Procurator of Judaea. But in almost less time than it took to notice it, this probing glance was switched off, and after casting a relaxed glance towards the entourage now assembling on the quay, Vitellius expressed his hope that neither Pilate nor the establishment in Caesarea would be incommoded by his having brought so large a number of retainers.

'This was necessary,' he added, lowering his voice to a whisper which Pilate found highly flattering by its suggestion that he alone should hear an important secret. 'For certain reasons my sojourn in Asia might be a lengthy one.' Was this, Pilate thought, a hint that those rumours in Antioch were to be confirmed? He waited, expectant, for further confidences from this man who, in that case, had been chosen to be his future overlord in Asia.

341

'However,' Vitellius went on, 'I can of course say no more about that until Caesar has himself publicly made known his intentions.' He had, he continued, taken the advantage of bringing with him several young men who had military ambitions and whose outstanding talent justified their high hopes. They were all, of course, of patrician family. He pointed his baton, first at the two youngsters flanking him and then at other uniformed dandies forming up behind him. And it had been necessary also, he continued, to bring with him the choicest of his household slaves: his invaluable steward, two physicians, three scribes, a librarian and assistants who were in charge of a prodigious collection of military manuals, his valet and body-slaves. 'Some cooks as well. They are experienced in my diet. Oh, and my masseur. Without him,' he sighed, flexing his strong wrists, 'I cannot *move*. Ah, and there is, of course, that wrestler I told you about.' He pointed to a blank-faced lad in a grey athletic cloak, his short blond hair bound with a leather band, accompanied by two swarthy porters. Vitellius beckoned the wrestler forward. 'The fellow has high hopes of carrying off laurels at the Games.' The hint of mockery in his voice indicated that the enthusiasm for the lad which he had expressed in his letter to Pilate had worn thin. 'But he'll need to get rid of some flesh,' he said, pushing aside the boy's cloak at the neck to grip a meaty chunk of his shoulder. 'He has been lying about too much.' He drew his hand away, and Pilate could see that under what must have been a quite fierce grip of that sinewy claw the flesh had flushed and showed the indentations left by the nails. 'He must put in some training and find some muscle again,' added Vitellius as he pushed the boy away with a sharp prod of the winged eagle on the tip of his baton.

The musicians were still playing. Oh, no, those were not part of his entourage. He had heard them perform in Cyprus. He had thought them good: one of them especially had seemed to possess attractive talent. So he had hired them to enliven the crossing. But they had been, on the whole, disappointing. They would be returning to Cyprus where this beautiful new trireme, newly built in Castellammare and put at his disposal by Caesar, was to be stationed.

His baggage? All of that must come ashore, of course, but he would take to the palace only such pieces as were needed for his use in Caesarea and Jerusalem. Those pieces were labelled accordingly. The rest could remain at the docks, in safe custody of course, until he proceeded to Antioch. For he intended to make the journey to Antioch by boat rather than have his wardrobes and furnishings trundled along that dusty northern road. Though there was one piece of baggage which he wished to see brought safely ashore before he left the quay. 'My personal secretary is attending to it at this moment,' he said, pointing his baton back towards the trireme where a surly brawny youth was going through the motions of performing that service, though doing little more than stamping his sandalled foot as he watched seamen man-handle a square crate from the lowest deck. 'It is a gift for you, Proconsul,' said Vitellius with a lordly nod, and it was then that Severus, who had been searching his memory, recalled where he had seen this distinguished military gentleman before. And it was also at this moment that Vitellius, casting his inspecting eyes over members of Pilate's escort, caught Severus's gaze, narrowed his eyes to look more closely at him, and then briefly nodded recognition. That capacious inexhaustible memory had not forgotten the sweat-smeared young soldier who had sprawled beside the gunwale of the boat from Puzzuoli, snoring inappropriately in sight of Caesar's Capri.

Pilate now presented Severus and his officers, and then, flanked by guards who had been specially picked out for this detail because of their physique and exceptionally immaculate turn-out, the Procurator and his guest ascended the staircases towards the palace, with the populous entourage drawn in their wake, rippling up the steps like a train woven from a peacock's tail and studded with burnished brass and ornaments of gold. Vitellius, his military gaze darting left and right, apparently noted everything: the spick-and-span soldiers marching alongside as escort, the fierce Syrian sentinels perched like hawks along the terraces, the garlanded statues on the esplanade, and even, further off, strings of whooping boys from the town who, darting between almond-trees heavy with blossom, tried to catch glimpses of the procession and the newcomer. He made no comment. Absence of comment apparently signified, with him, approval, except when he noticed, through a gateway giving access to a city street, a group of shawl-swathed young men who, withdrawn and silent, watched the Roman parade. These he described, to Pilate's surprise, as 'lean and lovely Jews', though it seemed he was quoting someone, and went on to explain that the sight of them reminded him more than anything else of the days of his youth when he had been so happily and energetically engaged in this province.

In the great courtyard of the palace, which this morning had been cleansed of its customary clutter of pastry-stalls and pickle-barrows and queuing suitors, scores of standards and banners gleamed and fluttered, and every balcony was burdened with swags of heavy fabric looped up with cords plaited from threads of gold and regal purple. Troops stood in a hollow square, forming with their brass-bossed shields a wall around the altar.

After the libations and sacrifices came the moment for Julius to step forward and perform a ceremony he had prepared as a means of taking special advantage of the arrival of Caesar's favourite: that of presenting to Vitellius a scroll expressing the city's appreciation of the honour of having so illustrious a patron for the forthcoming Games. Julius had decided that the most appropriate costume he could wear for the occasion was his athlete's robe. It was a becoming garment, unadorned and simple, but modest though the robe might appear to an uninformed eye, it was his favourite one, very costly and very precious, for it was made of wool from the sheep of the high plateaux above Miletus and was woven without seams in one piece, and in a circle so that it would hang in even and regular folds. To add to his dignity, Julius had marshalled a personal escort, each soldier carrying an emblem, such as a discus or knuckle-spikes or a staff, representative of a particular sport, and he was also attended by Ephir who had gleefully decked himself out in the costume of an Asian prince's body-slave, wearing Babylonian breeches and waistcoat fashioned from embroidered worsted, and calf-high boots of white kid, of skin so young and soft that the tops sagged even under the gentle weight of peacock-feather tassels knotted with silver thread.

The grave and haughty dignity with which Vitellius accepted the scroll endowed the ceremony with such high importance that the delighted Julius directed a frank and boyish smile of thanks full in the face of the important personage. But Julius was accorded no answering smile. The eyes now looking him over, eyes drilled for years to rigid concealment of desire, inspected him from head to toe with chilling deliberation. Though, for just one moment, it did seem that the lips, which had involuntarily parted for a sudden intake of breath, something between a sigh and a gasp, might widen into the candour of a smile, and it was then, under the threat of the possible smile, that Julius's innocent friendliness faltered, and sudden shyness, inexplicable, made him droop his head, so that Pilate saw, for the first time he had ever seen it on Julius's living features, that same downcast and troubled aspect which the Greek sculptor had apparently seen one day in his studio in Athens when he carved his over-sentimental statue of the boy. Vitellius broke off his inspection of Julius with an abruptness that looked almost like exasperation and turned to Pilate. 'I had not imagined, Proconsul,' he said, in a murmur, in a voice robbed of its usual self-confident yelp, 'I had not imagined that your son was already an accomplished young man,' and then he marched stiffly on towards the garlanded archway leading to the private apartments. Pilate, pleased that Julius had made so favourable an impression, stole a glance over his shoulder intending to smile approval at his son, but was disconcerted to see Julius standing there red-faced, and that idiotic Ephir unaccountably bent double and clutching his sides in unseemly but fortunately silent laughter.

Vitellius maintained his tight-lipped silence, that apparently approving silence, as Pilate conducted him past the doorways and arches and statues and freshly painted murals of the succession of rooms prepared for his stay in Caesarea. Even at the new mosaic on the floor of the vaulted balconied room adapted as his bedchamber he stared without comment. When this floor was being laid, architect Lucius had shown to local craftsmen his sketches of a notorious floor that had taken his youthful fancy years ago in Pompeii. At first the cavortings of nymphs and satyrs, more naughty than the prudish eastern minds of Caesarean workmen had ever dared to imagine, let alone illustrate with coloured marbles, had shocked them into timid giggles, but by the time they were actually laying the mosaic the sketches had inflamed them to reckless invention of embraces which even the Pompeian artist would have judged too outrageous for domestic decoration. Fortunately the marbles they had used were of such muted sea-green, sea-blue, and milky tints that a casual onlooker saw only a pleasing indeterminate pattern flowing across the vast floor, without noticing what was actually taking place under his feet. The curves and shadows of flanks and breasts and waists and the amorous exercises being performed by mouths and limbs and hands and other members became explicit only after a detailed examination of the floor. This examination, Pilate uneasily thought, Vitellius seemed on the point of devoting to it, whereupon he diverted Vitellius's attention to the adjoining dressing-room where, screened by cupboards, superbly carved from cedar-wood by Jewish carpenters, was the head of the stairway of grey marble which descended to the new steam baths.

After this Pilate led his guest out on to the bedroom's wide balcony which commanded a view of the harbour. Vitellius flung out his arms so wide in delighted appreciation that for a moment Pilate was tempted to launch there and then into the questions he was so anxious to ask. But now could be heard behind them the bustle of porters carrying in chests and bundles of baggage, and the voice of the palace steward explaining to Vitellius's steward the disposition of the various rooms; so Pilate, deciding that it might be precipitate to launch so soon on such a delicate operation, contented himself with saying, 'I thought you would be too tired after your voyage to face an official reception this evening, so I have arranged the banquet for tomorrow. However, I should be honoured if you would dine with me and my wife today. There will be no other guests.

'Of course. And your son too.'

Pilate smiled. 'Julius does not eat with us when we are entertaining guests. He is still at an age when he finds the presence of us old ones too restrictive.' When Vitellius looked somewhat vexed at this, Pilate added hurriedly, 'He has acquired a circle of friends of his own age, and when he is free of work he likes to spend time with them.'

'But the boy is the son of the Proconsul Procurator, so he should be encouraged to take advantage of that relationship and cultivate the company of politicians. And, my dear Pilate,' Vitellius went on with a seductive smile, 'I beg of you not to treat me as merely a guest. I should be happier to be thought of as one of the family.'

'Thank you, Vitellius.' Pilate, pleased even if somewhat disconcerted at the speed with which Caesar's favourite had become 'one of the family', said, 'I hope you will be happy with us.'

The view seemed to be satisfying Vitellius, for he remained standing on the balcony when Pilate took his leave and heard him calling his secretary to join him out there. Along the corridor the wrestler was sitting on an unpacked chest, berating his two swarthy slaves who, under his curses, stood drooping in the conventional attitude of upbraided slaves, but exchanging insolent and contemptuous grins. The wrestler, awaiting one of the doctors, kept breaking off his abuse to inspect, with that hysterical terror characteristic of athletes, a well-nigh invisible scratch on his angle which he had suffered, he wailingly protested, because of the clumsiness of those two slaves whose duty it was to protect and cherish his valuable body. As Pilate went down the stairway he heard Vitellius call out again, this time with an impatient bark, for his secretary, and saw the lad, just then crossing the stair, press his hands against his ears and let out a petulant sigh, although, as he hurried up to join his master, he began dutifully composing his features into that expression of admiration which Vitellius would think requisite when gazing out on yet another port.

Vitellius, staring haughtily out to sea, did not turn his head when the lad joined him at the balustrade. 'The choicest view in Asia,' he said with a proprietorial air. 'Finer than anything in Greece. Perhaps as fine as anything in Italy.' He now turned to see if his companion was suitably impressed, and his lips tightened with exasperation when he saw with what blank mindless and unselective eyes the fellow was gazing out on nothing.

Truth was the youth felt wearied to death, too weary by far to drag up any new expression, either of face or word. It felt to him that his very head was near to bursting with all the sights and views and monuments and temples that had been stuffed into it during the long voyage from Italy. What was it that he had to look at this time? There was a city; there was some sea; there were boats. There had been a city and sea and boats for weeks. However, he forced a nod, which, after all, was as much, though he was not to know that, as Vitellius had vouchsafed. Then with a shrug he turned away, but immediately he had done that he became conscious of the icy anger he had aroused. He attempted a gesture of apology. He mimed tiredness, passing the back of one heavy wrist over his sweaty forehead. Then he managed to summon up once again the rueful appealing smile which in the past had often saved him censure, and at that Vitellius reached out his brown hand, stretching it towards the brooch which pinned the youth's tunic at the shoulder. Hesitantly, retaining the smile, the youth glided forward until his shoulder came in contact with Vitellius's hand, and the strong fingers were able to lay themselves on the fabric of the tunic. It seemed to be the beginning of a friendly and familiar grasp, but Vitellius, using only thumb and forefinger, did no more than lift one of the folds. 'Your tunic is dirty, fellow. And get down to the baths. Your presence is a little more bearable when it has a little less stench.'

Vitellius was again staring at the view by the time the youth had reached the centre of the bedroom. His master's voice halted him there. 'And later go down to the port. In the crate marked "Trophies" you will find a bronze urn, the lid surmounted with a

347

Greek athlete. Strike it off the inventory on the lid of the crate and bring it to me.' Vitellius heard a murmur humbly acknowledging his order. He sighed. Compared with this youth, once so beautiful but now so tarnished and jaded in his service, that lovely Julius, son of Pilate, seemed bright and crisp as a new-cut gem. That urn from Olympia, with a Greek runner straddling the laurel-wreathed lid, in unashamed and impudently explicit nudity, would be an eminently suitable gift for the youthful major-domo of the Caesarea Games.

As Pilate walked to his study his thoughts glowed with memories of the colour, the sunlight, the magnificence, the success of the morning's ceremony. The glow was quickly doused. Marcellus was awaiting him. Marcellus was smiling. It was a satisfied smile, but savage and sunless, and Pilate found himself listening to a recital of the dark and dirty deeds performed in black corners below that glittering view Vitellius was enjoying on his balcony.

Names that had been dragged out of the traitor scribe, Marcellus was saying, had opened doors into the very heart of Zealot conspiracy. A man had been arrested in Jerusalem. He was not one of those insignificant hooligans such as the army rounded up in villages. Outwardly a rich and respectable cheese-merchant, he had turned out to be a treasurer in the Zealot organisation and a confidant of Zealot leaders. His house, 'almost on Annas's doorstep', had been the resort of terrorists, some of whom were actually Levites at the Temple. The house had also been the regular hideout of a Zealot leader.

Marcellus did not mention the name Barabbas. That important information was too precious to be scattered around, even to Pilate. Nor did Marcellus tell Pilate that the Jerusalem arrest had come dangerously near to failure. His agents, pretending to be Zealots, and supported in that pretence by a message giving them easy access to the merchant's house, had blundered. By some careless word they had aroused the suspicions of the man's wife. Terrified by thoughts of the punishment they would suffer at the hands of Marcellus if their blunder should send his carefully laid plot awry, they had panicked, with the result that the steps they had taken to silence the good lady had been hasty and excessive. By the time Marcellus reached the house the good lady's tongue, which might have been persuaded to wag, was beyond doing so. Nevertheless, the misadventure had in a way been advantageous;

the scene which had greeted the husband on his homecoming that night had so shocked him that he was more quickly than usual in a suggestible frame of mind.

But Pilate was asking a question. 'What has this merchant told you?'

'Oh, I have only just begun with him. He is old, so we dare not do too much to him at any one session. We don't want *his* tongue to die on us. After each interrogation we have to give him time to recover for the next. He is trying to be loyal to his criminal associates, and he is stubborn. But he is as full of facts as a pig is of fat, and he will squeal as loudly.'

With deliberate intent Marcellus began to enlarge on the kind of 'persuasion' one could use on an old man without killing him, and succeeded in drawing from Pilate another request not to be plagued with such unpleasant details. The gradual accumulation of such commands added up to assuring Marcellus that he would have complete freedom in future operations, and he saw the time fast approaching when he would more than ever need freedom to act without question. That time would be when he laid hands on Barabbas. This he felt sure of doing at Passover. That capture would herald a decisive stage in his strategy against the Zealots. It would be equivalent to seizing a general on the field of battle. He teased himself by speculating whether he would put Barabbas to death. One did not slaughter generals out of hand as one slaughtered lesser ranks. The crimes of generals were greater than the crimes of the poor wretches they had commanded, but generals were correspondingly more valuable alive. In fact, one sometimes accorded generals the honours of war. If, however, Barabbas was stubborn and had to be put to death, then that would be a crucifixion which would be best performed with the utmost publicity in order to dismay the Zealots with a spectacle of one of their leaders hanging on a cross like a miserable robber.

Marcellus felt confident that the Passover *coup* he was planning would be quick and clean and not too tumultuous, but he judged it unwise to reveal to Pilate what the Zealots were hoping to do at the festival. If Pilate knew that, he might be apprehensive about the safety of his important visitor, and change the programme for the inauguration of the aqueduct: that ceremony, Marcellus hoped, was to be the trap in which Barabbas would be caught.

Pilate began fussily arranging scrolls and documents across his desk. Marcellus took the hint and left.

Marcellus was highly satisfied with that brief conference. Pilate might have thought, and it was better that he should, that what had passed was merely routine approval of current actions, but Marcellus saw it as approval for unspecified future ones. It was one more step up the stairway, as private a stairway as that one he had tunnelled to Pilate's threshold, up which he was climbing to advancement. Marcellus was ambitious. He admitted it to himself. Yet his desires were not fixed on honours and high office. Such things could do no more than prove his success to others, whereas Marcellus wanted to prove his talents to himself. During his years as a serving soldier he had not dreamed dreams of becoming a general because he craved the uniforms and standards of generalship. His ambitions had never been so gaudy. Trappings of generalship could make the world gaze in awe on Marcellus; but Marcellus wanted not the world but Marcellus to gaze in awe, wanted to savour the exquisite joy of solving the puzzle in secret and spurning the prize. The fire of this desire, fierce enough to keep ambition on the boil even when his military future was crippled, had warmed him during his task in the dungeons. At last he had transmuted that menial labour into that of weaving the web of security which he considered essential in the conflict against terrorism and of which he alone could trace the threads. His old comrade-in-arms, Pontius Pilate, was welcome to enjoy the procuratorial pomp and ceremony which so obviously delighted him. Marcellus, for his part, was content to be the faceless one behind the throne, hugging in private happiness his secret power.

Actually Pilate did find, for some moments after Marcellus had left him, that several doubts aroused by the conversation kept intruding into his mind. But, he told himself, Marcellus had proved himself capable and inventive: if, later, he did exceed his brief, then he could be checked.

At the moment the immediate preoccupation was Vitellius. First of all and most of all, Pilate hoped to have from Vitellius's lips reassurance that the Sejanus débâcle had not prejudiced Pilate's future in Judaea nor blocked his prospect of higher office in Asia.

After working for a couple of hours, he sent a cordial message to Vitellius inviting him to a chat before dinner. News was sent back that Vitellius, after his bath, had gone to the secretariat, where he had spent some time with Julius and then invited the boy to take him to the hippodrome and show him the improvements being made to the twelve stalls for the chariot races, which architect Lucius hoped would be more efficient, even if less monumental, than those in the circuses of Rome or elsewhere.

Exasperated at the thought that Vitellius should seem more urgently interested in circuses and athletes than in matters of state, Pilate banged shut his desk and left his study. As he stalked to the balcony, he saw that the wrestler had taken possession of the patch of ground which Julius and Ephir used for their gymnastics and was showing off his oiled torso to members of the household staff, including Ephir. The audience, more bewildered than impressed by the spectacle of anyone doting so unashamedly on the ripple of his own muscles, whispered among themselves, but out of good manners restrained their giggles to those moments when the wrestler, his face somewhere out of sight in a knot of sweaty limbs, could not see them. Neither could he see Ephir's grotesque mimicry of his entwined poses. Pilate turned away and, still heavily frowning, walked along to the salon.

Claudia was there, lying on a rug and laughing appeals for mercy as Severus's son, flourishing bronze-painted wooden sword and tin shield, marched stumblingly upon her. She looked up. 'Isn't he like his father? So solid and serious.'

'I had hoped to see Vitellius. But he has sneaked off to the hippodrome, taking Julius with him.'

'I quite dread meeting that fabulous character,' said Claudia as she snatched out at the wooden sword but just failed to capture it.

'I hope to have some talk with him after dinner. Leave us alone as soon as possible.'

'He has sent a luxurious gift.' Claudia pointed towards an embrasure, and Pilate now noticed the glittering present which had been installed there. He walked over to look more closely at it. It was a statue of a pirouetting dancing boy heavily encrusted with enamel. Balanced on the tips of the raised hands was a bronze bowl. 'A costly piece I should guess,' he murmured.

'Julius thinks the figure is Greek and probably quite old. But the bowl, he says, is Roman and new and fastened on quite recently. Not too well fastened either, Julius noticed.'

Pilate tilted the statue. One of the hands had been slightly disfigured when the bowl had been welded on to it. 'I see what he means.' However, the obvious expensiveness of the gift could surely be seen as a comforting assurance of Vitellius's amiability.

'You must make sure of being lavish with your thanks though,' went on Claudia and then added with a laugh, 'He's given Julius a gift as well. A Greek urn which he claims is antique. Julius says it's a reproduction, fifty years old and bad at that.'

But Pilate was not listening. 'At the banquet tomorrow,' he said, 'we must seat Octavius near to us on the dais.'

'I suppose so.' Claudia sighed. 'Let us hope he stays sober.'

'Yes, let us hope so. But as Chamberlain he should be with us. And his wife. After all,' he added, also pulling a face, 'she is a Roman aristocrat. We must seat Albinus on the dais too. He's Roman enough for Vitellius.'

'I suppose so. Though I find Albinus's talk of poets and theatres only one shade less boring that Octavius's dogs and snares.' The boy, circling Claudia, whooped a laugh as once again he evaded her grasp. 'However, we have to show Caesar's favourite that we have culture here as well as in Rome.' She darted a hand out and this time managed to grab the boy's shoulders. 'Now you're my prisoner.' She gathered him towards her, and as he sobbed with laughter in her embrace said, 'Now I'll cut off your head.' The boy squealed and wriggled.

The commotion was at its height when the nurse came in from the anteroom. 'Come on, child. Time for bed.' She took the boy's hand. The boy pouted solemn disappointment at the interruption of his game, but obediently lisped good night to Aunt Claudia and submitted to being led away.

'I have invited ship-owner Accius too. Make a point of having a few words with him.'

'If I can get near him,' she said with another laugh. 'He went on that reducing treatment to Bauli, but his stomach is still vaster than his wealth.'

'The wealth is the more important,' said Pilate dryly, but then recollected the nurse who had taken the boy away. 'Why is that Luganese woman looking after the boy? Where is the Galilean woman?'

'She has gone home.'

'Home. You cannot mean Magdala?'

'Yes. To Magdala.'

'By whose permission?'

'I let her go. I told the secretary to give her a permit.'

His frown deepened. 'By what right, Claudia? Don't you realise that she was a prisoner and was brought here as a slave?'

'Surely after all this time . . .'

'She was a Galilean too,' he interrupted. 'Did you consult Marcellus?'

'No.' She acted a little shudder of repulsion. 'That is the last thing I should do. It was better for her, Pontius, and for her child, to join her family.'

'How did she go? Alone?'

'Two members of her family came for her.'

'Galilean baptists, no doubt. Perhaps even Zealots, for all you know. Please stand up.' She did so. 'I resent this very much. I find it intolerable that my wife should have acted without my authority.'

'Your wife!' She drew herself up. 'Indeed, I am your wife. Do not forget it. I am the wife of the Procurator of Judaea. Surely, in that lofty position, I can exercise my discretion in matters relating to the household. I have some rights.'

'Right, Claudia? Your rights are more restrained than those of the wife of a kitchen porter. In a lesser person stupidity can be overlooked: not in you. As the Procurator's lady you are obliged to be circumspect in all you do.'

'Like Caesar's wife!'

He flushed with anger at the mockery, but went on, 'In any case you should have shown the courtesy of discussing this matter with me first.'

'I have tried to do so. Not specifically, I admit. But I have tried to tell you about the Magdalene and her beliefs.'

'I know. And I have deplored your over-indulgent attitude to the woman and to those uncertain beliefs. I have refrained from taxing you with that. But now I find myself wishing that I had done so. If only to emphasise what you ought to know: that I dislike an official's wife intruding on his official affairs.'

'I cannot see that sending a woman and a child home to their family is an official affair.'

'Of course not. As a woman you can see only the emotional aspect of an action. But if you had given the matter intelligent thought you might have appreciated that the political situation in Judaea and the delicate state of affairs between my administration and that of Herod is more important than emotions.'

She shook her head. 'Pontius!' She came forward and in a less argumentative tone said, 'Perhaps a woman's view is sometimes wiser. There are moments when emotions, when human sentiment and the happiness of one person can be more important than politics.'

He drew back. 'A typically feminine remark! In making it you reveal how a woman lacks the logicality and objectivity essential to the conduct of public affairs. There are times, Claudia, when to grant what a woman sees as happiness to one person could destroy the happiness of a thousand. I do not think that the Magdala woman has such sinister importance. But, although she might be blameless in herself, she could be used by others, if for nothing more than passing on any information she has picked up in the palace.'

'She is too good to be used by anyone for evil. And the Galilean preacher . . .'

'I have heard enough. I am not prepared to listen to yet another sermon from the Sea of Galilee.'

'But I have learned so much, Pontius. I want to tell you . . .'

'No, I say. I am not prepared to listen. At this moment I do not find myself in a gentle or conciliatory mood. If you must tell me more, I beg you, my good lady, to choose your time carefully.'

Without attempting the formal words which he customarily used whenever he took leave of her, he turned abruptly and walked out. He went back to his study. There, deciding not to waste the two hours before dinner, he opened his desk and resumed work. After a few moments he jumped up again. He had felt, mildly but disturbingly suddenly, that little shaft of pain needling again at his stomach. He went to his bedroom, searched the cabinet for the medicine, took a gulp of it, grimaced at the repulsive taste, and went back to his desk.

Julius had promised Ephir and the soldiers who had acted as his escort that morning so well and with such good humour that they would enjoy a rollicking little feast of their own this evening, but now he had to tell them that he was commanded to dine with his parents and the old fellow from Rome. Pilate felt proud at the way his son now succeeded in concealing any trace of young and gauche embarrassment in the presence of Caesar's favourite, and the way in which he almost succeeded in wearing his adult toga, with which he had been so recently invested, as though it were his customary garb. But Pilate's pride was accompanied by a momentary spasm of sadness engendered by the thought of how soon the ebullient mischievousness of boyhood must be subdued under the gravity of manhood. For a moment he longed to be able to use those words spoken by that father in Plautus: 'No filial awe, my boy, for me. It's your love I want.' This sentimental thought Pilate sternly thrust aside. No proconsul father could use the words of a vulgarian comedian. Such sentimental utterances would diminish that *patria potestas* which a Roman son must ever observe.

Claudia responded to her son's bow with her accustomed grace, but her smile, Pilate noted, lacked its customary ease. Claudia seemed unusually subdued this evening. Perhaps she was tired, although he found himself admiring, as he always did on social occasions, her aristocratic grace. She was so accomplished. Somehow she managed to wear a resplendent gown and the whole wealth of Sextia's sapphires glittering on her neck and ears and bust and wrists with an air which implied that, although she was accustomed to costly luxury, this evening's exquisite toilette was a personal compliment to an honoured and welcome guest.

Pilate felt this evening the wish, so unusual for him, to indulge in wine. Wine, he thought, might relax the nervous tension which afflicted him at the prospect of having to gear himself throughout a whole evening to the task of nourishing the favour of Vitellius. So, although the nagging ache in his belly warned him to stick to water, he took some wine, and was soon astonished by a sensation that things were going quite well.

Vitellius, that severe tight-laced warrior politician, seemed determined this evening to be amazingly relaxed and amiable, and although his conversation with Pilate and Claudia was, of necessity, formal and dignified, he showed that amiable equality, one so unexpected in him, of softening his fierce wit to teasing amiability in his long interchanges with Julius. And the boy was responding, was becoming increasingly relaxed and frank under the kindly but never condescending questions directed on him by Caesar's famous intimate. In fact, Julius was being drawn out so much that he was emboldened even to contradict the politician on aspects of the Caesarea Games. To Pilate's immense surprise Vitellius took the boy's contrary arguments in great good humour – so much so that Pilate actually felt a twinge of jealously when he noticed that this Vitellius was more amiably disposed to the mere boy who wilfully contradicted him than he was to the Procurator who diplomatically agreed with him.

Vitellius, who had obviously inspected with appreciative interest the lists drawn up by Julius in the secretariat, commended the boy on his success in attracting so many famous athletes to Caesarea. He also approved the idea, seeing that the Games were being staged in Asia, of adopting the Greek custom of staging competitions also for poets and musicians. 'But,' he said, 'I fear your spectators are going to be grievously disappointed at the absence of gladiators.'

Julius shook his head in such candid disagreement that Pilate was uneasy.

But Vitellius only smiled and asked, 'You do not agree?'

No, Julius did not agree. The Caesarea Games, he pointed out, were taking place in a part of the world where people were known to have strong and religious prejudices against life-and-death spectacles being staged for mere entertainment.

'But fights to the death . . . ' Vitellius began with a strangely feverish leer, but then a quivering intake of breath interrupted his utterance.

'Caesar himself . . . ' began Julius.

'Ah, yes, my young friend!' Vitellius had got his breath back. 'You can, I admit, quote sentiments that Caesar has expressed against gladiatorial exhibitions. But I dare, as others dare, speculate that Caesar's main objection to them is because of the amount of money they spill rather than the amount of blood. And any true Roman must recognise that the slaughter of gladiators is not merely vulgar joy, for each dying gladiator represents that sacrifice which the living must willingly and honourably render to the spirits of the dead and to our deified Caesars. Also, as Cicero has so wisely observed, the spectators themselves receive an incomparable training in despising suffering and the pangs of death. Surely you, as a young Roman, will agree with that?'

No, Julius did not agree. Quite stubbornly he insisted that games staged in Asia should have more a Greek than a Roman flavour. 'The Caesarea Games,' he went on, 'should be more like the games in Athens – wrestling, boxing, foot races, chariot races, discus and javelin throwing, but also music and poetry: Greek poetry as well as Latin poetry. We would have had Hebraic, if the Jews could have been persuaded to compete.'

Vitellius shook his head. But his disagreeing was amiable, and he smiled quite broadly as he teasingly asked, 'Games without corpses, eh? Roman spectators always find Greek games rather colourless for that very reason.'

'The audience in Caesarea will not be Roman,' said Julius. There would be, he went on, only a minority of Romans, and it would be foolish to flout public opinion for the sake of pleasing that minority even more foolish to offend all his non-Roman friends, even some Jews in the secretariat, who had already done so much to help in preparing for the Games. 'We are not Roman

356

here,' the lad went on boldly. 'We are Asian. And probably all the more civilised because of it.'

Pilate was vastly relieved when, after the briefest silence, Vitellius actually applauded this. 'Excellent! For my own part I approve of local culture being encouraged. Under the patronage of Rome, of course.'

'Instead of human flesh being burned, we shall have a fish-fry for the prize-winners,' went on Julius with a grin. The grin was, Pilate had to confess, engagingly boyish, but surely too much so to be directed at a distinguished and so much older person.

Yet Vitellius seemed not the least put out. He laughed and actually leant forward and clapped the boy's shoulder. 'Like the one they have on the Vulcanal, eh? Excellent! And I must say the prizes you offer are generous.'

'I have my father to thank for that.'

Pilate beamed contentedly. 'I worked on the principle of thinking how much Herod offered at the Jerusalem Games and then doubled it.' But he went on to remark regretfully that, when that Tetrarch had built the hippodrome at Caesarea, he had not equipped it so generously with seats as hippodromes in Italy. At the Circus Maximus, he recalled, the Divine Julius had had tiers carved out to seat no fewer than one hundred and fifty thousand spectators.

'Phew!' exclaimed Julius admiringly. 'But in any case we could not hope for a crowd of that size in Caesarea. But we'll get a lot, because there will be prizes for the spectators as well.' Vitellius raised questioning eyebrows. 'Yes! We are going to have a booth selling raffle tickets,' Julius explained. 'I've already got three prizes offered: a shop, a house, and a farm.'

Vitellius turned to Pilate. 'I compliment you, Proconsul, on having appointed so inventive a master of ceremonies.' And in the smile he beamed upon Pilate was a hint of his surprise, somewhat uncomplimentary, that his host could have fathered so brilliantly attractive a son. 'I feel I should like the pleasure of contributing to the Games myself,' he went on.

'But of course you will,' said Pilate. 'That is if you are doing us the great honour of accepting our invitation to preside as praetor at the event.'

'Thank you. With this dear boy's assistance I hope I can perform that function adequately. But, no, I should also like to give something more lasting than my mere presence.' He pondered for a moment. 'I know. Let me donate the spina.'

357

'That is most generous, Vitellius. By my architect Lucius has already made a sketch of a spina and the marble is being quarried at Chios.'

'My idea is better.' Ignoring Pilate he turned to Julius to enlist his approval of the idea. 'I think it would be a nice compliment to the commonwealth status of the Games to procure an obelisk from Egypt. I know an agent who is the very man to buy a handsome antique one. I shall make the arrangements myself. And some new turning-posts for the chariot racing: yes, I'll buy those too.' Vitellius waved Pilate's thanks for this munificence aside. 'I am only too happy to help the Caesarea Games. Even more happy am I to encourage our young master of ceremonies in his ambitions.'

Pilate gave a satisfied nod. 'You will see tomorrow how fertile Julius is with ideas. I have entrusted to him the task of arranging the entertainment at the banquet. He has persuaded me that mere eating and conversation is not sufficient.' He laughed. 'He calls those "old men's pleasures". So he has hired a band of acrobats and jugglers. He assures me they are the most popular troupe in Palestine.'

'Excellent!' said Vitellius. 'I can add my contribution too.' For one dizzy moment Julius almost laughed. Was Vitellius going to sing? Or dance? But no! 'That wrestler I have brought. He delights in entertaining. He performs quite remarkable feats of strength.'

'There are rope-dancers among the acrobats,' said Julius. 'Also we have a marvellous dancer of our own at the palace.'

When Pilate now looked puzzled, Claudia at last emerged from her silence and explained to Vitellius that her sister-in-law, in a recent visit to Caesarea, had brought a dancer she had bought in Mauretania.

'But surely Sextia did not leave that Moor here!' exclaimed Pilate.

'No.' Julius laughed at his father's raised eyebrows. 'I am talking about Ephir.' He turned to Vitellius. 'Ephir is an Edomite slave. He saw Aunt Sextia's Moor rehearsing his act and he copied it. I've seen him do it in the mess. All the fellows say he does it better than the Moor did. He's super!'

'You make me all impatience,' gasped Vitellius, and, in what seemed to Pilate a kindly attempt to pretend to share Julius's enthusiasm, added in youthful slang, 'I look forward to a *super show*.'

358

Claudia caught Pilate's eye. She rose. 'Come, Julius.' They left together.

Vitellius reached for wine, and when a slave stepped forward to pour it he waved him away. Seeing this gesture, Pilate hastily dismissed all the slaves. He was delighted that Caesar's favourite apparently wanted to talk to him alone. Caesar's favourite yawned. The sparkle had gone from the evening.

Pilate began the *tête à tête* by expressing the hope that his guest was finding everything to his liking in his apartments and that . . .

'What a talented boy!' murmured Vitellius.

'I am looking forward,' Pilate said, 'to our having a discussion soon.' Vitellius looked blank. 'I was hoping that Tiberius Caesar might have given you some indication of his views . . .'

'All in good time, Proconsul,' snapped Vitellius.

'Ah! Am I to understand that I can expect comment from Caesar direct?'

'It is possible. Though it is far more likely that he will send any communication through me.' Vitellius sipped the wine. 'It is delightful to see mature comprehension in one so young.'

There was a long silence. Vitellius drained his goblet. He stirred as though about to take his leave, upon which Pilate hastily filled the goblet again. 'I should like very much to discuss that Paterculus incident with you.'

Vitellius looked ferociously bored. 'All in good time,' he repeated. 'Paterculus is hardly a pleasant subject for conversation. Do I understand you to say that Julius studied in Athens?'

'In Alexandria first. Then in Athens.' To keep Vitellius company Pilate filled his own goblet with neat wine. He wet his lips. 'I can understand the aversion felt at the treasonable activities of Paterculus.'

Vitellius shifted with impatience. This Pilate was too persistent. 'Paterculus is a name best forgotten, Proconsul,' he said and added harshly, 'Particularly by you. It recalls your indiscretion.'

'*My* indiscretion?'

'Yes. That of upsetting the Jews by raising Roman standards in their Holy City.'

'But surely it is known in Rome that Paterculus did that.'

'Whose hands actually raised the standards is irrelevant to Caesar. What registers in Capri is only that the offence was committed during your Procuratorship.' He laughed dryly. 'If ever the unfortunate incident should be recorded in future histories,

359

your name, because you are Procurator, would be the one mentioned: not the name Paterculus. So it always is, Pilate. When a pontiff is poisoned at a banquet it is the *host*, not the *cook* who is hanged.'

Pilate murmured protestingly. 'It is unjust to blame me for an offence committed without my knowledge and by a traitor.'

'Unjust? Caesars often are. So is public opinion. So is history. As with that later act of yours: the looting of the Temple treasure. In distant Capri that act of yours gives the impression that you are not sufficiently sensitive to the peculiar susceptibilities of a touchy race.'

'The Corban gold was not looted. It was borrowed to finance a project of benefit to the people. In fact, interest will be paid on it at a higher rate than is paid for loans which the Temple makes regularly to commercial enterprises.'

'I don't doubt it, Proconsul. I speak, as I have said, of how things are seen, not here on the spot, but in Capri. There it was seen as an anti-Jewish operation.'

'I had the support of Jews for my irrigation project.'

'One Jew! At least I know of only one. And he, so Capri sees it, was murdered by orthodox Jews who objected to his non-Jewish behaviour.'

There was another long pause, so nervous a one for Pilate that he drained the whole goblet of wine.

'I am fascinated to see how your son has developed an understanding of racial problems.'

'Yes,' said Pilate, covering a belch with his hand. 'It ought to be seen in Capri that the Jews who murdered Josephus were terorrists.'

'Indeed? How was it then that a Roman commander was put to death for the crime? Oh, yes, yes, yes, I do understand the circumstances, and I can sympathise with your situation. But there again, you see, it does appear in Capri that Romans of rank are suffering, even being crucified, as a result of political disorder in a province which is governed by Proconsul Pilate.' Vitellius rose. 'But, Pilate, it really would be better to leave further discussion until I am able to inform myself personally on the intricacies of Jewish affairs. Meanwhile I do assure you that in any communication I make to Caesar I shall not fail to bring to his notice the name of your talented son.'

Pilate accompanied him along the balcony to the entrance-hall of his apartments. The wrestler, with a bandaged ankle, was

360

squatting moodily on the rim of the fountain, making futile grabs at the goldfish.

'Good night, Proconsul.'

'Tomorrow,' said Pilate, 'I must show you the sketch-plans for the new aqueduct. I hope to persuade you to lay the stone at the inauguration ceremony. It is inscribed to Tiberius.'

'Nothing too laudatory, I hope,' warned Vitellius. 'The Caesar dislikes florid homage.'

'Merely name and date.'

'Excellent. If you have a copy of the sketch, it might be helpful to send it to Capri. At my recommendation Tiberius would pay special attention to it.' Pilate brightened. 'I can also mention Julius's work for the Games. I see Julius as a boy who stands in need of powerful patronage. He is worthy of it.' He looked at Pilate reflectively. 'I have an idea, Pilate. It occurs to me that it would profit the boy considerably and give him a wider knowledge of Asian affairs if he were to go to Antioch.'

'To Antioch?'

'Yes. With me.'

'Hm. I hardly think he is ready to enter public life just yet. I intend sending him to Rhodes.'

'For rhetoric?' Vitellius smiled understandingly. 'To follow in the steps of the Caesar whose names he bears? But I cannot believe that any rhetorician now existing in Rhodes has the stature of that Apollonius Maro at whose feet Julius Caesar wished to sit. Your son will learn more to his advantage in a few months amid the political disputes of Antioch than he could during years in the gardens of a provincial tutor in Rhodes.'

'I am not concerned so much with what knowledge he will actually acquire in Rhodes. What is more important at his age is to learn the discipline of study.'

'And remember, Pilate, that when Julius Caesar was on his way to Rhodes he was captured by pirates.' Vitellius drew a sharp breath. 'One imagines that Julius Caesar probably learned more in the embrace of pirates than he could ever learn from an ageing teacher of rhetoric.'

'But Antioch!' said Pilate doubtfully. 'Julius is rather young for such an atmosphere.'

'The younger the better.'

Pilate's reply to that ambiguous remark was an equally ambiguous nod. 'When do you think we might expect news from Capri?'

361

Vitellius shrugged irritation at the man's persistence. 'You should know, Proconsul, that Tiberius works slowly. He is a great procrastinator – in his wisdom of course. Lesser mortals are consumed with impatience: Tiberius Caesar more wisely broods a long time before he acts. Why, even in the lamentable affair of Sejanus, for instance, Tiberius has not reached his ultimate decision on certain aspects of the conspiracy. There are creatures of Sejanus still in prison. And there are other friends of his still at large, still occupying offices of state. About their future Tiberius has yet to decide. Good night, Pilate.'

An old colonial hand had told Pilate that Vitellius had soared so quickly up the ladder of power because his political baggage was so light: only two masks. His success on the stage of imperial politics had been achieved by the simple trick of always taking people by surprise: donning the mask of comedy when the audience expected tragedy, and vice versa.

Pilate recalled this as he watched Vitellius receiving guests at the banquet. In the great hall of the palace of Caesarea, where many torches had been lit to bring the semblance of comfort to its marble gloom, the principal actor, on a couch of honour on the dais, was playing his part impressively. Vitellius had arrived in sober style, austerely robed in a toga; his excessively black hair limp after the steam of his bath, his only jewellery a signet ring, and without any paint on his cheeks or any antimony on his eyes such as was affected by other ageing military men at the banquet.

Crowds had gathered in the great square outside the palace gates to watch the arrival of litters and carriages and chairs of slave-escorted dignitaries, and to peep into the courtyard where, at trestle tables built in rows, soldiers of the garrison and workers of the secretariat would celebrate the presence of Caesar's plenipotentiary at their own open-air banquet. Oxen were already dripping juice and crackling over the fires. Later soup and baked meats and other delicacies that had been pawed over and rejected in the great hall would be spread along the tables. There was enough Egyptian beer on hand to float a fleet. Greedy little urchins from the town were already planning how they could slip unseen through railings to sneak titbits of spitted beef. It was as good as a party in Rome itself.

Pilate thought the same. Sitting on the dais and looking down the length of the great hall he was content with the rich and populous scene; proud of the splendour of gowns, the piled hair and perfumes, the flash and clash of gold, and the procession of slaves carrying food and wine from busy kitchens.

Yet he was also ill at ease. Vitellius's reference to Sejanus had nagged him all day. The dropping of that disgraced name could have sinister import, though he attempted to reassure himself by recalling the expression that had accompanied the words. That expression could have been a sneer; but it might also have been a smile, the kind of smile that was exchanged between knowledge-able spectators who, standing outside a scandal, were unsullied by the scandal's treacheries and suspicions.

Vitellius had been almost unobtainable all day. Closeted with architect Lucius, he had discussed designs for the running-posts and written letters to his agent and carriers in Alexandria to arrange the purchase and transport of the obelisk. Pilate, when he had managed but the briefest meeting with him, had once again tried to initiate political discussion, but Vitellius had slid away from questions quick as a lizard darting from falling shadows, leaving Pilate clutching on words which, although at the time they seemed of high importance, on later inspection offered him no more enlightenment than a dead tail.

Pilate saw a similar process operating now. Guests who suc-ceeded in engaging the great man in conversation when presented were listened to with dignified geniality when they attempted to intrude their ambitions and ideas. They went away purring con-tentedly under the impression that the comments and compli-ments that had been showered upon them were heavy with glittering promise. Only later did they discover that these trophies seemed singularly light and, when inspected too closely, crumbled into glittering but insubstantial dust. Yet so accomplished was Vitellius in the political art of pleasing suitors that these dis-appointed suitors would blame themselves, not him, for failing to preserve gloriously intact the favours which they believed he had bestowed on them.

Well, they could still enjoy the food and wine. The steward, rising to the importance of the occasion, had coaxed the kitchens into devising dishes which would have won him praise even at a Roman banquet. In fact, the prodigal number of peacocks served with their spread tails skewered into their roasted flesh gave the banquet the atmosphere of a feast attended by Caesar himself, and some of the trenchers, on which were piled spiced and gleaming meats and poultry and game in multitudinous forms, all boiled or roasted or braised of stewed in sauces, were immense and so heavy that four slaves were needed to carry each one from table to table; and as soon as guests had rummaged for the choicest chunks, the remains were hustled out to be given to the soldiers in the courtyard, and fresh trenchers as prodigally piled were carried in.

The wine, Vitellius complimented Pilate, was superb. He could not remember having drunk better in Judaea. 'Judaean?' he asked. Pilate was on the point of nodding affirmatively when Claudia interposed quickly, 'Segona, from Galilee. It was sent to us by a dear old friend, Josephus the Cohen. It is very sad. He was assassinated at Sebaste.'

'Ah, yes,' said Vitellius, looking at Pilate over the rim of his goblet, 'I heard of that.' Then he poured more wine for Julius, whom he had flattered by making a place beside him on his couch. The boy's eyes shone, either with pride at being thus singled out for attention by the famous man or with the excess of wine pressed upon him.

Chamberlain Octavius's wife, leaning forward like a hen poised for a scatter of grain, awaited with itching eagerness for that gap in the conversation into which she would insert her customary monologue of life in Rome. It was an age since she had left that city as a young bride, and during the years of what she considered exile in Judaea her memories of her family and the capital had blossomed with ever richer and more improbable glories, and she wore her Roman birth like an oak-leaf crown which elevated her dizzily high above the wives of other Caesarea officials. For those wives were dowdy provincials who harked from Brindisi or Paestum or Syracuse or Bologna or other cities unfashionable and almost certainly ugly. 'My sister, the one who lives near the Palatine . . . ' she began, but her voice, made husky by anxiety, was overlaid by that of the chief secretary who, having captured the attention of Vitellius, was trying to interest him in the fortunes of his son in Rome. That poor lad, it appeared, was blocked from deserved advancement only because superiors were envious or afraid of his talent. Vitellius assured him that one of his constant preoccupations was to ensure that no youth of promise should be ignored, and then turned to answer a question put by a son of a Greek merchant. This young man had been arguing with Albanus about theatres. What shows, he asked Vitellius, were delighting Rome just now?

'A revival of Terence's *Mother-in-Law*,' said Vitellius, then

364

added, with a shrug, 'And Plautus, of course. In fact all those things which Aristophanes described as "small-man-and-woman affairs".'

Albinus, mistaking the reason for Vitellius's shrug, mumbled into his wine, 'Terence again. How old-fashioned can one get?'

'It is not antiquity I am objecting to,' said Vitellius primly. 'It is lack of art. Better a good old piece than a bad new one.'

'The best boar-hounds you can find in Tuscany,' declared the Chamberlain weightily.

'Well, I'm fond of Plautus,' ship-owner Accius boomed over his vast belly. 'I'm one who goes to the theatre for a laugh, not to think. The theatre should provide entertainment, not politics. Pantomimes for me. Music and laughter. There is too little fun in the world.'

'I grant you Plautus is rich in native humour,' said Vitellius. 'But nowadays even he is cut to please audiences who have been spoiled by short and slovenly modern farces.'

'I can just imagine my sister's table tonight!' the Chamberlain's wife had cleared her throat and was leaning eagerly towards Accius. She wanted to impress this wealthy man, for her mind was dazzled by the thought that she was addressing a descendant of that fabulous Marcius Censorinus whose will had bequeathed to his fortunate heir four thousand one hundred and sixteen slaves, three thousand six hundred pairs of oxen, two hundred and fifty-seven thousand other cattle, and more than sixty million sesterces. 'Red mullet from the Tyrrhenian,' she recited with glazed eyes. 'Baby lamb from the Alban hills. And, of course, Trebula cheese. My sister's husband, that is Tarquinius of course, brought up a whole valley of farms just to make sure there would always be Trebula cheese on the table.

Embarrassed by the winks aroused by this familiar menu, Pilate attempted to halt her recital, but Vitellius put him at ease. With a sharp silencing gesture in Pilate's direction, Caesar's favourite indicated that he was quite prepared to listen to the provincial lady's inanities. The Chamberlain's wife, misinterpreting this exchange of glances, stumbled into excuses. Her tactless praise of her sister's dinners, she explained breathlessly, was the result of the nostalgia engendered by this evening's sumptuous delicacies, which were every bit as good as anything one could find in Rome. Particularly, she said, popping one into her mouth and chewing it as she went on, these prawns which, she understood, had been towed to the port of Caesarea alive in sacks under water, just like those which were towed all the way from the coast of Ireland to Ostia and which her sister, the wife of Tarquinius of course, bought every day. However much did they cost in Caesarea? Claudia did not know. 'A king's ransom, I should think,' said the Chamberlain's wife chewing juicily on another.

Vitellius leaned towards Julius, put a hand on his shoulder and whispered. The boy nodded and made a sign to the musicians. The drums rattled impressively, and the wrestler came bouncing in. Choosing the spot where the light of the torches was most brightly bunched and would thus light up the contours of his muscles, he flexed his limbs. The graze on his ankle was now healed, but for heroic effect he had retained the heavy bandage: the whiteness of it set off the deep tan he had diligently cultivated on the beaches of his native Sicily. He wore a short kilt of leather straps over a white loin-cloth; his wrists were bound with leather like those of a charioteer. Aware under whose patronage the fellow appeared, the company emitted gasps of admiration when he rippled muscles, and bawled applause when he tossed balls of iron as though they were bladders, and bent metal bars into loops.

Eventually Vitellius, becoming weary of this toy, turned again to Julius and, with a smile which he intended Julius to see as mischievous but which enmeshed his eyes in disconcerting wrinkles, asked, 'When do we see your dancer?'

Floating in wine though he now was, Julius did not forget to ask permission of his parents to leave the dais, and then darted off to warn Ephir to be ready to take the floor.

The wrestler's act came to an end. The wrestler's slaves tripped in to enfold the precious body in a woollen cloak and then scuttled around gathering up gold coins thrown by guests who hoped that Vitellius would notice how liberal they had been to his protégé.

Now the musicians, changing suddenly their tune, launched into a barbaric eastern melody of squealing strings and thumping drums. Ephir came bounding in. In the torchlight his dark-skinned body, supple as a serpent's, gleamed almost black, and the only colours visible were those of the red-and-white grin he had painted grotesquely on his face and the long red claws he had fastened to his fingers. Other than these talons of painted ivory and a jewel in his navel, he wore nothing but a strap of black sequins and a naughty tassel. But he bore, balanced on his head, an immense brass tray on which were placed six jewel-studded goblets filled to the brim with wine, and, alternating with the goblets, six flaring candles. The swift glide and tap of his feet to the clashed commands of the cymbals and the swaying of his buttocks to the caresses of the pipes were hardly noticed by those of the spectators, who, holding their breath, they had their eyes glued to the tray and its load, and raised nervous fingers to their lips as they watched the tray spin round with him.

'Partridges,' said Octavius. 'On Tarquinius's estate the fattest you've ever seen. A thousand or more netted on one morning.'

'They put on Plautus at the house,' whispered Albinus. 'That comedy about the two old men and the two girls. They played it entirely nude. Not a stitch.'

The music quickened. Ephir's circling dance became more furious. The goblets shifted and swayed. But magically not a drop of wine was spilled.

'Tarquinius is my sister's husband,' the Chamberlain's wife informed Vitellius. He nodded acceptance of this information, but then stared keenly at her, as though daring her to add more. She looked quickly away, covering her confusion under expressions of surprised delight at the arrival of another dish of prawns. Now she wished she had not mentioned Tarquinius. Of course this personage from Rome would know all about that profligate's shamefully colossal bankruptcy.

Ship-owner Accius interrupted a murmured conversation with Claudia to stare enviously at Ephir's flat belly which, points of light sparkling from its navel, now undulated in slow circles to the weaving melody of pipes. 'I would give half my fleet if I could do that,' sighed ship-owner Accius. Then, turning back to Claudia, he chuckled, and the immense folds of fat rolled under his toga like sleepy dolphins.

Vitellius was looking towards the archway through which Julius had disappeared and wondering when the boy would be coming back. Then he sniffed. There was an unpleasant odour. Something burning?

Now Ephir was sinking to his knees, and then, as the tray rose and dipped and the goblets quivered, he was lying down. Yes, actually lying down, yet miraculously keeping the tray horizontal by edging it on to his brow and over his face, and all the time still moving his hands and feet to the coaxing of the pipes.

'But it's happening everywhere nowadays,' someone shouted across to Albinus. 'They have nude shows even in public theatres in Greece. Not in Athens yet. But in some places.'

The dancer was now full length on the floor. Now he was rolling over like a log, but incredibly, the wine-ladened tray, as the head rolled like a ball beneath it, floated over painted face and black head and painted face again like a boat breasting a heavy wave. The music swelled importantly: the climax of the act was drawing near. Ephir sprang erect. Only a few drops of wine dripped on to the tray.

Claudia looked worried. She had seen Vitellius's nostrils twitch again. She too smelled the reek of smoke. She looked around, then saw that one of the torches on the wall immediately behind the dais was dimming and sending up a spiral of oily smoke. She managed to catch the attention of the one slave who was not completely lost in contemplation of the spectacle. She pointed urgently to the offending torch.

The music grew more frenzied. Ephir, preparing for his finale, pirouetted further away down the hall, casting quick glances towards the entrance, to keep in sight the path for his astounding exit. Those who had seen him do the act in the mess were waiting with breathless smiles for that final stunning trick. From the spot Ephir had now chosen he would run from the scene, but would run so quickly that the candles would be blown out by the speed of his passing just before he reached the exit out of the hall and disappeared from sight.

The slave plucked down the offending torch and, keeping his eyes turned down to its smoking head, ran towards the archway.

Ephir and the tray reached that spot at the same time. The collision was spectacular. None of the guests was hit by the bouncing goblets; only slaves were splashed with wine and candle-fat; and with commendable presence of mind the musicians blew and beat so loudly that they almost succeeded in drowning the reverberations of the brass tray bouncing on the marble. But no music on earth could have been loud enough to drown completely the howl beyond the archway of Julius's unrestrained laughter, and his father, glowering in that direction, saw Ephir doubled up with mirth as he pulled himself to his feet and began searching for the jewel that had burst from his navel.

'I always say that the best boar-hounds are in Tuscany,' shouted the chamberlain belligerently, glaring round to challenge contradiction; and a moment later he was staring in puzzlement at the deep pits his wife's angry finger-nails had nipped into his forearm.

'The Galilean wine seems to have overcome your Chamberlain,' Vitellius whispered to Pilate.

Pilate nodded agitatedly. 'With your permission, Vitellius, I think we can dismiss the party.'

'No, no, Pilate!' For now the Caesarea troupe of acrobats and jugglers was pouring into the hall, cartwheeling, tumbling, leap-frogging, some tossing up to the high ceiling circles of beribboned staves, others balancing the points of long gaudy-hilted swords on their brows and chins. The air shuddered with a frenzy of cymbals, strings and pipes. 'Let your guests enjoy themselves. But, if you will excuse me, I shall go. I am sure no one will notice my leaving. My compliments to you, my Lady Claudia.'

He rose, and, as he had foreseen, amid the clamour of music and shouts and the downing of wine, the departure of Caesar's favourite was not noticed. Nor was that of Pilate and Claudia when, soon after, they slipped away.

'My sister, she's the wife of Tarquinius of course,' the Chamberlain's wife was continuing bravely in the ear of Accius, not noticing that the chins of the ship-owner were spread asleep over his chest and he was snoring gently.

Vitellius leaned over the balcony, peering down into the darkness. He thought he had caught a glimpse of Julius crossing the garden with the dancer. Yes, he could hear voices coming from near the Poseidon fountain. Was that Julius's voice? It was. But how thick it was, and how incoherent; and it finished in a disgusting splutter. Julius was being extravagantly and noisily sick. Vitellius heard a splash and then heard the dancing boy laugh as he ducked Julius's head deep under sobering water. Vitellius sighed and went to bed.

'I shall be sorry to see you go, Fabius,' said Pilate. 'You have done good work here.' He tapped his forefinger on the letter lying on his desk. 'As I have told your father in this.'

'Thank you, sir.'

'When do you intend to leave?'

'Tonight, with your permission, sir. There is a boat for Brindisi.'

'So quickly? Well, your father does ask you to make haste, and you are obviously a dutiful son, Fabius. Or,' he added teasingly, 'is it really that you cannot wait one moment longer to get out of this "backwater" of Judaea?'

Fabius shook his head. 'No. Honestly, Procurator, I now find myself sorry to be leaving you. And things promise to be quite interesting here.'

Pilate smiled wryly. 'Are they not already so?'

'I mean the war, sir.' Pilate's brows rose questioningly. 'If the Arabs should attack.'

'Ah, that!' Pilate shook his head. 'Aretas will not invade Palestine unless circumstances seem promising to him. And they will never seem so as long as Rome is strong and stable.'

'When Tiberius dies . . . '

Pilate waved down the brash interruption. 'The successor of Tiberius Caesar will also be Caesar, and Caesar will always, we hope, continue the Augustan policy of peaceful containment in Asia.'

'That is what I intended to say, sir. Caligula will certainly pursue that policy, even liberalise it,' said Fabius boldly, and despite Pilate's frown plunged deeper into politics. 'I think Vitellius will find his hopes dashed when Caligula assumes the diadem.' Pilate's frown deepened, but he waited questioningly. 'Caligula has no time for Vitellius, nor for any of the "old guard". My father is so sure about that that he thinks anyone would be well advised not to bother about cultivating Vitellius's patronage, but to wait for younger patrons.'

'You are becoming quite a politician, Fabius,' said Pilate stiffly. But then, because certain hopes had been encouraged in his own mind, admitted, 'Your father said the same in his letter to me. He promises to keep me informed.'

'I know he will, sir. And I have friends close to Caligula.'

'Thank you, Fabius. Even the most loyal servant of Caesar stands in need of friends at court. Your father has also told me that he is now quite confident of securing for me that little property, the villa and its scrap of land, in Tuscany. Convey to him my warmest thanks for handling the affair on my behalf and tell him how much I look forward to being his near neighbour.' He handed Fabius a letter. 'In this letter to your father I have asked yet another favour. I am hoping he will render me a similar service to the one which I have, successfully I hope, rendered him. In the same way that he sent *his* son to me for training I intend sending *my* son to him.'

'Julius?'

'Yes. I have come to the opinion that the boy can develop decent Roman virtues better in Italy than in this decadent east. And your father will, I know, protect him as lovingly as he would

370

his own son. I have decided to send Julius to Italy immediately after the Games.'

Pilate stood up and, stirred to affection by his talk of Julius, gave Fabius a fatherly parting embrace, accompanying him to the door with his arm around his shoulders and standing there watching him walk away along the corridor. He felt a twinge of sadness, a sadness shot through with what might have been envy, at the sight of a young man, elegant, beautiful, and, most enviable of all, aristocratic, marching off to the certainty of some glittering future in the heart of the empire.

'I shall quite miss that young dandy,' Pilate murmured to himself as he went back to his desk. Well, he knew that he would feel even more acutely the departure of Julius in a few months' time. He thrust these sad thoughts away, summoned Severus, and was soon immersed in discussing details for his Passover progress to Jerusalem.

On the Saturday before Passover Pilate rode in state into Jerusalem. Through the heart of the city, all the way from Herod's Gate to Herod's Palace, soldiers stood shoulder to shoulder along the route of his progress. It was late afternoon and the streets were crowded. Townsfolk were strolling about in their best clothes, and pilgrims from all the towns of Judaea and Samaria and Galilee and from cities beyond the Great Sea who had flocked down in their thousands from camps on Olivet and neighbouring hills to enjoy the Sabbath promenade. All pressed forward to gape at Pilate's impressive cavalcade. Knowledgeable spectators pointed out the figure of Procurator Pilate to country visitors, who gazed in awe on the pale stern profile of the governor whose name they had so often heard spoken in fear or anger. Some Jerusalem folk, recognising the Lady Claudia, hazarded the opinion that the boy riding beside her two-wheeled gig and bending attentively down to talk with her as she passed through the lovely city must be her son. Others made the wildest guesses at the identity of the stern-faced Roman in ancient but polished leather who rode amid the escort of centurions. The crowd was noisy but amiable. Prospects of the ten-day holiday for Passover, most joyous festival of the year, always put Jerusalem folk in a genial mood. In any case, Pilate's few hundred soldiers caused less confusion than the thousands of pilgrims. Scores of thousands of these were sleeping rough in olive-groves and gardens and fields around

371

the city. Thousands more were lodged with friends or relatives in the smart villas and apartments of the new suburb of Bezetha. In the old town, countless others were sleeping in corners of crowded bedrooms, on kitchen floors and in courtyards, or, if their hosts' homes were too small to provide one further inch of floor, were camping in the street where, tethered to the nearest doorposts, the paschal lambs they had carried from the country bleated and stumbled over babies and bedding. Amid this heaving mass of people, hawkers, almost invisible under loads of shawls and shoes, gowns and tunics, cheap jewellery and bottles and jars of scents and pomades, elbowed their bawling way. Donkeys stepped warily between the makeshift braziers of families dining on the paving. Children from hill villages loitered through the markets, gawping at the piled-up treasures of the world, while on the bridge below the Temple and up the staircase to the Court of the Gentiles the crowds were so dense that fathers had to swing children on to their shoulders, and timid country wives, keeping their faces covered and their eyes downcast, and clutching their husbands' robes, were drawn like rescued sailors through tumultuous waves of humans. And all the day, from sunrise to sunset, doves were selling in the 'bazaar of the sons of Annas' at forty to fifty times the usual price, and the coins pouring into the bowls of the money-changers rang an incessant carillon of profit.

Aemilius, commander of the Jerusalem cohort, had greeted Pilate and Vitellius at Herod's Gate and led them through the city to the Hasmonaean Palace. Pilate always felt that the sombre Antonia fortress, because it dominated the centre of the old city so powerfully, was the more appropriate setting for a Roman governor, but he adhered to the custom set by his predecessors of lodging in the Herodian palace during festival visits to Jerusalem. On this visit, however, he had allocated the more sumptuous of the apartments to Vitellius and planned to find sufficient official business to keep him occupied most of the day at the Antonia, and thus free himself from the nervous strain he suffered by too constant proximity to Caesar's favourite. The hundreds of slaves already at work in the palace gardens, sweeping terraces and clipping hedges and setting up canopies, indicated that Herod and Herodias had already arrived. Yes, said Aemilius, but they were resting after their progress from Galilee and would not be officially in residence until their two thousand pieces of baggage were unpacked and the state apartments were opened.

When these domestic chores had been executed, they would ceremonially welcome the Procurator and would give a banquet in honour of their beloved friend Vitellius.

Pilate accompanied Vitellius to the south pavilion and took leave of him in that same ornate room where he had last taken leave of Paterculus. Vitellius politely suggested that Pilate and Julius and, should she wish, the Lady Claudia might have supper with him, but when Pilate murmured of affairs he must attend to at the Antonia, Vitellius did not press his invitation, and, calling for valet and masseur, stalked away in the direction of the bath. Pilate sent Severus in search of Julius. 'The boy will stay at the Antonia. Find him some job to do. He can mess with the officers. That will be better than hanging about this place.'

With Aemilius and a small escort Pilate left the palace for the Antonia. Julius and Severus followed with the Jerusalem cohort, into which party Ephir had managed to intrude himself. With the air of one who knew every stone in the city he paraded his knowledge in whispers to Julius, halting him on the bridge to look down at the river, still swift and deep with its spring flood. 'It flows into the sea of salt,' he said. 'A sea so full of salt that a man can walk through it without sinking.' He pointed out to Julius the stairs leading to the Temple. At the top, he said, were stones carved with dire warnings against Gentiles.

'You daren't go past those,' he said with a fierce grin. 'If you do . . . ' He drew his finger like a knife across his throat. 'I can go though. I'm circumcised.'

Julius pulled a face. 'That's nothing to be proud of, Jew boy.' They laughed together.

'Come up on the battlements,' Ephir urged when they reached the entrance. 'You can see the whole city from there.' And they raced out of sight up the stair that spiralled through the thick wall.

Before sunset Pilate rode out with architect Lucius to inspect the pavilion erected for tomorrow's ceremony, at which the new aqueduct would be inaugurated and the gods besought to bestow their protection and favours on the project. It was a simple but impressive structure, square and windowless like a large tent, built of heavy beams of cedar with acanthus mouldings in plaster. The walls inside and the altar were painted with sylvan scenes and many waterfalls in which could be discerned the figures of Neptunes and, among less important river gods, Volturnus.

Some distance from the pavilion some blocks of stone had been stacked up ready for use. Each block was bored through, smooth and clean, and keyed to bind it to its neighbour when the conduit was laid. Beyond these pipes was the beginning of the trench. Pilate's eyes followed the line of it. Sharply shadowed by the low-slanting light of a sinking sun it stretched, a straight scar, over the hills, disappearing into the haze of evening. Workmen cooking their evening meal outside makeshift huts and tents stared at his and his officers incuriously. A party of pilgrims, tramping towards the city, halted to look at the workings and then moved on. Pilate could hear them murmuring among themselves. They were no doubt repeating the story that Procurator Pilate had stolen the Temple gold to pay for this work. But when they got to Jerusalem they would learn that all resentment against that deed had faded away. By now only Zealots and a few of the stiffer-necked Pharisees tried to keep the anger alive. Most Jerusalem folk, when they mentioned the project at all, talked only about the abundant water they hoped to enjoy 'so long as the Romans don't use it all for their baths'.

Pilate rode back to the city in a contented mood. He decided to stay at the Antonia for supper. He ate with Aemilius, Severus and Julius in the mess, discussing plans for the morrow's ceremony, the precedence to be observed in the procession, and the choice of officers to honour Vitellius with a suitably noble escort.

He asked after Marcellus. Aemilius shrugged. Marcellus, he said, had gone off on some 'cloak and dagger' business of his own devising.

'There is an enormous number of pilgrims this year,' said the commander. 'More than I ever remember.' Although, he went on reassuringly, there seemed no more fear of any tumult than at any previous Passover. The Jews seemed to be in a quite remarkably amiable mood. The aqueduct project was now actually welcomed. Traders and innkeepers in particular now saw it as a promising indication of Roman concern for the amenities of Jerusalem. As for pilgrims, well, the troops he would station at the customary strategic points tomorrow morning and for the rest of the festival were adequate to put down any trouble quickly and smartly.

Pilate returned to the palace and went to bed. He was tired and ready for sleep, but he succeeded in keeping awake long enough to luxuriate for a while in the memory of that long trench dug across the Judaean landscape. He felt wonderfully content. In the face of every opposition and despite the laggard indifference

374

of Rome, he had put his plan through. He had at last begun to make his mark on his province. No, the procuratorship of Pontius Pilate in Judaea would not be forgotten.

'Messiah!' The cry, ringing boldly from the building-site near the Pool of Siloam, could be heard inside the ceremonial pavilion. The orator, proclaiming praises of Caesar, stumbled over a phrase. A moment later shouts could be heard outside, followed by gasps and groans and the sound of running feet. Then, further away, from somewhere down the valley of the Kidron, came faintly an answer to the first call. 'Messiah! Messiah!'

Vitellius turned questioning eyes to Pilate. The guards, a statuesque frieze ranged against the painted walls, shifted hands to their daggers but did not draw. Obedient to the orders Marcellus had given at dawn, they made no move that might interrupt the ceremony or alarm those taking part. Pilate was surprised and disturbed by the unexpected sounds of disorder outside. But he too, ignoring Vitellius's questioning glance, kept his face stonily fixed on altar and braziers and priests. The ceremony had an hour to run. By that time, he hoped, Marcellus would have quelled the hooligans responsible for the demonstration outside. Happily at this moment the invocations spoken by the chorus swelled out with sudden fervour and drowned the noises now fading away further down the Kidron in the direction of the city gates.

'Messiah!' Crouching beside Barabbas behind building-rubble in the valley of the Kidron, Ishmael, his hand sweating and eager on the hilt of the Parthian dagger below his robe, had heard that first call coming from somewhere among the builders' cabins near the mounds of sandy-coloured blocks for the new aqueduct. At the sound of the call he and Barabbas leaped out and drew their daggers. As they did so, other Zealots sprang into sight from hiding-places around them and clambered up to the lip of the valley until they could see, ahead of them, the roof of the painted pavilion.

'Messiah! Messiah!' Barabbas yelled the answer. Yet as he advanced he muttered curses. Imeer had called too soon, for Pilate and his party had not yet emerged from the ceremony. However, perhaps Imeer had seen some need for attacking sooner than planned. It might be better so, because at that moment many of the guards were inside the pavilion. Outside was only a slender contingent. When those turned to defend themselves against

Zealots among the builders, they would fall easily to his attack at their rear.

Then with sudden dread Barabbas saw that the guards were not turning to attack the Zealot 'builders'. Instead they were facing him, forming up to repulse his attack. They had no need to look behind them. They had no need to protect themselves from attack from the building-sites. For at that spot the Zealots were themselves fighting for their lives.

The Zealots on the site had been thrown off balance from the start. For nearly an hour none of them had seen Imeer around, but shortly after Procurator Pilate and his party had marched into the pavilion, the battle-cry 'Messiah' was bawled in their midst. Loyally they responded to the call. It was their task to create a diversion by drawing upon themselves an attack from the guards outside the pavilion. They drew their Zealot daggers and grouped themselves to repulse the guards. But the enemies who struck them down were men in their own midst. 'Comrades' with whom they had mingled for days, men with whom they had shared sheepskins at night and whom they believed to be labourers from the hill villages of Judaea and fighters in a common cause, now drew daggers from under their robes and drove them into Zealot backs. Some of these sudden assassins even produced swords, and by the skill with which they wielded them and their fierce delight as they sliced into necks and shoulders and chopped off hands, revealed themselves as trained mercenaries of Pilate's army.

So the guards, free to attend to Barabbas and his men, spread out, forming above the Kidron an arc which could close like pincers on the Zealots in the valley. Barabbas, full length now behind rubble, saw the ring of spears like long grass against the sky. He waved to his comrades behind him to halt and also take cover.

Ishmael, even if he saw the command, did not heed it. After one savage stare at the pavilion into which he had earlier seen the murderer Pilate march in solemn procession, he darted leftward up the valley. There he had noticed, beyond the left tip of the enclosing Roman pincer, a low wall, half destroyed by recent excavations for the aqueduct. The remnants of the wall straggled behind the back of the pavilion near a cluster of ancient broad-trunked olive-trees which would provide cover for a waiting assassin. Sliding swiftly from each rock and pile of rubble to the next, his slim form, bent double, was not seen by the advancing guards whose eyes were fixed down to where they had first seen

Barabbas and his comrades spring into sight. Nor had Barabbas seen Ishmael go. At that moment, shielding his eyes against the sun, he had been peering towards Olivet, from which he hoped to see his reinforcements streaming down towards the Dung and Fountain Gates. He could send a runner to divert them and bring them to help him here. But even from this distance he could see that the treachery that had happened among the builders' cabins was happening also on Olivet. There also robed men were fighting hand-to-hand as Zealot 'pilgrims' were attacked by the daggers of Pilate's 'pilgrim' spies.

Trumpets shrilled from the Antonia. Looking back towards the city, Barabbas saw the flash of breastplates, the gleam of casques and the toss of plumes as the cohorts reached the gates and there halted, not advancing up the Kidron but forming a solid wall of cavalry and foot facing Gethsemane and ready to butcher any Zealots who might fight their way from the slaughter in the olive-groves and advance on the city.

Behind the wall near the pavilion Ishmael curled low among tumbled stones. Beyond a peaked rock he could see nail-studded beams and a portion of plaster acanthus-moulding on the roof of the pavilion which architect Lucius had designed to hide from Jewish eyes the Roman worship of Caesar and Gentile gods. The pavilion was larger than a tent. But it was as square as a tent, and its outer walls were dark and windowless, and so it recalled to Ishmael the tent he had looked down on years ago from the bluff of rock near his father's village. Below the roof of this blasphemous building was again that Roman who had condemned Uzziel to the cross. Ishmael knew that he would die in performing the deed, but it would be a noble death, for he would die driving into the heart of his father's murderer the Parthian dagger which he had vowed to bathe in that murderer's blood. He had but to wait here until the end of the ceremony, and when the Romans came out, flushed with their obscene rites, Ishmael son of Uzziel would avenge his father and join him gloriously in Sheol.

In the valley of the Kidron, Barabbas, lying amid rubble, his eyes watching the guards advancing warily down towards him, signalled back to his comrades still to lie low.

His plan had failed. They were betrayed. Imeer, in folly or in treachery, had called too soon, and Pilate's spies disguised as builders and pilgrims had wrought havoc on his Zealot force. Even so, all was not lost. The comrades behind him were the choicest of all his Zealot brethren, each one a beloved friend of proved and passionate courage. Even in retreat he and they could wipe out the few Romans menacing them.

He tried to count those Romans as they stepped cautiously between boulders down the side of the valley, seeking separate paths which, as they advanced, would tighten the pincer of attack. Barabbas had just finished counting the enemy when the Roman menace was suddenly heightened. Behind the spearmen appeared a posse of horsemen, cantering up from some spot where they had waited in ambush. Barabbas saw the flash of the swords they drew as they awaited the command to ride down in the wake of the spearmen and chop to pieces any fallen or wounded Zealot. Barabbas glanced back again. Down the valley to his right, only a little lower, were gardens and low walls. Just beyond there was a huddle of cottages. He waved to his comrades and pointed to their objective. They must fall back to that maze of alleys and yards into which horsemen could not ride.

At the building-site many of the Zealots had fallen to dagger-thrusts and were dead or dying. All the others, except two, were now contained, imprisoned in a wall of spies and auxiliary horse-men. The two, profiting by the confusion of a struggle between men robed alike, had cunningly escaped. Making furious and convincing pretence of one being the hunted and the other the dagger-wielding hunter, they had broken away and chased in the direction of a clump of olive-trees behind the ceremonial pavilion. They tumbled over a low wall. They saw Barabbas's boy, Ishmael, lying further along the wall and crawled over to him. He gave them one fierce stare and then fixed his eyes again on the pavilion. They saw the Parthian dagger flashing in his hand and, remembering how he had boasted at the desert rendezvous, guessed his intent. Barabbas would never forgive them if they allowed his beloved Ishmael to throw his life away. In whispers they tried to argue him out of it. When he refused to listen they grabbed him. He resisted furiously, but the burlier of the two flung himself on to him with all his weight and knocked the wind out of him. The other seized his hands, and eventually they dragged him, weeping with rage, into the cover of the olive-trees. There they lay panting, and when they had recovered their breath they tumbled downhill into the excavations and, by a circuitous route through nearby olive-groves, reached a path lead-ing to the Bethany road. There, with their daggers now hidden below their robes, they sat for a time amid a knot of old men and

378

women pilgrims who had fled from their tents on Olivet and were now praying for the riot to end without their being caught up in it.

In the valley of the Kidron three auxiliaries and two Zealots, who had fought beside Barabbas and surrendered inch by inch as they covered the retreat of the others, lay dead among the tumbled stones. The rest of the band, except for Barabbas and one comrade, were now safe amid the shelter of the gardens and cottages. Barabbas and his comrade had almost reached the first low wall when two of Pilate's auxiliaries charged down on them.

One of the soldiers thrust at Barabbas with his spear. Barabbas dodged the head of the spear and moved in with his dagger. The dagger-blade skidded on the breastplate, but under the weight of Barabbas's rushing body the man went down with Barabbas astride him. Barabbas lifted his dagger high to drive it clean into the man's throat, but at that moment the other soldier, who had used his spear more successfully and impaled Barabbas's comrade, now flung himself on Barabbas's back and wound his leather-bound forearms around his neck. Barabbas twisted round, broke the man's grip, and slashed air with his dagger. The man was leaning back to avoid the blade, but was still standing menacingly over him. Barabbas, on his knees, looked up at the legs. He thrust his dagger upward. The point, entering the smooth dark skin on the inner part of the Syrian's thigh, gouged upward. It folded back a forearm's length of flesh in a deep carmine-dripping smile, and it slid into the groin as smoothly as though it were cutting silk, and the same luxuriant hiss.

The man gulped. His spear clattered on stones as he dropped his hands to clutch his loins. His mouth hung open. He stared down at Barabbas in doltish surprise. Frothing blood spurted between his fingers.

The auxiliary under Barabbas tried to wrench himself free. Barabbas drove the blade into his throat; he felt the point grate on bone or on stone at the back of the man's neck. But now the other soldiers were around him, and the hooves of horses thudding nearby. Senseless now to fight on, but Barabbas did fight on, battling now in that desperate rage of defeat, exulting in that lust to wound and kill as many as can be wounded or killed before one is killed oneself. His dagger found flesh in flanks and breasts and bellies, and once, before he was overpowered, it gouged from eye to chin a cleft which filled an enemy face with a grin that gibbered blood.

'Alive! Alive! Take him alive!' The command came from some-one on horseback high and cool above the blood-and-earth-smeared brawl.

Alive Barabbas was taken. Shamefully unwounded, except for fierce scratches and huge bruises, he lay spread-eagled, his only physical agony that caused by a pointed rock digging into his spine as the weight of soldiers stretched him on the ground, pressing the back of his jewelled hands into the earth. Others were at his legs. A soldier stamped into his groin; another slapped him across the eyes with the slashed hand which Barabbas had savaged with the last shrug of his Zealot dagger.

The horseman who had commanded Barabbas's living capture coaxed his pawing mount closer and looked down at his prize. Barabbas, blinking blood and sweat away, looked up. He saw a hand, gauntleted in leather and metal, clutching the reins. Behind was another horse. Across its back lay Imeer, trussed, moaning against the bite of the savage cords with which they had bound him one hour before an impostor Zealot had falsely called 'Messiah!'

By the time Pilate and Vitellius emerged from the pavilion, most of the corpses had been carried away and the rest dragged out of sight behind piled-up earth. Marcellus had spared no effort to keep from the eyes of Caesar's plenipotentiary evidence that a battle had been fought so close to him. All soldiers bearing obvious wounds had been sent to the Antonia and the guards now lined up to escort the procession back to the city had cleaned every speck of blood and dust from their swords and trappings. But Vitellius, with the eyes of a seasoned campaigner, noticed that soldiers down the valley were lifting bodies, dead or wounded, and further away, around the walls of some gardens and cottages, casques and spears bobbed into sight as auxiliaries combed the area for Zealots. However, riding back to the city ahead of Pilate, he had no opportunity of questioning him, and when they reached the palace they were immediately engulfed in the feverish pomp of the reception arranged by the Tetrarch.

The priests of the Sanhedrin had already arrived. In a corner of the audience-chamber Caiaphas, a dumb corralled ox, was encircled by colleagues urgently whispering around him and clawing arguments from the air with feverish fingers. That they were discussing the events of the morning was immediately evident to Pilate by the way they swung faces exceptionally flushed with anger and dark with accusation in his direction when he entered, though the gaze Caiaphas cast at him over the cordon of agitated shoulders was one of terrified helplessness: his bulbous eyes watered with vexation, and his plump fingers flopped in the torrent of his beard. Annas strode in. As soon as he saw Pilate he marched towards him, his wrinkles puckering urgently. But at that moment the Tetrarch made his appearance.

Herod, as soon as he had reached that position on the threshold where he was visible to all his guests, came to an ostentatious halt, standing dramatically still under a canopy borne by four slaves in resplendent livery with scimitars slanting in their girdles, and then, having netted all eyes, Herod could endow with regal significance even the unremarkable gesture of raising a hand brilliantly burdened with rings and resting it on the collar of gold half-moons which hung like a corselet over shoulders and chest. Holding this pose, indolent and bored but undeniably princely, he rolled his jasper gaze around the assembly until it rested, with excellent timing, last of all on Vitellius; upon which, stretching his yellow visage in a wolfish smile and gesturing to the slaves to remain where they were, he stepped free of his canopy's oppressively regal shadow and glided, still sumptuously but with a host's kindly disregard of regal protocol, to greet Caesar's favourite first of all. 'My dear friend,' he lisped, throwing forward his braceleted arms, 'what pleasure it gives me to welcome you back to Asia!' Then, tossing the remaining crumbs of his smile to the rest of the company, and a frown at Pilate, he laid a hand on Vitellius's forearm and led him to a couch.

Had the visitor been Caesar himself, Herod could have been no more ingratiating than he was to Vitellius. Not until he had made a dozen solicitous inquiries about his visitor's family and journey and comfort did he speak to Pilate. To do that he switched off the smile. 'I am distressed by news that there has been trouble in the Holy City again,' he said sombrely, 'and that on the eve of Passover.'

Conscious that Vitellius was turning upon him a face full of questions, Pilate shrugged. 'Nothing of great consequence.'

'Nothing of great consequence!' Herod's lisp added venom to the sarcasm. 'Of no great consequence except for those who died. Some three score, I am informed. At Siloam and on Olivet.'

Pilate stared stonily at him. 'I am awaiting a full report.'

'I am told that some Galilean pilgrims were among those who suffered.'

'I should have been the more surprised had there been *no* Galileans.'

Herod sighed extravagantly. 'I shall await information, Procurator, at a more appropriate time.' He turned from Pilate and assumed the smile again to address himself to Vitellius.

Herodias and Claudia could be seen outside. The Tetrarch's consort had done the Procurator's wife the honour of going in person to the Procurator's apartments to accompany her to the reception and now, on shoes so heightened by thick soles of cork that she appeared as tall as Claudia, she was tottering gingerly along the terrace, flapping one fold of her jewel-dusted oriental veil coquettishly over white enamelled cheeks and murmuring pleasantries to her dear Lady Claudia. Pilate used his wife's appearance as an excuse to go on to the terrace, but, after exchanging the briefest formal greetings with the Tetrarch's consort, slipped hurriedly away to his apartments.

Severus was awaiting him there with news that Marcellus was anxious to report to the Procurator at his convenience. 'Shall I send for him, sir?'

'No. I prefer to see him at the Antonia.' Pilate welcomed the excuse to escape from the hysterical atmosphere of Herod's court and also from Vitellius's questions. Those he could not answer until he knew something about this morning's disturbance. Sixty dead? If that were so, the event was worse than he had imagined. Yet the city did not seem immoderately agitated. The crowds swarming across the bridge and up the staircase to the Temple esplanade were dense, of course, and the noise in the Court of Gentiles deafening, but those were features of Passover; and those people whom his escort had to thrust aside to clear his way made no more than the scowling response they usually made to rough handling by Roman guards whose presence in the Holy City was an insult by now so habitual that it had lost its sting.

When Pilate reached the top of the stairway leading to the entrance of the Antonia, a slight figure in centurion's uniform detached itself from the guards who were leaning over the balustrade and staring down at the Jewish multitude, and stepped towards him. It was Julius, his grin of welcome almost submerged below a helmet miles too big for him. He carried a centurion's staff, vine-embossed, and Pilate's frown moved up from that to the bloodied bandage on the boy's elbow. 'What have you been doing?' he asked sharply, but before the boy had time to speak, Aemilius, coming out of the fortress, answered, 'Not fighting,

Procurator. Though I guess he was itching to be out with us today.'

'Only a graze,' said Julius, smoothing the bandage. 'I slipped.'

'On the battlements,' said Aemilius, pointing upward.

'I went up with Ephir to watch the fighting,' said Julius, but now Pilate was glaring at a cut on the commander's chin and a darkening bruise across one red cheek.

'Were you up there too?'

'No.' Aemilius fingered his chin tenderly. 'I got this on Olivet. A stone. Though it was a frantic old fool who threw it; not a Zealot. But,' he added with relish, 'we get plenty of those,' and murmured, 'Thanks to Marcellus.'

If Aemilius could be moved to compliment Marcellus, then this morning's operation must have been singularly successful, though this did not rid Pilate of a sense of resentment at it having happened outside his command.

'Tell Marcellus I wish to see him immediately,' he said and then turned to Julius. 'What are you doing in that uniform?'

'I got it from the quartermaster. Aemilius lent me the staff.'

'Uniform is not fancy dress. It is worn only by men who have earned the right to it. Take it back.'

'Yes, sir.'

As Pilate walked into the fortress, his heels rapping along the stony corridor, Julius took off the crested helmet, replied to Aemilius's friendly wink with a half-smile, and went disconsolately down to divest himself of martial finery.

Tearing the last leaves from a sprig of rosemary and crushing them against his leather fingers to savour their aroma, Marcellus came up from the mess, tossed the crumpled twig away as he crossed the audience-chamber, and went in to the Procurator. His slanted visage was fierce with triumph. Before Pilate had time to put a question he declared, 'We have nipped a Zealot revolt in the bud.'

'How many were killed? Was it really sixty?'

'Five bodies were handed to families who asked for them. Others were disposed of without trouble.'

'How many?'

'No count was made. We lost six auxiliaries.'

'Were there Galileans killed?'

'It is possible. We have captured Barabbas.'

'The Zealot leader?'

'The same. He organised the attack. The plan was to assassinate you, Pontius.'

Pilate shrugged. 'Not for the first time.'

'True. But this time they hoped to spark off a rebellion in the city. When we caught Barabbas and other ringleaders the spirit went out of them. There must be thousands who never dared even to draw their daggers.'

'You acted very expeditiously,' Marcellus nodded. Then he became aware of Pilate's stony frown: the words were a question, not a commendation. 'You must have been aware that the attack was to be attempted.' Marcellus murmured non-committally. 'Why was I not informed?'

'Because the attack was no more than suspected. No more. There was always the possibility that the Zealots might learn that their plan had been discovered and call off the attack.'

'There was also the possibility that not I but Vitellius might have been victim in the assassination attempt.'

'There never was that possibility,' insisted Marcellus confidently. 'We captured the terrorists before they got near the pavilion.'

'Herod says three people were killed.'

'When you have the opportunity, Pontius, you can tell the Fox that we also saved him today. Aretas was prepared to invade Palestine if the Zealot rebellion showed signs of being successful.'

'Is there proof of that?'

'I expect Barabbas to provide that proof.'

'Where is he?'

Marcellus pointed a leather finger to the floor. 'Safe.'

Pilate got up from his chair and paced about. 'The problem is whether to execute him before Vitellius leaves Jerusalem or after.' Marcellus waited. 'Before,' Pilate said with sudden decision. 'Vitellius seems already restive that there should have been disorder in the city. It would be as well to demonstrate to him with what little fuss we can net Zealot leaders.'

'Yes,' said Marcellus, but without enthusiasm. 'I agree that on this occasion a crucifixion might be salutary. It would teach this Passover rabble a lesson. We could put up three. Barbabas and two others: the old cheese-merchant, and another important Zealot, a Jerichoan called Imeer. But, no. I have still to work on Barabbas.'

'In the dungeons?' asked Pilate with the familiar grimace.

'Oh no. Torture is useless with a Barabbas. He is not in the

384

dungeons. He is lodged in apartments.'

'But he is not a soldier; he is a rebel.'

'In our eyes, yes. But it could be to our advantage to accord him the status of an honourable enemy. If, of course, he pays a price high enough for the honour.'

'I cannot treat with a terrorist.'

'*You* cannot, of course. But I can. Leave Barabbas to me. Having spent so much time finding him, it would be foolish to waste him. If we use him properly, we can cut the ground from under the Zealots.'

'Hm! But I insist that you keep me informed.'

'Of course. As always. Incidentally, Aemilius is preparing a report on today's engagement. A formal report: an army one.'

'He seems well pleased.'

'He has reason to be. The city will now be a quiet for Passover.'

'What the Jews call quiet!' Pilate tilted a sour face towards the high window.

The din of the Passover crowd below was billowing up more strongly than ever, for now rumours of what had happened at the Pool of Siloam and on Olivet had filtered into the city. There had been brawls. Zealots had been arrested. Some had been killed. In taverns and eating-houses there were whispers that pilgrims had been brutally struck down. Some declared that far more had been killed than had been counted, because scores of corpses had been dragged away unidentified and hastily buried, even burned, in secret.

For a time the holiday crowds, stubbornly clinging to the festival spirit, dismissed these alarmist tales as gossip. It was not until reports came that Barabbas the Zealot had been taken prisoner that anyone believed that a crucial battle had been fought and a cause lost. Barabbas a prisoner! That was hard to believe. Yet two men who appeared among the crowd in the Court of the Gentiles claimed that they had seen Barabbas seized and bound and thrown on to a horse and covered with a cloak to be brought to the dungeons of the Antonia fortress. One of the men raised his fist and shook it up at soldiers standing guard on the staircase of the hated building, and a boy at his side, his face smeared with dust and tears, yelled, 'Release Barabbas!' The two men and others nearby raised the same cry, 'Release Barabbas!'

At that moment the crowds around the Temple were parted by the staves of Levites clearing a path for the priests returning to the Temple for a meeting of the Sanhedrin. Spectators in the front rank were vouchsafed the honour of a nod from High Priest Caiaphas who, drawing aside with his fat fingers the curtains of his palanquin, smiled benignly on the pilgrims. After the priestly procession had passed, the crowd surged forward again, the hawkers resumed their bawling, coins rattled into the bowls, and the mutinous cry of 'Release Barabbas!' was overlaid by the clamour of the festival crowd. The men and the boy attempted to gather another audience to listen to the fierce demand to 'Release Barabbas!' but now another cry was sounding along the streets.

'Messiah!'

Newly arriving pilgrims streaming down on the city from the Bethany road were raising that cry at the Fountain Gate. The Galilean had arrived! Jesus of Nazareth, the miracle-worker from the north, was entering Jerusalem.

News of this fresh excitement ran through the city like a flame, burning away those squalid rumours of death and defeat which, although one tried to ignore them, had clouded everyone's thoughts. Townsfolk and pilgrims ran from the markets and side-streets to see the prodigy, and as they ran they took up the cry, careless of what it meant or whether they believed it.

'Messiah!'

'Messiah!' they yelled as they joined the multitude hailing the man who, just like the Messiah promised by the Book, had entered the city riding an ass and was now advancing on the Temple.

Julius and Ephir, leaning through one of the crenellations on the roof of the Antonia, watched the approach of the Galilean. From that high point they could stare over the whole city. They could see torrents of robed figures surge down the streets and alleys towards the Fountain Gate and there break like a wave and draw back to leave, ahead of the rider, a narrow path along which his comrades, bunched like a guard about him and waving palms as though they flourished the banners of a king, escorted him to the Temple.

'What is it that they are shouting?' Julius asked.

'Hosannah! Messiah!' said Ephir. He laughed excitedly. 'They say the King of the Jews lives again and has returned to the Holy City!'

More and more voices took up the cry. It became a rhythmic chant, a vast salutation that overwhelmed completely the bawling of hawkers and bleating of sheep in the Court of the Gentiles, where the dense crowd had now turned to watch the procession approaching the bridge.

'Messiah!'

The cry, now distinctly heard, penetrated into Pilate's room. He flung out his hands in exasperation. 'Can that mean . . . ?' he began, and then walked out of the room and across the audience-chamber to the balcony from which he could look towards the Court of the Gentiles. Marcellus joined him. They saw the crowds drawing aside to allow entry to the Court of a group of robed men. In the centre of them walked a man dangling a drover's whip in one hand.

'Messiah! Messiah!'

'So Herod's preacher's arrived at last,' said Pilate. 'That must be the Galilean.'

The crowd in the Court of the Gentiles parted, leaving a broad avenue along which the Galilean walked the length of the Court to one of the staircases leading to the doors of the Temple. It was uncanny how still the crowd was becoming. Movement slowed; voices died away; everyone gazed spellbound on the figure with a whip who marched resolutely but without haste towards the Temple. He began climbing the steps. But on the third one he halted and turned to face his vast audience. By now they were completely still and silent. He held up his hands, palms outward and high. He began speaking.

'What is he saying?' asked Pilate. But the man was speaking far too softly for his words to be heard up there on the high balcony. He was not bellowing in the usual manner of a preacher lashing a crowd. He seemed instead to be engaged in a colloquy with his comrades. This softness of speech had more effect on the crowd than any shouted words could have had, for those nearest to him, pressing closer to hear the better, waved commands for quiet to those moving up behind them. So that from the knot of listeners at the foot of the steps a vast hush flowed out, submerging the whole Court in a sea of expectant silence on the far shores of which those ecstatic cries of 'Messiah!' drowned and died, and the hawkers and vendors muffled the clappers of their bells, and even the clinking of coins ceased.

'What is he saying?' Pilate asked again. 'Can you make it out?' Marcellus shook his head.

The speaker had lifted the whip. He pointed it towards a rank of money-lenders' stalls, then to another rank, and then to the tethered beasts and the piled crates of pigeons. As he pointed, the heads of his audience, stirring together like grasses pressed by the breath of an approaching storm, turned this way and that, and

387

then, as though suddenly feeling the full blast of the threatened tempest, the crowd heaved into violent life. Hands were waved aloft in gestures of defiance and determination, and once again thousands of voices cried out. The crowd turned away from the speaker, and now flowed like a tide towards the stalls, each man thrusting ahead of him any who stood in his way. The money-lenders, jumping up from their stools, stared in aghast disbelief into the eyes of those who, when flung against the counters by pressure from behind, tried to keep their balance but sprawled, stretching helpless sliding hands across swaying boards on which the scales rocked and tumbled, and coins, first in trickles then in cascades, flowed from tilted bowls. Screaming piteous protests, the money-lenders flung themselves to the ground, circling frantic arms like scoops over the paving or wrapping themselves like nursing mothers around their bags of treasure.

Marcellus turned quickly, intending to hurry from the balcony, but Pilate shaking his head, grasped his forearm and drew him back. On the staircase below, Aemilius came into sight, leading reinforcements on to the staircase.

'Aemilius!' Pilate called down. 'Keep your men back. Take no action unless anyone tries to enter the fortress.'

Checked, the soldiers leaned over the balustrades and stared at the scene below, laughing at the spectacle. Even down there, in the thick of the confusion, many were laughing; laughing at money-lenders who, crawling after money across the paving, were now buffeted by frantic sheep and oxen whose tethering ropes had been slashed and under whose hoofs bounced and flashed the coins that had been traded for their flesh. Above the cries and the laughter there could be heard at a corner of the court the snapping and splintering of wood as crates were hacked apart. Suddenly the air was streaked and noisy with the whir of massed wings as pigeons, saved from the threat of sacrificial knife, swept aloft and, after fluttering dazedly around the marble towers of the Temple and the stony flanks of the Antonia, gained the freedom of the morning and headed north for their native valleys.

Watching the wheeling patterns made by pigeons against the sky, Pilate smiled with savage satisfaction. 'There goes the profit that the Pigeon-fancier has made this Passover,' he said and then, noticing with what fierce interest Marcellus was looking towards the Temple, followed that gaze.

The Galilean was now ascending the staircase to the Temple. At the top of the steps, ranging along the terrace and blocking access to the great doors, stood Levite guards who had burst out to protect the sacred edifice. Armed with staves and swords they formed up rank on rank to repel threatened invasion of the House of God by the mob.

But the Galilean was alone. His comrades had remained at the foot of the staircase, standing there with many others who had climbed the lower steps to gain a better view of the sudden and unexpected cleansing of the Court of the Gentiles. Now, bombarded with lusty laughter and contemptuous coins, the money-lenders and the dealers in sacrificial flesh were scuttling from the scene, clutching to their sobbing breasts dung-smeared bags and purses, woefully thin, into which they had scrabbled paltry remnants of a morning's trade.

With his back to that scene the Galilean walked with confident, unhurried steps towards the great door of the Temple. And the massed ranks of the Levite guards did not halt him! For when he came to within an arm's length of the foremost rank, he lifted the whip again free of the folds of his robe and gently, more gently than one would have flicked a butterfly aside, switched it right and left; and in the face of that casually confident gesture the Levites parted ranks, drawing back right and left and leaving before him a broad path along which he walked alone and un-molested, out of the sunlight into the incense-clouded glittering murk of the Temple.

Once again Marcellus turned to hurry away.

'Stay!' commanded Pilate. Despite the sharpness in his voice he was smiling broadly, and Marcellus saw creases of laughter around eyes happier than he had seen for years. 'Stay, Marcellus. Leave the Jews to handle this affair for themselves. The Galilean is their problem. Caiaphas's problem. Or Herod's. Not ours.' He rubbed his hands together like one luxuriating in the feel of triumph. 'We have everything to gain by not getting mixed up in this affair. Yes, I can wash my hands of that man.'

XI

Sunrise of a new day. Pilate awoke in his room in the Antonia, where he had chosen to spend the night. He saw pale yellow light brushing the high window, then heard the dawn greeted with shrill of trumpets and the pompous rumble of Temple doors. He had not slept well. The room was chilly, the coverlet felt damp, the pain in his guts had nagged him even in his dreams, and there was a foul taste in his mouth. He shivered. He got up from his pallet and wrapped himself in his toga, then found his way through the dark of the audience-chamber and went out on to the balcony. As yet the sunlight was touching only the tips of the Temple spires and the gaudy crenellations on the towers of Herod's Palace. The Court of the Gentiles was still sunk in shadow, and in its half-light the throng of robed figures padding across the paving looked vague and rather sinister.

Pilate had never known the Court so quiet. So quiet it was that it seemed to him that even up here on the balcony, high above the scene, he could hear the separate slap of each sandal and the separate hiss of each whisper. For on this morning no traders were bawling, nor hawkers ringing bells, nor money rattling into bowls. There were no benches or stalls either: cleaners from the Temple staff had tidied those away during the night, and they had also swept the paving clean of dung, and pocketed such coins as yesterday's happy crowd had not found.

Marcellus appeared, as though apprised by some sixth sense that his master was awake, and joined Pilate on the balcony.

'No money-lenders this morning,' said Pilate.

Marcellus laughed. 'They are too scared at the moment. They are sending a delegation to the Sanhedrin demanding that they be protected by Levite guards and that the preacher be denied entrance to the Temple. They are also asking recompense for their losses.'

'Of course! And payment for lost pigeons, no doubt. What happened to the Galilean?'

Pilate had retired early the evening before. Feeling the onset of his stomach pains he had used this indisposition as an excuse for not dining at the palace, and, after taking a double dose of the doctor's concoction, had curled himself up in the damp coverlet. The Galilean, Marcellus now told him, had come out of the Temple just before the doors were closed for the night. There had been quite a crowd around him, many of whom had been trying for hours to get a word with him, and, when they still pressed questions on him, the preacher had sat down on the steps, and his audience gathered around his feet like scholars sitting before a teacher. At that hour of the evening, people would normally have been hurrying through darkening streets and lanes to their homes or camps, but the group round the Galilean seemed more intent on talking than on supper, and stayed on, questioning him; and all the time the Levite guards stalked along the terraces glowering uneasily down but keeping their distance.

'They made no move to clear him off then?'

'No,' said Marcellus. It was late before the Galilean at last stood up and, promising to return next day, left the Court. The crowd dispersed. The arguments and laughter of disputing groups could be heard trickling away along the streets of the city and the lanes leading to the hills.

'Where did he go?' asked Pilate.

'After he left the Temple he was seen crossing the Kidron.'

'And then?'

'He was apparently making his way to the Bethany road. But I did not have him followed, because you said that . . . '

'Yes, quite right. Let him be. He is not our problem. I wonder if he will come back today.'

'I think so. I should imagine he'll stay in Jerusalem for the Passover.'

'Good!' Pilate rubbed his hands; then, noticing that Marcellus seemed surprised at his pleasure, he explained it. 'Don't you see? This fellow has popped up at the right moment. Had he not arrived just now the Zealots could have found it easy to stir up trouble about the terrorists we killed. But by now the mob is so entranced with this Galilean's performance that they have almost forgotten Barabbas and the Zealot defeat. And, even better, this man from Galilee does not seem intent on causing trouble. Trouble for us, I mean. Yes, Marcellus, as long as this preacher can keep the crowd listening to him and attract their interest from the Zealots, the more hope there is of a peaceful Passover.'

Marcellus nodded. It sounded reasonable. 'But,' he mused, 'can Annas put up with it? That clean-up of his traders was bad enough, but the way the man has taken possession of the Temple must seem even worse to him. It's a challenge to his authority.'

'Yes. Those pigeons meant more than lost shekels to Annas: he must have seen their flight as a symbol of revolt against him and his bazaar. Yet dare Annas move against a man who has proved so popular with the pilgrims? Oh, how he must wish we would do the job and rid him of the rebel! Annas and his Temple cronies would far rather have Zealots than this man. Zealots threaten Rome, but the Galilean threatens the Temple.'

'In which case why did not Annas order his arrest? The Temple was stiff with Levite guards.'

'Arrest him?' Pilate gave Marcellus a smug smile. 'You must learn more Jewish law. Levite police cannot *arrest*. By Jewish law an arrest must be made by a witness, by one who "bears witness" against a malefactor. And woe betide the witness who cannot prove his accusation. If he "bears false witness" on a capital charge, he suffers what he expected the other to suffer: he is stoned to death.'

'Then Annas will need to buy some witnesses.'

'Instead of pigeons.' Pilate shivered, for although the sun was now flooding all the stony face of the Antonia he still felt cold. 'I have to go back to the palace,' he grumbled. 'Keep me informed of any developments. In the case of anything of real importance come yourself.'

When he reached the palace he paid his respects to Vitellius.

'You are still unwell, Procurator?' Pilate nodded. 'Yes, you look so,' added Vitellius. The inspection which might have been intended as sympathetic conveyed an impression of ghoulish joy.

'The events of yesterday were probably a greater strain than you realise.'

It was the third or fourth time that Vitellius had referred in some way to the battle at the Pool of Siloam. Each time he had done so he had managed to convey the displeasure he felt at being, as he described it, 'kept in the dark' about his proximity to a Zealot attack.

Pilate had not confessed that he too had been kept in the dark. He dodged away from the subject. 'We were to dine with Herod tomorrow,' he reminded Vitellius. 'If it suits you, I should prefer to put it off until Wednesday.'

'That suits me admirably. I was myself hoping to postpone the visit because, somewhat to my surprise, I have been invited to the house of Annas tomorrow.'

Pilate grimaced. 'I don't welcome the prospect of making that visit. If I am not hearty enough to endure the Fox and his vixen, I certainly cannot face Annas and son-in-law.'

'You, my dear Procurator, are not invited,' said Vitellius with acid emphasis. 'Annas wants me to meet certain chosen members of the Sanhedrin in an atmosphere free from the restraint of the Procurator's presence.'

Pilate shrugged. At the moment his craving to be alone and quiet was so intense that neither insult nor suspicion could register.

On his way to his bedroom he heard Claudia talking in her room and a woman replying. The visitor's voice sounded familiar to him. He went in. Claudia, sitting on a couch, swung round to welcome him. Instead of looking worried and asking about his health she smiled radiantly. A woman who had been standing in an attitude of submissive obedience before her also turned to him and prostrated herself.

'You recognise her?' asked Claudia brightly.

'Of course!' said Pilate grimly. It was the woman from Magdala. 'And I suppose she came to Jerusalem along with the Galilean.'

'Exactly!' Claudia seemed irrationally overjoyed by a slave-woman's visit. 'She tells me she saw the preacher healing the sick at Bethany.'

Pilate scowled. He was on the point of ordering the woman out and then berating Claudia for chattering nonsense with a slave. But he was too weary to bother about feminine inanities. 'I wish to be alone today,' he said curtly and went to his room. He sum-

moned Dumb Black to massage him, then ordered broth and
extra braziers to be brought in. Wrapping himself in a fur mantle
he lay on his couch and, after dozing for an hour, felt well enough
to sit up and reach for a scroll of the *Commentaries*.

Meanwhile Marcellus was busying himself zestfully at the
Antonia. From the balcony he saw the Galilean return and the
crowd surge in high excitement into the Temple after him. The
man was again surrounded by his comrades. These, an informer
reported to Marcellus, were the same men who had accompanied
the Galilean as a kind of bodyguard when he arrived in Jerusalem.
There were twelve of them. Eleven were Galilean. The other was
a Judaean, a man called Judas. That one's father was a banker in
Jericho, an influential Sadducee and formerly a member of the
Sanhedrin.

'And who are the Galileans?' asked Marcellus.

The spy knew next to nothing about them. They were only
typical men of Galilee: a tough bunch – fishermen types, and one
customs official. Marcellus grumbled at such inadequate information. He wanted their names, and all the information possible.
Among his 'pilgrim' spies, he said, there were a number of
Galileans. Surely one of those could insinuate himself into the
company of the preacher's gang. 'And that Judas might be important. Find out what a person of such standing is doing in the
company of a rabble-rouser.'

Having no official office of his own at the Antonia, Marcellus
had commandeered Pilate's room, so Severus, who did not know
that Pilate was remaining at the palace that morning, was surprised, when he hurried in to report for duty, to find Marcellus
installed at the Procurator's desk.

'The Old Man is a bit off colour today,' said Marcellus casually.
'He has asked me to keep watch on what is happening at the
Temple.' The explanation struck Severus as reasonable enough,
although, when he noticed that the map which Marcellus had
spread before him across Pilate's desk was the map of the frontiers
of Judaea and Galilee, he wondered what old Twisted Neck could
be up to. He wondered even more soon afterwards when he saw
the Zealot prisoner, Barabbas, being escorted up to the room,
and a slave carrying up from the mess wine and bread and cold
meat for two.

Marcellus felt he was making good progress with the Zealot
leader. Yesterday he had written the name 'Barabbas' boldly
across one of the three crucifixion blanks signed by Pilate and

then laid the warrant prominently on the table between them. The sight had loosened the Zealot's tongue. Realising he had nothing to lose, the man had become bravely impudent. Marcellus encouraged that impudence. From the man's unguarded taunts he sifted grains of useful information. Particularly interesting were hints of links between the Zealots and the Arabian king, Aretas. Over wine this morning he had pursued these hints for an hour, and then, when Barabbas showed signs of realising that he had spoken too freely or committed himself too far, broke off the session.

Sunning himself briefly on the balcony in the afternoon, Marcellus had noticed much agitated coming and going of dignitaries and Levite messengers between the Temple and the house of Annas, and soon afterwards his 'pilgrim' informer came with news that a group of priests and rabbis and scribes were questioning the Galilean. The meeting was remarkable in that the dignitaries had arrived in the manner of a formal deputation, obsequious to the preacher and scared of the company around him. In fact they had actually presented themselves to him as though it were he who was the power in the Temple and they who were being granted the favour of an audience with him. There had been a lengthy dispute.

'What about?' asked Marcellus. 'Zealots? Romans?'

No, there had been nothing of that nature. It had been all about Jewish law and God and trivial things like that. What it all added up to only a Jew could say, though some hot-heads in the crowd were spreading the tale that the Galilean had threatened to tear down the Temple.

'Well,' said Marcellus with a laugh, 'at least he's not doing that today.'

It was just before sunset. The preacher and his comrades could be seen emerging from the Temple. Once again they left the city and disappeared in the direction of the Bethany road.

On the following day, Tuesday, the Galilean appeared once again. So did the flock of priests and scribes. But today those came in even more formidable array. And today, the spy told Marcellus, the Galilean's utterances were being written down, and the scribes were sending a constant flow of dispatches to the house of Annas.

'Ah! So Annas is collecting his evidence,' said Marcellus. 'And no doubt witnesses as well.'

A number of prominent members of the Sadducee party who

were visiting Jerusalem for the Passover, the spy went on, had been summoned to the house of Annas. Heated discussions were going on there.

A testy note came from the Procurator. Pilate, who had become so depressingly weak that he had not summoned up enough strength to defy his doctor and leave his bed, had written to complain that Marcellus was not keeping him posted regularly.

Instead of writing a reply, Marcellus thought it would calm the Old Man down if he sent Severus to the palace to assure the Procurator personally that there had been no change in the situation. 'Tell the Procurator,' Marcellus added, 'that Vitellius has visited Annas and been introduced to a pack of eminent Sadducees.'

When Severus arrived at the palace he was not immediately allowed access to Pilate. A scribe in the ante-chamber said the Procurator's indisposition had become worse during the afternoon. The Tetrarch had offered the services of his physicians. So had Vitellius. But Pilate had preferred to stick to his army doctor, the old Greek whom he had bought in Pannonia and who knew the channels of his body as well as his road home.

'The Procurator must be very sick,' went on the scribe dolefully. 'Because the doctor, as soon as he saw him, called in the astrologer.'

Severus could hear the murmur of voices in Pilate's bedroom and caught the whiff of incense. The Greek doctor had also called in a priest to make an offering to Aesculapius.

Inside the room, the doctor, while awaiting the findings of the astrologer who was poring over his charts of mystic numbers, continuing his examination of his patient. The old Greek had optimistically brought along his battery of instruments, the very latest of forceps and pincers and knives, and a slave was industriously sharpening and cleaning them with river-sand and pumice. But the doctor had reluctantly come to the decision that his patient's illness was not something simple. Not gall-stones, for instance, which he had first suspected and which could be cured quickly with a knife, given a dexterous surgeon and a courageous patient. No, Pilate had complained that during the afternoon he had felt alternately icy cold and scorchingly hot, and this indicated fever. Perhaps it was that very fever described by the great Varro, the fever caused by minute animals which breed in swampy ground and, invisible to the eye, reach the inside of the body through the mouth and nose. With this diagnosis in mind he asked Pilate to describe the dreams he had experienced during the preceding night. Ah yes! The images which Pilate managed to recall were certainly disordered enough to convince the doctor that those little animals were there. Swamp fever! Little doubt about it. For had not Pilate served for years in those foetid damp valleys in Pannonia? The little animals must have been breeding in him ever since and now, having become a multitude, they were on the rampage. Well, this knowledge made clear the way to cure. So the doctor could confidently resort to his scrolls, and, having found the required paragraphs, refresh his memory with those words which, although they were of such antiquity and had become outlandishly garbled through the centuries by generations of careless copyists that they seemed to mean nothing to present-day ears, were nevertheless a certain specific against the little monsters. He rehearsed the phrases several times and then, pressing his thin brown fingers excruciatingly deep into Pilate's midriff, that place which the ancients said was the seat of melancholy and was assuredly the centre of many ills, he murmured the incantations particularly prescribed for banishing alien and poisonous creatures from the blood.

'Now,' he said, with a satisfied nod, 'a dose of medicine, and all will be well,' and padded off to compound the recipe which he had used successfully on hundreds of sick soldiers in the past. He came back with a large phial. The contents were steaming. He kept his thumb clamped over the mouth of the phial until he handed it to Pilate and said, as cheerfully as he could, 'Drink it quickly. But you'd better hold your nose while you do so.'

Pilate downed it immediately in one convulsive gulp. Even when empty the phial sent a nauseating stench through the room, and the priest, also holding his nose, hurried to the embers and sprinkled upon them a prodigious shower of incense.

'Whatever is it?' asked Pilate, his lips writhing.

'A wonderful specific,' replied the doctor. But he did not tell Pilate the ingredients: they were too disgusting.

When the doctor, astrologer, priests and slaves had gone, Severus came in to give Pilate the message from Marcellus.

'Good,' said Pilate in a weak voice. 'But do tell Marcellus that he must keep in constant touch. How did the Annas-Vitellius meeting go?' Severus did not know. Pilate moved fretfully. 'Tell Marcellus to make discreet inquiries. I want to know all that was said.'

Soon afterwards Claudia peeped into the room and, seeing that

Pilate was awake, came to his bed. His eyes looked sunken, and there were dark lines of pain round them. She touched his forehead with cool fingers. 'You look better,' she lied.

He pulled the towel over his lips, feeling ashamed of the stench which he thought must be still rising from his throat. 'The doctor says I shall soon be better,' he murmured below the towel. He forced a thin smile. 'If not, then you will have to summon the Galilean.'

'He has cured greater ills,' she said. Pilate, exasperated at her having taken his attempted joke seriously, waved her away.

An hour later he vomited violently. Sweat burst out and flowed down his face and chest. He fell back weakly, but within minutes he felt better. Weak and emptied, yes, but undeniably better. 'As Cicero said, some god has worked a cure,' he thought and fell asleep quickly.

On the following morning, Wednesday, the pain had gone. He still felt weak, but in a not unpleasant way. The doctor was so pleased that he suggested another dose of the medicine which had been so miraculously successful. The suggestion made Pilate feel queasy. He resisted the invitation, but the conscientious Greek did persuade him to submit to another laying on of hands and the intoning of further incantations which, the doctor assured him, were specifically necessary to establish a cure so profitably initiated.

This ceremony, accompanied by suitable offerings to the god, was in progress when Marcellus arrived from the Antonia. He had come in person because Pilate had insisted that he should do so if he had news of particular importance. The Negro body-slave, hovering gigantically at the entrance to Pilate's bedroom, motioned to him to wait and succeeded in telling him in dumb show that the doctor and astrologer were with the Procurator. As Marcellus was pacing about the anteroom, Vitellius stalked in from his apartments, wearing a stiffly satisfied air of haughty good health.

'Who's outside?' They could hear Pilate ask the question in a weak but irritated voice.

The doctor peeped out and, on seeing Marcellus stride past the doorway, said, 'Only Captain Marcellus.' Pilate pulled himself to a sitting position. As he did so a flicker of pain deepened the lines around his mouth. The doctor frowned. It was plain that agitation was his patient's worst enemy. 'Be quiet,' he said sharply.

'The evil humours have been expelled, but now your body needs rest.'

Waiting in the anteroom, Vitellius looked Marcellus over. It was the first time he had met the crippled campaigner. Pilate had spoken highly of him, and Vitellius had sufficiently analysed current gossip to guess that Marcellus had been the principal architect of Sunday morning's successful operation against the Zealots.

The astrologer came out of the bedroom and walked across the anteroom, nodding vaguely to everyone in sight. His smile indicated that all was going well, but when Marcellus was stepping hurriedly into the bedroom the doctor barred his entry. 'Not yet!' he said. 'Just a moment.'

Marcellus turned back, and began his pacing backwards and forwards across the anteroom, smacking the palm of his hand against his clenched gauntlet with obvious impatience.

'Urgent business?' asked Vitellius in a confidential whisper.

Marcellus halted and eyed him warily. 'Only a local matter.'

'A local matter!' Vitellius assumed his bland mask. 'What you call local matters in Jerusalem seem to have a tendency to be quite perilous. That *local matter* at the Pool of Siloam, for instance.'

Marcellus, thinking it advisable to continue the comedy, grinned. 'Zealots are not our worry today. Only a crazy Galilean preacher.'

'*Only!* I am relieved to hear you describe him as merely crazy. The Sanhedrin sees him as a menace. But I imagine you will be able to deal with him adequately, crazy or otherwise.' Vitellius faced Marcellus's questioning stare with his customary head-to-toe inspection. 'From what I have learned about your operation at the Pool of Siloam . . . ' He broke off, glanced towards the door of Pilate's room, and then, stepping closer to Marcellus, spoke in a lower tone. 'Procurator Pilate is wise in imposing such trust in you. You are obviously one who acts quietly and expeditiously.' Marcellus accepted the compliment with a nod, and Vitellius went on, 'A governor whose main concern is general political administration is fortunate when he has someone who can take decisive action without troubling him with details.' The blandness had disappeared, and Marcellus had the sense of being, in the space of a second, critically assessed. 'Anticipating my future duties in Asia,' Vitellius added in an even lower tone, 'I am happy to hope that, if the need should arise, I might rely upon similar devoted service.'

At that moment the doctor came out of the bedroom and announced that the Procurator was now able to receive visitors. 'But please don't tire him. Do persuade him to rest.'

Marcellus was striding towards the bedroom, but Vitellius laid a detaining hand on his shoulder. 'Just a moment, Captain,' he murmured. 'I shall not be long,' and stalked in to Pilate, expressing pleasure at his speedy recovery and reminding him that, if he felt fit enough, they were to dine with Herod at midday. Marcellus thus had time to ponder, alone in the anteroom, over the glittering hints dropped into his ears by Caesar's future legate in Asia.

'Fortunately I now feel hungry enough to face the Tetrarch's table,' said Pilate. 'Though I'll avoid his wine.'

'In an hour's time then,' said Vitellius, turning to leave, but Pilate could not resist asking, 'What had Annas to say yesterday?'

Vitellius stared above Pilate's head. 'Nothing of immediate importance. We discussed politics in general. His other guests were interesting. Particularly the priests. One imagines priests as being immured in the Temple, cut off from the world of affairs. But no! They are wonderfully knowledgeable politically. And Annas I found very understanding and amiable. Admittedly a little harsh occasionally. About you, I mean. Of course, he must be upset about the present trouble at the Temple, and that was probably what made him so tetchy.' It seemed almost that a smile might take shape. 'Indeed, had one not known better, one could have imagined that Annas does not like you very much.' The smile did come: it cracked open to let out a high-pitched bray.

'Whereas, of course, Annas and I are most devoted friends,' Pilate said icily. 'I suppose he will enlarge on the affair at the Temple when I receive him tomorrow.'

'You are meeting him tomorrow?'

'When I perform the ceremony of handing over the festival vestments.'

'Ah, of course. Actually we discussed that business. Keeping Jewish trappings under Roman lock and key does seem to me a somewhat archaic procedure.'

'Did Annas say that?'

'Hm! Indirectly. He spoke generally of the irritant of out-of-date repressive measures.'

'The vestments were taken into Roman custody after a most bloody Jewish revolt. Since then they have remained in our hands as a kind of symbolic pledge against excesses of that kind.'

'I do not stand in need, Procurator, of lessons in Judaic history. But a statesman shows his wisdom not in *knowing* history but in *making* it. I have promised Annas that at some convenient time in the future the question of the vestments may be reviewed, among other reforms.' Upon which, not allowing Pilate time to reply, he marched out, calling back over his shoulder, 'In an hour's time, Procurator,' and bestowing upon Marcellus, as he glided past him, a particularly collusive glance.

Marcellus came in. 'What has brought you here?' asked Pilate.

'I felt I must warn you. It looks as though there might be developments at the Temple today.'

'What developments? Is the preacher whipping up trouble?'

'No. He is there again, but his audience seems peaceful enough. The trouble I am thinking of might come from Annas. I've managed to get inside the Sanhedrin.' He stroked his gauntlet lovingly and smiled with deep satisfaction. 'I have enlisted two Levites on the pay-roll. Oh, I don't trust them much: they are prepared to sell too much for too little money. I could even suspect that the Sanhedrin or the Temple has encouraged them to collaborate with me in the hope they might have their own spies in our camp. Nevertheless I can use them. If one sifts lies well enough one always finds a few grains of truth in the sieve.'

'Just a moment, Marcellus,' Pilate interrupted. 'I am anxious to know about yesterday. Do you know what was said at the Annas–Vitellius encounter?'

Marcellus grinned. 'It was trying to find out that which got me in touch with the two Levites. Annas seems to have staged the meeting merely to make contact with the future Legate of Asia. He was cautious.'

'As usual.'

'Vitellius was vague.'

'As usual.'

'And Caiaphas . . .'

' . . . said nothing. But,' Pilate went on, 'I gather Vitellius did discuss future policy in Judaea.'

'In vague terms. A lot about friendly co-operation between Rome and the Jews. He spoke of the possibility, if the Zealot problem could be solved, of Judaea having a greater measure of autonomy in civil affairs. Annas talked about you.' Marcellus waited for the inevitable pout.

Pilate gave it. 'Don't bother to tell me. I can recite all Annas said without a script. Anything else?'

Marcellus shook his head. 'Except that the meeting finished with the two of them hand in hand exchanging airy promises. Annas thinks he has won Vitellius over completely.'

'And Vitellius thinks he has won over Annas. Some day he may find out the truth. Though will he? Flattered by incense in Antioch, he'll be too far away from the stink of reality here.' He sighed. 'Anyhow what do your Levites report about today?'

'That Annas has decided, come what may, the Galilean must be arrested.'

'On what charge?'

'Annas says the man has condemned himself from his own mouth. Yesterday priests and lawyers bombarded him with questions designed to incriminate him.'

'I can guess what kind of questions Annas would design. "Answer me yes or no, Nazarene, have you stopped breaking the law?" ' He shrugged. 'However, I suppose Annas is forced to make some move. He can hardly allow this man from the streets of Galilee to take over the Temple and hold forth day after day.'

'Even so, Caiaphas is against taking action. According to the Levites, he is in a state of terror.'

'He would be. The son-in-law is the timid one.'

'The son-in-law is also the Chief Priest. Consequently he is terrified of seeming to "bend the law".'

Pilate nodded. 'The greatest crime any Jew can commit, eh? Bearing false witness. But no one is going to bury Caiaphas under a pile of stones.'

'No. But Caiaphas is afraid the charges won't stick. Some of the Sadducees think the same, or say they think so. There's a split in the party. It seems that quite a few of them rather welcome Annas being pulled down a peg, and that group is arguing against the arrest of the Galilean.'

Pilate laughed. 'That's the best news I've heard in a long time. If Annas's witnesses drag the man before the court of the Sanhedrin and then the case collapses, Caiaphas and Annas will have to let the Galilean go free. What a comedy! What fools they'll look! They deserve it.'

'Annas has said the man must not go free on any account. Annas is determined to destroy a man who has openly defied him. But my concern at the moment is that, if the man is seized, we might have a full-scale riot in the city, with Zealots still thick as leaves in the olive groves. I've tried to warn Aemilius. But he insists that he will take orders only from you. I suggest you instruct him to put the cohorts on full alert. Just in case.'

At that moment they heard a voice in the anteroom asking for Marcellus. Marcellus went to the door. 'Come in!' he commanded. A centurion entered and handed a message to Marcellus. 'A Jew fellow brought it, Captain. He said it was urgent.'

'From one of my Levites,' Marcellus said excitedly and unrolled the papyrus. His face fell. 'Curse him. It's in Aramaic. Or Hebrew.'

'Give it to me.' Pilate reached out his hand. The message was not in Aramaic; it was in Hebrew, scribbled in haste, not easy to read. Pilate worked it out patiently. He looked up. 'Annas is making his next move, Marcellus.' He called out for Dumb Black. 'Bring a toga!' Pulling the coverlet around his shoulders he swung his legs over the edge of the bed and sat up. 'It appears, Marcellus, that Annas is trying to drag us into his quarrel. He is coming to the Antonia to demand Roman aid against a heretic.'

Not until Pilate was descending the staircase through the gardens did he remember his promise to accompany Vitellius to dine with Herod. He sent one of his escort back to convey his apologies to both and to explain that unforeseen circumstances demanded his presence at the Antonia.

The journey to the fortress took longer than usual. The holiday crowds were denser and more disorderly than ever. Thousands of people were converging on the Temple, all of them excited by the hope of catching a glimpse of the preacher. The man's presence in the Temple had become the most enthralling feature of this year's Passover. Beyond the bridge progress was made all the more difficult by the fact that Levite guards were halting the crowds and pressing them back to clear the way for another party. Pilate could see a a bouquet of parasols bobbing up the steps to the Court of the Gentiles. Accompanied by an immense court of priests and lawyers and Levite guards, Chief Priest Caiaphas and Annas were proceeding in portentous state to a meeting of the Sanhedrin at the Temple. This procession attracted so much attention that the arrival of Pilate and his escort at the Antonia was almost unnoticed.

Aemilius, puffing cheeks redder than usual, greeted the Procurator at the foot of the steps. At last the size and tumult of the crowd had disturbed him. 'I have put the cohorts on the alert,' he said.

Pilate nodded. 'Good. But keep them out of sight. There must be no provocation.'

Aemilius bridled. 'There never is!'

As Pilate climbed the steps he felt annoyingly weak, and by the time he reached the audience-chamber he was sweating profusely. He had to halt for a moment to wipe the drips from his brow, and also to shake away a slight dizziness. Then he walked out on to the balcony. The crowd outside the Temple was noisy. There was a lot of laughter, yet there seemed to be anger in it, and fists were being shaken at members of the Sanhedrin who, arriving later than the chief priest's party, had to be protected by sturdy rings of Levite guards as they were shepherded through the multitude towards the safety of the Temple.

'Have you some of your agents down there?' Pilate asked Marcellus sharply. Marcellus nodded. 'I hope you have made it clear beyond all possible doubt that they must not stir up any trouble. On no account shall we interfere.' Pilate walked back into the audience-chamber. 'We shall take necessary action only if we are attacked,' he went on. 'Otherwise . . . ' He made a pushing-away gesture with his hands. 'Let these Jews tear themselves to bits if they wish. Let preachers deal with preachers. Whatever Annas says I wash my hands of this rebel.' A storm of yells thundered through the window. He covered his ears. 'What an unearthly din!' Marcellus signalled urgently to a guard to close the shutters. Pilate belched. 'I shall wait in my room until Caiaphas and company arrive,' he said. He pressed a hand on his stomach and grimaced. 'I should have brought my medicine. Send to the palace for it.' He went into his room and lay down on his couch to regain some strength to face Annas.

When Pilate's message excusing himself from Herod's invitation arrived, Vitellius had been enjoying the stimulating ministrations of his masseur. He was rather pleased that Pilate would not be joining the party. The little man's absence would make it easier to establish closer contact with young Julius. Pilate had not even thought of the boy being invited. Vitellius had not mentioned that oversight to Pilate; he had spoken, instead, to Claudia. 'My dear lady, it is wrong for so talented a boy to be immured all the time with a crowd of soldiers. He should be allowed to enjoy the world a little more, and profit from it.' Claudia thanked Vitellius for his thoughtfulness.

Vitellius decided to wear uniform for the occasion. In muted magnificence of gallant leather and historic brooches he marched along the terrace towards the portico of the royal apartments. He looked across the valley to the old city and could see the grey surge of crowds lapping around the walls of the Temple esplanade. Even here the hubbub of the unruly city was loud enough to sound menacing. Annas had reason to be worried. One hoped that Pilate adequately appreciated the explosive nature of a hysterical mob. Anyhow, that fellow Marcellus, not an unattractive fellow in a crooked way, was undoubtedly more decisive and competent than Pilate, and would no doubt have prepared plans to deal with any outbreak. Vitellius saw a fairhaired figure standing near the aviary and quickened his steps.

'Julius! You have already arrived!'

'Yes, sir.'

The boy wore a simple tunic of undyed linen, fashioned in Greek style and undecorated except for the silver clasp that fastened it on one shoulder, and a Roman kilt of strips of soft leather with gilded points. His hair had been cropped so short that some of the attractive waves were lost, but probably the style showed more to advantage his square smooth brow.

'And the Lady Claudia?'

'She is on her way, sir. She waited for an escort.'

'Then did you come without escort?'

'Oh, yes!' The boy grinned.

'Alone?'

'Yes. Except for Ephir.' Julius directed a friendly smile towards the staircase, Ephir, disposed comfortably on the sunny side of the clipped hedge, had already sunk into the contented doze he would enjoy until his young master was ready to return to the Antonia.

'But two boys,' protested Vitellius, 'coming alone through those crowds!'

'It was no trouble. Everybody was very jolly.'

'Hm! Well, fortunately they would not know who you were.'

'Oh, but Ephir told everyone!' Julius laughed. 'Make way for the son of the Procurator!' he mimicked. But then, feeling that somehow the old Roman's stare was oppressively intense, his laughter died away. He looked down at his feet.

In his niche below the hedge Ephir had heard his name and Julius's laugh. He leaned out to see who was there. He saw it was that battered old Roman, and he grinned, but just as he was about to close his eyes and doze again he saw Vitellius step closer to Julius, lifting a persuasive hand. At that Ephir kept his eyes open, though not impudently staring: merely narrowed, but cunningly intent.

'Julius,' said Vitellius in a dry whisper. 'Julius!' The whisper was now commanding. Obediently the boy looked up. 'Did your father think it wise for you to come unaccompanied?'

'I did not ask him.'

'Ah!' The reply seemed to please the staring personage. 'You are, of course, now old enough not to need your father's permission for things you wish to do.'

'I do not worry him, sir. In any case, he is here at the palace.'

'He is not, Julius. The Procurator was called to the Antonia.' The raised hand hovered nearer. Vitellius had taken a step, almost unnoticed, closer to Julius. 'Well, as he is absent, I suppose . . . ' He laid the hand on Julius's shoulder. The tips of the fingers toyed with the silver clasp. 'I suppose I must assume a father's responsibility. Eh?'

Slowly and most politely, the boy slid away from the increasing weight of the brown hand. He stepped towards the aviary and peered between the gilded bars. Vitellius followed. 'Are you interested in birds?' he gasped, close behind.

'Welcome, Vitellius!' The lisping voice startled both of them. Herod had glided up behind them so discreetly that neither of them had heard either the tinkle of his bracelets or the whisper of golden fringes over the mosaic.

'Ah, Herod!' exclaimed Vitellius. 'Allow me to present the Procurator's son, Julius.'

The agate eyes looked Julius over. 'Welcome, Julius,' said Herod with a stiff smile. He had acceded to Vitellius's request to invite the boy, but he did not altogether relish acting host to youngsters. Boys were inappropriate in adult company, except, of course, as slaves or toys. Now something seemed to amuse him; and, with a quick swivelling of the fox eyes from Julius to Vitellius and then back to Julius, he managed to pass on his amusement so plainly that Julius flushed. The boy turned his attention back to the birds.

'You will have received the Procurator's regrets . . . ' began Vitellius.

'I did,' said Herod. 'I was not surprised that he was unable to join us. Indeed, I expected no guests at all, considering the turn of events over there.' He nodded in the direction of the Temple.

'Yes. The crowds are noisy,' said Vitellius.

'I was not thinking of the crowds. I meant the Sanhedrin. They are meeting in special session.'

'To discuss the Galilean?'

'Yes, and to frame a request to Pilate. Annas will shortly be having audience with the Procurator. Which is why we are not to have the pleasure of Pilate's company. Which is also why I had quite expected to be deprived of the pleasure of yours.'

'I?'

'Well, Vitellius, I had thought, indeed hoped, that you might . . . how can I put it? . . . that you might buttress Pilate with your wise advice. For it does seem that events may be now moving towards a crisis. Annas is pressing for some decisive action, but there is a split among the Sadducees. Pilate might react inappropriately.' Vitellius stared dolefully at the Temple. 'However, you obviously think Pilate can . . . ' He waved a hand heavy with rings towards the portico. 'Shall we go in?'

Vitellius did not move. 'I had not known that Annas was to see Pilate,' he murmured. He looked at Julius. Julius was peering into the aviary and had his back to him. The boy seemed exasperatingly indifferent to the discussion. He sighed. 'Yes, Herod, you are right. It would be as well for me to be there. Julius! We must return to the Antonia.'

'Oh, Vitellius, there's no need to deprive the boy of, as you would say, a glimpse of the world. He can partner his mother at dinner. Herodias is at this moment awaiting the arrival of the Lady Claudia.'

Vitellius sighed again and took his leave, an erect soldierly figure marching away in arrogant exasperation.

Herod waited until Vitellius was out of sight and then looked across to Julius. But the boy, still staring intently in at the birds, had his back to him, and was leaning against the cage, gripping the bars with raised hands, in a posture which made the fingers seem singularly defenceless, as submissive as one waiting to be flogged. To Herod the sight seemed to be a moving one. He shook his head slowly, almost sadly; or perhaps he was pondering on that mysterious capacity which innocence has of wearing unmentionable wickedness like a charm. But then, brightening up, he said suddenly, 'Julius, let me introduce you to my parrots,' and his yellow face now creased with mischief, he took the boy by the arm and led him into the aviary.

At the Antonia, Pilate, lying on his pallet, had just finished reading a letter. It was from Sextia. He was still quivering with exasperation. It disquieted him to think that she or anyone could be indiscreet enough to send such a missive by casual courier. True enough she had made an attempt, an inept one, to bury her gossip under scatterings of irrelevant chit-chat, but any public informer or inquisitive spy could have extracted the kernel of her information in less than five minutes. And the most stupid dolt could not have failed to guess who was the distinguished military personage she cryptically referred to as 'V'. However, the seal looked not to have been tampered with, and certainly the information she sent was useful.

Sextia had written from Baia, where she had gone, she said, 'to take the waters'; and take, Pilate felt sure, more than that. At a party there – no doubt she was referring to one of those midnight gatherings on the beach – she had made the acquaintance of the son of a former lover. The youth, she hinted with naughty pride, seemed flatteringly desirous of following in his father's footsteps. With him had been some young companions including a close friend of Caligula. It was common enough for young socialites to claim friendship with Caesar's heir, but she had used her own resources to check up on the youngster's claims. They were substantiated. In fact his friendship with Caligula was staggeringly intimate. But loyal. So much so that the young man was not given to retailing Capri stories, and it was only during a moment of particular intimacy and under the influence of hospitable wine that the young man had lifted slightly the veil of secrecy which was now shrouding everything that happened on Capri.

It seemed that there were conferences on policy nearly every day. Tiberius Caesar; still smarting with memories of the treachery of his trusted Sejanus, was determined to make a clean sweep throughout the whole administration, at home and abroad. Caligula was not only enthusiastically assisting in this cleaning of the stables, but was urging his uncle to go even further than the old man had intended, particularly begging him to get rid of the 'old gang' and bring new young blood into government: men with foresight, men with vision, men with liberal tendencies.

What would particularly interest Pilate, however, Sextia continued, was that one of the personages Tiberius was thinking of raising to high office was one whom Caligula considered particularly old-fashioned, worn out, and reactionary, as well as being of dubious and ambivalent character. 'That man,' Sextia recklessly explained, 'is someone you are entertaining in Judaea.' More than a month ago, Sextia continued, Tiberius had drawn up the instruments appointing 'V' to an administrative post in Asia. Against Caligula's protests he had actually signed the documents. But, at the very last minute, Caligula had succeeded in at least persuading old Caesar not to announce the appointment publicly.

No, the documents had not been destroyed. They had been placed for the time being in safe deposit in Capri, but it was always possible that they could lie there until the old man died, and then, along with many other unratified promises, go up in a cloud of smoke. We must pension off men like 'V', Caligula had argued. We need men who can do more than rule subject races: we need men who can enthuse those subject races to become proud, independent, prosperous partners in a great commonwealth and teach those partners how to develop their own wealth and their own countries. Pilate stood up. He felt suddenly stronger. His heart swelled with ambition.

If Sextia's information was correct, it changed the whole situation of Vitellius's presence. But it was dangerous to jump to conclusions. He must tread with infinite caution the narrow line which divided Caesar's possible favourites from Caesar's possible rejects.

He had just burned the letter when Severus, looking at the Old Man worriedly to see what shape he was in, came to announce that Vitellius was on his way. Pilate groaned extravagantly, but grinned at Severus to indicate that he felt equal to the visit. When he emerged from his room, Vitellius was marching in portentous haste through the audience-chamber.

'The priests have not arrived yet?' asked the Roman. He seemed somewhat breathless from his dash across the city. Pilate shook his head. At that moment the yells outside rose to such a crescendo that they seemed to rattle the shutters. 'The situation is disturbing!' Vitellius declared.

'Jews are given to wailing,' said Pilate wearily. 'Their howls are fiercer than their teeth.'

'To me it sounds as though they are on the verge of riot. I am not altogether with you, Procurator, in taking it so lightly. Nor is the Sanhedrin. I think we shall have to help them to root out the cause of this disorder.'

'The Galilean, you mean? But he has not put in an appearance today.'

'Annas fears he might come back. On Passover Day! On which day, he thinks, the mob might be inflamed to greater excesses. Even the Tetrarch is worried.'

'As he should be! After all, the man is one of the Fox's country-men.'

'All the more reason, perhaps, why we should consult Herod also.'

'With respect, Vitellius, I advise you to suspect any word Herod speaks. I am certain he seeks only profit for himself in the present situation. He sees it as an admirable opportunity for dragging Rome into a Jewish domestic quarrel. In a somewhat similar way the Sanhedrin, who are frightened of taking action against the Galilean themselves, would be delighted to see Rome suffer the odium of doing so.'

'I am myself a politician,' Vitellius snapped. 'I am not an innocent who can be gulled by the duplicity of others. For your part, Procurator, you must not allow prejudices, racial or personal, to influence you. You should not take sides in this quarrel.'

'I am glad to hear you confirm my own opinion. I am keeping my hands clean of the whole affair. By standing aside I make it plain that Rome does not interfere in religious disputes.'

'But such forbearance could be seen as weakness. This Galilean is creating a disturbance. The Sanhedrin has therefore some justification for asking us to take action against him.'

'On what grounds? It is not an offence against Roman law for a man from Galilee to say naughty things about Jewish priests.'

'You showed no hesitation in taking action on Sunday,' retorted Vitellius. 'You, or Marcellus, did not discuss grounds for action at the Pool of Siloam.'

'The circumstances on Sunday were completely different. Then we were operating against Zealot terrorism. But the Galilean has not attacked Rome. He is not a Zealot.'

'No, he is not a Zealot. I think he is something much worse, Pilate. He is an idea.'

An officer came in and handed a roll of papyrus to Pilate. As Pilate was reading, Vitellius, noticing the clamour outside had much abated, pushed open one of the shutters and went out on to the balcony. Yes, the crowd had quietened down considerably. Now everyone was staring expectantly towards the staircases of the Antonia. When he came back into the room Pilate was giving orders to the officer. 'Detail two scribes and ask Severus to attend with a full report. Have the graven images veiled.'

'They are quiet outside,' said Vitellius. 'The wolf no longer howls outside the door.'

'The wolf is not outside the door,' said Pilate with a grim smile. 'He is inside. He has arrived with his son-in-law. That is why the crowd is quiet. Having seen the high priests come up to Pilate they are waiting for them to come down, as once they waited for Moses to come down from Sinai.'

'Moses came down from *god*,' commented Vitellius with haughty sarcasm.

'Well, at the moment Caiaphas is coming up to Caesar,' retorted Pilate, then added hastily, 'at least coming up to Caesar's servant in Judaea.'

'I hope that Caesar's servant will try to be as wise as a Jewish god.'

Slaves came in to shift table and stools and chairs into position. One climbed up to draw the curtains over the Caesars. Severus appeared with the guards and posted them in a frieze along the walls.

Vitellius took Pilate by the elbow and steered him away from this bustle into one of the embrasures. He adopted the flattering air of conspiring with an equal. 'In this part of the world,' he said, 'I am, for the moment, only an unofficial observer. However . . . ' He paused, waiting for the weight of that ponderous 'however' to plumb his listener's depths. 'However, I can speak in Caesar's name.'

Pilate shifted uneasily, and the persuasive hand fell from his elbow. 'The Procurator,' he said with a show of stubbornness, 'must do more than *speak* in in Caesar's name: he must *govern* in Caesar's name.'

Pompous little man! But Vitellius repressed his irritation. 'Of course. You are Procurator and I am only the Procurator's guest. But it does seem to me that you think of the Jews as an inferior race?'

'Inferior? No. But different. After all they are not exactly Romans, are they?'

'No. But neither are many other peoples who are members of our commonwealth of nations. Jews are different, but because of that we should not assume they are naturally enemies. To put it bluntly, Pilate . . . ' Studying Pilate's averted profile, he broke off and held back his decisive blow until Pilate turned to receive it in the face. 'To put it bluntly, Pilate, the days of Sejanus are over.' He saw Pilate flinch. He also saw, he thought, a tremor of alarm in the sick and tired eyes. 'As we know, most of those who were infected with the racialist opinions of that detestable would-be-regicide have been purged from the councils of the commonwealth. Those remaining, will, we pray, eventually be dealt with according to their deserts.'

Avoiding Vitellius's eyes, Pilate gazed along the audience

chamber towards where Severus stood waiting for the signal to open the doors. He hoped his preoccupied stare would remind Vitellius that the priests were waiting, and put an end to a disquieting conversation.

But Vitellius went on. 'Now, I do agree that, as far as Rome is concerned, the fact that a rabble-rouser is causing trouble in a Jewish temple is neither here nor there. But the situation can be turned to Caesar's advantage. What the Sanhedrin wants you to do is really very little: nothing more than preventing this rebellious preacher from returning to the Temple to cause further trouble. You and Marcellus would not find such an operation all that difficult. And if you perform it, you make not *one* but *three* political gains. First, by helping the Sanhedrin out of a difficulty you put them in your debt and can expect in return their more compliant collaboration. Second, you establish that it is Rome's right to have its voice heard in even the religious councils of Judaean government. Third, and this is of personal importance to you, you give incontestable proof, not only to the Jews but also to Tiberius Caesar, that you are not tainted with the anti-Jewish policy for which your former patron was notorious. Have I made myself clear?'

Pilate nodded dismissively and turned to walk towards the dais, but Vitellius clutched at him. 'A moment, Pilate! I wish to sit in at this audience. As an observer, or, I might say, as Caesar's ear.'

'If you insist,' murmured Pilate. 'Excuse me a moment.' He went into his room. He poured water into a bowl and plunged his hands into it. The water was stingingly cold. He sluiced his brows and felt somewhat refreshed. He washed his hands, towelled himself energetically, combed his hair, and, for safety's sake, took a dose of his medicine.

When he returned to the audience chamber he saw that an extra chair had been placed on the dais beside his. Vitellius was already standing on the dais. Pilate seated himself magisterially on his high chair, smoothed his hair with his palms, arranged the folds of his toga, rested his hands on the acanthus carvings and pulled himself erect. He nodded to Severus. The doors swung open. Caiaphas and Annas entered.

They were, unexpectedly, alone. No train of Levite guards and scribes attended them, and Annas, as he marched ahead of Caiaphas through the long room, glowered disapprovingly at the frieze of soldiers and the scribes at the table. 'I had hoped this discussion would be informal,' he said. 'And private.'

'But, of course!' exclaimed Vitellius. 'The better so.' He stood up and, stepping down from the dais greeted Annas and Caiaphas in an informal social manner.

'Severus! Dismiss your men,' said Pilate, and, 'You go too,' he said to the scribes. But before the scribes left, Vitellius had them drag chairs into a circle around the table, and Pilate had to surrender the eminence of his high chair. Now that he had stepped down from the dais he looked, thought Annas, frail and sickly.

'Please be seated, gentlemen,' said Pilate.

Caiaphas, his plump face so puckered with distress that he seemed on the verge of tears, sank into the nearest chair. Annas remained standing. He grasped the back of a chair. His knuckles showed white above his brown and hairy fingers. He scowled at Pilate. 'You are aware, are you not, of the situation at the Temple?' he asked in a tone of heavy reproach.

'We are,' interposed Vitellius. 'We share your concern.'

This reply seemed to take the edge off the anger Annas had built up, for he now sat down and grumbled, 'A heretic preacher has seized the Temple.'

'Seized?' asked Pilate as he sat down opposite the two priests. 'I did see the man enter the Temple on Sunday, but his entry was not, it seemed to me, a forcible entry.'

'He was allowed unopposed access only because opposition would have created unseemly tumult in the House of God. He has already created riot. He encouraged a mob of ignorant pilgrims to attack the money-changers and the dealers in sacrificial flesh.'

'Yes. I saw flocks of pigeons.'

Annas stiffened. 'As a Gentile, sir, you might see offences committed in the House of God as no more than amusing. But as Caesar's procurator you have a duty . . .'

Vitellius interposed hurriedly. 'I assure you, High Priest, that the Procurator is conscious of his duties. But to us the situation is confused by what seems a divergence of opinion among the Jews. The Tetrarch tells me that many Jews applaud what happened in the Court of the Gentiles. They have described it as a "cleansing of the Temple".'

'Those who speak in that way have been corrupted by the Galilean. He is a blasphemer.' Caiaphas nodded. 'Chief Priest Joseph has declared himself on that point. The manner in which the man entered Jerusalem condemns him. He rode into the city "mounted on the foal of an ass". He did so to persuade the ignorant that prophecy was being fulfilled and that he is the Messiah. A number of foolish people actually acclaimed him as such.'

'But has he made that claim himself?' asked Pilate.

'Yes, he has. He did so when he was questioned in the Temple yesterday. The claim is blasphemous, for, by assuming the title, the man is professing himself to be the final exponent of the divine meaning of the religion of Israel.'

Pilate looked bewildered. 'I regret, High Priest, that I am insufficiently versed in the complexity of your religion to judge on such a point.'

Vitellius interrupted. 'But I do not think you are being asked to judge on religious points, Procurator. I suggest we accept the learned opinion of the high priests that the man has committed a religious offence. What concerns us is how far it lies within the competence of the Roman administration to assist the Sanhedrin in preventing sacrilege leading to riot.'

'Thank you, sir,' said Annas. 'That is the reason for our presence here. It is said that the man intends to return on Passover Day. He has made wild threats to destroy the Temple, and certainly his return on Passover Day could lead to a tumult of destruction. That return must be prevented.'

'I fail to see how a Roman Procurator can prevent a Jew from entering the Temple of his god,' said Pilate.

'He could be arrested. We have sufficient witnesses against him.'

'Then why have you not used them?'

'Because the man has a bodyguard of Galileans. Those men are armed. Illegally so, but armed, and the witnesses are men of peace, some of them aged.'

'Then what do you suggest?'

'That he be arrested by you . . . by the Roman administration.'

Vitellius was nodding agreement. Pilate frowned dubiously. 'But surely, High Priest, the arrest of a Jewish preacher by Romans would incense the pilgrims more than his arrest by Jewish witnesses. His arrest by my soldiers would seem flagrant interference by Rome with Jewish religious affairs.'

'Not if you made the arrest secretly,' said Annas. 'As has been done with others.'

'With Zealots, you mean? But Zealots are avowed enemies of Rome. Zealots commit crimes against Rome. Whereas this man . . .'

'He has created public mischief.'

'Yes,' Pilate agreed. 'Perhaps on grounds of inciting to riot I might justifiably have him rounded up and imprisoned.'

'Imprisoned!' Annas exclaimed. 'More than imprisoned. A blasphemer must be . . . ' He broke off abruptly, checked in full gallop and turned a questioning glance on Caiaphas. Pilate saw, beyond the rim of the table, a plump hand tugging urgently at Annas's sleeve. Caiaphas shook his head. When he faced Pilate again, Annas continued in more persuasive tones, 'But, Procurator, the first problem is the arrest.'

'Yes. But if the charge is, as you maintain, blasphemy, then the arrest must be made by the Jewish witnesses,' persisted Pilate.

Vitellius leaned forward. 'You can understand, High Priest, the Procurator's reluctance to involve the Roman administration in a religious quarrel.' He turned to Pilate. 'But would you agree, Procurator, that that difficulty could be surmounted if the Romans did not themselves make the arrest but merely assisted the Sanhedrin to make it quietly?'

It was an ingenious suggestion. Pilate pondered over it. Vitellius smiled encouragingly at the priests.

'Agreed!' Pilate said at last. 'We are prepared to help. The arrest must be made by the Jewish witnesses. But those witnesses will be protected against the illegally armed Galileans by a military escort from the Antonia fortress.'

'Though,' interrupted Annas, 'it must be understood that the man will not be taken to the Antonia. He will be brought before the Sanhedrin. He must face trial.'

'Of course that is understood,' said Pilate sternly. 'Any arrested man must be tried by the competent tribunal. And the arrest must take place outside the city.'

'Indeed,' agreed Annas. 'And, on that point, I hope your assistance may also include that of helping to find the man. He has left Bethany and gone into hiding somewhere with his fellows.'

Vitellius leaned towards Pilate. 'Have you any information about his movements?' Pilate shook his head. 'Marcellus?'

'It is possible,' said Pilate.

Vitellius turned to Annas. 'We need not trouble the Procurator with such minor details, High Priest. We are fortunate in having in Jerusalem an officer perfectly capable of carrying out the operation. He will be instructed to attend on you. The man is Marcellus.'

'Did you see Caiaphas tugging at father-in-law's sleeve?' Pilate asked Vitellius when the priests had left. 'He was frightened of

Annas saying too much.'

'It might be so.'

'I am sure of it. There is a split in the Sanhedrin, and even Caiaphas thinks Annas is going to extremes.'

Vitellius sniffed. 'Internal wrangles in the Sanhedrin are not our concern.'

'Unless I am dragged into them, Vitellius.'

'Oh, of course, you must stand apart. But your only concern is to see that the man is quietly rounded up and handed over to the Sanhedrin. And surely Marcellus can attend to that?' Pilate nodded. 'Then the trouble is over, and there is no fear of a riot on Passover Day. Incidentally, the Tetrarch has invited me to join him and Herodias at their Passover Eve supper. He suggests you should come. A pleasing Jewish festival. It should be amusing.' The invitation did not seem to lighten Pilate's mood. He was still frowning dubiously. 'Are you feeling unwell again, Pilate?' asked Vitellius in the accusing tone of one who never indulged in the luxury of ill-health.

'I am much better,' said Pilate unconvincingly.

Vitellius nodded. 'Things went very well this morning, thanks to you, Procurator. You handled the situation excellently,' he said and, aglow with the charity of bestowing an undeserved compliment, marched proudly out.

Pilate went to his room and flung himself on his pallet. When Marcellus appeared, he pulled himself from a fevered doze and began giving instructions relative to the arrest of the Galilean. But Marcellus interrupted. Vitellius, he said, had already briefed him. Pilate wearily waved him away and drifted off to sleep.

Marcellus interrupted Severus on his way to Pilate's room. 'Don't disturb the Old Man. He needs sleep,' he said and took Severus downstairs to discuss strategy and the detailing of a select posse of soldiers for an important arrest.

Pilate did sleep most of the day and when he awoke late in the afternoon felt stronger. When dusk was falling over the city he went out on to his balcony and, wrapped in a fur mantle, watched the crowds leave the Court of the Gentiles and make for the lighted streets and markets. Then he went back into his room to await the return of Marcellus from the house of Annas.

When Marcellus appeared he looked none too pleased.

'The Levites are not very efficient,' he grumbled. 'All they know is that the man is in hiding. Somewhere on Olivet, they say. I intend to send out a patrol myself to trace him.'

'But the *Jews* must do the arresting. Don't forget that.'

'I shan't. I've already met some of the witnesses. And a party of Temple guards have been put at my disposal.'

'How did Annas receive you?'

'He didn't. He was sitting in council with Sadducee party leaders. But his steward was very amiable. He kept pressing wine on me – very good wine too. There was a good coming and going. One of the Levites told me there was quite a row going on behind closed doors. So far as I can understand, it seems that the witnesses can't agree on their charges against the man. Annas is trying to make them agree.'

'He will have to,' said Pilate with a satisfied nod. 'Under Jewish law, the least discordance between the evidence of witnesses destroys the value of all the evidence. In that case Annas would lose his victim.'

'And apparently he is pressing for a sentence of death.'

'Are you sure?'

'The Levite said so. Annas has warned the Sanhedrin to be ready to attend a trial tomorrow night. The Galilean is expected to come into the city for supper and ... '

'Tomorrow *night*?' interrupted Pilate.

'Yes. If the man's to be executed, it must be done on Friday morning, before Passover.'

'You must be mistaken, Marcellus. If not, then Annas also needs some lessons in Jewish law. If he is wanting a death sentence, the court cannot sit at *night*. Only civil disputes, not capital charges, can be tried at night.'

Marcellus shrugged. 'I suppose Annas will find some way round that.'

Pilate shook his head. 'Jews are strict about their law. To them law is the word of god, and even an Annas dare not ignore that. What your Levite says suggests that some of the Sadducees are insisting on rigorous observance of the law. That is why Annas is so eager to drag me into the dispute on his side.'

'The Levite said that Annas hoped the Galilean might be crucified on Friday morning along with the Zealots.'

'Indeed!' said Pilate angrily. 'The Zealots who are to be crucified on Friday are being crucified for offences against Rome. I am not going to dance to Annas's tune to the extent of putting his religious offender among them. The crucifixion of Barabbas and his accomplices bears no relation at all to the affair of the

Galilean and Annas's pigeons. By the way, I have not seen the warrants for Friday's executions.'

'I used those three blanks you signed. I needed them for the interrogations.' Marcellus paced around the room for a while and then, 'I'm still wondering about Barabbas.'

'Wondering what?'

'As I see it, now that we have identified him he is no danger to us. I have been thinking of ways we could use him. If we crucify him, we lose the chance of doing that.'

Pilate's mouth set in stubborn lines. 'I am not prepared to treat with rebels.'

'Not *treat* with him, Pontius. *Use* him. His contacts with Petra could be used to our advantage.'

'The best use that can be made of Barabbas is to hang him on a cross on Passover Day to show the Zealots what happens to terrorists.'

'He could be more useful alive,' persisted Marcellus.

Pilate stood up. 'I am afraid you would find it difficult to convince me of that, Marcellus. Anyhow, the immediate problem is the Galilean. Keep me informed at the palace of any developments.'

When Pilate reached the palace he was surprised to find Vitellius ensconced with Claudia. 'Pilate!' Vitellius exclaimed. 'I have been waiting for you.' He sprang up and advanced on Pilate with uncharacteristic affability. Pilate winced. In his weak state, this unexpected geniality assailed him like a gust of wind.

'The Lady Claudia and I have been talking about Antioch!' Vitellius's voice rose to its lightest yap. 'I have insisted that she shall pay me a visit. She says she will, particularly as Julius will be there. No, you cannot pack the boy off to Rome. There is now every prospect of a brilliant future for him in Asia.' His voice dried to a whisper. 'I have something to tell you. In confidence.' Unbending so far into amiability as to lay a hand on Pilate's elbow, he steered him out of the room to the portico. In the half light his angular visage was a mask of sharp triangular shadows. 'I am reliably informed from Capri that Tiberius Caesar has made his decision.

'Antioch?'

'Yes. Lamia is to be honorably retired, and I . . . ' He left his future luxuriously unsaid.

'When the appointment is ratified I shall be the first to congratulate you,' said Pilate fervently.

Vitellius gave a satisfied nod. 'So, Pilate, I am now in a position to offer prospects of advancement to your son.'

'Thank you, Vitellius. Though we must of course wait until your appointment . . . ' His voice trailed off.

Vitellius shrugged impatiently. 'As Lamia is remaining in Rome,' he said in confident clipped tones, 'I think I can expect Caesar to ratify any appointments I make out here.' He inspected Pilate intently. 'Or any dismissals either,' he added sharply. 'Good night, Pilate.'

'Release Barabbas!' The cry had nagged Judas for days, and now, as he sat alone, withdrawn from the circle of Galileans in the darkness of an olive grove in Olivet, it branded his thoughts again. 'Release Barabbas!' He recalled how when he first heard the cry it had come from afar off, rising like a prayer above the tumult in the Court of the Gentiles and then dying away, but at that moment his ears and perhaps even his mind had been deafened by the Galilean's entry into Jerusalem. 'Release Barabbas!' It had seemed a prayer that would in all good time be answered, as many prayers were to be answered in the City of David. The freeing of the faithful was but one of the deeds of salvation promised.

But tonight on Olivet, with that flood-tide of promises ebbed and his hopes lying like wrecked things on a dry shore, that unanswered prayer tolled through his mind like an accusation of betrayal. Judas a betrayer? That was a damnable thought. But it was true that a brave friend had fought for the freedom and glory of Judah and now lay in a Roman dungeon, and he, Judas, had deserted him to indulge in giddy dreams.

The first day, the day of the Galilean's entry into Jerusalem, had been one of joyous hope. It had seemed like a day for miracles, a day when prophecy was to be fulfilled. On the shores of the Sea of Galilee Jesus, like Micah of old, had denounced priests and false prophets. Like Jeremiah he had called upon people to repent their sins and turn away evil. And, like both those prophets, he had prophesied that the Temple would be destroyed. With these prophecies fresh on his lips, the Galilean had entered Jerusalem as promised: in triumph. All the people of the Holy City and the multitude of pilgrims from every town and hill in Judaea had hailed him as Messiah and Saviour. The Court of the Gentiles had been swept clean of its stinking commerce. The priests and

Levites had fallen back impotent before him. No one had dared to oppose the man who had come to claim a throne. The Temple was surrendered into his hands. With passionate impatience Judas had awaited the command to draw the sword and cleanse the House of God of perjured priests as thoroughly as the Court had been cleansed of beasts. But that command had not been made. The brilliant moment withered.

The preacher who had entered the Temple like a king stayed in it like a preacher: the man who might have conquered was content to prate. That man was holding forth now under the olive-trees. Judas could hear the sonorous Galilean voice. That voice could be wondrously persuasive and comforting. For the Galilean was a good man. Yes, grant him so much. A wise man, too, and possessed of mysterious powers.

But what was he doing here, sitting humbly on the earth? Did a king, did a Messiah, hold court at night under an olive-tree?

For three days Jesus had held the Temple as his own. Yet each day he had meekly surrendered the prize. Yesterday, the third day, had been the most humiliating. Yesterday the creatures sent by Caiaphas and Annas had become bolder. They had dared to show their anger. But the Galilean, smiling mildly in the face of their insults, had given them soft answers. Instead of lashing them with contempt like the conqueror and king he could have been, he seemed content, like a Galilean lawyer, to weigh word against word and meaning against meaning.

By what right, his questioners had asked, did he set himself up as one to cleanse the Temple? 'By my right as God's chosen king!' That was the reply he should have made. Instead he had mildly asked them to consider similarly what credentials John the Baptist had possessed, and then he had launched into an argument, dressing it up, in that style which he favoured, as a parable. Any man who rejected God's messenger, he argued, would be himself rejected by God.

Caiaphas's interrogators thought up more tricky questions. What was the true name and title of the Messiah? Would he be announced by God or declare himself? What was meant by resurrection? Question followed question. Argument followed argument. But no action. It was all words; nothing but words. Jesus had even said he had no quarrel against the Romans! And once again, for the third time, the Temple had been surrendered. Indeed it seemed that yesterday it had been surrendered for ever, for Jesus announced his intention of staying out of Jerusalem until Passover Eve, when they would gather for supper at the house of friends in the city.

Judas sighed. He got to his feet quietly and stole away from the Galileans. He walked moodily through the olive-plantations. Every few yards there were groups of pilgrims: men and women squatting on bedding-rolls, and children sleeping on rugs with their fingers laced into the fleece of petted lambs blinking without foreboding into fires sparkling under the cooking pots. Lower down the hill, near the Bethany road, the camps were more thickly clustered. On the road itself shopkeepers from the city had set up stalls, and throughout all the day and late into the night did a brisk trade in butcher's meat and vegetables, cheeses, cooked meats and stew, sweetmeats and pastries. There was always a crowd around the stalls, for lots of folk who did not intend to buy anything came down to gossip, particularly at nightfall when the unlighted camps higher up the hill seemed dreary and lonely.

At the point where Judas reached the road was an inn. The tumbledown place probably did more trade in the few days before Passover than it did all the year round. To make certain of not losing any custom the innkeeper had opened his window as well as his door, so that those who did not wish to go inside could squat on the roadside and be served by the innkeeper's two sons who handed out beer and wine over the window-sill. Judas joined fellows who were drinking there and bought wine at the window. He asked for a flask of it; enough for four. He felt need of it. The son serving him did not ask for the payment, but merely called the price, and Judas, following the example of those who had ordered ahead of him, tossed the necessary coin into the brass bowl balanced on the sill.

Two fellows sitting below the window drew nearer together to make room for him, but he did not sit with them. He nodded his thanks and moved away. The jolly chatter of those around made his black thoughts blacker. He would drown those thoughts, or at least stupefy them, in wine. But alone. A few feet beyond the glow of light around the window was the deep shadow of the doorway of the inn. There he could drink unnoticed and not be latched on to by some gossip hungry for ears. He drank greedily. The wine was rough and vinegary stuff, but refreshingly chilled. Certainly the pilgrims seemed to like it. Were they drinking so much to celebrate Passover or because the wine was absurdly cheap?

The call of orders at the window was constant. So was the

clinking of mites in the brass bowl, though there came a pause in that clinking when one of the sons, passing a filled jar through the window to a boy outside called the price, and the boy tossed back no coin. Instead he craned over the sill and murmured something. The son nodded as though accepting a promise the boy had made about payment, but, keeping his fingers laced into the handle of the jar, sought his father's attention and repeated the boy's message, mouthing it extravagantly so that the father could translate it above the hubbub around the window.

Of the message Judas had heard only one word. Even then he doubted that he could have heard correctly. Was he already so fuddled with cheap wine that he could hear nothing on every hand except, tauntingly, the name 'Barabbas!'? For that name was the word Judas had heard, and it seemed that it could be accepted as a token for a jar of wine, because the innkeeper, after brushing a cautionary finger across his lips and peering in the direction of the boy, nodded. The innkeeper's son released his grip on the wine-jar, and the boy snatched it over the sill and, calling out thanks over his shoulder, darted across the road and hurried uphill towards the darkness of the olive-groves.

When the boy had swung sharply away to leave the window, Judas had seen below the cowl enough of the face to stir memories of a face seen before. When the boy's voice rang out those memories coalesced. The boy was Ishmael, nephew of his friend Simeon of Jericho. Judas planted his half-emptied flask at the feet of the men sitting below the window and hurried after him.

He could see the boy pacing up the hill ahead of him. Despite the darkness, the boy was swiftly treading a trickily twisting track between rocks and trees, as though well accustomed to the difficult route. Now and again the slim robed figure went out of sight beyond a terrace wall or a clump of trees or a bluff of the hill, and only by plunging ahead heedless of roots and rocks did Judas manage to get sight of him again. Once, when Judas slipped and sent gravel showering behind him, the boy halted as though startled by the sound of someone near to him, and dodged out of sight behind trees, and waited there.

Judas was on the point of calling out; then checked himself. He was curious to see where the boy would go. If he caught up with him now, perhaps he would refuse to go further or to tell Judas where he was making for.

After a few moments the boy stepped into sight again and continued along the brow of the hill. But he was going more slowly now, and Judas, fearing to get too close to him, also slowed his pace. Then the boy surprised him by turning sharply to the left and disappearing from sight down a gully choked with undergrowth. Judas plunged after him, briars scratching his wrists and ankles and plucking at his mantle, and stumbled out of the gully on to level sandy ground. He found himself in a small clearing. On the farther side the boy stood facing him. The wine-jar was on the ground near his feet, and he had drawn from under his robe a dagger whose hilt was so richly studded with gems that it glittered like fire even in the dim light.

'Ishmael!' Judas held out his hands palm upward to show he came in peace and stepped forward, but he had moved only a pace from the trees when he was seized from behind. Two men who had been crouching in ambush, one on either side of the gully, flung themselves at him. They grasped his arms, wrenching them behind his back to force him to his knees, and one of them seized his neck in an excruciating grip to drag his head back and bare his throat defenceless for the dagger. His hood had fallen over his face. He heard Ishmael say, 'A Pilate spy, I think. He followed me from the road.'

The hood was pulled back and one of the men, dragging on Judas's hair, twisted his face up to the night sky.

'Ah!' sighed Ishmael. 'It is Judas of Jericho!' He lowered the dagger. 'Release him,' he said with indifference. 'He's harmless.'

Judas got to his feet. Massaging his bruised neck he smiled at Ishmael. But the face which Judas remembered glowing with friendship over the supper-table at his father's house, stared back at him now with narrowed eyes. The boy looked him over slowly, then turned away. How like Barabbas! From boyhood, for as far back as Judas could remember, Barabbas had used that same narrow-eyed stare to disconcert an antagonist; and Barabbas had also that habit of swinging away, turning his back on you, just as Ishmael was doing now.

'So this is Judas of Jericho,' said one of the men. He strode across to the wine-jar and, as he lifted it, asked Judas mockingly, 'You are the Galilean's treasurer, are you not?'

'I remember you in Jericho,' said the other. 'You were once a friend of Barabbas.'

'I still am.'

At that statement Ishmael darted a glance over his shoulder at Judas, then switched his eyes away and spat.

'If you are not with him,' said the first man, wiping his lips after drinking, 'you are no friend of Barabbas. While you and your Galilean have been enjoying yourselves chatting to Caiaphas, Barabbas has been lying in the dungeons of the Antonia. The Romans will break his body and then hang it on a cross.'

'Unless we release him!' Ishmael said with a groan.

The man grunted and shook his head to dismiss the futile plea he had heard too often. 'The boy would have us storm the Antonia and tear Barabbas from Pilate's arms. A thousand men . . . no, two thousand or more would die in the attempt.'

The one who remembered Judas in Jericho strode towards him. 'Unless your Galilean performs one of his miracles,' he said with a brutal laugh. 'When will your Messiah keep his promise to free the Sons of Judah?'

The other guffawed brutally. 'The Galilean will do nothing against the Romans. They are his friends. What was it he said in the Temple yesterday? When the priests questioned him he said he was no enemy of Rome. His mission, he said, is not against Rome. And the Romans know it. They crucify Zealots. But they give their friend from Nazareth the freedom of the city.'

'Perhaps the Galilean has bewitched the Romans,' said the other. 'As he has bewitched this Judas.' He peered into Judas's face. 'Friend of Barabbas!' He spat. 'A true man is loyal to his friends, not to words.'

Judas stepped past the man. 'Ishmael!' When the boy turned to face him, Judas again held out his hands in a gesture of friendship. Ishmael drew back sharply, as though the thought of being touched by Judas revolted him. 'Traitor!' he hissed.

The man grasped Judas by the shoulder and swung him round. 'Go!' he growled. 'Your kind are no use to us. When next you sit in the Temple discussing the Law think of Barabbas hanging on a Roman cross. Now leave us. Leave us before I change my mind and use a dagger in the guts of one Barabbas once called friend.'

Judas left them. He walked back down the hill. His path took him past the group of Galileans still talking under the trees. But he did not join them. Instead he went back to the road and followed the curve of it around the lower slopes of Olivet until he came to where the road ran above the Kidron valley. From there he could look down on the Fountain Gate. The gate was closed, but a Roman guard was checking the papers of some late travellers who were seeking access to the city after nightfall. Beyond the gate he could see, outlined against the night, the palely gleaming marble towers of the Temple, and, behind those, the sullen slab of the Antonia fortress.

He stood there for a long time. He thought of Barabbas. He recalled their childhood and boyhood together. They had grown up sharing the dream of a free Judaea. They had parted only when each of them had chosen a different path towards that dream. The path chosen by Barabbas had led to defeat and prison. The path chosen by Judas had led . . . Where? To something more bitter than a cross. Barabbas would not in death be burdened with the guilt of betrayal. Barabbas would suffer; but there would be nobility in his suffering. Barabbas would die as a soldier dies in a good fight, with the sure knowledge that others would come in his wake and, in honour of him, fight the same battle until, in his name, victory was achieved.

It was time to forget the Galilean's soft words and to think instead of the words Barabbas had said to him on their last meeting beside the ancient walls of Jericho. 'If your Jesus dares to come to Jerusalem, then we shall see whether he is a leader or not. You will join us sooner or later, when you have seen your Messiah put to the test.' That was a prophecy that had been fulfilled. That was truth.

And Barabbas had given more than words for Judah: he had given his life. The brutish fellow hiding on Olivet had been right. 'A true man is loyal to his friends, not to words.'

It was almost dawn. A Roman patrol, accompanied by four Jews, was tramping wearily down the road towards the city. When the soldiers saw the lonely figure sitting on a rock and staring towards the city, they slowed their gait, and the officer in charge of the party eyed him suspiciously. But during the night-search on Olivet the patrol had seen scores of fellows like this one, pilgrims awaiting Passover, and in any case the man they had been seeking would not be alone. So, thinking of the soup and wine that would be waiting in the mess, the officer motioned his men to step on towards the gate. Two of the Jews, however, moved on for only a few paces, then stopped and, looking back at Judas, whispered between themselves. They turned and walked towards him.

'It is Judas of Jericho, is it not?' asked one of them, and Judas recognised one of the Levites who had questioned Jesus so closely in the Temple yesterday. 'Where is the preacher?' Judas shrugged. 'What are you doing here alone?' Judas turned away. Such indifference to his questions brought a look of surprised delight to the man's face. He looked at his companion, raising his eyebrows. The other nodded. 'Judas,' said the Levite. 'Come into the city. Yes, come along. We can get you past the guards.'

'Why should I come into the city?'

'Why not? For a drink. For a talk. To meet friends.'

Like every home in Jerusalem, rich or poor, the magnificent house of Annas was filled with warmth and joy and good smells on Passover Eve. The great hall, where Annas, children on his knee, sat facing a recently arrived and elderly visitor, was redolent with the aromas floating in from the busy kitchen: scents of bread drawn from the ovens, and lamb roasting on the spits, and spices in savoury stews. And every room and corridor echoed with the laughter of scampering feet of children riotous with the presents and excitements of the festival. The light cast by candles flaring in many-branched stands and pendant oil-lamps struck gleams from the freshly polished gold and silver and enamel of bowls and ornaments.

Annas sat on a high-backed chair. Astride one of his knees a grandson bounced like a jockey; on the other a granddaughter, balanced precariously on tiptoe, strained up to capture the tassel of his homely knitted cap. Annas stole a glance at his visitor and, deciding to give the old man a little more time to compose himself and, perhaps, be comforted by the happiness of the domestic scene, continued teasing the little girl, jerking his head to bob the tassel away from her grasp. Of all his numerous brood this little redhead was his favourite. His darkest-skinned and blackest-haired son had taken as his first concubine an astonishingly fair-haired girl from Sinai, and the blessed result of the union had been this child whose locks flamed as red as leaves after the first frosts of autumn. All his children, thanks be to God, had been abundantly fertile, except the wife of Joseph known as Caiaphas. Perhaps Joseph was empty of passion, or too fat to give passion a chance. Yet one must console oneself with the thought that lack of children afforded Caiaphas freedom from family cares and gave him more time to devote to the service of God and the Temple. The little redhead tugged at the tassel. Annas uncurled her pretty grasp, repeating his game of gently nibbling each mischievous finger in turn between his yellow teeth. She squealed with pleasure. At her laughter his wrinkled mask of a face creased like crumpled parchment to which she, undaunted by its ugliness,

426

pressed her lips, covering it with kisses.

It was time to compose his face into graver lines. It was not kind to indulge himself too openly in family happiness in the face of a visitor behind whose eyes the pain of nagging sorrow was all too visible. Annas kissed the children, swung them from his knees, planted them on their feet and smacked them away. They toddled off to join the others, who were now darting around the feet of slaves carrying in candlesticks and bowls and napkins to dress the big table for the paschal feast.

'It was good of you to come,' said Annas, 'on this day of all days, from Jericho. What a pity you could not bring your wife . . . '

'Oh, Sarah would not have left the house on the eve of Passover. There'll be more than a score around the table. All the slaves and some of the poor. And,' he added with a sigh, 'even today she hoped that Judas might be with us.'

'Would that he were,' said Annas sombrely. 'But, God be praised, you can hope to see him here tonight.'

'So your messenger told me. Did you invite him?'

'He is invited.'

'After what has happened at the Temple! You show great charity, High Priest, to allow him here, on this day of all days.'

'What better day could there be for receiving an erring son?' Annas beckoned a slave and whispered an order. The slave brought goblets and a beaker of wine. 'Some wine, my friend,' Annas invited, and after they had both sipped wine in silence for a while he said, 'Judas is the only Judaean among the Galilean's followers.'

'The more shame of it.'

'And the more hope,' said Annas fervently. 'Judas, I hear, is the treasurer of the band of Galileans,' he went on and then, with a smile added, 'Like his father, he is a man of money.'

The other did not smile. 'I had hoped he would follow me in other ways,' he murmured.

'He will. Yes, tonight I find myself confident that you will live to see Judas do honour to your name. Oh, yes, we know he has been in error. But you must remember that as a boy he was always dreaming and questioning and arguing. It is easy for a young mind to be infected with wild ideas. But such fevers pass, as the heat of the blood passes.' When the visitor, staring at the smouldering logs, shook his head in mournful doubt, Annas declared, 'And already Judas has had a change of heart.' Now the other looked up at him. Annas nodded sagely. 'Yes. He has talked of the change. He sees now that he has been led away from the truth. He needs to be led back to it.'

'Has he said that?'

'His actual words I do not know. But what has been reported to me shows that Judas is suffering an agony of doubt, and that is where you, his father, can help. His love of you and his duty to your authority will be decisive in resolving his doubts. Tonight you must stand beside him to help him cleanse himself of the influence of the heretic.'

The man sighed. 'I have tried to do that so many times.'

'This is the time when you shall succeed. Tonight you will lead your son back to God.'

'I pray for God's help. And yours.' Judas's father clenched his fists. 'But the Galilean! He should be expelled from the city. He should be driven out of Judaea!'

'He must suffer more than that,' said Annas. 'He must . . .' He broke off and poured wine. 'But he must be brought to trial. Those who have been led astray by him must see him shown up for the impostor that he is.' He sipped the wine. 'A good wine, is it not? My own pressing. The Galilean is in the city tonight. After supper he goes to Olivet. We plan to arrest him there. That is where Judas can help us.'

'You mean . . . ? Judas will be asked to . . . ?' He could not go on.

Annas stood up, walked across the hearth and placed a hand on the man's bowed shoulders. 'You are thinking of betrayal, are you not? But, no, my friend! To point a finger to one who has sinned is not betrayal. It is an act of courage. It is a service to God.'

To the soldiers gazing down upon it from the staircases and battlements of the Antonia fortress the city of Jerusalem on Passover Eve looked like a treasure-chest of gems flung open to the sky. Lamps and candles gleamed in doors and windows, and the joyous streets were ribands of light. South of the city, above the shadow of the Garden of Gethsemane, the dark brow of Olivet was lit tonight with festival stars and fire burning below the spitted lambs. Behind the old city the Palace of Herod glowed sumptuously from the peaks of its three towers to the lowest depths of its gardens. Light blazed in every portico and a forest of torches flared amid shrubs and flowers on every terrace.

At their favourite vantage point on the battlements, Julius and Ephir stared down on the fabulous sight. Julius had hoped to accompany his father and mother to the palace this evening. But Pilate had not approved that idea and, at his dictation, Julius had written a polite note regretting his inability to accept the Tetrarch's gracious invitation. Julius, the note explained, was in duty bound, as son of the Procurator, to attend the supper being given to the soldiers at the Antonia.

Pilate had thought the rough military ambience of the fortress was far more suitable for a young Roman than the Asian frolics customarily staged by Herod on festival occasions. And the boy was far better in the company of the trustworthy Severus than in the too flattering presence of Vitellius.

Julius sniffed the night air. 'It smells like one big oven,' he said.

Ephir licked his lips. 'I'm hungry.'

The roasting in the kitchens of the Antonia was this evening so prodigious that its rich aroma reached them even up here. They raced down to the mess together.

Aemilius had laid on a Passover treat for the Jerusalem cohorts with his usual liberality. 'When the Jews feast,' he said, 'we might as well join in.' He said the same every Passover. And always he insisted that the feast should be in the Jewish tradition: paschal lamb and unleavened bread for everyone. Romans, Greeks, Gauls, Syrians and Jews alike, though the lamb was swathed, Roman-fashion, so thickly in rosemary that it came from the spits in crusty juicy jackets of the herb. As for the bread, the army bakers usually ended up by making it as hard as biscuits, though it was not all that bad when soused in wine.

All afternoon the cooks had been roasting an army of lambs, slaking immoderate thirsts with such gallons of wine that by evening they could hardly tell whether they or the spits were spinning the more furiously. The first roasts were being carried in as Julius and Ephir reached the mess-hall. A Gaul, staggering from the kitchen, brandished a lamb aloft on its spit like a baby on a spear. 'Come and get it, you uncircumcised dogs,' he bawled, and the Romans roared laughter and banged tankards, splashing wine across the tables.

Marcellus, passing through the mess-hall on his way upstairs, grabbed a chunk of steaming meat, and then caught sight of one convivial bunch of soldiers into whose brimming goblets a centurion was sloshing wine. He beckoned Severus aside. 'Those men are the detail for tonight's arrest, aren't they?' he asked.

Severus, chewing on lamb, wiped grease from his broad chin and nodded.

'Then don't let them overdo the wine. You don't want to be taking a lot of drunks on that job.'

Severus swallowed the meat. 'There's no fear of that. That centurion has a head like a rock.'

'Hm! Have a word with him in any case. It'll be your funeral, Severus, if anything goes wrong.'

Aemilius, red cheeks blazing like beacons and already reeling, pulled Marcellus convivially towards a table for a drink. Marcellus sipped from a tankard.

'Good wine, no?' spluttered Aemilius.

'Old Annas serves better,' said Marcellus, and managed to slip away before Aemilius's eyes had opened from the choking laughs that had closed them.

Even the guards at the entrance to the fortress were chewing joints of lamb, and there were tankards beside them.

'Drinking on duty?' growled Marcellus.

'On commander's orders!' retorted one of them cheekily. 'Aemilius sent it out.'

Marcellus shrugged. After all, the garrison was not under his command. 'Well, try to keep your eyes open for visitors. I'm expecting two. Jews. They'll probably have an escort of Temple guards with them. Severus will take charge of those, but bring the two Jews to me immediately. I shall be in the Procurator's room.'

It was two hours before the Jews arrived. They had come in haste. They were breathless and flung back their hoods to wipe sweat from their foreheads as they came into the room.

Marcellus sprang up and pushed past the desk. 'Everything fixed? Are the guards here?'

'No! No!' The Galilean of the two answered both questions.

Marcellus glared at the other. 'But you said one of the band was to lead us to Olivet. Which one is it?'

It was again the Galilean who answered. 'The Judaean, of course,' he sneered. 'But now even he is being stubborn.'

'His father is trying to talk him round,' said the other. 'But . . . Well, he insists on seeing you. Annas sent us to ask you to come.'

'He's a Judaean,' insisted the Galilean. 'I guess he's wanting a higher price.'

'A higher price!' exclaimed Marcellus. 'What price?'

The Galilean looked away. 'I'm not sure. Perhaps you can guess.'

Marcellus stared thoughtfully. 'Perhaps I can,' he said softly. He swung away and paced about the room for some moments, then halted at the desk, staring down at it, tracing the whorls in the wood with a leather finger as he tracked down the possibilities forming in his mind. At last he looked up, tightened his scarf over his scarred neck, and said, 'Let's go.'

As they left the fortress, Marcellus sent a guard to tell Severus to bring the centurion and the detail to the house of Annas.

The house of Annas was hushed. Few lights were burning. All the children were in bed, except for a red-haired tot who, cradled in the arms of a nurse and whimpering a weak protest at being denied admittance to grandfather's room, was being carried off.

When Marcellus entered the room, Annas had his hands raised in declamatory appeal. When he saw Marcellus he lowered them and shook his head in vexation and despair. In the whole vast room there was only one candelabra lit. It stood on a long table. A scribe sat in its glow. Lying before him was a sheet of parchment, still dusted with the sand that had dried the ink of the heavy Hebrew characters. One corner of the parchment curled against a little sack of soft leather. Standing beside the table, leaning on his knuckles, was an old man. Tears were trickling into his whiskers.

In the shadows beyond the table stood a young man. He was facing Annas, and the light fell on one hand as he extended it and pointed to the sack on the table. The hand was quivering.

As Marcellus stepped forward, this young man glanced at him, but only momentarily, and then glared back at Annas. The young man moved into the light. He was a handsome black-haired fellow with fierce eyes.

'A bribe!' he exclaimed. 'A bag of gold to pay for betrayal!'

'My son!' The old man at the table groaned. 'That is not so, Judas. The High Priest has explained. It is a token: a mere formality.'

'A formality!' The young man laughed wildly. 'And that formality to be inscribed on the parchment of Temple records. And for all time the people of Judah will read how Judas of Jericho sold a man for a sack of gold. It should be silver. Thirty pieces of silver. That would be the proper tariff for such a deal: that's the current rate for a male slave.'

'No!' Annas's voice quavered with anger. But, restraining himself, he paused; then lifted his begging-bowl hands piteously and pleaded, persuasion thick as oil on his tongue. 'The payment is merely in accordance with Temple procedure. And the document! That is a noble one, for it records a service to the Temple, my son. A service to God.'

The young man laughed again, this time even more shrilly. Marcellus recognised that laugh. It was one he had heard from others lips. A body teased with pincers sometimes laughed that way: a mind torn with agony always did. He waited.

Judas darted forward and snatched up the bag. He tossed it clinking in one hand. 'How heavy is your token, Annas? The sons of Annas always ask a high price for the flesh of beasts in the Temple. How much do they pay for the heart of a man?' He swung round and ran contemptuous eyes over Marcellus. 'And this cripple? I suppose he is the Roman you have hired? Or your ally? Or your master?' He looked around the room, seeming to search for something. At last his eyes fell on what he had looked for. Near the door was a tall box, a richly gilded antique, trumpet-shaped and placed at that strategic spot so that those leaving the presence of High Priest Annas would be reminded by its hungry gape of the offering they should render for the honour of the audience they had enjoyed in that room. Judas pushed past Marcellus, strode to the box and unleashed the cord of the bag. He held the bag mouth down, and the gold poured out. The coins clattered down the trumpet's wooden throat and then clinked softly on to the velvet lining of its belly. Judas walked back to the table, screwing up the empty bag and tossing it away. It slid over the polished wood, pushing the parchment askew. He faced Annas with folded arms. Now he spoke very quietly. 'The price you offered is not enough.'

Annas stepped forward, raising his hands as a prelude to argument, but was silenced when Judas raised a fiercely restraining hand. 'I demand more!' Judas went on. 'Much more. I am a man of Judah. I am a faithful Jew. I believe in the Law. I demand what the Law demands: a life for a life.'

'A life for a life?' Annas shook a bewildered head. 'How?'

'A life for a life,' repeated Judas. 'I shall deliver Jesus of Nazareth into your hands only if you deliver Barabbas the Zealot into the hands of my people.'

'Judas!' His father pushed himself from the table and beat his hands together.

Annas pushed the old man aside as he advanced on Judas.

'Judas! This is madness. Impossible! The Romans hold Barabbas.'

'The Romans are your allies. Tell them to free him.'

'Barabbas is sentenced to death,' said Annas. He looked for confirmation to Marcellus.

Marcellus spoke at last, choosing his Aramaic carefully. 'Barabbas is to be crucified tomorrow.' He saw how the words made Judas shudder. He spoke slowly, turning each word like a knife. 'On the hill of Golgotha. With two other terrorists. The poles and cross-bars are ready.'

Judas pressed his hands to his eyes. He seemed to be praying. Then, uncovering his face, he said, 'So be it, Annas! So be it. You must find the Galilean yourself. That is easy enough. He will come to the Temple tomorrow. You can take him then. And the bazaar of the Sons of Annas will flow with Jewish blood for your Passover sacrifice.'

Annas groped behind him for the arm of his chair and sank down sighing. 'You ask what is not possible, Judas. You promised to serve God; now you betray us.'

Marcellus strode into the circle of light. He picked up the document. 'Ah.' He looked disappointed. 'It is in Hebrew.'

The scribe scrabbled for his bag in the shadow of the table. 'There is a Greek translation here, prepared for the Procurator. You may read it.'

'I shall *take* it,' said Marcellus flatly, pulling it roughly from the scribe's hand and rolling it into his gauntlet's grasp. He looked down at Annas, bowed in his chair. 'The rebel Galilean will be arrested tonight,' he said.

Annas looked up. 'But how?'

'Leave it to me. And to Judas.' He turned to Judas. 'Young man, we must discuss your suggestion.' He looked around at the others. 'But not here. You will accompany me to the Antonia fortress.' Judas eyed him suspiciously. 'As a guest, under safe conduct.' Judas made no reply. 'Are you afraid?'

'Afraid?' Judas glared at him. Then laughed. The laugh was the kind Marcellus had expected. It complemented the look in the young fellow's eyes, a look equally wild, with the thoughts behind it stretching to that point when reason snaps. He must be handled gently, this Judas. 'What should I be afraid of? Of you? Of Rome? What can you or Rome do to me more than I can do to myself?'

'Then come,' urged Marcellus quietly. 'If you want to help your friend Barabbas.'

Crazy hope flared in the black eyes. 'Shall I see him?'

'That could be possible.'

The hope dimmed. 'Alive? Or dead?'

'That could depend on you.'

When Judas made his decision, he made it in the manner Marcellus guessed he would. Sudden and tense, like a man jumping into the void with a noose round his neck, he swung round and walked out of the room and stood in the hall, not looking back but quivering with impatience for Marcellus to follow. Six Levite guards were in the hall. Severus, the centurion and five auxiliaries had just joined them. Severus stood erect, his helmet cradled in the crook of his arm. The centurion and auxiliaries, full of wine, lounged clumsily around, pawing at the rich hangings and Jewish ornaments. The Levites clustered together and looked Judas over. Wondering if he had the right to leave the house, they kept cautious eyes on the outer door.

In the big room the silence that had fallen after Judas's abrupt exit was so intense that the crackling of parchment in the gauntleted hand brought all eyes on Marcellus. Marcellus kept them waiting luxuriously enjoying for a spell their helpless gaze. At last he swivelled his slanting visage towards Annas. He did not speak: he merely nodded. Yet Annas seemed to find that nod sufficient. He stepped up to Marcellus. 'It is understood, is it not,' he whispered, 'that the Nazarene will be brought here? It is proper that he should be delivered to the Sanhedrin.' Marcellus nodded again, swung round and marched into the hall.

Annas lifted his hands high in silent thanksgiving, then went to Judas's father and took his hands in his. 'Your son fights bravely for what he believes. But have no fear. God, who has endowed him with courage, will fashion that courage into an instrument of divine will. Judas tonight will do in his own way the service demanded of him.'

'But Barabbas?' murmured the scribe. 'If Bárabbas were freed . . . ?'

'What of it?' Annas silenced the man testily. 'Barabbas is not an enemy of the Temple. Barabbas is Pilate's problem: not ours.'

'You will accompany us to the Antonia,' Marcellus said to the Levites as he walked to the outer door. Shouldering their staves they fell in behind the Roman escort.

The streets were deserted, but from many windows lights still streamed from rooms where families were sitting late over supper. Marcellus, walking beside Judas, saw the young man's profile sharp as an engraving against the glow of festival candles. Becoming aware of this inspection, Judas swung an angry glance at his twisted Roman companion.

Marcellus was accustomed to seeing pain in men's eyes: the pain in the eyes of Judas was singularly exquisite.

Marcellus did not speak to Judas until they had reached Pilate's room and, ordering Severus and the escorts, Roman and Levite, to wait in the audience chamber, he had closed the door. He was alone with Judas.

'Sit down, Judas,' he said. 'There is wine there.' Marcellus took his place in Pilate's chair and faced Judas across the desk. 'I said there is wine there. Drink! And rest for a moment.' He sipped wine himself, to put the man at ease, and, seeing him staring wildly down at the desk, withdrew his gauntleted hand and laid it out of sight on his knee. The fellow laughed again. This one must be driven delicately. The crack in that laugh and the crack which threatened to splinter the man's thoughts were symptoms Marcellus knew well. His skill was that of knowing how to prise them a little wider, with instrument or word, and probe the subject's mind without utterly destroying his reason. So, speaking calmly and without looking in the man's face, he asked in most casual and gentle tones, 'Now, Judas, why do you so much desire the release of Barabbas?'

'He is my friend.'

'Yes. Then, are you also a Zealot?'

'No!'

'You wear a dagger under that robe?'

'I do not deny it.'

'Does the Galilean wear a dagger too?' Judas shook his head. 'Yet his followers are armed. Why?'

'We bought swords because . . . ' Judas went silent.

'Because this Jesus of Nazareth ordered you to buy swords. I am well informed, you see. So you came into Jerusalem armed. Why? It must be because the Galilean thought there would be need to use weapons for some purpose. How did you expect them to be used?'

'I am not an assassin.'

Marcellus nodded. 'You mean that you did not intend to use your dagger in secret, as a Zealot would. You expected open battle?' He smiled, as one soldier might smile to another.

Judas stared boldly. 'I was prepared to fight. To restore the House of David, to establish the Kingdom of God.'

'A high ambition! Was that the Galilean's plan?'

'It is prophesied.'

'But the Galilean has not brought it to pass.' The bold stare fell. 'Do you think Barabbas might?'

'Barabbas is not a prophet.'

'No. He is a man. He has courage. Would you carry a dagger for him? If he were freed ...'

'Could he be freed?' Judas interrupted.

That glow of hope in the fellow's eyes was crazy. Marcellus adopted a musing tone. 'One never knows. Barabbas is a dangerous fellow. But resourceful. So who knows? He could even escape.' He laughed softly; then called in one of the guards. 'Bring more wine. And take this key to Severus. Ask him to send up my box. He knows which one.' He emptied the jug into the goblet and pushed it towards Judas. 'It is good Judaean,' he said, and then, while they waited, he bent his head over the Greek translation.

Eventually he felt Judas's eyes on him. His scarf had slipped. He drew it over the scar. Keeping his eyes down, pretending to be reading the document, he repeated the word Judas had used. 'Crippled!' He said it softly but savagely. 'Though I was crippled in battle, Judas. In Pannonia. We don't have battles in Judaea.' He looked up now, straight into Judas's eyes. 'There is no shame in battle, man. There is joy in it. There is love in it, too. Only in battle can any man love his enemies. In battle you meet men who fight with swords, not men who trick you with words.'

The guard came in with a long box made of battered wood and bound with iron straps from which a padlock dangled. Marcellus pushed a finger down the wrist of his gauntlet and drew out a key. He unlocked the box and from the top of a stack of documents lifted three that were rolled together. He peeled off the first and laid it on the desk, smoothing it flat and then swinging it round for Judas to read. Written in bold Hebrew characters after a preamble in Greek was the name 'Barabbas'. At the foot of the warrant for crucifixion was the signature 'Pilate'.

Trembling, Judas turned his eyes away, but, as though fascinated by the horror of the thing, had to turn and stare down at the document again.

Marcellus took a small knife from the pen-rack. He bent his head intently over the warrant. He splayed two fingers around the name 'Barabbas' and began scratching the knife carefully over the first letter. The letter faded away flake by flake.

Marcellus gave Judas a mischievous grin. 'It could be done, you see.' How easy it was to switch on that crazy light in the fellow's eyes. 'Barabbas would be a good exchange for the Galilean,' he laughed. 'A good exchange for you, I mean. A bargain. Then we hand the fellow from Galilee over to the Sanhedrin. They'll drive him out of town, and Barabbas . . . ' He pointed to the warrant. 'His name will not be there.' He waited just long enough before he said, 'You have already persuaded me to scratch out one letter. I can scratch it all out later. But first let's go to Olivet.' He stood up abruptly. 'Let us get the job done.' He walked to the door.

'You said I should see Barabbas,' said Judas.

'I said that would be possible. But now I say you *can* see Barabbas. I give you my word. You can see him at the Dung Gate, free, and beyond the walls of the city, as soon as you have fulfilled your part of the bargain.'

To anyone looking down on it from the Antonia the city now looked asleep. Few of the festival lights were still glowing. The palace of Herod was, of course, still ablaze, but the brow of Olivet was in darkness, lamps and candles snuffed and the camp fires trodden out. Soon, however, there came into sight below Olivet a string of lights from the torches carried by Romans and Levites hurrying through the night to the Garden of Gethsemane.

News that the Galilean had been arrested and taken to the house of Annas was awaiting Pilate when he awoke in his apartments at the palace. Dumb Black had padded in silently during the night and laid the note from Marcellus beside his bed. There had been, Marcellus wrote, some difficulties, but the operation had been performed without causing any disturbance in the city. Marcellus had told the Negro there was no reason to awake his master. Pilate was grateful for such consideration. He had enjoyed his best night's sleep for more than a week. Soundly insulated behind the succession of doors between his bedroom in the south pavilion and the great hall of the palace, he had slept undisturbed by the twanging harps, clashing cymbals, wailing pipes and the roars of a wine-swilling audience applauding the erotic contortions of dancing girls and the sometimes even more outrageous posturings of dancing boys. It had been a cosmopolitan party. Herod had a gaggle of Idumean relatives and favourites staying at the palace for Passover, and lots of Jews, Jerusalem bankers and merchants and the more important shopkeepers, had also attended. There were even some distinguished members of the Sadducean party bibbing wine and blinking over the goblets at the circling bellies and bouncing breasts. It was not, Pilate thought, the kind of Passover party which Annas and his austere cronies at the Temple would have considered suitable for celebrating a sacred festival.

Vitellius and Pilate had been walking through the torchlit gardens together on their way to that banquet when Vitellius's burly secretary caught up with them. A courier had just arrived, he said, and his usually sulky eyes lit with a smile expectant of his master's pleasure as he added, 'From Capri! With this!' He handed Vitellius a package on which Caesar's seal stood out big and bold as the boss of a shield.

'You must excuse me, Pilate,' Vitellius gasped. 'Go on ahead. I must attend to this first.'

Pilate could not but admire the man for not actually breaking into a run to get back to his study with the precious document, though one could well imagine that, as Vitellius stalked beneath the lights, he had drawn himself at least another inch taller.

He was still quiveringly erect when he did appear at the banquet, but he seemed to have lost that extra inch, and responded to Herod's greetings with austere nods.

'Important news?' asked Pilate as soon as he had the opportunity.

'Any news from Caesar is always important, Procurator,' he said snubbingly, then stared coldly at the guests on the dais. 'I see that your son is not with us this evening.' He seemed to welcome the opportunity that then arose to leave Pilate. Herodias, creaking enamelled smiles, claimed his attention, begging the great man towards a couch where her reprehensible but undeniably beautiful daughter Salome was diverting a gaggle of tittering female cousins by putting through its dancing and tumbling paces the new pet which her father had bought for her from an Egyptian merchant. This pet was a Negro, possibly male, but a dwarf of such horrible malformation that it looked like nothing but a bouncing lunatic head with no body at all between its chin and its crumpled but agile feet. The creature attracted so much attention to that corner of the hall that Pilate was able to steal away unnoticed to his bed. So, after all, he told himself,

Sextia had possibly been right. He was soon asleep.

Now, in the morning light, he stretched in bed and looked around. The room was immense, vast as an eastern emperor's and just as gaudy. The Herods were good builders, but they did overdo the decoration. And they overdid the scent too. All the scrubbing by slaves and the polishing by Dumb Black had not rid the room of its sickly stink. The cedar panels had been steeped in perfume for a generation before they were pegged to the beams. He preferred his stark cell at the Antonia, preferred even more his rooms at Caesarea.

Well, he need endure this decadent Herodian luxury for only one more day and then he could turn his back on Jerusalem until his next festival visit. He looked forward to the ride back over the hills and down to the Plain of Sharon. Though perhaps he might make a detour. It would be a good idea to let Julius see some of the country. Just he and Julius and a small escort, with Severus, perhaps. It would be a good idea to let Julius see Sebaste. A bit sad to go there, remembering Josephus, but the boy would certainly find the city interesting. It would be nice to be alone with his son for a few days: he saw far too little of him.

He yawned contentedly and got up. He pushed open the shutters and stepped on to the balustraded roof. Dawn was just breaking. Sure enough, at that moment the Temple was greeting the sun with its usual morning din. Slaves were already tidying up the gardens, sweeping terraces and staircases, and carting away the stumps of the burned-out torches.

Dumb Black had heard him stirring and came in, towels slung over his shoulder, grasping scissors and razor in a folded corner of his garish kilt. Was that length of cloth the same that he had worn for years, or had he brought bales of the same pattern from Africa? It never seemed to wear out. Nor did his smile, a tongue-less grin interminably draped over his vast black face. Yes, Pilate thought, as the black hands scoured his shoulders, the Negro was a good servant. But it was time that lazy young rascal, the Young Barber, returned to duty instead of spending all his time capering around Julius. Though perhaps that boy should be made over to Julius officially as his property: he was probably as suitable as any body-slave that could be bought elsewhere.

After his bath Pilate felt even fitter. Strange to remember that only a few mornings ago, when the Negro had been painting the red spot below his left ribs, he had found himself wondering whether any sword could hurt more than the pain already piercing under there like a death thrust. Whereas, as the Negro breathed on the paint to dry it, he felt full of life. Indeed he felt fit enough to do what he had not had heart to do all this week. 'Send for Severus. An escort and my horse immediately.'

By the time Severus arrived at the palace the Procurator was already pacing about on the lower terrace, looking impatient yet smiling. He swung himself lightly on to his horse. 'I am going to look at the aqueduct,' he said. 'In case I do not have time later today.'

After they had ridden out of the city, the route chosen by Pilate took them near a cluster of tombs behind which was the hill Golgotha. Pilate spurred his horse off the road to avoid a group of Jews who were standing on the road looking up to the crest of the low hill. They were watching soldiers planting three upright beams in the sandy soil. At the sight of Roman helmets, one of the group, a crazed old woman, raised her fists and screeched at Pilate. Her companions pulled her arms down and bustled her away.

'A pity that business had to be this morning,' said Pilate. 'But executions must be performed before Passover begins.' He made a wry smile. 'The corpses will no doubt be seen as proof that Pilate has visited Jerusalem.'

Over the brow of the next hill they came in sight of the far-stretched furrow of the aqueduct. Pilate cantered happily forward. Despite the holiday, the Jew labourers had worked well. It was deeply satisfying to ride along the course of the great stone pipes. Here were the first strokes of his signature on the face of Judaea. He rode out as far as the site of one of the siphons which, made of stone blocks so carefully joined as to be watertight, would lift the water over a hill. Far ahead pegs and roughly piled cairns marked the long length of future digging.

'Severus! When we get back find the engineer. We might as well discuss the sketch for the next accqueduct now.' He rode back to the city feeling proud and happy.

His content was puffed away when they came within sight of the Antonia. Spears bristling thick above the balustrades and the glint of hurrying helmets signalled some new excitement. This fractious city! Was even his last day in Jerusalem to be vexatious?

As he mounted the staircases of the fortress, he saw Levite guards drawn up in the Court of the Gentiles in more than usual force, and scores of them standing in two files to keep a corridor clear from the Temple doors and across the Court.

Aemilius met him at the top of the stairs. The commander's cheeks were pale this morning. His bleary eyes showed the cause: Aemilius had as usual indulged himself too copiously at his Passover supper.

'What is going on?' snapped Pilate, but just then Marcellus appeared and Pilate turned to him for information.

'Annas is requesting an audience. He is waiting at the Temple for your return,' Marcellus said. 'The Galilean business.'

'Again?' Pilate marched to his room in ill humour. 'What now?'

'Annas says the man should be brought before you for trail.'

'Before *me*?' Pilate sat down, pettishly pushing aside waiting documents and laying clasped hands on the cleared space. 'What do I try him for? Blasphemy against a Jewish god? Or releasing pigeons? What nonsense is this?'

'The charge is treason: treason against Rome.'

'How treason? What is Annas up to?'

'They wrangled most of the night. Finally they called in a Sadducee who is said to be an expert on Roman law. He helped them to frame an accusation. This fellow Jesus, he said, had declared himself king without Caesar's authority. Jesus of Nazareth has flouted this law. Hence he has committed treason. That's their case.'

'That snake Annas!' Pilate hissed. He leaned back. 'You can see what's happened, can't you, Marcellus? There *was* a split in the Sanhedrin, and Annas has failed to heal it. Those Sadducees who wanted to stick to the letter of the law refused to support his charges of blasphemy and suchlike against the Galilean. But Annas has thought up a new way to get rid of the problem, a way of tossing the man into our hands.' He slapped the desk angrily. 'And, oh, how pleased he will be if it is we who rid Judaea of the man! He hopes the Romans will have to crucify the preacher, and his hands will be clean. Well, I am not going to play Annas's game.' He brooded. 'Did the man actually call himself King of the Jews?' he asked. Marcellus nodded. 'Is that the whole substance of the charge?'

'It is the one the Temple are laying. They add that his plot to destroy the Temple was a preliminary step to declaring himself king.'

'Have you questioned the man?'

Marcellus shook his head. 'He was taken straight from Gethsemane to the house of Annas. The Levites questioned him in the cellar there. My man kept guard. He was beaten up.'

441

'Why?'

'He was beaten by Levites trying to make him confess. They got nothing out of him.' Marcellus sneered. 'From what the centurion says, Levites don't seem very skilled.'

'I suppose you would have done better,' said Pilate, sarcastic in his irritation.

Marcellus nodded. 'It would have been interesting. Apparently the man has some talent for argument.'

'How did the arrest go?'

Marcellus dropped his eyes and fiddled with the lacings of his gauntlet and said, 'There was a difficulty.'

'So you said. What was it?'

'Judas, the man who was to lead us to the Galilean's hide-out, nearly backed out of the job. He refused to help Annas. He threw Annas's gold in his face.'

'Something to his credit, at any rate. But he helped you?'

'At a price.'

Pilate nodded. 'How much?'

'More than gold.' Marcellus braced himself. 'He asked for an exchange of prisoners. He demanded the release of Barabbas.'

'Nonsense!' exclaimed Pilate. 'The man must be mad.'

'I agreed to the exchange,' said Marcellus quietly. He looked up and faced Pilate's astonished stare. 'There was no time to lose, Pontius. In your absence I agreed to the bargain.'

'But, why exchange Barabbas for this . . . ? What is the man's name? I can never remember it. Letting an important Zealot leader go free just to let Annas get his hands on a country preacher!'

'He is not quite an innocent preacher. At his arrest one of our soldiers had his ear sliced off.'

'Do you mean the Galilean was armed?'

'His men were. They drew swords.'

'Then they are Zealots after all?'

'No. But possibly more dangerous than Zealots. I am beginning to think so now. More secret. More clever.'

'Were they arrested?'

'No. The guards had been ordered to take only the Galilean. The others made off. Anyhow, I imagine that without their leader they'll be no trouble. We can be pleased that we have him.'

'At the cost of Barabbas!' Pilate scowled.

'Not much of a cost, really. We know Barabbas now, so we can always pull him in at the first sign of trouble. But I am hoping he will be more value than trouble to us. We can use his contacts with Petra to good advantage.'

'So you have set him free?'

'Not yet. Not until the Galilean has been dealt with, one way or the other, will Barabbas be freed. Actually it occurs to me that you could make him a kind of Passover present to the Jews. Freeing Barabbas on Passover Day could be built up as an act of clemency on your part.' Marcellus watched Pilate brooding over that, and was eventually relieved to see him nod reflectively. 'And the act of freeing Barabbas will also take some attention away from the Galilean.'

Pilate was nodding again. Voices outside the audience chamber interrupted his thoughts. Severus came in. High Priest Annas had been informed of the Procurator's return and was on his way to the Antonia.

'I've not yet said that I shall grant him audience,' Pilate said stiffly, but added, 'All right! But make it clear that I am granting him a favour by receiving him. And, as he is coming to beg favours, leave the graven images uncovered. If he is asking Caesar's help, then he must be prepared to see Caesar's face.'

When Severus had left Pilate asked, 'What does Vitellius think of this new development.'

'I don't know. Should I have told him?'

'You best know that, Marcellus. He seems to have been close to you of late.'

Marcellus noted the reproach. He let it pass. 'I should imagine he will still be asleep. Herod's Passover frolic went on until almost dawn. Before the end even some of the guests were dancing.'

'Led by Salome, no doubt. She was wearing as little as a dancing girl.'

The tart remark made Marcellus feel more at ease: the Old Man had been steered well away from the touchy question of Barabbas.

Pilate was already enthroned in his high chair on the dais when Annas came into the audience-chamber, but when he saw that Annas was completely alone he condescended to step down, dismissed Severus and drew a chair up to the table.

'Is the High Priest Caiaphas not coming?' he asked.

'High Priest Joseph cannot now leave the Temple. He has already retired into the Holy of Holies.'

'Ah, of course. He will be officiating at the service.'

'But I have authority to speak in his name, Procurator.'

443

'I am sure he has granted you that. I understand you have tried the Galilean.'

'He was brought before the Sanhedrin.'

'The Sanhedrin! But I understood he was questioned at your *house?*'

'The Sanhedrin was sitting in extraordinary session, Procurator. The house of a high priest can be used for an extraordinary session.'

'But the man was accused of a capital offence. Surely I am right in saying that in that case trial at night would not be legal?'

'I am aware of your knowledge of Jewish law, Procurator,' said Annas bowing ironically. 'But this was not a trial. It was merely an interrogation.'

'Accompanied by blows?'

'That happened in the cellar. I was not present.'

'Ah, well, I suppose priests might think the man deserved a beating for causing so much trouble at the Temple, and for losing so many pigeons.'

'I note your point, Procurator,' Annas said tartly. 'But actually it was the Roman guards who were most angry with the man. His gang had attacked and wounded them. Incidentally your Roman soldiers were, as usual, drunk. I should think they were as free with their fists as were the Temple guards.'

Pilate scowled. 'If that is so, then they will suffer for it.'

'In any case, the man is more properly held prisoner by Romans,' Annas said hurriedly. 'The crime he has committed . . . '

'Just a moment.' Pilate held up a restraining hand. 'At the moment I am worried about the manner in which this affair has been conducted. Will you tell me if the man was questioned by the Sanhedrin or not?'

'He was. He was brought before us twice.'

'So you were sitting as judges?'

'Of course.'

'And you cross-examined him?'

Annas hesitated, then attempted to brush the question aside. 'This is irrelevant . . . '

'It is not irrelevant, High Priest. I can see you understand what I am getting at. I have reliable information that your witnesses failed to agree on the charges. Their testimony had broken down. Now for a little more Jewish law: it is illegal for judges to cross-examine an accused man after testimony has broken down.'

Annas bowed again. 'I compliment you, Procurator. You are

444

indeed well versed in our laws. But, as I have been trying to say, these legal arguments have now no relevance. We are no longer attempting to press our charges against the man. We are handing him over to you as a rebel. We are doing so in accordance with Roman law, not Jewish law, and also in accordance with the terms of Judaea's treaty with Rome. That treaty demands that we must not harbour or give comfort to enemies of Rome. Under that treaty we are bound to surrender traitors or rebels, Jews or others, into your hands for punishment. This man has committed treason against Rome. We have taken legal advice on the matter. We are assured that his claim to be King of the Jews without Caesar's sanction is a treasonable act.'

'Did he proclaim himself as such?'

'He was asked, in the name of the Living God, if he was Christ, the Messiah, the Son of God. He replied, "I am!"' Annas made a gesture of distaste. 'That is all he said. "I am."'

'That is a religious point,' said Pilate brusquely. 'It is of no relevance to me. What I asked is whether he proclaimed himself, from his own mouth, King of the Jews.'

Annas waved this aside as a quibble. 'He has allowed himself so to be proclaimed. That, our advisers say, is enough.' He flung out his hands. 'In any case, Procurator, I cannot understand your reluctance to assist us in this matter. The man is a plain menace to public order. That trouble in the Court of the Gentiles . . . ' He laughed wryly. 'Even the loss of a few pigeons is not all that important. What is important is the rebellious following he has built up.'

Pilate shook his head. 'No! I still see it as a religious dispute. You are trying to persuade me to exercise Roman law against one who has done no more than argue on religious matters and suggest reforms in your church. That is not a Roman affair. If what this Jesus of Nazareth is doing offends you, surely you can find some way of punishing him? Exclude him from your Temple. Bar him from your religious ceremonies. But do not ask Rome to punish him. Ask your God to do it. From all I hear, your Jewish God is a mighty severe one when it comes to punishing.'

'You crucify Zealots out of hand. Why hesitate with this man?'

'Because, as I have said before, I have no proof that he has committed offences against Rome. I hear that superstitious people say that he has healed the sick by laying on of hands. Some declare he has healed a man of leprosy. One says he has actually raised a dead man to life. None of those wonders are crimes

445

against Rome, even if they are crimes against your Temple.'

Annas scowled against these taunts. 'He is as much a Zealot as those you have executed. His gang are also dagger-men. Procurator! Not only for the sake of the Temple but for the sake of peace in Judaea, you must take action against this man from Galilee.'

Pilate fingered his chin. 'This man from Galilee!' He murmured the words reflectively. Then suddenly he smiled. 'Where is the man now?'

'Still in my house. Under Roman guard,' said Annas, and added eagerly, 'He can be brought here within minutes.'

Pilate nodded. 'All right! I am busy today, but I can find time to question this man.'

'Question!' Annas gasped. 'He must be more than questioned. He must be crucified.'

'Please, High Priest. Think of the law. Roman law is as just as Jewish law. We Romans do not dictate sentence before evidence has been heard. Have the man sent over.'

When Annas had left him Pilate went back to his study, and the engineer, who had been waiting around fretfully rolling and unrolling his disputed plans, bustled in. The two were soon immersed in happy argument.

At ground level in the Antonia fortress was a long low-ceilinged chamber which on the occasion of public ceremonies could serve conveniently as an anteroom for the Procurator, because the wide arches at its northern end opened on to that stretch of the Temple esplanade locally known as 'the Pavement'. The Pavement, being an extension of the Court of the Gentiles, was considered orthodox enough ground to be used by Jews assembling to hear Roman proclamations or trials without risking defilement by stepping into a Gentile fortress. At the other end of the room a heavy door gave access to barrack rooms at the foot of one of the staircases. On the eastern side of this gloomy cavern of a room were two windows, but the walls at the base of the fortress were so immensely thick that these windows were more like long square tunnels through which the morning sunshine, creeping weakly, brought little light and no warmth.

On Passover Eve the room had been filled with feasting soldiers overflowing from the crowded mess, and the slaves, tired after a night's labour, had intended to begin clearing up the litter later in the day. But this morning they were suddenly rounded up and bullied into hasty preparation of the room for the Procurator's use.

Out on the Pavement other slaves began laying rugs and setting up that high chair used by the Procurator when he made pronouncements or delivered judgement. A crowd, drawn to the Court of the Gentiles by rumours of an impending public event, began building up. Soldiers with tired eyes and sore heads trooped out, grumbling, to line up for unexpected ceremonial duty. Four soldiers, buckling cuirasses and straightening helmets and still chewing bread, gathered in the room to serve as guards there when the Procurator descended.

Marcellus, also awaiting Pilate, paced around in his usual impatient way. He knew this room well. He approved of it. Its chill ugliness made a suitable setting for interrogation. He had discovered that here, in these stony bowels of the fortress, the fervour of the hottest rebel was quickly chilled. Even the door, the one leading to the stair, the one through which prisoner would enter, enhanced the room's impression of unrelenting power. It was a brutally ugly door, ill-proportioned, its solid timbers embossed with a ferocious display of bolts and bars. At eye-level in the door was a peep-hole furnished with a sliding wooden shutter which, when drawn open, enabled an observer to peer into the room through a grid of interlaced iron bars. Marcellus had found the device useful. He could slide the shutter quietly open and, looking in unseen on the lonely waiting prisoner, choose the moment, when the man's fears had reached their peak, in which to stride in upon him.

Across the centre of the room was a long battered table. Slaves pulled away the benches that had been used by the soldiers and put in their stead the ornate but rather shabby stool which the Procurator or any presiding official customarily used. They placed it so that the Procurator could look across the table towards the door and face the prisoner when he entered. The slaves arranged a group of other stools at the end of the table for the use of scribes.

The door swung open, and Pilate, unexpectedly early, stalked in, accompanied by the engineer who carried, flapping open in his hands, plans of the course for the new aqueduct which had now become the foremost preoccupation in the Procurator's mind. The four guards leaped, startled, to their posts and stood quiveringly erect. One of them, when the Procurator had passed, wiped a breakfast smear from his chin and surreptitiously adjusted his kilt. Another ran his fingers through the iron-tipped thongs of the scourging whip which, on occasions, had to be used down here, especially on prisoners condemned to crucifixion.

Marcellus walked towards Pilate, but Pilate waved him away and, still talking to the engineer about aqueducts, went to the table, where two slaves were scooping up in desperate haste the last mugs and platters, and another was wiping crumbs and driblets of wine from the scarred surface They scuttled out. The engineer laid the plans on the table and continued his argument about some point in his scheme. Pilate pondered over it, then nodded. 'All right,' he said. 'But let me have draft estimates before I leave Jerusalem.'

The engineer went out. Pilate seated himself on the stool. 'Has the Galilean been sent for?' he asked Marcellus.

'Yes.'

A scribe came in, laid some written folios before Pilate, and then took a chair at the end of the table and busied himself preparing pens, stylus and tablets. Unhurriedly Pilate read through the folios. As he read, he overheard Marcellus ordering the opening of the doors leading to the Pavement. 'No!' he said. 'This is not a public trial: it is an interrogation. If there is any necessity for a pronouncement, I shall make it outside. If Annas or any Temple officials have anything to say, they can say it out there.' He read on. 'Thank you, Marcellus,' he said when he had finished. 'A useful report. Well drawn up. Your Levite spies seem to have reported every word exchanged in the Temple and also in the house of Annas. I shall question him alone, Marcellus.'

Marcellus was unconcerned. This interrogation was not one that required his particular skills. This prisoner was not a terrorist, only a nuisance, and by all accounts he spoke freely without torture.

'You had better keep your eye on things outside,' went on Pilate. 'Warn the men that they must not be provocative. The crowds seem quiet enough.'

But, as though choosing that moment to deny him, shouting began outside. It was not, however, the united roar of a crowd. Only one or two voices were raised.

'What are they shouting for now?' As Pilate asked the question the answer came more clearly through the tunnelled windows.

'Release Barabbas!' the voices chanted. 'Release Barabbas!'

'Well, thanks to you, Marcellus,' said Pilate, 'that prayer is one we are now forced to grant. I shall announce that act of clemency from the Pavement at the appropriate time. You can go, Marcellus. I'll tell the guard when to bring in the man.'

Marcellus went out and closed the door, then, peering through the peep-hole, saw Pilate fiddle with the folios, shove them aside and lean back, deep in thought. Then he looked up suddenly. 'Find Severus,' he commanded a scribe. 'Ask him to give you that map of Judaea. Bring it down to me.' When the scribe had gone, Pilate reached along the table for a pen. He turned one of the folios face down and began writing a column of figures. He was still engrossed in this task when the scribe came back with the map. He studied the map intently. 'Yes,' he murmured. 'That fool engineer is wrong. Totally wrong. The original route is miles shorter.'

One of the guards shifted and then, failing to hold it back, let out a sneeze. Pilate looked across at him, but abstractedly, as though not at first seeing him. Then the helmet and cuirass reminded him of the business in hand. 'Ah yes! Have the prisoner brought in,' he said, but while commands were being shouted along the corridor he began adding up mileages again. 'Totally wrong!' The thud of feet as guards marched towards the table roused him. He looked up.

The morning sun, still low in the sky, had risen to the height at which its rays beamed directly into the squat windows and laid a riband of dusty light across the room. The haze dazzled Pilate, making it difficult for him to see distinctly the man who stood between the glinting cuirasses of the escort. He beckoned testily.

'Come forward!' he said in Aramaic.

The man stepped through the light. Pilate had seen him only once before, from a distance, on the Sunday morning when the Galilean had walked so boldly into the Temple with his body-guard of twelve. Since then the picture of him that had built up in Pilate's mind had been that of a rebel leader, a reckless rabble-rouser, with armed followers, and a man doughty enough to strike terror into the heart of Annas. The man before him did not fit that picture at all. Or did he? Was that quiet composure part of the man's reputed magic? Was it assumed in order to endow with conviction the wild words and outrageous prophecies detailed in the report now lying on the table between them?

One of the guards seemed to think that the Procurator's thoughts were elsewhere. It was the guard's duty to name the prisoner. 'Jesus of Nazareth!' he barked, and the scribe duly wrote the name. Pilate dropped his eyes to the report. The one folio was still lying face down, his calculations scribbled on the back of it. He turned it over. A phrase from the Sanhedrin's accusation caught his eye and made him smile. He stared up at the man again.

Where had he seen the face before? He felt sure he had. Or at least he had seen the same expression. A memory teased him, but he thrust that aside and, with the smile conjured up by Annas's exaggeration still on his lips, read out the phrase, 'King of the Jews!'

Poor devil! The face was bruised. Dried sweat, or tears, had gathered dust that stained the cheeks. There was a blood-encrusted weal across one brow. The eyes were agonisingly tired. 'Are *you* the King of the Jews?' Pilate asked with not unkindly irony.

'You say it.'

An ambiguous reply, yet not made in the evasive, pleading manner commonly used by prisoners trying to dodge away from an accusation: merely a calm statement in a deep Galilean voice.

There was blood on the man's hands also. They were lightly clasped before him, and Pilate, noticing the cords just visible below the sleeves of the man's torn and muddy mantle, became aware that the prisoner was bound.

'Untie him,' Pilate ordered sharply.

A guard fumbled at the tight knots. Failing to untie them, he drew his dagger and sliced the hands apart.

The prisoner smiled thanks for that relief.

Where *had* he seen that smile before? It was exasperating not to be able to remember something so undeniably compelling.

'It is said you have claimed to be King of the Jews,' said Pilate. 'That is not an accusation made by Romans. Your own people, the Jews, have said so.'

The prisoner did not speak. The silence irritated Pilate. He had been prepared for either fear or anger from the man: the fear of a prisoner threatened with death, or the anger of the fanatical rebel he was reported to be. Either fear or anger in a prisoner could be played on to weave a web of guilt around him. But silence! That was something it took a Marcellus to break.

'Galilean? Can you read Greek?'

The prisoner smiled, then winced a little, and Pilate noticed that one of the man's lips had split against his teeth when a blow had caught him there. The wide smile had pulled at the wound.

'I am a rabbi,' the prisoner said. 'Yes, I can read Greek.'

'Then read this.' Pilate beckoned him nearer the table and swung the report round for him to look down on it. The prisoner read it. At one point he read a sentence aloud, and then, looking at Pilate, patiently corrected the mistakes in the syntax. Pilate nodded appreciatively.

'Is the report correct?' asked Pilate when the prisoner reached the end of the last folio.

'It is a report only of what was said.'

'What else could it be?'

'He who wrote it deals only with words as they were spoken. He shows no understanding of their meaning.'

'All right, then. If you dispute the report, if you have anything to say in your defence, say it, and say it quickly. If you do not, you could risk facing trial for treason. For it is treason, Galilean, for a man to proclaim himself king without the sanction of Caesar.' The man was rubbing his wrists where the cords had chafed them. With his eyes on his hands, Pilate said, 'And you know the punishment for treason, don't you?'

The prisoner lifted his hands and for a moment held them with their palms facing Pilate; then nodded. But Pilate scarcely noticed that significant gesture. For his mind was straining, as though trying to hear an echo, to recapture the words he had just spoken: 'You know the punishment for treason, don't you?' Ah, yes! He remembered. He had used those same words during the interrogation he had conducted in his black tent in the shadows of an escarpment north of Jerusalem. And on that occasion, when he had said those words, he had added, 'Caesar crucifies traitors!' Remembering that, he now said the same to the Galilean.

Again the prisoner nodded. 'So be it. Caesar makes laws in his kingdom. But Caesar is only a man, as I am on earth. But Caesar set himself above other men. I do not. For my kingdom is not of this world. If it were then it would a kingdom to be fought for, as men do fight for worldly kingdoms. But those who believe in the Kingdom of God do not fight for earthly thrones.'

'Galilean! This is no time for preaching. Law is not built up of parables. Nor does my writ run in kingdoms that are not of this world. It is in this world that I am governor. It is the only world I know. In this world I do my duty. My duty is to Caesar and to my office as Procurator of Judaea. I ask you again: do you claim to be king?'

'It is you who say it.'

451

'I say nothing,' Pilate retorted. 'I read what is here.' He pulled the report back. 'Most of what you are reported to have said is of no offence to me or to Caesar. You are accused of having threatened to destroy the Temple within three days. Well, for all I know, that is another of your Jewish parables. Look, fellow! I am a Roman and I do not relish interfering in Jewish religious squabbles.' He smiled up at the prisoner and, dropping his voice, said, 'Nor does a Roman governor relish doing for the Sanhedrin something it dare not do itself. Can't you see the chance I am offering you? In this report I find no offence in you. But I am forced to take some note of an accusation made against you, a Jew, by your own Jewish high priest. He says you have committed treason against Rome. You, a Galilean, should know that that does not really worry him. All he wants to do is get rid of you, and he wants Rome to do that for him. So, what do you say in reply to that charge of treason? You need but deny it, and you can go free, and I can wash my hands of the affair. *Deny it!*

'I cannot take back words I have spoken. Everything I have said is written there.'

Pilate gathered up the folios and held them up between his hands. 'And can be torn up, and forgotten.'

'No! For everything I have said there is prophecy. And prophecy is the word of God. It is not for me to deny the word of God.'

Pilate flung his arms wide, letting the folios shower on to the desk. 'We are not talking of *god*, man. The god you believe in is of no interest to me, nor are his prophecies. We are talking of Caesar!'

'And also of kingdoms,' said the prisoner. 'But different ones.'

'Parables! Parables!' Pilate stared down exasperated at the litter of evidence. He sighed. 'When you have thought out a clear answer you will be brought back. Guard! Take the man away!'

There was some dignity in the fellow. Even though so humiliatingly handled he retained dignity. This also reminded Pilate of some earlier occasion, and, suddenly feeling that he was on the verge of remembering where he had seen the face before, he called, 'Galilean!'

The scribe, who had thought the interrogation at an end, seized the stylus again, but Pilate gestured him not to make further notes. The guards swung the prisoner round to face Pilate again.

'Man,' Pilate found himself saying. 'Do you wish to die? Is that what you wish? Death?'

In the face of that question the prisoner was silent for so long that it seemed it was a question which would be answered only with silence, but at last he said, 'It is not what *I* wish. Nor what *you* wish, Procurator.' He held out his hands and laid the wrists together so that the cords seemed to be again tied. 'To this end I was born. For this cause I came into the world: that I should bear witness of the truth.'

Pilate gestured to the guards. They grabbed the prisoner's arms and led him through the haze of light and through the door.

'Witness of the truth!' Pilate repeated the man's words. 'What truth? God's truth or Caesar's truth?' He slid the folios together. 'What is truth?'

Then he did remember. It was understandable why it had been so hard to remember whom the Galilean resembled. The faces were so utterly different: a bruised, black-haired Jewish face, and a shaved, grey-haired Roman one. But the expression, that expression of calm resignation in the presence of destiny, was the same. The Galilean bore it, and so had that Roman he had interrogated in the black tent and sent to the cross. To that Roman also Pilate had said, 'Caesar crucifies traitors!' And both the prisoners, both the Roman and Galilean, had made the threat seem banal. He had asked that Roman the same question. 'Do you wish to die?' The Roman had answered, 'It is not what *I* wish, or what *you* wish, Procurator. If I must die on the cross, then I shall die as a witness of truth.' And when the guards had led that Roman out of the black tent he too had walked out with grace and dignity, and Pilate, left alone at his desk, had asked, 'What is truth?'

When the scribe came hurrying out of the chamber Marcellus halted him. 'What's the decision?' Marcellus asked.

The scribe shook a bewildered head. 'No decision. He merely told me to go.'

Marcellus slid open the shutter and peered through the peephole. Immediately behind the door was a guard. Seeing Marcellus peering at him, the guard stood aside so that Marcellus had a clear view through to the table. Pilate was still sitting there. His head was bent over the report, but he was not reading it, for his hands were clasped on it.

Marcellus began pushing the door open, but the guard hissed, 'No!' Obviously the Procurator had given orders he was not to be disturbed. Marcellus went along the corridor and stared at the prisoner standing between the two guards. 'Tie his hands,' commanded Marcellus, and then began pacing up and down the corridor, waiting for Pilate to send for him. The crowd outside remained for the most part sullenly quiet, though now and again some voices took up the chant, 'Release Barabbas!' The call came regularly. Perhaps some Zealot chorus-master was occasionally urging sympathisers to bleat it, or paying them to do so.

The door opened at last, and Pilate appeared. 'Marcellus! This report is vague on one most important point. The prisoner's place of birth? It is suggested here that it could be Bethlehem.'

'There seems to be some doubt . . . '

'Yes, there does. It is a doubt I shall take advantage of. He has always been described as a Galilean, coming from a town called . . . '

'Nazareth.'

'Yes, that's it. So it is judicious to consider him a Galilean subject.' When Marcellus made no comment Pilate snapped, 'Do you agree?'

Marcellus shrugged. 'Of course, if it makes any difference.'

'It makes a great deal of difference. It frees me from performing a distasteful act for Annas's benefit. I find no fault in the man. The accusations are ill-founded. However, we cannot overlook that he has been the cause of unrest. But he is a Galilean. Therefore complaints about him should justifiably be made to Galilee. It is convenient that the Tetrarch of Galilee is at present in Jerusalem. So Herod can deal immediately with his own troublesome countryman. Have my request that the Tetrarch should do this drawn up in proper form for my signature, and send the document to the palace. The Galilean can be sent at the same time. That, I hope, will be the end of the matter.' He caught sight of Severus on the stair and called him down. 'Send the engineer up to my room. Tell him to bring his plans again.'

He was at his desk, disputing mileages with the engineer, when Marcellus brought Pilate's letter to Herod for signature. It was composed in appropriately diplomatic terms. It emphasised how reluctant the Procurator was to sit in judgement on one of the Tetrarch's subjects. It ended with a request that the authorities in Galilee should take more stringent steps to discourage dissident factions in Galilee, and prevent Zealots and others from crossing the frontier to create trouble in Judaea. Nicely put! Pilate signed it with a flourish and returned to his aqueducts. A few minutes later his calculations were interrupted by the roar of the crowd in the Court of the Gentiles.

He walked through the audience chamber to the balcony. A posse of guards, the prisoner in the midst, was leaving for the palace. The crowd began flowing in the same direction. As he was returning to his room, Marcellus appeared in the audience chamber.

'They are still yelling for the release of Barabbas,' said Marcellus.

'So I heard.' Pilate noticed him fiddling with his gauntlet. The habit usually indicated some problem. 'What's worrying you now?' he asked sharply.

'The Jews!' said Marcellus with a grin. 'They always think of bargaining. The idea seems to have got around that you are deciding which one of two men is to be crucified. They think you have to make a choice: Jesus or Barabbas. So the Zealots are whipping up the crowd to demand that it is Jesus who goes to the cross and Barabbas who goes free.'

'The Jews must learn that justice is not on auction for the mob,' said Pilate and stalked back to his plans.

Once again he was interrupted. This time it was Severus who came into the room. 'What is it now?' Pilate asked petulantly, his pen posed over the engineer's draft of labour costs.

'The Lady Claudia has arrived.'

'Claudia! At the Antonia?' He gestured to the engineer to go. 'No, leave the plans. Come back in a few minutes, when the Lady Claudia has left.'

He stepped out of his room to greet Claudia. As he walked towards him along the audience-chamber he saw, a few paces behind her, the Magdalene slave. Pilate led Claudia into his room saying, 'No! Alone!' as he closed the door in the Magdalene's face. 'Why have you come here, Claudia? You had an escort?' She nodded. 'What do you want?'

'I am worried, Pontius. About the Galilean.'

He flung up his hands in exasperation. 'And you have come across the city to tell me that? Do you think you are the only one worried? Annas is worried. So is Caiaphas. So are the Sadducees! And listen to that crowd.'

'You must not do the man wrong.'

He frowned. 'I do no man wrong. Has that Magdala woman put you up to this?'

'It is not she who has told me. Pontius. My dreams have told

455

me. You must do nothing against that righteous man.'

'Dreams!' Pilate turned on her angrily. 'After listening to parables I am now to be plagued with women's nonsense. This, Claudia, is what comes from dabbling with religions. Do you, or that woman out there, now believe that you have the competence to interpret dreams? That can be done only by an experienced astrologer. You had better consult one. He will show you that your dreams are merely muddled thoughts engendered by the superstitions you have been playing about with.'

She shook her head. 'I am sure my dreams are warnings,' she said stubbornly. 'I am frightened.'

'Frightened? Of whom? Of the Jews? Of Annas? Or of me?'

'Not *of* you, Pontius. *For* you.' She tried to clasp his shoulders. He pushed her away. 'In my dream a voice seemed to be saying you must beware of doing anything against this righteous man.'

'A voice!' He gritted his teeth. He knew what voice. The Magdala woman would have been planting words of that kind in Claudia's head for days. 'I do not persecute righteous men. If any man is righteous, if any man is innocent, he does not suffer at the hands of justice.'

'The Galilean has done no more than preach peace. Yet now the mob is crying "Crucify him!" and demanding that the robber Barabbas be released. Pontius, if the Galilean is crucified and Barabbas set free, it is a triumph of evil over good. You must not allow yourself to be the instrument of such evil. If you do, you will suffer.'

He curbed his anger. Perhaps it was his fault for being weak or indifferent, and indulging her desire for the company of that Galilean woman. That unpleasant association must be terminated quickly. Herod must have the woman carted back to Galilee. She would be fit company for the preacher.

He took Claudia's hands. 'Listen, Claudia,' he said firmly. 'Go back to the palace. I shall join you there soon. We are to dine with Vitellius. In the meantime consult the astrologer. Herod also has a clever one. Let them analyse your dreams and examine the omens.'

He led her firmly to the door. Seeing the woman from Magdala standing beside one of the pillars in the audience chamber, Pilate addressed Claudia, in a voice loud enough for the Magdalene to hear, 'I adhere to the law, my lady. Justice is not a whim that can be dictated at the behest of women's dreams. Or,' he added as he pushed her away, 'should not be.'

456

He watched the two women walk down the audience-chamber towards the escort gathered in a gossiping inquisitive group near the entrance. Feeling uneasy at having surrendered Claudia again to the woman, he called Severus to his side. 'Accompany the Lady Claudia back to the palace,' he whispered. 'At a convenient moment have the Magdala woman detached from her presence and have her confined somewhere quietly. Be discreet.'

Severus nodded dubiously. 'I was to accompany Julius to the palace later,' he reminded Pilate.

'Ah, yes! Well, go with the Lady Claudia now. Julius can accompany me, or another escort.'

It was another hour before Pilate and the engineer had completed the revised estimates. When the man had gone, Pilate relaxed. He was well satisfied with his new plan. Despite the immense cost of the Caesarea Games there would still be sufficient funds in the treasury to initiate the new aqueduct immediately after that event. He reached for a sheet of papyrus and wrote the day's date boldly on the top of it. It was always a good idea to record events while they were hot and fresh in the mind. This page would be useful for those who in the future would write the history of Pronconsul Pontius Pilate, Procurator of Judaea. From this page they would learn that this day, a day known to the Jews as Passover Day, was an important one in the history of Judaea. On this day in this year of the reign of the Caesar, His August Highness Tiberius Claudius Nero, he, Pontius Pilate, had initiated yet another stage in the irrigation scheme designed to enrich the province he governed.

He was just finishing his record of this important fact when Vitellius was announced. The would-be legate of Asia came in angrily.

'You have precipitated quite a scene at the palace Procurator!' he said. Pilate continued writing. 'Pilate!'

Pilate carefully wrote the last sentence and closed it with his initials and date. Then he put the folio carefully aside and at last looked up. Vitellius found the bland smile insulting. There was something other than the smile which offended him: a certain smug self-assurance which the fellow had not shown in his presence before.

'A scene?' asked Pilate, mildly inquiring.

'Sending that preacher to Herod was bound to provoke confusion.'

'I should have thought that sending the man to the Tetrarch of

Galilee was a proper disposal of a Galilean.'

'That is a quibble! The man caused trouble here in Judaea. It is in Judaea, not in Galilee, that he had proclaimed himself king.'

'A crazy act.'

'Maybe. Yet, crazy or not, the act was treasonable.'

'Is that what Herod is saying?'

'It is what I am saying. Herod has not deigned to argue the point. He no doubt sees your decision to shift responsibility as a sign of your weakness. He is making great sport of the Galilean's arrival at the palace. Making a farce of it, in fact. He is prancing around addressing the man as "King of the Jews" and inviting him to show his guests a few miracles. Yes, Herod is playing the fool, but it is not really comedy. Actually Herod is making game of you, Pilate. Herod puts on his display as an insult to you. As such it is an insult to Rome.'

'Did you tell him so?'

'I deemed it better to ignore it. But I shall ask the Tetrarch to send the man back to you.'

Pilate laid his right hand on his breast, as though to reassure himself that his badge of office was still there. 'Am I to understand that you are assuming authority already, sir?'

Vitellius flushed. 'I am merely *advising* you not to antagonise the Jewish government.'

He had no doubt promised Annas his aid. Winning friendship of the Sanhedrin could sound quite a victory in Capri.

'Are you representing the Sanhedrin in this quarrel, Vitellius?'

'I speak in the best interests of Rome, and in your interests, Pilate. Failure to act quickly and firmly in this matter makes you appear impotent. There are many ready to take advantage of what they see as weakness. Have you seen that crowd out there? Before the public clamour gets out of hand you must end the affair with a decisive act.'

'What act?'

'The answer is obvious, Pilate. This man is accused of treason.'

'Accused, yes. But I have not found him guilty.'

The roar of the crowd was rising again. 'Listen to that, Pilate!' The cries became louder, and Pilate followed Vitellius as he strode agitatedly across the audience-chamber to the balcony. Rising above the confused bellowing of the excited crowd, came the now familiar chant, 'Release Barabbas!' But there was now another cry. 'Crucify him. Crucify him.'

'Listen, Pilate. Whether you think the Galilean guilty or not

458

the Jews have decided that he is.'

'Are you actually suggesting, Vitellius, that we allow Roman justice to be decided by the yells of a mob?'

Vitellius shrugged. 'We are in Judaea. You should know by now that Jewish criminal law rests on the principle of public denunciation. Why, even capital punishment is carried out by the public.'

'All right! If the Jews think this man guilty, let them do their Jewish duty: let them stone him to death.'

'No, Pilate.' Vitellius shook his head. 'This man is guilty of treason against Caesar. If you do not punish him for that, you show that, despite all your protestations, you are no friend of Caesar.' He turned and walked back into the audience-chamber. 'I am now returning to the palace. When I can put an end to the folly there, I shall give it as your order that the man must be brought back here. I trust you to act appropriately.'

Vitellius strode quickly out of the audience-chamber. When he reached the entrance of the fortress he saw Julius also about to leave with an escort. 'Ah, Julius! Are you on your way to the palace?' Julius nodded. 'Then you can accompany me.' As they descended the staircase, Julius glanced back to assure himself that Ephir had managed to intrude himself into the escort.

There was great confusion on the bridge. Some men with laden donkeys, traders far more concerned with getting their wares across the city than with the religious passions of the crowd, were pressed against the balustrades, cursing Romans and Jews alike. The pressure of hawkers and spectators forced the escort to thin out until it was almost nipped in two by the crowd. Julius, laughing at the excitement of it all, turned to look back to see how Ephir was making out, and was surprised to see him now raised above the crowd, mounted on a glossy pony and leading another pony on a leading rein. Then he realised it was not Ephir, though the boy did look very much like Ephir: all wild black hair and glowing eyes. But Ephir was further behind, trying, along with three or four auxiliaries, to break his way through the file of donkeys. Ahead, things were just as muddled. Vitellius, by now some fifty strides ahead, had been forced to a halt and, flushed with offended authority, was commanding his escort to use their spears if necessary and cut a way through the stubborn idiots who blocked his path. The boy on the pony forced through the crowd and came up alongside Julius.

'Son of Pilate!' said the boy. 'You should be mounted.'

Julius was proud to show off his Aramaic. 'You have beautiful ponies,' he said.

'Arab!' said the boy. 'Get on this one. Just try him.'

Ephir, pushing through the file of donkeys, was surprised to see Julius suddenly lifted high into view as he vaulted on to a pony.

Just then the pressure on the bridge was released. Vitellius's escort had broken through. Ephir could see Julius laughing as the ponies broke into a trot. Julius and the boy appeared to be shouting at each other and joking together. The boy was waving one arm and pointing towards the stretch of waste ground which curved around the end of the palace in the direction of the Pool of Siloam. He seemed to be inviting Julius to ride in that direction, or challenging him to a race. And Julius seemed to accept the challenge, for they cantered off. Ephir made up his mind quickly. He vaulted on to the balustrade at the end of the bridge, swung over and dropped down to the bank of the stream. Julius and his new-found friend were obviously heading for the Pool of Siloam, and Ephir knew a short cut.

Meanwhile Vitellius had reached the gates of the palace. Quivering with indignation at the indignity of pushing through an unruly mob, he flapped dust off his cloak, glanced round to make sure the rest of the escort was following, and gathering his breath, stepped quickly up the first of the many staircases.

Pilate sat alone in his room with his angry thoughts. The folio on which he had written his sanguine thoughts of this day's work lay before him. He tried to find comfort in reading through it. For a moment he actually became so absorbed in it that he scored out a word and carefully wrote a substitute. But then he pushed the folio aside and sat staring at the blank desk.

Vitellius's words rankled in his mind. What Vitellius had said was not advice: it was a command, and thinly disguised at that. Harder to take was the threat behind it.

'You are not Caesar's friend!' As he brooded over those words Pilate tried to analyse his attitude towards the Galilean. After all, the preacher was, of himself, of trivial importance. A man bemused with ideas. Yes, like that Roman, the Galilean had shown nearly contemptuous disregard of the fate he might suffer. That indifference, that almost insolent disregard for the Procurator's authority, was the feature that had always figured most vividly in Pilate's memory of the encounter in the black tent. He remembered how strong had been the temptation to try to break down that indifference by detailing the agonies the man would suffer under crucifixion. But Pilate had rejected the idea of resorting to such crude tactics, rejected it not because to do so was only one step removed from the dirtiness of torture, but because he sensed that the Roman's composure, mysteriously intact even on the eve of brutal death, was so impregnable that with one more of his condescending pitying smiles he would have reduced Pilate's threats to banality. Just like the crazy Galilean. So, having failed to probe the man's thoughts, having failed to unearth anything that bore any resemblance to the truth. Pilate had let the Roman go to the cross.

But sending the Roman to his death had been his, Pilate's, own decision, made in his own right as Procurator. He had not been steered or bullied into it by others. That was the difference in the Galilean's case. In this case it was Annas and his cronies, a pack of withered fanatical Jews, who were demanding a man's death; and, of course, Vitellius, who thought it promised political gain to make them his allies. Yet Vitellius's political hopes could seem petty to those Pilate could realise if he turned the tables on them all. If only he could reach out to the crowd, capture their ears and their imagination with a staggering act of clemency that would deprive Annas and his Sadducees of victory! Could that be engineered?

His mind was clenched around this problem of tactics when the voice of Marcellus broke into his thoughts. The prisoner, Marcellus reported, had been sent back. He was in the Court of the Gentiles. Annas also had arrived there, said Marcellus. The High Priest had descended, in self-satisfied pomp, from Temple to Pavement to hear Pilate pronounce sentence of crucifixion.

Pilate smiled. 'So far so good,' he said. 'I shall make Annas beg me to do that. All Jerusalem will hear Annas ask for the Galilean's death. And all Jerusalem will hear Pilate say no.'

Despite the impatient clamour of the expectant crowd Pilate made an unhurried toilet. He examined his cuirass minutely, and after it had been strapped on, insisted on Dumb Black breathing on it and polishing it again. He drew himself up as the helmet was lowered on to his head; the plumes, he felt, made him look majestically tall. He set his face into an impassive mask and walked through the great audience-chamber and along the stony corridors.

As he approached the top of the steps the bellowing of the crowd buffeted his ears. Seeing harsh sunlight ahead, he closed his eyes before stepping into it. When he opened them he saw

461

Severus standing before him. His forearms were coated with blood and dust. He was holding a boy's body. Blood dripped from the head cradled in the crook of his arm.

Pilate stepped aside to let Severus pass with his burden and then walked after him into the fortress. Severus laid the boy on a couch in the ante-chamber. 'The doctor!' he said to one of the escort. 'Quickly!'

One of the boy's legs swung loose, bent at a grotesque angle, a spear of splintered bone sticking out white through bloody flesh. Severus laid the leg straight. Not until he had gently disposed the head on a cushion and taken from the face the rag that had protected it from the sun was Pilate sure that the wounded boy was really the Young Barber. The boy was unconscious, and his right eye was closed as though in sleep. But his left eye . . . where that had been was a well of pulpy flesh, splattered with flecks of bone, from which the blood oozed thick and lazy.

'By the gods!' sighed Pilate. 'How did this happen?'

Severus was afraid of looking at Pilate, afraid of speaking too. He fussed over the boy.

'What happened?' hissed Pilate angrily.

The doctor hurried in and knelt to examine the wounded boy.

'He was trying to save . . . ' Severus sobbed. Then, still looking down at Ephir, said, 'He was fighting for your son, sir.'

'For my . . . ?' Pilate's voice croaked. 'Julius!' he wailed. 'Where is Julius?'

Severus kept his face bent. Even when the couch had been carried out, he kept his eyes turned to the spot where it had been.

'Severus!' Pilate pleaded. 'Tell me. Please! Where is my son?'

'He is dead, sir.'

Severus heard Pilate groan. He waited. Pilate made no other sound. But sunlight streaming in through the outer door cast a shadow of the Procurator across the stone paving, and Severus saw the shadow's helmet fall forward and its hands rise. Severus kept his eyes turned away, decently avoiding the spectacle of the Procurator's distress.

At last he heard Pilate's voice, dry and thin.

'Where is the . . . ? Where is my son now?'

'He is being carried here,' said Severus.

'Leave me. For a moment. Leave me.'

Severus heard the Procurator walk along the audience-chamber towards his room.

When the footsteps had faded away he went to the dormitory

into which they had carried Ephir. 'Nothing vital is severed,' the doctor was saying. 'The boy will live. With one eye, of course. The leg? It will heal. Fairly straight. Though I don't think he'll dance again.'

Marcellus came in. 'How did all this happen? Severus, come on! Snap out of it! Tell me!'

'A Zealot murdered Julius. A mere boy. The Zealot, I mean.'

'Come, Severus. Leave the doctor to his work. I also have work to do now and I need information.'

Over a table in the mess-hall Severus told the story. A villager, an old man living near the Pool of Siloam, had seen the murder. He had been quite near. Yes, he could describe the Zealot. A young boy.

'We've got the dagger he used,' said Severus.

'I've seen it,' said Marcellus. 'Covered with jewels. An eastern one, probably Parthian. Go on.'

Julius had been on a pony. The Zealot was on another pony, a few lengths ahead of him. As they reached the valley of the Kidron, the Zealot boy reined his mount, wheeled round, and, when Julius galloped up to him, leaped on Julius and attacked him. When they first tumbled from their mounts, the old man had thought they were playing some rough game or, at the most, merely quarrelling. Then he saw the lifted dagger flash in the sunlight and saw it driven down. He saw Julius trying to pull himself up from the ground, reaching for his sword. But he was swaying, and blood began gushing from his belly. The Zealot went at him again. Julius fell prone. Then, astride his body, the Zealot boy started work with the dagger. He was shouting.

'Shouting what?'

'The usual. "A life for a life!" But also, as far as I can make out, something like "A son for a father".'

'But where was Ephir?'

Ephir had been running uphill from the city. He must have still been scrambling up the Kidron banks when he saw the Zealot astride the body. Although unarmed, Ephir had flung himself on the Zealot, and the old man was screaming for anyone to come and help. Some villagers and three soldiers came running down from the camp near the aqueduct. Before they got near the scene, Ephir had actually managed, though so horribly wounded, to tear the dagger out of the Zealot's hands. When the Zealot saw the soldiers he bolted, managed to round up one of the ponies, and rode off. Yes, Severus said, the soldiers had seen what direction

463

he had taken. Some mounted men had set off after him. But the Zealot had a long start on them.

Marcellus hurried out. Severus went into the wash-room to sluice blood off his arms. Yes, he thought, Marcellus would round up spies for another anti-Zealot operation. But the cleverest spies known to the gods could only avenge, and the most fearful vengeance known could never bring back Julius and his smile.

Severus was in his dormitory changing into a clean vest when Marcellus hurried in.

'Severus! The Old Man's asking for you,' he said. 'I am having Julius's body coffined. It must be sent to Caesarea immediately. The embalmer there is clever. He might be able to do something with it before the Old Man sees it.'

'But Pilate has asked already.'

'Tell him it has already gone. Tell him anything. You can say I did it without asking. But he must not be allowed to see the boy's body in the state it is in now. The sight's too horrible: it would send Pilate mad.'

Pilate was standing in the audience-chamber. Dumb Black was on his knees beside him, polishing his greaves. The grey face under the high helmet stared implacably.

'Severus! I am awaited below. To deliver sentence. Come.' They walked together along the audience-chamber. As they neared the entrance Pilate laid a hand on Severus's arm and halted him. 'I have been told about the . . . about my son's corpse. One of the soldiers told me. He also was a father. Once. And lost his son. I shall do as that man says. I shall not look upon Julius dead: I shall remember him as he was.' His voice trembled and choked to silence. Then, recovering himself, he went on firmly, 'I shall leave for Caesarea immediately after the business below. I shall ride. You and a small escort will accompany me. The Lady Claudia has been informed of the event. She will follow tomorrow, by carriage, with the Caesarea troops. Come Severus.'

Again Pilate stepped into the sunlight and the roar of the crowd.

As he descended to the Pavement he saw the great sea of faces gazing up at him. Were they staring at him so fixedly because they were trying to detect in his attitude some clue to the sentence their Governor might or might not pronounce from his high chair? Were they speculating, 'Jesus or Barabbas'? Or were they offensively curious, wanting to see his wounds? Had they heard the news that, in the last hour, the life of this Procurator of Judaea, now to be seen marching down armoured from his fortress, had ended?

There was Annas under his parasol, tall and thin and black, like a stake for a burning, with a wrinkled leer at the top of it. Was he smiling in triumph? Or was he smiling at what he would assuredly see as the judgement of God on a Gentile sinner?

The toe of Pilate's gilded bootee ruffled the fringe of one rug. A soldier tidied it in his wake. He mounted the high chair. 'Release Barabbas!' shouted someone. 'Crucify the Galilean!' shouted another. But the cries trailed away, and a hush descended. The crowd held its voice and breathed heavily, like a greedy beast slavering over meat.

A group of guards unfolded, and from their midst pushed forward the prisoner. He was in a sorrier state than before. Although not yet scourged, as he would have to be prior to his crucifixion, he was bloodied, and from that ugly bruise on his brow there now stretched a line of fresh scars, marking where Herod, in mockery, had had the 'king' crowned with a circlet of thorns. King of the Jews. Pilate looked down at him. King or not was of little account. But Jew he certainly was: one of a doomed race. Calm he looked, even now. And mild. A man of peace? No. A Jew. True, there was no dagger hidden under that torn and blood-splotched gown, but there was worse: there was a Jewish soul. That condemned him.

An accursed race bound together by their dark blood and their worship of a terrible god. All of them accursed. All? What of Josephus? And Mattathias? Yes, even they. For virtuous though they tried to be, like the prisoner before him, and preaching peace and love as he had done, they were Jews; tainted, doomed brothers of a doomed race. So, although this prisoner wore no Zealot dagger, what did that matter? He was a Jew and thus could die like a Jew or Zealot, it did not matter which, on one of those three crosses waiting on the Hill of Golgotha.

And down there was the priest: High Priest Annas, the Jew who was privy to the mysteries of the Holy of Holies, a Jew who communed between Jews and their racial god, and a Jew who sold for profit the flesh that fed him.

Annas, his hands clutching the folds of his black shawl, was waiting for Pilate to speak.

'I find no fault in this man!' said Pilate.

The words, so different from those Annas had been encouraged to expect, shocked the high priest. 'The man is guilty of treason!' he shouted. 'He has been proved guilty by his own words. He must be crucified.' That word fanned the hungry crowd. Annas waited for the shouts to die away. Then, 'Pilate! If you do not crucify this man,' he declaimed, 'you are no friend of Caesar.'

As he went on Pilate stared bleakly around. In what corner did Vitellius stand, pulling the strings of this puppet who mouthed the same words?

No friend of Caesar! Neither had Sejanus been a friend of Caesar. But Sejanus had found the truth. Sejanus had known the Jews better than Caesar knew them.

'Silence!' Annas stopped his babbling, shocked to silence by the Procurator's suddenly powerful and malign authority. 'I said I find no fault in this man. But listen. He is a Jew. He is one of you. He is of your blood. He speaks your tongue. He is your prophet. He is your victim, and because he is so you can demand his death. Therefore, do as you wish with him. Take him away. Crucify him.'

'Release Barabbas!' The single voice soared, clear and shrill, above the dense crowd. It was a boy's voice. Was there really a Jew who wanted anyone to live?

'Rome made the promise that Barabbas would be released. Therefore Barabbas will be released.' A murmur in the crowd, but it died quickly away when he raised his hand in stern authority. 'And if perhaps he also becomes a prophet in your midst, I shall still be here to judge over him when you bring him also before me to be crucified.'

He stood up, a little unsteadily, and blindly descended from the high chair. By the time he was mounting the staircase to the entrance of the fortress they were hustling the Galilean away, a Roman guard grinning behind him and fluttering the metal-tipped thongs of the short-handled whip that would be used for the scourging, and a whole satisfied mob of Jews surging exultant down the steps, a few of them, the young ones, snatching up handfuls of dung from the paving and throwing clods of it at the false disgraced Messiah, but all of them making their way eagerly towards Golgotha for the spectacle that was to excite them there before the more solemn hour of Passover.

Vitellius halted Marcellus. 'The warrant? Make sure he signs it before he leaves for Caesarea.'

466

'The warrant is already signed.'

'Thank you, Marcellus. You think of everything.'

On the upper steps Pilate felt the fit of giddiness assaulting him again, but then felt Severus's broad peasant hand, hidden discreetly under his cloak, gripping his elbow, steadying him, secretly helping him to walk erect, dignified, Roman, until he was out of sight of gaping Jews.

'Do you want your doctor?' asked Severus.

'No. Leave me, Severus.'

His eyes so dazed that he saw little of the audience-chamber, Pilate walked by instinct through the long avenue of its squat pillars, found his room, banged the door shut behind him and flung himself on his pallet groaning with sorrow but finding no tears.

XII

Everyone agreed that this year's Games at Caesarea were the most spectacular the city had ever enjoyed. In fact, the Caesareans almost believed their boast that Rome itself could not have staged a finer show. That, of course, was an exaggeration, an expression of provincial pride, but even Romans attracted to the city by programmes listing names of famous athletes from every country of the commonwealth were heard expressing admiration of Caesarea's Games before a single competitor appeared. For it was admitted on all sides that the refurbished stadium was a triumph. The athletes' village, with its Asian luxury of arcaded pavilions, was much acclaimed, but particular praise was accorded the new stalls for the chariots. There were the customary twelve, representing the constellation of the zodiac, and each was flanked by two impressive Hermes carved in Pentelic marble with bronze heads, and between them were slung the heavy multi-coloured ropes which would fall to signal the start of each race. Among the horses brought to Caesarea from Italy, Greece, Africa and Spain were stallions so famous that their names were household words through all the commonwealth. As for the darling charioteers, each one of them the petted idol of a flock of adoring fans, they were so impressed with the opulence of Caesarea that they vied with each other in equipping their horses with accoutrements of the utmost lavishness.

The race tracks – there were seven to represent the seven days of the week – were beautified by the new turning-posts and, ennobling the whole scene and delighting the eye of sophisticated travellers, was that new feature of the Caesarea landscape, the magnificent Egyptian obelisk which the great Vitellius had donated as the spina for the stadium. Some spectators said they had never seen a more fervent waving of more thousands of handkerchiefs than that which welcomed this distinguished personage when he appeared at the opening of the Games. Rumour had it that the Roman was soon to be appointed Caesar's legate in Asia, and some cynics declared, as cynics naturally would, that the popularity he had bought with his open-mouthed generosity in Caesarea was certain to influence Caesar in his favour and pave gloriously his road to Antioch.

The cheers raised at that inaugural procession were loud enough, some said, to be heard over the whole extent of the Plain of Sharon. Cheers were obligatory, of course, to the statues of Augustus and Tiberius and other deities carried ceremoniously in the parade. But those dutiful cheers swelled to a roar, a roar of sheer delight, when the audience saw in the parade the living presence of all the performers whose marvellous exploits were to delight them during the ensuing days, and thousands of enthusiasts yelled the names of favourite charioteers, horses, wrestlers, boxers and runners.

Before the Games were finished, reports and letters of commendation were flowing from Caesarea, many to Rome and even some to Capri, recounting the success of the event. In all these reports Vitellius came in for unbounded praise, the more so because he had so conscientiously taken on the burden of presiding at an event at which the only shadow, the only feature that seemed a little off-key, though slight and not very important, was Proconsul Pilate's seeming indifference to the glory happening in the capital of his province. Some events Pilate had not even honoured with his presence, and on those days when he did attend, guests in his immediate company found his grey silence chillingly discomfiting.

However, the Procurator's lack of spirit was more than compensated for by the presence of the energetic Vitellius. It was indeed a lucky accident that the progress to Antioch of this amiable patron of sport should have brought him to Asia so fortuitously at the time of the Games. This coincidence seemed a most happy augury for the future. All eyes were on him as, glorious on the tribune in scarlet tunic and embroidered toga, and wielding an ivory baton surmounted with a flying eagle and a wreath of leaves in solid gold, he rose to give the signal for the first chariot race. He held out the white napkin for just long enough to get the whole crowd quivering with gasping expectation. The napkin fell.

At that signal the trumpets sounded, the cords between the Hermes were snatched away, and the twelve chariots roared into sight. Horses with knotted tails erect and manes plaited with pearls; charioteers, glitteringly helmeted, their muscled thighs sheathed with leggings, and, flashing at their waists, the jewel-hilted daggers with which they could slash the reins in case of accident. As the chariots roared off, each separate charioteer's entourage of trainers, masseurs, grooms, stable-boys, veterinary surgeons, saddlers, tailors, dressers and waterers flocked out from behind the stalls to clamber up to the nearest vantage point and add their yells to those of enthusiasts in the stands who were bellowing encouragement to their chosen team.

Each day the excitement mounted. As a result of representations from Rome, mainly from owners of gladiators who had financial interest in their performances, the original programme for the Games had been changed to include some gladiatorial fight-to-the-death combats, despite murmurs of protest from Jews, and even some criticism by Greeks. But these bloody spectacles, exciting though they were, were outshone in excitement by the feats of the jockeys in their seven-lap races. The marvels performed by these riders, particularly those fierce slit-eyed men from the northern plains, were breathtaking. Riding two horses at once at a gallop, they leaped from one to the other, snatched scraps of cloth from the track and, one foot on either horse, leaped over obstacles of tremendous height, including a chariot harnessed to four horses. Those interested in recording such things claimed that some champion athletes had raced in shorter times or boxed and wrestled more superbly than they had done at Games in other cities.

There were many good-humoured jokes made about the Sicilian wrestler who had been brought to Caesarea by the sport-loving Vitellius. In his first bout the lad had put up a very disappointing show. On the following day, however, he slipped on the marble rim of the pool at the palace and, fortunately for his reputation, sprained his shoulder. So, full of lamentations that an accident had deprived him of the highest award, he was shipped home to Sicily before the Games finished. He went without his two slaves: those Vitellius took from him to give to the wrestler eventually judged champion at the Games, a blond and handsome German fellow.

In addition to the pleasures of the Games themselves, the citizens of Caesarea enjoyed the vast increase in business caused by the presence of so many free-spending visitors. Not only in the arcades around the stadium but also in every street in Caesarea and along the waterfront, wine-merchants, caterers, pastry cooks, astrologers and prostitutes did a roaring trade. Among the prostitutes were a number of especially pretty girls shipped from Athens, even a few exotic ones who had been brought from Alexandria, as well as, for those who liked such things, boys, black and blond, and children much below the age of puberty.

Pilate did, of course, attend on the first day, but although his eyes followed the course of the races his blank gaze registered neither interest nor excitement. He had intended to attend also on the second day, when a large party of Herodian royals, invited by the Tetrarch, were to be among the audience. To assure himself that they would be given places of appropriate honour at the stadium, he asked the secretariat to send up the seating plan. It was an old one upon which Julius had scribbled names. Across two of the neat squares which represented chairs on the tribune, were scribbled the names 'Vitellius' and 'Herod'. On a third chair Julius had written merely, 'Father'. With a convulsive sob Pilate thrust the plan away. He was thankful no one was in the room. After a while he found strength to scratch out the 'Father', and then called Severus and told him to take the plan to Vitellius, ask him for his advice on the seating of the Herod family and to accept the Procurator's apologies for not attending today owing to a sudden indisposition.

Pilate knew that those who had personal sympathy for him, faithful members of his staff like Severus, certain scribes, and others of the secretariat staff, and some slaves, including of course Dumb Black, believed that daylong he mourned the death of his son. The diffident and gentle hints which they insinuated into conversation to comfort him indicated that they must often talk among themselves about his continued mourning. They were wrong. He could remember awaking one morning from a dream in which he had been walking along the terrace and seen Julius,

471

laughing and beautiful, demonstrating wrestling holds on the patch of bare ground in the garden. The dream reminded him that during two whole days, immersed as he had been in official business, he had not so much as thought of Julius. He felt guilty at thus forgetting his son. But later there were many other days when he again forgot. Even when, alone in his bedroom, he opened the cupboard which enshrined the statue of Julius, he began to find himself looking on a boy in an athlete's cloak with only tender sentiment instead of that agonising sense of loss which had first tortured him. No, the tragedy had shifted. The son had been murdered; but it was he, the father, who had died. Also, it seemed, his capacity to feel grief had died. He had heard it said that grief comes to one every day, like salt at meals. Yes, grief was a condiment of life, and if he, Pilate, were still alive, he might feel it. But now his being was too numb to taste salt.

Inevitably the Games aroused some vivid memories of the work Julius had done for them, like the word 'Father' scribbled on the seating plan. That had shocked him.

The palace was very quiet that day. It was almost deserted. All the guests, and practically the entire staff, had gone to the Games. He bathed himself, but then, feeling that he would like to be refreshed with a shave and massage, he sent for Dumb Black. He lay on his couch awaiting him. The shutters had been closed to shut out as much as possible the roar of the joyous crowd south of the city. So the room was deeply shadowed, only a few hazy ribbons of light falling across the mosaic floor. But, finding even so gentle a light a strident intrusion on his sadness, he flung his napkin over his eyes.

At last he heard feet padding softly across the floor. When they reached his couch he wearily uncovered his eyes. Staring down at him, with one dark and beautiful eye and one puckered socket, was the Young Barber holding his instruments wrapped in a creamy towel.

It was the first time Pilate had seen the boy since his ravaged body had been carried into the Antonia in Severus's arms. Pilate pulled himself up. Quivering with shock, he pointed urgently to the door. 'Go! Go! Go away!' he gasped, choking on the words. The boy's mouth twisted into a grimace of fear and sorrow. Then he turned and, sobbing, ran from the room.

Pilate sank back trembling. Because he had known that the sight of the Young Barber would always bring back in full the searing pain of that moment at the Antonia, he had given strict orders that the boy should never be allowed into his presence. This afternoon's confrontation had brought back the agony of the first days after Julius's murder. Better death, Pilate had thought then, than this torture of loss. Those whose bodies died or were killed were to be envied: those whose lives died but whose bodies lived on existed always in torment.

A slave came in to ask when he wished to dine. Dismissing him, he asked where Dumb Black was. At the Games, of course.

A woman slave came with the Lady Claudia's respects. Would he dine with her? 'No. My regrets. I wish to be alone.'

He still found the presence of the woman who had borne his son only a shade less agonising than the presence of Ephir. During the first days after the murder she had tried to comfort him. Julius, she had said, was not forever dead. Death in this world was not the end. There was a life hereafter. Julius would enjoy that eternal life. Julius would arise, in all his beauty and joy, from the grave. For one happy moment, when Pilate heard these words, his mind, his very heart, soared upward towards a wondrous vision. The horror of his fall, from that dizzy height of hope to the black pit of truth, ravaged every particle of his being. For an intemperate moment he found himself hating the wife whose womanly imaginings had tricked him into such idiot behaviour.

Easier to bear than such agony of intermittent hope and despair was the brutality of reality. Julius was lost forever. That was truth. An immensely beautiful sarcophagus held all that remained of him. Behind the light and glory of exquisitely carved marble and moulded bronze was darkness, the black interior in which the charred remains of a mangled body crumbled to dust. Anything that said differently, all prayers and promises and comfortings, were lies. Truth, the fierce spear which impales the mind and presses its point, each year, nearer the vitals of mortal existence, was all. Face it, Pilate! Face it! Reject, reject superstitious imaginings and baseless yearnings!

The Games ended. Now the official reports were drawn up. They lauded the name Vitellius with special commendation. They were sent to Rome and Capri; and Vitellius himself, after a succession of brilliant banquets, sailed north expectantly to Antioch.

Marcellus, coming back from duties in Jerusalem, attended on Pilate to report on his investigations into the murder of Julius. Pilate silenced him. He did not wish to hear. Marcellus felt relieved at that, for he had not much to report. An impressive number of Zealots had been rounded up in the hills, and by now coveys of vultures flapped exultant on a glut of corpses. Their flesh afforded a grisly feast for the son of Pilate; their crosses adorned the landscape of a score of villages. But no trace had been found of the boy Zealot who had murdered Julius.

One captured Zealot did seem to promise a likelihood of providing clues to the young murderer's whereabouts, but the information gathered from this man by torture, during which he lost four fingers, some toes, other portions of his body, and his eyes, was scanty. When it was thought that at last he was on the brink of saying vital words he unfortunately expired.

However, it was plain to Marcellus that Pilate was not interested. Not interested even in revenge! Well, Marcellus, for his part, thought time and energy enough had been spent in the search for a boy who, despite the importance of his victim, was after all only one frenzied little savage. Marcellus was needing his network of agents for more significant operations. By keeping careful track on comings and goings between Barabbas and Petra he was building up a valuable armoury of intelligence concerning the Arab king and his expansionist ambitions. Because of this, Barabbas and his immediate entourage of Zealot fanatics were allowed to enjoy their desert meetings and journeys, under the delusion that their activities were unknown to the Romans. Even to all this Pilate was indifferent.

'I leave it to you, Marcellus,' he said in a thin tired voice. 'Don't plague me with such details ever again.'

At last! These were the words Marcellus had awaited so long. Most readily he accepted them as his ultimate command, ceased his regular reporting to Pilate, and, now unhindered, strengthened in secret his campaign against terrorists and Jewish freedom groups.

Increasingly Pilate reduced his interests in Judaea to his proper procuratorial function of controlling the finances of the province. He cut down his appearances and progresses as much as possible and was seen in public less and less. He moved out of the palace of Caesarea only when necessary. In accordance with custom he went regularly in state to Jerusalem on the occasion of Jewish religious feasts. As Caesar's governor he had also to appear in public to proclaim Caesar's law. But he left it to the army commanders to administer that law.

The cost of the Games had left less in the treasury than the finance officers had expected, with the result that the new aqueduct progressed only slowly. Even that left him indifferent. He startled his council at one meeting by breaking off a discussion on irrigation with the words, 'If the Jews are short of water, they can always be driven into the sea.'

He spent much of his time, even on winter days, sitting on his balcony looking westward over the Great Sea. Often when Dumb Black came to signal that the bed in his room was made up for the night, he would wave the slave away and spend the night on his couch outdoors.

On one of these nights he was aroused from his half sleep by an unexpected shower of rain blown on to him by the gust of a suddenly rising wind. He got up fretfully and made his way, barefoot and silently and unnoticed by the slaves who dozed in dark corners, to his bed. The startled gasp of someone in his room surprised Pilate when he opened his door. The door of the cupboard enshrining the statue of Julius was swinging open, and a figure that had been on its knees before the statue sprang to its feet. Its limping progress as it tried to run past him betrayed who it was.

'Ephir!' he exclaimed. He intercepted the youth, and, not at first understanding why he should do so, he grabbed and held on to his shoulders. The youth, expecting blows and flinching, bowed his head. How much taller the Young Barber had grown, thought Pilate. He released him. Uncertain what awaited him, the youth stood before him.

'Light the lamps,' said Pilate.

Ephir obeyed, finding the flint on the table beside the bed and lighting the lamps one by one. The last was the lamp standing on a bracket below the cupboard, and now the pensive marble head could be seen gazing down into its rays. The flickering light moved shadows over its cheeks and eyes, making the features smile.

Ephir, as though no longer aware of Pilate's presence in the room, dropped to his knees. He reached up and timidly put his finger tips to the statue. In doing so his hand brushed the casket holding the whiskers of Julius's first shave. At that he buried his wounded face in his hands and sobbed.

Pilate laid his hands on the youth's strong young shoulders. He pressed down on them, trying to still the shudders of weeping. 'Ephir,' he murmured. He stroked the youth's hair. He slid his hands down the cheeks and turned the boy's face and lifted it up towards him, as he had once done, he now remembered, with the face of a gentle frightened Jewish boy in his tent on the morning of some crucifixion.

He looked down into the dark face, a face of such sadness but also of such unutterable manly beauty that even the puckered socket where an eye should have been could not destroy its radiance. Pilate smiled. 'Ephir, my son,' he sighed. 'My son!'

The youth prostrated himself and clasped Pilate's ankles. 'Father!' he murmured, and kissed his feet. 'Father!'

Pilate felt the tears on his feet. His own eyes were pricking. The tears flowed. Pilate wept.

This morning, a brick which Tiberius had been laying on a new wall, that wall which the peach-garden of the Villa Lucullus had for too long deplorably lacked, slipped from his grasp. Stooping, he peered down at it, shaking and spluttering with vexation. Then, as was his habit, he saw himself: bent, weak, ludicrous, and impotently angry. But angered not by the paltry accident of cement spattering his gown and plopping on his toes. No. Angered by the affectionate concern on the faces of the young slaves who stood around, ready to spring to his side if he tottered, though their human pity for his enfeebled state could not entirely hide that amusement which the lusty young always find in the comic doddering of the old.

Any one of these lads could die in a quick moment, be drowned from a boat, be gored by a boar, be hacked in two on a field of battle, or be choked by the disaster of inexplicable disease. Yet, much as any one of them might not like the act of dying, not one of them would be aware of the immensity of their loss. They were too young to know that. Only an old man, because he has seen so many years, knows how precious years are; knows that each year can be studded with joys and glories or, more adorably, endowed with interest. Thus, the longer an old man lives, the sharper becomes his greed for years, the more avariciously he hangs on to the thin breath to avoid death which, in youth, had no terrors for him. For when one is young, excitement, ambition and love sharpen the sword, making death a short brave ecstasy. But when one is old, death kills slowly with blunt mean weapons, as it was doing to him, the life of each limb and organ being sucked away each minute of day and night by a slavering insatiable sickness, and his sovereign grasp on the world being loosened, finger by finger. He bent towards the brick.

A youngster darted forward to retrieve it. Tiberius, creaking down, stretching an uncertain hand for it, spat him away like an angered snake. Yet he could not reach the brick. He saw his hand. He saw on it the cords of enlarged veins which now stood out bolder than the atrophying muscles. His fingertips were only inches away from the brick. But those inches seemed arduous as miles. And he could feel the heavy ring that bore Caesar's signet sliding down his emaciated finger. That golden circle must know the time had come to desert a hand which, though it ruled a world, had not strength enough to pick up a brick.

His hood fell forward. Good! For it covered his face and hid his contorted features. He was ashamed of anyone, even his doctors, seeing Caesar's visage confess to pain. Forcing himself erect, he tossed the trowel aside, pretending sudden indifference to the work. but actually needing that hand free so that he could press it, under his robe, against the seat of his bursting agony.

He turned to walk up to the terrace where his litter waited, and his body-slave hurried to his side, offering the aid of his golden German arm. Tiberius waved him aside. Years ago, in the years when Caesar could have walked unaided anywhere, on the floor of the Senate or across corpses on a battlefield, it had been part of the imperial act to favour a slave or honour a general by resting Caesar's hand upon an obedient arm. But now it was part of the act to show that Caesar still had strength to walk alone.

As he walked up the path, pain halted him occasionally. But when it did, he made pretence of halting only to examine planted shrubs and winter greens, so that the gasps and grimaces of his illness could be seen merely as sighs and frowns of displeasure at the poor quality of the gardening here at Misenum compared with that at his villas on Capri. He reached the litter at last. He slumped backwards into it and swung his legs in and on to the cushions. Not until he had jerked the curtains closed did he lie back, moan under his breath, and give way to pain.

The litter tilted and swayed as its bearers picked their way between the untidy oleanders below the villa. A breeze stirred the curtains. The air smelled damp and grey. Winter still had its grip on this draughty corner of Italy, and still the channel between here and Capri was lashed every day with sad and sodden winds. In his present state he had not the heart to endure such seas. He had not, he must confess, even much wish to return to Capri. Perhaps when the calm spring days did come he might, even then, find it more convenient to stay on the mainland. It would be easier, this much nearer to Rome, to keep his hands on shorter reins of power. Thus could he be sure of keeping intact to the end the empire he would, as he died, hand over to Gaius. That young heir was now bounding down the villa steps to meet him.

Caligula, poor lad, must surely find it boring to be cooped up in this lonely rainswept corner of Italy, waiting for the death of an old man who seemed too stubborn to die. One could almost forgive a talented youngster if, in impatience, he should press a pillow on the old face, or toss the withered hulk into the sea; though, if he did that, he must remember, of course, to drag the signet off the thin finger first.

Certainly Caligula had betrayed himself as cruelly impatient to inherit the diadem. But the lad had been encouraged to that indiscretion by that pernicious young rascal, Herod Agrippa, nephew of the Tetrarch of Galilee. When Tiberius's son Drusus had died, this scion of the Herods, cunningly attaching himself to Caligula, had eventually made himself the bosom pal of the expected heir to the empire. But, as could be expected of any man who was a spendthrift and enmeshed in debt, Herod Agrippa was not satisfied with future certainties; he tried to hasten his advantages by playing on the young prince's ambitions.

One evening, at one of those low dinner parties at which, in these days, noble youngsters enjoyed boozing in the company of boxers and charioteers and prostitutes, male and female, Herod Agrippa, so deep in his cups that he was careless of the nearby ears of Eutychus, a blockheaded but loyal charioteer, had enlarged on what a brilliant absolute monarch Caligula would make when indecisive old Tiberius was out of the way. Eutychus reported that conversation in the right quarters, and Herod Agrippa was quickly clapped in jail.

Caligula had, after all, been only the listener to and not the speaker of the seditious diatribe, but Tiberius had to take him to task and, plucking him out of the tavern society of Rome, insist that he should in future remain in constant and obedient attendance on the Caesar in Capri and, now, in Misenum. Tiberius tempered this exile with the wry comment that perhaps he might not have too long to wait to achieve his ambition. He also added that if the young man was all that eager for succession he had best be at Caesar's elbow to learn how burdensome was the weight of the imperial diadem. For although Caligula showed promise of being good, like his father, at military strategy, and was also clever enough in winning friends and sniffing out enemies, he had still a lot to learn about the more demanding tasks involved in dreary day-to-day administration.

As Caligula helped him out of the litter, Tiberius stole a glance at his face. He was relieved to see confirmed there the impression he had gathered when the young man had run down the steps to greet him. He was in an amiable mood today, more like his old self. It was good to see him so. Though one had to admit that these good days got fewer and fewer as the months passed. It was natural enough that Caligula had sulked for a while after Herod Agrippa's arrest and imprisonment, and he must have been irked by the suspicions of wished-for regicide that underlay the scandal. But there was more to Caligula's malaise than that. In fact, there were occasions when Tiberius was near to suspecting some deep-seated illness in the young man's mind. Tiberius had told his doctor to examine the young man thoroughly when he got a chance. Old Charicles had taken that opportunity when Gaius was suffering stomach-ache after eating shell-fish. He had peered into Caligula's mouth and into his other orifices, and listened to his heart and poked his midriff. He had found no physical ills, and the astrologers whom he had consulted had cast favourable horoscopes. Though they did say, as Charicles had said, that the young man's sexual appetites were alarmingly greedy. Maybe, but that could be expected in a lusty hairy youngster. Admittedly his choice of partners was a little bizarre. The licentiousness of his panting frolics with his sisters could possibly indicate a tendency to incest. Well, in some kingdoms of the empire such family goings-on were royal privilege, and what Tiberius found much more disturbing were those black moods which seemed to assail his nephew with increasing frequency. In these moods he would either flare up in sudden and often irrational angers, or sit utterly motionless, staring ahead for an hour or more, the pupils of his eyes hardening to points. The stare could look, to an observer, intense and earnestly concentrated, but Tiberius had the suspicion that the eyes collected no sense at all from whatever they were seeing.

Anyhow, it was now far too late to go rooting around for another heir. Rome would have to make do with the one he had chosen, well or sick. After all it was Rome, not Tiberius, who had insisted on continuing the concept of kingship. And perhaps the gruelling labour of actually ruling the world would put a curb on Gaius's native wildness. Today's jobs were admirably suited for giving him another taste of the varied problems that would one day be his to solve. There was the business of the Aventine refugees, and there was that latest dispatch, only one step short of alarming, from Antioch.

'Are you feeling bad, uncle?' Caligula asked.

Tiberius warmed to a trace of the old affection in the voice and in the affectionate grip on his forearm as they mounted the steps arm in arm like bosom friends. 'A few minutes ago I felt damnably bad,' admitted Tiberius. 'But the pain's almost gone. Fortunate, because we've work to do. You and I have accounts to do, and we must also send instructions to Antioch. Attend me in the library in an hour's time. Meanwhile, send Charicles to me.'

The old doctor bustled in immediately. He frowned triumphantly when he saw Tiberius bent over the back of a chair and snappily reminded him that he had warned his patient against going out on a January day to muck about with his interminable bricks.

'Stop blathering, Charicles. Mix a draught.'

The medicine soon gave him relief, and he dozed for a while until it was time to go to the library.

First the Aventine accounts. Tiberius was giving one hundred million sesterces to those rendered homeless by the fires which had devastated the Aventine and surrounding regions. He and Gaius had to devise some scheme which would prevent local barons and bureaucrats from lining their nests with cash and materials allocated to those in real need.

Next Antioch. Tiberius pulled his chair round so that he was facing Augustus's map of the Roman world. The map was engraved on gold; exquisitely rare gems represented the principal cities. He asked Caligula also to face the map while he read aloud extracts from a dispatch sent by Vitellius.

That name elicited the usual grimace from Caligula. Yes, thought Tiberius, Vitellius was, as the young prince said, old-fashioned and reactionary. But what did those words imply? 'Old-fashioned' indicated experience; 'reactionary' indicated love of the past and the determination to maintain law and order. None of Caligula's bright sparks could handle the vast complexities of Asian administration so well as did that power-greedy rascal Vitellius. And Vitellius knew it. In a private note he had included with the dispatch, he had shown an impatience almost insulting. He suffered all the toil and woe of high office, he complained, without the support of a title. If Tiberius still favoured Lamia as legate of Asia, then let Lamia be prised out of Rome and sent to Antioch to do the job. Offended, as Tiberius always was by anyone hastening him towards a decision, for after all he had not been many years hesitating over this one, he had to admit that Vitellius was right. Well, the instruments of appointment were already sealed by Caesar. They must be sent in the next Antioch bundle. Caligula need be told that only after they had gone.

He resumed his reading of the Antioch dispatch. At the end of each extract Tiberius bent his leathery visage towards his heir and waited for comments. The young man was quick: the comments were shrewd and almost on target. After the reading, Tiberius began dictating his reply, and as he did so he flattered the young man by incorporating into it some of the words, even whole phrases, which Gaius had used.

The immediate issue in Asia was the threatened invasion by Aretas. It was obvious that the Arab king was on the point of launching another all-out attack on Galilee, and, if that went well, invading the rest of Palestine. This time, Tiberius argued, Rome could not hold back. 'As soon as Aretas moves,' he dictated, 'attack.' He winced at that word. In this context 'attack' could only mean war with the Arabs again, and this time who knew what the Parthian tribes further east might do? At the first whiff of battle they might reconcile their internal dissensions and join to support Aretas. Asia engulfed in war? What then? Well, perhaps Armegeddon could be postponed for a few more years. By that time it would be Caligula's job to deal with this ferocious nibbling on the eastern fringe of the Augustan commonwealth of peace.

However, what Vitellius had to do at the moment, apart from building up an army to smash Aretas back into his deserts, was to ensure the peace and obedience of all the provinces of Syria. Tetrarch Herod of Galilee could be trusted to fight alongside Rome to repel a second Arab attack on his kingdom, for he knew well enough what he would suffer if his former father-in-law, offended by his daughter having been insulted by divorce, got his hands on him.

Samaria and Judaea were more uncertain. Much as the Jews hated the Arabs, it was beginning to appear they hated Romans more. They might even, in their mad hatred, go as far as putting their suicidal heads in an Arab noose, if those hangmen would help them to drive Rome out of the Jewish homeland. So Tiberius had at last to make his mind up about that man . .

'What's the governor's name, Gaius?'

'Pontius Pilate.'

'Ah, yes.'

For four, or five – why, it could be even six years – he had delayed making up his mind what to do about that fellow. A creature of Sejanus of hateful memory, but not, it appeared, one who had sympathy with the Sejanus plot. Nevertheless, the stink of anti-Semitism seemed still to hang about this Pilate, also some inability to be sufficiently sensitive. For had he not at one time actually crucified a Roman who shared Jewish sympathies? And surely it was Pilate who had, on the other hand, inconsistently freed a notorious Zealot and robber. Worse than such deeds, however, was his apparent indifference to the dangers of new cults. Such indifference, or loose administration, had been revealed by the ridiculous carelessness of his officers in the case of the crucified body of one Jewish rabbi.

Despite the established convention that the corpse of anyone executed by Roman sentence became automatically the legal property of Rome, Pilate, or his officers, had allowed the Jews to take this body from the cross for burial. The Jews had taken quick advantage of that. Within three days they were spreading the story that the rabbi had walked out of the tomb, rejoined his followers and, wrapped in a cloud, ascended to some heaven of Jewish design. Tittle-tattle about this supposed miracle had encouraged imaginative and dissident Jews to laud this resurrected prophet, and hundreds of ignorant and superstitious folk had begun fabricating garbled versions of the sayings and sermons of their supposed Messiah. It would have been bad enough if that legend had circulated only in Judaea. But Jews, moving as they did freely throughout the whole empire, had carried the tale across the whole world. As far away as Spain, idiots were chattering about it. Yes, with one bizarre crucifixion Pilate had done more than create a new religious myth: he had made that myth an imperial export.

'But enough,' said Tiberius. 'Let this dispatch be confined merely to the question of Aretas. Tomorrow, or the day after, I shall make some decision about our man in Judaea.'

A Caesar must never rush things. He did not wish to be remembered as a reckless hasty ruler. *Remembered?* Such a thought was surely a premonition of approaching dissolution. It was a symptom that a man was accepting the nearness of death when he began to worry more about what men would say about him tomorrow than what they said about him today.

So weeks passed before Tiberius made any decision about Pilate. And, as was always the case with the decisions of Tiberius, it was made the more drastic by the severity of the event which forced him at last to make up his mind. That event was reported in one of the first dispatches Vitellius had sent under his new imprimatur as legate in Asia. News had reached Antioch of a wholesale massacre of Jews in Samaria.

The Jews had been trooping northward. They were, admittedly, in large numbers, but they were not an army of enemies: they were a multitude of peaceful pilgrims lured to Mount Gerizum, a mountain in Samaria, by false reports that treasure and sacred relics of the Jewish King Solomon had been unearthed there. At a place called Tirathana, auxiliary cohorts under the command of Roman officers from Caesarea had swooped on the Jews and butchered hundreds of them. Roused to frenzy by this racial murder, the people of Judaea were on the verge of rebellion. Jerusalem was in turmoil. Vitellius felt it his duty to go to Caesarea in person and demand an explanation from the Procurator of Judaea for this reckless act.

'Explanations are not enough,' raged Tiberius as he dictated. 'Yes, go to Judaea. But move on this man Pilate suddenly and discreetly. Make sure of depriving him of adherents and any protection that he may enjoy. And then send him back to Italy. Here he will answer charges of gross maladministration. Also, Vitellius, while you are in Judaea, and when passing through Galilee, take the opportunity of gathering information there regarding any movements of Arab troops on the eastern frontier.'

Pilate was paying a festival visit to Jerusalem when news of the slaughter of Jewish pilgrims at Tirathana burst on the city. When he first heard of the massacre he had suspected that it might be the result of some anti-Zealot operation engineered by Marcellus. But Marcellus himself came hot-foot from Caesarea full of complaint against the stupidly provocative engagement. It had been the work of Antonius, Commander of the Horse, who had for years despised the un-Roman tactics of Marcellus and had always dreamed of sword-brandishing glory on the field of battle.

Marcellus quickly marshalled every spy at his command, infiltrated a veritable army of disguised auxiliaries into Jerusalem, and thus managed to split the enraged crowds into useless ineffective brawling segments. At last the city simmered down.

But the pompous state arrival of Vitellius, Legate in Asia, weeks later made it boil up again. Jerusalem folk in general and Annas in particular remembered Vitellius as the man who on at least one occasion had bludgeoned Pilate into acting in accordance with Jewish law. So the crowds flocked out to acclaim the distinguished Roman as a saviour come to right their wrongs, and took the opportunity of shrieking, amid their acclamations, execrations of the brutal and perfidious Pilate. Two whole cohorts of soldiers, making barriers of their spears and waving threatening swords, were hardly sufficient to clear a passage for the legate to the entrance of the Antonia.

Pilate was waiting in the audience-chamber to welcome the overlord of Syria.

The Procurator, Vitellius thought, had not altered in the last five years: not the slightest thinning in the short-cropped grey hair, not an extra inch of bulk on the slight trim figure. The cold grey stare was also just the same; the smile just as contrived. The formal greetings they exchanged were almost inaudible because of the cries welling up from the court and pouring through the windows, and Pilate indicated they should seek the quiet of his room.

Vitellius accepted the invitation with a nod. There was no reason to be fierce with the man. He could, during this last encounter, afford to be magnanimous. Indeed, when they were walking past the dais with its imposing chair, he was magnanimous enough to lay his hand on Pilate's shoulder, gently but firmly, as a sympathetic gaoler might lay a hand to sustain a man not without honour who was being led to execution.

Vitellius beckoned forward the scribe who had accompanied him, held out his hand for a scroll, then entered Pilate's room, closed the door, and seated himself judicially.

'Pray be seated, Procurator. I am sorry to inform you that I come to you on an unpleasant errand. For some time Caesar has been gravely disturbed by what appeared to him as dangerous tendencies in the three provinces under your administration: Judaea, Samaria and Idumaea. For years he has been approaching the opinion that the fault for continual unrest here lay with you, and that your incapacity to maintain peace in this region could be the result of your insensitivity to the Jews and their peculiarly racial sensitivities. It is regrettable, but inevitable, that he should still suspect that, despite the passage of some five years or more, you are still infected, apparently incurably, with the anti-Jewish prejudices of your late patron, Sejanus. This latest incident in Samaria, the massacre of pilgrims, seems to have confirmed those suspicions.'

'I am taking appropriate disciplinary action against those responsible for that deed.'

'So I understand. And I have also learned that the stupidity was committed without your orders or your knowledge. But, Pilate, you are Procurator. As such you cannot throw blame on your servants. I cannot but say, as I believe I said to you many years ago, that when a pontiff is poisoned at a banquet, it is the host, not the cook, who is hanged.'

'I have not forgotten, Vitellius.'

Vitellius unrolled the scroll. 'Here,' he said, 'is my précis of the comments and commands which Caesar made in his latest dispatch to me.' He handed it to Pilate. 'I should really read it to you. But I do you the honour of allowing you to read it yourself.'

Pilate remembered having used such words himself on a nearly similar occasion. He read Tiberius's caveat with mingled anger and humiliation: anger because Caesar's strictures and barbed sarcasms were so often unjust, humiliation because the man sitting opposite him was privy to the insults.

Vitellius eagerly waited for Pilate's eyes to reach the last phrase, the climactic one conveying Caesar's demand that Proconsul Pilate, Procurator of Judaea and Samaria and Idumaea, be removed from his office, deprived of personal honours and personal officers, and sent back under Roman guard to face charges in Rome of maladministration throughout the ten years of his governorship. But when they did reach that passage Pilate's eyes did not waver. He rolled the scroll and laid it back on the desk.

'You may keep that, Pilate,' said Vitellius. 'It is only a copy.' And for the first time that he could remember he found himself near to admiring this little-minded petty governor for his impenetrable calm. Blood of slaves there might be in that frail frame: there was also the slightest trace of Roman stoicism.

'Do I compliment Caesar on his exact memory for Jewish names?' asked Pilate dryly.

Vitellius smirked. 'Oh, those! No, it is I who corrected Caesar's spelling.'

'I guessed so,' said Pilate. 'But Caesar's contradictory argu-

485

ments you could not correct. And contradictory they certainly are.'

'Ah, Pilate!' Vitellius shrugged. 'It is the prerogative of Caesars, as it is of gods, to *appear* inconsistent. But what might appear to us lesser mortals as inconsistencies are often actually subtleties, the inner meaning of which our intelligences fail to grasp.'

'So you find it subtle of Caesar to accuse me on the one hand of "unnecessary and anti-Jewish savagery" and then, I think it is four lines later, to accuse me of handling Jews too timidly and irresolutely?'

Vitellius put on his politician's mask. 'I deduce that when Caesar talks of savagery he is referring to such acts as this recent massacre in Samaria. He also remembers your high-handed seizure of Temple funds.'

'And also, no doubt, my defiling of Jerusalem with graven images.'

'He does not refer to that incident.'

'And my weaknesses?' asked Pilate with a tired and somewhat impatient smile.

'Political weaknesses. In the actual dispatch Tiberius expresses himself more forcibly, and I might say, more vulgarly . . . well, you know his style . . . than in my précis. He feels you have been weak *politically*. You have encouraged the wrong people and offended the powerful ones. You made a friend of, for instance, a man like that renegade Jew, the banker Josephus, but you were antagonistic to the conservative elements in the Sanhedrin; to Annas in particular, and the Sadducee party in general.'

Pilate nodded. He sighed. 'I am a stubborn man, Vitellius. You know that, don't you? And here, at the end of my career, I remain stubborn. I am stubborn in my belief that I have been right. Those who follow me will learn. I have kept the Jews divided. I have played one against the other. Any radical change in that policy could lead to the Jews uniting. Once they are united, they will begin to dream again their dreams of nationhood. Then, and I thank the gods I shall not be here to deal with it, they will rise together against Rome. When that happens Rome will be able to subdue them only in the way in which Jews have been subdued again and again in their sorry history.'

'How, Pilate?'

'By dispersal. By being driven out. Broken up.'

'But Jews always come back,' said Vitellius teasingly.

'Oh, yes! Give Jews their due, they always survive. More than

Egyptians, more than Persians, perhaps even more than Romans, Jews can survive. The gods alone know how, or why, these Jews can so hang on. If you put the whole lot of them into one vast camp, piled every Jew on to one pyre and tried to burn the lot, some remnant of them would escape, or rise from the flames, and survive, and, eventually, return to their "promised land".' Pilate shrugged. 'Anyhow, they are no longer my problem, are they?'

'No, Pilate. They are your successor's problem.'

'Has Caesar named that lucky man?'

'No. He has left it to me.'

'It needs a person of some stature and possessed of some political sagacity. Such a one is difficult to find immediately. Until he is found, it is necessary to replace you with someone who has an intimate knowledge of the present situation in the country and of its people. Someone, also, who is capable of putting neecssary changes into effect discreetly, even secretly. I have decided . . . '

'On Marcellus,' interrupted Pilate, and grinned boldly at Vitellius's frown at having his pronouncement anticipated. 'I compliment you on an admirable choice.'

A compliment from Pilate did not seem to impress Vitellius. 'The appointment will be provisional. Marcellus will occupy the post only until a personage of more appropriate character and better presence can be found.'

'But I know,' said Pilate, 'why you should think him particularly valuable to you at this moment. Marcellus is the only Roman in Asia who is privy to every move that Aretas is making in his projected invasion of Syria.'

Vitellius waved these comments aside. Politics were not something one discussed with a displaced governor. Though, to demonstrate to the disgraced Procurator how things would now be changed in Judaea, he could not restrain himself from saying, 'I am receiving High Priest Annas shortly in the audience-chamber. I have news for him. Good news, and bad news. The good news is . . . '

'That at long last the sacred Jewish vestments are to be removed from Roman custody in the Antonia and handed over to the Temple,' said Pilate, impudently interrupting. 'You are also to remit unpopular market taxes.'

Vitellius flushed. 'How did you know that?'

'And the bad news is that son-in-law Caiaphas is to be removed from his throne as high priest of the Temple. But the bad news will be tinctured by you, Vitellius, with a grain of consolation,

487

You will appoint one of Annas's sons, either Jonathan or Theophilus, as high priest.'

Vitellius stood up angrily. 'I made those decisions in council at Antioch. I am disturbed to learn that they are common knowledge.'

'Not *common* knowledge. Only Marcellus and I know these things. You see, Marcellus has sources of information also in Antioch. In fact he appropriated my own informant there. Oh, yes, Vitellius, you have chosen a good man.'

Vitellius frowned heavily. He looked down at Pilate. 'Caesar commands that you return to Italy to face trial when you have settled your personal affairs.'

'So your précis tells me.'

'Do you intend to go?' whispered Vitellius. 'I am not a vindictive person. If you should desire it, I could grant you the liberty to . . . '

Pilate laughed sharply. 'Thank you, Vitellius. Do you think I want to do what Procurator Mela did? He fell on his sword rather than face trial at the hand of Tiberius. I am not that kind of man. I am, as I said, a stubborn man. So, still stubbornly believing that what I have done is right, I am determined to tell Tiberius, face to face, even with the strangler's cord on my neck, that what I have done I have done for the honour and glory of Rome.'

Lucius Gnaeus Marcellus, Procurator of Judaea, ordered that Pontius Pilate could retain his personal apartments in the palace of Caesarea until the time came when he could be shipped to Italy. The storms of an unusually prolonged winter were still raging over the Great Sea; so it would have been unduly severe to cast old Pontius on such perilous waters, even had there been suitable craft available. Hardly any boats were putting out from Caesarea, and only a few were arriving – navy vessels, which, bringing necessary armaments and reinforcements for the build-up against the Arabs, had sneaked eastwards from port to port between the storms until they reached snug safety behind the mole at Caesarea and tied up in the harbour. It was desirable also that any boat chosen for the shipment of the deposed Procurator should be one bound for Ostia, which port was near enough to Rome to avoid his being carried through the whole length of Italy as Caesar's prisoner.

But above all it was useful to Marcellus to have Pilate near at hand for as long as possible. There were many details of civil administration about which Marcellus knew little and Pilate knew a lot. So Pilate attended on the new Procurator each day to enlighten him on such matters.

Sitting in a high chair and laying his gauntlet on the table, Marcellus could not avoid giving these conferences the character of interrogations. He kept on the table a stack of documents representing outstanding administrative and military affairs. Daily he rearranged the papers in sequence of each subject's importance or urgency. Because of impending conflict on the frontiers, military matters assumed precedence at the top of the pile, whereas that folder which contained estimates and plans for aqueducts went lower and lower in the pile until, after some weeks, it reached the bottom.

When the days lengthened and spring sunshine flooded the courtyard, Pilate spent more and more time in the gardens, sitting beside the pool and reading the *Commentaries* of Julius Caesar. At first, those members of the secretariat who passed along the balcony and saw him there were embarrassed by his presence, uncertain as to what measure of attention they should give to their former master. Some gave him a slight nod of recognition and looked away as they bustled along to the office of Procurator Marcellus. Eventually, however, they began not to notice Pilate at all.

For hours his only companion in the garden was Ephir, whom Pilate had freed from slavery but who persisted in devoting his days to service on his 'father', sitting quietly on the ground beside Pilate's bench and awaiting any opportunity to answer a command. The youth now knew enough Latin to be able to find amid the books in Pilate's chest any needed volume of the *Commentaries*. He would run upstairs to find the volume and could even find, on his way downstairs, the chapter Pilate was wanting to read, and would have the scroll open at the proper place. Sometimes his choice of a passage was wrong, and for a while Pilate did not correct him, but then decided that it was wrong not to point out the mistake. It was better for the boy's education to guide him to the proper page. Ephir, his dark hair swinging luxuriantly over the scroll as he bent his gaze to follow Pilate's finger, read aloud, word by word, stories of battles long ago in a strange and far distant world of bogs and snow and wild blond men who lived in wattle huts. Pilate became conscious that the

Commentaries had taken on, for him, a different flavour. Always falling across the austere grandeur of these reports of Caesar's victory over great odds seemed to be the shadow of the noble writer's mortal destiny, a presage of the bloody end of all triumph.

Sometimes, when he lifted his eyes from the scroll to reflect on such thoughts, his reflective gaze fell on the statue of Poseidon. That beautiful piece troubled his consience. It did seem something of a betrayal of the memory of old Josephus that the statue would not, after all, be taken to grace the villa of Pilate's retirement. But the cost of transporting so heavy and valuable a piece to Italy was more than he could afford. Nor could he now hope to realise his dream of honourable retirement amid the Tuscan hills. In fact, he had terminated his negotiations for that property, and had added the money recovered to the pitiably slender fortune he had managed to smuggle into Claudia's possession before the trial which would certainly lead to his disgrace and the sequestration of his property. Not that Claudia should ever be in financial need. Sextia would see her all right on that score. Claudia's personal safety was of greater concern. He had insisted that she should not return to Italy with him. It would be better, he said, for her to stay in Asia for a time. Hoping that she would not guess his sombre fears for his own future, he had tried to keep from her, as much as he possibly could, news of how dangerously severe was Caesar's displeasure, and advised her to stay in Judaea. 'Until I can make decisions about our future,' he added. She had agreed. Later she had asked his permission to spend that time waiting in Galilee.

'In Magdala?'

She nodded.

He pondered over this. The idea of her becoming even more deeply involved with the Galilean religious sect worried him. Some of its preachers, building up supernatural legends about their crucified leader, were considered as wilful trouble-makers and were being reviled by orthodox Jews. But a woman should not be in much danger, for, after all, womenfolk were allowed their womanish dreams. Nor did he feel the desire, one common with too many husbands, to extend his authority over his wife from the grave. Herod, who had always liked and admired Claudia, had been most obliging. He had promised to take her under his protection in Galilee, and, should she still decline his offer of a home at Tiberias, he would help her to find suitable property in or near Magdala.

Severus, when not engaged in duties for Marcellus, often came into the garden with his son. The little boy was growing up sturdy and frank-faced, an absolute miniature of his father. Even his voice, when he spoke Latin, had the same guttural Celtic accent. But the youngster also spoke Aramaic, already more than his father. When Ephir was beside Pilate, the boy always ran over to embrace the young Edomite who had taught him Aramaic and further enriched it with a wealth of Edomite dialect, as well as training his infant body to all manner of agility in wrestling and tumbling and dancing.

On Pilate's fall from office the loyal Severus, despite the new Procurator's promises of advancement, had immediately volunteered to accompany his master to Rome.

'And then?' asked Pilate.

'To serve you in some capacity.'

'But if I am not able to employ you, or, let's face it, not even there to do so?'

'I shall go home to Lugano.

'No, Severus. Hitch your wagon to a rising star. Your career is now more important than ever, young man, for you have a son!'

So Severus had been persuaded to accept Marcellus's offers.

Severus had been of help, in an amusing fashion, in the matter of Dumb Black. When Pilate had freed this faithful slave he discovered that the Negro's ambition had always been, if he should become a freed man, to set himself up as a brothel-keeper. Severus had been able to find a modest house of pleasure for sale on the waterfront at Caesarea. It was going cheap because the girls in it were not all that attractive, and the place itself lacked any semblance of luxury.

'But it's a beginning for him,' said Severus. 'He can improve it. And at least Dumb Black's clients won't have any fear that he'll chatter about their performances.'

'What is more,' added Pilate, 'Dumb Black will be able to enjoy for free what he has had to pay for so often in the past.'

'Pontius!' said Marcellus abruptly, at the end of a session of discussions one afternoon. 'You will be leaving tomorrow. A boat is sailing for Ostia. Fortunately it will have some retiring officers aboard. So your escort will be a dignified one.'

'Thank you.'

'It would have been my wish, as a friend, to accompany you to the quay. But in view of my office I can hardly do that.'

'I understand, Procurator,' said Pilate.

Marcellus's gaze fell to his gauntlet. The metal parts, Pilate noticed, were now chased silver, cleverly jointed. 'Also,' murmured Marcellus, 'a quiet unattended departure will, I think, be less embarrassing for you. Severus has requested permission to see you aboard and to give orders ensuring your comfort and freedom from molestation during the voyage.'

Pilate stood up. 'So we part!' Marcellus nodded. 'A long career we have had together. And it is a happy conclusion to a partnership when the fall of one results in the elevation of the other. I wish you well, and thank you for all your past service.'

'Good day, Pontius.'

'Goodbye, Procurator.'

Pilate went back to his apartments, but not to the grand salon. He went instead to the austere little study made dear to him by ten years of labour. His desk was empty and closed. Official papers had long since been taken from it and handed over to Marcellus. All his private papers had been burned. Pompey's oil-lamp had been given to Severus. But his armour still hung glittering on its ebony stalk. He would wear that tomorrow, when he left Caesarea. And he would wear it also when he confronted his accusers. Tiberius Caesar alone had the power of stripping him of its glittering honour.

He sent a message to Dumb Black to ask him, though a freedman, to serve him one last time. It was the first time, Pilate thought, that he had seen the Negro without his grin: without the light of that smile the black face looked blacker than ever.

For the last time Dumb Black painted the red circle below Pilate's left rib. 'Give me the brush and paint,' said Pilate when the operation had been performed. 'I shall pack it. I must learn to do that job for myself. I think I know the spot well enough by now.' He honoured the Negro's new status by clasping the great pink-palmed hands when they parted.

He sent for Ephir. 'Cut my hair, my son, for the last time.'

'Not the last time, Father. I am going with you.'

'No! That you cannot, Ephir.'

The boy prostrated himself, clasping Pilate's ankles, imploring permission to serve him for ever. Pilate blinked away tears and pulled the boy to his feet. He looked into the wounded but still beautiful face with passionate tenderness.

'Ephir! You must stay here. Severus will keep you under his protection. Help your little friend Severus Secundus to grow happily and strong to boyhood. And you, Ephir, live on. Live bravely and well, in memory of me, and in memory of Julius.'

The boy, weeping, gathered up the instruments which had scattered from the towel when he flung himself down to offer his life in service to his master and father. This time he had remembered to bring the pomade.

'Now,' said Pilate crisply, 'do as I tell you. Cut my hair. And cut it short. So that it will never need cutting again . . . Until I reach Rome.'

When that was done he led Ephir into his bedroom. The doors of the cupboard were open; the cupboard was empty. Pilate pointed to a crate. 'The statue is there. Also . . . ' He smiled. ' . . . also Julius's whiskers. The box will be taken to Severus's apartments. But the statue, and the whiskers, are my gift to you, Ephir. There is money in the crate too. Some day you will have a home of your own, and I trust you will then accord Julius a place of honour under your roof.'

Claudia insisted on accompanying Pilate to the boat in the morning. On the quay she embraced him. 'Good voyage, my beloved,' she said, 'and good luck. I shall pray for you.'

Pray? She looked nowadays more like a priestess than ever: austerely gowned, and without jewels or paint. The simplicity suited her. She looked like one of those Roman matrons whose statues reminded one of the frugal dignities of the Republic. That air of quiet authority which she had assumed years ago as appropriate to those mystical beliefs of her had deepened, so much so that now it seemed to flow outward from her inner being, instead of being something laid upon her. Dedicated. Yes, that was the word. Her gaze was like that of someone to whom mysteries had been revealed, someone who had been summoned to a presence and, answering the summons, had dedicated herself to that service.

'When I send for you . . . ' he began, in an attempt to reassure her, but her loving smile, full of a sad but triumphant acceptance of truth, checked him. Her smile rejected the lying hope he had proffered as a solace. And that smile, he knew, dismissed him, as a living husband, forever. Oh, true it was that she had never kissed him with a more fervent attitude of love than she did now. She even ran her fingertips over his brow in the familiar caress which recalled that first moment of the passion that had united them and borne them their son. But yet her love dismissed him. A love so universal went beyond him, making him only one of a whole world who shared its forgiveness and understanding: a vast love, all embracing and pure: so pure that to his human lips it seemed cold as marble. So, after he had turned away, he did not, as he walked up the gangplank, look back at her. He knew that he had seen the Lady Claudia Procula for the last time.

One chest had been big enough to hold all Pilate's possessions. All life, he thought, in one corded box. That had been taken aboard earlier.

Severus came aboard with him and introduced him to the officers appointed to accompany him to Ostia, where they would hand him over to gaolers sent from Rome.

'Good luck, Severus,' said Pilate as the mooring ropes were being untied. 'And look after Ephir.'

At this request Severus shifted his gaze in an embarrassed way. Why? Was this stolid fellow frightened of showing emotions? So Pilate went on, 'Ephir will be good company for Secundus. Your son is old enough now to be free of a nurse. It isn't good for boys to be cooped up with women. Let Ephir . . . let my son Ephir look after your son.'

Pilate remained on deck until the coastline of Judaea receded into the shimmering glow of a spring morning, and the land which he had, in some way, loved had disappeared like a dream, and all his life went with it. He went below then to the modestly comfortable cabin which Severus had ordered to be improvised for him. It was somewhat crowded because in it were two bunks. Both the bunks, he noticed, were dressed with covers. So, after all, they had decided that a guard must be with him day and night. So be it.

He opened his chest, where, on the top of the packed possessions, was a scroll of the *Commentaries*, the ebony bar enwrapped within it to mark the passage he had chosen to sustain him, during the first hours of this departure, against the natural sadness of the wrench of leaving Caesarea. He read for an hour or so, and then, feeling tired, for he had not slept during his last night in the palace, he tossed the scroll on to the second bunk, turned his face to the wall, pulled a coverlet over his ears and, lulled by the dip and swing of the boat, was soon asleep.

The noise of the bar of ebony clattering to the floor awakened him. He pulled himself round. Seated on the other bunk, the scroll lying open across his knees, was Ephir, mischievously making pretence of being engrossed in a finger-by-finger study of the *Commentaries*.

'Ephir!'

'Father!' With a gasp of joy and a great smile the youth flung himself into Pilate's arms and, made bold by happiness, covered his cheeks and neck and chest with kisses.

Severus, it was explained when at last the two of them emerged from joy sufficiently to speak, had arranged this. Ephir, with the connivance of the officers detailed to guard Pilate, had been smuggled aboard at dawn, and secreted with instructions not to reveal his presence until the boat was far enough away from Caesarea to eliminate any possibility of the captain turning back with the stowaway. The crate with the statue had been left in Severus's keeping. 'It will be waiting for us when we come back,' said Ephir.

'And the money?' asked Pilate.

'That also can wait. Severus gave me some; enough for food and things. And he got me this.' With a swagger of pride he handed a document to Pilate. It was a firman permitting freedman Ephir Iphtahel Bar-Hadad Oholibaham unhindered voyaging through all the principalities and provinces ruled by His August Highness Tiberius Claudius Nero. It was imposingly sealed. It was signed by Marcellus, Procurator of Judaea, Samaria and Idumaea. That signature removed the hurt Pilate had felt since his last chilly session with Marcellus. 'Thank you, Marcellus,' he murmured.

'Well, he owed me something. I did catch that scribe for him. And that led to Barabbas and everything else,' Ephir reminded him.

'Yes indeed,' said Pilate and smilingly repeated that 'Barabbas and everything else'.

'And you brought no baggage?' asked Pilate.

Ephir shook his head. His woolly hooded robe was all he needed: that was his whole wardrobe, his bed, his tent, his home. His only other possession he wore under his robe: it was something he had never shown to Pilate. Marcellus had given it to him after the search for Julius's murderer had been abandoned. It was the jewelled Parthian dagger which Ephir had wrested from the hands of that evil boy who had carved the corpse of Julius so obscenely.

For a long time after Julius's death Ephir had hoped that some fortunate chance, a chance as fortunate as that which had helped him to uncover the treachery of the spying scribe at the palace, might lead him to Julius's murderer. For months, whenever he had seen, in the streets of Caesarea or Jerusalem, a boy of that same slight build and long black hair, he would run after him, clutching his hand to the jewelled hilt below his robe, hoping that he could bury the dagger in the heart of its murderous owner. During the years the hope had faded. But still he wore the dagger. He wore it in memory of Julius. It was a pledge to Julius, a promise that some time his murder would be avenged with the blade that had committed it. One day Pilate came unexpectedly into the cabin when Ephir had dragged off his robe to track down a pesky flea. He saw the dagger hanging at the boy's hip. Even as he asked where Ephir had picked up so gaudy and costly a weapon he guessed the truth. He closed his eyes when Ephir answered. After a while he asked, 'But how can you wear it?'

'I wear it to avenge my brother,' said Ephir, letting his robe fall over it.

In all their weeks together on the boat that was the only moment when unease crept between them.

For the boat and its captain the voyage from Caesarea was one long series of unlucky incidents. At their first port of call, Cyprus, they were to take on board the retiring governor and his family. But when they berthed he was still in the hills, rounding up recruits for sending to Judaea, and the boat left Cyprus nearly two weeks late. At Ephesus some of the crew went down with fever or food poisoning, and, because every trading vessel was still trying to make up for the months lost during that particularly stormy winter, it took a long time to find a new complement of oarsmen, with the result that by the time they reached Piraeus supplies were running short. Merchants, knowing the boat was long overdue, tried to take advantage of the captain's dilemma and asked exorbitant prices, whereupon supplies were commandeered as military stores. But an astute lawyer from Athens declared the seizure illegal and sued the captain. The legal wrangle went on for two weeks. At Sicily, because the captain had secured the oarsmen at Ephesus only by pledging they would be freed on arrival at Sicily to bring a trading-vessel from there, he had to find more crew.

For Pilate, on the other hand, the voyage was a period of sad but placid content. Each day he told himself that it was an unexpected bonus to any life that its last weeks should be so rich with happiness. He had indeed been blessed by the gods: the blessing came somewhat late, but it was very welcome. He luxuriated in the devoted affection of his young companion. A youth's determination to serve him, to place his life and destiny in his father's hands so unreservedly, warmed Pilate to a love he had never had for anyone except his own son. But in the case of his son the discipline of his office and the call of the duty to educate his son had kept Julius so often out of his embrace, whereas now the cramped confines of the boat enfolded him and Ephir into happy intimacy. For them the little cabin was the whole world. The fact that this world would end at Ostia and life itself would end in Rome was a truth which Pilate contemptuously tossed aside.

On a summer evening when the boat was sailing up the coast of Italy to Ostia, Ephir insisted on barbering Pilate in preparation for his landing. 'It is a good thing I came, isn't it?' he said boastfully. During the operation a swift little vessel from the mainland, with soldiers aboard, came alongside. The two captains exchanged messages. When the vessels parted, the little vessel darting swiftly back to the mainland, the captain came below to tell Pilate something. But then, seeing Ephir with him, he hesitated, and, after an uncertain pause, apparently decided that what he had to say might better not be said. He stalked importantly away. Pilate sought him out later.

'What is your news?' he asked.

The captain pondered, but eventually said, 'The escort meeting you at Ostia will tell you. Rome is to be informed of the time of your arrival. You will not disembark until the escort arrives.'

They berthed at Ostia late that evening, at the hour when lights were springing up along the waterfront and amid the maze of its populous markets. Next morning, just before dawn, the captain roused Pilate 'Your escort has arrived.' Pilate went on deck, and, when Ephir joined him, he pointed through the early morning haze to four guards of the imperial household grouped around a tall motionless officer. 'My gaolers,' he said. 'They will take me to Rome. I shall petition for permission to take you with me. But, Ephir, I dare not hope they will allow it. The captain of the boat has promised to find you a cheap lodging in Ostia and to take you back to Caesarea when he returns.'

'I shall come to Rome. If I cannot go with you, then I shall follow you. I have Caesar's permission to travel where I wish.'

They embraced as the boat berthed. Pilate put on his helmet. With barber's fingers Ephir coaxed its plumes to their full height and buckled the straps of the cuirass. Pilate strode to the gang-plank leading up from the deck to the quay. At that moment the tall officer detached himself from the group of guards and

497

marched into the light. When he had first seen this officer from a distance, Pilate had thought how like he was, in height and debonair carriage, to Fabius. Now he saw that it really was Fabius, whose joyous smile as he ran down to the deck contradicted Pilate's sadness.

'Welcome home, Pilate,' he cried. 'I requested Caesar that my father might have the honour of offering you hospitality in Rome. Caesar will grant you audience at the basilica as soon as he recovers from his illness.'

'Then is Tiberius in Rome?'

Fabius stepped back amazed. 'Tiberius! Have they not told you? Or is this another boat that has missed the news? Tiberius is dead, Pilate. And our new Caesar will receive you honourably as a retired and faithful servant of Rome.' He lowered his voice. 'Caligula that is,' he added with a grin. 'The little boots now walk beneath the diadem.'

Pilate had braced himself to face arrest. He felt so weakened by the sudden and happy relief that, finding Ephir standing beside him, he supported himself on the boy's shoulders. 'How kind of you to come, Fabius. And your father? Is he well?'

'Yes, sir. Except for a few old man's aches in his joints. He is waiting for you eagerly. We are lodging with the Prefect Macro, for our house on the Tiber is in a mess. Father has decided to add more rooms to it before he sells it and retires to Tuscany.'

As he helped Pilate on to the quay the guards formed up in honourable escort. Ephir ran gaily ashore. Fabius looked at the wounded face. 'But isn't this Young Barber of years ago?'

'Captain Fabius, allow me to present my adopted son, Ephir Iphtahel Bar-Hadad Oholibamah.'

Fabius laughed. 'Oh, I remember trying to get my tongue round that one. No other Roman but you, sir, could ever do it. I think it would be better to stick to Young Barber.'

'No. He is no longer a barber, except to his father. Call him Ephir.'

As they rode along the wide villa-lined avenue leading out of Ostia in the direction of Rome, Fabius told Pilate about Tiberius's death. The end had come at the Villa Lucullus at Misenum on March 16. The Old Man had died 'on his feet'. Feeling his strength failing, he had taken off his ring to hand it over, but then, as though at the last moment reluctant to surrender the world, had snatched it back and folded it in his palm. He staggered forward a few more paces and fell. He was dead, and they had to prise open his stubborn grip on the imperial signet.

But, went on Fabius, the sequel was happy. Twelve days later Gaius Germanicus, 'Baby-boots', entered Rome. After being ruled by an old recluse whom they had had not set eyes on, and consequently had suspected, for years, the Romans now had a Caesar they could see. They flocked out in millions to bless him. They threw spring flowers and called him 'Darling!' Immediately he had assumed the diadem, Caligula had begun fulfilling his promises, went on Fabius. He initiated schemes for reforms; prisoners were released; exiles were recalled; officials who had grown corrupt during the years of Caesar's absence from Rome were replaced; histories and writing that had been banned and burned were copied again for public sale. 'And, more important to you, sir, all prosecutions initiated by Tiberius have been annulled.'

Yes, Caligula was living up to all the hopes Rome had entertained. It was a nuisance that in the middle of this beneficent revolution he had fallen ill. His adoring public declared that their beloved young Caesar had made himself ill with overwork.

'There may be something in that,' said Fabius. 'Though the doctors are secretive. Perhaps that's just their self-importance. They pad about without a word and for days they cordon him off from the outside world. Even Macro cannot get audience with him sometimes. Caesar, they say, must have rest and quiet. '

At the villa of Prefect Macro beside the Tiber, Pilate's old comrade-in-arms, was awaiting him with affectionate greetings. They sat up all night talking.

Often, during the weeks that followed, Pilate asked himself if fortune could ever have been more mischievously indulgent than she had been to him. Having snatched him back from the very brink of dishonourable death she had made him her pet.

So sanguine did he become that he hardly heeded the first events that heralded the end of Caligula's illness. Of these events the only one that interested him was the arrival in Rome of Herod and his consort. The Tetrarch had been persuaded, or bullied, by the frenziedly ambitious Herodias, to grab immediately any advantage possible from the change of Caesars. They hoped to play on the new Caesar's friendship with their cousin Herod Agrippa and further their claims to richer suzerainty in Asia.

Herodias wanted Herod to be crowned as a king. She would then be a queen, instead of only a Tetrarch's consort. Pilate considered calling on them. He rather looked forward to meeting Herod in the guise of a distinguished retired Roman gentleman. But he never managed to see them. Within days Caesar cast them down. For instead of helping them, their cousin Agrippa had ruined them. While they were sending petitions to Caesar he was busily uncovering documents which proved that, five years earlier, Herod had been in correspondence with Sejanus, of hateful memory, treasonably offering his assistance in Asia for a coup against Tiberius. It was revealed, too, that Herod had also been intriguing with the Parthian king, Artabanus. The documents could not be disproved. Nor could Herod deny that in Galilee he had amassed a vast accumulation of arms: and his arguments that he had done this to protect his country from threatened Arab invasion were dismissed. The young Caesar was convalescing at Baia, recovering from his sickness amid the pleasures of that notorious resort, when Herod was summoned for audience. He was deposed from the Tetrarchy, but he escaped with his life. He was banished to Lyons. Herodias, showing unexpectedly noble devotion, decided to go with him and share his exile.

Disquieting gossip came from Baia. Caligula, enjoying his freedom from sickroom and doctors, was indulging himself in all the exotic pleasures available in a place renowned, among its delights, for extravagant and licentious midnight bathing-parties. But, a loving populace declared, one must view this phase with tolerant understanding. After all, he was a young and lusty fellow. He had been confined to his bed for weeks with no company other than hectoring doctors and dried-up astrologers. Also, it had to be remembered, he had lived for years with that old Tiberius at his elbow, watching everything he did and censoring youth's natural excesses. And, if it were true that he was seducing his sisters in quick succession, there was no sign that the girls themselves were bewailing his lusts.

Later, however, acts of a less private nature began to cast their shadow. The promises of reform withered away, and Caesar's rule became a succession of strangely unconnected and wilful edicts. The Egyptian cults banished by Tiberius were welcomed back to Rome, and sacred water was fetched from Meroe to sprinkle at the Temple of Isis. The few politicians of repute admitted to Caesar's presence came out of it shaking mournful heads. 'He is too impatient to wait for deification after death,' said one. 'He talks as though the living Caesar can be a living god.' That careless senator was the same who later chattered too openly of his increasing disgust with Rome and his intention to retire as soon as possible from public life to the decency of a country estate. He was one of the first of the many to be arrested at his home. His property was sequestrated and his family impoverished.

Caligula, revitalised by his convalescence beside the sea, returned to Rome. His presence in the capital was signalled by the great glow of light on the Palatine where torches burned, often till dawn, on the terraces of his palace. Troops of guests, responding dutifully to imperious invitation, were entertained lavishly and then, dazed with wine, were bullied into performing at Caesar's command simulations of lust, which exhibitions Caligula felt might rouse his fading appetite.

Suddenly the light went out again on the Palatine. The palace was hushed and dark, a shadowy sinister weight pressing down on a whispering city. Caesar was sick again.

Fabius's father confessed his fears to Pilate. 'Caesar, they say, is being nursed back to health. For a time, they say, they feared for his reason. I do not think I shall stay in Rome until the house is sold. The sooner I can leave the better.'

The lights came on again. On the first evening of Caligula's fresh recovery he invited Macro and his wife Ennia to supper. 'An intimate party,' he intimated. It was. He received them in his bedroom, sitting up, swathed in sheets, on his golden couch. He talked at length to Macro about the Prefect Sejanus, whom Macro had succeeded five years ago. Then he suddenly ceased talking. His face settled into a blank stare which he fixed rigidly on a point beyond his guests. It seemed as though he were listening to other voices than theirs. Thinking Caesar had wearied of their presence Macro begged permission to leave. Caligula started, as though the sound of Macro's voice had broken in on those other voices.

'Oh, you must not go,' he said. A ghost of that impish smile which had characterised him in his youth flickered over his white invalid face. 'There is something you must do for me tonight which it would be more decent to do here than in the presence of your children.' Ennia drew away from him and took her husband's arm. Caligula looked her over slowly and sneered at her presumptuous fears. Then, in a flat level voice he denounced Macro as a traitor and commanded that he and his wife commit suicide.

'I had feared Caesar would command an act less clean than suicide,' said Macro boldly, and Ennia laughed with relief. They obeyed.

A banquet had been arranged at the palace for the following evening to celebrate Caesar's return to work. He had decided that appropriate sacrifice must be made to the gods to thank them for his restoration to health. Prisoners who were awaiting execution in the gaols and a number of disobedient slaves and other offenders would be offered. He, or one of his intimates, had thought up an ingenious method to sacrifice them. It was a method which would serve three purposes: it would applaud the gods, it would execute the condemned, and it would cast an extra glow over the celebration. This banquet was to be used as the setting for an announcement of new measures of Caesar's imperial policy. Consequently it was to be attended by his principal officers of state. Also to be invited were all foreign legates, tetrarchs, governors, and civil servants of provinces beyond the seas who were in Rome awaiting audience of the new Caesar. Two officers of Caesar's household attended on Pilate in the evening. Hospitable Caesar had put a carriage at the disposal of the retired Procurator.

Rome had a brooding air that evening. Shops and taverns and brothels were open and a number of people about, yet the streets seemed more dark than usual, perhaps because their lights were so much dimmer than the sumptuous glare up the flanks of the Palatine. Yet even up there, Pilate thought as he mounted the stairway to the outer court, it was quieter than he had expected. That, one of the officers explained, was because Caesar had not yet descended to join his guests on the terrace where the banquet was to be held.

In the outer court the antique walls of a former fountain had been removed and replaced by raw new stone on which nymphs and satyrs, carved in full-bosomed and tumescent marble, grossly entwined their limbs and spouted jets of water at the central figure in the bowl. The central figure was an older piece: the statue of a handsome youth in heroic pose holding sword and shield aloft and naked except for his boots.

'Caesar himself,' said Pilate's companion. 'A good likeness.' At which Pilate halted and examined intently the features of the Caesar he was to meet. 'It was carved at the home of the Divine Tiberius in Capri,' the man went on. 'It will have to be cleaned, though. The water's made a mess of it.'

Through the years a deposit or some salts in the spraying water had streaked the statue with grey-green stains. The cheeks and mouth and chin were lightly smeared with this green, but the eyes had escaped it and stared out bald and blank and white. It was, however, the body which was more thickly bedewed with smears. As though marble could exude a foul disease, the loins and thighs were scabbed.

Pilate walked up towards the banqueting terrace. Surprisingly it was almost dark, with only a few niggardly lamps disposed on the tables. Guests were finding places on the benches, seeking out friends or allies with whom to sit. They were a subdued company; many of them old grave men accompanied by severe wives, yet mingling incongruously with them and crushing themselves on to occupied couches beside them without a by-your-leave were heavily painted slave girls who wore thin shifts and tipsily crooked wreaths. A major-domo was already banging the floor of the dais with his staff to announce the imminent arrival of Caesar. Beyond the entrance, trumpets shrilled as Caesar left his apartments. A party of shaven-pated priests in Egyptian skirts sidled in. In the dim light Pilate had not at first identified the objects to which the company around the table at which he had chosen to sit were directing their doom-laden gaze. High on the wall, branching out above each arch of the arcade, were what looked liked brands of torches, but extravagantly immense. It was not until Pilate's eyes became accustomed to the gloom that he saw that each torch had a head. The torches were humans fastened by cocoons of bandages to metal bars. The bandages were drenched in wax to make a human candle of each being who was to be sacrified in thank-offering for Caesar's recovery. As Caesar's litter approached, the torches borne by the slaves preceding it illumined the faces of those candles. Most of the faces were brutish or wounded, faces of slaves or soldiers condemned to death for some wickedness. Among them, however, were also noble faces; faces wise and scholarly and elegant. But all wore the same expression of expectant horror imposed upon them by the pressure of the wax that, encasing them, had congealed cool around their limbs and members and would release its pressure only when it melted in spluttering rivulets of flame.

Caesar's litter was his golden bed. And the Caesar who claimed to have been restored to health reared himself unsteadily on it in his sheets. His features were still as brilliantly handsome as when portrayed by the sculptor on Capri, and the gold leaves of his wreath were numerous enough to hide the baldness his family had suffered and hated. But his eyes were also like those of the statue. They were blind and blank and seemed paralysed of movement, so that in order to see his guests he had to swivel the whole white funereal mask of his face from side to side. The startled guests stared, appalled and speechless.

Caesar opened his mouth. It gaped, silent, for a moment. Then a laugh screeched out of it. 'What ails you Romans?' he cried, in his young clear beautiful voice. 'Are you dumb? No word of joy, no acclaim for your Caesar and your god?' At this his guests forced out cheers. Caesar waited until the adulation had sounded long enough to satisfy him. He lifted a goblet. 'Drink!' he commanded. They drank. 'Now laugh, you solemn folk. Be joyful. Let me hear each laugh. Let me share each joy.'

They laughed. To drown their fears they poured wine wildly down their throats. They guffawed. And behind their grins fear flickered back and forth.

Caesar called intimates to join him at tables on the dais. Whenever his youthful voice rang out, those who were speaking dutifully stopped their murmuring tongues to listen to the words of the ruler who, like a god, held power of life and death over them. Pilate could hear the voice joyously describing the last act Prefect Macro had performed in obedience to Caesar. Then Pilate heard, repeated several times, the name of Sejanus. At last he heard his own name, and soon a serving-man found him out and told him that Caesar had honoured him with an invitation to the dais.

'Proconsul Pilate, former Procurator of Judaea,' he said when he stood beside the bed, bowing to the staring Caesar.

'Welcome, Pilate!' said Caligula. 'Pilate protégé of Sejanus. Pilate, uncle's naughty servant. Come nearer.' Pilate obeyed. Then, in a herald's voice, plunging the company into waiting silence, he bawled, 'Procurator Pilate!' Again the voice fell to a whisper. 'Crucifier Pilate. Surely that's a better title? Pilate the Crucifier! Step nearer! Nearer!' Pilate was now inches away from the staring mask. From it issued, in a tone that could have been either approval or accusation, 'You crucify my Jews. You even, is it not true, crucify Romans? Pilate the Crucifier!' He laughed. 'Would you like to go back to Judaea, Pilate? Would you like to take me back with you? You can. You can convey the god Gaius to Asia. For I am having a statue of myself carved at Sidon and sent to Jerusalem. I want even Jews to share my divine joy, so I shall show myself to them as a living god.'

'As Caesar wishes!' Those were the words that Pilate should have spoken. But he could not. For truth, inescapable truth had come to him at last and silenced him. The night air closed on him, hanging around him as dark as the black worsted of a tent, as solid as the walls of the Antonia, and in a shaft of light that slanted through the recesses of memory stood a figure which first he thought was a pale shaved Roman smiling against the threat of death but then recognised as a prisoner whose hands were bound and whose lips were bruised but whose calm regard was radiant with compassion and forgiveness for the judge who in blindness or in error could not see the light of truth; and this one faced Pilate as Pilate should now face Caesar, should face the doomed and tortured wearer of the diadem with the same compassion; and face him also with that same courage which, born of truth, was divinely indifferent to the fierce cruelties and petty injustices of human judges.

When Pilate, indescribably inspired and comforted, emerged from that vision he saw that Caesar had recoiled from him. Pulling petulantly at the sheets, he was glaring at him with distaste. 'You fail in your duty to Caesar, Pilate. You insult Us with your silence. It criticises Our intentions. Caesar is offended, Pilate. It appears to Us that Pilate is not Caesar's friend.'

The others on the dais peered in wonder at this modest grey-haired man when, even at this extremity, he made no reply. Why, the fellow did not so much as bow his head!

Caligula turned his senseless gaze away. 'Leave Our company, Pilate. It is Our pleasure, on this evening of Our restoration from a grievous sickness, to be supported by the company only of joyous friends. Surrender your sword! Now, go back to your lodging in the house of the traitor Macro. We shall let you know Our pleasure. We must study carefully what We can design for those who are not Caesar's friends.'

Pilate turned his back on Caesar and walked the length of the terrace. As he was descending the staircase to the outer court and neared the diseased statue, he heard the clear young voice shouting happily, 'Let there be light! Light the torches! Light the torches!'

The house beside the Tiber was deserted except for Pilate and Ephir. Fabius and his father and all the household slaves had left.

On their estate in Tuscany they might, for a time at least, be far enough away to be forgotten by Caesar's anger. Outside, a rising wind shrieked around, as crazy as Caesar's laugh.

'Ephir! My letters are finished. And now the city is quiet enough for you to leave. Here is a wallet with all the money you will ever need for the longest journey' He smiled. 'Enough to pay for all haircuts, in this world and the next. And two letters. One is for the Lady Sextia in Pompeii. You remember her?' Sad though Ephir was, his one eye brightened and his lips parted with a grimace at memories of the Lady Sextia. 'She will be easy to find in Pompeii. She will see you aboard a safe boat to Judaea. The other letter you will take yourself to the Lady Claudia in Galilee. Do you understand?' Ephir nodded. 'Then come with me. There is one last service you must perform for me.' He hesitated. 'My son, I beg you not to be saddened by what I must ask you. Believe me, it is the noblest duty you could ever perform for me. I ask you to do it only because I find myself at this moment old and timid, and I fear I might not do the deed in proper style. When you have done what is necessary you must leave, at once, for Pompeii.'

They left the house not by the porticoed street door but by a side door which led into the kitchen garden. Beyond was an alley running down to the bank of the Tiber, near to the half-built walls of the extensions to the house of Pilate's friend. Through rain-sodden scaffolding and planking that gleamed in fitful moonlight, Pilate led Ephir below newly cemeted arches to a niche formed from stacks of planking and roughly fashioned templates for window arches. At this point the path along the river's bank was narrow and greasy with mud. The river surged heavy and yellow. Pilate halted at its brink and turned. He stood with his back to the river and faced Ephir. 'Draw that beautiful dagger, Ephir. Now do as I command. Do it in obedience, but also in love, and in honour of my name and my memory.' He undid his corselet and bared part of his chest. 'You know the spot. Direct the blade truly, as once in Caesarea you pointed your scissors, but this time drive the blade to the end.'

'No!' The boy turned his head away, wrenching it so violently to the right that it dragged the scarred folds around his eye and the blind socket seemed to be weeping.

'Ephir Bar-Hadad! My Iphtahel! It is my last command. It is my dearest wish. Come, my son! Courage!'

It was not, despite what the surgeons had told him, as quick a death as he had hoped. The poor lad weakened at the crucial moment. Nor had Pilate fallen, as he planned, into the river so that his corpse would escape the indignities that Caesar would inflict on it. So he was still alive when Ephir, thinking he was dead, turned and ran, and could hear the youth's sobs and slapping feet fading away along the deserted street. And he was still not dead when Caligula's men found him collapsed and retching blood against a couple of naked planks. They saw there was no hope of a living prisoner, so they used their daggers to rip off his clothes and reduce him to writhing nakedness. His body, striped with gouts of his blood and torn by careless daggers, looked as though it had been scourged. One of the men used his dagger to lop off a finger to take the signet ring. At that Pilate died.

The other man thought it was a fitting jest to tie the corpse, before tossing it into the river, to the two planks which were already nailed together in a rough cross. Laughing, he thrust the dagger point through each palm to heighten the effect.

Borne on that cross the body floated downstream until it was nudged aside by reeds and lodged on a spit of mud. Two gardeners found it there next day: the body of an apparently crucified man. Thieves, they thought, must have been at it after the crucifying for the finger where a signet ring could have been was missing. Poverty-stricken thieves they must have been: they had apparently taken even the nails.

Pontius Pilate: Saint in the Canon of the Orthodox Church of Ethiopia. (June 25.)

Claudia Procula: Saint in the Canon of the Eastern Orthodox Church. (October 27.)

RICH MAN, POOR MAN
by Irwin Shaw

From the author of THE YOUNG LIONS and TWO
WEEKS IN ANOTHER TOWN comes the greatest novel
to appear in post-war America. Truly global in the scope
of its humanity and passion, RICH MAN, POOR MAN is
the story of a generation at war with the values of its past,
the hypocrisy and tension of its present and the
terrifying inevitability of a shipwrecked future.

Rudolph is the romantic, who learns to live with doubt
and make a fortune at 30. His brother Tom is the brute,
whose acid-scarred American dream is coloured with
boiling blood. Their sister, Gretchen, seduced by the small
town's leading citizen, is the beauty in urgent search of a
man – the only man – who can save her from herself.

'By the end of it we know America from coast to coast.'
— **Daily Telegraph**

NEW ENGLISH LIBRARY

THE JUDAS TREE
by A. J. Cronin

In a story of wide and fascinating detail A. J. Cronin tells
of Dr David Morey who tries to atone for his desertion
of the woman he loved.

Beguiled by the prospect of riches he goes on to marry
Dottie, a spoiled but beautiful neurotic who brings him
almost constant misery, until a chance remark makes him
seek retribution in memories of the past and a return to
his native Scotland.

In the great tradition of A. J. Cronin's THE STARS LOOK
DOWN and THE CITADEL.

THE NEW ENGLISH LIBRARY

THE CRUSADER'S TOMB

by A. J. Cronin

Stephen Desmonde, a graduate of Oxford, has been
brought up to follow in his father's footsteps and,
eventually, to succeed him as rector of Stillwater. But
instead, despite all entreaties to prevent him, he chooses
to become an artist in Paris.

In the face of life's despairs, privations, ostracisation and
humiliation, his struggle for recognition never wavers.

A remarkable, gripping, often tender novel in the mould
of A. J. Cronin's classic bestsellers.

THE NEW ENGLISH LIBRARY

NEL BESTSELLERS

War

T027 066	COLDITZ: THE GERMAN STORY	*Reinhold Eggers*	50p
T009 890	THE K BOATS	*Don Everett*	30p
T020 584	THE GOOD SHEPHERD	*C. S. Forester*	35p
T012 999	PQ 17 – CONVOY TO HELL	*Lund & Ludlam*	30p
T026 299	TRAWLERS GO TO WAR	*Lund & Ludlam*	50p
T025 438	LILLIPUT FLEET	*A. Cecil Hampshire*	50p
T020 495	ILLUSTRIOUS	*Kenneth Poolman*	40p
T018 032	ARK ROYAL	*Kenneth Poolman*	40p
T027 198	THE GREEN BERET	*Hilary St George Saunders*	50p
T027 171	THE RED BERET	*Hilary St George Saunders*	50p

Western

T017 893	EDGE 12: THE BIGGEST BOUNTY	*George Gilman*	30p
T023 931	EDGE 13: A TOWN CALLED HATE	*George Gilman*	35p
T020 002	EDGE 14: THE BIG GOLD	*George Gilman*	30p
T020 754	EDGE 15: BLOOD RUN	*George Gilman*	35p
T022 706	EDGE 16: THE FINAL SHOT	*George Gilman*	35p
T024 881	EDGE 17: VENGEANCE VALLEY	*George Gilman*	40p

General

T017 400	CHOPPER	*Peter Cave*	30p
T022 838	MAMA	*Peter Cave*	35p
T021 009	SEX MANNERS FOR MEN	*Robert Chartham*	35p
T019 403	SEX MANNERS FOR ADVANCED LOVERS	*Robert Chartham*	30p
T023 206	THE BOOK OF LOVE	*Dr David Delvin*	90p
P002 368	AN ABZ OF LOVE	*Inge & Stan Hegeler*	75p
W24 79	AN ODOUR OF SANCTITY	*Frank Yerby*	50p

Mad

S006 086	MADVERTISING	40p
S006 292	MORE SNAPPY ANSWERS TO STUPID QUESTIONS	40p
S006 425	VOODOO MAD	40p
S006 293	MAD POWER	40p
S006 291	HOPPING MAD	40p

NEL P.O. BOX 11, FALMOUTH, TR10 9EN, CORNWALL.

For U.K.: Customers should include to cover postage, 18p for the first book plus 8p per copy for each additional book ordered up to a maximum charge of 66p.

For B.F.P.O. and Eire: Customers should include to cover postage, 18p for the first book plus 8p per copy for the next 6 and thereafter 3p per book.

For Overseas: Customers should include to cover postage, 20p for the first book plus 10p per copy for each additional book.

Name ....

Address ....

....

....

Title ....
(JANUARY)

Whilst every effort is made to maintain prices, new editions or printings may carry an increased price and the actual price of the edition supplied will apply.